Harlan
COBEN

Darkest Fear

No Second Chance

D0532414

ALSO BY HARLAN COBEN

Deal Breaker
Drop Shot
Fade Away
Back Spin
One False Move
The Final Detail
Tell No One
Gone for Good
Just One Look
The Innocent
Promise Me

Harlan
COBEN

Darkest Fear

No Second Chance

Darkest Fear
First published in Great Britain by Orion in 2002

No Second Chance
First published in Great Britain by Orion in 2003

This omnibus edition published in 2011
by Orion Books Ltd
Orion House, 5 Upper St Martin's Lane
London WC2H 9EA

An Hachette UK Company

A CIP catalogue record for this book is available
from the British Library.

ISBN 9781407234182

Printed and bound in Great Britain by Clays Ltd, St Ives plc

www.orionbooks.co.uk

Darkest Fear

When a father gives to his son, they both laugh.
When a son gives to his father, they both cry.

Yiddish Proverb

—

This one is for your father. And mine.

When a father gives to his son, they both laugh.
When a son gives to his father, they both cry.

—Yiddish proverb

This one is for your father. And mine.

1

An hour before his world exploded like a ripe tomato under a stiletto heel, Myron bit into a fresh pastry that tasted suspiciously like a urinal cake.

"Well?" Mom prompted.

Myron battled his throat, won a costly victory, swallowed. "Not bad."

Mom shook her head, disappointed.

"What?"

"I'm a lawyer," Mom said. "You'd think I'd have raised a better liar."

"You did the best you could," Myron said.

She shrugged and waved a hand at the, uh, pastry. "It's my first time baking, *bubbe*. It's okay to tell me the truth."

"It's like biting into a urinal cake," Myron said.

"A what?"

"In men's public bathrooms. In the urinals. They put them there for the smell or something."

"And you eat them?"

"No—"

"Is that why your father takes so long in there? He's having a little Tastykake? And here I thought his prostate was acting up."

"I'm joking, Mom."

She smiled through blue eyes tinged with a red that Visine could never hope to get out, the red you can only get through slow, steady tears. Normally Mom was heavily into histrionics. Slow, steady tears were not her style. "So am I, Mr. Smarty Pants. You think you're the only one in this family with a sense of humor?"

Myron said nothing. He looked down at the, uh, pastry, fearing or perhaps hoping it might crawl away. In the thirty-plus years his mother had lived in this house, she had never baked—not from a recipe, not from scratch, not even from one of those Pillsbury morning croissant thingies that came in small mailing tubes. She could barely boil water without strict instructions and pretty much never cooked, though she could whip up a mean Celeste frozen pizza in the microwave, her agile fingers dancing across the numerical keypad in the vein of Nureyev at Lincoln Center. No, in the Bolitar household, the kitchen was more a gathering place—a Family Room Lite, if you will—than anything related to even the basest of the culinary arts. The round table held magazines and catalogs and congealing white boxes of Chinese takeout. The stovetop saw less action than a Merchant-Ivory production. The oven was a prop, strictly for show, like a politician's Bible.

Something was definitely amiss.

They were sitting in the living room with the dated pseudo-leather white modular couch and aqua-tinged rug whose shagginess reminded Myron of a toilet-seat cover. Grown-up Greg Brady. Myron kept stealing glances out the picture window at the For Sale sign in the front yard as though it were a spaceship that had just landed and something sinister was about to step out.

"Where's Dad?"

Mom gave a weary wave toward the door. "He's in the basement."

"In my room?"

"Your *old* room, yes. You moved out, remember?"

He did—at the tender age of thirty-four no less. Childcare experts would salivate and tsk-tsk over that one—the prodigal son choosing to remain in his split-level cocoon long after the deemed appropriate deadline for the butterfly to break free. But Myron might argue the opposite. He might bring up the fact that for generations and in most cultures, offspring lived in the familial home until a ripe old age, that adopting such a philosophy could indeed be a societal boom, helping people stay rooted to something tangible in this era of the disintegrating nuclear family. Or, if that rationale didn't float your boat, Myron could try another. He had a million.

But the truth of the matter was far simpler: He liked hanging out in the burbs with Mom and Dad—even if confessing such a sentiment was about as hip as an Air Supply eight track.

"So what's going on?" he asked.

"Your father doesn't know you're here yet," she said. "He thinks you're not coming for another hour."

Myron nodded, puzzled. "What's he doing in the basement?"

"He bought a computer. Your father plays with it down there."

"Dad?"

"My point exactly. The man can't change a lightbulb without a manual—all of a sudden he's Bill Gates. Always on the nest."

"The Net," Myron corrected.

"The what?"

"It's called the Net, Mom."

"I thought it was nest. The bird's nest or something."

"No, it's Net."

"Are you sure? I know there's a bird in there somewhere."

3

"The Web maybe," Myron tried. "Like with a spider."

She snapped her fingers. "That's it. Anyway your father is on there all the time, weaving the Web or whatever. He chats with people, Myron. That's what he tells me. He chats with complete strangers. Like he used to do with the CB radio, remember?"

Myron remembered. Circa 1976. Jewish Dads in the suburbs checking for "smokeys" on the way to the delicatessen. Mighty convoy of Cadillac Sevilles. Ten-four, good buddy.

"And that's not all," she went on. "He's typing his memoirs. A man who can't scribble down a grocery list without consulting Strunk and White suddenly thinks he's an ex-president."

They were selling the house. Myron still could not believe it. His eyes wandered about the overly familiar surroundings, his gaze getting snagged on the photographs running up the stairwell. He saw his family mature via fashion—the skirts and sideburns lengthening and shortening, the quasi-hippie fringes and suede and tie-dyes, the leisure suits and bell-bottoms, the frilly tuxedos that would be too tacky for a Vegas casino—the years flying by frame by frame like one of those depressing life insurance commercials. He spotted the poses from his basketball days—a sixth-grade suburban-league foul shot, an eighth-grade drive to the hoop, a high school slam dunk—the row ending with *Sports Illustrated* cover shots, two from his days at Duke and one with his leg in a cast and a large-fonted IS HE FINISHED? emblazoned across his knee-cast image (the answer in the mind's eye being an equally large-fonted YES!).

"So what's wrong?" he asked.

"I didn't say anything was wrong."

Myron shook his head, disappointed. "And you a lawyer."

"Setting a bad example?"

"It's no wonder I never ran for higher office."

She folded her hands on her lap. "We need to chat."

Myron didn't like the tone.

"But not here," she added. "Let's take a walk around the block."

Myron nodded and they rose. Before they reached the door, his cell phone rang. Myron snatched it up with a speed that would have made Wyatt Earp step back. He put the phone to his ear and cleared his throat.

"MB SportsReps," he said, silky-smooth, professional-like. "This is Myron Bolitar speaking."

"Nice phone voice," Esperanza said. "You sound like Billy Dee ordering two Colt 45s."

Esperanza Diaz was his longtime assistant and now sports-agent partner at MB SportsReps (M for Myron, the B for Bolitar—for those keeping score).

"I was hoping you were Lamar," he said.

"He hasn't called yet?"

"Nope."

He could almost see Esperanza frown. "We're in deep doo-doo here," she said.

"We're not in deep doo-doo. We're just sucking a little wind, that's all."

"Sucking a little wind," Esperanza repeated. "Like Pavarotti running the Boston Marathon."

"Good one," Myron said.

"Thanks."

Lamar Richardson was a power-hitting Golden Glove shortstop who'd just become a free agent—"free agent" being a phrase agents whisper in the same way a mufti might whisper "Praise Allah." Lamar was shopping for new representation and had whittled his final list down to three agencies: two supersized conglomerates with enough office space to house a Price Club and the aforementioned pimple-on-the-buttocks but oh-so-personal MB SportsReps. Go, pimple-butt!

Myron watched his mother standing by the door. He switched ears and said, "Anything else?"

"You'll never guess who called," Esperanza said.

"Elle and Claudia demanding another ménage à trois?"

"Oooo, close."

She would never just tell him. With his friends, everything was a TV game show. "How about a hint?" he said.

"One of your ex-lovers."

He felt a jolt. "Jessica."

Esperanza made a buzzing noise. "Sorry, wrong bitch."

Myron was puzzled. He'd only had two long-term relationships in his life: Jessica on and off for the past thirteen years (now very off). And before that, well, you'd have to go back to . . .

"Emily Downing?"

Esperanza made a *ding-ding* noise.

A sudden image pierced his heart like a straight-blade. He saw Emily sitting on that threadbare couch in the frat basement, smiling that smile at him, her legs bent and tucked under her, wearing his high school varsity jacket that was several sizes too big, her gesturing hands slipping down and disappearing into the sleeves.

His mouth went dry. "What did she want?"

"Don't know. But she said that she simply *had* to talk to you. She's very breathy, you know. Like everything she says is a double entendre."

With Emily, everything was.

"She good in the sack?" Esperanza asked.

Being an overly attractive bisexual, Esperanza viewed everyone as a potential sex partner. Myron wondered what that must be like, to have and thus weigh so many options, and then he decided to leave that road untraveled. Wise man.

"What did Emily say exactly?" Myron said.

"Nothing specific. She just spewed out a colorful assortment of breathy teasers: urgent, life-and-death, grave matters, etceteras, etceteras."

"I don't want to talk to her."

"I didn't think so. If she calls back, you want me to give her the runaround?"

"Please."

"*Más tarde* then."

He hung up as a second image whacked him like a surprise wave at the beach. Senior year at Duke. Emily so composed as she dumped the varsity jacket onto his bed and walked out. Not long after that, she married the man who'd ruin Myron's life.

Deep breaths, he told himself. In and out. That's it.

"Everything okay?" Mom asked.

"Fine."

Mom shook her head again, disappointed.

"I'm not lying," he said.

"Fine, right, sure, you always breathe like an obscene phone call. Listen, if you don't want to tell your mother—"

"I don't want to tell my mother."

"Who raised you and . . ."

Myron tuned her out, as was his custom. She was digressing again, taking on a past life or something. It was something she did a lot. One minute she was thoroughly modern, an early feminist who marched alongside Gloria Steinem and became proof that—to quote her old T-shirt—A Woman's Place Is in the House . . . and Senate. But at the sight of her son, her progressive attire slid to the floor and revealed the babushka-clad yenta beneath the burned bra. It made for an interesting childhood.

They headed out the front door. Myron kept his eyes on the For Sale sign as though it might suddenly brandish a gun. His mind flashed onto something he had never actually seen—the sunny day when Mom and Dad had arrived here for the first time, hand in hand, Mom's belly swelling with child, both of them scared and exhilarated realizing that this cookie-cut three-bedroom split-level would be their life vessel, their SS *American Dream*. Now, like it or not, that journey was coming to an end. Forget that "close one door, open another" crap. That For Sale sign marked the end—the end of youth, of middle age, of a family, the universe of two people who'd started here and fought here and raised kids here and worked and carpooled and lived their lives here.

They walked up the street. Leaves were piled along the curb, the surest sign of suburban autumn, while leaf blowers shattered the still air like helicopters over Saigon. Myron took the inside track so his path would skim the piles' edges. The dead leaves crackled under his sneakers and he liked that. He wasn't sure why.

"Your father spoke to you," Mom said, half-question. "About what happened to him."

Myron felt his stomach tense up. He veered deeper into the leaves, lifting his legs high and crunching louder. "Yes."

"What did he say exactly?" Mom asked.

"That he'd had chest pains while I was in the Caribbean."

The Kaufman house had always been yellow, but the new family had painted it white. It looked wrong with the new color, out of place. Some homes had gone the aluminum-siding route, while others had built on additions, bumping out the kitchens and master bedrooms. The young family who'd moved into the Miller home had gotten rid of the Millers' trademark overflowing flower boxes. The new owners of the Davis place had ripped out those wonderful shrubs Bob Davis had worked on every weekend. It all reminded Myron of an invading army ripping down the flags of the conquered.

"He didn't want to tell you," Mom said. "You know your father. He still feels he has to protect you."

Myron nodded, stayed in the leaves.

Then she said, "It was more than chest pains."

Myron stopped.

"It was a full-blown coronary," she went on, not meeting his eyes. "He was in intensive care for three days." She started blinking. "The artery was almost entirely blocked."

Myron felt his throat close.

"It's changed him. I know how much you love him, but you have to accept that."

"Accept what?"

Her voice was gentle and firm. "That your father is getting older. That I'm getting older."

He thought about it. "I'm trying," he said.

"But?"

"But I see that For Sale sign—"

"Wood and bricks and nails, Myron."

"What?"

She waded through the leaves and took hold of his elbow. "Listen to me. You mope around here like we're sitting shiva, but that house is not your childhood. It isn't a part of your family. It doesn't breathe or think or care. It's just wood and bricks and nails."

"You've lived there for almost thirty-five years."

"So?"

He turned away, kept walking.

"Your father wants to be honest with you," she said, "but you're not making it any easier."

"Why? What did I do?"

She shook her head, looked up into the sky as though willing divine inspiration, continued walking. Myron stayed by her side. She snaked her arm under his elbow and leaned against him.

"You were always a terrific athlete," she said. "Not like your father. Truth be told, your father was a spaz."

"I know this," Myron said.

"Right. You know this because your father never pretended to be something he wasn't. He let you see him as human—vulnerable even. And it had a strange effect on you. You worshipped him all the more. You turned him into something almost mythical."

Myron thought about it, didn't argue. He shrugged and said, "I love him."

"I know, sweetheart. But he's just a man. A good man. But now he's getting old and he's scared. Your father always wanted you to see him as human. But he doesn't want you to see him scared."

Myron kept his head down. There are certain things you cannot picture your parents doing—having sex being the classic example. Most people cannot—probably should not even try to—picture their parents in flagrante delicto. But right now Myron was trying to conjure up another taboo image, one of his father sitting alone in the dark, hand on his chest, scared, and the sight, while achievable, was aching, unbearable. When he spoke again, his voice was thick. "So what should I do?"

"Accept the changes. Your father is retiring. He's worked his whole life and like most moronically macho men of his era, his self-worth is wrapped up in his job. So he's having a tough time. He's not the same. You're not the same. Your relationship is shifting and neither one of you likes change."

Myron stayed silent, waiting for more.

"Reach out to him a little," Mom said. "He's carried you your whole life. He won't ask, but now it's his turn."

When they turned the final corner, Myron saw the Mercedes parked in front of the For Sale sign. He wondered for a moment if it was a Realtor showing the house. His father stood in the front yard chatting with a woman. Dad was gesturing wildly and smiling. Looking at his father's face—the rough skin that always seemed in need of a shave, the prominent nose Dad used to "nose punch" him during their giggling fun-fights, the heavy-lidded eyes à la Victor Mature and Dean Martin, the wispy hairs of gray that held on stubbornly after the thick black had fled—Myron felt a hand reach in and tweak his heart.

Dad caught his eye and waved. "Look who stopped by!" he shouted.

Emily Downing turned around and gave him a tight smile. Myron looked back at her and said nothing. Fifty minutes had passed. Ten more until the heel crushed the tomato.

2

Too much history.

His parents made themselves scarce. For all their almost legendary butting in, they both had the uncanny ability to trample full tilt through the Isle of Nosiness without tripping any gone-too-far mines. They quietly disappeared into the house.

Emily tried a smile, but it just wasn't happening. "Well, well, well," she said when they were alone. "If it isn't the good one I let get away."

"You used that line last time I saw you."

"Did I?"

They had met in the library freshman year at Duke. Emily had been bigger then, a bit fleshier, though not in a bad way, and the years had definitely slimmed her down and toned her up, though again not in a bad way. But the visual whammy was still there. Emily wasn't so much pretty as, to quote *SuperFly*, foxy. Hot. Sizzlingly so. As a young coed, she'd had long, kinky hair that always had that just-did-the-nasty muss to it, a crooked smile that could knock a movie up a rating, and a subconsciously undulating body that continuously flickered out the word *sex* like an old movie projector. It didn't matter that she wasn't beautiful; beauty had little to do with it, in fact. This was an innate thing; Emily couldn't turn it off if she donned a muumuu and put roadkill on her head.

The weird thing was, they were both virgins when they met, somehow missing the perhaps overblown sexual revolution of the seventies and early eighties. Myron always believed that the revolution was mostly hype or, at the very least, that it didn't seep past the brick façades of suburban high schools. But then again, he was pretty good at self-rationalization. More likely, it was his fault—if you could consider not being promiscuous a fault. He'd always been attracted to the "nice" girls, even in high school. Casual affairs never interested him. Every girl he met was gauged as a potential life partner, a soul mate, an undying love, as though every relationship should be a Carpenters song.

But with Emily it had been complete sexual exploration and discovery. They learned from each other in stuttering, though achingly blissful, steps. Even now, as much as he detested her very being, he could still feel the tightening, could still recall the way his nerve endings would sing and surge when they were in bed. Or the back of a car. Or a movie theater or a library or once even during a poly sci lecture on Hobbes's *Leviathan*. While he may have yearned to be a Carpenters man, his first long-term relationship had ended up more like something off Meat Loaf's *Bat Out of Hell* album— hot, heavy, sweaty, fast, the whole "Paradise by the Dashboard Light."

Still, there had to have been more to it. He and Emily had lasted three years. He had loved her, and she'd been the first to break his heart.

"There a coffee bar near here?" she asked.

"A Starbucks," Myron said.

"I'll drive."

"I don't want to go with you, Emily."

She gave him the smile. "Lost my charms, have I?"

"They lost their effect on me a long time ago." Half lie.

She shifted her hips. Myron watched, thinking about what Esperanza had said. It wasn't just her voice or her words—even her movements ended up a double entendre. "It's important, Myron."

"Not to me."

"You don't even know—"

"It doesn't matter, Emily. You're the past. So is your husband—"

"My *ex*-husband. I divorced him, remember? And I never knew what he did to you."

"Right," Myron said. "You were just the cause."

She looked at him. "It's not that simple. You know that."

He nodded. She was right, of course. "I always knew why I did it," Myron said. "I was being a competitive dumbass who wanted to get one up on Greg. But why you?"

Emily shook her head. The old hair would have flown side to side, ending up half covering her face. Her new coif was shorter and more stylized, but his mind's eye still saw the kinky flow. "It doesn't matter anymore," she said.

"Guess not," he said, "but I've always been curious."

"We both had too much to drink."

"Simple as that?"

"Yes."

Myron made a face. "Lame," he said.

"Maybe it was just about sex," she said.

"A purely physical act?"

"Maybe."

"The night before you married someone else?"

She looked at him. "It was dumb, okay?"

"You say so."

"And maybe I was scared," she said.

"Of getting married?"

"Of marrying the wrong man."

Myron shook his head. "Jesus, you're shameless."

Emily was about to say more, but she stopped as though her last reserves had suddenly been zapped away. He wanted her gone, but with ex-loves there is also a pulling sadness. There before you stands the true road untraveled, the lifetime what-if, the embodiment of a totally alternate life if things had gone a little different. He had absolutely no interest in her anymore, yet her words still drew out his old self, wounds and all.

"It was fourteen years ago," she said softly. "Don't you think it's time we moved on?"

He thought about what that "purely physical" night had cost him. Everything, maybe. His lifelong dream, for sure. "You're right," he said, turning away. "Please leave."

"I need your help."

He shook his head. "As you said, time to move on."

"Just have coffee with me. With an old friend."

He wanted to say no, but the past had too strong a pull. He nodded, afraid to speak. They drove in silence to Starbucks and ordered their complicated coffees from an artist-wannabe *barista* with more attitude than the guy who works at the local record store. They added whatever condiments at the little stand, playing a game of Twister by reaching across one another for the non-fat milk or Equal. They sat down in metal chairs with too-low backs. The sound system was playing reggae music, a CD entitled *Jamaican Me Crazy*.

Emily crossed her legs and took a sip. "Have you ever heard of Fanconi anemia?"

Interesting opening gambit. "No."

15

"It's an inherited anemia that leads to bone marrow failure. It weakens your chromosomes."

Myron waited.

"Are you familiar with bone marrow transplants?"

Strange line of questioning, but he decided to play it straight. "A little. A friend of mine had leukemia and needed a transplant. They had a marrow drive at the temple. We all went down and got tested."

"When you say 'we all'—"

"Mom, Dad, my whole family. I think Win went too."

She tilted her head. "How is Win?"

"The same."

"Sorry to hear that," she said. "When we were at Duke, he used to listen to us making love, didn't he?"

"Only when we pulled down the shade so he couldn't watch."

She laughed. "He never liked me."

"You were his favorite."

"Really?"

"That's not saying much," Myron said.

"He hates women, doesn't he?"

Myron thought about it. "As sex objects, they're fine. But in terms of relationships . . ."

"An odd duck."

She should only know.

Emily took a sip. "I'm stalling," she said.

"I sorta figured that."

"What happened to your friend with leukemia?"

"He died."

Her face went white. "I'm sorry. How old was he?"

"Thirty-four."

Emily took another sip, cradling the mug with both hands. "So you're listed with the bone marrow national registry?"

"I guess. I gave blood and they gave me a donor card."

She closed her eyes.

"What?" he asked.

"Fanconi anemia is fatal. You can treat it for a while with blood transfusions and hormones, but the only cure is a bone marrow transplant."

"I don't understand, Emily. Do you have this disease?"

"It doesn't hit adults." She put down her coffee and looked up. He was not big on reading eyes, but the pain was neon-obvious. "It hits children."

As though on cue, the Starbucks soundtrack changed to something instrumental and somber. Myron waited. It didn't take her long.

"My son has it," she said.

Myron remembered visiting the house in Franklin Lakes when Greg disappeared, the boy playing in the backyard with his sister. Must have been, what, two, three years ago. The boy was about ten, his sister maybe eight. Greg and Emily were in the midst of a bloody take-no-prisoners custody battle, the two children pinned down in the crossfire, the kind no one walks away from without a serious hit.

"I'm sorry," he said.

"We need to find a bone marrow match."

"I thought siblings were an almost automatic match."

Her eyes flicked around the room. "One-in-four chance," she said, stopping abruptly.

"Oh."

"The national registry found only three potential donors. By potential I mean that the initial HLA tests showed them as possibilities. The A and B match, but then they have to do a full blood and tissue workup to see—" She stopped again. "I'm getting technical. I don't mean to. But when your kid is sick like this, it's like you live in a snow globe of medical jargon."

"I understand."

"Anyway, getting past the initial screening is like winning a second-tier lottery ticket. The chance of a match is still slim. The blood center calls in the potential donors and runs a battery of tests, but the odds they'll be a close enough match to go through with the transplant are pretty low, especially with only three potential donors."

Myron nodded, still having no idea why she was telling him any of this.

"We got lucky," she said. "One of the three was a match with Jeremy."

"Great."

"There's a problem," she said. Again the crooked smile. "The donor is missing."

"What do you mean, missing?"

"I don't have the details. The registry is confidential. No one will tell me what's going on. We seemed to be on the right track, and then all of a sudden, the donor just pulled out. My doctor can't say anything—like I said, it's protected."

"Maybe the donor just changed his mind."

"Then we better change it back," she said, "or Jeremy dies."

The statement was plain enough.

"So what do you think happened?" Myron asked. "You think he's missing or something?"

"He or she," Emily said. "Yes."

"He or she?"

"I don't know anything about the donor—age, sex,

where they live, nothing. But Jeremy isn't getting any better and the odds of finding another donor in time are, well, almost nonexistent." She kept the face tight, but Myron could see the foundation starting to crack a bit. "We have to find this donor."

"And that's why you've come to me? To find him?"

"You and Win found Greg when no one else could. When he disappeared, Clip went to you first. Why?"

"That's a long story."

"Not so long, Myron. You and Win are trained in this sort of thing. You're good at it."

"Not in a case like this," Myron said. "Greg is a high-profile athlete. He can take to the airwaves, offer rewards. He can buy private detectives."

"We're already doing that. Greg has a press conference set up for tomorrow."

"So?"

"So it won't work. I told Jeremy's doctor we would pay anything to the donor, even though it's illegal. But something else is wrong here. I'm afraid all the publicity might even backfire—that it may send the donor deeper into hiding or something, I don't know."

"What does Greg say to that?"

"We don't talk much, Myron. And when we do, it's usually not very pretty."

"Does Greg know you're talking to me now?"

She looked at him. "He hates you as much as you hate him. Maybe more so."

Myron decided to take that as a no. Emily kept her eyes on him, searching his face as though there were an answer there.

"I can't help you, Emily."

She looked like she'd just been slapped.

"I sympathize," he went on, "but I'm just getting

over some major problems of my own."

"Are you saying you don't have time?"

"It's not that. A private detective would have a better chance—"

"Greg's hired four already. They can't even find out the donor's name."

"I doubt I can do any better."

"This is my son's life, Myron."

"I understand, Emily."

"Can't you put aside your animosity for me and Greg?"

He wasn't sure that he could. "That's not the issue. I'm a sports agent, not a detective."

"That didn't stop you before."

"And look how things ended up. Every time I meddle, it leads to disaster."

"My son is thirteen years old, Myron."

"I'm sorry—"

"I don't want your sympathy, dammit." Her eyes were smaller now, black. She leaned toward him until her face was scant inches from his. "I want you to do the math."

He looked puzzled. "What?"

"You're an agent. You know all about numbers, right? So do the math."

Myron tilted back, giving himself a little distance. "What the hell are you talking about?"

"Jeremy's birthday is July eighteenth," she said. "Do the math."

"What math?"

"One more time: He's thirteen years old. He was born July the eighteenth. I was married October tenth."

Nothing. For several seconds, he heard the mothers chatting over one another, one baby cry, one *barista* call out an order to another, and then it happened. A cold gust blew across Myron's heart. Steel bands wrapped around his chest, making it almost impossible to breathe. He opened his mouth but nothing came out. It was like someone had whacked his solar plexus with a baseball bat. Emily watched him and nodded.

"That's right," she said. "He's your son."

3

You can't know that for sure," Myron said.

Emily's whole persona screamed exhaustion. "I do."

"You were sleeping with Greg too, right?"

"Yes."

"And we only had that one night during that time. You probably had a whole bunch with Greg."

"True."

"So how can you possibly know—?"

"Denial," she interjected with a sigh. "The first step."

He pointed a finger at her. "Don't hand me that psychology-major crap, Emily."

"Moving quickly to anger," she continued.

"You can't know—"

"I've always known," she interrupted.

Myron sat back. He stayed composed but underneath he could almost feel the fissure widening, his foundation starting to shift.

"When I first got pregnant, I figured like you: I'd slept with Greg more, so it was probably his baby. At least, that's what I told myself." She closed her eyes. Myron stayed very still, the knot in his stomach tightening. "And when Jeremy was born, he favored me, so who was to say? But—and this is going to sound so goddamn stupid—a mother knows. I can't tell you how. But I knew. I tried to deny it too. I told myself I was just feeling guilty over what we'd done, and that this was God's way of punishing me."

"How Old Testament of you," Myron said.

"Sarcasm," she said with almost a smile. "Your favorite defense."

"Your maternal intuition hardly counts as evidence, Emily."

"You asked before about Sara."

"Sara?"

"Jeremy's sister. You wondered about her matching as a donor. She didn't."

"Right, but you said there was only a one-in-four chance with siblings."

"For *full* siblings, yes. But the match wasn't even close. Because she's only Jeremy's half sister."

"The doctor told you this?"

"Yes."

Myron felt the stone footing beneath his feet give way. "So . . . Greg knows?"

Emily shook her head. "The doctor pulled me aside. Because of the divorce, I'm Jeremy's primary custodian. Greg has custody too, but the children live with me. I'm in charge of the medical decisions."

"So Greg still believes . . . ?"

"That Jeremy is his, yes."

Myron was floundering in deep water with no land in sight. "But you said you've always known."

"Yes."

"Why didn't you tell me?"

"Are you kidding? I was married to Greg. I loved him. We were starting our life together."

"You still should have told me."

"When, Myron? When should I have told you?"

"As soon as the baby was born."

"Aren't you listening? I just told you I wasn't sure."

"A mother knows, you said."

"Come on, Myron. I was in love with Greg, not you. You with your corny sense of morality—you would have insisted I divorce Greg and marry you and live some suburban fairy tale."

"So instead you chose to live a lie?"

"It was the right decision based on what I knew then. With hindsight"—she stopped, took a deep sip—"I probably would have done a lot of things differently."

He tried to let some of it sink in, but it was a no-go. Another group of stroller-laced soccer moms entered the coffee shop. They took a corner table and started jabbering about little Brittany and Kyle and Morgan.

"How long have you and Greg been separated?" Myron's voice sounded sharper than he intended. Or maybe not.

"Four years now."

"And you were no longer in love with him, right? Four years ago?"

"Right."

"Earlier even," he went on. "I mean, you probably fell out of love with him a long time ago, right?"

She looked confused. "Right."

"So you could have told me then. At least four years ago. Why didn't you?"

"Stop cross-examining me."

"You're the one who dropped this bombshell," he said. "How do you expect me to react?"

"Like a man."

"What the hell does that mean?"

"I need your help. Jeremy needs your help. That's what we should be concentrating on."

"I want some answers first. I'm entitled to that much."

She hesitated, looked like she might argue, then

nodded wearily. "If it'll help you get past this—"

"Get past this? Like it's a kidney stone or something?"

"I'm too tired to fight with you," she said. "Just go on. Ask your questions."

"Why didn't you tell me before now."

Her eyes drifted over his shoulder. "I almost did," she said. "Once."

"When?"

"Do you remember when you came to the house? When Greg first vanished?"

He nodded. He had just been thinking about that day.

"You were looking out the window at him. He was in the yard with his sister."

"I remember," Myron said.

"Greg and I were going through that nasty custody battle."

"You accused him of abusing the children."

"It wasn't true. You realized that right away. It was just a legal ploy."

"Some ploy," Myron said. "Next time accuse him of war atrocities."

"Who are you to judge me?"

"Actually," Myron said, "I think I'm just the person."

Emily pinned him with her eyes. "Custody battles are war without the Geneva Accords," she said. "Greg got nasty. I got nasty back. You do whatever you have to in order to win."

"And that includes revealing that Greg wasn't Jeremy's father?"

"No."

"Why not?"

"Because I won custody anyway."

"That's not an answer. You hated Greg."

"Yes."

"Still do?" he asked.

"Yes." No hesitation.

"So why didn't you tell him?"

"Because as much as I loathe Greg," she said, "I love Jeremy more. I could hurt Greg. I'd probably enjoy it. But I couldn't do that to my son—take away his father like that."

"I thought you'd do anything to win."

"I'd do anything to Greg," she said, "not Jeremy."

It made sense, he guessed, but he suspected she was holding something back. "So you kept this secret for thirteen years."

"Yes."

"Do your parents know?"

"No."

"You never told anyone?"

"Never."

"So why are you telling me now?"

Emily shook her head. "Are you being purposely dense, Myron?"

He put his hands on the table. They weren't shaking. Somehow he understood that these questions came from more than mere curiosity; they were part of the defense mechanism, the internal barbed wire and moat he'd lavishly built to keep Emily's revelation from reaching him. He knew that what she was telling him was life altering in a way nothing he'd ever heard before was. The words *my son* kept floating through his subconscious. But they were just words right now. They'd get through eventually, he guessed, but for now the barbed wire and moat were holding.

"You think I wanted to tell you? I practically begged you to help, but you wouldn't listen. I'm desperate here."

"Desperate enough to lie?"

"Yes," she said, again with no hesitation. "But I'm not, Myron. You have to believe that."

He shrugged. "Maybe someone else is Jeremy's father."

"Excuse me?"

"A third party," he said. "You slept with me the night before your wedding. I doubt I was the only one. Could be one of a dozen guys."

She looked at him. "You want your pound of flesh, Myron? Go ahead, I can take it. But this isn't like you."

"You know me that well, huh?"

"Even when you got angry—even when you had every right to hate me—you've never been cruel. It's not your way."

"We're in uncharted waters here, Emily."

"Doesn't matter," she said.

He felt something well up, making it hard to breathe. He grabbed his mug, looked into it as though it might have an answer on the bottom, put it back down. He couldn't look at her. "How could you do this to me?"

Emily reached across the table and put her hand on his forearm. "I'm sorry," she said.

He pulled away.

"I don't know what else to say. You asked before why I never told you. My main concern was always Jeremy's welfare, but you were a consideration too."

"Bull."

"I know how you are, Myron. I know you can't just shrug this off. But for now you have to. You have to find the donor and save Jeremy's life. We can worry about the rest after that."

27

"How long has"—he almost said *my son*—"Jeremy been ill?"

"We learned about it six months ago. When he was playing basketball. He started getting bruised too easily. Then he was short of breath for no reason. He started falling down . . ." Her voice tailed off.

"Is he in the hospital?"

"No. He lives at home and goes to school and he looks fine, just a little pale. But he can't play competitive sports or anything like that. He seems to be doing well, but . . . it's just a matter of time. He's so anemic and his marrow cells are so weak that something will get him. Either he'll contract a life-threatening infection or if he manages to get past that, malignancies will eventually develop. We treat him with hormones. That helps, but it's a temporary treatment, not a cure."

"And a bone marrow transplant would be a cure?"

"Yes." Her face brightened with an almost religious fervor. "If the transplant takes, he can be completely cured. I've seen it happen with other kids."

Myron nodded, sat back, crossed his legs, uncrossed them. "Can I meet him?"

She looked down. The sound of the blender, probably making a frappuccino, exploded while the espresso maker shrieked its familiar mating call to the various lattes. Emily waited for the noise to die down. "I can't stop you. But I'm hoping you'll do the right thing here."

"That being?"

"It's hard enough being thirteen years old and almost terminally ill. Do you really want to take away his father too?"

Myron said nothing.

"I know you're in shock right now. And I know you have a million more questions. But you have to forget that for now. You have to work through your confusion, your anger, everything. The life of a thirteen-year-old boy—our son—is at stake. Concentrate on that, Myron. Find the donor, okay?"

He looked back toward the soccer moms, still cooing about their children. Listening to them, he felt an overwhelming pang.

"Where can I find Jeremy's doctor?" he asked.

4

When the elevator doors opened into the reception area of MB SportsReps, Big Cyndi reached out to Myron with two arms the approximate circumference of the marble columns at the Acropolis. Myron almost leaped out of the way—involuntary survival reflex and all—but he stayed still and closed his eyes. Big Cyndi embraced him, which was like being wrapped in wet attic insulation, and lifted him into the air.

"Oh, Mr. Bolitar!" she cried.

He grimaced and rode it out. Eventually she put him back down as though he were a porcelain doll she was returning to a shelf. Big Cyndi is six-six and on the planetoid side of three hundred pounds, the former intercontinental tag-team wrestling champion with Esperanza, aka Big Chief Mama to Esperanza's Little Pocahontas. Her head was cube shaped and topped with hair spiked to look like the Statue of Liberty on a bad acid trip. She wore more makeup than the cast of *Cats*, her clothing form-fitted like sausage casing, her scowl the stuff of sumos.

"Uh, everything okay?" Myron ventured.

"Oh, Mr. Bolitar!"

Big Cyndi looked like she was about to hug him again, but something stopped her, perhaps the stark terror in Myron's eyes. She picked up luggage that in her manhole-paw resembled a Close'N Play phonograph from the early seventies. She was that kind of big, the kind of big where the world around her always looked like a bad B-monster movie set and she was walking through a miniature Tokyo, knocking over power lines and swatting at buzzing fighter planes.

Esperanza appeared in her office doorway. She folded her arms and rested against the frame. Even after her recent ordeal, Esperanza still looked immensely beautiful, the shiny black ringlets still falling over her forehead just so, the dark olive skin still radiant—the whole image a sort of gypsy, peasant-blouse fantasy. But he could see some new lines around the eyes and a slight slouch in the perfect posture. He'd wanted her to take time off after her release, but he knew she wouldn't. Esperanza loved MB SportsReps. She wanted to save it.

"What's going on?" Myron asked.

"It's all in the letter, Mr. Bolitar," Big Cyndi said.

"What letter?"

"Oh, Mr. Bolitar!" she cried again.

"What?"

But she didn't respond, hiding her face in her hands and ducking into the elevator as though entering a tepee. The elevator doors slid closed, and she was gone.

Myron waited a beat and then turned to Esperanza. "Explanation?"

"She's taking a leave of absence," Esperanza said.

"Why?"

"Big Cyndi isn't stupid, Myron."

"I didn't say she was."

"She sees what's going on here."

"It's only temporary," Myron said. "We'll snap back."

"And when we do, Big Cyndi will come back. In the meantime she got a good job offer."

"With Leather-N-Lust?" Big Cyndi worked nights as a bouncer at an S&M bar called Leather-N-Lust.

Motto: Hurt the ones you love. Sometimes—or so he had heard—Big Cyndi was part of the stage show. What part she played Myron had no idea nor had he worked up the courage to ask—another taboo abyss his mind did its best to circumvent.

"No," Esperanza said. "She's returning to FLOW."

For the wrestling uninitiated, FLOW is the acronym for the Fabulous Ladies of Wrestling.

"Big Cyndi is going to wrestle again?"

Esperanza nodded. "On the senior circuit."

"Excuse me?"

"FLOW wanted to expand its product. They did some research, saw how well the PGA is doing with the senior golf tour and . . ." She shrugged.

"A senior ladies' wrestling tour?"

"More like retired," Esperanza said. "I mean, Big Cyndi is only thirty-eight. They're bringing back a lot of the old favorites: Queen Qaddafi, Cold War Connie, Brezhnev Babe, Cellblock Celia, Black Widow—"

"I don't remember the Black Widow."

"Before our time. Hell, before our parents' time. She must be in her seventies."

Myron tried not to make a face. "And people are going to pay money to see a seventy-year-old woman wrestle?"

"You shouldn't discriminate on the basis of age."

"Right, sorry." Myron rubbed his eyes.

"And professional women's wrestling is struggling right now, what with the competition from Jerry Springer and Ricki Lake. They need to do something."

"And grappling old ladies is the answer?"

"I think they're aiming more for nostalgia."

"A chance to cheer on the wrestler of your youth?"

"Didn't you go see Steely Dan in concert a couple of years ago?"

"That's different, don't you think?"

She shrugged. "Both past their prime. Both mining more on what you remember than what you see or hear."

It made sense. Scary sense maybe. But sense. "How about you?" Myron asked.

"What about me?"

"Didn't they want Little Pocahontas to return?"

"Yep."

"Were you tempted?"

"To what? Return to the ring?"

"Yes."

"Oh, sure," Esperanza said. "I busted my shapely ass working full-time while getting my law degree, so I could once again don a suede bikini and grope aging nymphs in front of drooling trailer trash." She paused. "Still, it is a step above being a sports agent."

"Ha-ha." Myron walked over to Big Cyndi's desk. There was an envelope with his name scrawled across the top in glow-in-the-dark orange.

"She wrote it in crayon?" Myron said.

"Eye shadow."

"I see."

"So are you going to tell me what's wrong?" she asked.

"Nothing," Myron said.

"Bullshit," she said. "You look like you just heard Wham split up."

"Don't bring that up," Myron said. "Sometimes, late at night, I still suffer flashbacks."

Esperanza studied his face a few more seconds. "This have something to do with your college sweetheart?"

"Sort of."

"Oh Christ."

"What?"

"How do I say this nicely, Myron? You are beyond moronic in the ways of women. Exhibits A and B are Jessica and Emily."

"You don't even know Emily."

"I know enough," she said. "I thought you didn't want to talk to her."

"I didn't. She found me at my parents' place."

"She just showed up there?"

"Yep."

"What did she want?"

He shook his head. He still wasn't ready to talk about it yet. "Any messages?"

"Not as many as we'd like."

"Win upstairs?"

"I think he went home already." She picked up her coat. "I think I'll do likewise."

"Good night."

"If you hear anything from Lamar—"

"I'll call you."

Esperanza put on her coat, flipping the glistening black flow out of the collar. Myron headed into his office and made a few phone calls, mostly of a recruiting nature. It was not going well.

Several months ago, a friend's death had sent Myron into a tail-spin, causing him to—and we're using complex psychiatric jargon here—wig out. Nothing overly drastic, no nervous breakdown or institutional commitment. He had instead fled to a deserted Caribbean island with Terese Collins, a beautiful TV anchorwoman he didn't know. He had told no one—not Win, not Esperanza, not even Mom and Dad—where he was going or when he'd be back.

As Win put it, when he wigged out, he wigged out in style.

By the time Myron was forced to return, their clients were scattering into the night like kitchen help during an immigration bust. Now Myron and Esperanza were back, attempting to revive the comatose and perhaps dying MB SportsReps. This was no easy task. The competition in this business was a dozen starving lions, and Myron was one heavily limping Christian.

The MB SportsReps office was nicely situated on Park Avenue and Forty-sixth Street in the Lock-Horne Building, owned by the family of Myron's college-and-current roommate, Win. The building was in primo midtown location and offered up some semi-dazzling views of the Manhattan skyline. Myron soaked it in for a moment and then looked down at the suits speeding below. The sight of the working ants always depressed him, a chorus of "Is That All There Is?" playing in his head.

He turned now toward his Client Wall, the one with action shots of all the athletes represented by MB SportsReps, which now looked as spotty and sparse as a bad hair transplant. He wanted to care, but unfair as it was to Esperanza, his heart wasn't really in it. He wanted to go back, to love MB and have that old hunger, but no matter how much he tried to stoke the old fire, it wouldn't flame up.

Emily called about an hour later.

"Dr. Singh doesn't have office hours tomorrow," Emily said. "But you can hook up during rounds tomorrow morning."

"Where?"

"Babies and Children's Hospital. It's part of Columbia Presbyterian on 167th Street. Tenth floor, south."

"What time?"

"Rounds start at eight," Emily said.

"Okay."

Brief silence.

"You okay, Myron?"

"I want to see him."

It took her a few seconds. "Like I said before, I can't stop you. But sleep on it, okay?"

"I just want to see him," Myron said. "I won't say anything. Not yet, at least."

"Can we talk about this tomorrow?" Emily asked.

"Yeah, sure."

She hesitated again. "Do you have Web access, Myron?"

"Yes."

"We have a private URL."

"What?"

"A private Web address. I take photos with the digital camera and post them there. For my parents. They moved to Miami last year. They check it out every week. Get to see new pictures of the grandkids. So if you want to see what Jeremy looks like . . ."

"What's the address?"

She gave it to him and Myron typed it in. He hung up before hitting the return button. The images came up slowly. He drummed his fingers on the desk. On top of the screen was a banner saying HI, NANA AND POP-POP. Myron thought about his parents and shook it off.

There were four photographs of Jeremy and Sara. Myron swallowed. He placed the arrow on Jeremy's image and clicked the mouse, zooming in closer, enlarging the boy's face. He tried to keep his breathing steady. He stared at the boy's face for a long time without really registering anything. Eventually his vision blurred, his own face reflecting on the monitor over the boy's, blending the images together, creating a visual echo of he knew not what.

5

Myron heard the cries of ecstasy through the door.

Win—real name: Windsor Horne Lockwood III—was letting Myron temporarily crash at his apartment in the Dakota on Seventy-second Street and Central Park West. The Dakota was an old New York landmark whose rich and lush history had been totally eclipsed by the murder of John Lennon twenty-some-odd years ago. Entering meant crossing over the spot where Lennon had bled to death, the feeling not unlike trampling over a grave. Myron was finally getting used to it.

From the outside, the Dakota was beautiful and dark and resembled a haunted house on steroids. Most apartments, including Win's, had more square footage than a European principality. Last year, after a lifetime of living in Mom and Dad's suburban sprawl, Myron had finally moved out of the basement and into a SoHo loft with his ladylove, Jessica. It was a huge step, the first sign that after more than a decade, Jessica was ready to—gasp!—commit. So the two lovers clasped hands and took the live-together plunge. And like so many plunges in life, it ended in an ugly splat.

More cries of ecstasy.

Myron pressed his ear against the door. Cries, yes, and a soundtrack. Not live action, he decided. He used his key and pushed open the door. The cries were coming from the TV room. Win never used that room for, uh, filming. Myron sighed and stepped through the portal.

Win wore his casual WASP uniform: khakis, shirt with a color so loud you couldn't look at it straight on except through a pinhole, loafers, no socks. His blond locks had been parted with the precision of old ladies dividing up a lunch check; his skin was the color of white china with dabs of golf-ruddy red on both cheeks. He sat yoga-lotus-style, his legs pretzeled to a point man was never supposed to achieve. His index fingers and thumbs formed two circles, the hands resting against the knees. Yuppie Zen. Old World European clashing heads with Ancient Oriental. The sweet smell of Main Line mixed with the heavy Asian incense.

Win breathed in for a twenty count, held it, breathed out for a twenty count. He was meditating, of course, but with a Win-like twist. He did not, for example, listen to soothing nature sounds or chimes; no, he preferred meditating to the sound tracks of, uh, skin flicks from the seventies, which basically sounded like a bad Jimi Hendrix impersonator making wah-wah-wah noises on an electric kazoo. Just listening to it was enough to make you rush out for a shot of antibiotics.

Win did not close his eyes either. He did not visualize a deer sipping water by a lapping stream or a gentle waterfall against green foliage or any of that. His gaze remained fixed on the television screen; more specifically, on homemade videotapes of himself and a potpourri of females in the throes of passion.

Myron stepped fully into the room. Win turned one of his finger-Os into a flat-palm stop sign, then lifted the index finger up to indicate he wanted another moment. Myron risked a glance at the screen, saw the writhing flesh, turned away.

A few seconds later, Win said, "Hello."

"I'd like my disgust noted for the record," Myron said.

"So noted."

Win moved fluidly from the lotus position to a full stand. He popped out the tape and put it in a box. The box was labeled *Anon 11*. *Anon*, Myron knew, stood for *Anonymous*. It meant Win had either forgotten her name or never learned it.

"I can't believe you still do this," Myron said.

"Are we moralizing again?" Win asked with a smile. "How nice for us."

"Let me ask you something."

"Oh, please do."

"Something I always wanted to know."

"My ears are all atwitter."

"Putting aside my repugnancy for a moment—"

"Not on my account," Win said. "I so enjoy when you're superior."

"You claim this"—Myron motioned vaguely at the videotape and then the TV screen—"relaxes you."

"Yes."

"But doesn't it also . . . I mean, sick as it is . . . doesn't it also arouse you?"

"Not at all," Win replied.

"That's the part I don't understand."

"Viewing the act does not arouse me," Win explained. "Thinking about the act does not arouse me. Videos, dirty magazines, *Penthouse Forum*, cyberporn—none of them arouse me. For me, there is no substitute for the real thing. A partner must be present. The rest has the same effect as tickling myself. It's why I never masturbate."

Myron said nothing.

"Problem?" Win asked.

"I'm just wondering what possessed me to ask," Myron said.

Win opened a Ming dynasty cabinet that had been converted into a small fridge and tossed Myron a Yoo-Hoo. He poured himself a snifter of cognac. The room was lush antiques and rich tapestries and Oriental carpets and busts of men with long, curly hair. If not for the state-of-the-art home entertainment system, the room could have been something you'd stumble across on a tour of a Medici palace.

They grabbed their usual seats.

Win said, "You look troubled."

"I have a case for us."

"Ah."

"I know I said we weren't going to do this anymore. But this is sort of a special circumstance."

"I see," Win said.

"Do you remember Emily?"

Win did that swirl thing with his snifter. "College girlfriend. Used to make monkey noises during sex. Dumped you in the beginning of our senior year. Married your archenemy Greg Downing. Dumped him too. Probably still makes monkey noises."

"She has a son," Myron said. "He's sick." He quickly explained the situation, leaving out the part about possibly being the kid's father. If he couldn't talk about it with Esperanza, there was no way he could raise the subject with Win.

When he finished, Win said, "It shouldn't be too difficult. You're going to talk to the doctor tomorrow?"

"Yes."

"Find out what you can about who handles the records."

Win picked up the remote and flicked on the television. He flipped the channels because there were a lot of commercials on and because he was male. He stopped at CNN. Terese Collins was anchoring the news.

"Is the lovely Ms. Collins visiting us tomorrow?" Win asked.

Myron nodded. "Her flight comes in at ten."

"She's been visiting quite a bit."

"Yep."

"Are you two"—Win crinkled his face as if someone had just flashed him a particularly nasty case of jock rot— "getting serious?"

Myron looked at Terese on the screen. "Still too new," he said.

There was an *All in the Family* marathon on cable, so Win flipped to it. They ordered in some Chinese food and watched two episodes. Myron tried to get lost in the bliss of Archie and Edith, but it wasn't happening. His thoughts naturally kept returning to Jeremy. He managed to deflect the paternity issue, concentrating, as Emily had asked, on the disease and task at hand. Fanconi anemia. That was what she said the boy had. Myron wondered if they had anything about it on the Web.

"I'll be back in a little while," Myron said.

Win looked at him. "The Stretch Cunningham funeral episode is up next."

"I want to check something on the Web."

"The episode where Archie gives the eulogy."

"I know."

"Where he comments that he never thought Stretch Cunningham was Jewish because of the 'ham' in his last name."

"I know the episode, Win."

"And you're willing to miss it for the sake of the Web?"

"You have it on tape."

"That's not the point."

The two men looked at each other, comfortable in the silence. After some time passed, Win said, "Tell me."

He barely hesitated. "Emily said I'm the boy's father."

Win nodded and said, "Ah."

"You don't sound surprised."

Win used the chopsticks to grab another shrimp. "You believe her?"

"Yes."

"Why?"

"For one thing, it's a hell of a thing to lie about it."

"But Emily is good at lying, Myron. She's always lied to you. She lied to you in college. She lied to you when Greg disappeared. She lied in court about Greg's behavior with the children. She betrayed Greg the night before their wedding by sleeping with you. And, if you will, if she is telling the truth now, she lied to you for the better part of thirteen years."

Myron thought about it. "I think she's telling the truth about this."

"You *think*, Myron."

"I'm going to take a blood test."

Win shrugged. "If you must."

"What does that mean?"

"I'll let the statement speak for itself."

Myron made a face. "Didn't you just say I should find out for sure?"

"Not at all," Win said. "I was merely pointing out the obvious. I didn't say it made a difference."

Myron thought about it. "You're confusing me."

"Simply put," Win said, "so what if you are the boy's biological father? What difference does it make?"

"Come on, Win. Not even you can be that cold."

"Quite the opposite. As strange as this might sound, I am using my heart on this one."

"How do you figure?"

Win swirled the liquid again, studied the amber, took a sip. It colored his cheeks a bit. "Again I'll put it simply: No matter what a blood test might indicate, you are not Jeremy Downing's father. Greg is. You may be a sperm donor. You may be an accident of lust and biology. You may have provided a simple microscopic cell structure that combined with one slightly more complex. But you are not this boy's father."

"It's not that simple, Win."

"It is that simple, my friend. The fact that you insipidly choose to confuse the issue does not change the fact. I'll demonstrate, if you'd like."

"I'm listening."

"You love your father, correct?"

"You know the answer to that."

"I do," Win said. "But what makes him your father? The fact that he once grunted on top of Mommy after a few drinks—or the way he has cared for you and loved you for the past thirty-five years?"

Myron looked down at the can of Yoo-Hoo.

"You owe this boy nothing," Win continued, "and equally important, he owes you nothing. We will try to save his life, if that is what you wish, but that should be where it ends."

Myron thought about it. The only thing scarier than Win irrational was when Win made sense. "Maybe you're right."

"But you still don't think it's that simple."

"I don't know."

On the television, Archie approached the pulpit, a yarmulke on his head. "It's a start," Win said.

6

Myron mixed childlike Froot Loops and very adult All-Bran into a bowl and poured on skim milk. For those not reading the Cliffs Notes, this act denotes that there is still a great deal of boy in the man. Heavy symbolism. How poignant.

The Number 1 train took Myron to a platform on 168th Street so far below ground that commuters had to take a urine-encapsulated elevator to reach the surface. The elevator was big and dark and shaky and brought on images of a PBS documentary on coal mining.

Located in Washington Heights, a quick stone's toss from Harlem and directly across Broadway from the Audubon Ballroom where Malcolm X was gunned down, Columbia Presbyterian Medical Center's famed pediatric building was called Babies and Children's Hospital. It used to be called just Babies Hospital, but a committee of learned medical experts was formed and after hours of intense study, they decided to change the name from Babies Hospital to Babies and Children's Hospital. Moral of the story: Committees are really, really important.

But the name, while not exactly Madison Avenue, does adequately reflect the reality of the situation—the hospital is strictly pediatric and deliveries, a well-worn twelve-floor edifice with eleven of them devoted to sick children. There was something very wrong with that, but probably nothing beyond the theologically obvious.

Myron stopped before the entranceway and looked up at the pollution-brown brick. Lots of misery in the city and much of it ended up here. He ducked inside and checked in at the security desk. He gave his name to a guard. The guard tossed him a pass, almost glancing up from his *TV Guide* in the process. Myron waited a long time for the elevator, reading the Patient's Bill of Rights, which was printed in both English and Spanish. There was a sign for the Sol Goldman Heart Center right next to a sign for the hospital's Burger King. Mixed messages or assuring future business—Myron wasn't sure which.

The elevator opened on the tenth floor. Directly in front of him, there was a rainbow-hued "Save the Rain Forest" mural, painted, according to the sign, by the "pediatric patients" of the hospital. Save the Rain Forest. Oh, like these kids didn't have enough on their plate, right?

Myron asked a nurse where he might find Dr. Singh. The nurse pointed to a woman leading a dozen interns through the corridor. Myron was a little surprised to see that Dr. Singh was of the female persuasion, mostly because he had somehow imagined her being a man. Terribly sexist, but there you go.

Dr. Singh was, as her name strongly implied, Indian, from-India Indian as opposed to Native American Indian. Mid-thirties, he figured, her hair a lighter brown than what he was used to seeing on India Indians. She wore a white doctor coat, of course. So did all the interns, most of them appearing to be about fourteen years of age, their white coats more like smocks, like they were about to finger-paint or maybe dissect a frog in a junior high biology class. Some wore grave expressions that were almost laughable on their cherubic faces, but most emanated that medical-intern exhaustion from too many nights on call.

Only two of the interns were men—boys really—both sporting blue jeans, colorful ties, and white sneakers like waiters at Bennigan's. The women—to call them girls would use up Myron's anti-PC quota for the week—favored hospital scrubs. So young. Babies taking care of babies.

Myron followed the group at a semi-discreet distance. Every once in a while he glanced in a room and immediately regretted it. The corridor walls were festive and brightly painted, jammed with Disney/Nick Junior/PBS kiddie images and collages and mobiles, but Myron only saw black. A floor filled with dying children. Bald little boys and girls in pain, their veins blackened by toxins and poisons. Most of the children looked so calm and unafraid and unnaturally brave. If you wanted to see the stark terror, you had to look in the eyes of the parents, as though Mom and Dad were sucking the horror toward them, taking it on so that their child wouldn't have to.

"Mr. Bolitar?"

Dr. Singh met his eye and held out her hand. "I'm Karen Singh."

Myron almost asked her how she did this, how she stayed on this floor day in and day out, watching children die. But he didn't. They exchanged the usual pleasantries. Myron had expected an Indian accent, but the only thing he picked up was a little Bronx.

"We can talk in here," she said.

She pushed open one of the superheavy, superwide doors endemic to hospitals and nursing homes, and they stepped into an empty room with stripped beds. The barrenness ignited Myron's imagination. He could almost see a loved one rushing into the hospital, repeatedly pushing the elevator call button, diving inside, pushing more buttons, sprinting down the corridor into this silent room, the bed being stripped by a nurse, then the sudden cry of anguish . . .

Myron shook his head. He watched too much TV.

Karen Singh sat on the corner of the mattress, and Myron studied her face for a moment. She had long sharp features. Everything pointed down—her nose, her chin, her eyebrows. Sort of harsh.

"You're staring," she said.

"I don't mean to."

She pointed to her forehead. "You were maybe expecting a dot?"

"Er, no."

"Very good, then let's get to it, shall we?"

"Okay."

"Mrs. Downing wants me to tell you whatever you want to know."

"I appreciate your taking the time."

"Are you a private investigator?" she asked.

"More like a family friend."

"Did you play basketball with Greg Downing?"

Myron was always surprised by the memory of the public. After all these years, people could still recall his big games, his big shots, sometimes with more clarity than Myron could. "You're a fan?"

"Nope," she said. "Can't stand sports actually."

"So how did you—"

"Just a deduction. You're tall and about the right age and you said you were a family friend. So . . ." She shrugged.

"Nice deduction."

"It's what we do here when you think about it. Deduce. Some diagnoses are easy. Others must be deduced from the evidence. You ever read Sherlock Holmes?"

"Sure."

"Sherlock said that you should never theorize before you have facts—because then you twist facts to suit theories rather than twisting theories to suit facts. If you see a misdiagnosis, nine times out of ten they ignored Sherlock's axiom."

"Did that happen with Jeremy Downing?"

"As a matter of fact," she said, "it did."

Somewhere down the hall, a machine started beeping. The sound hit the nerves like a police taser.

"So his first doctor screwed up?"

"I won't get into that. But Fanconi anemia isn't common. And because it looks like other things, it's often misdiagnosed."

"So tell me about Jeremy."

"What's to tell? He has it. Fanconi anemia, that is. In simple terms, his bone marrow is corrupted."

"Corrupted?"

"In layman's term, it's shit. It makes him susceptible to a host of infections and even cancers. It commonly turns into AML." She saw the puzzled look on his face and added, "That's acute myelogenous leukemia."

"But you can cure him?"

" 'Cure' is an optimistic word," she said. "But with a bone marrow transplant and treatments with a new fludarabine compound, yes, I believe his prognosis is excellent."

"Fluda-what?"

"Not important. We need a bone marrow donor that matches Jeremy. That's what counts here."

"And you don't have one."

Dr. Singh shifted on the mattress. "That's correct."

Myron felt the resistance. He decided to back off, test another flank. "Could you take me through the transplant process?"

"Step by step?"

"If it's not too much trouble."

She shrugged. "First step: find a donor."

"How do you go about that?"

"You try family members, of course. Siblings have the best chance of matching. Then parents. Then people of similar background."

"When you say people of similar background—"

"Blacks with blacks, Jews with Jews, Latino descent with Latino descent. You'll see that quite often in marrow drives. If the patient is, for example, a Hasidic Jew, the donation drives will take place within their shuls. Mixed blood is usually the hardest to match."

"And Jeremy's blood or whatever you need to match—it's fairly rare?"

"Yes."

Emily and Greg were both of Irish descent. Myron's family came from the usual potpourri of old Russia and Poland and even a little Palestine thrown in. Mixed blood. He thought about the paternity implications.

"So after you exhausted the family, how do you search for the match?"

"You go to the national registry."

"Where are they located?"

"In Washington. You listed?"

Myron nodded.

"They keep computer records there. We search for a preliminary match in their banks."

"Okay, now assuming you find a match in the computer—"

"A *preliminary* match," she corrected. "The local

center calls the potential donor and asks them to come in. They run a battery of tests. But the odds of matching are still fairly slim."

Myron could see that Karen Singh was relaxing, comfortable with the familiar subject matter, which was exactly what he wanted. Interrogations are a funny thing. Sometimes you go for the full frontal attack, and sometimes you sidle up, friendly-like, and sneak in the back. Win put it simpler: Sometimes you get more ants with honey, but you should always pack a can of Raid.

"Let's suppose you find a full-fledged donor," Myron said. "What then?"

"The center acquires the donor's permission."

"When you say 'center,' do you mean the national registry in Washington?"

"No, I mean the local center. Do you have your donor card in your wallet?"

"Yes."

"Let me see it."

Myron took out his wallet, flipped through about a dozen supermarket discount cards, three video club memberships, a couple of those buy-a-hundred-coffees-get-ten-cents-off-the-hundredth coupon, that sort of thing. He found the donor card and handed it to her.

"See here," she said, pointing to the back. "Your local center is in East Orange, New Jersey."

"So if I was a preliminary match, the East Orange center would call me?"

"Yes."

"And if I ended up being a full match?"

"You'd sign some papers and donate marrow."

"Is that like donating blood?"

Karen Singh handed the card back to him and shifted

again. "Harvesting bone marrow is a more invasive procedure."

Invasive. Every profession has its own buzzwords. "How so?"

"For one thing, you have to be put under."

"Anesthesia?"

"Yes."

"And then what do they do?"

"A doctor sticks a needle through the bone and sucks the marrow out with a syringe."

Myron said, "Eeuw."

"As I just explained, you're not awake during the procedure."

"Still," Myron said, "it sounds much more complicated than giving blood."

"It is," she said. "But the procedure is safe and relatively painless."

"But people must balk. I mean, most probably signed up the same way I did: They had a friend who was sick and ran a drive. For someone you know and care about, sure, you're willing to make a sacrifice. But for a stranger?"

Karen Singh's eyes found his and settled in hard. "You are saving a life, Mr. Bolitar. Think about that. How many opportunities do you get to save a fellow human being's life?"

He had hit a nerve. Good. "Are you saying people don't balk?"

"I'm not saying it never happens," she said, "but most people do the right thing."

"Does the donor get to meet the person he or she is saving?"

"No. It's totally anonymous. Confidentiality is very important here. Everything is held in the utmost secrecy."

They were getting to it now, and Myron could sense that her defenses were starting to slide back up like a car window. He decided to pull back again, let her resettle on comfy ground. "What's the patient going through during all this?" he asked.

"At what point?"

"While the marrow is being harvested. How do you prep the patient?" Prep. Myron had said "prep." Like a real doctor. Who said watching *St. Elsewhere* was a waste of time?

"It depends on what you're treating," Dr. Singh said. "But for most diseases, the recipient goes through about a week's worth of chemotherapy."

Chemotherapy. One of those words that hush a room like a nun's scowl. "They get chemo before the transplant?"

"Yes."

"I would think that would weaken them," Myron said.

"To some degree, yes."

"Why would you do it, then?"

"You have to. You're giving the recipient new bone marrow. Before you do that, you have to kill the old marrow. With leukemia, for example, the amount of chemo is high because you have to kill off all the living marrow. In the case of Fanconi anemia, you can be less aggressive because the marrow is already very weak."

"So you kill off all the bone marrow?"

"Yes."

"Isn't that dangerous?"

Dr. Singh gave him the steady eyes again. "This is a dangerous procedure, Mr. Bolitar. You are in effect replacing a person's bone marrow."

"And then?"

"And then the patient is infused with new marrow through an IV. He or she is kept isolated in a sterile environment for the first two weeks."

"Quarantined?"

"In effect. Do you remember the old TV movie *The Boy in the Plastic Bubble*?"

"Who doesn't?"

Dr. Singh smiled.

"Is that what the patient lives in?" Myron asked.

"A bubble chamber of sorts, yes."

"I had no idea," Myron said. "And this works?"

"Rejection is always a possibility, of course. But our success rate is quite high. In the case of Jeremy Downing, he can live a normal, active life with the transplant."

"And without it?"

"We can keep treating him with male hormones and growth factors, but his premature death is inevitable."

Silence. Except for that steady mechanical beep coming from down the hall.

Myron cleared his throat. "When you said that everything involving the donor is confidential—"

"I meant totally."

Enough wading. "How does that sit with you, Dr. Singh?"

"What do you mean?"

"The national registry located a donor who matched Jeremy, didn't they?"

"I believe so, yes."

"So what happened?"

She tapped her chin with her index finger. "May I speak candidly?"

"Please."

"I believe in the need for secrecy and confidentiality. Most people don't understand how easy, painless, and important it is to put their name in the registry. All they have to do is give a little blood. Just a little tube of the stuff, less than you would for any blood donation. Do that simple act—and you can save a life. Do you understand the significance of that?"

"I think so."

"We in the medical community must do all we can to encourage people to join the bone marrow registry. Education, of course, is important. So, too, is confidentiality. It has to be honored. The donors have to trust us."

She stopped, crossed her legs, leaned back on her hands. "But in this case, something of a quandary has developed. The importance of confidentiality is bumping up against the welfare of my patient. For me, the quandary is easy to resolve. The Hippocratic oath trumps all. I'm not a lawyer or a priest. My priority must be to save the life, not protect confidences. My guess is that I'm not the only doctor that feels that way. Perhaps that's why we have no contact with the donors. The blood center—in your case, the one in East Orange—does everything. They harvest the marrow and ship it to us."

"Are you saying that you don't know who the donor is?"

"That's right."

"Or if it's a he or she or where they live or anything?"

Karen Singh nodded. "I can only tell you that the national registry found a match. They called and told me so. I later received a call telling me that the donor was no longer available."

"What does that mean?"

"My question exactly."

"Did they give you an answer?"

"No," she said. "And while I see things on the micro level, the national registry has to remain macro. I respect that."

"You just gave up?"

She stiffened at his words. Her eyes went small and black. "No, Mr. Bolitar, I did not give up. I raged against the machine. But the people at the national registry are not ogres. They understand that this is a life-or-death situation. If a donor backs out, they try their best to bring them back into the fold. They do everything I would do to convince the donor to go through with it."

"But nothing worked here?"

"That seems to be the case."

"The donor would be told that he's sentencing a thirteen-year-old boy to death?"

She didn't hesitate. "Yes."

Myron threw up his hands. "So what do we conclude here, Doctor? That the donor is a selfish monster?"

Karen Singh chewed on that one for a moment. "Perhaps," she said. "Or perhaps the answer is simpler."

"For example?"

"For example," she said, "maybe the center can't find the donor."

Hello. Myron sat up a bit. "What do you mean, 'can't find'?"

"I don't know what happened here. The center won't tell me, and that's probably how it should be. I'm the patient's advocate. It's their job to deal with the donors. But I believe they were"—she stopped, searching for the right word—"perplexed."

"What makes you say that?"

"Nothing concrete. Just a feeling that this might be more than a donor with cold feet."

"How do we find out?"

"I don't know."

"How do we find the donor's name?"

"We can't."

"There has to be a way," Myron said. "Play pretend with me. How could I do it?"

She shrugged. "Break into the computer system. That's the only way I know."

"The computer in Washington?"

"They network with the local centers. But you'd have to know codes and passwords. Maybe a good hacker could get through, I don't know."

Hackers, Myron knew, worked better in the movies than in real life. A few years ago, maybe—but most computer systems nowadays were secure against such invasions.

"How long do we have here, Doctor?"

"There's no way of telling. Jeremy is reacting well to the hormones and growth factors. But it's only a question of time."

"So we have to find a donor."

"Yes." Karen Singh stopped, looked at Myron, looked away.

"Is there something else?" Myron asked.

She did not face him. "There is one other remote possibility," she said.

"What?" Myron asked.

"Keep in mind what I said before. I'm the patient's advocate. It's my job to explore every possible avenue to save him."

Her voice was funny now.

"I'm listening," Myron said.

Karen Singh rubbed her palms on her pant legs. "If Jeremy's biological parents were to conceive again, there is a twenty-five percent chance that the offspring would be a match."

She looked at Myron.

"I don't think that's a possibility," he said.

"Even if it's the only way to save Jeremy's life?"

Myron had no reply. An orderly walked by, looked in the room, mumbled an apology, left. Myron stood and thanked her.

"I'll show you to the elevator," Dr. Singh said.

"Thank you."

"There's a lab on the first floor in the Harkness Pavilion." She handed him a slip of paper. Myron looked at it. It was an order form. "I understand you might want to take a certain confidential blood test."

Neither of them said anything else as they walked toward the elevators. There were several children being wheeled through the corridor. Dr. Singh smiled at them, the pointed features softening into something almost celestial. Again the children looked unafraid. Myron wondered if the calmness spawned from ignorance or acceptance. He wondered if the children did not understand the gravity of what was happening to them or if they possessed a quiet clarity their parents would never know. Such philosophical queries, Myron knew, were best left to those more learned. But maybe the answer was simpler than he imagined: The children's suffering would be relatively short; their parents' would be eternal.

When they reached the elevator, Myron said, "How do you do it?"

She knew what he meant. "I could say something fancy about finding solace in helping, but the truth is, I block and I compartmentalize. It's the only way."

The elevator door opened, but before Myron could move he heard a familiar voice say, "What the hell are you doing here?"

Greg Downing stepped toward him.

7

Too much history. Again.

The last time the two men had been in the same room, Myron was straddled over Greg's chest, trying to kill him, punching him repeatedly in the face until Win—Win of all people—pulled him off. Three years ago. Myron hadn't seen him since, except on highlight films during the evening news.

Greg Downing glared at Myron, then at Karen Singh, then back at Myron as though he expected him to have evaporated by then.

"What the hell are you doing here?" he asked again.

Greg was clad in a flannel shirt over some waffle knit you'd buy at Baby Gap, faded jeans, and preternaturally scuffed work boots. The Suburban Lumberjack.

Something sparked hot in Myron's chest, ignited, took flight.

From the day they first battled for a rebound in the sixth grade, Greg and Myron were the pure definition of cross-town rivals. In high school, where their competitive cup truly runneth over, Greg and Myron met up eight times, splitting the games evenly. Rumor had it that there was bad blood between the budding superstars, but that was just standard sports hyperbole. The truth was, Myron barely knew Greg off the court. They were killer competitors, sure, willing to do just about anything to win, but once the final buzzer sounded, the two boys shook hands and the rivalry hibernated until the next opening tap.

Or so Myron had always thought.

When he accepted a scholarship at Duke and Greg chose the University of North Carolina, basketball fans rejoiced. Their seemingly innocent rivalry was ready for ACC prime time. Myron and Greg did not disappoint. The Duke-UNC matchups drew fantastic television ratings, no game decided by more than three points. Both had spectacular college careers. Both were named first-team All-Americans. Both were on covers of *Sports Illustrated*, once even sharing it. But the rivalry stayed on the court. They would do battle until bloody, but the competition never overlapped into their personal arenas.

Until Emily.

Before the start of senior year, Myron broached the subject of marriage with Emily. The next day she came to him, held his hands, looked into his eyes, and said, "I'm not sure I love you." Bam, like that. He still wondered what happened. Too much too soon, he guessed. A need to spread the proverbial wings a bit, play the proverbial field, what have you. Time passed. Three months, by Myron's count. Then Emily took up with Greg. Myron publicly shrugged it off—even when Greg and Emily got engaged just before graduation. The NBA draft took place right about then too. Both went in the first round, though Greg was surprisingly picked before Myron.

That was when it all unraveled.

The end result?

Almost a decade and a half later, Greg Downing was winding down an All-Star pro basketball career. People cheered him. He made millions and was famous. He played the game he loved. For Myron, his lifelong dream had ended before it had begun. During his first preseason game with the Celtics, Big Burt Wesson had slammed into him, sandwiching Myron's knee between himself and another player. There was a snap, crackle, pop—and then a hot, ripping pain, as though metal talons were shredding his kneecap into thin strips.

His knee never recovered.

A freak accident. Or so everyone thought. Including Myron. For more than ten years, he'd believed that the injury was merely a fluke, the fickle work of the Fates. But now he knew better. Now he knew the man who stood in front of him had been the cause. Now he knew that their seemingly innocent childhood rivalry had grown monstrous, had feasted upon his dream, had slaughtered Greg and Emily's marriage, and had in all probability led to the birth of Jeremy Downing.

He felt his hands tighten into fists. "I was just leaving."

Greg put a hand on Myron's chest. "I asked you a question."

Myron stared at the hand. "One good thing," he said.

"What?"

"No transportation time," Myron said. "We're already at the hospital."

Greg sneered. "You sucker-punched me last time."

"You want to go again?"

"Pardon me," Karen Singh said. "But are you guys for real?"

Greg kept glaring at Myron.

"Stop it," Myron said, "or I'll wet myself."

"You're a son of a bitch."

"And you're not on my Christmas card list either, Greggy-poo." Greggy-poo. Very mature.

Greg leaned closer. "You know what I'd like to do to you, Bolitar?"

"Kiss me on the lips? Buy me flowers?"

"Flowers for your grave maybe."

Myron nodded. "Good one, Greg. I mean, ouch, I'm wounded."

Karen Singh said, "Just because this is a children's floor doesn't mean you two have to act like ones."

Greg took a step back, his eyes never leaving Myron. "Emily," he spat suddenly. "She called you, right?"

"I have nothing to say to you, Greg."

"She asked you to find the donor. Like you found me."

"You always were a bright boy."

"I'm calling a press conference today. I'm going to make a direct appeal to the donor. Offer a reward."

"Good."

"So we don't need you, Bolitar."

Myron looked at Greg, and for a moment they were back on the court, faces drenched with sweat, the crowd cheering, the clock ticking down, the ball bouncing. Nirvana. Gone forever. Snatched away by Greg. And by Emily. And maybe most of all, when he looked at it honestly, by Myron's own stupidity.

"I've got to go," Myron said.

Greg took a step back. Myron moved past him and pressed the elevator button.

"Hey, Bolitar."

He faced Greg.

"I came here to talk to the doc about my son," Greg said, "not rehash our past."

Myron said nothing. He turned back to the elevator.

"You think you can help save my boy?" Greg asked.

Myron's mouth went dry. "I don't know."

The elevator dinged and opened. There were no good-byes, no nods, no further communication of any sort. Myron stepped inside and let the doors close. When he reached the first level, he went to the lab. He rolled up his sleeve. A woman drew his blood, untied the tourniquet, and said, "Your doctor will be in touch with you about the results."

8

Win was bored, so he drove Myron to the airport to pick up Terese. His foot pushed down on the gas pedal as though it had offended him. The Jag flew. As was his custom when driving with Win, Myron kept his eyes averted.

"It would appear," Win began, "that our best option would be to locate a satellite marrow clinic in a somewhat remote area. Upstate maybe or in western Jersey. We would then break in at night with a computer expert."

"Won't work," Myron said.

"Por qua?"

"The Washington center shuts down the computer network at six o'clock. Even if we were to break in, we couldn't bring up the mainframe."

Win said, "Hmm."

"Don't fret," Myron said. "I have a plan."

"When you talk like that," Win said, "my nipples harden."

"I thought only the real thing aroused you."

"This isn't the real thing?"

They parked in JFK Airport's short-term parking and reached the Continental Airlines gate ten minutes before the flight touched down. When the passengers began to appear, Win said, "I'll stand over in the corner."

"Why?"

"I wouldn't want to cast a shadow on your greeting," he said. "And standing over there affords me a better view of Ms. Collins's derrière."

Ah, Win.

Two minutes later, Terese Collins—to use a purely transportational term—disembarked. She was casually decked out in a white blouse and green slacks. Her brown hair was up in a ponytail. People lightly elbowed one another, whispering and subtly gesturing, giving her that surreptitious glance, the one that says "I recognize you but don't want to appear fawning."

Terese approached Myron and offered up her breaking-to-commercial smile. It was small and tight, trying to be friendly but reminding viewers that she was telling them about war and pestilence and tragedy and that maybe a big happy smile would be somewhat obscene. They hugged a little too tightly, and Myron felt the familiar sadness overwhelm him. It happened to him every time they hugged—a sense that something inside of him was crumbling anew. He sensed that the same thing happened to her.

Win came over.

"Hello, Win," she said.

"Hello, Terese."

"Checking out my ass again?"

"I prefer the term 'derriere.' And yes."

"Still choice?"

"Grade A."

"Ahem," Myron said. "Please wait for the meat inspector."

Win and Terese looked at each other and rolled their eyes.

Myron had been wrong before. Emily was not Win's favorite. Terese was—though it was strictly because she lived far away. "You are the pitiful, needy type who feels incomplete without a steady girlfriend," Win had told him. "Who better than a career woman who lives a thousand miles away?"

Win headed for his Jag while they waited for her luggage. Terese watched Win walk away.

Myron said, "Is his ass better than mine?"

"No ass is better than yours," she said.

"I know that. I was just testing you."

Terese kept looking. "Win is an interesting fellow," she said.

"Oh yeah," Myron agreed.

"On the outside, he's all cold and detached," she said. "But underneath that—way down deep inside— he's all cold and detached."

"You read people well, Terese."

Win dropped them off at the Dakota and returned to the office. When Myron and Terese got inside the apartment, she kissed him hard. Always an urgency with Terese. A desperation in their love-making. Pleasant, sure. Awesome even. But there was still the aura of sadness. The sadness didn't go away when they made love, but for a little while it lifted like cloud cover, hovering above instead of weighing them down.

They had hooked up at a charity function a few months back, both dragged there by well-meaning friends. It was their mutual misery that drew them, as though it were one of those psychic crowns only they could spot on each other. They met and ran away that very night to the Caribbean on a let's-just-flee dare. For the usually predictable Myron, the spontaneous act felt surprisingly right. They spent a numbingly blissful three weeks alone on a private island, trying to stave off the flow of pain. When Myron was finally forced to return home, they'd both assumed it was over. They'd assumed wrong. At least, it appeared that way.

Myron recognized that his own healing was finally under way. He wasn't back to full strength or normal or any of that. He doubted he ever would be. Or even wanted to be. Giant hands had twisted him and then let go, and while his world was slowly untwisting, he knew that it would never fully return to its original position.

Again with the poignant.

But whatever had happened to Terese—whatever had brought on the sadness and twisted her world, if you will—still held firm, refusing to let go.

Terese's head lay on his chest, her arms wrapped around him. He could not see her face. She never showed him her face when they finished.

"You want to talk about it?" he asked.

She still hadn't told him, and Myron rarely asked. Doing so, he knew, was breaking an unspoken though cardinal rule.

"No."

"I'm not pushing," he said. "I just wanted you to know that if you're ever ready, I'm here."

"I know," she said.

He wanted to say something more, but she was still at a place where words were either superfluous or they stung. He stayed quiet and stroked her hair.

"This relationship," Terese said. "It's bizarre."

"I guess."

"Someone told me you're dating Jessica Culver, the writer."

"We broke up," he said.

"Oh." She did not move, still holding him a little too tightly. "Can I ask when?"

"A month before we met."

"And how long were you two together?"

"Thirteen years, on and off."

"I see," she said. "Am I the recovery?"

"Am I yours?"

"Maybe," she said.

"Same answer."

She thought about that a little. "But Jessica Culver is not the reason you ran away with me."

He remembered the cemetery overlooking the school yard. "No," he said, "she's not the reason."

Terese finally turned to him. "We have no chance. You know that, right?"

Myron said nothing.

"That's not unusual," she went on. "Plenty of relationships have no chance. But people stay in them because it's fun. This isn't fun either."

"Speak for yourself."

"Don't get me wrong, Myron. You're a hell of a lay."

"Could you put that in a sworn affidavit?"

She smiled but there was still no joy. "So what do we have here?"

"Truth?"

"Preferably."

"I always overanalyze," Myron said. "It's my nature. I meet a woman, and I immediately picture the house in the burbs and the white picket fence and the two-point-five kids. But for once I'm not doing that. I'm just letting it happen. So, to answer your question, I don't know. And I'm not sure I care."

She lowered her head. "You realize that I'm pretty damaged."

"I guess."

"I have more baggage than most."

"We all have baggage," Myron said. "The question is, does your baggage go with mine?"

"Who said that?"

"I'm paraphrasing from a Broadway musical."

"Which one?"

"Rent."

She frowned. "I don't like musicals."

"Sorry to hear that," Myron said.

"You do?"

"Oh yeah."

"You're in your mid-thirties, single, sensitive, and you like show tunes," she said. "If you were a better dresser, I'd say you were gay."

She pressed a hard, quick kiss to his lips, and then they held each other a little more. Once again he wanted to ask her what had happened to her, but he wouldn't. She would tell him one day. Or she wouldn't. He decided to change subjects.

"I need your help with something," Myron said.

She looked at him.

"I need to break into a bone marrow center's computer system," he said. "And I think you can help."

"Me?"

"Yup."

"You got the wrong technophobe," she said.

"I don't need a technophobe. I need a famous anchorwoman."

"I see. And you're asking for this favor postcoital?"

"Part of my plan," Myron said. "I've weakened your will. You cannot refuse me."

"Diabolical."

"Indeed."

"And if I refuse?"

Myron wiggled his eyebrows. "I'll once again use my brawny body and patented lovemaking technique to make you succumb."

" 'Succumb,' " she repeated, pulling him closer. "Is that one word or two?"

9

It took a shockingly short time to set up.

Myron told Terese his plan. She listened without interruption. When he finished, she started placing calls. She never asked why he was looking for the donor or how he and the donor were connected. The unspoken rule again, he guessed.

Within the hour a news van complete with a hand-held television camera was delivered to the Dakota. The director of the Bergen County Blood Center—a nearby New Jersey bone marrow center—had agreed to drop everything for an immediate interview with Terese Collins, anchorwoman extraordinaire. The power of the idiot box.

They took the Harlem River Drive up to the George Washington Bridge, crossing the Hudson and exiting onto Jones Road in Englewood, New Jersey. After they parked, Myron hoisted up the camera. Heavier than he thought. Terese showed him how to hold it, how to lean it against his shoulder and aim. There was something bazooka-like about the whole thing.

"Do you think I should wear a disguise?" Myron asked.

"Why?"

"People still recognize me from my playing days."

She made a face.

"I'm rather famous in certain circles."

"Get real, Myron. You're an ex-jock. If someone by some miracle recognizes you, they'll think you got lucky and didn't end up in a gutter like most ex-jocks."

He thought about it. "Fair enough."

"One other thing," she said. "And this will be nearly impossible for you."

"What?"

"You have to keep your big mouth shut," Terese said.

"Egads."

"You're just the cameraman here."

"We prefer to be called 'photographic artists.' "

"Just play your part. Trust me to handle him."

"Can I at least use a pseudonym?" He put the camera to his eye. "You can call me Lens. Or Scoop."

"How about Bozo? No, wait, that would be a synonym."

Everyone's a wise guy.

When they entered the clinic's lobby, people turned toward Terese and did that surreptitious stare again. Myron realized that today was the first time he had been with her in public. He had never quite thought about how famous she was.

"You get these stares wherever you go?" he whispered.

"Pretty much."

"Does it bother you?"

She shook her head. "That's horseshit."

"What is?"

"Celebrities who complain about people staring at them. Want to really piss off a celebrity? Let him go someplace and not be recognized."

Myron smiled. "You're so self-realized."

"That a new way of saying cynical?"

The receptionist said, "Mr. Englehardt will see you now."

She led them down a corridor with thin plaster walls

and a bad paint job. Englehardt sat behind a plastic-wood desk. He was probably late twenties with a slight build and a chin weaker than machine-dispensed coffee.

Myron quickly noted the computer setup. Two of them. One on his desk. One on the credenza. Hmm.

Englehardt jumped up as though he'd just been passed a note that his chair had cooties. His eyes were wide and fixed on Terese. Myron was ignored and felt like, well, the cameraman. Terese smiled brightly at Englehardt, and he was lost.

"I'm Terese Collins," she said, extending her hand. Englehardt did everything but take a knee and kiss it. "This is my cameraman, Malachy Throne."

Myron sort of smiled. After the Broadway-musical debacle, he had worried. But Malachy Throne? Genius. Pure genius.

They all exchanged quick pleasantries. Englehardt kept touching his hair, trying very hard to look subtle about it and not like he was prepping for the camera. Not happening, bub. Finally Terese signaled that they were ready to begin.

"Where would you like me to sit?" Englehardt asked.

"Behind the desk would be nice," she said. "Don't you agree, Malachy?"

"Behind the desk," Myron said. "Yeah, that's the ticket."

The interview began. Terese kept her gaze on her subject; Englehardt, trapped in the beam, could look nowhere else. Myron put his eye to the camera. The consummate professional. Very Richard Avedon.

Terese asked Englehardt how he'd gotten started in this business, his background, general crap, relaxing him, putting him on that comfy ground, not all that different from the technique Myron had used with Dr.

Singh. She was in on-air mode now. Her voice was different, her eyes steadier.

"So the national registry in Washington keeps track of all donors?" Terese asked.

"That's correct."

"But you can access the records?"

Englehardt tapped the computer on his desk. The screen faced him, the back of the monitor toward them. Okay, Myron thought, so it was the one on his desk. That would make it more difficult, but not impossible.

Terese looked at Myron. "Why don't you get a back shot, Malachy?" Then turning to Englehardt, "If that's okay with you."

"No problem at all," Englehardt said.

Myron started moving into position. The monitor was off. No surprise.

Terese continued to hold Englehardt's gaze. "Does everyone in the office have access to the national registry's computer?"

Englehardt shook his head firmly. "I'm the only one."

"Why's that?"

"The information is confidential. We don't breach the secrecy under any circumstance."

"I see," she said. Myron was in place now. "But what's to stop someone from coming in here when you're not around?"

"I always lock my office door," Englehardt said, up on his haunches and eager to please. "And you can only access the network with a password."

"You're the only one who knows the password?"

Englehardt tried not to preen, but he didn't try too hard. "That's correct."

Ever see those hidden-camera stories on *Dateline* or

74

20/20? They always shoot from some strange angle and in black-and-white. Truth is, it's easy for any layperson to buy one and it's even easy to get one that films in color. There are stores that sell them right in Manhattan, or you can go online and search under "spy stores." You'll see hidden cameras in clocks, pens, briefcases and, most common of all, smoke detectors—available to anyone with the proper buckage. Myron had one that looked like a film case. He dropped it now on the window ledge with the lens pointing toward the computer monitor.

When it was in place, Myron tapped his nose with his finger, à la Redford in *The Sting*. Their signal. *Bolitar. Myron Bolitar. A Yoo-Hoo. Shaken not stirred.* Terese picked up her cue. The smile dropped off her face like an anvil.

Englehardt looked startled. "Ms. Collins? Are you okay?"

For a moment she could not bear to face him. Then: "Mr. Englehardt," Terese said, her voice Gulf Wargrave, "I must confess something."

"I'm sorry?"

"I am here under somewhat false pretenses."

Englehardt looked confused. Terese was so good, Myron almost looked confused.

"I sincerely believe you are doing important work here," she continued. "But others are not so sure."

Englehardt's eyes were widening. "I don't understand."

"I need your help, Mr. Englehardt."

"Billy," he corrected.

Myron made a face. Billy?

Terese didn't miss a beat. "Someone is trying to disrupt your work, Billy."

"My work?"

"The national registry's work."

"I'm still not sure what you—"

"Are you familiar with the case of Jeremy Downing?"

Englehardt shook his head. "I never know the names of patients."

"He's the son of Greg Downing, the basketball star."

"Oh, wait, yes, I heard about this. His son has Fanconi anemia."

Terese nodded. "That's correct."

"Isn't Mr. Downing supposed to hold a press conference today? To track down a donor?"

"Exactly, Billy. And that's the problem."

"What is?"

"Mr. Downing has found the donor."

Still confused. "That's a problem?"

"No, of course not. If the person is the donor. And if the person is telling the truth."

Englehardt looked at Myron. Myron shrugged and moved back to the front of the desk. He left the film case on the windowsill.

"I'm not following you, Ms. Collins."

"Terese," she said. "A man has come forward. He claims that he is the matching donor."

"And you think he's lying?"

"Let me finish. He not only claims he's the donor, but he says that the reason he refused to donate his marrow was because of the terrible treatment he received from this center."

Englehardt nearly tipped back. "What?"

"He claims he was treated shabbily, that your staff was rude, and that he's even debating leveling a lawsuit."

"That's ridiculous."

"Probably."

"He's lying."

"Probably," she said again.

"And he'll be found out," Englehardt continued. "They'll test his blood and see he's a phony."

"But when, Billy?"

"What?"

"When will they do that? A day from now? A week from now? A month? But by then the damage is done. He's going to appear at the press conference today with Greg Downing. The media will be there in force. Even if it ends up being false, no one remembers the retraction. They just remember the allegation."

Englehardt sat back. "Jesus."

"Let me be frank, Billy. A number of my colleagues believe him. I don't. I smell a publicity hound. I'm having some of my best investigators dig into this man's past. So far they've come up with nothing, and time is running short."

"So what can I do?"

"I need to *know* it's not true. I can't stop it merely because I *believe* it's not true. I have to know for certain."

"How?"

Terese chewed on her lower lip. Deep thought. "Your computer network."

Englehardt shook his head. "The information in here is confidential. I explained that before. I can't tell you—"

"I don't need to know the name of the donor." She leaned forward. Myron moved as far away from the action as possible, trying to be no threat whatsoever. "I need to know what's *not* the name."

Englehardt looked hesistant.

"I'm sitting over here," she said. "I can't see the monitor. Malachy is by the door." She turned to Myron. "Your camera is off, Malachy?"

"Yes, Terese," Myron said. He put it down for emphasis.

"So here is what I suggest," Terese said. "You look up Jeremy Downing in your computer. It will list a donor. I give you a name. You tell me if the name matches. Simple?"

Englehardt still looked hesistant.

"You wouldn't be violating anyone's confidentiality," she said. "We can't see your screen. We can even leave the room while you look it up, if you'd like."

Englehardt said nothing. Terese said nothing either. Waiting him out. The perfect interviewer. She finally turned to Myron. "Grab your stuff," she said to him.

"Wait." Englehardt's eyes slid left, then right, up then down. "Jeremy Downing, you say?"

"Yes."

He did another quick series of eye-slides. When he saw that the coast was clear, he hunched over the keyboard and typed quickly. A few seconds later, he asked, "What's the name of this supposed donor?"

"Victor Johnson."

Englehardt looked at the monitor and smiled. "That's not him."

"You're sure?"

"Absolutely."

Terese matched the smile. "That's all we needed to know."

"You'll stop him?"

"He won't even get to the press conference."

Myron grabbed the film case and camera, and they

hurried down the corridor. Once outside he turned to her and said, "Malachy Throne?"

"You know who he is?"

"He played False Face on *Batman*."

Terese smiled and nodded. "Very good."

"Can I tell you something?"

"What?"

"It turns me on when you talk *Batman*," he said.

"And even when I don't."

"Are you trying to make a point?"

Five minutes later they were watching the tape in the van.

10

Mr. Davis Taylor
221 North End Ave
Waterbury, Connecticut

The social security and phone numbers were there too. Myron took out his cell phone and dialed. After two rings, a machine picked up and a robotic voice, the default greeting, asked him to leave a message at the tone. He left his name and mobile number and asked Mr. Taylor to return his call.

"So what are you going to do?" Terese asked.

"I guess I'll drive up and try to talk to Mr. Davis Taylor."

"Hasn't the clinic already tried that?"

"Probably."

"But you're more persuasive?"

"Questionable."

"I have to cover the Waldorf tonight," she said.

"I know. I'll go alone. Or maybe I'll bring Win."

She still would not face him. "This boy who needs the transplant," she said. "He's not a stranger, is he?"

Myron was not sure how to answer that. "I guess not."

Terese nodded in a way that told him not to say any more. He didn't. He picked up the phone and called Emily. She answered halfway through the first ring.

"Hello?"

"When is Greg doing the news conference?" he asked.

"In two hours," Emily said.

"I need to reach him."

He heard a hopeful gasp. "Did you find the donor for Jeremy?"

"Not yet."

"But you have something."

"We'll see."

"Don't patronize me, Myron."

"I'm not patronizing you."

"This is my son's life we're talking about here."

And mine? "I have a lead, Emily. That's all."

She gave him the number. "Myron, please call me if—"

"The moment I know something."

He hung up and called Greg.

"I need you to put off the press conference," Myron said.

"Why?" Greg asked.

"Just give me till tomorrow."

"You have something?"

"Maybe," Myron said.

"Maybe nothing," Greg said. "Do you have something or not?"

"I have a name and address. It might be our man. I want to check it out before you make a public plea."

"Where does he live?" Greg asked.

"Connecticut."

"You driving up?"

"Yes."

"Right now?"

"Pretty much."

"I want to go with you," Greg said.

"That's not a good idea."

"He's my kid, dammit."

Myron closed his eyes. "I understand that."

"So then you'll understand this: I'm not asking your permission. I'm going. So stop dicking around and tell me where you want me to pick you up."

Greg drove. He had one of those fancy SUV four-by-fours that are all the rage with New Jersey suburbanites whose idea of "off-road" is a speed bump at the mall. Très truck chic. For a long while neither man spoke. The tension in the air was more than the cut-with-a-knife variety; it pressed against the car windows, weighed Myron down, made him tired and gloomy.

"How did you get this name?" Greg asked.

"It's not important."

Greg left it alone. They drove some more. On the radio, Jewel earnestly insisted that her hands were small, she knew, but they were hers and not someone else's. Myron frowned. Not exactly "Blowing in the Wind," was it?

"You broke my nose, you know," Greg said.

Myron kept quiet.

"And my vision hasn't been the same. I'm having trouble focusing on the basket."

Myron could not believe what he was hearing. "You blaming me for your crappy season, Greg?"

"I'm just saying—"

"You're getting old, Greg. You've played fourteen seasons, and sitting out the strike didn't help you."

Greg waved a hand. "You wouldn't understand."

"You're right." Myron's knob turned from Simmer to Boil. "I never got to play pro ball."

"Right, and I never fucked my friend's wife."

"She wasn't your wife," Myron said. "And we weren't friends."

They both stopped then. Greg kept his eyes on the road. Myron turned away and stared out the passenger window.

Waterbury is one of those cities you bypass to reach another city. Myron had probably taken this stretch of 84 a hundred times, always remarking that at a distance Waterbury was a butt-ugly city. But now that he had the opportunity to see the city up close, he realized that he had underestimated the city's offensiveness to the eyes, that indeed the city had a butt-ugly quality to it that you just couldn't appreciate from afar. He shook his head. And people make fun of New Jersey?

Myron had gotten directions from the MapQuest Web site. He read them off to Greg in a voice he barely recognized as his own. Greg followed them in silence. Five minutes later, they pulled up to a dilapidated clapboard house in the middle of a street of dilapidated clapboards. The houses were uneven and crammed so close together, they looked like a set of teeth needing extensive orthodontic work.

They got out of the car. Myron wanted to tell Greg to stay back, but that would be pointless. He knocked on the door and almost immediately a gruff voice said, "Daniel? That you, Daniel?"

Myron said, "I'm looking for Davis Taylor."

"Daniel?"

"No," Myron said, yelling through the door. "Davis Taylor. But maybe he calls himself Daniel."

"What are you talking about?" An old man opened the door, already in full-suspicious squint. He wore glasses too small for his face, so that the metal earpieces were embedded into the folds of skin beneath both temples, and a bad yellow wig, like something Carol Channing wore once too often, adorned his crown. He had on one slipper and one shoe, and his bathrobe looked as if it'd been trampled over during the Boer War.

"I thought you was Daniel," the old man said. He tried to readjust the glasses, but they wouldn't move. He squinted again. "You look like Daniel."

"Must be the clouds in your eyes," Myron said.

"What?"

"Never mind. Are you Davis Taylor?"

"What do you want?"

"We're looking for Davis Taylor."

"Don't know no Davis Taylor."

"This is 221 North End Drive?"

"That's right."

"And there's no Davis Taylor living here?"

"Just me and my boy Daniel. But he's been away. Overseas."

"Spain?" Myron asked. He pronounced it Spahhheeeeen. Elton would have been proud.

"What?"

"Never mind." The old man turned to Greg, tried again to readjust the glasses, gave another squint. "I know you. You play basketball, right?"

Greg gave the old man a gentle if not superior smile—Moses gazing down at a skeptic after the Red Sea parted. "That's right."

"You're Dolph Schayes."

"No."

"You look like Dolph. Helluva shooter. Saw him play in St. Louis last year. What a touch."

Myron and Greg exchanged a glance. Dolph Schayes had retired in 1964.

"I'm sorry," Myron said. "We didn't catch your name."

"You're not wearing uniforms," the old man said.

"No, sir, he only wears it on the court."

"Not that kind of uniform."

"Oh," Myron said, though he had no idea why.

"So you can't be here about Daniel. That's what I mean. I was afraid you were with the army and . . ." His voice drifted off then.

Myron saw where this was going. "Your son is stationed overseas?"

The old man nodded. "Nam."

Myron nodded, feeling bad now about the Elton John teasing. "We still didn't catch your name."

"Nathan. Nathan Mostoni."

"Mr. Mostoni, we're looking for someone named Davis Taylor. It's very important we find him."

"Don't know no Davis Taylor. He a friend of Daniel's?"

"Might be."

The old man thought about it. "Nope, don't know him."

"Who else lives here?"

"Just me and my boy."

"And it's just the two of you?"

"Yep. But my boy is overseas."

"So right now you live here alone?"

"How many different ways you gonna ask that question, boy?"

"It's just that it's a pretty big house," Myron said.

"So?"

"Ever take in any boarders?"

"Sure. Had a college girl just moved out of here."

"What was her name?"

"Stacy something. I don't remember."

"How long did she live here?"

"About six months."

"And before that?"

That one took some thought. Nathan Mostoni scratched his face like a dog going after his own belly. "A guy named Ken."

"Did you ever have a tenant named Davis Taylor?" Myron asked. "Or something like that?"

"Nope. Never."

"Did this Stacy have a boyfriend?"

"I don't think so."

"Do you know her last name?"

"My memory ain't so good. But she's at the college."

"Which college?"

"Waterbury State."

Myron turned to Greg and another thought hit him. "Mr. Mostoni, have you heard the name Davis Taylor before today?"

Another squint. "What do you mean?"

"Has anybody else visited you or called you and asked about Davis Taylor?"

"No, sir. Never heard the name before."

Myron looked at Greg again, then turned back to the old man. "So no one from the bone marrow center has been in touch with you?"

The old man cocked his head and put a hand to his ear. "The bone what?"

Myron asked a few more questions, but Nathan Mostoni started time-traveling again. There was nothing more to get here. Myron and Greg thanked him and headed back down the cracked pathway.

When they were back in the car, Greg asked, "Why didn't the bone marrow center contact this guy?"

"Maybe they did," Myron said. "Maybe he just forgot."

Greg didn't like it. Neither did Myron. "So what's next?" Greg asked.

"We run a background check on Davis Taylor. Find out everything we can about him."

"How?

"It's easy nowadays. Just a few keystrokes and my partner will know it all."

"Your partner? You mean that violent wacko you used to room with in college?"

"A, it is unhealthy to refer to Win as a violent wacko, even when he appears not to be in the vicinity. B, no, I mean my partner at MB SportsReps, Esperanza Diaz."

Greg looked back at the house. "What do I do?"

"Go home," Myron said.

"And?"

"And be with your son."

Greg shook his head. "I don't get to see him until the weekend."

"I'm sure Emily wouldn't mind."

"Yeah, right." Greg smirked, shook his head. "You don't know her too well anymore, do you, Myron?"

"I guess not, no."

"If she had her way, I'd never get to see Jeremy again."

"That's a bit harsh, Greg."

"No, Myron. If anything, it's being generous."

"Emily told me that you're a good father."

"Did she also tell you what she charged in our custody battle?"

Myron nodded. "That you abused the kids."

"Not just abused them, Myron. *Sexually* abused them."

"She wanted to win."

"And that's an excuse?"

87

"No," Myron said. "It's deplorable."

"More than that," Greg said. "It's sick. You have no idea what Emily's capable of doing to get her way."

"For example?"

But Greg just shook his head and started up the car. "I'll ask you again: What can I do to help?"

"Nothing, Greg."

"No good. I'm not sitting around while my kid is dying, you understand?"

"I do."

"You have anything besides this name and address?"

"Nope."

"Fine," Greg said. "I'll drop you off at the train station. I'm staying up here and watching the house."

"You think the old man is lying?"

Greg shrugged. "Maybe he's just confused and forgot. Or maybe I'm wasting my time. But I got to do something."

Myron said nothing. Greg continued to drive.

"You'll call me if you hear something?" Greg asked.

"Sure."

During the train ride back to Manhattan, Myron thought about what Greg had said. About Emily. And about what she'd done—and what she'd do—to save her son.

11

Myron and Terese started out the next morning showering together. Myron controlled the temperature and kept the water hot. Prevents, er, shrinkage.

When they stepped out of the steamy stall, he helped Terese towel off.

"Thorough," she said.

"We're a full-service operation, ma'am." He toweled her off some more.

"One thing I notice when I shower with a man," Terese said.

"What's that?"

"My breasts always end up squeaky clean."

Win had left several hours ago. Lately he liked to get to the office by six. Overseas markets or something. Terese toasted a bagel while Myron fixed himself a bowl of cereal. Quisp cereal. They didn't have it in New York anymore, but Win had it shipped in from a place called Woodsman's in Wisconsin. Myron downed an industrial-size spoonful; the sugar rush came at him so fast he nearly ducked.

Terese said, "I have to go back tomorrow morning."

"I know."

He took another spoonful, feeling her eyes on him.

"Run away with me again," Terese said.

He glanced up at her. She looked smaller, farther away.

"I can get us the same house on the island. We can just hop on a plane and—"

"I can't," he interrupted.

"Oh," she said. Then: "You need to find this Davis Taylor?"

"Yes."

"I see. And after that . . . ?"

Myron shook his head. They ate some more in silence.

"I'm sorry," Myron said.

She nodded.

"Running away isn't always the answer, Terese."

"Myron?"

"What?"

"Do I look in the mood for platitudes?"

"I'm sorry."

"Yeah, you said that already."

"I'm just trying to help."

"Sometimes you can't help," she said. "Sometimes all that's left is running away."

"Not for me," he said.

"No," she agreed. "Not for you."

She wasn't angry or upset, just flat and resigned, and that scared him all the more.

An hour later Esperanza came into Myron's office without knocking.

"Okay," she began, grabbing a seat, "here's what we've got on Davis Taylor."

Myron leaned back and put his hands behind his head.

"One, he's never filed a tax return with the IRS."

"Never?"

"Glad you're paying attention," Esperanza said.

"Are you saying he's never shown any income?"

"Will you let me finish?"

"Sorry."

"Two, he has virtually no paperwork. No driver's license. One credit card, a Visa recently issued by his bank. It has very little activity. Only one bank account, with a current balance of under two hundred dollars."

"Suspicious," Myron said.

"Yes."

"When did he open the account?"

"Three months ago."

"And before that?"

"Nada. At least nada that I've been able to come up with so far."

Myron stroked his chin. "No one flies that far below the radar screen," he said. "It has to be an alias."

"I thought the same thing," Esperanza said.

"And?"

"The answer is yes and no." Myron waited for the explanation. Esperanza tucked some loose tresses behind both ears. "It appears to be a name change."

Myron frowned. "But we got his social security number, right?"

"Right."

"And most records are kept by social security number, not name, right?"

"Another right."

"So I don't get it," Myron said. "You can't change your social security number. A name change might make you harder to find, but it wouldn't wipe out your past. You'd still have tax returns and stuff like that."

Esperanza turned both palms upward. "That's what I mean by yes and no."

"There's no paperwork under the social security number either?"

"That's correct," Esperanza said.

Myron tried to digest this. "So what's Davis Taylor's real name?"

"I don't have it yet."

"I would have thought it'd be easy to locate."

"It would," she said, "if he had any records at all. But he doesn't. The social security number has no hits. It's as though this person hasn't done a thing in his whole life."

Myron thought about it. "Only one explanation," he said.

"That being?"

"A fake ID."

Esperanza shook her head. "The social security number exists."

"I don't doubt that. But I think someone pulled the classic tombstone-fake-ID trick."

"That being?"

"You go to a graveyard and find the tombstone of a dead child," Myron said. "Someone who would be about your age if he'd lived. Then you write and request his birth certificate and paperwork and *voilà*, you've set up the perfect fake ID. Oldest trick in the book."

Esperanza gave him the look she saved for his most idiotic moments. "No," she said.

"No?"

"You think the police don't watch TV, Myron? That doesn't work anymore. Hasn't worked in years, except maybe on cop shows. But just to make sure, I double-checked."

"How?"

"Death records," she said. "There's a Web site that has the social security numbers of all the deceased."

"And the number isn't there."

"Ding, ding, ding," Esperanza said.

Myron leaned forward. "This makes absolutely no sense," he said. "Our phony Davis Taylor has gone to a great deal of trouble to create this phony ID—or at least to fly below the radar, right?"

"Right."

"He wants no records, no paperwork, nothing."

"Right again."

"Even changes his name."

"You go, boy."

Myron put his arms out. "Then why would he sign up to be a bone marrow donor?"

"Myron?"

"Yeah."

"I don't know what you're talking about," Esperanza said.

True enough. He'd called last night and asked her to check out Davis Taylor. He had not yet told her why.

"I guess I owe you an explanation," he said.

She shrugged.

"I sort of promised you I wouldn't be doing this anymore," he said.

"Investigating," she said.

"Right. And I meant it. I wanted this to be a straight agency from now on."

She didn't respond. Myron glanced at the wall behind her. The sparse Client Wall again reminded him of a hair transplant that hadn't taken. Maybe he should paint on a couple of coats of Rogaine.

"You remember Emily's call?" he said.

"It was yesterday, Myron. My memory can sometimes go back a whole week."

He explained it all. Some men—men Myron grudgingly admired—keep it all inside, bury their secrets, hide the pain, the whole cliché. Myron rarely did. He was not one to walk down the mean streets alone—he liked Win to be his backup. He didn't grab a bottle of whiskey and drown his sorrows—he discussed them with Esperanza. Not very macho, but there you have it.

Esperanza stayed silent as he spoke. When he got to the part about being Jeremy's father, she let out a small groan and closed her eyes and kept them shut for a very long time. When she finally opened them, she asked, "So what are you going to do?"

"I'm going to find the donor."

"That's not what I meant."

He knew that. "I don't know," he said.

She thought about it, shook her head in disbelief. "You have a son."

"Seems so."

"And you don't know what you're going to do about it?"

"That's right."

"But you're leaning," she said.

"Win made a pretty good case for not saying anything."

She made a sound. "Win would."

"Actually he claims to be using his heart."

"If only he had one."

"You don't agree?"

"No," she said. "I don't agree."

"You think I should tell Jeremy?"

"I think first and foremost you should put aside your Batman complex," she said.

"What the hell does that mean?"

"It means you always try a little too hard to be heroic."

"And that's bad?"

"Sometimes it clouds your thinking," she said. "The

heroic thing is not always the right thing."

"Jeremy already has a family. He has a mother and a father—"

"He has," Esperanza interrupted, "a lie."

They sat there and stared at each other. The phone, usually so active, was silent, as it had been for too long now. Myron wondered how he could explain it so that she would understand. She stayed still, waiting.

"We were both lucky when it came to parents," Myron said.

"Mine are dead, Myron."

"That's not what I mean," he said. He took a deep breath. "How many days pass that you don't still miss them?"

"None," she said without hesitation.

He nodded. "We were both loved unconditionally and we both loved our parents the same way."

Esperanza's eyes started misting. "So?"

"So—and this was what Win said—isn't that what makes a mother or father? Isn't it about who raised us and loved us and not simply an accident of biology?"

Esperanza leaned back. "Win said that?"

Myron smiled. "He has his moments."

"That he does," she said.

"And think about your father—the one who raised and loved you. What happens to him?"

Her eyes were still misty. "My love for him is strong enough to survive the truth. Isn't yours?"

He tilted back as though the words were jabs at his chin. "Sure," he said. "But it would still hurt him."

"Your father would be hurt?"

"Of course."

"I see," Esperanza said. "So now you're worried about poor Greg Downing?"

"Hardly. You want to hear something awful?"

"Love to."

"When Greg constantly refers to Jeremy as 'my son,' I want to yell out the truth. Right in his smug face. Just to see his reaction. Just to watch his world crumble."

"So much for your Batman complex," Esperanza said.

Myron held out his hands. "I have my moments too," he said.

Esperanza stood and headed for the door.

"Where you going?"

"I don't want to talk about this anymore," she said.

He sat back.

"You're blocking," she said. "You know that?"

He nodded slowly.

"When you move past it—and you will—we'll talk about it again. Otherwise, we're wasting our time here, okay?"

"Okay."

"Just don't be stupid."

" 'Don't be stupid,' " he repeated. "Check."

Her departing smile was brief.

12

Myron spent the rest of the day working the phones. He strapped on his Ultra Slim headset and paced the office. He talked up college coaches, mining for potential free agents. He touched base with his clients and listened to their problems, both real and imagined, therapist-style, which was a large part of his job. He sifted through his Rolodex of companies, trying to conjure up a few endorsement deals.

One serious lead came a-knocking on its own.

"Mr. Bolitar? I'm Ronny Angle from Rack Enterprises. Are you familiar with us?"

"You run a bunch of topless bars, right?"

"We prefer they be called upscale exotic nightclubs."

"And I prefer to be called a well-endowed stallion," Myron said. "What can I do for you, Mr. Angle?"

"Ronny please. Can I call you Myron?"

"Myron please."

"Great, Myron. Rack Enterprises is entering a new venture."

"Uh-huh."

"You've probably read about it. A chain of coffee-houses called La, La, Latte."

"For real?"

"Pardon?"

"Well, I think I did see something about this, but I figured it was a joke."

"It's no joke, Mr. Bolitar."

"So you guys are really going to open up topless coffee bars?"

"We prefer they be called upscale erotic coffee experiences."

"I see. But you're, uh, *baristas* will be topless, correct?"

"Correct."

Myron thought about it. "Makes asking for milk something of a double entendre, don't you think?"

"That's very funny, Myron."

"Thanks, Ronny."

"We're going to open with a big splash."

"That another milk joke, Ronny?"

"No, Myron, but you're a pretty funny guy."

"Thanks, Ronny."

"Let me cut right to it, okay? We like Suzze T." Suzze T was Suzze Tamirino, a journeyman (or is it journeywoman?) on the pro tennis circuit. "We saw her picture in the *Sports Illustrated* swimsuit issue, and, well, we were very impressed. We'd like her to do a cameo for our grand opening."

Myron rubbed the bridge of his nose with his thumb and forefinger. "When you say cameo—"

"A brief performance."

"How brief?"

"No more than five minutes."

"I don't mean brief in terms of time. I mean in terms of clothing."

"We'd require full frontal nudity."

"Well, thanks for thinking of us, Ronny, but I don't think Suzze will be interested."

"We're offering two hundred thousand dollars."

Myron sat up. Easy to hang up, but with this kind of dough, he had a responsibility to follow up. "How about if she wears a small top?"

"No."

"A bikini?"

"No."

"An itsy-bitsy, teeny-weeny bikini?"

"Like in the song?"

"Exactly," Myron said. "Like in the song."

"I'm going to state this as plainly as I can," Ronny said. "There must be nipple visibility."

"Nipple visibility?"

"This point is nonnegotiable."

"So to speak."

Myron promised to call him back later in the week. The two men hung up. Negotiating nipple visibility. What a business.

Esperanza came in without knocking. Her eyes were wide and bright.

"Lamar Richardson is on line one," she said.

"Lamar himself?"

She nodded.

"No relative or personal manager or favorite astrologer?"

"Lamar himself," Esperanza repeated.

They both nodded. This was a good thing.

Myron picked up the phone. "Hello."

"Let's meet," Lamar said.

"Sure," Myron said.

"When?"

"You name it."

"When are you free?"

"You name it," Myron said.

"I'm in Detroit right now."

"I'll catch the next plane out."

"Just like that?" Lamar said.

"Yup."

"Shouldn't you pretend you're really busy?"

"We going to date, Lamar?"

Lamar chuckled. "No, I don't think so."

"Then I'll skip the playing-hard-to-get stage. Esperanza and I want you to sign up with MB Sports-Reps. We'll do a good job. We'll make you a priority. And we won't play mind games with you."

Myron smiled at Esperanza. Was he good or what?

Lamar said he was going to be in Manhattan later in the week and would like to meet then. They set up a time. Myron hung up. He and Esperanza sat there and smiled at each other.

"We have a chance," she said.

"Yep."

"So what's our strategy?"

"I thought I'd impress him with my nimble mind," he said.

"Hmm," Esperanza said. "Maybe I should wear something low cut."

"I was kinda counting on that."

"Hit him with brains and beauty."

"Yes," Myron said. "But which one of us is which?"

When Myron got back to the Dakota, Win was heading out with his leather gym bag and Terese was gone.

"She left a note," Win said, handing it to Myron.

Had to go back early. I'll call.
Terese

Myron read the note again. It didn't change. He folded it up and put it away.

"You going to Master Kwon's?" Myron asked. Master Kwon was their martial arts instructor.

Win nodded. "He's been asking for you."

"What did you tell him?" Myron asked.

"That you wigged out."

"Thanks."

Win gave a slight bow and lifted his gym bag. "May I make a suggestion?"

"Shoot."

"You haven't been to the *dojang* in a long while."

"I know."

"You have a great deal of stress in your life," Win said. "You need an outlet. You need some focus. Some balance. Some structure."

"You're not going to make me snatch a pebble from your hand, are you?"

"Not today, no. But come with me."

Myron shrugged. "I'll grab my stuff."

They were halfway out the door when Esperanza called. He told her they were just on their way out.

"Where?" she asked.

"Master Kwon's."

"I'll meet you there."

"Why? What's up?"

"I got some information on Davis Taylor."

"And?"

"And it's more than a little strange. Is Win going with you?"

"Yes."

"Ask him if he knows anything about Raymond Lex's family."

Silence. "Raymond Lex is dead, Esperanza."

"Duh, Myron. I said *family*."

"This has something to do with Davis Taylor?"

"It'll be easier to explain in person. I'll see you down there in an hour."

She hung up.

One of the doormen had already fetched Win's Jag. It sat waiting for them on Central Park West. The rich. Myron settled into the lush leather. Win hit the accelerator pad. He was big with the accelerator pad; he had a bit more trouble when it came to the brake.

"Do you know Raymond Lex's family?"

"They used to be clients," Win said.

"You're kidding?"

"Oh yes, I'm a regular Red Buttons."

"Were you directly involved in this inheritance squabble?"

"Calling this a squabble would be similar to calling nuclear Armageddon a campfire."

"Hard to divide up billions, huh?"

"Indeed. So why are we discussing the Lex clan?"

"Esperanza is going to meet us down at the *dojang*. She has some information on Davis Taylor. Somehow the Lex family is connected."

Win arched his eyebrow. "The plot doth thicken."

"So tell me a little about them."

"Most of it was in the media. Raymond Lex writes a controversial bestseller called *Midnight Confessions*. Said bestseller becomes an Oscar-winning blockbuster. Suddenly he goes from obscure junior-college instructor to millionaire. Unlike most of his artistic brethren, he understands business. He invests and amasses private holdings with a substantial yet confidential net worth."

"The papers place it in the billions."

"I won't argue."

"That's a lot of money."

"He never wrote another book?"

"No."

"Odd."

"Not really," Win said. "Harper Lee and Margaret Mitchell never wrote another book. And at least Lex kept busy. It's hard to build one of the largest privately held corporations and do book signings."

"So now that he's dead, his family is—how to say it?—nuclear Armageddoning?"

"Close enough."

Master Kwon had moved his headquarters and main *dojang* into the second floor of a building on Twenty-third Street near Broadway. Five rooms—studios really—with hardwood floors, mirrored walls, high-tech sound system, sleek and shiny Nautilus equipment—oh, and some of those rice-paper Oriental scroll-posters. Gave the place a real Old World Asia feel.

Myron and Win slipped into their *dobok*, a white uniform, and tied their black belts. Myron had been studying tae kwon do and *hapkido* since Win had first introduced him to them in college, but he hadn't been to a *dojang* more than five times in the past three years. Win, on the other hand, remained devoutly lethal. Don't tug on Superman's cape, don't spit in the wind, don't pull the mask off the ol' Lone Ranger, and you don't mess around with Win. Bah, bah, dee, dee, dee, dee, dee.

Master Kwon was in his mid-seventies but could easily pass for two decades younger. Win had met him during his Asian travels when he was fifteen. As near as Myron could tell, Master Kwon had been a high priest or some such thing at a small Buddhist monastery straight out of a Hong Kong revenge flick. When Master Kwon emigrated to the United States, he spoke very little English. Now, some twenty years later, he spoke almost none. As soon as the wise master hit our shores, he opened up a chain of state-of-the-art tae kwon do schools—with Win's financial backing, of course. Once he saw the *Karate Kid* movies, Master Kwon started playing the old wise man to the hilt. His English disappeared. He started dressing like the Dalai Lama and began every sentence with the words "Confucius say," ignoring the small fact that he was Korean and Confucius was Chinese.

Win and Myron headed to Master Kwon's office. At the entrance, both men bowed deeply.

"Please in," Master Kwon said.

The desk was fine oak, the chair rich leather and orthopedic looking. Master Kwon was standing near a corner. He held a putter in his hands and wore a splendidly tailored suit. His face brightened when he saw Myron, and the two men embraced.

When they broke apart, Master Kwon said, "You better?"

"Better," Myron agreed.

The old man smiled and grabbed his own lapel. "Armani," he said.

"I thought so," Myron said.

"You like?"

"Very nice."

Satisfied, Master Kwon said, "Go."

Win and Myron bowed deeply. Once in the *dojang*, they fell into their customary roles: Win led and Myron followed. They started with meditation. Win loved meditating, as we already graphically witnessed. He sat in the lotus position, palms tilted up, hands resting on knees, back straight, tongue folded against the upper teeth. He breathed in through his nose, forcing the air down, letting his abdomen do all the work. Myron tried to duplicate—had been trying for years—but he had never quite gotten the hang of it. His mind, even during less chaotic times, wandered. His bad knee tightened. He got fidgety.

They cut down the stretching to only ten minutes. Again Win was effortless, executing splits and toe touches and deep bends with ease, his bones and joints as flexible as a politician's voting record. Myron had never been a naturally limber guy. When he was training seriously, he could touch his toes and complete a hurdle stretch with little problem. But just then, that felt like a long time ago.

"I'm already sore," Myron said through a grunt.

Win tilted his head. "Odd."

"What?"

"That's precisely what my date said last night."

"You weren't kidding before," Myron said. "You really are another Red Buttons."

They did a little sparring, and Myron immediately realized how out of shape he was. Sparring is the most tiring activity in the world. Don't believe it? Find a punching bag and pretend-box with it for one three-minute round. Just a bag that can't fight back. Try it, just one round. You'll see.

When Esperanza came in, the sparring mercifully ceased and Myron grabbed his knees, sucking wind. He bowed to Win, threw a towel over his shoulder, grabbed some Evian. Esperanza folded her arms and waited. A group of students walked past the door, saw Esperanza, did a double take.

Esperanza handed Myron a sheet of paper. "The birth certificate of Davis Taylor né Dennis Lex."

"Lex," Myron repeated. "As in . . . ?"

"Yep."

Myron scanned the photocopy. According to the

document, Dennis Lex would be thirty-seven years old. His father was listed as one Raymond Lex, his mother as Maureen Lehman Lex. Born in East Hampton, New York.

Myron handed it to Win.

"They had another child?"

"Apparently so," Esperanza said.

Myron looked at Win. Win shrugged.

"He must have died young," Win said.

"If he did," Esperanza said, "I can't find it anywhere. There's no death certificate."

"No one in the family ever mentioned another child?" Myron asked Win.

"No one," Win said.

He turned back to Esperanza. "What else you got?"

"Not much. Dennis Lex changed his name to Davis Taylor eight months ago. I also found this." She handed him a photocopy of a news clipping. A small birth announcement from the *Hampton Gazette* dated thirty-seven years ago:

Raymond and Maureen Lex of Wister Drive in East Hampton are delighted to announce the birth of their son, Dennis, six pounds eight ounces on June 18th. Dennis joins his sister Susan and his brother Bronwyn.

Myron shook his head. "How could no one know about this?"

"It's not all that surprising," Win said.

"How do you figure?"

"None of the Lex family holdings are public. They are fiercely protective of their privacy. Security around them is around-the-clock and the best money can buy.

Everyone who works with them must sign confidentiality agreements."

"Even you?"

"I don't do confidentiality agreements," Win said. "No matter how much money is involved."

"So they never asked you to sign one?"

"They asked. I refused. We parted ways."

"You gave them up as clients?"

"Yes."

"Why? I mean, what would have been the big deal? You keep everything confidential anyway."

"Exactly. Clients hire me not only because of my brilliance in the ways of finance but because I am the very model of discretion."

"Don't overlook your startling modesty," Myron added.

"I don't need to sign a contract saying I won't reveal anything. It should be a given. It's the equivalent of signing a document saying that I won't burn down their house."

Myron nodded. "Nice analogy," he said.

"Yes, thank you, but I'm trying to illustrate how far this family will go to maintain their privacy. Until this inheritance feud erupted, the media had no idea how extensive Raymond Lex's holdings were."

"But come on, Win. This is Raymond Lex's son. You'd know about a son."

Win pointed to the top of the clipping. "Notice when the child was born—*before* Raymond Lex's book came out, when Lex was just a typical small-town professor. It wouldn't make news."

"You really buy that?"

"Do you have a better explanation?"

"So where is the kid now? How can the son of one of

America's wealthiest families have no paperwork? No credit cards, no driver's license, no IRS filings, no trail at all? Why did he change his name?"

"The last one is easy," Win said.

"Oh?"

"He's hiding."

"From?"

"His siblings perhaps," Win said. "As I said before, this inheritance battle is rather nasty."

"That might make sense—and I stress the word 'might'—if he'd been around before. But how can there be no paperwork on him? What is he hiding from? And why on earth would he put his name in the bone marrow registry?"

"Good questions," Win said.

"Very good," Esperanza added.

Myron reread the article and looked at his two friends. "Nice to have a consensus," he said.

13

The mobile phone blew him out of his sleep like a shot-gun blast. Myron's hand reached up blindly, his fingers bouncing along the night table until they located the phone.

"Hello?" he croaked.

"Is this Myron Bolitar?"

The voice was a whisper.

"Who is this?" Myron asked.

"You called me."

Still whispering, the sound like leaves skittering across pavement.

Myron sat upright, his heartbeat picking up a little steam. "Davis Taylor?"

"Sow the seeds. Keep sowing. And open the shades. Let the truth come in. Let the secrets finally wither in the daylight."

Ooookay. "I need your help, Mr. Taylor."

"Sow the seeds."

"Yes, of course, we'll sow away." Myron flicked on the light. 2:17 A.M. He checked the LCD display on the phone. The Caller ID was blocked. Damn. "But we have to meet."

"Sow the seeds. It's the only way."

"I understand, Mr. Taylor. Can we meet?"

"Someone must sow the seeds. And someone must unlock the chains."

"I'll bring a key. Just tell me where you are."

"Why do you wish to see me?"

What to say? "It's a matter of life and death."

"Whenever you sow the seeds, it's a matter of life and death."

"You donated blood for a bone marrow drive. You're a match. A young boy will die if you don't help."

Silence.

"Mr. Taylor?"

"Technology cannot help him. I thought you were one of us." Still whispering but sad now.

"I am. Or at least I want to be—"

"I'm hanging up now."

"No, wait—"

"Good-bye."

"Dennis Lex," Myron said.

Silence, except for the sound of breathing. Myron wasn't sure if the sound was coming from him or the caller.

"Please," Myron said. "I'll do whatever you ask. But we have to meet."

"Will you remember to sow the seeds?"

Small chunks of ice dropped down his back.

"Yes," Myron said, "I'll remember."

"Good. Then you know what you must do."

Myron gripped the receiver. "No," he said. "What must I do?"

"The boy," the voice whispered. "Say one last good-bye to the boy."

14

"Sow the seeds?" Esperanza said.

They were in Myron's office. The morning sun striped the floor with Venetian slits, two cutting across Esperanza's face. She didn't seem to mind.

"Right," Myron said. "And something about that phrase keeps gnawing at me."

"It was a Tears for Fears song," Esperanza said.

" 'Sowing the Seeds of Love.' I remember."

"Wasn't that the name of the tour too? We saw them at the Meadowlands in, what, 1988?"

"Eighty-nine."

"What happened to those guys?"

"They broke up," Myron said.

"Why do they all do that?"

"Got me."

"Supertramp, Steely Dan, the Doobie Brothers—"

"Not to mention Wham."

"They break up and then they never make anything decent on their own. They flounder around and end up a segment of VH-1's *Where Are They Now?*"

"We're getting off the subject."

Esperanza handed him a slip of paper. "Here's the office number for Susan Lex, Dennis's older sister."

Myron read the number like it was in code and might mean something. "I had another thought."

"What's that?"

"If Dennis Lex exists, then he had to have gone to school, right?"

"Maybe."

"So let's see if we can find out where the Children Lex schooled—public, private, whatever."

Esperanza frowned. "You mean like college?"

"Start there, yes. Not that siblings go to the same school, but maybe they did. Or maybe they all went to Ivy League schools. Something like that. You might want to start with high school. It's more likely that they all went to the same one."

"And if I don't find any record of him in high school?"

"Go back even further."

She crossed her legs, folded her arms. "How far?"

"As far as you can."

"And what good will this exercise in futility do us?"

"I want to know when Dennis Lex fell off the radar screen. Did people know him in high school? In college? In grad school?"

She did not look impressed. "And assuming I somehow manage to find, say, his elementary school, what exactly is that going to do for us?"

"Damn if I know. I'm grasping at straws here."

"No, you're asking *me* to grasp at straws."

"Then don't do it, Esperanza, okay? It was just a thought."

"Nah," she said with a wave of her hand. "You may be right."

Myron put his palms on his desk, arched his back, looked left, looked right, looked up, looked down.

"What?" she said.

"You said I may be right. I'm waiting for the world as we know it to end."

"Good one," Esperanza said, standing. "I'll see what I can dig up."

She left the room. Myron picked up the telephone and dialed Susan Lex's number. The receptionist transferred the call, and a woman identifying herself as Ms. Lex's secretary picked it up. She had a voice like a steel-wool tire over gravel.

"Ms. Lex does not see people she doesn't know."

"It's a matter of grave importance," Myron said.

"Perhaps you did not hear me the first time." Classic Battle-ax. "Ms. Lex does not see people she doesn't know."

"Tell her it's about Dennis."

"Excuse me?"

"Just tell her that."

Battle-ax put Myron on hold without another word. Myron listened to a Muzak version of Al Stewart's "Time Passages." Myron had thought the original was Muzak-y enough, thank you very much.

The battle-ax came back with a snap. "Ms. Lex does not see people she doesn't know."

"I've been thinking about that, but it doesn't really make sense."

"Excuse me?"

"I mean, at some time she must see people she doesn't know—otherwise she'd never meet anybody new. And if we follow my logic, how did you ever get to see her for the first time? She was willing to see you before she knew you, right?"

"I'm hanging up now, Mr. Bolitar."

"Tell her I know about Dennis."

"I just—"

"Tell her if she doesn't agree to see me, I'll go to the press."

Silence. "Hold." A click and then the Muzak came back on. Time passed. So, mercifully, did "Time Passages," replaced by the Alan Parsons Project's "Time." Myron nearly slipped into a coma.

Battle-ax returned. "Mr. Bolitar?"

"Yes?"

"Ms. Lex will give you five minutes of her time. I have an opening on the fifteenth of next month."

"No good," Myron said. "It has to be today."

"Ms. Lex is a very busy woman."

"Today," Myron said.

"That simply will not be possible."

"At eleven. If I'm not let in, I go immediately to the press."

"You're being terribly rude, Mr. Bolitar."

"To the press," Myron repeated. "Do you understand?"

"Yes."

"Will you be there?"

"What possible difference could that make?"

"All this sexual tension is driving me batty. Maybe afterward we could get together for a nice cool latte."

He heard the phone go click and smiled. The charm, he thought. It's baaaaack.

Esperanza buzzed in. "Topless tennis, anyone?"

"What?"

"I got Suzze T on line one."

He hit a button. "Hey, Suzze."

"Hey, Myron, what's shaking?"

"I got an offer for you to refuse."

"You mean you're going to hit on me?"

The charm suffers a setback. "Where are you going to be this afternoon?"

"Same place as now," she said. "The Morning Mosh. You know it?"

"No."

She gave him the address, and Myron agreed to meet her there in a few hours. He hung up the phone and leaned back.

" 'Sow the seeds,' " he said out loud.

He stared at the wall. An hour to kill before he headed over to the Lex Building on Fifth Avenue. He could sit here and think about life and maybe contemplate his navel. No, too much of that already. He swiveled his seat to the computer, double-clicked the proper icon, connected to the Net. He tried Yahoo first and typed *sow the seeds* into the search field. Only one hit: a Web site for the San Francisco League of Urban Gardeners. They went by the acronym SLUG. Tough guys probably. A gang. Probably wore green bandannas and engaged in drive-by waterings.

He tried Alta Vista's search engine next, but they listed 2,501 Web pages. It was kinda like Goldilocks and the Three Bears. Yahoo's search was toooo small. Alta Vista's was toooo big. They didn't have LEXIS–NEXIS at the office, but Myron tried a less powerful media engine. He typed in the same three words and pressed the return key, and bammo.

http://www.nyherald.com/archives/9800322

Myron hit the link and the article came up:

New York Herald
THE MIND OF TERROR—YOUR DARKEST FEAR
by Stan Gibbs

Whoa, hold the phone. Myron knew the name. Stan Gibbs had been a big-time newspaper columnist, the kind of guy who regularly pontificated (read: pimped) on the cable news talk shows, though he'd been less annoying than most, which is like saying syphilis is less annoying than gonorrhea. But that had all been before the scandal gutted him like Ted Nugent over a fallen moose. Myron read:

The phone call comes out of the blue.

"What is your darkest fear?" the voice whispers. "Close your eyes now and picture it. Can you see it? Do you have it yet? The very worst agony you can imagine?"

After a long pause, I say, "Yes."

"Good. Now imagine something worse, something far, far worse . . ."

Myron took a deep breath. He remembered the series of articles. Stan Gibbs had broken a story about a bizarre kidnapper. He'd told the heart-wrenching tale of three abductions that the police had supposedly wanted to keep quiet, out of, Stan Gibbs claimed, embarrassment. No names were mentioned. He had spoken with the families under the condition of anonymity. And, the coup de grâce, the kidnapper had granted Gibbs access:

I ask the kidnapper why he does it. Is it for the ransom?

"I never pick up the ransom money," he says. "I usually leave explosives at the spot and burn it. But sometimes money helps me sow the seeds. That is what I'm trying to do. Sow the seeds."

Myron felt his blood stop.

"You all think you're safe," he continues, "in your technological cocoon. But you're not. Technology has made us expect easy answers and happy endings. But with me, there is no answer and there is no end."

He has kidnapped at least four people: the father

of two young children, age 41; a female college student, age 20; and a young couple, newlyweds ages 28 and 27. All were abducted while in the New York City area.

"The idea," he says, "is to keep the terror going. Let it grow, not with gore or obvious bloodletting, but with your own imagination. Technology is trying to destroy our ability to imagine. But when someone you love is taken away, your mind can conjure up horrors darker than any machine—than anything even I can do. Some minds won't go that far. Some minds stop and put up a barrier. My job is to push them through that barrier."

I ask him how he does that.

"Sow the seeds," he repeats. "You sow the seeds over time."

He explains that sowing the seeds means giving hope and taking it away over a sustained period of time. His first call to the victim's family is naturally devastating, but merely the beginning of a long and torturous ordeal.

He begins the call, he claims, with a normal hello and asks the family member to please hold. After a pause, the family member hears their loved one give a blood-curdling shriek. "Just one," he says, "and it's very short. I cut them off in mid-scream.

"This is the last they'll ever hear from their loved one," he continues. "Imagine how that scream echoes."

But for the victim's family, it does not end there. He demands a ransom that he has no intention of claiming. He calls after midnight and asks the family to imagine their darkest fear. He convinces them that this time, he will really let their loved one go, but he is only

extending hope to those who no longer have it, rekin-
dling their agony.

"Time and hope," he says, "sow the seeds of
despair."

The father of two has been missing for three years.
The young premed college student has been missing
for twenty-seven months. The newlyweds were married almost two years ago this weekend. To date, not a
trace of any of them has been found. Rarely does a
week pass when the families don't get a call from their
tormentor.

When I ask him if his victims are alive or dead, he is
coy. "Death is closure," he explains, "and closure
stops the sowing."

He wants to talk about society, how computers and
technology are doing our thinking for us, how what he
does lets us see the power of the human brain.

"That is where God exists," he says. "That is where
all things valuable exist. True bliss can only be found
inside of you. The meaning of life is not in your new
home entertainment system or sports car. People must
see their limitless potential. How do you make them
see? Right now imagine what these families are going
through."

His voice soft, he invites me to try.

"Technology could never conjure up the horrors you
are now imagining. Sow the seeds. Sowing the seeds
shows us the potential."

Myron's heart pounded in big thuds. He sat back,
shook his head, started reading again. The crazed
kidnapper ranted on, his theories feverishly demented,
sort of Symbionese Liberation Army by way of Ted
Kaczynski. Stan Gibbs's column continued into the next

day's paper. Myron hit the link and read on. During the second day, Gibbs opened with some heartbreaking quotes from the family of the victims. Then he questioned the kidnapper some more:

I ask him how he has managed to keep these kidnappings out of the media.

"By sowing the seeds," he repeats yet again.

I ask for an example.

"I tell his wife to go to the garage and open the red Stanley toolbox on the third shelf. I tell her to pick out the black pliers with the bubble grip. Then I send her to the basement. I tell her to stand in front of the Mission chair they bought the previous summer at that tag sale on the Cape. Imagine, I say, your husband tied naked to that chair. Imagine those pliers in my hand. And finally, imagine what I'll do if I see anything about him in the newspaper."

But he does not stop there.

"I ask her about the children. I mention their names. I mention their schools and their teachers and their favorite breakfast cereal."

I ask him how he knows these things.

His answer is simple. "Daddy tells me."

Myron fell back. "Jesus," he uttered.

Deep breaths, he told himself again. In and out. That's it. Think it through. Slowly now. Carefully. Okay, first off: Horrible as this is, what does it have to do with Davis Taylor né Dennis Lex? Probably nothing. The worst sort of long shot. And again, horrible as this is, Myron knew that there was more to the story. More—and in a sense, less.

The Gibbs columns drew weeks' worth of nationwide attention and criticism—until, Myron remembered, it all blew up in the most public way possible. What had happened exactly? Myron hit some keys and clicked the mouse. He started a search of articles where Stan Gibbs was the subject. They came up in date order:

FEDS DEMAND GIBBS'S SOURCE

The Federal Bureau of Investigation, which in recent weeks has been denying the allegations listed in Stan Gibbs's columns, took a new tack today. They demanded his notes and information.

Dan Conway, a spokesman for the FBI, began by saying, "We know nothing about these crimes," then added, "But if Mr. Gibbs is being truthful, he has important information on a possible serial kidnapper and killer, perhaps even harboring or aiding him. We have a right to that information."

Stan Gibbs, a popular columnist and television journalist, has refused to reveal his sources. "I'm not protecting a killer here," Mr. Gibbs said. "The families of the victims as well as the perpetrator of the crimes spoke to me under the strict condition of confidentiality. It's a cry as old as our country: I will not reveal my sources."

The *New York Herald* and American Civil Liberties Union have already denounced the FBI and plan on backing Mr. Gibbs. The judge has ordered the case sealed from the public.

Myron read on. The arguments on both sides were pretty standard. Gibbs's attorneys naturally wrapped themselves in the First Amendment, while the feds equally naturally countered that the First Amendment was not an absolute, that you can't yell "Fire!" in a crowded theater, and that freedom of expression does not include protecting possible criminals. The country also argued the issue. It played well on CNBC and MSNBC and CNN and a bunch of other cable letters, lighting up the phone lines like a radio giveaway. The judge was about to render a verdict when the whole story exploded in a way no one expected.

Myron hit the link:

GIBBS FIBS?
Reporter accused of plagiarism

Myron read the endgame shocker: Someone had found a mystery novel published by a tiny press with a minuscule print run in 1978. The novel, *Whisper to a Scream*, by F. K. Armstrong, closely mirrored Gibbs's story. Too closely. Certain snippets of dialogue were pretty much copied verbatim. The crimes in the novel—kidnappings with no resolution—were too similar to what Gibbs had written to be dismissed as coincidence.

The plagiaristic spectres of Mike Barnicle and Patricia Smith and the like rose from the grave and would not disperse. Heads rolled. There were resignations and hand-wringing. For his part, Stan Gibbs refused to comment, which didn't look good. Gibbs ended up "taking a leave of absence," a modern-day euphemism for *getting fired*. The ACLU issued an ambiguous statement and retreated. The *New York Herald* quietly retracted the story, saying that the matter "was under internal review."

After some time passed, Myron reached for the phone and dialed.

"News desk. Bruce Taylor speaking."

"How about meeting me for a drink?"

"I know this is out nowadays, Myron, but I'm strictly hetero."

"I have the ability to change you."

"I don't think so, pal."

"Several women I've dated started out hetero," Myron said. "But one date with me and whammo, they switched teams."

"I love it when you're self-deprecating, Myron. It's just so real."

"So what do you say?"

"I'm on deadline."

"You're always on deadline."

"You buying?"

"To quote my brethren during Passover seders, why should this night be different from any other night?"

"I buy sometimes."

"Do you even own a wallet?"

"Hey, I'm not the one asking for favors," Bruce said. "Four o'clock. The Rusty Umbrella."

15

The Lex Building's wrought-iron gates lined a Fifth Avenue façade with vegetation so dense you wouldn't see light through it if a supernova burst on the other side. The famed edifice was a converted Manhattan mansion with a European courtyard and a regal art deco exterior and enough security to handle a Tyson boxing match. The building had wonderful old lines and detailed Venetian touches, except that for the sake of privacy, the windows had been converted into the smoky-limo variety. It made for a distracting and unnatural mix.

Four blue-blazered, gray-slacked guards stood at the entrance—real guards, Myron noted, with cop eyes and KGB facial tics, not the rent-a-uniforms you saw at department stores or airports. The four of them stood silently, eyeing Myron like he was wearing a tube top in the Vatican.

One of the guards stepped forward. "May I see some ID please?"

Myron took out his wallet and showed him a credit card and driver's license.

"There's no photo on the driver's license," the guard said.

"New Jersey doesn't require them."

"I need a photo ID."

"I have my picture on my health club membership card."

Cop-patient sigh. "That won't do, sir. Do you have a passport?"

"In midtown Manhattan?"

"Yes, sir. For the purposes of ID."

"No," Myron said. "Besides, it's a terrible picture. Doesn't fully capture the radiant blue in my eyes." Myron batted them for emphasis.

"Wait here, sir."

He waited. The other three guards frowned, crossed their arms, studied him as though he might start drinking from a toilet. Myron heard a whirring noise and looked up. A security camera was on him now, focusing in. Myron waved, smiled into the lens, performed a few flexes he had picked up from watching he-man events on ESPN 2. He ended with a pretty dramatic back lat spread and waved to the appreciative crowd. The blue-blazers looked unimpressed.

"All natural," Myron said. "I've never taken steroids."

No replies.

The first guard came back. "Follow me, please."

Stepping into the courtyard was like stepping into C. S. Lewis's wardrobe, another world, the other side of the shrubbery, so to speak. Here in the middle of Manhattan, the street noises were suddenly very far away, muted. The garden was lush, the tile walkways forming a pattern not unlike an Oriental carpet. There was a sprouting fountain in the middle with a statue of a horse rearing back its head.

A new set of blue-blazers greeted him by the ornate front door. This place, Myron thought, must rack up a hell of a dry-cleaning bill. They made him empty his pockets, confiscated his cell phone, frisked him by hand, ran a metal wand over his person so thoroughly he almost asked for a condom, walked him through a metal detector twice, again frisked him with a little too much gusto.

"If you touch my wee-wee one more time," Myron said, "I'm telling my mommy."

More no replies. Maybe the Lexes demanded not only confidentiality but a discriminating sense of humor.

"Follow me, sir," the talking blue-blazer said.

The stillness of the place—a building in the middle of Manhattan, for chrissake—was unnerving, the only sound now the steady echo of their footsteps against the cool marble. It was like walking through an old museum at night, the whole experience like something out of *From the Mixed-up Files of Mrs. Basil E. Frankweiler*. The guards formed a poor man's presidential motorcade—the talking blue-blazer and a buddy three paces in front of him, two other blue-blazers three paces back. Just for fun, Myron would slow down or speed up and watch the guards do likewise. Like a really bad line dance, which was something of a redundancy. At one point he almost did a moonwalk, à la Michael Jackson, but these guys were already viewing him as a potential pedophile.

The mahogany staircase was wide and smelled a bit like lemon Pledge. There were enormous tapestries on the wall, the kind with swords and horses and hedonistic feasts of suckling pig. There were two more blue-blazers on the second floor. Now it was their turn to inspect Myron as though they'd never seen a man before. Myron twirled for their benefit. They too seemed unimpressed.

"You should have seen me flex before," Myron said.

The double doors opened and Myron entered a room slightly larger than a sports arena. Two guards followed him and took up positions in the back corners. There was a big man sitting to the right in a wing chair. At least he looked big in the chair. Or maybe the chair was tiny. The man was probably in his mid-forties. His head and neck formed a near-perfect trapezoid, the top buzzed into a military crew cut. He had a flat nose and ham-hock hands and knockwurst fingers. Ex-boxer or ex-marine or probably both. A man of ninety-degree angles and granite blocks.

Granite Man gave Myron more hard eyes, though his were more relaxed, as though Myron amused him in the way a little kitty nipping at his pant leg might. He didn't stand, choosing instead to stare at Myron and crack his knuckles one at a time.

Myron looked at Granite Man. Granite Man cracked another knuckle.

"Shiver," Myron said.

No one asked him to take a seat. Hell, no one spoke. Myron stood there and waited with the three sets of eyes weighing on him.

"Okay," Myron said. "I'm intimidated. Can we get past this, please?"

Granite Man nodded at the two blazers. They both left. Almost simultaneously, a door on the other side of the room opened and two women appeared. They were pretty far away, but Myron guessed that the first one was Susan Lex. Her hair was done up in an impossibly neat, semi-shellacked bun, and her lips were pursed as if she'd just swallowed a live beetle. The other woman— she looked no more than eighteen or nineteen—had to be her daughter, a carbon copy with the same pursed lips and twenty-five years less wear and tear, not to mention better hair.

Myron started to cross the room with his hand extended, but Susan Lex held up her palm in a stop gesture. Granite Man sat forward, nearly leaning into Myron's path. He gave Myron a small shake of the head, which was no easy task when you have no neck. Myron stayed where he was.

"I don't like being threatened," Susan Lex called from across the room.

"I apologize for that. But I had to see you."

"And that makes it right to threaten and blackmail me?"

Myron had no quick answer to that. "I need to talk to you about your brother Dennis."

"So you said on the phone."

"Where is he?"

Susan Lex looked at Granite Man. Granite Man frowned and cracked his knuckles again. "Just like that, Mr. Bolitar?" Susan Lex said. "You call my office. You threaten me. You insist I alter my schedule to accommodate you. And then you come in here and make demands?"

"I don't mean to be abrupt," Myron said. "But this is a matter of life and death."

Whenever he said "a matter of life and death," he expected to hear that melodramatic *dum-dum-duuuummm* music.

"That's hardly an explanation," Susan Lex said.

"Your brother registered with the national bone marrow center," Myron said. "His marrow matched a sick child's." After the creepy say-good-bye-to-the-boy conversation last night, Myron had decided to stop being gender specific. "Without that transplant, the child will die."

Susan Lex arched an eyebrow. The rich are really good at that, at arching eyebrows without altering anything else on their face. Myron wondered if they learned it at rich-people summer camp. Susan Lex looked at Granite Man again. Granite Man was trying to smile now. "You're mistaken, Mr. Bolitar," she said.

Myron waited for her to say more. When she didn't, he said, "Mistaken how?"

"If you're telling the truth, you've made a mistake. I will say no more."

"With all due deference," Myron said, "that's not good enough."

"It will have to be."

"Where is your brother, Ms. Lex?"

"Please leave, Mr. Bolitar."

"I can still go to the press."

Granite Man crossed his legs and started cracking his knuckles again.

Myron turned to him. "Yes, but can you do this?" Myron patted his head with one hand and rubbed his belly with the other.

Granite Man didn't like that one.

"Look," Myron said, "I don't want to cause any trouble here. You're private people. I understand that. But I need to find this donor."

"It's not my brother," Susan Lex said.

"Then where is he?"

"He's not your donor. More than that is none of your concern."

"Does the name Davis Taylor mean anything to you?"

Susan Lex repursed the lips as though a fresh beetle had sneaked through. She turned and walked out. Her daughter did likewise. Again on cue, the door behind Myron opened and the two blue-blazers filled it. More glares. They stepped fully into the room. Granite Man finally stood, which took some time. He was indeed big. Very big.

The men approached Myron.

"Let's go to the judges," Myron said. "Charles Nelson Reilly, your score?"

Granite Man stepped in front of him, shoulders square, eyes calm.

"The not introducing yourself," Myron said, doing his best Charles Nelson Reilly lisp, which was not very good. "I thought that was really very macho. And that whole silent persona combined with the amused glare. Very nicely done, really. Professional. But—and here's where you kinda lost me—the knuckle cracking, well, Gene, that was overkill, don't you think? Overall score: an 8. Comment: stick with the subtle."

Granite Man said, "You finished?"

"Yes."

"Myron Bolitar. Born in Livingston, New Jersey. Mother Ellen, father Al—"

"They like to be called El-Al," Myron interjected. "Like the Israeli airline."

"Basketball All-American at Duke University. Picked eighth in the NBA draft by the Boston Celtics. Blew out your knee in your first preseason game, ending your career. Currently owns MB SportsReps, a sports representation firm. Dated the novelist Jessica Culver since you graduated college, but you two recently parted ways. Should I go on?"

"You left off the part about my being a snazzy dancer. I can demonstrate if you like."

Granite Man smirked. "You want my score on you now?"

"Suit yourself."

"You wisecrack too much," Granite Man said. "I know you do it to look confident, but you're trying too hard. And since you raised the issue of subtlety, your story about a dying kid needing a bone marrow transplant was touching. The only thing missing was the string quartet."

"You don't believe me?"

"No, I don't believe you."

"So why am I here, then?"

Granite Man spread his satellite-dishes excuse for hands. "That's what I'd like to know."

The three men formed a triangle, Granite in front, the two blue-blazers in back. Granite made a small nod. One of the blazers produced a gun and aimed at Myron's head.

This was not good.

There are ways of disarming a man with a gun, but there's an inherent problem: It might not work. If you miscalculate or if your opponent is better than you think—something not unlikely in an opponent who knows how to handle a gun—you could get shot. That's a serious drawback. And in this particular situation there were two other opponents, both of whom looked good and were probably armed. There is a word expert fighters use for a sudden move at this juncture: *suicide*.

"Whoever did your research on me left something out," Myron said.

"What might that be?"

"My relationship with Win."

Granite Man didn't flinch. "You mean Windsor Horne Lockwood the Third? Family owns Lock-Horne Security and Investments on Park Avenue. Your college roommate from Duke. Since moving out of the Spring Street loft you shared with Jessica Culver, you've been living at his apartment in the Dakota. You have close business and personal ties, might even be called best friends. That relationship?"

"That would be the one," Myron said.

"I am aware of it. I am also aware of Mr. Lockwood's"—he paused, searching for the word—"talents."

"Then you know that if that bozo gets itchy"—Myron head-gestured toward the blazer with the gun—"you die."

Granite Man wrestled with his facial muscles and this time he achieved a smile, though not without effort. Heart's song "Barracuda" played in Myron's head. "I am not without my own, uh, talents, Mr. Bolitar."

"If you really believe that," Myron said, "then you don't know enough about Win's, uh, talents."

"I won't debate the point. But I will point out that he doesn't have an army like this at his disposal. Now, are you going to tell me why you're asking about Dennis Lex?"

"I told you," Myron said.

"You're really going to stick with the dying-child story?"

"It's the truth."

"And how did you get Dennis Lex's name?"

"From the bone marrow center."

"They just gave it to you?"

Myron's turn. "I too am not without my own, uh, talents." It somehow didn't sound right when he said it about himself.

"So you're saying that the bone marrow center told you that Dennis Lex was a donor—that about right?"

"I'm not saying anything," Myron said. "Look, this is a two-way street here. I want some information."

"Wrong," Granite Man said. "It's a one-way street. I'm a Mack truck. You're like an egg in the road."

Myron nodded. "Cutting," he said. "But if you're not going to give me anything, I'm not giving you anything."

The guy with the gun stepped closer.

Myron felt a quiver in his legs, but he didn't blink. Maybe he did overplay the wisecracks, but you don't show fear. Ever. "And let's not pretend you're going to shoot me over this. We both know you won't. You're not that stupid."

Granite Man smiled. "I might beat on you a bit."

"You don't want trouble, I don't want trouble. I don't care about this family or its fortune or any of that. I'm just trying to save a kid's life."

Granite Man played air violin for a moment. Then he said, "Dennis Lex is not your salvation."

"And I'm just supposed to believe you?"

"He's not your donor. That much I personally guarantee."

"Is he dead?"

Granite Man folded his arms across his paddleball-court chest. "If you're telling the truth, the bone marrow people either lied to you or made a mistake."

"Or you're lying to me," Myron said. Then added, "Or you're making a mistake."

"The guards will show you out."

"I can still go to the press."

Granite Man walked away then. "We both know you won't," he said. "You're not that stupid either."

16

Bruce Taylor was in print-journalist garb—like he'd gone to his laundry hamper and dug out whatever was on the bottom. He sat at the bar, scooped up the free pretzels, and pushed them into his mouth as though he were trying to swallow his palm.

"Hate these things," he said to Myron.

"Yeah, I can see that."

"I'm at a bar, for crying out loud. I gotta eat something. But nobody serves peanuts anymore. Too fattening or some such crap. Pretzels instead. And not real pretzels. Little tiny buggers." He held one up for Myron to see. "I mean, what's up with that?"

"And the politicians," Myron said. "They spend all that time on gun control."

"So what do you want to drink? And don't ask for that Yoo-Hoo crap here. It's embarrassing."

"What are you having?"

"The same thing I always have when you pay. Twelve-year-old Scotch."

"I'll just have a club soda with lime."

"Wuss." He ordered it. "What do you want?"

"You know Stan Gibbs?"

Bruce said, "Whoa."

"What whoa?"

"I mean, whoa, you get involved in some hairy-ass shit, Myron. But Stan Gibbs? What the hell could you possibly have to do with him?"

"Probably nothing."

"Uh-huh."

"Just tell me about him, okay?"

Bruce shrugged, took a sip of Scotch. "Ambitious s.o.b. who went too far. What else do you need to know?"

"The whole story."

"Starting with?"

"What exactly did he do?"

"He plagiarized a story, the dumbass. That's not unusual. But to be so stupid about it."

"Too stupid?" Myron asked.

"What do you mean?"

"I mean we both agree that stealing from a published novel is not only unethical but idiotic."

"So?"

"So I'm asking if it's *too* idiotic."

"You think he's innocent, Myron?"

"Do you?"

He chucked down a few more pretzels. "Hell no. Stan Gibbs is guilty as sin. And as stupid as he was, I know plenty stupider. How about Mike Barnicle? The guy steals jokes from a George Carlin book. George Carlin, for chrissake."

"Does seem pretty stupid," Myron agreed.

"And he's not the only one. Look, Myron, every profession's got their dirty laundry, right? The stuff they want swept under the rug. Cops got their blue line when one of them pounds a suspect into the earth. Doctors cover each other's asses when they take out the wrong gallbladder or whatever. Lawyers . . . well, don't even get me started on their dirty little secrets."

"And plagiarism is yours?"

"Not just plagiarism," Bruce said. "Wholesale fabrication. I know reporters who make up sources. I know guys who make up dialogue. I know guys who make up whole conversations. They run stories about crack mothers and inner-city gang leaders who never existed. Ever read those columns? Ever wonder why so many drug addicts, say, sound so friggin' poignant when they can't even watch *Teletubbies* without a tutor?"

"And you're saying this happens a lot?"

"Truth?"

"Preferably."

"It's epidemic," Bruce said. "Some guys are lazy. Some are too ambitious. Some are just pathological liars. You know the type. They'll lie to you about what they had for breakfast just because it comes so naturally."

The drinks came. Bruce pointed at the empty pretzel bowl. The bartender replaced it.

"So if it's so epidemic," Myron said, "how come so few get caught?"

"First off, it's hard to catch. People hide behind anonymous sources and claim people moved, stuff like that. Second, it's like I said before. It's our dirty little secret. We keep it buried."

"I'd think you'd want to clean house."

"Oh, right. Like cops want to. Like doctors want to."

"You're not the same thing, Bruce."

"Let me give you a scenario, Myron, okay?" Bruce finished up his drink, and now he pointed to his glass for a refill. "You're an editor with, say, the *New York Times*. A story is written for you. You print it. Now it's brought to your attention that the story was fabricated or plagiarized or maybe just totally inaccurate, whatever. What do you do?"

"Retract it," Myron said.

"But you're the editor. You're the dumbass responsible

for its publication. You're probably the dumbass who hired the writer in the first place. Who do you think the higher-ups are going to blame? And do you think the higher-ups are going to be happy to hear that their paper printed something false? You think the *Times* wants to lose business to the *Herald* or the *Post* or whatever? And hell, the other papers don't even want to hear about it. The public already doesn't trust us as an institution, right? If the truth gets out, who gets hurt? Answer: everyone."

"So you quietly fire the guy," Myron said.

"Maybe. But, again, you're this editor for the *New York Times*. You fire, say, a columnist. Don't you think a higher-up is going to want to know why?"

"So you just let it go?"

"We're like the church used to be with pedophiles. We try to control the problem without hurting ourselves. We transfer the guy to another department. We pass the problem to someone else. Maybe we team him up with another writer. Harder to make shit up with someone looking over your shoulder."

Myron took a sip of his club soda. Flat. "Okay, let me ask the obvious question then. How did Stan Gibbs get caught?"

"He was dumb, dumber and dumbest. It was too high profile a piece to plagiarize like that. Not only that, but Stan rubbed the feds' face in a public crapper and flushed. You don't do that if you don't have the facts, especially to the feds. My guess is he thought he was safe because the novel had a negligible print run from some shitass vanity press in Oregon. I don't think they published more than five hundred copies of the thing, and that was more than twenty years ago. And the author was long dead."

"But someone dug it up."

"Yup."

Myron thought about it. "Strange, don't you think?"

"Most of the time I'd say yes, but not when it's this high-profile. And once the truth was uncovered, boom, Stan was done. Every media outlet got an anonymous press release about it. The feds held a press conference. I mean, there was almost a campaign against him. Someone—probably the feds—were out for their pound of flesh. And they got it."

"So maybe the feds were so pissed they set him up."

"How do you figure?" Bruce countered. "The novel exists. The passages Stan copied exist. There is no way around that."

Myron mulled that one over, looking for a way around it. Nothing came to him. "Did Stan Gibbs ever defend himself?"

"He never commented."

"Why not?"

"The guy's a reporter. He knew better. Look, stories like these become the worst kind of brushfire. Only way to get the fire out is to stop feeding the flame. No matter how bad, if there's nothing new to report—nothing new to feed the flame—it dies out. People always make the mistake of thinking they can douse the flame with their words, that they're so smart, their explanations will work like water or something. It's always a mistake to talk to the press. Everything—even wonderfully worded denials—feed the flames and keep it stoked."

"But doesn't silence make you look guilty?"

"He *is* guilty, Myron. Stan could only get himself in more trouble by talking. And if he hung around and tried to defend himself, someone would dig into his past too. Mainly his old columns. All of them. Every fact, every quote, everything. And if you've plagiarized one story, you've plagiarized others. You don't do it for the first time when you're Stan's age."

"So you think he was trying to minimize the damage?"

Bruce smiled, took a sip. "That Duke education," he said. "It wasn't wasted on you." He grabbed more pretzels. "Mind if I order a sandwich?"

"Suit yourself."

"It'll be worth it," Bruce said with a suddenly big smile. "Because I haven't yet mentioned the last little tidbit that convinced him to keep quiet."

"What's that?"

"It's big, Myron." The smile slid off his face. "Very big."

"Fine, order fries too."

"I don't want this to become public knowledge, you understand?"

"Come on, Bruce. What?"

Bruce turned back to the bar. He picked up a cocktail napkin and tore it in half. "You know the feds took Stan to court to find his sources."

"Yes."

"The court documents were kept sealed, but there was a bit of nastiness. See, they wanted Stan to provide some sort of corroboration. Something to show he didn't totally make the story up. He wouldn't offer any. For a while he claimed that only the families could back him and he wouldn't give them up. But the judge pressed. He finally admitted that there was one other person who could back his story."

"Back up his made-up story?"

"Yes."

"Who?"

"His mistress," Bruce said.

"Stan was married?"

"Guess the word 'mistress' gave it away," Bruce said. "Anyway, he was. Still is, technically, but now they're separated. Naturally Stan was hesitant about naming her—he loved his wife, had two kids, the backyard, whatever—but in the end he gave the judge her name under the condition that it stay sealed."

"Did the mistress back him?"

"Yes. This mistress—one Melina Garston—claimed to have been with him when he met the Sow the Seeds psycho."

Myron's brow creased. "Why does that name ring a bell?"

"Because Melina Garston is dead now. Tied and tortured and you don't want to know what."

"When?"

"Three months ago. Right after the shit hit Stan's fan. Worse, the police think Stan did it."

"To keep her from telling the truth?"

"Again that Duke education."

"But that makes no sense. She was killed after the plagiarism was discovered, right?"

"Right after, yeah."

"So it was too late by then. Everyone thinks he's guilty already. He's lost his job. He's disgraced. If his mistress now comes out and says 'Yeah, I lied,' it wouldn't really change a thing. What would Stan have gained by killing her?"

Bruce shrugged. "Maybe her retraction would have removed any doubt."

"But there's not much doubt there anyway."

The bartender came over. Bruce ordered a sandwich. Myron shook him off. "Can you find out where Stan Gibbs is hiding?"

Bruce waved down the bartender again. "I already know."

"How?"

"He was my friend."

"Was or is?"

"Is, I guess."

"You like him?"

"Yeah," Bruce said. "I like him."

"Yet, you still think he did it."

"Murder, probably not. Plagiarize . . ." He shrugged. "I'm a cynical guy. And just because a guy is a friend of mine doesn't mean he can't do dumb things."

"Will you give me his address?"

"Will you tell me why?"

Myron sipped his flat club soda. "Okay, this is the part where you say you want to know what I have. Then I say I have nothing and when I do, you'll be the first to know. Then you get kinda huffy and say I owe you and that's not good enough, but in the end you take the deal. So why don't we skip all that and just give me the address?"

"Will I still get my sandwich?"

"Sure."

"Fine, then," Bruce said. "Doesn't matter. Stan hasn't talked to anyone since he resigned—not even his close friends. What makes you think he'll talk to you?"

"Because I'm a witty dinner companion and natty dresser?"

"Yeah, that." He turned to Myron and looked at him heavily. "Now, this is the part where I tell you that if you find anything, anything, that suggests that Stan Gibbs is being set up, you tell me because I'm his friend and I'm a reporter hungry for a big story."

"Not to mention a sandwich."

No smile. "You got me?"

"Got you."

"Anything you want to tell me now?"

"Bruce, I got less than nothing. It's just a thread I need to snip away."

"You know Cross River in Englewood?"

"A mid-eighties condo development that looks like something out of *Poltergeist*."

"Twenty-four Acre Drive. Stan just came back to the area. He's renting there."

17

The Morning Mosh was not really the establishment's name. Located in a converted warehouse downtown on the West Side, the Mosh had a neon sign that changed as the day went on. The word *Mosh* stayed lit all the time, but in the morning it blinked *Morning Mosh*, then *Mid-Day Mosh* (as it now read) and later on, *Midnight Mosh*. And that's *Mosh*, not *Nosh*. Myron had expected a bagel store. But the letter was *M*, not *N*, and this place was *Mosh*. As in *Mosh Pit*. As in some retro heavy-metal band minus the talent blaring sounds that could strip paint while kids danced—and we're using that term in its loosest form here—in a pit, careening off one another like a thousand pinballs released into the machine at the same time.

A sign by the front door read FOUR BODY PIERCE MINIMUM TO ENTER (EARS DON'T COUNT).

Myron stayed on the sidewalk and used his cell phone. He called the Mosh's number. A voice answered, "Go for it, dude."

"Suzze T please."

"Dig."

Dig?

Suzze came on two minutes later. "Hello?"

"It's Myron. I'm out on the curb."

"Come in. No one bites. Well, except for that guy who bit the legs off a live frog last night. Man, that was so cool."

"Suzze, please meet me out here, okay?"

"What-ev-er."

Myron hung up, feeling old. Suzze came out less than a minute later. She wore bell-bottom jeans with a gravity-defying waist that stayed up south of her hips. Her top was pink and much too small, revealing not only a flat stomach but a bottom-side hint of what interested the fine folks at Rack Enterprises. Suzze sported only one tattoo (a tennis racket with a snake's head grip) and no piercings, not even her ears.

Myron pointed to the sign. "You don't meet the minimum piercing requirement."

"Yeah, Myron, I do."

Silence. Then Myron said, "Oh."

They started walking down the street. Another strange Manhattan neighborhood. Kids and the homeless hung out together. There were bars and nightclubs alongside daycare centers. The modern city. Myron passed a storefront with a sign: TATTOOS WHILE U WAIT. He reread the sign and frowned. Like how else would you do it?

"We got a weird endorsement offer," Myron said. "You know the Rack Bars?"

Suzze said, "Like, upscale topless, right?"

"Well, topless anyway."

"What about them?"

"They're opening up a chain of topless coffee bars."

Suzze nodded. "Cool," she said. "I mean, taking the popularity of Starbucks and mixing it with Scores and Goldfingers, well, it's totally wise."

"Uh, right. Anyway, they're having this big grand opening and they're trying to generate excitement and media attention and all that. So they want you to make a, uh, guest appearance."

"Topless?"

"Like I said on the phone, I had an offer I wanted you to refuse."

"Totally topless?"

Myron nodded. "They insist on nipple visibility."

"How much they willing to pay?"

"Two hundred thousand dollars."

She stopped. "Are you shitting me?"

"I shit you not."

She whistled. "Lots of cha-ching."

"Yes, but I still think—"

"This was, like, their first offer?"

"Yes."

"Do you think you could get them up?"

"No, that would be your job."

She stopped and looked at him. Myron shrugged his apology.

"Tell them yes," she said.

"Suzze . . ."

"Two hundred grand for flashing a bit of booby? Christ, last night I think I did it in there for free."

"That isn't the same thing."

"Did you see what I wore in *Sports Illustrated?* I might as well have been naked."

"That isn't the same thing either."

"This is Rack, Myron, not some sleazoid place like Buddy's. It's upscale topless."

"Saying 'upscale topless' is like saying 'good toupee,' " Myron said.

"Huh?"

"It might be good," he said, "but it's still a toupee."

She cocked her head. "Myron, I'm twenty-four years old."

"I know that."

"That's like 107 in women-tennis years. I'm ranked

thirty-one in the world right now. I haven't made two hundred grand over the past two years on tour. This is a big score, Myron. And man, will it change my image."

"Exactly my point."

"No, listen up, tennis is looking for draws. I'll be controversial. I'll get tons of attention. I'll suddenly be a big name. Admit it, my appearance fees will quadruple."

Appearance fees are the money paid to the big names just to show up, win or lose. Most name players make far more in appearance fees than prize money. It's where the potential major *dinero* is, especially for a player ranked thirty-first.

"Probably," Myron said.

She stopped and grabbed his arm. "I love playing tennis."

"I know that," he said softly.

"Doing this will extend my career. That means a lot to me, okay?"

Christ, she looked so young.

"All of what you're saying may be true," Myron said. "But at the end of the day, you're still appearing at a topless bar. And once it's done, it's done. You will always be remembered as the tennis player who app-eared topless."

"There are worse things."

"Yes. But I didn't become an agent to get in the stripping business. I'll do what you want. You're my client. I want what's best for you."

"But you don't think this is best for me?"

"I have trouble advising a young woman to appear topless."

"Even if it makes sense?"

"Even if it makes sense."

She smiled at him. "You know something, Myron?

You're cute when you're being a prude."

"Yeah, adorable."

"Tell them yes."

"Think about it for a few days, okay?"

"It's a no-brainer, Myron. Just do what you do best."

"What's that?"

"Get the number up. And tell them yes."

18

Cross River Condos was one of those complexes that looked like a movie façade, like whole buildings might topple over if you pushed against any one wall. The development was sprawlingly cramped, with every building looking exactly the same. Walking through it was like something out of *Alice in Wonderland*, all avenues mirroring the others, until you got dizzy. Have too much drink and you're bound to stick your key in the wrong lock.

Myron parked near the complex pool. The place was nice but too close to Route 80, the major artery that ran from, well, here in New Jersey to California. The traffic sounds sloshed over the fence. Myron located the door to 24 Acre Drive and then tried to figure out which windows belonged to it. If he had it right, the lights were on. So was the television. He knocked on the door. Myron saw a face peer through the window next to the door. The face did not speak.

"Mr. Gibbs?"

Through the glass, the face said, "Who are you?"

"My name is Myron Bolitar."

A brief pause. "The basketball player?"

"At one time, yes."

The face looked through the window for a few more seconds before opening the door. The odor of too many cigarettes wafted through the opening and happily nested inside Myron's nostrils. Not surprisingly, Stan Gibbs had a cigarette in his mouth. He had a gray stubble-to-beard going, too far gone for retro *Miami Vice.* He wore a yellow Bart Simpson sweatshirt, dark green sweatpants, socks, sneakers, and a Colorado Rockies baseball cap—the standard fashion fare shared with equal fervor by joggers and couch potatoes. Myron suspected the latter here.

"How did you find me?" Stan Gibbs asked.

"It wasn't difficult."

"That's not an answer."

Myron shrugged.

"It doesn't matter," Stan said. "I have no comment."

"I'm not a reporter."

"So what are you?"

"A sports agent."

Stan took a puff of the cigarette, didn't remove it from his mouth. "Sorry to disappoint you, but I haven't played competitive football since high school."

"May I come in?"

"No, I don't think so. What do you want?"

"I need to find the kidnapper you wrote about in your article," Myron said.

Stan smiled with very white teeth, especially when you considered the smoking. His skin was sort of clumpy and winter-colorless, his hair thin and tired, but he had those bright eyes, superbright eyes, the kind that look like supernatural beacons are shining out from within. "Don't you read the papers?" he asked. "I made the whole thing up."

"Made it up or copied it from a book?"

"I stand corrected."

"Or maybe you were telling the truth. In fact, maybe the subject of your articles called me on the phone last night."

Stan shook his head, the growing ash on the cigarette

holding on like a kid on an amusement park ride. "This is not something I want to revisit."

"Did you plagiarize the story?"

"I already said I wouldn't comment—"

"This isn't for public consumption. If you did—if the story was a fake—just tell me now and I'll go away. I don't have time to waste on false leads."

"Nothing personal," Stan said, "but you're not making a whole lot of sense here."

"Does the name Davis Taylor mean anything to you?"

"No comment."

"How about Dennis Lex?"

That threw him. The dangling cigarette started to slip from Stan's lips, but he caught it with his right hand. He dropped it on the walkway and watched it sizzle for a moment.

"Maybe you better come in."

The condo was a duplex centered with that staple of new American construction, the cathedral ceiling. Plenty of light came in from the big windows, splashing down on a decor straight out of a Sunday circular. A blond-wood entertainment center took up one wall, a matching coffee table not far from it. There was also a white-and-blue-striped couch—Myron would bet his lunch money it was a Serta Sleeper—and matching love seat. The carpeting was the same neutral as the exterior, a sort of inoffensive tan, and the place was clean yet disorderly in a divorcé way, newspapers and magazines and books piled here and there, nothing really put in a specific place.

He had Myron sit on the couch. "Want something to drink?"

"Sure, whatever," Myron said. The coffee table had one photograph on it. A man had his arms around two boys. All three were smiling too hard, like they'd just come in second place and didn't want to appear disappointed. They were standing in a garden of some sort. Behind them loomed a marble statue of a woman with a bow and arrow over her shoulder. Myron picked up the frame and studied it. "This you?"

Gibbs lifted his head while scooping a handful of ice into a glass. "I'm on the right," he said. "With my brother and my father."

"Who's that a statue of?"

"Diana the Huntress. You familiar with her?"

"Didn't she turn into Wonder Woman?"

Stan chuckled. "Sprite okay?"

Myron put the photograph down. "Sure."

Stan Gibbs poured the drink, brought it out to Myron, handed it to him. "What do you know about Dennis Lex?"

"Just that he exists," Myron said.

"So why mention his name to me?"

Myron shrugged. "Why did you react so strongly to hearing it?"

Gibbs took out another cigarette, lit it. "You're the one who came to me."

"True."

"Why?"

No secret. "I'm looking for a man named Davis Taylor. He's a bone marrow donor who matched a kid and then vanished. I traced him to an address in Connecticut, but he's not there. So I dug a little more and found out that Davis Taylor is a name change. His real name is Dennis Lex."

"I still don't see what this has to do with me."

"This might sound a little nutty," Myron said. "But I left a voice mail message for Davis Taylor né Dennis

Lex. When he called back, he made little sense. But he kept telling me to 'sow the seeds.' "

A small quake ran through Stan Gibbs. It passed quickly. "What else did he say?"

"That was pretty much it. I should sow the seeds. I should say good-bye to the child. Stuff like that."

"It's probably nothing," Gibbs said. "He probably just read my article and decided to have a little fun at your expense."

"Probably," Myron said. "Except that wouldn't really explain your reaction to Dennis Lex's name."

Stan shrugged, but there wasn't much behind it. "The family is famous."

"If I said Ivana Trump, would you have reacted the same?"

Gibbs stood. "I need some time to think about this."

"Think out loud," Myron said.

Stan just shook his head.

"Did you make up the story, Stan?"

"Another time."

"Not good enough," Myron said. "You owe me something here. Did you plagiarize the story?"

"How do you expect me to answer that?"

"Stan?"

"What?"

"I don't care about your situation. I'm not here to judge you or tell on you. I don't give a rat's ass if you made up the story or not. All I care about is finding the bone marrow donor. Period. End of story. *El Fin*."

Stan's eyes started to well up. He took another puff of the cigarette. "No," he said. "I never plagiarized. I never saw that book in my life."

It was like the room had been holding its breath and finally let go.

"How do you explain the similarities between your article and that novel?"

He opened his mouth, stopped, shook his head.

"Your silence makes you look guilty."

"I don't have to explain anything to you."

"Yeah, you do. I'm trying to save a kid's life here. You're not that wrapped up in your problems, are you, Stan?"

Stan moved back into the kitchen. Myron stood and followed him. "Talk to me," Myron said. "Maybe I can help."

"No," he said. "You can't."

"How do you explain the similarities, Stan? Just tell me that, okay? You must have thought about it."

"I don't need to think about it."

"Meaning?"

He opened the refrigerator and grabbed another can of Sprite. "Do you think all psychotics are original?"

"I'm not following you."

"You received a call from a guy who told you about sowing the seeds."

"Right."

"There are two possibilities that explain why he did that," Stan said. "One, he is the same killer I wrote about. Or two?" Stan looked at Myron.

"He just repeated what he'd read in the article," Myron said.

Stan snapped and pointed at Myron.

"So you're saying that the kidnapper you interviewed read this novel and it, what, influenced him somehow? That he copied it?"

Stan took a swig from the can. "That's a theory," he said.

And a damn good one, Myron thought. "So why

didn't you say that to the press? Why didn't you defend yourself?"

"None of your goddamn business."

"Some people say it's because you were afraid they'd look closer at your work. That they'd find other fabrications."

"And some people are morons," he finished.

"So why didn't you fight?"

"I spent my whole life being a journalist," Stan said. "Do you know what it means for a journalist to be called a plagiarist? It's like a daycare worker being called a child molester. I'm done. No words can change that. I've lost everything to this scandal. My wife, my kids, my job, my reputation—"

"Your mistress?"

He shut his eyes suddenly, tightly, like a child trying to make the bogeyman go away.

"The police think you killed Melina," Myron said.

"I'm well aware of that."

"Tell me what's going on here, Stan."

He opened his eyes and shook his head. "I have to make some calls, check out some leads."

"You can't just cut me loose."

"I have to," he said.

"Let me help."

"I don't need your help."

"But I need yours."

"Not right now," Stan said. "You'll have to trust me on this."

"I'm not big on trust," Myron said.

Stan smiled. "Neither am I," he said. "Neither am I."

19

Myron pulled out. So, too, he noticed, did two men in a black Oldsmobile Ciera. Hmm.

The cell phone rang.

"Have you learned anything?" It was Emily.

"Not really," Myron said.

"Where are you?"

"Englewood."

"Do you have any plans for dinner?" Emily asked.

Myron hesitated. "No."

"I'm a good cook, you know. We dated in college, so I didn't have much chance to demonstrate my culinary skills."

"I remember you cooking for me once," Myron said.

"I did?"

"In my wok."

Emily chuckled. "That's right, you had an electric wok in your dorm, right?"

"Yep."

"I almost forgot about that," Emily said. "Why did you have one, anyway?"

"To impress chicks."

"Really?"

"Sure. I thought I'd invite a girl up to my room, slice up some vegetables, add a little soy sauce—"

"To the vegetables?" she asked.

"For starters."

"So how come you never pulled that one on me?"

"Didn't have to."

"You calling me easy, Myron?"

"How exactly does one answer that," Myron asked, "and maintain possession of both testicles?"

"Come on over," Emily said. "I'll make us some dinner. No soy sauce."

Another hesitation.

"Please don't make me ask again," Emily said.

He wanted very much to say no. "Okay."

"Just take Route 4—"

"I know the way, Emily."

He hung up then and checked the rearview mirror. The black Oldsmobile Ciera was still following. Better safe than sorry. Myron hit the preprogrammed number on his cell phone. After one ring, Win answered.

"Articulate," Win said.

"Got a tail, methinks."

"License plate?"

Myron read it off to him.

"Where should we coordinate?"

"Garden State Plaza mall," Myron said.

"On my way, fair maiden."

Myron stayed on Route 4 until he saw a sign for the Garden State Plaza. He took a rather complicated cloverleaf overpass and veered into the mall's lot. The black Olds followed, dropping back a bit. Stall time. Myron circled a few times before finding a parking space. The Olds kept its distance. He turned off the car and headed for the "Northeast Entrance."

The Garden State Plaza had all the artificial elements endemic in malls—the mall ear-pop when you enter, the stale mall air, the mall hollow acoustics, as though all sound were traveling through a high-volume distorter— the audial equivalent of a shower door, voices somehow rendered both loud and incomprehensible. Too much with the high ceilings and faux marble, nothing soft to cushion the sound.

He strolled through the nouveau riche section of the Garden State Plaza, past several barren shoe stores, the kind that display maybe three pairs of shoes on the ends of what look like deer antlers. He reached a store called Aveda, which sold wildly overpriced cosmetics and lotions. The Aveda saleswoman, a starving young thang in tourniquet-tight black, informed Myron that they were having a sale on face moisturizers. Myron refrained from crying out "Yippee!" and went on his way. Victoria's Secret was next, and Myron did that male surreptitious glance at the lingerie window displays. Most of your more sophisticated heterosexual males are well versed in this art, awarding the racily clad supermodels the most casual of once-overs, feigning a lack of interest in the blown-up, blown-clear images of Stephanie and Frederique in Miracle Bras. Myron, of course, did the same thing—and then he thought, why pretend? He stopped short, squared his shoulders, ogled in earnest. Honesty. Shouldn't a woman respect that in a man too?

He checked his watch. Not yet. More stall. The plan, as it were, was fairly simple. Win drives to the Garden State Plaza. When he arrives, he calls Myron on the cell phone. Myron then goes back to his car. Win looks for the black Olds and follows the followee. Super clever, no?

Myron hit Sharper Image, one of the few places in the world where people use the words *shiatsu* and *ionic* and nobody laughs. He tried out a massage chair (setting: Knead) and debated purchasing a $5,500 life-size statue of a *Star Wars* star-trooper that had been reduced to a mere $3,499. Talk about redefining nouveau riche.

Here's a little tip for you: If you've purchased a Sharper Image life-size *Star Wars* star-trooper, take out your platinum-est charge card, hand it to the nearest cashier, and buy a life.

The cell phone rang. Myron picked it up.

"They're feds," Win said.

"Yikes."

"Yes."

"No reason to follow them, then."

"No."

Myron spotted two men in suits and sunglasses behind him. They were studying the fruit-flavored shampoos in the Garden Botanica store window a little too closely. Two men in suits and sunglasses. Oh, like that happens. "I think they're following me in here too."

"If they arrest you with lingerie," Win said, "tell them it's for your wife."

"That what you do?"

"Keep the phone on," Win said.

Myron did as he asked. An old trick of theirs. Myron kept his cell phone on, thereby freeing Win to listen in. Okay, fine, now what? He kept strolling. Two more men in business suits were window-shopping up ahead. They turned as Myron approached, both staring him down. Some tail. Myron glanced behind him. The first two feds were right there.

The two feds in front of him stepped directly into his path. The other two came up behind him, boxing him in.

Myron stopped, looked at all four feds. "Did you guys check out the facial moisturizer sale at Aveda?"

"Mr. Bolitar?"

"Yes."

One of them, a short guy with a severe haircut, flashed a badge. "I'm Special Agent Fleischer with the Federal Bureau of Investigation. We'd like a word with you, sir."

"What about?"

"Would you mind coming with us?"

They had the standard-issue stone expressions; Myron would get nothing out of them. Probably didn't even know anything themselves. Probably just delivery boys. Myron shrugged and followed them out. Two got into a white Olds Ciera. The other two stayed with Myron. One opened the back door of the black Ciera and head-gestured for Myron to get in. He did so. The interior was very clean. Nice, smooth seats. Myron ran his hand over it.

"Corinthian leather?" he asked.

Special Agent Fleischer turned around. "No, sir, that would be the Ford Granada."

Touché.

No one spoke. No radio played. Myron settled back. He debated calling Emily and postponing their soy-sauce-less encounter, but he didn't want the feds to hear him. He sat tight and kept his mouth shut. He didn't do that often. It felt odd and somehow right.

Thirty minutes later, he was in the basement of a modest high-rise in Newark. He sat at a table with his hands on a semi-sticky table. The room had one barred window and cement walls the color and texture of dried oatmeal. The feds excused themselves and left Myron alone. Myron sighed and sat back. He'd figured that this was the old soften-him-up-by-making-him-wait bit, when the door flew open.

The woman was first. She wore a pumpkin-orange blazer, blue jeans, sneakers, and ball-and-chain earrings. The word that came to mind was *husky*. Not big really.

Husky. Everything was husky—even her hair, a sort of canned-corn yellow. The guy riding in on her fumes was geeky thin with a pointy head and a small, greased shock of black hair. He looked like an upside-down pencil. He spoke first.

"Good afternoon, Mr. Bolitar," Pencil said.

"Good afternoon."

"I'm Special Agent Rick Peck," he said. "This is Special Agent Kimberly Green."

The orange-blazered Green did a caged-lion pace. Myron nodded at her. She nodded back but grudgingly, like her teacher had just told her to apologize for something she didn't do.

Pencil Peck continued. "Mr. Bolitar, we'd like to ask you a few questions."

"What about?"

Peck kept his eyes on his notes and spoke like he was reading. "Today you visited one Stan Gibbs at 24 Acre Drive. Is that correct?"

"How do you know I didn't visit two Stan Gibbs?"

Peck and Green exchanged a glance. Then Peck said, "Please, Mr. Bolitar, we'd appreciate your cooperation. Did you visit Mr. Gibbs?"

"You know I did," Myron said.

"Fine, thank you." Peck wrote something down slowly. Then he looked up. "We'd very much like to know the nature of your visit."

"Why?"

"You are the first visitor Mr. Gibbs has had since moving to his current residence."

"No, I mean, why do you want to know?"

Green crossed her arms. She and Peck looked at each other again. Peck said, "Mr. Gibbs is part of an ongoing investigation."

Myron waited. No one said anything. "Well, that pretty much clears it up."

"That's all I can say for the moment."

"Same here."

"Pardon?"

"If you can't say any more, I can't say any more."

Kimberly Green put her hands on the table, gave a toothy grimace—husky teeth?—and leaned down like she might take a bite out of him. The canned-corn hair smelled like Pert Plus. She eyeballed him—must have read a memo on intimidating glares—and then spoke for the first time. "Here's how we're going to play it, asshole. We're going to ask you questions. You're going to listen to them and then you're going to answer them. You got it?"

Myron nodded. "I want to make sure I got this straight," he said to her. "You're playing bad cop, right?"

Peck picked up the ball. "Mr. Bolitar, no one is interested in making trouble here. But we'd very much like your cooperation in this matter."

"Am I under arrest?" Myron asked.

"No."

"Bye then."

He started to stand. Kimberly Green gave him a shove mid-rise and he fell back into the chair. "Sit down, asshole." She looked over at Peck. "Maybe he's part of it."

"You think so?"

"Why else would he be so reluctant to answer questions?"

Peck nodded. "Makes sense. An accomplice."

"We can probably arrest him now," Green said. "Lock him up for the night, maybe leak it to the press."

Myron looked up at her. "Gasp," he said. "Now. I. Am. Really. Scared. Second gasp."

She narrowed her eyes. "What did you say?"

"Don't tell me," Myron said. "Maybe I'm guilty of aiding and abetting. That's my personal favorite. Does anyone actually get prosecuted for that?"

"You think we're playing games here?"

"I do. And by the way, how come you're all called 'special' agent? Doesn't that sound like something someone made up one day? Like a kid's game to raise self-esteem. 'We're promoting you from agent to special agent, Barney,' and then what, super-special agent?"

Green grabbed his lapels and leaned his chair back. "You're not funny."

Myron looked at her hands gripping him. "Are you for real?"

"You want to try me?" she said.

Peck said, "Kim."

She ignored him and kept her glare on Myron. "This is serious," she said.

Her tone aimed for angry but came out more like a frightened plea. Two more agents entered. With the four delivery boys, that made eight. This was something big. What, Myron had no idea. The murder of Melina Garston maybe. But that was doubtful. The locals usually handled murders. You don't call in the feds.

The new guys came at Myron in different ways, but there were only so many routes to travel and Myron knew them all. Threatening, friendly, flattering, insulting, building up, belittling, hard, soft, every sell. They denied him the bathroom, they made excuses to keep him longer, all the while they're working him and he's working them and neither one is giving. Sweat started flowing, mostly from them, the stains and stench filling the air, metastasizing into something Myron could swear was genuine fear.

Kimberly Green came in and out and she kept shaking her head at him. Myron wanted to cooperate, but here's the pertinent cliché: Once the genie is out of the bottle, you can't put it back in. He didn't know what they were investigating. He didn't know if it would benefit Jeremy to talk or hurt him. But once he spoke, once his words were in the public domain, he couldn't take them back. Any leverage he might later be able to apply would be gone. So, for now, even if he might want to help, he wouldn't. Not until he learned more. He had the contacts. He could find out quickly enough, make an informed decision.

Sometimes, negotiating meant shutting up.

When things wound down, Myron got up to leave. Kimberly Green blocked his path. "I'm going to make your life hell," she said.

"That your way of asking me out?"

She leaned back as if he'd slapped her. When she recovered, she shook her head slowly. "You have no idea, do you?"

Shutting up, he reminded himself. Myron pushed past her and headed outside.

20

He called Emily from the car.

"I thought I was being stood up," she said.

Myron checked out the rearview mirror and spotted what might be another fed tail. No matter. "Sorry," he said. "Something came up."

"Involving the donor?"

"I don't think so."

"You still in Jersey?" Emily asked.

"Yes."

"Come on over. I'll reheat dinner."

He wanted to say no. "Okay."

Franklin Lakes was about sprawling. Everything sprawled. The houses were mostly new construction, big brick mansions on eternal cul-de-sacs, little gates at the front of the driveways that opened with push-button or intercom, like that would really protect the owners from what lay outside the lush lawns and pedicure-clipped hedges. The interiors were sprawling too, dining rooms big enough to house helicopters, remote-controlled blinds, Sub-Zero/Viking Stove kitchens with marble islands that overlooked family rooms the size of movie theaters, always with complicated state-of-the-art entertainment centers.

Myron rang the bell and the door opened and for the first time in his life, Myron was face-to-face with his son.

Jeremy smiled at him. "Hi."

Strong, totally alien surges ricocheted haphazardly

through Myron, his nervous system melting down and in overdrive all at once. His diaphragm contracted and his lungs stopped. So, he was sure, did his heart. His mouth weakly opened and closed like a dying fish on a boat deck. Tears headed up and pushed toward the eyes.

"You're Myron Bolitar, right?" Jeremy said.

An ocean-shell rushing filled Myron's ears. He managed a nod.

"You played ball against my dad," Jeremy said, still with the smile that ripped at the corners of Myron's heart. "In college, right?"

Myron found his voice. "Yes."

The kid nodded back. "Cool."

"Yeah."

A horn honked. Jeremy leaned to the right and looked behind Myron. "That's my ride. Later."

Jeremy leaped past Myron. Myron numbly turned and watched the boy jog down the driveway. Imagination maybe, but that gait was oh-so-familiar. From Myron's old game films. More surges. *Oh Christ . . .*

Myron felt a hand on his shoulder, but he ignored it and watched the boy. The car door opened and swallowed Jeremy into the darkness. The driver's window slid down and a pretty woman called out, "Sorry I'm late, Em."

From behind him, Emily said, "No problem."

"I'll take them to school in the morning."

"Great."

A wave and the pretty woman's window slid back into place. The car started on its way. Myron watched it disappear down the road. He felt Emily's eyes on him. He slowly turned to her.

"Why did you do that?"

"I thought he'd be gone by now," Emily said.

"Do I really look that stupid?"

She stepped back into the house. "I want to show you something."

Trying to get his legs back, his head wobbly and his internal referee still giving him the eight count, Myron followed her silently up the stairway. She led him down a darkened corridor lined with modern lithographs. She stopped, opened a door, and flipped on the lights. The room was teenage-cluttered, as if someone had put all the belongings in the center of the room and dropped a hand grenade on them. The posters on the walls—Michael Jordan, Keith Van Horn, Greg Downing, Austin Powers, the words *YEAH, BABY!* across his middle in pink tie-dye lettering—had been hung askew, all tattered corners and missing pushpins. There was a Nerf basketball hoop on the closet door. There was a computer on the desk and a baseball cap dangling from a desk lamp. The corkboard had a mix of family snapshots and construction-paper crayons signed by Jeremy's sister, all held up by oversized pushpins. There were footballs and autographed baseballs and cheap trophies and a couple of blue ribbons and three basketballs, one with no air in it. There were stacks of computer-game CD-ROMs and a Game Boy on the unmade bed and a surprising amount of books, several opened and facedown. Clothes littered the floor like war wounded; the drawers were half open, shirts and underwear hanging out like they'd been shot mid-escape. The room had the slight, oddly comforting smell of kids' socks.

"He's a slob," she said. Leaving off the obvious "like you."

Myron stayed still.

"He keeps Oxy 10 in his desk drawer," Emily said. "He thinks I don't know. He's at that age where crushes keep him up all night, but he's never even kissed a girl." She walked over to the corkboard and snatched up a photograph of Jeremy. "He's beautiful, don't you think?"

"This isn't helping, Emily."

"I want you to understand."

"Understand what?"

"He's never been kissed. He is going to die and he's never even kissed a girl."

Myron held up his hands. "I don't know what you want me to say here."

"Try to understand, okay?"

"I don't need melodrama. I understand."

"No, Myron, you don't. You look back at the night and see it as some sort of Gothic blunder. We did something sinful and for that we all paid a heavy price. If we could just go back and erase that tragic mistake, well, it's all so *Hamlet* and *Macbeth*, isn't it? Your ruined basketball career, Greg's future, our marriage—all laid to waste in that one moment of lust."

"It wasn't lust."

"Let's not go through that argument again. I don't care what it was. Lust, stupidity, fear, fate. Call it whatever the hell you want to—but I would never want to go back. That 'mistake' was the best thing that ever happened to me. Jeremy, our son, came out of that mess. Do you hear what I'm saying? I'd destroy a million careers and marriages for him."

She looked at him, challenging. He said nothing.

"I'm not religious and I don't believe in fate or destiny or any of that," she went on. "But maybe, just maybe, there had to be a balance. Maybe the only way to produce something so wonderful was to surround the event with so much destruction."

Myron started backing out of the room. "This isn't helping," he said again.

"Yes," she said, "it is."

"You want me to find the donor. I'm trying to do that. But this kind of distraction doesn't help. I need to stay detached."

"No, Myron, you need attachment. You need to get emotional. You have to understand the stakes—your son, that beautiful boy who opened the door—is going to die before he's even kissed a girl." She moved closer to him and looked into his eyes and Myron thought that her eyes had never looked so clear before.

"I watched you play every game at Duke," she said. "I fell in love with you on that court—not because you were the team star or because you were graceful or athletic. You were so open out there, so raw and emotional. And the more emotional you got, the more pressure there was, the better you played. If the game was a blowout, you lost interest. You needed it to matter. You needed to be double-teamed with only a few seconds on the clock. You needed to lose control a little."

"This isn't a game, Emily."

"Right," she said. "The stakes are higher. The emotion should be higher. I want you desperate, Myron. That's when you're at your best."

He looked at the photograph of Jeremy, and he knew that he was feeling something that he had never felt before. He blinked, caught the expression on his face in the closet-door mirror, and for a moment he saw his own father staring back.

Emily hugged him then. She buried her face in his shoulder and started to cry. Myron held on tight. They stood that way for several minutes before making their way downstairs. Over dinner, Emily told him about Jeremy, and he soaked in every story. They moved to the couch and broke out the photo albums. Emily tucked her legs under her, her elbow on the top of the couch, her head leaning on the heel of her hand, and told him more. It was nearly two in the morning when she walked him to the door. They were holding hands.

"I know you spoke to Dr. Singh," she said in the open door.

"Yes."

She let loose a deep breath. "I'm just going to say this, okay?"

"Okay."

"I've been keeping track. I bought one of those home tests. The, uh, optimum conception day will be Thursday."

He opened his mouth but she stopped him with her hand.

"I know all the arguments against this, but it might be Jeremy's only chance. Don't say anything. Just think about it."

She closed the door. Myron stared at it for a few moments. He tried to conjure up the moment Jeremy had opened it, the crooked smile on the boy's face, but already the image was hazy and fading fast.

21

First thing in the morning, Myron called Terese. Still no answer. He frowned at the phone. "Am I getting the big kiss-off?" he asked Win.

"Doubtful," Win said. He was reading the newspaper and wearing silk pajamas with a matching bathrobe and slippers. Give him a pipe and he could have been something Noël Coward created on an off day.

"What makes you say that?"

"Our Ms. Collins appears to be rather direct," Win said. "If you were being tossed into the dung heap, you'd know the smell."

"And then there's the part about my being irresistible to women," Myron said.

Win turned the page.

"So what's she up to?"

Win tapped his chin with his index finger. "What's the term you relationship people use? Oh, yes. Space. Perhaps she needs some space."

" 'Needing space' is usually a code phrase for the big kiss-off."

"Yes, well, whatever." Win crossed his legs. "You want me to look into it?"

"Into what?"

"What Ms. Collins might be up to."

"No."

"Fine," Win said. "Let's move on, shall we? Tell me about your encounter with the Federal Bureau of Investigation."

Myron recapped the interrogation.

"So we don't know what they wanted," Win said.

"Correct."

"Not a clue?"

"Nothing. Except that they were scared."

"Curious."

Myron nodded.

Win took a sip of tea, pinky up. Oh, the horrors that pinky had witnessed, partaken in, even. They sat in Win's formal dining room and used a silver tea set. Victorian mahogany table with lion-paw feet, silver tea set, silver milk pitcher, boxes of Cap'n Crunch and some new cereal called Oreo, which is exactly what you would imagine. "Theorizing at this juncture is a waste of time. I'll make some calls, see what I can find out."

"Thanks."

"I'm still not sure I see a connection between Stan Gibbs and our blood donor."

"It's a long shot," Myron agreed.

"More than that. A newspaper columnist makes up a story about a serial kidnapper and now—what?—we think the fictional character is the donor?"

"Stan Gibbs claims the story is real."

"Does he now?"

"Yes."

Win rubbed his chin. "Pray tell, why does he not defend himself?"

"No clue."

"Presumably because he is guilty," Win said. "Man is, above all, selfish. He's into self-preservation. It's instinctive. He does not martyr himself. He cares about one thing above all else: saving his hide."

"Assuming I agree with your sunny view of human

nature, wouldn't you agree that man would lie to save himself?"

"Of course," Win said.

"So armed with this pretty decent defense—the idea that the serial kidnapper copycatted the novel—why wouldn't Stan use it to defend himself, even if he was guilty of plagiarism?"

Win nodded. "I like the way you're thinking."

"Cynically, yes."

The intercom buzzed. Win pressed the button, and the doorman announced Esperanza. A minute later, she swept into the room, grabbed a chair, and poured herself a bowl of Oreo cereal.

"Why do they always say it's 'part of this complete breakfast'?" Esperanza asked. "Every single time, every single cereal. What's all that about?"

Nobody replied.

Esperanza took a spoonful, looked at Win, head-gestured toward Myron. "I hate it when he's right," she said to Win.

"A bad omen," Win agreed.

Myron said, "I was right?"

She turned her gaze to Myron. "I did that school check on Dennis Lex. I tracked down any and all educational institutions any of his siblings or parents had gone to. Nothing. College, high school, middle school—even grammar school. No trace of Dennis Lex."

"But?" Myron said.

"Preschool."

"You're kidding me."

"Nope."

"You found his preschool?"

"I'm more than just a great piece of ass," Esperanza said.

171

Win said, "Not to me, my dear."

"You're sweet, Win."

Win bowed his head slightly.

"Miss Peggy Joyce," Esperanza said. "She still teaches and runs the Shady Wells Montessori School for Children in East Hampton."

"And she remembers Dennis Lex?" Myron said. "From thirty years ago?"

"Apparently." Esperanza shoved in another spoonful and tossed Myron a sheet of paper. "This is her address. She's expecting you this morning. Drive safely now, ya hear?"

22

The car phone rang.

"The old man is a lying sack of shit." It was Greg Downing.

"What?"

"The geezer is lying."

"You mean Nathan Mostoni?"

"Jesus Christ, what other old man have I been watching?"

Myron switched ears. "What makes you think he's lying, Greg?"

"Lots of things."

"Like?"

"Like starting with Mostoni never hearing from the bone marrow center. Does that sound logical to you?"

He thought of Karen Singh and her dedication and the stakes. "No," Myron said, "but it's like we said before—he might be confused."

"I don't think so."

"Why not?"

"Nathan Mostoni goes out plenty on his own, for one thing. Sometimes he acts loony, but other times, he seems just fine. He shops himself. He talks to people. He dresses like a normal person."

"That doesn't mean anything," Myron said.

"No? An hour ago he went out, right? So I got close to the house, right up against the back window, and I dialed that number, the one you got for the donor."

"And?"

"And I hear a phone inside the house ringing."

That made Myron pause.

"So what do you think we should do?" Greg asked.

"I'm not sure. Have you seen anybody else at the house?"

"Nobody. Mostoni goes out but nobody's been here. And I tell you something else. He looks younger now. I don't know how else to explain it. It's weird. You making any headway on your end?"

"I'm not sure."

"That's some answer, Myron."

"The only one I got."

"So what do you think we should do about Mostoni?"

"I'll have Esperanza do a background check. In the meantime, stay on him."

"Time's a-ticking away here, Myron."

"I know that. I'll be in touch."

He disconnected the call and flipped on the radio. Chaka Khan was singing "Ain't Nobody Love You Better." If you can listen to that one without moving your feet, you got some serious rhythm issues. He took the Long Island Expressway east, which was shockingly clear today. Usually the road was more or less a parking lot that swayed forward every couple of minutes.

People always tell you that the Hamptons, the swanky Long Island summer spot where Manhattanites get away from it all by being with other Manhattanites, is best in the off season. You always hear that about vacation spots. People, mostly vacationers themselves, whine through the high-season months, waiting to reach this apex of a theoretically swarmless nirvana. But—and this was the part Myron never understood—no one is ever in the Hamptons in the off months. No one. Downtown is dead to the point of craving tumbleweeds.

Shop owners sigh and discount nothing. The restaurants are less crowded, sure, but they're also closed. And hey, let's be honest here, the weather and beaches and even the people-watching are big draws here. Who goes to a Long Island beach in the winter?

The school was in a residential neighborhood with older, more modest homes—a place where the true Long Island regulars, none of whom hang out with Alec and Kim at Nick and Toni's, resided. Myron parked in a church lot and followed the signs down the steps into the rectory's basement. A young woman, a hall monitor of sorts, greeted Myron at the landing. He gave her his name and said he was here to see Ms. Joyce. The young woman nodded and told him to follow her.

The corridor was silent. Strange when one considered that this was a preschool. *Preschool.* Another new term. In Myron's day, they had called them nursery schools. Myron wondered when the name had changed and what group had considered the term *nursery school* somehow discriminatory. Professional RNs? Breast-feeding mothers? Bottle-fed infants maybe?

Still silent. Perhaps it was vacation or naptime. Myron was about to ask the young hall monitor when she opened a door. He looked in. Wrong-a-mundo. The room was chock full of small children, probably twenty give or take, and they were all working independently and in total silence. The older teacher smiled at Myron. She whispered to the little boy she was working with—he was doing something with blocks and letters—and stood.

"Hello," she said to Myron, speaking softly.

"Hi," Myron whispered back.

She leaned toward the young monitor. "Miss Simmons, will you help Mrs. McLaughlin?"

"Of course."

Peggy Joyce wore an open yellow sweater over a buttoned-at-the-neck blouse. The collar was frilly. She had half-moon glasses dangling from a chain around her neck. "We can chat in my office."

"Okay." He followed her. The place was silent as, well, a place without children. Myron asked, "Do you give those kids Valium?"

She smiled. "Just a little Montessori."

"A little what?"

"You don't have children, do you?"

The question caused a pang, but he answered in the negative.

"It's a teaching philosophy created by Dr. Maria Montessori, Italy's first female physician."

"It seems to work."

"I suppose."

"Do the children act like this at home?"

"Good Lord, no. Truth be told, it doesn't translate into the real world. But few things do."

They moved into the office, which consisted of a wooden desk, three chairs, one file cabinet.

"How long have you taught here?" Myron asked.

"I'm in my forty-third year."

"Wow."

"Yes."

"I guess you've seen lots of changes?"

"In kids? Almost none. Children don't change, Mr. Bolitar. A five-year-old is still a five-year-old."

"Still innocent."

She cocked her head. " 'Innocent' isn't the word I would use. Children are total id. They are perhaps the most naturally vicious creatures on God's green earth."

"Strange outlook for a preschool teacher."

"Just an honest one."

"So what word would you use?"

She thought about it. "If pressed, I'd say 'unformed.' Or maybe 'undeveloped.' Like a picture you've already taken but haven't processed yet."

Myron nodded, though he had no idea what she meant. There was something about Peggy Joyce that was a little, well, scary.

"Do you remember that book *All I Really Need to Know I Learned in Kindergarten?*" she asked him.

"Yes."

"It's true, but not in the way you think. School removes children from their warm parental cocoon. School teaches them to bully or be bullied. School teaches them how to be cruel to one another. School teaches them that Mommy and Daddy lied to them when they told them that they were special and unique."

Myron said nothing.

"You don't agree?"

"I don't teach preschool."

"That's sidestepping, Mr. Bolitar."

Myron shrugged. "They learn socialization. That's a hard lesson. And like every hard lesson, you have to get it wrong before you can get it right."

"They learn boundaries, in other words?"

"Yes."

"Interesting. And perhaps true. But you remember when I was giving the film-processing example earlier?"

"Yes."

"School only processes the picture. It doesn't snap it."

"Okay," Myron said, not wanting to follow her train of thought.

"What I mean is, everything is pretty much decided

by the time these children leave here and enter kindergarten. I can tell who will be successful and who will fail, who will end up happy and who will end up in prison, and ninety percent of the time I'm right. Maybe Hollywood and video games have an influence, I don't know. But I can usually tell which kid will be watching too many violent movies or playing too many violent games."

"You can tell all this by the time they're five years old?"

"Pretty much, yes."

"And you feel that's it? That they don't have the ability to change?"

"The ability? Oh, probably. But they're already on a path, and while they may still be able to change it, the majority do not. Staying on the path is easier."

"So let me ask you the eternal question: Is it nature or nurture?"

She smiled. "I get asked that all the time."

"And?"

"I answer nurture. Know why?"

Myron shook his head.

"Believing in nurture is like believing in God. You might be wrong, but you might as well cover your bases." She folded her hands and leaned forward. "Now, what can I do for you, Mr. Bolitar?"

"Do you remember a student named Dennis Lex?"

"I remember all my students. Does that surprise you?"

Myron didn't want her going off on another tangent. "Did you teach the other Lex children?"

"I taught them all. Their father made a lot of changes after his book became a bestseller. But he kept them here."

"So what can you tell me about Dennis Lex?"

She sat back and regarded him as though seeing him for the first time. "I don't want to be rude, but I'm wondering when you're going to tell me what this is all about. I'm talking to you, Mr. Bolitar—and breaching confidences, I suspect—because I think you're here for a very specific reason."

"What reason is that, Ms. Joyce?"

Her eyes had a steely glint. "Don't play games with me, Mr. Bolitar."

She was right. "I'm trying to find Dennis Lex."

Peggy Joyce kept still.

"I know this sounds weird," he went on. "But as far as I can tell, he fell off the earth after preschool."

She stared straight ahead, though Myron had no idea at what. There were no photographs on the walls, no diplomas, no drawings by little hands. Just cold wall. "Not after," she said finally. "During."

There was a knock on the door. Peggy Joyce said, "Come in." The young hall monitor, Miss Simmons, entered with a little boy. His head was down and he'd been crying. "James needs a little time," Miss Simmons said.

Peggy Joyce nodded. "Let him lie on the mat."

James eyed Myron and left with Miss Simmons.

Myron turned to Peggy Joyce. "What happened to Dennis Lex?"

"It's a question I've been waiting for someone to ask for more than thirty years," she said.

"What's the answer?"

"First, tell me why you're looking for him."

"I'm trying to find a bone marrow donor. I think it might be Dennis Lex." He gave her as few details as he could. When he finished, she put a bony hand to her face.

"I don't think I can help you," she said. "It was so long ago."

"Please, Ms. Joyce. A child will die if I don't find him. You're my only lead."

"You spoke to his family?"

"Only his sister Susan."

"What did she tell you?"

"Nothing."

"I'm not sure what I can add."

"You could start by telling me what Dennis was like."

She sighed and neatly arranged her hands on her thighs. "He was like the other Lex children—very bright, thoughtful, contemplative, perhaps a bit too much so for so young a child. With most students, I try to get them to grow up a bit. With the Lex children, that was never an issue."

Myron nodded, trying to encourage.

"Dennis was the youngest. You probably know that. He was here the same time as his brother Bronwyn. Susan was older." She stopped, looked lost.

"What happened to him?"

"One day he and Bronwyn didn't come to school. I got a call from their father saying that he was taking them on an unplanned vacation."

"Where?"

"He didn't say. He wasn't being very specific."

"Okay, go on."

"That's pretty much it, Mr. Bolitar. Two weeks later, Bronwyn came back to school. I never saw Dennis again."

"You called his father?"

"Of course."

"What did he say?"

"He told me that Dennis wouldn't be coming back."

"Did you ask him why?"

"Of course. But . . . did you ever meet Raymond Lex?"

"No."

"You didn't question a man like that. He mentioned something about home schooling. When I pressed, he made it clear it was none of my concern. Over the years, I've tried to keep track of the family, even when they moved out of the area. But like you, I never heard anything about Dennis."

"What did you think happened?"

She looked at him. "I assumed he was dead."

Her words, though not all that surprising, worked like a vacuum, sucking the room dry, forcing out the air.

"Why?" Myron asked.

"I figured that he was ill, and that was why he was pulled out of school."

"Why would Mr. Lex try to hide something like that?"

"I don't know. After his novel became a bestseller, he became private to the point of paranoia. Are you sure this donor you're looking for is Dennis Lex?"

"Not sure, no."

Peggy Joyce snapped her fingers. "Oh, wait, I have something you may find interesting." She stood and opened a file drawer. She sifted through it, pulled something out, studied it for a moment. Her elbow smacked the drawer closed. "This was taken two months before Dennis left us."

She handed him an old class photograph, the color not so much fading as greening from age. Fifteen kids flanked by two teachers, one a far younger Peggy Joyce. The years had not been unkind to her, but they'd passed anyway. A small black sign with the white lettering read SHADY WELLS MONTESSORI SCHOOL and the year.

"Which one is Dennis?"

She pointed to a boy sitting in the front row. He had a Prince Valiant cut and a face-splitting smile that never quite hit his eyes. "Can I have this?"

"If you think it will help."

"It might."

She nodded. "I better get back to my students."

"Thank you."

"Do you remember your preschool, Mr. Bolitar?"

Myron nodded. "Parkview Nursery School in Livingston, New Jersey."

"How about your teachers? Do you remember them at all?"

Myron thought about it. "No."

She nodded as though he'd answered correctly. "Good luck," she said.

23

AgeComp. Or age-progression software, if you prefer.

Myron had learned a bit about it when searching for a missing woman named Lucy Mayor. The key was in the digital imaging. All Myron had to do—or in the case of their office, all Esperanza had to do—was take the class photograph and scan it into the computer. Then, using common software programs like Photoshop or Picture Publisher, you blow up the face of young Dennis Lex. AgeComp, a software program constantly being retooled and perfected by missing-children organizations, does the rest. Using advanced mathematical algorithms, AgeComp stretches, merges, and blends digital photographs of missing children and produces a color image of what they might look like today.

Naturally, a lot is left to chance. Scarring, facial fractures, facial hair, cosmetic surgery, hairstyle or, in the case of some of the older ones, male pattern baldness. Still, the class photo could be a serious lead.

When he was back in Manhattan, the cell phone rang.

"I spoke to the feds," Win said.

"And?"

"Your impression is correct."

"What impression?"

"They are indeed frightened."

"Did you speak to PT?"

"I did. He put me onto the right person. They requested a face-to-face."

"When?"

"Pretty pronto. We are, in fact, waiting in your office."

"The feds are in my office right now?"

"Affirmative."

"Be there in five."

More like ten. When the elevator opened, Esperanza was sitting at Big Cyndi's desk.

"How many?" he asked.

"Three," Esperanza said. "One blond woman, one extra-strength dork, one nice suit."

"Win's with them?"

"Yep."

He handed her the photograph and pointed to Dennis Lex's face. "How long before we could get an age progression on this?"

"Jesus, when was this taken?"

"Thirty years ago."

Esperanza frowned. "You know anything about age progression?"

"Some."

"It's mostly used to find missing kids," she said. "And it's usually used to age them five, maybe ten years."

"But we can get something, right?"

"Something very rough, yeah maybe." She flicked on the scanner and placed the photo facedown. "If they're in the lab, we'll probably have it by the end of the day. I'll crop it and e-mail it over."

"Do it later," he said, gesturing toward the door. "Mustn't keep the feds waiting. Our tax dollars and all that."

"You want me in there?"

"You're a part of everything that goes on here,

Esperanza. Of course I want you in there."

"I see," she said. Then: "Is this the part where I blink back tears because you're making me feel oh-so-special?"

Wiseass.

Myron opened his office door. Esperanza followed. Win sat behind Myron's desk, probably so that none of the feds would. Win could be territorial—just one of the ways he was like a Doberman. Kimberly Green and Rick Peck rose with lack-of-sleep-luggage eyes and squared-off smiles. The third fed stayed in his seat, not moving, not even turning to see who'd entered. Myron saw his face and felt a jolt.

Whoa.

Win watched Myron, an amused smile curling the ends of his mouth. Eric Ford, deputy director of the Federal Bureau of Investigation, was the man in the suit. His presence meant one thing: This was serious big-time.

Kimberly Green pointed at Esperanza. "What's she doing in here?"

"She's my partner," Myron said. "And it's not polite to point."

"Your partner? You think this is a business transaction?"

"She stays," Myron said.

"No," Kimberly Green said. She was still wearing the ball-and-chain earrings, still the jeans and black turtleneck, but the jacket now was spearmint green. "We're not exactly thrilled talking to you and Cheekbones boy over there"—she gestured toward Win—"but at least you have some clearance. We don't know her. She goes."

Win's smile spread and his eyebrows did a quick up-and-down. Cheekbones. He liked that.

"She goes," Green said again.

Esperanza shrugged. "No biggie," she said.

Myron was about to say something, but Win shook his head. He was right. Save it for the important battles.

Esperanza left. Win got up and gave Myron the chair. He stood on Myron's right, arms crossed, totally at ease. Green and Peck fidgeted. Myron turned to Eric Ford. "I don't think we've met."

"But you know who I am," Ford said. He had one of those smooth soft-rock-DJ voices.

"Yes."

"And I know who you are," he said. "So what would be the point?"

Oookay. Myron glanced back at Win. Win shrugged.

Ford nodded at Kimberly Green. She cleared her throat. "For the record," she said, "we don't think we should have to go through this."

"Through what?"

"Telling you about our investigation. Debriefing you. As a good citizen, you should be willing to cooperate with our investigation because it's the right thing to do."

Myron looked at Win and said, "Oh boy."

"Some aspects of an investigation need to be contained," she continued. "You and Mr. Lockwood should understand that better than most. You should be anxious to cooperate with any federal investigation. You should respect what we're trying to do here."

"Right, okay, we respect. Can we skip ahead, please? You looked us up. You know we'll keep our mouths shut. Otherwise none of us would be here."

She folded her hands and put them in her lap. Peck kept his head down and scribbled notes, Lord knew on what. Myron's decor maybe. "What we say here cannot leave this room. It is classified to the highest—"

"Skipping," Myron said with an impatient hand roll. "Skipping."

Green slid her eyes toward Ford. He nodded again. She took a deep breath and said, "We have Stan Gibbs under surveillance."

She stopped, settled back. Myron waited a few seconds and then said, "Label me surprised."

"That information is classified," she said.

"Then I'll leave it out of my diary."

"He isn't supposed to know."

"Well, that's usually implied with words like 'classified' and 'surveillance.' "

"But Gibbs does know. He loses us whenever he really wants. Because when he's out in public, we can't get too close."

"Why can't you get too close?"

"He'll see us."

"But he already knows you're there?"

"Yes."

Myron looked up at Win. "Wasn't there an Abbott and Costello skit that went like this?"

"Marx Brothers," Win said.

"If we were out in the open about tailing him," Green said, "the fact that he's a target could become public knowledge."

"And you're trying to contain that?"

"Yes."

"How long has he been under surveillance?"

"Well, it's not that simple. He's been out of range a lot—"

"How long?"

Again Green looked at Ford. Again Ford nodded. She balled her hands into fists. "Since the first article on the kidnappings appeared."

Myron sat back, feeling something akin to a head rush. He shouldn't have been surprised, but damned if he wasn't. The article came flooding back to him—the sudden disappearances, the awful phone calls, the constant, eternal anguish, the picket-fenced lives suddenly bulldozed over by inexplicable evil.

"My God," Myron said. "Stan Gibbs was telling the truth."

"We never said that," Kimberly Green said.

"I see. So you've been tailing him because you don't like his syntax?"

Silence.

"The articles were true," Myron said. "And you've known it all along."

"What we did or did not know is not your concern."

Myron shook his head. "Unbelievable," he said. "So let me see if I got this straight. You have a serial psycho out there who snatches people out of the blue and torments their families. You want to keep a lid on it because if word got out to the public, you'd have a panic situation. Then the psycho goes directly to Stan Gibbs and suddenly the story is in the public domain . . ." Myron's voice died off, seeing that his logic trail had hit a major pothole. He frowned and forged ahead. "I don't know how that old novel or the plagiarism charges tie in. But either way, you decided to ride it. You let Gibbs get fired and disgraced, probably in part because you were pissed off that he upset your investigation. But mostly"—he spotted what he thought was a clearing—"but mostly you did it so you could watch him. If the psycho contacted him once, you figured, he'd probably do it again—especially if the articles had been discredited."

Kimberly Green said, "Wrong."

"But close."

"No."

"The kidnappings Gibbs wrote about took place, right?"

She hesitated, gave Ford an eye check. "We can't verify all of his facts."

"Jesus, I'm not taking a deposition here," Myron said. "Was his column true, yes or no?"

"We've told you enough," she said. "It's your turn."

"You haven't told me squat."

"And you've told us less."

Negotiating. Life is being a sports agent—constant negotiating. He had learned the importance of leverage, of doling out, of being fair. People forget that last one, and it always costs you in the end. The best negotiator isn't the one who gets the whole pie while leaving scant crumbs behind. The best negotiator is the one who gets what he wants while keeping the other side happy. So normally, Myron would dole out a little something here. Classic give-and-take. But not this time. He knew better. Once he told them the reason for his visit to Stan Gibbs, his leverage would be zippo.

The best negotiator, like the best species, also knows how to adapt.

"First answer my question," Myron said. "Yes or no, was the story Stan Gibbs wrote true?"

"There is no yes-or-no answer to that," she said. "Parts were true. Parts were not true."

"For example?"

"The young couple was from Iowa, not Minnesota. The missing father had three children, not two." She stopped, folded her hands.

"But there have been kidnappings?"

189

"We knew about those two," she said. "We had no information about the missing college student."

"Probably because the psycho got to her parents. They probably never reported it."

"That's our theory," Kimberly Green said. "But we don't know for sure. Still, there are major discrepancies. The families swear they never spoke to him, for example. Many of the phone calls and events don't match what we know to be true."

Myron saw more clearing. "So you asked Gibbs about it? About his sources?"

"Yes."

"And he refused to tell you anything."

"That's right."

"So you destroyed him."

"No."

"The one part I don't get is the plagiarism," Myron said. "I mean, did you guys somehow set that up? I can't see how. Unless you made up a book and . . . no, that's too far-fetched. So what's the deal with that?"

Kimberly Green leaned forward. "Tell us why you went to his apartment."

"Not until—"

"For several months we couldn't find Stan Gibbs," she interrupted. "We think maybe he left the country. But since he's moved into that condo, he's always alone. As I said before, he loses us sometimes. But he never accepts visitors. Several people have tracked him down. Old friends even. They come to his door or they call on the phone. And you know what always happens, Myron?"

Myron didn't like her tone of voice.

"He sends them away. Every single time. Stan Gibbs sees no one. Except you."

Myron looked up at Win. Win nodded very slowly. Myron took a look at Eric Ford before going back to Kimberly Green. "You think I'm the kidnapper?"

She leaned back with a partial shrug, looking satiated. Turning the tables and all that. "You tell us," she said.

Win started for the door. Myron rose and followed.

"Where the hell are you two going?" Green asked.

Win grabbed the knob. Myron headed around the desk and said, "I'm a suspect. I'm not talking until I have an attorney present. If you'll excuse me."

"Hey, we're just talking here," Kimberly Green said. "I never said I thought you were the kidnapper."

"Sounded that way to me," Myron said. "Win?"

"He snatches hearts," Win told her, "not people."

"You got something to hide?" Green said.

"Just his fondness for cyber pornography," Win said. Then: "Oops."

Kimberly Green stood and blocked Myron's path. "We think we know about the missing college student," she said, her eyes locked hard on his. "Do you want to know how we found out about it?"

Myron kept still.

"Through her father. He got a call from the kidnapper. I don't know what was said. He hasn't said a word since. He's catatonic. Whatever that psycho said to that girl's father put him in a padded room."

Myron felt the room shrink, the walls closing in.

"We haven't found any bodies yet, but we're pretty sure he kills them," she went on. "He kidnaps them, does Lord knows what, and makes the families suffer interminably. And you know he won't stop."

Myron kept his eyes steady. "What's your point?"

"This isn't funny."

"No," he said. "It's not. So stop playing stupid games."

She said nothing.

"I want to hear it from your mouth," Myron said. "Do you think I'm involved in this, yes or no?"

Eric Ford took this one. "No."

Kimberly Green slid back into her chair, her eyes never leaving Myron's. Eric Ford made a big hand gesture. "Please sit down."

Myron and Win moved back to their original positions.

Eric Ford said, "The novel exists. So do the passages Stan Gibbs plagiarized. The book was sent to our office anonymously—more specifically, to Special Agent Green here. We admit that we found that issue confusing at first. On the one hand, Gibbs knows about the kidnappings. On the other hand, he doesn't know everything and he clearly copied excerpts from an old, out-of-print mystery novel."

"There's an explanation," Myron said. "The kidnapper might have read the book. He might have identified with the character, become a copycat of sorts."

"We considered that possibility," Eric Ford said, "but we don't believe that's the case here."

"Why not?"

"It's complicated."

"Does it involve trigonometry?"

"You still think this is a joking manner?"

"You still think it's smart to play games?"

Ford closed his eyes. Green looked on edge. Peck continued scribbling notes. When Ford opened his eyes, he said, "We don't believe Stan Gibbs made up the crimes," he said. "We believe he perpetrated them."

Myron felt a pow. He looked up at Win. Nothing.

"You have some background in the criminal mind, do you not?" Ford asked.

Myron might have nodded.

"Well, here we have an old pattern with a new twist. Arsonists love to watch firemen put out the blaze. Ofttimes they're even the ones who report the fire. They play the good Samaritan. Murderers love to attend the funerals of their victims. We videotape funerals. I'm sure you know this."

Myron nodded again.

"Sometimes killers make themselves part of the story." Eric Ford was gesturing a lot now, his knotted hands rising and falling as though this were a press conference in too big a room. "They claim to be witnesses. They become the innocent bystanders who happened to find the body in the brush. You're familiar with this moth-near-the-flame phenomenon, are you not?"

"Yes."

"So what could be more enticing than being the only columnist to report the story? Can you imagine the high? How mind-bogglingly close to the investigation you'd be. The brilliance of your deception—for a psychotic, it's almost too delicious. And if you are perpetrating these crimes to get attention, then here you get a double dose. Attention as the serial kidnapper, one. Attention as the brilliant reporter with the scoop and possible Pulitzer, two. You even get the bonus attention of a man bravely defending the First Amendment."

Myron was holding his breath. "That's a hell of a theory," he said.

"You want more?"

"Yes."

"Why won't he answer any of our questions?"

"You said it yourself. First Amendment."

"He's not a lawyer or psychiatrist."

"But he is a reporter," Myron said.

"What kind of monster would continue to protect his source in this situation?"

"I know plenty."

"We spoke to the victims' families. They swore they never spoke to him."

"They could be lying. Maybe the kidnapper told them to say that."

"Okay, then why hasn't Gibbs done more to defend himself against the charges of plagiarism? He could have fought them. He could have even provided some detail that would have proved he was telling the truth. But no, instead he goes silent. Why?"

"You think it's because he's the kidnapper? The moth flew too close to the flame and is licking his wounds in darkness?"

"Do you have a better explanation?"

Myron said nothing.

"Lastly, there's the murder of his mistress, Melina Garston."

"What about it?"

"Think it through, Myron. We put the screws to him. Maybe he expected that, maybe he didn't. Either way, the courts don't see everything his way. You don't know about the court findings, do you?"

"Not really, no."

"That's because they were sealed. In part, the judge demanded that Gibbs show some proof he had been in contact with the killer. He finally said that Melina Garston would back him."

"And she did, right?"

"Yes. She claimed to have met the subject of his story."

"I still don't understand. If she backed him up, why would he kill her?"

"The day before Melina Garston died, she called her father. She told him that she lied."

Myron sat back, tried to take it all in.

Eric Ford said, "He's back now, Myron. Stan Gibbs has finally surfaced. While he was gone, the Sow the Seeds kidnapper was gone too. But this brand of psycho never stops on his own. He's going to strike again and soon. So before that happens, you better talk to us. Why were you at his condominium?"

Myron thought about it but not for long. "I was looking for someone."

"Who?"

"A missing bone marrow donor. He could save a child's life."

Ford looked at him steadily. "I assume that Jeremy Downing is the child in question."

So much for being vague, but Myron was not surprised. Phone records probably. Or maybe there had indeed been a tail when he visited Emily's. "Yes. And before I go on, I want your word that you will keep me in the loop."

Kimberly Green said, "You're not a part of this investigation."

"I'm not interested in your kidnapper. I'm interested in my donor. You help me find him, I'll tell you what I know."

"We agree," Ford said, waving Kimberly Green silent. "So how does Stan Gibbs fit in with your donor?"

Myron reviewed it for them. He started with Davis Taylor and then moved on to Dennis Lex and then the cryptic phone call. They kept their faces steady, Green and Peck scratching on their pads, but there was a definite jolt when he mentioned the Lex family.

They asked a few follow-up questions, like why he got involved in the first place. He said that Emily was an old friend. He wasn't about to go into the patrimony issue. Myron could see Green getting antsy. He had served his purpose. She was anxious to get out and start tracking things down.

A few minutes later, the feds snapped their pads closed and rose. "We're on it," Ford said. He looked straight at Myron. "And we'll find your donor. You stay out."

Myron nodded and wondered if he could. After they left, Win took a seat in front of Myron's desk.

"Why do I feel like I was picked up at a bar and now it's the next morning and the guy just handed me the 'I'll call you' line?" Myron asked.

"Because that's precisely what you are," Win said. "Slut."

"Think they're holding something back?"

"Without question."

"Something big?"

"Gargantuan," Win said.

"Not much we can do about it now."

"Nope," Win said. "Nothing at all."

24

Myron's mom met him at the front door.

"I'm picking up the takeout," Mom said.

"You?"

She put her hands on her hips and shot him her best wither. "There a problem with that?"

"No, it's just . . ." He decided to drop it. "Nothing."

Mom kissed his cheek and fished through her purse for the car keys. "I'll be back in a half hour. Your father is in the back." She gave him the imploring eyes. "Alone."

"Okay," he said.

"No one else is here."

"Uh-huh."

"If you catch my drift."

"It's caught."

"You'll be alone."

"Caught, Mom. Caught."

"It'll be an opportunity—"

"Mom."

She put her hands up. "Okay, okay, I'm going."

He walked around the side of the house, past the garbage cans and recycling bins, and found Dad on the deck. The deck was sanded redwood with built-in benches and resin furniture and a Weber 500 barbecue, all brought to being during the famed Kitchen Expansion of 1994. Dad was bent over a railing with a screwdriver in his hand. For a moment, Myron fell back to those "weekend projects" with Dad, some of which lasted almost an entire hour. They would go out with toolbox in tow, Dad bent over like he was now, muttering obscenities under his breath. Myron's sole task consisted of handing Dad tools like a scrub nurse in the operating room, the whole exercise boring as hell, shuffling his feet in the sun, sighing heavily, finding new angles from which to stand.

"Hey," Myron said.

Dad looked up, smiled, put down the tool. "Screw loose," he said. "But let's not talk about your mother."

Myron laughed. They found molded-resin chairs around a table impaled by a blue umbrella. In front of them lay Bolitar Stadium, a small patch of green-to-brown grass that had hosted countless, oft-solo football games, baseball games, soccer games, Wiffle ball games (probably the most popular sport at Bolitar Stadium), rugby scrums, badminton, kickball, and that favorite pastime for the future sadist, bombardment. Myron spotted Mom's former vegetable garden—the word *vegetable* here being used to describe three annual soggy tomatoes and two flaccid zucchinis; it was now slightly more overgrown than a Cambodian rice paddy. To their right were the rusted remnants of their old tetherball pole. Tetherball. Now, there was a really dumb game.

Myron cleared his throat and put his hands on the table. "How you feeling?"

Dad gave a big nod. "Good. You?"

"Good."

The silence floated down, puffy and relaxed. Silence with a father can be like that. You drift back and you're young and you're safe, safe in that all-encompassing way only a child can be with his father. You still see him hovering in your darkened doorway, the silent sentinel to your adolescence, and you sleep the sleep of the naive, the innocent, the unformed. When you get older, you realize that this safety was just an illusion, another child's perception, like the size of your backyard.

Or maybe, if you're lucky, you don't.

Dad looked older today, the flesh on his face more sagged, the once-knotted biceps spongy under the T-shirt, starting to waste. Myron wondered how to start. Dad closed his eyes for a three count, opened them, and said, "Don't."

"What?"

"Your mother is about as subtle as a White House press release," Dad said. "I mean, when was the last time she picked up the takeout instead of me?"

"Has she ever?"

"Once," Dad said. "When I had a fever of a hundred and four. And even then she whined about it."

"Where's she going?"

"She has me on a special diet now, you know. Because of the chest pains." *Chest pains*. Euphemism for *heart attack*.

"Yeah, I figured that."

"She's even tried cooking a little. She told you?"

Myron nodded. "She baked something for me yesterday."

Dad's body went stiff. "By God," he said. "Her own son?"

"It was pretty scary."

"The woman has many, many talents, but they could airdrop that stuff into starving African nations and no one would eat it."

"So where's she going?"

"Your mother is high on some crazy Middle Eastern health food place. Just opened in West Orange. Get this, it's called Ayatollah Granola."

Myron gave him flat eyes.

"Hand to God, that's the name. Food is almost as dry as that Thanksgiving turkey your mother made when you were eight. You remember that?"

"At night," Myron said. "It still haunts my sleep."

Dad looked off again. "She left us alone so we could talk, right?"

"Right."

He made a face. "I hate when she does stuff like that. She means well, your mother. We both know that. But let's not do it, okay?"

Myron shrugged. "You say so."

"She thinks I don't like growing old. News flash: No one does. My friend Herschel Diamond—you remember Heshy?"

"Sure."

"Big guy, right? Played semipro football when we were young. So Heshy, he calls me and he says now that I'm retired, I can do tai chi with him. I mean, tai chi? What the hell is that anyway? If I want to move slowly, I have to drive down to the Y to do it with a bunch of old yentas? I mean, what's that about? I tell him no. So then Heshy, this great athlete, Myron, he could hit a softball a country mile, this marvelous big ox, he tells me we can walk together. Walk. At the mall. Speedwalk, he calls it. At the mall, for chrissake. Heshy always hated the place—now he wants us to trot around like a bunch of jackasses in matching sweatsuits and expensive walking shoes. Pump our arms with these little *faigelah* barbells. Walking shoes, he calls them. What the hell is that anyway? I never had a pair of shoes I couldn't walk in, am I right?"

He waited for an answer. Myron said, "As rain."

Dad stood up. He grabbed a screwdriver and feigned

working. "So now, because I don't want to move like an old Chinaman or walk around a godforsaken mall in overpriced sneakers, your mother thinks I'm not adjusting. You hear what I'm saying?"

"Yes."

Dad stayed bent, fiddling a little more with the railing. In the distance, Myron heard children playing. A bike bell rang. Someone laughed. A lawn mower purred. Dad's voice, when he finally spoke again, was surprisingly soft. "You know what your mother really wants us to do?" he said.

"What?"

"She wants you and I to reverse roles." Dad finally looked up through his heavy-lidded eyes. "I don't want to reverse roles, Myron. I'm the father. I like being the father. Let me stay that, okay?"

Myron found it hard to speak. "Sure, Dad."

His father put his head back down, the gray wisps upright in the humidity, his breathing tool-work heavy, and Myron again felt something open up his chest and grab hold of his heart. He looked at this man he'd loved for so long, who'd gone without complaint to that damn muggy warehouse in Newark for more than thirty years, and Myron realized that he didn't know him. He didn't know what his father dreamed about, what he wanted to be when he was a kid, what he thought about his own life.

Dad kept working on the screw. Myron watched him.

Promise me you won't die, okay? Just promise me that.

He almost said it out loud.

Dad straightened himself out and studied his handiwork. Satisfied, he sat back down. They started talking about the Knicks and the recent Kevin Costner movie and the new Nelson DeMille book. They put away the toolbox. They had some iced tea. They lounged side by side in matching molded-resin chaises. An hour passed. They fell into a comfortable silence. Myron fingered the condensation on his glass. He could hear his father's breathing, moderately wheezy. Dusk had settled in, bruising the sky purple, the trees going a burnt orange.

Myron closed his eyes and said, "I got a hypothetical for you."

"Oh?"

"What would you do if you found out you weren't my real father?"

Dad's eyebrows went skyward. "You trying to tell me something?"

"Just a hypothetical. Suppose you found out right now that I wasn't your biological son. How would you react?"

"Depends," Dad said.

"On?"

"How you reacted."

"It wouldn't make a difference to me," Myron said.

Dad smiled.

"What?" Myron said.

"Easy for both of us to say it wouldn't matter. But news like that is a bombshell. You can't predict what someone will do when a bomb lands. When I was in Korea—" Dad stopped, Myron sat up. "Well, you never knew how someone would react . . ." His voice tailed off. He coughed into his fist and then started up again. "Guys you were sure would be heroes completely lost it—and vice versa. That's why you can't ask stuff like this as a hypothetical."

Myron looked at his father. His father kept his eyes

on the grass, taking another deep sip. "You never talk about Korea," Myron said.

"I do," Dad said.

"Not with me."

"No, not with you."

"Why not?"

"It's what I fought for. So we wouldn't have to talk about it."

It didn't make sense and Myron understood.

"There a reason you raised this particular hypothetical?" Dad asked.

"No."

Dad nodded. He knew it was a lie, but he wouldn't push it. They settled back and watched the familiar surroundings.

"Tai chi isn't so bad," Myron said. "It's a martial art. Like tae kwon do. I've been thinking of taking it up myself."

Dad took another sip. Myron sneaked a glance. Something on his father's face began to quiver. Was Dad indeed getting smaller, more fragile—or was it like the backyard and safety, again the shifting perception of a child turned adult?

"Dad . . . ?"

"Let's go inside," his father said, standing. "We stay out much longer, one of us is going to get misty and say, 'Wanna play catch?'"

Myron bit off a laugh and followed him inside. Mom came home not long after that, lugging two bags of food as though they were stone tablets. "Everybody hungry?" she called out.

"Starving," Dad said. "I'm so hungry I could eat a vegetarian."

"Very funny, Al."

"Or even your cooking . . ."

"Ha-ha," Mom said.

". . . though I'd prefer the vegetarian."

"Stop it, Al, I'm going to phlegm up, you keep making me laugh like this." Mom dropped the bags onto the kitchen counter. "See, Myron? It's a good thing your mother is shallow."

"Shallow?" Myron asked.

"If I judged a man on brains or sense of humor," Mom continued, "you'd have never been born."

"Right-o," Dad said with a hearty smile. "But one look at your old man in a bathing suit and whammo—all mine."

"Oh please," Mom said.

"Yes," Myron said. "Please."

They both looked at him. Mom cleared her throat. "So did you two, uh, have a nice talk?"

"We talked," Dad said. "It was very life-affirming. I see the errors of my ways."

"I'm being serious."

"So am I. I see everything differently now."

She put her arms around his waist and nuzzled him. "So you'll call Heshy?"

"I'll call Heshy," he said.

"Promise."

"Yes, Ellen, I promise."

"You'll go to the Y and do jai alai with him?"

"Tai chi," Dad corrected.

"What?"

"It's called tai chi, not jai alai."

"I thought it was jai alai."

"Tai chi. Jai alai is the game with the curved rackets down in Florida."

"That's shuffleboard, Al."

"Not shuffleboard. The other thing with the sticks. And the gambling."

"Tai chi?" Mom said, testing it for sound. "Are you sure?"

"I think so."

"But you're not positive?"

"No, I'm not positive," Dad said. "Maybe you're right. Maybe it is called jai alai."

The name debate continued for a while. Myron didn't bother correcting them. Never cut in on that strange dance known as marital discourse. They ate the health food. It was indeed nasty. They laughed a lot. His parents must have said "You don't know what you're talking about" to each other fifty times; maybe it was a euphemism for "I love you."

Eventually Myron said good night. Mom kissed his cheek and made herself scarce. Dad walked him to the car. The night was silent save a lone dribbling basketball somewhere on Darby Road or maybe Coddington Terrace. A nice sound. When he hugged his father good-bye, Myron again noticed that his father felt smaller, less substantial. Myron held on a little longer than usual. For the first time he felt like the bigger man, the stronger man, and he suddenly remembered what Dad had said about reversing roles. So he held on in the dark. Time passed. Dad patted his back. Myron kept his eyes closed and held on tighter. Dad stroked his hair and shushed him. Just for a little while. Just until the roles reversed themselves again, returning both of them to where they belonged.

25

Granite Man was waiting outside the Dakota.

Myron spotted him from his car. He picked up the cell phone and called Win. "I have company."

"A rather large gentleman, yes," Win said. "Two cohorts are parked across the street in a corporate vehicle owned by the Lex family."

"I'll leave the cell phone on."

"They confiscated it last time," Win said.

"Yes."

"Likely they'll do the same."

"We'll improvise."

"Your funeral," Win said, and hung up.

Myron parked in the lot and approached Granite Man.

"Mrs. Lex would like to see you," Granite Man said.

"Do you know what she wants?" Myron asked.

Granite Man ignored the question.

"Maybe she saw me flexing on the security tape," Myron said. "Wanted to get to know me better."

Granite Man did not laugh. "You ever think about doing this comedy thing professionally?"

"There have been offers."

"I bet. Get in the car."

"Okay, but I have a curfew, you know. And I never French-kiss on the first date. Just so we understand each other."

Granite Man shook his head. "Man, I'd like to waste you."

They got in the car. Two blue-blazers sat in front. The car ride was silent except for Granite Man and His Magic Cracking Knuckles. The Lex building emerged grudgingly through the dark. Myron traveled through the security travail again. As Win predicted, they confiscated his phone. Granite Man and the two blazers turned left this time instead of right. They escorted him into an elevator. It opened into what appeared to be living quarters.

Susan Lex's office had been done sort of Renaissance palatial, but the apartment up here—it looked like an apartment anyway—did a one-eighty. Modern and minimalism were the major themes. The walls were painted stark white and had nothing on them. The floors were a pigeon-gray wood. There were black and white bookshelves made of fiberglass, most empty, some with indistinct figurines. The couch was red and shaped like two lips. There was a well-stocked see-through bar constructed out of Lucite. Two metallic swivel stools were painted red on the base, looking about as inviting as rectal thermometers. A fire danced lazily in the fireplace, fake logs casting an unnatural glow over the black mantel. The whole place had a feel and aura about as warm as a cold sore.

Myron strolled, feigning interest. He stopped at a crystal statue with a marble base. Something modern or cubist or what-have-you. Symmetrical Bowel Movement maybe. Myron put his hand on it. Substantial. He looked out the one-way glass. Too low for much of a view beyond the hedges lining the front gate. Hmm.

The two blue-blazers did the Buckingham Palace Guard thing on either side of the door. Granite Man followed Myron, his hands clasped behind his lower back. A door on the other side of the room opened. Myron was not surprised to see Susan Lex enter, again keeping her distance. There was a man with her this time. Myron did not bother approaching.

"And you are?" he called out.

Susan Lex answered this one. "This is my brother Bronwyn."

"Not the brother I'm interested in," Myron said.

"Yes, I know. Please sit down."

Granite Man gestured toward the lips-couch. Myron sat on the lower lip, waiting to be swallowed. Granite Man sat right next to him. Cozy.

"Bronwyn and I would like you to answer some questions, Mr. Bolitar," Susan Lex said.

"Could you move a little closer?"

She smiled. "I think not."

"I showered."

She ignored the remark. "I understand that you occasionally do some investigative work," Susan Lex said.

Myron did not reply.

"Is that correct?"

"Depends on what you mean by investigative work."

"I'll take that as a yes," Susan Lex said.

Myron gave her a suit-yourself shrug.

"Is that why you're searching for our brother?" she asked.

"I already told you why I was searching for him."

"That bit about him being a bone marrow donor?"

"It's not a bit."

"Please, Mr. Bolitar," Susan Lex said with that rich-people air. "We both know that's a lie."

Myron started to rise. Granite Man put a hand on Myron's knee. It felt like a cinder block. Granite Man shook his head. Myron stayed where he was. "It's not a lie," he said.

"We're wasting time," Susan Lex said. She flicked her eyes at Granite Man. "Show him the pictures, Grover."

Myron turned to him. "Grover is the name of my very favorite *Sesame Street* character. I want you to know that."

"We've been following you, *Myron*." Granite Man handed him a pile of photographs. Myron looked at them. They were eight-by-tens of him at the condo with Stan Gibbs. The first one showed him knocking on the door. The second one showed Stan sticking his head out. The third one showed them both heading inside the condo.

"Well?"

Myron frowned. "I have no knack for accessorizing."

"We know that you're working for Stan Gibbs," Susan Lex said.

"Doing what exactly?" Myron asked.

"Investigating. As I stated earlier. So now that we understand your true motive, tell me how much it will cost for you to go away."

"I don't know what you're talking about."

"Simply put, how much will it cost to have you cease and desist?" Susan Lex asked. "Or are you going to force us to destroy you too?"

Too?

Brain click.

Myron turned his attention to the silent brother. "Let me ask you something, Bronwyn," he said. "You and Dennis were both going to nursery school. You both disappeared. Two weeks later, only you came back. How come? What happened to your brother?"

Bronwyn's mouth opened and closed, marionette style. He looked to his sister for help.

"It's like he disappeared off the face of the earth after

that," Myron went on. "For thirty years, he's totally off the radar. But now, well, it's like he's come back for some reason. He changed his name, opened a small checking account, donated blood to a bone marrow center. So what gives, Bron? You got a clue?"

Bronwyn said, "That simply cannot be!"

His sister silenced him with a look. But Myron felt something in the air. He mulled the feeling over and another thought hit him: Maybe the Lex siblings didn't know the answer themselves. Maybe they were looking for Dennis too.

It was while he was lost in that thought that Granite Man punched him deep in the stomach. The fist followed through to the point where it seemed the knuckles must have reached the fabric of the couch. Myron snapped closed at the waist. He dropped to the floor, struggled to regain a breath, suffocating from within. He lowered his head to his knees, consumed with one thought: air. He needed air.

Susan Lex's voice boomed in his ears. "Stan Gibbs knows the truth. His father is a disgusting liar. His accusations are totally without merit. But I'll defend my family, Mr. Bolitar. You tell Mr. Gibbs he has not yet begun to suffer. What has happened to him so far is nothing compared to what I will do to him—and you—if he doesn't stop. Do you understand?"

Air. Gulps of air. Myron managed not to throw up. He took his time, looked up, met her eye. "Not even a little," he said.

Susan Lex looked at Grover. "Then make him."

With that, she left the room. Her brother took one last look and followed.

Myron gathered his breath a hitch at a time. "Nice sucker punch, Grover," he said.

Grover shrugged. "I went easy on you."

"Next time, go easy when I'm looking, tough guy."

"Won't change the outcome."

"We'll see." Myron sat up. "So what the hell is she talking about?"

"I thought Ms. Lex made herself very clear," he said. "But because you appear to be a little vacant between the ears, I'll restate her position. She doesn't like people interfering with her affairs. Stan Gibbs, for example, interfered. You can see what happened to him. You interfered. You're about to see what's going to happen to you."

Myron struggled to his feet. The blue-blazers stayed by the door. Granite Man started cracking his knuckles again. "Listen closely, please," he said. "I'm going to break your leg. Then you're going to limp your sorry ass out of here and tell Gibbs that if he sniffs around again, I will exterminate you both. Any questions?"

"Just one," Myron said. "Don't you think leg breaking is a tad cliché?"

Grover smiled. "Not the way I do it."

Myron looked around the room.

"Nowhere to run, my friend."

"Who wants to run?" Myron countered.

Without warning, he grabbed the heavy bowel-movement statue. The blue-blazers drew their guns. Granite Man ducked. But Myron wasn't going for them. He heaved the statue, straightened his arms, spun around like a discus thrower, and hurled it marble-base-forward at the plate-glass window. The window exploded.

And that was when the gunfire began.

"Hit the deck!" Myron shouted.

The blue-blazers obeyed. Myron dove. The bullets

continued. Sniper fire. One took out the overhead light. One hit the lamp.

Gotta love that Win.

"You want to live," Myron shouted, "stay down."

The bullets stopped. One of the blue-blazers started rising. A bullet sang out, nearly parting the man's hair. The blazer dropped back down, flattening himself into a bearskin rug.

"I'm getting up now," Myron said. "And I'm leaving. I'd advise you guys to stay down. And, Grover?"

"What?"

"Radio downstairs. Tell them not to stop me. I can't be certain but I'm pretty sure my friend will lob in grenades if I'm unduly delayed."

Granite Man made the call. No one moved. Myron stood up. He almost whistled as he walked out.

26

It was midnight when Myron knocked on the door of Stan Gibbs's condo.

"Let's take a walk," Myron said to him.

Stan threw down his cigarette, smothered it with his toe. "A drive might be better," he countered. "The feds use long-range amplifiers."

They got into Myron's Ford Taurus, aka the Chick Trawler. Stan Gibbs flicked on the radio and started playing with the stations. Commercial for Heineken. Does anyone really care that it's imported by Van Munchin and Company?

"Are you wearing a wire, Myron?"

"No."

"But the FBI spoke to you," Stan said. "After you left."

"How did you know?"

"They're watching me," he said with a shrug. "It would only be logical to assume they questioned you."

"Tell me about your connection with Dennis Lex," Myron said.

"I already told you. I don't have one."

"A big guy named Grover picked me up tonight. He and Susan Lex gave me a very stern warning not to play with you anymore. Bronwyn was there too."

Stan Gibbs closed his eyes and rubbed them. "They knew about your visit here."

"Had eight-by-ten glossies."

"And they concluded that you're working for me."

"Bingo."

Stan shook his head. "Get out of this, Myron. You don't want to mess with these people."

"Is that advice you wished someone had given you earlier?"

His smile had nothing behind it. Exhaustion came off him like heat squiggles on a hot sidewalk. "You have no idea," he said.

"Tell me about it."

"No."

"I can help," Myron said.

"Against the Lexes? They're too powerful."

"And being powerful, you wanted to do a story on them, right?"

He said nothing.

"And they didn't like that. In fact, they took exception."

More nothing.

"You started digging where they didn't want you to. You learned that there was another brother named Dennis."

"Yes."

"And that really pissed them off."

Stan started biting a hangnail.

"Come on, Stan. Don't make me drag this out of you."

"You've pretty much got it."

"Then tell me."

"I wanted to do a story on them. An exposé, really. I even had a publisher all lined up for a book deal. But then the Lexes got wind of it. They warned me to stay away. A big man came to my apartment. I didn't catch his name. Looked like Sergeant Rock."

"That would be Grover."

"He told me that I could stop or I could be destroyed."

"And that only made you more curious."

"I guess."

"So you found out about Dennis Lex."

"Just that he existed. And that he vanished into thin air when he was a young child." Stan turned to him. Myron slowed the car and felt something creep along the top of his scalp.

"Like the Sow the Seeds victims," Myron finished.

"No."

"Why not?"

"It's different."

"How?" Myron asked.

"This is going to sound silly," Stan said, "but the family doesn't have that same sense of terror that the other families have."

"The rich are good with façades."

"It's more than that," Stan said. "I can't put my finger on it exactly. But I'm sure Susan and Bronwyn Lex know what happened to their brother."

"But they want to keep it a secret."

"Yes."

"Do you have a guess why?"

"No," Stan said.

Myron glanced back. The feds were following at a discreet enough distance.

"Do you think Susan Lex is responsible for that novel surfacing?"

"The thought has crossed my mind."

"But you never looked into it?"

"I started to. After the scandal hit. But I got a call from the big guy. He told me that it was just the beginning. That he was just flicking his finger and next time he would crush me between both palms."

"He can be a poetic fellow," Myron said.

"Yes."

"But I still don't get something."

"What?"

"You don't scare easily. When they warned you away the first time, you ignored it. After what they did to you, I'd have thought you'd fight back even harder."

"You're forgetting something," Stan said.

"What?"

"Melina Garston."

Silence.

"Think about it," Stan said. "My mistress, the only person who can back up my meeting with the Sow the Seeds kidnapper, ends up dead."

"Her father claims she retracted that."

"Oh, right. In some bizarre before-death confession."

"You think the Lexes arranged that too?"

"Why not? Look at what happened here. Who's the lead suspect in Melina's murder? I am, right? That's what the feds told you. They think I killed her. We know that the Lexes have enough juice to dig up this novel I supposedly plagiarized. Who knows what else they can do?"

"You think they could frame you for the murder?"

"At the very least."

"Are you saying they killed Melina Garston?"

"Maybe. Or it could have been the Sow the Seeds kidnapper. I don't know."

"But you think Melina was a warning."

"She was definitely a warning," Stan Gibbs said. "I just don't know who sent it."

On the radio, Stevie sang out about a landslide coming down. Oh yeah.

"You're leaving something out, Stan."

Stan kept his eyes forward. "What's that?"

"There's a personal connection here," Myron said.

"What do you mean?"

"Susan Lex mentioned your father. She said he was a liar."

Stan shrugged. "She might be right."

"What does he have to do with this?"

"Take me back."

"Don't hold back on me now."

"What do you really want here, Myron?"

"Excuse me?"

"What's your interest here?"

"I told you."

"That boy who needs a bone marrow transplant?"

"He's thirteen years old, Stan. He'll die without it."

"And what if I don't believe you? I did a little research of my own. You used to do government work."

"A long time ago."

"And maybe now you're helping the FBI. Or even the Lex family."

"No."

"I can't take that chance."

"Why not? You're telling me the truth, right? The truth can't hurt you."

He snorted. "You really believe that?"

"Why did Susan Lex mention your father?"

Nothing.

"Where is your father?" Myron said.

"That's just it."

"What?"

Stan looked at him. "He vanished. Eight years ago."

Vanished. That word again.

"I know what you're thinking and you're wrong. My father wasn't a well man. He had been in and out of institutions all his life. We've always assumed he ran off."

"But you never heard from him."

"That's right."

"Dennis Lex vanishes. Your father vanishes—"

"More than twenty years apart," Stan interjected. "It's not connected."

"So I still don't get it," Myron said. "What does your father or his disappearance have to do with the Lexes?"

"They think he's the reason I wanted to do the story. But they're wrong."

"Why would they think that?"

"My father was a student of Raymond Lex's. Before *Midnight Confessions* came out."

"So?"

"So my father claimed the novel was his. He said that Raymond Lex stole it from him."

"Jesus Christ."

"No one believed him," Stan added quickly. "Like I said, he wasn't right in the head."

"Yet you suddenly decided to investigate the family?"

"Yes."

"And you're telling me that's just a coincidence? That your own investigation had nothing to do with your father's accusations?"

Stan leaned his head against the car window like a little kid longing for home. "No one believed my father. That includes me. He was a sick man. Delusional even."

"So?"

"So at the end of the day, he was still my father," Stan said. "Maybe I owed it to him to at least give him the benefit of the doubt."

"Do you think Raymond Lex plagiarized your father?"

"No."

"Do you think your father is still alive?"

"I don't know."

"There has to be a connection here," Myron said. "Your story, the Lex family, your father's accusations—"

Stan closed his eyes. "No more."

Myron switched tracks. "How did the Sow the Seeds kidnapper get in touch with you?"

"I never reveal sources."

"Come on, Stan."

"No," he said firmly. "I may have lost a lot. But not that part of me. You know I can't say anything about my sources."

"You know who it is, don't you?"

"Take me home, Myron."

"Is it Dennis Lex—or did the same kidnapper take Dennis Lex?"

Stan crossed his arms. "Home," he said.

His face closed down. Myron saw it. There would be no more give tonight. He took a right and started heading back. Neither man spoke again until Myron stopped the car in the front of the condominium.

"Are you telling the truth, Myron? About the bone marrow donor?"

"Yes."

"This boy is someone close to you?"

Myron kept both hands on the wheel. "Yes."

"So there's no way you'll walk away from this?"

"None."

Stan nodded, mostly to himself. "I'll do what I can. But you have to trust me."

"What do you mean?"

"Give me a few days."

"To do what?"

"You won't hear from me for a little while. Don't let that shake your faith."

"What are you talking about?"

"You do what you have to," he said. "I'll do the same."

Stan Gibbs stepped out of the car and disappeared into the night.

27

Greg Downing woke Myron early the next morning with a phone call. "Nathan Mostoni left town," he said. "So I came back to New York. I get to pick up my son this afternoon."

Goody-goody for you, Myron thought. But he kept his tongue still.

"I'm going to the Ninety-second Street Y to shoot around," Greg said. "You want to come?"

"No," Myron said.

"Come anyway. Ten o'clock."

"I'll be late." Myron hung up and rolled out of bed. He checked his e-mail and found a JPEG image from Esperanza's contact at AgeComp. He clicked the file and an image slowly appeared on the screen. The possible face of Dennis Lex as a man in his mind to late thirties. Weird. Myron looked at the picture. Not familiar. Not familiar at all. Remarkable work, these age-enhanced images. So lifelike. Except in the eyes. The eyes always looked like the eyes of the dead.

He clicked on the print icon and heard his Hewlett-Packard go to work. Myron checked the clock on the bottom right-hand corner of the screen. Still early in the morning, but he didn't want to wait.

He called Melina Garston's father.

George Garston agreed to meet Myron at his penthouse at Fifth Avenue and Seventy-eighth Street, overlooking Central Park. A dark-haired woman answered the door.

She introduced herself as Sandra and led him silently down the corridor. Myron looked out a window. He could see the Gothic outline of the Dakota all the way across the park. He remembered reading somewhere how Woody and Mia would wave towels from their respective apartments on either side of Central Park. Happier days, no doubt.

"I don't understand what you have to do with my daughter," George Garston said to him. Garston wore a collared blue shirt nicely offset by a shock of white neck-to-chest hairs sprouting out like a troll doll's. His bald head was an almost perfect sphere jammed between two boulder-excuses for shoulders. He had the proud, burly build of a successful immigrant, but you could see that he'd taken a hit. There was a slump there now, the stoop of the eternally grieving. Myron had seen it before. Grief like his breaks your back. You go on, but you always stoop. You smile, but it never really reaches the eyes.

"Probably nothing," Myron said. "I'm trying to find someone. He may be connected to your daughter's murder. I don't know."

The study was too-dark cherry-wood with drawn curtains and one lamp giving off a faint yellow glow. George Garston turned to the side, staring at the rich paisley wallpaper, showing Myron his profile. "We've worked together once," he said. "Not us personally. Our companies. Did you know that?"

"Yes," Myron said.

George Garston had made his fortune with a chain of Greek quasi-restaurants, the kind that work best as mall stands in crowded food courts. The chain was called Achilles Meals. For real. Myron had a Greek hockey player who endorsed the chain regionally, in the upper Midwest.

"So a sports agent is interested in my daughter's murder," Garston said.

"It's a long story."

"The police aren't talking. But they think it's her boyfriend. This reporter. Do you agree?"

"I don't know. What do you think?"

He made a scoffing noise. Myron could barely see his face anymore. "What do I think?" he said. "You sound like one of those grief counselors."

"Didn't mean to."

"Spewing all that sensitivity garbage. They're just trying to distract you from reality. They say they want you to face it. But really, it's the opposite. They want you to dig so far into yourself you won't be able to see how terrible your life is now." He grunted and shifted in his chair. "I don't have an opinion on Stan Gibbs. I never met him."

"Did you know he and your daughter were dating?"

In the dark, Myron saw the big head silently go back and forth. "She told me she had a boyfriend," he said. "She didn't tell me his name. Or that he was married."

"You wouldn't have approved?"

"Of course I wouldn't have approved," he said, trying to sound snappish, but he was beyond petty indignation. "Would you approve if it was your daughter?"

"I guess not. So you knew nothing about her relationship with Stan Gibbs?"

"Nothing."

"I understand that you spoke to her not long before she died."

"Four days before."

"Can you tell me about the conversation?"

"Melina had been drinking," he said in that pure

monotone you get when the words have been ricocheting around your brain too long. "A lot. She drank too much, my daughter. Got that from her papa—who got it from his papa. The Garston family legacy." He made a chuckling sound that sounded far closer to a sob than anything in the neighborhood of a laugh.

"Melina talked to you about her testimony?"

"Yes."

"Could you tell me what she said exactly?"

" 'I made a mistake, Papa.' That's what she said. She said that she lied."

"What did you say?"

"I didn't even know what she was talking about. It's as I told you before—I didn't know about this boyfriend."

"Did you ask her to explain?"

"Yes."

"And?"

"And she didn't. She said to forget about it. She said she'd take care of it. Then she told me she loved me and hung up."

Silence.

"I had two children, Mr. Bolitar. Did you know that?"

Myron shook his head.

"A plane crash killed my Michael three years ago. Now an animal has tortured and killed my girl. My wife, her name was Melina too, passed away fifteen years ago. There is no one. Forty-eight years ago, I thought I came to this country with nothing. I made a lot of money. And now I truly have nothing. You understand?"

"Yes," Myron said.

"Is that all, then?"

"Your daughter had an apartment on Broadway."

"Yes."

"Are her personal belongings still there?"

"Sandra—that's my daughter-in-law—she's been packing her things. But it's all still there. Why?"

"I'd like to go through them, if it's okay with you."

"The police already did that."

"I know."

"You think you might find something they didn't?"

"I'm almost positive I won't."

"But?"

"But I'm attacking this thing from a different perspective. It gives me a fresh set of eyes."

George Garston flicked on his desk lamp. The yellow from the bulb painted his face a dark jaundice. Myron could see that his eyes were too dry, brittle like fallen acorns in the sun. "If you find whoever killed my Melina, you will tell me first."

"No," Myron said.

"Do you know what he did to her?"

"Yes. And I know what you want to do. But it won't make you feel any better."

"You say this like you know it for a fact."

Myron kept silent.

George Garston flicked off the light and turned away. "Sandra will take you over now."

"He sits in that study all day," Sandra Garston told him, pressing the elevator button. "He won't go out anymore."

"It's still new," Myron said.

She shook her head. Her blue-black hair fell in big, loose curls, like thermal fax paper fresh out of the machine. But despite the hair color, her overall effect was almost Icelandic, the face and build of a world-class speed skater. Her features were sharp and ended rather abruptly. Her skin had the red of raw cold.

"He thinks he has no one," she said.

"He has you."

"I'm a daughter-in-law. He sees me and it's like a tether to Michael. I don't have the heart to tell him I finally started dating."

When they reached the street, Myron asked, "Were you and Melina close?"

"I think so, yes."

"Did you know about her relationship with Stan Gibbs?"

"Yes."

"But she never told her father."

"Oh, she would never. Papa didn't approve of most men. A married one would have sent him off the ledge."

They crossed the street and into the mid-city wonder known as Central Park. The park was packed on this rather spectacular day. Asian sketch artists hustled business. Men jogged by in those shorts that look suspiciously like diapers. Sunbathers lazed around on the grass, crowded together yet totally alone. New York City is like that. E. B. White once said that New York bestows the gift of loneliness and the gift of privacy. Damn straight. It was like everyone was plugged into their own internal Walkman, each playing a different tune, bopping obliviously to his or her own beat.

A yah-dude with a bandanna around his head tossed a Frisbee and yelled "Fetch," but he had no dog. Hard-bodied women skated by in black jogging bras. Lots of men with various builds had their shirts off. Examples: A guy thick with flab that looked like wet Play-Doh jiggled past him. Behind him, a well-built guy skidded to a stop and arrogantly flexed a bicep. Actually flexed. In public. Myron frowned. He didn't know which was worse: guys who shouldn't take their shirts off and do, or guys who should take their shirts off and do.

When they reached Central Park West, Myron asked, "Did you have a problem with her dating a married man?"

Sandra shrugged. "I worried, of course. But he told Melina he would leave his wife."

"Don't they all?"

"Melina believed it. She seemed happy."

"Did you ever meet Stan Gibbs?"

"No. Their relationship was supposed to be a secret."

"Did she ever tell you about lying in court?"

"No," she said. "Never."

Sandra used her key and swung the door open. Myron stepped inside. Colors. Lots of them. Happy colors. The apartment looked like the Magical Mystery Tour meets the Teletubbies, all bright hues, especially greens, with hazy psychedelic splashes. The walls were covered with vivid watercolors of distant lands and ocean voyages. Some surreal stuff too. The effect was like an Enya video.

"I started throwing her stuff in boxes," Sandra said. "But it's hard to pack up a life."

Myron nodded. He started walking around the small apartment, hoping for a psychic revelation or something. None came. He ran his eyes over the artwork.

"She was supposed to have her first show in the Village next month," Sandra said.

Myron studied a painting with white domes and crystal blue water. He recognized the spot in Mykonos. It was wonderfully done. Myron could almost smell the salt of the Mediterranean, taste the grilled fish along the beach, feel the night sand clinging to a lover's skin. No clue here, but he stared another minute or two before turning away.

He started going through the boxes. He found a high school yearbook, class of 1986, and flipped through it until he found Melina's picture. She'd like to paint, it said. He glanced again at the walls. So bright and optimistic, her work. Death, Myron knew, was always ironic. Young death most ironic of all.

He turned his attention back to her photograph. Melina was looking off to the side with the hesitant, unsure smile of high school. Myron knew it well. Don't we all. He closed the book and headed to her closets. Her clothes were neatly arranged, lots of sweaters folded on the top shelf, shoes lined up like tiny soldiers. He moved back to the boxes and found her photographs in a shoebox. A shoebox of all things. Myron shook his head and started going through them. Sandra sat on the floor next to him. "That's her mother," she said.

Myron looked at the photograph of two women, clearly mother and daughter, embracing. There was no sign of the unsure smile this time. This smile—the smile in her mother's arms—soared like an angel's song. Myron stared at the angel-song smile and imagined that celestial mouth crying out in hopeless agony. He thought about George Garston alone in that jaundice-lit study. And he understood.

Myron checked his watch. Time to pick up the pace. He thumbed through pictures of her father, her brother, Sandra, family outings, the norm. No pictures of Stan Gibbs. Nothing helpful.

He found makeup and perfume in another box. In another, he stumbled across a diary, but Melina hadn't written anything in it for two years. He paged through it, but it felt like too much of an unnecessary violation. He found a love letter from an old boyfriend. He found some receipts.

He found copies of Stan's columns.

Hmm.

In her address book. All the columns. There were no markings on them. Just the clippings themselves, held together by a paper clip. So what did that mean? He checked them again. Just clippings. He put them aside and did some more flipping. Something fell out near the back. Myron picked up a piece of cream-colored or aged-white paper torn along the left edge, more a card really, folded in half. The outside was totally blank. He opened it. On the upper half, the words *With Love, Dad* had been written in script. Myron thought again about George Garston sitting alone in that room and felt a deep burn flush his skin.

He sat on the couch now and tried again to conjure up something. That might sound weird—sitting in this too empty room, the sweet smell of a dead woman still hovering, feeling not unlike that tiny old lady in the *Poltergeist* movies—but you never knew. The victims didn't speak to him or anything like that. But sometimes he could imagine what they'd been thinking and feeling and some spark would hit the edges and start to flame. So he tried it again.

Nothing.

He let his eyes wander across the canvases and the burn under his skin started up again. He scanned the bright colors, let them assault him. The brightness should have protected her. Nonsense, but there you have it. She'd had a life. Melina worked and she painted and she loved bright colors and had too many sweaters and stored her precious memories in a shoebox and someone had snuffed that life away because none of that meant anything to him. None of that was important. It made Myron mad.

He closed his eyes and tried to turn the anger down a notch. Anger wasn't good. It clouded reason. He'd let that side of him out before—his Batman complex, as Esperanza had called it—but being a hero seeking justice or vengeance (if they weren't the same thing) was unwise, unhealthy. Eventually you saw things you didn't want to. You learned truths you never should have. It stings and then it deadens. Better to stay away.

But the heat in his blood would not leave him. So he stopped fighting it, let the heat soothe him, relax his muscles, settle gently over him. Maybe the heat wasn't such a bad thing. Maybe the horrors he'd seen and the truths he'd learned hadn't changed him, hadn't deadened him, after all.

Myron closed the boxes, took one last, lingering look at the sunkissed isle of Mykonos, and made a silent vow.

28

Greg and Myron met up on the court. Myron strapped on his knee brace. Greg averted his eyes. The two men shot for half an hour, barely speaking, lost in the pure strokes. People ducked in and pointed at Greg. Several kids came up to him and asked him for autographs. Greg acquiesced, glancing at Myron as he took pen in hand, clearly uncomfortable getting all this attention in front of the man whose career he had ended.

Myron stared back at him, offering no solace.

After some time, Myron said, "There a reason you wanted me here, Greg?"

Greg kept shooting.

"Because I have to get back to the office," Myron said.

Greg grabbed the ball, dribbled twice, took a turn-around jumper. "I saw you and Emily that night. You know that?"

"I know that," Myron said.

Greg grabbed the rebound, took a lazy hook, let the ball hit the floor and slowly bounce toward Myron. "We were getting married the next day. You know that?"

"Know that too."

"And there you were," Greg said, "her old boyfriend, screwing her brains out."

Myron picked up the ball.

"I'm trying to explain here," Greg said.

"I slept with Emily," Myron said. "You saw us. You

wanted revenge. You told Big Burt Wesson to hurt me during a preseason game. He did. End of story."

"I wanted him to hurt you, yes. I didn't mean for him to end your career."

"You say tomato, I say tomahto."

"It wasn't intentional."

"Don't take this the wrong way," Myron said in a voice that sounded awfully calm in his own ears, "but I don't give two shits about your intentions. You fired a weapon at me. You might have aimed for a flesh wound, but that didn't happen. You think that makes you blameless?"

"You fucked my fiancée."

"And she fucked me. I didn't owe you anything. She did."

"Are you telling me you don't understand?"

"I understand. It just doesn't absolve you."

"I'm not looking for absolution."

"Then what do you want, Greg? You want us to clasp hands and sing 'Kumbaya'? Do you know what you did to me? Do you know what the one moment cost me?"

"I think maybe I do," Greg said. He swallowed, put out a pleading hand as though he wanted to explain more, and then he let the hand drop to the side. "I'm so sorry."

Myron started shooting but he felt his throat swell.

"You don't know how sorry I am."

Myron said nothing. Greg tried to wait him out. It didn't work.

"What else do you want me to say here, Myron?"

Myron kept shooting.

"How do I tell you I'm sorry?"

"You've already done it," Myron said.

"But you won't accept it."

"No, Greg. I won't. I live without playing pro ball. You live without my accepting your apology. Pretty good deal for you, you ask me."

Myron's cell phone rang. He ran over, picked it up, said hello.

A whisper asked, "Did you do as I instructed?"

His bones turned to solid ice. He swallowed away something thick and said, "As you instructed?"

"The boy," the voice whispered.

The stale air pressed against him, weighed down his lungs. "What about him?"

"Did you say one last good-bye?"

Something inside of Myron withered up and blew away. His knees buckled as the realization seeped into his chest. And the voice came on again:

"Did you say one last good-bye to the boy?"

29

Myron snapped his head toward Greg. "Where's Jeremy?"

"What?"

"Where is he?"

Greg saw whatever it was on Myron's face and dropped the basketball. "He's with Emily, I guess. I don't get him until noon."

"Got a cell phone?"

"Yes."

"Call her."

Greg was already heading toward his gym bag, the athlete with the wonderful reflexes. "What's going on?"

"Probably nothing."

Myron explained about the call. Greg did not slow down to listen. He dialed. Myron started running toward his car. Greg followed, the phone pressed against his ear.

"No answer," Greg said. He left a message on the machine.

"Does she have a cell phone?"

"If she does, I don't have the number."

Myron hit a stored number as they walked. Esperanza picked up.

"I need Emily's cell phone number."

"Give me five," Esperanza said.

Myron hit another stored number. Win answered and said, "Articulate."

"Possible trouble."

"I'm here."

They reached the car. Greg was calm. That surprised Myron. On the court, when the pressure mounted, Greg's modus operandi was to get freaky, start screaming, psych himself into a frenzy. But of course, this was not a game. As his father had recently told him, when real bombs drop, you never know how someone will react.

Myron's phone rang. Esperanza gave him Emily's cell phone number. Myron dialed it. After six rings, Emily's voice mail picked up. Damn. Myron left a message. He turned to Greg.

"Any clue where Jeremy might be?" Myron asked.

"No," Greg said.

"How about a neighbor we can call? Or a friend?"

"When Emily and I were married, we lived in Ridgewood. I don't know the neighbors in Franklin Lakes."

Myron gripped the steering wheel. He hit the accelerator. "Jeremy's probably safe," Myron said, trying to believe it. "I don't even know how this guy would know his name. It's probably a bluff."

Greg started shaking.

"He'll be all right."

"Jesus, Myron, I read those articles. If that guy has my kid . . ."

"We should call the FBI," Myron said. "Just in case."

"You think that's the way to go?" Greg asked.

Myron looked at him. "Why? You don't?"

"I just want to pay the ransom and get my boy back. I don't want anybody screwing it up."

"I think we should call," Myron said. "But it's your decision."

"There's something else we have to consider," Greg said.

"What?"

"There's a good chance this wacko is our donor, right?"

"Yes."

"If the FBI kills him, it's over for Jeremy."

"First things first," Myron said. "We have to find Jeremy. And we have to find this kidnapper."

Greg kept shaking.

"What do you want to do, Greg?"

"You think we should call?"

"Yes."

Greg nodded slowly. "Call," he said.

Myron dialed Kimberly Green's number. He felt waves pounding in his head, the blood flowing to his ears. He tried not to think about Jeremy's face, what his smile had looked like when he opened that door.

Did you say one last good-bye to the boy?

A voice said, "Federal Bureau of Investigation."

"Myron Bolitar calling Kimberly Green."

"Special Agent Green is unavailable."

"The Sow the Seeds kidnapper may have taken somebody else. Put her on."

The hold was longer than Myron expected.

Kimberly Green started with a bark. "What the hell are you ranting about?"

"He just called me." Myron filled her in.

"We're on our way," she said.

They hit a patch of traffic where Route 4 met Route 17, but Myron went up on the grass and knocked over several orange construction buckets. He broke off at Route 208 and exited near the synagogue. Two miles later, they made the final turn onto Emily's street. Myron could see two FBI cars making the turn at the same time.

Greg, who had gone into something of a trance, woke up and pointed. "There she is."

Emily was putting her key in the front door. Myron started honking madly. She looked back confused. He turned the car and skidded. The FBI car followed. Myron and Greg were both out the door almost before the car had stopped.

"Where's Jeremy?" they both said in unison.

Emily had her head tilted to the side. "What?" she called back. "What's going on here?"

Greg took it. "Where is he, Emily?"

"He's with a friend—"

From inside the house, the phone started ringing. Everyone froze. Emily snapped out of it first. She ran inside and picked up the phone. She put the phone to her ear, cleared her throat, and said, "Hello."

Through the receiver, they could all hear Jeremy's scream.

30

There were six federal agents in all. Kimberly Green was the task force leader. They set up with quiet efficiency. Myron sat on one couch, Greg the other. Emily paced between them. There was probably something symbolic in that, but Myron was not sure what. He tried to push himself past the numb so he could get to a place where he could do some good.

The phone call had been brief. After the scream, the whispery voice had said, "We'll call back." That was it. No warnings not to contact the authorities. No telling them to prepare funds. No setting up another time to call. Nothing.

They all sat there, the boy's scream still echoing, mauling, shredding, conjuring up images of what could have made a thirteen-year-old boy scream like that. Myron shut his eyes and pushed hard. That was what the bastard wanted. Unwise to play into that.

Greg had contacted his bank. He was not a risky investor, and so most of his assets were liquid. If ransom money was needed, he'd be ready. The various feds, all male except for Kimberly Green, put traces on all the possible phones, including Myron's. She and her men were doing a lot of sotto voce. Myron hadn't pressed them yet. But that wasn't going to last.

Kimberly caught his eyes and waved him over. He stood and excused himself. Greg and Emily paid no attention, still lost in the vortex of that scream.

"We need to talk," she said.

"Okay," Myron said. "Start by telling me what happened when you checked out Dennis Lex."

"You're not family," she said. "I could throw you out."

"This isn't your house," he said. "What happened with Dennis Lex?"

She put her hands on her hips. "It's a dead end."

"How so?"

"We traced it down. He's not involved in any of this."

"How do you know that?"

"Myron, come on. We're not stupid."

"So where is Dennis Lex?"

"It's not relevant," she said.

"The hell it's not. Even if he's not the kidnapper, we still have him as the bone marrow donor."

"No," she said. "Your donor is Davis Taylor."

"Who changed his name from Dennis Lex."

"We don't know that."

Myron made a face. "What are you talking about?"

"Davis Taylor was an employee in the Lex conglomerate."

"What?"

"You heard me."

"So why did he donate blood for a bone marrow drive?"

"It was a work thing," she said. "The plant boss had a sick nephew. Everyone at the plant gave."

Myron nodded. Something finally made sense. "So if he didn't give a blood sample," he said, "it would have been conspicuous."

"Right."

"You got a description on him?"

"He worked on his own, kept to himself. All anyone

remembers is a man with a full beard, glasses, and long blond hair."

"A disguise," Myron said. "And we know Davis Taylor's original name was Dennis Lex. What else?"

Kimberly Green raised her hand. "Enough." She sort of hitched herself up, trying to alter momentum. "Stan Gibbs is still our top suspect here. What did you talk about last night?"

"Dennis Lex," Myron said. "Don't you get it?"

"Get what?"

"Dennis Lex is connected into all this. He's either the kidnapper, or maybe he was the first victim."

"Neither," she said.

"Then where is he?"

She shook it off. "What else did you two talk about?"

"Stan's father."

"Edwin Gibbs?" That got her attention. "What about him?"

"That he vanished eight years ago. But you already know about that, don't you?"

She nodded a little too firmly. "We do," she said.

"So what do you think happened to him?" Myron asked.

She hesitated. "You believe that Dennis Lex may be Sow the Seeds' first victim, correct?"

"I think it's something to look into, yes."

"Our theory," she went on, "is that the first victim may have been Edwin Gibbs."

Myron made a face. "You think Stan kidnapped his own father?"

"Killed him. And the others. We don't believe any of them are still alive."

Myron tried not to let that sink in. "You have any evidence or motive?"

"Sometimes the apple doesn't fall far from the tree."

"Oh, that'll go over big with a jury. Ladies and gentlemen, the apple doesn't fall far from the tree. And you should never put the cart before the horse. Plus every dog has his day." He shook his head. "Are you listening to yourself?"

"On its own, I admit it doesn't make sense. But put it all together. Eight years ago, Stan was starting out on his own. He was twenty-four, his father forty-six. By all accounts, the two men did not get along. Suddenly Edwin Gibbs vanishes. Stan never reports it."

"This is silly."

"Maybe. But then add back everything else we already know. The only columnist to get this scoop. The plagiarism. Melina Garston. Everything that Eric Ford discussed with you yesterday."

"It still doesn't add up."

"Then tell me where Stan Gibbs is."

Myron looked at her. "Isn't he at the condo?"

"Last night, after you two talked, Stan Gibbs slipped surveillance. He's done that before. We usually pick him up a few hours later. But that hasn't happened this time. He's suddenly out of sight—and by coincidence, Jeremy Downing has been snatched by the Sow the Seeds kidnapper. You want to explain that one to me?"

Myron's mouth felt dry. "You're searching for him?"

"We got an APB. But we know he's good at hiding. You got any clue where he went?"

"None."

"He said nothing to you about it?"

"He mentioned that he might go away for a few days. But that I should trust him."

"Bad advice," she said. "Anything else?"

Myron shook his head. "Where is Dennis Lex?" he tried again. "Did you see him?"

"I didn't have to," she said. But her voice had a funny monotone to it. "He's not involved in this."

"You keep saying that," Myron said. "But how do you know?"

She slowed down. "The family."

"You mean Susan and Bronwyn Lex?"

"Yes."

"What about them?"

"They gave us reassurances."

Myron almost stepped back. "You just took their word for it?"

"I didn't say that." She glanced around, let loose a sigh. "And it's not my call."

"What?"

She looked straight through him. "Eric Ford handled it personally."

Myron could not believe what he was hearing.

"He told me to stay away," she said, "that he had it covered."

"Or covered up," Myron said.

"Nothing I can do about it." She looked at him. She had stressed the word *I*. Then she walked away without another word. Myron dialed his cell phone.

"Articulate," Win said.

"We're going to need help," Myron said. "Is Zorra still working freelance?"

"I'll call her."

"Maybe Big Cyndi too."

"Do you have a plan?"

"No time for a plan," Myron said.

"Ooo," Win said. "Then we're going to get nasty."

"Yes."

"And here I thought you weren't going to break the rules anymore."

"Just this once," Myron said.

"Ah," Win countered. "That's what they all say."

31

Win, Esperanza, Big Cyndi, and Zorra were all in his office.

Zorra wore a yellow monogrammed sweater (the monogram being one letter: Z), large white pearls à la Wilma Flintstone, a plaid skirt, and white bobby socks. Her—or if you want to be anatomically correct, his— wig looked like early Bette Midler or maybe Little Orphan Annie on methadone. Shiny red high-heel shoes like something stolen from a trampy Dorothy in Oz adorned the men's-size-twelve feet.

Zorra smiled at Myron. "Zorra is happy to see you."

"Yeah," Myron said. "And Myron is happy to see you too."

"This time, we're on the same side, yes?"

"Yes."

"Zorra pleased."

Zorra's real name was Shlomo Avrahaim, and she was a former Israeli Mossad agent. The two had had a nasty run-in not long ago. Myron still carried the wound near his rib cage—a scar-shaped Z made by a blade Zorra hid in her heel.

Win said, "The Lex Building is too well guarded."

"So we go with Plan B," Myron said.

"Already in motion," Win said.

Myron looked at Zorra. "You armed?"

Zorra pulled a weapon out from under her skirt. "The Uzi," Zorra said. "Zorra likes the Uzi."

Myron nodded. "Patriotic."

"Question," Esperanza said.

"What?"

Esperanza settled her eyes on his. "What if this guy doesn't cooperate?"

"We don't have time to worry about it," Myron said.

"Meaning?"

"This psycho has Jeremy," Myron said. "You understand that? Jeremy has to be the priority here."

Esperanza shook her head.

"Then stay behind," he said.

"You need me," she said.

"Right. And Jeremy needs *me*." He stood. "Okay, let's go."

Esperanza shook her head again, but she went along. The group—a sort of cut-rate Dirty (One-Third of a) Dozen—broke off when they reached the street. Esperanza and Zorra would walk. Win, Myron, and Big Cyndi headed into a garage three blocks away. Win had a car there. Chevy Nova. Totally untraceable. Win had a bunch of them. He referred to them as disposable vehicles. Like paper cups or something. The rich. You don't want to know what he does with them.

Win drove, Myron took the front passenger seat, and Big Cyndi squeezed into the back, which was a little like watching a film of childbirth on rewind. Then they were off.

The Stokes, Layton and Grace law firm was one of the most prestigious in New York. Big Cyndi stayed in reception. The receptionist, a skinny skirt-suit of gray, tried not to stare. So Big Cyndi stared at her, daring her not to look. Sometimes Big Cyndi would growl. Like a lion. No reason. She just liked to do it.

Myron and Win were ushered into a conference room

that looked like a million other big Manhattan law firm conference rooms. Myron doodled on a yellow legal pad that looked like a million other big Manhattan law firm legal pads, watched through the window the smug, pink, fresh-scrubbed Harvard grads stroll by, again all looking exactly the same as the ones at a million other big Manhattan law firms. Reverse discrimination maybe, but all young white male lawyers looked the same to him.

Then again, Myron was a white Harvard law school graduate. Hmm.

Chase Layton trollied in with his rolly build and well-fed face and chubby hands and gray comb-over, looking like, well, a name partner at a big Manhattan law firm. He wore a gold wedding band on one hand and a Harvard ring on the other. He greeted Win warmly—most wealthy people do—and then gave a firm, I'm-your-guy hand-shake to Myron.

"We're in a rush," Win said.

Chase Layton shoved the big smile out of the room and strapped on his best battle-ready face. Everyone sat. Chase Layton folded his hands in front of him. He leaned forward, putting a bit of a belly push on the vest buttons. "What can I do for you, Windsor?"

Rich people always called him Windsor.

"You've been after my business for a long time," Win said.

"Well, I wouldn't say—"

"I'm here to give it to you. In exchange for a favor."

Chase Layton was too smart to snap-bite at that. He looked at Myron. An underling. Maybe there'd be a clue how to play on this plebeian's face. Myron kept up the neutral. He was getting better at it. Must be from hanging around Win so much.

"We need to see Susan Lex," Win said. "You are her attorney. We'd like you to get her to come here immediately."

"Here?"

"Yes," Win said. "At your office. Immediately."

Chase opened his mouth, closed it, checked on the underling again. Still no clue. "Are you serious, Windsor?"

"You do that, you get the Lock-Horne business. You know how much income that would generate?"

"A great deal," Chase Layton said. "And yet not even a third of what we receive from the Lex family."

Win smiled. "Talk about having your cake and eating it too."

"I don't understand this," Chase said.

"It's pretty straightfoward, Chase."

"Why do you want to see Ms. Lex?"

"We can't divulge that."

"I see." Chase Layton scratched a ham-red cheek with a manicured finger. "Ms. Lex is a very private person."

"Yes, we know."

"She and I are friends."

"I'm sure," Win said.

"Perhaps I can set up an introduction."

"No good. It has to be now."

"Well, she and I usually conduct business at her office—"

"Again no good. It has to be here."

Chase rolled his neck a bit, stalling for time, trying to sort through this, find an angle to play. "She's a very busy woman. I wouldn't even know what to say to get her here."

"You're a good attorney, Chase," Win said, steepling his fingers. "I'm sure you'll come up with something."

Chase nodded, looked down, studied his manicure. "No," he said. He looked back up slowly. "I don't sell out clients, Windsor."

"Even if it meant landing a client as big as Lock-Horne?"

"Even then."

"And you're not doing this just to impress me with your discretion?"

Chase smiled, relieved, as though he finally got the joke. "No," he said. "But wouldn't that be having my cake and eating it too?" He tried to laugh it off. Win didn't join him.

"This isn't a test, Chase. I need you to get her here. I guarantee that she won't find out you helped me."

"Do you think that's all that concerns me here—how it would look?"

Win said nothing.

"If that's the case, you've misread me. The answer is still no, I'm afraid."

"Think about it," Win said.

"Nothing to think about," Chase said. He leaned back, crossing one leg over the other, making sure the crease sat right. "You didn't really think I'd go along with this, did you, Windsor?"

"I hoped."

Chase again looked at Myron, then back at Win. "I'm afraid I can't help you, gentlemen."

"Oh, you'll help us," Win said.

"Pardon me?"

"It's just a matter of what we need to do to get your cooperation."

Chase frowned. "Are you trying to bribe me?"

"No," Win said. "I already did that. By offering you our business."

"Then I don't understand—"

Myron spoke for the first time. "I'm going to make you," he said.

Chase Layton looked at Myron and smiled. Again he said, "Pardon me?"

Myron rose. He kept his expression flat, remembering what he'd learned from Win about intimidation. "I don't want to hurt you," Myron said. "But you will call Susan Lex and get her to come here. And you'll do it now."

Chase folded his arms and sat them atop his belly. "If you wish to discuss this further—"

"I don't," Myron said.

Myron walked around the table. Chase did not back away. "I will not call her," he said firmly. "Windsor, would you tell your friend to sit down?"

Win feigned a helpless shrug.

Myron stood directly over Chase. He looked back at Win. Win said, "Let me handle it."

Myron shook his head. He loomed over Chase and let his gaze fall. "One last chance."

Chase Layton's face was calm, almost amused. He probably saw this as a bizarre put-on—or perhaps he was just certain that Myron would back down. That was how it was with men like Chase Layton. Physical violence was not a part of the Layton equation. Oh, sure, those uneducated animals on the street might engage in it. They might knock him on the head for his wallet. Other people—lesser people, really—yes, they solved problems with physical violence. But that was another planet—one filled with a more primitive species. In Chase Layton's world, a world of status and position and lofty manners, you were untouchable. Men threatened. Men sued. Men cursed. Men schemed behind one another's backs. Men never engaged in face-to-face violence.

That was why Myron knew that no bluff would work here. Men like Chase Layton believed that anything remotely physical was a bluff. Myron could probably point a gun at him, and he wouldn't budge. And in that scenario, Chase Layton would be right.

But not this one.

Myron boxed Chase Layton's ears hard with his palms.

Chase's eyes widened in a way they probably never had before. Myron put his hand over the lawyer's mouth, muffling the scream. He cupped the back of the man's skull and pulled him back, knocking him off his chair and onto the floor.

Chase lay on his back. Myron looked him straight in the eye and saw a tear roll down the man's cheek. Myron felt ill. He thought about Jeremy and that helped keep his face neutral. Myron said, "Call her."

He slowly released his hand.

Chase's breathing was labored. Myron glanced at Win. Win shook his head.

"You," Chase said, spitting out the word, "are going to jail."

Myron closed his eyes, made a fist, and punched the lawyer up and under the ribs, toward the liver. The lawyer's face fell into itself. Myron held the man's mouth again, but this time there was no scream to smother.

Win eased back in his chair. "For the record, I am the sole witness to this event. I'll swear under oath that it was self-defense."

Chase looked lost.

"Call her," Myron said. He tried to keep the pleading

out of his voice. He looked down at Chase Layton. Chase's shirttail was out of his pants, his tie askew, his comb-over unraveling, and Myron realized that nothing would ever be the same for this man. Chase Layton had been physically assaulted. He would always walk a little more warily now. He would sleep a little less deeply. He would always be a little different inside.

Maybe so too would Myron.

Myron punched him again. Chase made an *oof* noise. Win stood by the door. Keep your face even, Myron told himself. A man at work. A man who won't stop no matter what. Myron cocked his fist again.

Five minutes later, Chase Layton called Susan Lex.

32

'Would have been better," Win said, "if you let me hurt him."

Myron kept walking. "It would have been the same," he said.

Win shrugged. They had an hour to set up. Big Cyndi was now in the conference room with Chase Layton, supposedly going over her new professional-wrestling contract. When she entered the room, all six-six, three hundred pounds of her wearing her Big Chief Mama costume, Chase Layton barely looked up. The pain from the punches, Myron was sure, was ebbing. He had not struck the man in any place that would do lasting damage, except maybe to the obvious.

Esperanza was set up in the lobby. Myron and Win met Zorra two levels down, on the seventh floor. Zorra had staked out the lower floors and decided that this would be the quietest and easiest to contain. The office suites on the northern side were empty, Zorra noted. Anyone entering or leaving had to do so from the west. Zorra was stationed there with one cell phone. Esperanza had the other one downstairs. Win held the third. They were on a three-way line with one another. Myron and Win were in position. In the last twenty minutes, the elevator had stopped at their floor only twice. Good. Both times the door opened, Myron and Win feigned conversation, just two guys waiting for an elevator heading in the opposite direction. Real undercover commandos.

Myron hoped like hell no one happened upon the scene when it all went down. Zorra would warn them, of course, but once the operation was under way, it couldn't be stopped. They'd have to come up with some excuse, say it was a drill maybe, but Myron was not sure he could stomach hurting any more innocents today. He closed his eyes. Can't back down now. Too far gone.

Win smiled at him. "Wondering yet again if the ends justify the means?"

"Not wondering," Myron said.

"Oh?"

"I know they don't."

"And yet?"

"I'm not in the mood for introspection right now."

"But you're so good at it," Win said.

"Thanks."

"And knowing you as well as I do, you'll save it for later—for when you have more time. You'll gnash your teeth over what you just did. You'll feel ashamed, remorseful, guilty—though you'll also be oddly proud that you didn't have *moi* do your dirty work. You'll end up making a clear declaration that it will never happen again. And perhaps it won't—not, at least, until the stakes are this high."

"So I'm a hypocrite," Myron said. "Happy?"

"But that is my point," Win said.

"What?"

"You're not a hypocrite. You aim toward lofty heights. The fact that your arrow cannot always reach them does not make you a hypocrite."

"So in conclusion," Myron said, "the ends do not justify the means. Except sometimes."

Win spread his hands. "See? I just saved you hours of soul-searching. Perhaps I should consider penning one of those how-to-manage-your-time manuals."

Esperanza broke in through the phone. "They're here," she said.

Win put the phone to his ear. "How many?"

"Three coming in. Susan Lex. That granite guy Myron keeps talking about. Another bodyguard. Two more staying parked outside."

"Zorra," Win said into the phone. "Please keep an eye on the two gentlemen outside."

Zorra said, "And if they move?"

"Detain them."

"With pleasure." Zorra giggled. Win smiled. Welcome to the Psycho Hotline. Only $3.99 per minute. First call is free.

Myron and Win waited now. Two minutes past. Esperanza said, "Middle elevator. All three are inside."

"Anyone else with them?"

"No . . . wait. Damn, two businessmen are going in."

Myron closed his eyes and cursed.

Win looked at him. "Your call."

Panic squeezed Myron's chest. Innocent people in the elevator. There was sure to be violence. Witnesses now.

"Well?"

"Hold the phone." It was Esperanza. "The granite guy blocked their path. Looks like he told them to wait for another elevator."

"Top-notch security," Win said. "Good to see we're not dealing with amateurs."

"Okay," Esperanza said. "Just the three of them are inside now."

The relief in Myron's face was palpable.

Esperanza said, "Elevator closing . . . now."

Myron pressed the Up button. Win took out his forty-four. Myron pulled out a Glock. They waited.

Myron kept the gun by his thigh. It felt heavy in a terrible, comforting way. Myron kept glancing down the corridor. No one. He hoped their luck would hold. He felt his pulse start to race. His mouth was dry. The room suddenly felt warmer.

A minute later, the light above the middle elevator dinged.

Win's face was in the zone, semi-euphoric. He wriggled his eyebrows and said, "Showtime."

Myron tensed his muscles, leaned in a bit. The elevator's whirring noise stopped. There was a delay and then the doors started sliding open. Win didn't wait. He was inside before the opening had reached a foot. He found Grover and stuck the gun in the big man's ear. Myron did the same with the other guard.

"Waxy ear buildup a problem, Grover?" Win said in his best voice-over. "Smith and Wesson has the solution!"

Susan Lex started to open her mouth. Win cut her off with a finger against her lip and a gentle "Shh."

Win frisked and disarmed Grover. Myron followed his lead with the second guard. Grover glared daggers at Win. Win took them on and said, "Please—no, pretty please—make a sudden move."

Grover didn't budge.

Win stepped back. The elevator door started closing. Myron stopped it with his foot. He pointed the weapon at Susan Lex. "You're coming with me," Myron said.

"Don't you want revenge first?" Grover said.

Myron looked at him.

"Go ahead." Grover spread his hands. "Hit me in the gut. Go ahead, give it your best shot."

"Pardon *moi*," Win said. "But does that offer apply to me too?"

Grover looked at the smaller man like a tasty leftover. "I heard you're not bad," he said.

Win looked back at Myron. " 'Not bad,' " he repeated. "Monsieur Grover heard I was 'not bad.' "

"Win," Myron said.

Win snapped his knee deep into Grover's groin. He followed through, driving the man's testicles all the way into his stomach. Grover did not make a sound. He simply folded like a bad hand of poker.

"Oh, wait, you said 'gut,' didn't you?" Win looked down at him, frowned. "Must work on my aim. Perhaps you're right. Perhaps I am merely 'not bad.' "

Grover was on his knees, his hands between his legs. Win kicked him in the head with his instep. Grover toppled over like a bowling pin. Win looked over at the other guard, who was putting his hands up and backing quickly into a corner.

"Will you tell your friends I was 'not bad?' " Win asked him.

The guard shook his head.

"Enough," Myron said.

Win picked up the cell phone. "Zorra, report."

"They are not moving, handsome."

"Come back up then. You can help me clean up."

"Clean up? Ooo, Zorra will hurry."

Win laughed.

"No more," Myron said. Win did not reply, but Myron hadn't really expected him to. Myron grabbed Susan Lex's arm. "Let's go."

He pulled her into the stairwell. Zorra bounded into view—on high heels no less. Leaving two unarmed men alone with Win and Zorra. Talk about scary. But he had no choice here. Myron turned to Susan Lex, keeping tight hold of her elbow.

"I need your help," he said to her.

Susan Lex looked at him, head high, not backing off.

"I promise not to say anything," he went on. "I have no interest in hurting you or your family. But you're going to take me to see Dennis."

"And if I say no?"

Myron just looked at her.

"You'd hurt me?" she said.

"I just beat up an innocent man," Myron said.

"And you'd do the same to a woman?"

"I wouldn't want to be accused of sexism."

Her expression remained defiant, but unlike Chase Layton, she seemed to understand how the real world worked. "You know what sort of power I have."

"I do."

"Then you know what I'll do to you when this is all over?"

"I don't much care. A thirteen-year-old boy has been kidnapped."

She almost smiled. "I thought you said he needed a bone marrow transplant."

"I don't have time to explain."

"My brother isn't involved in this."

"I keep hearing that."

"Because it's true."

"Then prove it to me."

Something in her face shifted then, changing her features, relaxing them into something strangely approaching tranquility. "Come," she said. "Let's go."

33

Susan Lex directed him north on the FDR to the Harlem River Drive and then north again to 684. Once they were in Connecticut, the roads grew quieter. Woods thickened. Buildings grew scarce. Traffic was pretty much nonexistent.

"We're almost there," Susan Lex said. "I'd like the truth now."

"I'm telling you the truth."

"Fine," she said. Then: "How do you plan on getting away with this?"

"With what?"

"Are you going to kill me when this is all over?"

"No."

"Then I'll come back after you. I'll press charges, if nothing else."

"I told you before. I don't much care. But I've thought of something."

"Oh?"

"Dennis will save me."

"How?"

"If he is the Sow the Seeds kidnapper—"

"He's not."

"—or somehow involved with him, then what I'm doing here will be small potatoes by comparison."

"And if he's not?"

Myron shrugged. "Either way, I'm going to learn whatever it is you want to hide. We make a deal. I never tell what I saw. In exchange, you leave me alone."

"Or I can simply kill you."

"I don't believe you'd do that."

"No?"

"You're not a killer. And even if you were, it would be too complicated. I'd leave evidence behind. I have Win covering my back. It would be too messy."

"We'll see," she said, but there was no starch there. She pointed up ahead. "Turn off up here."

She pointed to a dirt road that seemed to materialize from nowhere. There was a guardhouse fifty yards down and to the left. Myron pulled up. Susan Lex leaned over and smiled. The guard waved her through. There were no signs, no identification marks, nothing. The whole setup looked like some sort of militia compound.

After the gatehouse, the dirt road stopped and a paved one began. New pavement from the looks of it colored the dark black-gray of heavy rain. Trees crowded the sides like parade watchers. Up ahead, the road narrowed. The trees closed in too. Myron veered the car to the left and passed through wrought-iron gates guarded by two stone falcons.

"What is this?" Myron asked.

Susan Lex did not reply.

A mansion seemed to push out of the green, elbowing its way forward. The exterior was classic off-white Georgian but on an oversized scale. Palladian windows, pilasters, fancy pediments, curved balconies, brick cornering and what looked like real stone masonry were all garnished with hints of green ivy. A set of oversized double doors were dead center, the entire edifice perfectly symmetrical.

"Park in the lot over there," Susan Lex said.

Myron followed her finger. There was indeed a paved

lot. Myron figured it contained close to twenty cars. Various makes. A BMW, a couple of Honda Accords, three Mercedes of different lineage, Fords, SUVs, one station wagon. Your basic American melting pot. Myron glanced back at the oversized manor. He noticed ramps now. Lots of them. He checked the cars. Several had MD license plates.

"A hospital," he said.

Susan Lex smiled. "Come along."

They headed up the brick path. Gloved gardeners were on their knees, working on the flower beds. A woman walked by in the opposite direction. She smiled politely but said nothing. They passed through an arched entranceway and into a two-story foyer. A woman seated behind the desk stood, slightly startled.

"We weren't expecting you, ma'am," she said.

"That's fine."

"I don't have security set up."

"That's fine too."

"Yes, ma'am."

Susan Lex barely broke stride. She took the sweeping staircase on her left, staying in the middle, not touching a handrail. Myron followed.

"What did she mean about security?" Myron asked.

"When I visit, they make sure the hallways are kept clear and that no one else is present."

"To keep your secret?"

"Yes," she said. She did not stop moving. "Perhaps you noticed that she called me 'ma'am.' That's part of the discretion here. They never use names."

When they reached the top level, Susan turned to the left. The corridor had raised wallpaper in a classic floral design and nothing else. No small tables, no chairs, no pictures in frames, no Oriental runners. They passed by maybe a dozen rooms, only two with doors open. Myron noticed that the doors were extra wide and he remembered his visit to Babies and Children's Hospital. Extra wide doors there too. For wheelchairs and stretchers and the like.

When they reached the end of the corridor, Susan stopped, took a deep breath, looked back at Myron. "Are you ready?"

He nodded.

She opened the door and stepped inside. Myron followed. A four-poster antique bed, like something you'd see on a tour of Jefferson's Monticello, overwhelmed the room. The walls were warm green with woodwork trim. There was a small crystal chandelier, a burgundy Victorian couch, a Persian rug with deep scarlets. A Mozart violin concerto was playing a bit too loudly on the stereo. A woman sat in the corner reading a book. She too started upright when she saw who it was.

"It's okay," Susan Lex said. "Would you mind leaving us for a few moments?"

"Yes, ma'am," the woman said. "If you need anything—"

"I'll ring, thank you."

The woman did a semi-curtsy/semi-bow and hurried out. Myron looked at the man in the bed. The resemblance to the computer rendering was uncanny, almost perfect. Even, strangely enough, the dead eyes. Myron moved closer. Dennis Lex followed him with the dead eyes, unfocused, empty, like windows over a vacant lot.

"Mr. Lex?"

Dennis Lex just stared at him.

"He can't talk," she said.

Myron turned to her. "I don't understand," he said.

"You were right before. It's a hospital. Of sorts. In

another era, I suppose one would have called it a private sanitarium."

"How long has your brother been here?"

"Thirty years," she said. She moved toward the bed, and for the first time, she looked down at her brother. "You see, Mr. Bolitar, this is where the wealthy store unpleasantness." She reached down and stroked her brother's cheek. Dennis Lex did not respond. "We're too cultured not to give our loved ones the best. All very humane and practical, don't you know."

Myron waited for her to say more. She kept stroking her brother's cheek. He tried to see her face, but she kept it lowered and away from him.

"Why is he here?" Myron asked.

"I shot him," she said.

Myron opened his mouth, closed it, did the math. "But you were only a child when he disappeared."

"Fourteen years old," she said. "Bronwyn was six." She stopped stroking the cheek. "It's an old story, Mr. Bolitar. You've probably heard it a thousand times. We were playing with a loaded gun. Bronwyn wanted to hold it, I said no, he reached for it, it went off." She said it all in one breath, staring down at her brother, still stroking the cheek. "This is the end result."

Myron looked at the still eyes in the bed. "He's been here since?"

She nodded. "For a while I kept waiting for him to die. So I could officially be a murderer."

"You were a child," Myron said. "It was an accident."

She looked at him and smiled. "My, that means so much coming from you, thank you."

Myron said nothing.

"No matter," she said. "Daddy took care of it. He

arranged for my brother to have the best care. He was a very private person, my father. It was his gun. He'd left it where his children could play with it. His business and reputation were both growing. He had political aspirations at the time. He just wanted it all to go away."

"And it did."

She tilted her head back and forth. "Yes."

"What about your mother?"

"What about her?"

"What did she say?"

"My mother hated unpleasantness, Mr. Bolitar. After the incident, she never saw her son again."

Dennis Lex made a sound, a guttural scrape, nothing remotely human. Susan gently shushed him.

"Did you and Bronwyn ever get help?" Myron asked.

She cocked an eyebrow. "Help?"

"Counseling. To help you through it."

She made a face. "Oh please," she said.

Myron stood there, his mind circling nowhere over nothing.

"So now you know the truth, Mr. Bolitar."

"I guess," he said.

"Meaning?"

"I wonder why you told me all this. You could have just shown Dennis to me."

"Because you won't talk."

"How can you be so sure?"

She smiled. "After you shoot your own brother, shooting strangers becomes so easy."

"You don't really believe that."

"No, I suppose not." Susan Lex turned and faced him. "The fact is, you really don't have much to tell. As you said earlier, we both have reasons to keep our mouths shut. You'll be arrested for kidnapping and Lord knows what. The evidence of my crime—if indeed it was a crime—is nonexistent. You'd be worse off than I."

Myron nodded, but his mind still whirred. Her story might be true or just something she told him to gain sympathy, to contain the damage. Still, there was the ring of truth in her words. Maybe her reason for talking was simpler. Maybe, after all this time, she just needed someone who'd listen to her confession. Didn't matter. None of it mattered. There was nothing here. Dennis Lex was truly a dead end.

Myron looked out the window. The sun was starting to dip away. He checked his watch. Jeremy had been missing five hours now—five hours alone with a madman—and Myron's best lead, his *only* lead, was lying brain-damaged in a hospital room.

The sun was still strong, bathing the expansive garden in white. Myron saw what looked like a maze made of shrubbery. He spotted several patients in wheelchairs, legs covered with blankets, sitting by a fountain. Serene. The rays reflected off a pool of water and a statue in the middle of—

He stopped. The statue.

Myron felt the blood in his veins turn to crystal. He shaded his eyes with his hand and squinted again.

"Oh Christ," he said.

Then he sprinted toward the stairs.

34

Susan Lex's helicopter was starting to descend toward the sanitarium's landing pad when Kimberly Green called him on the cell phone.

"We've caught Stan Gibbs," she said. "But the boy wasn't with him."

"That's because he isn't the kidnapper."

"You know something I don't?"

Myron ignored the question. "Has Stan told you anything?"

"Nope. He lawyered up already. Says he won't talk to anyone but you. You, Myron. Why don't I find that particularly surprising?"

Had Myron responded, the helicopter's propeller would have drowned it out. He backed off a few steps. The copter touched down. The pilot stuck his head out and waved to him.

"I'm on my way," Myron shouted into the phone. He switched it off and turned to Susan Lex. "Thank you."

She nodded.

He ducked and ran toward the helicopter. As they rose, Myron looked back down. Susan Lex's chin was tilted up, her eyes still on him. He waved. And she waved back.

Stan was not in a holding cell because they had nothing to hold him on. He sat in a waiting room with his eyes on the table and let his attorney, Clara Steinberg, do the talking. Myron had known Clara—he called her Aunt

Clara though there was no familial relationship—since he was too young to remember. Aunt Clara and Uncle Sidney were Mom and Dad's closest friends. Dad had gone to elementary school with Clara. Mom had roomed with her in law school. Aunt Clara, in fact, had set up Mom and Dad on their first date. She liked to remind Myron with a wink that "you wouldn't be here if it weren't for your aunt Clara." Then she'd wink again. Subtle, that Clara. During the holidays, she always pinched Myron's cheeks in admiration of his *punim*.

"Let me set up the ground rules, *bubbe*," she said to him. Clara had gray hair and a pair of oversized glasses that magnified her eyes to Ant-Man size. She looked up at him and the giant eyes seemed to reel in everything all at once. She wore a white blouse with a gray vest, matching skirt, a kerchief around her neck, and teardrop pearl earrings. Think Shtetl Barbara Bush.

"One," she said, "I am Mr. Gibbs's attorney of record. I have requested that this conversation not be overheard. I have changed rooms four times to make sure the authorities don't listen in. But I don't trust them. They think your aunt Clara is an old dodo bird. They think we're going to chat right here."

"We're not?" Myron said.

"We're not," she repeated. There was little hint of the cheek pincher here; if she were an athlete, you'd say that she'd strapped on her game face. "What we're going to do first is stand up. Got me?"

"Stand up," Myron repeated.

"Right. Then I'm going to lead you and Stan outside, across the street. I'm going to remain on the other side of the street with all those friendly agents. We do this right now, quickly, so they won't have a chance to set up surveillance. Understood?"

Myron nodded. Stan kept his eyes on the Formica.

"Good, just so we're all on the same page here." She knocked on the door. Kimberly Green opened it. Clara walked past her without speaking. Myron and Stan followed. Kimberly rushed up behind them.

"Where do you think you're going?"

"Change of plans, doll."

"You can't do that."

"Sure I can. I'm a sweet little old lady."

"I don't care if you're the Queen Mother," Kimberly said. "You're not going anywhere."

"You married, hon?"

"What?"

"Never mind," Clara said. "Try this on for size. See how it fits. My client demands privacy."

"We already promised—"

"Shh, you're talking when you should be listening. My client demands privacy. So he and Mr. Bolitar are going to take a little walk somewhere. You and I will watch from a distance. We will not listen in."

"I already told you—"

"Shh, you're giving me a headache." Aunt Clara rolled her eyes and kept walking. Myron and Stan followed. They reached the doorway. Clara pointed to a bus depot across the street. "Sit over there," she said to them. "On the bench."

Myron said okay. Clara put a hand on his elbow.

"Cross at the corner," she said. "And wait for the light."

The two men walked to the corner and waited for the light before crossing the street. Kimberly Green and her fellow agents fumed. Clara took them by the hand and led them back toward the building's entrance. Stan and Myron sat on the bench. Stan watched a New Jersey

Transit bus go by like it carried the secret to life.

"We don't have time to enjoy the scenery, Stan."

Stan leaned forward, put his elbows on his knees. "This is difficult for me."

"If it makes it any easier," Myron said, "I know that the Sow the Seeds kidnapper is your father."

Stan's head fell into his hands.

"Stan?"

"How did you find out?"

"Through Dennis Lex. I found him in a private sanitarium in Connecticut. He's been there for thirty years. But you already knew that, didn't you?"

Gibbs said nothing.

"At the sanitarium, there's a big garden in the back. With this statue of Diana the Huntress. There's a picture in your condo of you and your father standing in front of that same statue. He was a patient there. You don't have to confirm or deny it. I was just there. Susan Lex has pull. An administrator told us Edwin Gibbs had been in and out of there for fifteen years. The rest is fairly obvious. Your father was there a long time. It'd be easy to learn who else was there, no matter how strict the so-called security. So he knew about Dennis Lex. And he stole his identity. It's a hell of a twist, I'll give him that. Fake IDs used to be somewhat pretty easy to come by. You'd visit a graveyard, find a child who died, request his social security card, bingo. But that doesn't work anymore. Computers closed down that loophole. Nowadays when you die, your social security number dies with you. So your father took the identity of someone still alive, someone who has no use for it, someone committed permanently. In other words, he used the ID of a living person who has no life. And to go deeper undercover, he changed the person's name.

Dennis Lex became Davis Taylor. Untraceable."

"Except you traced it."

"I got lucky."

"Go on," Stan said. "Tell me what else you know."

"We don't have time for this, Stan."

"You don't understand," he said.

"What?"

"If you're the one who says it—if you figure it out on your own—it's not as much a betrayal. You see?"

No time to argue. And maybe Myron did see. "Let's start with the question every reporter wanted to know: why you? Why did the Sow the Seeds kidnapper choose you? The answer: because the kidnapper was your father. He knew you wouldn't turn him in. Maybe part of you hoped someone would figure it out. I don't know. I also don't know if you found him or he found you."

"He found me," Stan said. "He came to me as a reporter. Not as a son. He made that clear."

"Sure," Myron said, "double protection. He gets you with the fact that you'd be turning in your own father—plus he gives you an ethical foundation for remaining silent. The beloved First Amendment. You couldn't name a source. It gave you a very neat out—you could be both moralistic and the good son."

Stan looked up. "So you see that I had no choice."

"Oh, I wouldn't be so easy on myself," Myron said. "You weren't being totally altruistic. Everyone says you were ambitious. That played a part here. You got fame out of this. You were handed a monster story—the kind that propels careers into the stratosphere. You were on TV and got your own cable show. You got a big raise and invited to fancy parties. You want to tell me that wasn't a part of it?"

"It was a by-product," Stan said. "It wasn't a factor."

"You say so."

"It's like you said—I couldn't turn him in, even if I wanted to. There was a constitutional principle here. Even if he wasn't my father, I had an obligation—"

"Save it for your minister," Myron said. "Where is he?"

Stan did not reply. Myron looked across the street. Lots of traffic. The cars started blurring and through them, standing on the other side of the street with Kimberly Green, he saw Greg Downing.

"That man over there," Myron said, pointing with his chin. "That's the boy's father."

Stan looked, but his face didn't change.

"There's a kid in danger," Myron said. "That trumps your constitutional cover."

"He's still my father."

"And he's kidnapped a thirteen-year-old boy," Myron said.

Stan looked up. "What would *you* do?"

"What?"

"Would you give up your father? Just like that?"

"If he was kidnapping children? Yeah, I would."

"Do you really think it's that easy?"

"Who said anything about easy?" Myron said.

Stan put his head back in his hands. "He's sick and he needs help."

"And there's also an innocent boy out there."

"So?"

Myron looked at him.

"I don't mean to sound callous, but I don't know this boy. He has no connection to me. My father does. That's what matters here. You hear about a plane crash, right? You hear about how two hundred people die and you sigh and you go on with your life and you thank God it wasn't your loved one in the plane. Don't you do that?"

"What's your point?"

"You do that because the people on the plane are strangers. Like this boy. We don't care about strangers. They don't count."

"Speak for yourself," Myron said.

"Are you close to your father, Myron?"

"Yes."

"And in your heart of hearts, in your deepest, most honest moments, if you could sacrifice his life to save those two hundred people on the airplane, would you do it? Think about it. If God came down to you and said, 'Okay, that plane never crashed. Those people all arrive safely. In exchange, your father will die.' Would you make that trade?"

"I'm not into playing God."

"But you're asking me to," Stan said. "I turn my father in, they'll kill him. He'll get the lethal injection. If that's not playing God, I don't know what is. So I'm asking you. Would you trade those two hundred lives for your father's?"

"We don't have time—"

"Would you?"

"Okay, if it was my father shooting down the plane," Myron said, "yes, Stan, I would make that trade."

"And suppose your father wasn't culpable? If he was sick or deranged?"

"Stan, we don't have time for this."

Something in Stan's face dropped. He closed his eyes.

"There's a boy out there," Myron said. "We can't let him die."

"And if he's already dead?"

"I don't know."

"You'll want my father dead."

"Not by my hand," Myron said.

Stan took a deep breath and looked over at Greg Downing. Greg stared back, stared right through him. "Okay," he said at last. "But we go alone."

"Alone?"

"Just you and me."

Kimberly Green had a major conniption. "Are you insane?"

They were back inside, sitting around the Formica table. Kimberly Green, Rick Peck, and two other faceless feds were hunched together as one. Clara Steinberg sat with her client. Greg sat next to Myron. Jeremy's kidnapping had siphoned all the blood from Greg's face. His hands looked sucked dry, his skin almost crisp, his eyes too solid and unblinking. Myron put a hand on his shoulder. Greg didn't seem to notice.

"You want my client to cooperate or not?" Clara asked.

"I'm supposed to let my number one suspect go?"

"I'm not running away," Stan said.

"How am I supposed to know that?" Kimberly countered.

"It's the only way," Stan said, his voice a plea. "You'll go in with guns blazing. Someone is going to get hurt."

"We're professionals," Green countered. "We don't go in with guns blazing."

"My father is unstable. If he sees a lot of cops, I can guarantee there will be bloodshed."

"Doesn't have to be that way," she said. "It's up to him."

"Exactly," Stan said. "I'm not taking that chance with my father's life. You let us go. You don't follow us. I'll have him surrender to you. Myron will be with me the whole time. He's armed and he has a cell phone."

"Come on," Myron said. "We're wasting time here."

Kimberly Green chewed on her lower lip. "I don't have the authorization—"

"Forget it," Clara Steinberg said.

"Excuse me?"

Clara pointed a meaty finger at Kimberly Green. "Listen up, missy, you haven't arrested Mr. Gibbs, correct?"

Green hesitated. "That's correct."

Clara turned to Stan and Myron and waved the backs of both hands at them. "So shoo, go, good-bye. We're talking nonsense here. Hurry along. Shoo."

Stan and Myron slowly rose.

"Shoo."

Stan looked down at Kimberly. "If I spot a tail, I'm calling this off. You got me?"

She stewed in silence.

"You've been trailing me for three weeks now. I know what one of your tails looks like."

"She won't tail you."

It was Greg Downing. He and Stan locked eyes again. Greg stood. "I want to go with you too," Greg said. "And I probably have the strongest interest in keeping your father alive."

"How do you figure?"

"Your father's bone marrow can save my son's life. If he dies, so does my son. And if Jeremy has been hurt . . . well, I'd like to be there for him."

Stan didn't waste a lot of time thinking about it. "Let's hurry."

35

Stan drove. Greg sat in the front passenger seat, Myron in the back.

"Where are we going?" Myron asked.

"Bernardsville," Stan said. "It's in Morris County."

Myron knew the town.

"My grandmother died three years ago," Stan said. "We haven't sold the house yet. My father sometimes stays there."

"Where else does he stay?"

"Waterbury, Connecticut."

Greg looked back at Myron. The old man, the blond wig. It clicked for both of them at the same time.

"He's Nathan Mostoni?"

Stan nodded. "That's his main alias. The real Nathan Mostoni is another patient at Pine Hills—that's what we call that fancy loony bin, Pine Hills. Mostoni was the one who came up with the idea of using the identification of the committed, mostly for scams. He and my father became close friends. When Nathan slipped into total delirium, my father took his identity."

Greg shook his head, made two fists. "You should have turned the crazy bastard in."

"You love your son, don't you, Mr. Downing?"

Greg gave Stan a look that could have bored holes through titanium. "What the hell does that have to do with anything?"

"Would you want your son to turn you in one day?"

"Don't hand me that. If I'm a raving psychopathic

maniac, yeah, my son can turn me in. Or better, he can put a bullet in my head. You knew your old man was sick, right? The least you could have done was get him help."

"We tried," Stan said. "He was in institutions most of his adult life. It didn't do any good. Then he ran off. When he finally called me, I hadn't seen him in eight years. Imagine that. Eight years. He calls me and tells me he needs to talk to me as a reporter. He made that clear. As a reporter. No matter what he told me, I couldn't reveal the source. He made me promise. I was confused as all hell. But I agreed. And then he told me his story. What he'd been doing. I could barely breathe. I wanted to die. I wanted to just dry up and die."

Greg put his fingers to his mouth. Stan concentrated on the road. Myron stared out the window. He thought about the father of three young children, age forty-one; the female college student, age twenty; and the young newlyweds, ages twenty-eight and twenty-seven. He thought about Jeremy's scream over the phone. He thought about Emily waiting at the house, her mind sowing the seeds, sick and blackening.

They got off Route 78 and took 287 north. They exited onto winding streets with no straightaways. Bernardsville was about old money and rustic wealth, a town of converted mills and stone houses and waterwheels. There were fields of long brown grass swaying in death, everything a little too old and too neatly overgrown.

"It's on this road," Stan said.

Myron looked out. His mouth was dry. He felt a tingle deep in his belly. The car traveled down another corkscrew of a street, the loose gravel crunching under the tires. There were deeply wooded lots commingling, with your standard suburban front lawns. Plenty of center-hall colonials and those mid-seventies ranches that aged like milk left out on the counter. A yellow sign warned about children at play, but Myron saw none.

They pulled into a cake-dried driveway with weeds poking up through the cracks. Myron lowered his window. There was plenty of burnt-out grass, but the sweet summer smell of lillies still loomed and even cloyed. Crickets droned. Wildflowers blossomed. Not a hint of menace.

Up ahead Myron spotted what looked like a farmhouse. Black shutters stood out against the white clapboards. There were lights coming from inside, giving the house a glow that was big and soft and oddly welcoming. The front porch was the type that craved a swinging settee and a pitcher of lemonade.

When the car reached the front of the house, Stan shifted into park and turned off the ignition. The crickets eased up. Myron almost waited for someone to note that it was "Quiet" and for someone else to add, "Yeah, too quiet."

Stan turned to them. "I think I should go in first," he said.

Neither man argued. Greg stared out the window at the house, probably conjuring up unspeakable horrors. Myron's left leg started jackhammering. It often did when he was tense. Stan reached for the door handle.

That was when the first bullet smashed through the front passenger-side window.

The glass exploded, and Myron saw Greg's head fly back at a rate it was never supposed to achieve. A thick gob of crimson smacked Myron in the cheek.

"Greg!"

No time. Instincts took over. Myron grabbed Greg,

pushed him down, trying to keep his own head down too. Blood. Lots of it. From Greg. He was bleeding, bleeding heavily, but Myron couldn't tell from where. Another bullet rang out. Another window shattered, raining shards of glass down on Myron's head. He kept his hand on top of Greg, tried to cover him, protect him. Greg's own hand fumbled absently on his chest and face, calmly searching for the bullet hole. Blood kept flowing. From the neck. Greg's neck. Or collarbone. Whatever. He couldn't see through the blood. Myron tried to stop the flow with his bare hand, pushing the sticky liquid away, finding the wound with his finger, applying pressure with his palm. But the blood slipped through the cracks between his fingers. Greg looked up at him with big eyes.

Stan Gibbs put his hands over his head and ducked into a quasi-emergency-landing position. "Stop!" he yelled, almost childlike. "Dad!"

Another bullet. More glass shards. Myron reached into his pocket and pulled out his gun. Greg grabbed his hand and pulled it down. Myron looked at him.

"Can't kill him," Greg said to Myron. There was blood in his mouth now. "If he dies . . . Jeremy's only hope."

Myron nodded, but he didn't put the gun away. He looked over at Stan. In the distance, they heard a heli-copter. Then sirens. The feds were on their way. No surprise. There was no way they weren't going to follow. By air, at the very least.

Greg's breathing was short spurts. His eyes were going hazy-gray.

"We got to do something here, Stan," Myron said.

"Just stay down," Stan said. Then he opened the car door and shouted, "Dad!"

No reply.

Stan got out of the car. He raised his hands and stood. "Please," he shouted. "They'll be here soon. They'll kill you."

Nothing. The air was so motionless that Myron thought he could still hear the echoes from the gun blasts.

"Dad?"

Myron lifted his head a little and risked a glance. A man stepped out from behind the side of the house. Edwin Gibbs wore full army fatigues with combat boots. He had an ammunition belt hanging off his shoulder. His rifle was pointed toward the ground. Myron could see it was Nathan Mostoni, though he looked twenty years younger. His head was high, chin up. His back was straight.

Greg made a gurgling sound. Myron ripped off his shirt and pushed it against the wound. But Greg's eyes were closing. "Stay with me," Myron urged. "Come on, Greg. Stay here."

Greg did not reply. His eyes fluttered and closed. Myron felt his heart slam into his throat. "Greg?"

He felt for a pulse. It was there. Myron was no doctor, but it didn't feel strong. Oh damn. Oh come on.

Outside the car, Stan moved closer to his father. "Please," Stan said. "Put down the rifle, Dad."

The fed cars poured into the driveway. Brakes squealed. Feds jumped out of their vehicles, took position using the open doors as shields, aimed their weapons. Edwin Gibbs looked confused, panicked, Frankenstein's monster suddenly surrounded by angry villagers. Stan hurried toward him.

The air seemed to thicken, molasses-like. It was hard to move, hard to breathe. Myron could almost feel the officers tense up, fingers itchy, tips touching the cold metal of the trigger. He let go of Greg for a moment and shouted, "You can't shoot him!"

A fed had a megaphone. "Put down the rifle! Now!"

"Don't shoot!" Myron shouted.

For a moment nothing happened. Time did that in-and-out motion where everything rushes and freezes all at one time. Another fed car skidded up the driveway. A news van followed, screeching when it hit the brakes. Stan kept walking toward his father.

"You are surrounded," the megaphone said. "Drop the rifle and put your hands behind your head. Drop to your knees."

Edwin Gibbs looked left, looked right. Then he smiled. Myron felt the dread rise up in his chest. Gibbs lifted his rifle.

Myron rolled out of the car. "No!"

Stan Gibbs broke into a sprint. His father spotted him, his face calm. He aimed the rifle at his approaching son. Stan kept running. Time did stop this time, waiting for the blast of gunfire. But it didn't come. Stan had gained on him too fast. Edwin Gibbs closed his eyes and let his son tackle him. The two men fell to the ground. Stan stayed on top of his father, blanketing him, leaving no space open.

"Don't shoot him," Stan yelled. His voice sounded hurt, again so childlike. "Please don't shoot him."

Edwin Gibbs lay on his back. He let go of the rifle. It dropped into the grass. Stan pushed it away, still on top of his father, still shielding him from harm. They stayed there until the officers took over. They gently removed Stan and then rolled Edwin Gibbs onto his stomach, cuffing his hands behind his back. The news camera caught it all.

Myron turned back to the car. Greg's eyes were still closed. He wasn't moving. Two of the officers ran toward the car, calling into their radios for an ambulance. Nothing Myron could do for Greg now. He looked back at the farmhouse, his heart still lodged in his throat. He ran toward the house and grabbed the knob. The door was locked. He used his shoulder. The door came down. Myron stepped into the foyer.

"Jeremy?" he called out.

But there was no reply.

36

They didn't find Jeremy Downing.

Myron checked every room, every closet, the basement, the garage. Nothing. The feds streamed in with him. They started knocking down walls. They used a heat sensor to check for underground caves or hidden places. Nothing. In the garage, they found a white van. In the back of it, they found one of Jeremy's red sneakers.

But that was it.

News vans, lots of them, gathered at the end of the driveway. What with the kidnapped boy, his famous father shot and in critical condition, a potential serial killer in custody, the connection to Stan Gibbs and the famed plagiarism charges—the story was getting the full, round-the-clock, give-it-a-banner-and-theme-music, death-of-Diana coverage. Stiffly coiffed correspondents flashed their best grim-news teeth and led with phrases like "the vigil continues" or "the search is reaching its xth hour" or "behind me lurks the lair" or "we'll be here until."

A recent photograph of Jeremy, the one Emily had on the Web, ran continuously on all the stations. Brokaw, Jennings and Rather interrupted their programming. Viewers called in tips, but so far none amounted to anything.

And the hours passed.

Emily drove to the scene. It played on all the usual outlets, her head lowered, hurrying toward a waiting car like an arrested felon, the flashbulbs creating a grotesque strobe effect. Cameramen elbowed each other out of the way to capture a glimpse of the stricken mother collapsing in the back of the car. They even got a shot of her through the passenger seat crying. Great TV.

Nightfall brought out searchlights. Volunteers and law officials scoured the nearby grounds for signs of recent graves or digging. Nothing. They brought in dogs. Nothing. They spoke to neighbors, some of whom "never trusted that family" but most gave the standard "seemed like nice folk, real quiet neighbors" spiel.

Edwin Gibbs had been taken into custody. They tried to question him at the Bernardsville Police Station, but he wasn't talking. Clara Steinberg became his attorney. She stayed with him. So did Stan. They pleaded with Edwin, Myron guessed, but so far, he hadn't talked.

Back at the farmhouse, the wind picked up. Myron's bad knee ached, each step giving him a fresh jolt of pain. The pain was unpredictable, arriving whenever it damn well pleased, staying on like the most unwelcome houseguest. There was no side benefit to the knee pain, no weather forecasting or anything like that. Some days it just ached. Nothing he could do about it. He approached Emily and put his arm around her.

"He's still out there," Emily said to the dark.

Myron said nothing.

"He's all alone. And it's night. And he's probably scared."

"We'll find him, Em."

"Myron?"

"Hmm."

"Is this more payback for that night?"

Another search party returned, their shoulders slumped in resignation, if not defeat. Odd thing, these search parties. You wanted to find something, yet you didn't want to find something.

"No," Myron said. "I think you were right. I think our mistake was the best thing that could have happened. And maybe there's a price to pay to have something so good."

She closed her eyes, but she did not cry. Myron stayed next to her. The wind howled, scattering the surrounding voices like dead leaves, whipping branches, and whispering in your ear like the most frightening lover.

37

Myron and Win looked through the one-way glass at Clara Steinberg's back and the faces of Stan and Edwin Gibbs. Kimberly Green stood with them. So did Eric Ford. Emily had gone to the hospital to sit vigil while Greg was in surgery. No one seemed to know if he'd make it.

"Why aren't you listening in?" Myron asked.

"Can't," Ford replied. "Attorney-client."

"How long they been at it?"

"On and off since we took him into custody."

Myron checked the clock behind his head. Nearly three in the morning. Evidence collection teams had leveled the house, but still no clue where Jeremy was. Fatigue lined everyone's face, except maybe Win's. Fatigue never registered on his face. Win must internalize it. Or maybe it had something to do with having little to no conscience.

"We don't have time for this," Myron said.

"I know," Eric Ford said. "It's been a long night for all of us."

"Do something."

"Like what?" Ford snapped. "What exactly would you like me to do?"

Win picked up that one. "Perhaps you could speak to Ms. Steinberg in private."

That hooked Ford's attention. "What?"

"Take her into another room," Win said, "and leave me alone with your suspect."

Eric Ford looked at him. "You shouldn't even be here. He"—a gesture toward Myron—"represents the Downing family, as much as I don't like it. But you got no reason to be here."

"Make a reason," Win said.

Eric Ford waved his hand as if this wasn't worth his time.

Win kept the voice at a low, soothing level. "You don't have to be a part of it," he said. "Simply talk to his attorney. Leave Gibbs alone in the room. That's all. Nothing unethical about that."

Ford shook his head. "You're crazy."

"We need answers," Win said.

"And you want to beat them out of him."

"Beating leaves marks," Win said. "I never leave marks."

"That's not how it works, pal. Ever heard of the U.S. Constitution?"

"It's a document," Win said, "not a trump card. You have a choice. The obscure rights of that subhuman"— Win gestured through the glass—"or a young boy's right to live."

Ford leaned his forehead against the glass.

"If the boy dies while we're standing here," Win said, "how will you feel then?"

Ford shut his eyes. In the holding room, Clara Steinberg rose from her chair. She turned, and for the first time, Myron saw her face. He knew that she had represented bad people before—very, very bad people— but whatever horrors she was now hearing had washed away her skin tone and etched in something that would probably never leave. She approached the one-way mirror and knocked. Ford hit the sound switch.

"We need to talk," she said. "Let me out."

Eric Ford met Clara and Stan by the door. "Let's head down this way," he said.

"No," Clara said.

"Pardon me?"

"We'll talk in here," she said, "where I can watch my client. Wouldn't want an accident, now, would we?"

There were no chairs so they all stood by the one-way window—Kimberly Green, Eric Ford, Clara Steinberg, Stan Gibbs, Myron and Win. Stan kept his head down and plucked at his lower lip with his fingers. Myron tried to meet his eyes. Stan never gave him the chance.

"Okay," Clara said. "First off, we need a D.A."

"What for?" Eric Ford asked.

"Because we want a deal."

Ford tried to snicker. "Are you out of your mind?"

"No. My client is the only one who can tell you where Jeremy Downing is. He'll only do so under specific conditions."

"What conditions?"

"That's why we need a D.A."

"A D.A. will back whatever I agree to," Eric Ford said.

"I'll still want it in writing."

"And I want to hear what you're looking for here."

"Okay," Clara said, "here's the deal. We help you find Jeremy Downing. In exchange, you guarantee not to seek the death penalty for Edwin Gibbs. You also agree to psychiatric tests. You then recommend he be placed in a proper mental health facility, not a prison."

"You have to be kidding me."

"There's more," Clara said.

"More?"

"Mr. Edwin Gibbs will also agree to donate bone marrow to Jeremy Downing if the need arises. I understand that Mr. Bolitar is representing the family here. For the record, we should note that he is present as a witness to this agreement."

No one said anything.

"So we clear?" Clara said.

"No," Ford said, "we're not."

Clara adjusted her eyeglasses. "This deal is nonnegotiable." She turned to leave, her gaze snagging on Myron's. Myron just shook his head.

"I'm his attorney," she said to him.

"And you'll let a boy die for him?" Myron said.

"Don't start," Clara said, but her voice was soft.

Myron studied her face again, saw no give. He turned to Ford. "Agree," he said.

"Are you nuts?"

"The family cares about retribution. But they care more about finding their son. Agree to her terms."

"You think I'm taking orders from you?"

Myron's voice was soft. "Come on, Eric."

Ford frowned. He rubbed his face with his hands and then dropped them back to his side. "This agreement assumes, of course, that the boy is still alive."

"No," Clara Steinberg said.

"What?"

"Alive or dead does not change the state of Edwin Gibb's mental health."

"So you don't know if he's alive or—"

"If we did, it would be an attorney-client communication and thus confidential."

Myron looked at her in stark horror. She met his eyes and would not blink. Myron tried Stan, but his head was still lowered. Even Win's face, usually the model of neutrality, was on edge. Win wanted to hurt somebody. He wanted to hurt somebody badly.

"We can't agree to that," Ford said.

"Then there's no deal," Clara said.

"You have to be reasonable—"

"Do we have a deal or not?"

Eric Ford shook his head. "No."

"See you in court, then."

Myron moved into her path.

"Step aside, Myron," Clara said.

He just looked down at her. She raised her eyes.

"You think your mother wouldn't be doing the same thing?" Clara said.

"Leave my mother out of this."

"Step aside," she said again. Aunt Clara was sixty-six. For the first time since he'd known her, she looked older than her age.

Myron turned back to Eric Ford. "Agree," he said.

He shook his head. "The boy is probably dead."

"Probably," Myron repeated. "Not definitely."

Win spoke up this time. "Agree," he said.

Ford looked at him.

"He won't get off easily," Win said.

Stan's head finally rose at that one. "What the hell is that supposed to mean?"

Win gave him flat eyes. "Absolutely nothing."

"I want this man kept away from my father."

Win smiled at him.

"You don't get it, do you?" Stan said. "None of you get it. My father is sick. He's not responsible. We're not making this up. Any competent psychiatrist in the world will agree. He needs help."

"He should die," Win said.

"He's a sick man."

"Sick men die all the time," Win said.

"That's not what I mean. He's like someone who has

a heart condition. Or cancer. He needs help."

"He kidnaps and probably kills people," Win said.

"And it doesn't matter why he does it?"

"Of course it doesn't matter," Win said. "He does it. That's enough. He should not be put in a comfortable mental hospital. He should not be allowed to enjoy a wonderful film or read a great book or laugh again. He should not be able to see a beautiful woman or listen to Beethoven or know kindness or love—because his victims never will. What part of that don't you understand, Mr. Gibbs?"

Stan was shaking. "You agree," he said to Ford. "Or we don't help."

"If the boy dies because of this negotiation," Win said to Stan, "you will die."

Clara stepped into Win's face. "You threatening my client?" she shouted.

Win smiled at her. "I never threaten."

"There are witnesses."

"Worried about collecting your fee, Counselor?" Win asked.

"That's enough." It was Eric Ford. He looked at Myron. Myron nodded. "Okay," Ford said slowly. "We agree. Now, where is he?"

"I'll have to take you," Stan said.

"Again?"

"I wouldn't be able to give you directions. I'm not even sure I can find it after all these years."

"But we come along," Kimberly Green said.

"Yes."

There was an empty space, a sudden stillness that Myron didn't like.

"Is Jeremy alive or dead?" Myron asked.

"Truth?" Stan said. "I don't know."

38

Eric Ford drove with Kimberly Green riding shotgun and Myron and Stan in the backseat. Several cars' worth of agents followed them. So too did the press. Nothing they could do about that.

"My mother died in 1977," Stan said. "Cancer. My father was already unwell. The one thing in his life that mattered to him—the one good thing—was my mother. He loved her very much."

The time on the car clock read nearly 4:03 A.M. Stan told them where to turn off Route 15. A sign read DINGSMAN BRIDGE. They were heading into Pennsylvania.

"Whatever sanity was still there, my mother's death stripped away. He watched her suffer. Doctors tried everything—used all their technological advances—but it only made her suffer more. That's when my father started with the strength of the mind. If only my mother hadn't relied on technology, he thought. If only she used her mind instead. If only she'd seen its limitless potential. Technology killed her, he said. It gave her false hope. It stopped her from using the one thing that could save her—the limitless human brain."

No one had a comment.

"We had a summerhouse out here. It was beautiful. Fifteen acres of land, walking distance to a lake. My father used to take me hunting and fishing. But I haven't been out here in years. Haven't even thought about the place. He took my mother out here to die. Then he buried her in the woods. See, it's where her suffering finally ended."

The obvious question hung in the air, unasked: *And who else's?*

Myron would later remember nothing about the drive. No buildings, no landmarks, no trees. Outside his window was total night, the black folding over black, eyes squeezed shut in the darkest of rooms. He sat back and waited.

Stan told them to stop at the foot of a wooded area. More crickets sounded. The other cars pulled up alongside them. Feds got out and started combing the area. Beams from powerful flashlights revealed uneven earth. Myron ignored them. He swallowed and ran. Stan ran with him.

Before morning broke, the federal officers would find graves. They'd find the father of three children, the female college student, and the young newlyweds.

But for now, Myron and Stan kept running. Branches whipped Myron's face. He tripped over a root, curled into a roll, stood back up, kept running. They spotted the small house, barely visible in the faint moonlight. There were no lights on inside, no hint of life. Myron did not bother trying the knob this time. He took it full on, crashing the door down. More darkness. He heard a cry, turned, fumbled for the light switch, flipped it up.

Jeremy was there.

He was chained to a wall—dirty and terrified and still very much alive.

Myron felt his knees buckle, but he fought them and stayed upright. He ran to the boy. The boy stretched out his arms. Myron embraced him and felt his heart fall and shatter. Jeremy was crying. Myron lifted his hand and stroked the boy's hair and shushed him. Like his father. Like his father had done to him countless times. A sudden, beautiful warmth streamed through his veins, tingling his fingers and toes, and for a moment, Myron thought that maybe he understood what his father felt. Myron had always cherished being on the son side of the hug, but now, for just the most fleeting of moments, he experienced something so much stronger—the intensity and overwhelming depth of being on the other side—that it shook every part of him.

"You're okay," Myron said to him, cupping the boy's head. "It's over now."

But it wasn't.

An ambulance came. Jeremy was put inside. Myron called Dr. Karen Singh. She didn't mind being woken at five in the morning. He told her everything.

"Wow," Karen Singh said when he finished.

"Yes."

"We'll get someone to harvest the marrow right away. I'll start prepping Jeremy in the afternoon."

"You mean with chemo."

"Yes," she said. "You done good, Myron. Either way, you should be proud."

"Either way?"

"Come by my office tomorrow afternoon."

Myron felt a thumping in his chest. "What's up?"

"The paternity test," she said. "The results should be in by then."

Jeremy was on his way to the hospital. Myron wandered back outside. The feds were digging. The news vans were there. Stan Gibbs watched the mounds of earth grow, his face now beyond emotion. No sound, not even the crickets now, except for shovel hitting dirt.

Myron's knee was acting up. He felt bone-weary. He wanted to find Emily. He wanted to go to the hospital. He wanted to know the results of that test and then he wanted to know what he was going to do with them.

He climbed back up the hill toward the car. More media. Someone called out to him. He ignored them. There were more federal officers working in silence. Myron walked past them. He didn't have the heart to hear what they'd found. Not just yet.

When he reached the top of the landing—when he saw Kimberly Green and the lifeless expression on her face—his heart took one more plummet.

He took another step. "Greg?" he said.

She shook her head, her eyes hazy and unfocused. "They shouldn't have left him alone," she said. "They should have watched him. Even after a careful search. You can never search too carefully."

"Search who?"

"Edwin Gibbs."

Myron was sure he'd heard wrong. "What about him?"

"They just found him," she said, having trouble with the words. "He committed suicide in his cell."

39

Karen Singh summed it up for them: You can't get bone marrow from a dead man.

Emily did not collapse when she heard the news. She took the blow without blinking and immediately segued to the next step. She was on a calmer plane now, somewhere just outside panic.

"We have incredible access to the media right now," Emily said. They were sitting in Karen Singh's hospital office. "We'll make pleas. We'll set up bone marrow drives. The NBA will help. We'll get players to make appearances."

Myron nodded, but the enthusiasm wasn't there. Dr. Singh mimicked his motion.

"When will you have the paternity results?" Emily asked.

"I was just about to call for them," Dr. Singh said.

"I'll leave you two alone, then," Emily said. "I have a press conference downstairs."

Myron looked at her. "You don't want to wait for the results?"

"I already know the results."

Emily left without a backward glance. Karen Singh looked at Myron. Myron folded his hands and put them in his lap.

"You ready?" she asked.

He nodded.

Karen Singh picked up the phone and dialed. Someone on the other end answered. Karen read off a reference number. She waited, tapping a pencil on the desk. Someone on the other end said something. Karen said, "Thank you," hung up, focused her eyes on Myron.

"You're the father."

Myron found Emily in the hospital lobby, giving the press conference. The hospital had set up a podium with their logo perfectly positioned behind it, sure to be picked up by any and all television cameras. Hospital logo. Like they were McDonald's or Toyota, trying to sleaze some free advertising. Emily's statement was direct and heartfelt. Her son was dying. He needed new bone marrow. Everyone who wanted to help should give blood and get registered. She plucked the strings of societal grieving, making sure it rang personal in the same way that Princess Diana's and John Kennedy Jr.'s deaths rang personal, wanting the public to mourn as if they actually knew him. The power of celebrity.

When she finished her statement, Emily hurried off without answering questions. Myron caught up to her in the closed-off area near the elevators. She glanced at him. He nodded, and she smiled.

"So now what are you going to do?" she asked him.

"We have to save him," Myron said.

"Yes."

Behind them the press were still yelling out questions. The sound trickled and then faded into the background. Someone ran by with an empty gurney.

"You said Thursday was the optimum day," Myron said.

Hope lit her eyes. "Yes."

"Okay, then," he said. "We try it on Thursday."

*

The bullet that had struck Greg had entered in the lower part of his neck and traversed toward his chest. It had stopped short of the heart. But it had done plenty of damage anyway. He survived surgery but remained unconscious in "critical" and "guarded" condition. Myron looked in on him. Greg had tubes in his nose and a frightening assortment of machinery Myron hoped never to understand. He looked like a corpse, waxen and gray-white and sucked dry. Myron sat with him for a few minutes. But not very long.

He returned to the offices of MB SportsReps the next day.

"Lamar Richardson is coming in this afternoon," Esperanza said.

"I know."

"You okay?"

"Dandy."

"Life goes on, huh?"

"Guess so."

Special Agent Kimberly Green came semi-bouncing by a few minutes later. "It's all wrapping up," she told him, and for the first time he saw her smile.

Myron sat back. "I'm listening."

"Edwin Gibbs, under his Dennis Lex/Davis Taylor identity, still had a locker at work. We found the wallets of two of his victims, Robert and Patricia Wilson, in there."

"They were the honeymoon couple?"

"Yes."

They both took a moment, out of respect for the dead, Myron guessed. He pictured a healthy young couple beginning their life, coming to the Big Apple to see some shows and do a little shopping, walking the bustling streets hand in hand, a little scared about the future but ready to give it a go. *El fin.*

Kimberly cleared her throat. "Gibbs also rented a white Ford Windstar using the Davis Taylor credit card. It was one of those automatic reservations. You just make a call, walk straight to the rental, and drive off. No one sees you."

"Where did he pick up the van?"

"Newark Airport."

"I assume that's the van we found in Bernardsville," Myron said.

"The very."

"Tidy," he said, using a Win word. "What else?"

"Preliminary autopsies reveal that all the victims were killed with a thirty-eight. Two shots to the head. No other signs of trauma. We don't think he tortured them or any of that. His modus operandus seemed to involve the early scream and then he just killed them."

"He ends the seed sowing for them," Myron said, "but not the families."

"Right."

"Because for his victims, the terror would be real. He wanted it all in the mind." Myron shook his head. "What did Jeremy tell you about his ordeal?"

"You didn't talk to him about it?"

Myron shifted in his chair. "No."

"Edwin Gibbs wore the same disguise he used at work—the blond wig and beard and glasses. He blindfolded Jeremy as soon as he had him in the van and drove straight to that cabin. Edwin told him to scream into the phone—even made him practice first to make sure he had it right. After the call, Edwin chained him up and left him alone. You know the rest."

Myron nodded. He did.

"What about the plagiarism charge and the novel?"

She shrugged. "It was like you and Stan said. Edwin read it, probably right after his wife was dying of cancer. It influenced him."

Myron stared at her for a moment.

"What?" she said.

"You guys figured that part out when you first got the novel," Myron said. "That Stan hadn't plagiarized. That the book influenced the killer."

She shook her head. "No."

"Come on. You knew that the kidnappings had taken place. You just wanted to put pressure on Stan so he'd talk. And maybe you wanted to embarrass him a little."

"That's not true," Kimberly Green said. "I'm not saying some of our agents didn't take it personally, but we believed that he was the Sow the Seeds kidnapper. I already told you some of the reasons why. Now we know that a lot of the same evidence pointed to his father."

"What same evidence?"

She shook her head. "It's not important anymore. We knew Stan was more here than just a reporter. And we were right. We even thought he was getting stuff wrong on purpose—that he was using the book rather than what he'd really done just to throw us off."

Her words didn't resonate the way the truth does, but Myron didn't argue the point. He scanned his Client Wall and tried to bring his focus around to Lamar Richardson's visit. "So the case is closed."

She smiled. "Like legs in a nunnery."

"You make that one up?"

"Yup."

"Good thing you carry a gun," Myron said. "So are you going to get a big promotion?"

She rose. "I think I get to be a super-secret-special agent now."

Myron smiled. They shook hands. Kimberly left then. Myron sat alone for a while. He rubbed his eyes and thought about what she'd said and what she hadn't said and realized that something was still very wrong.

Lamar Richardson, shortstop extraordinaire, showed up on time and by himself. Positively shocking. The meeting went well. Myron gave his standard spiel, but the standard spiel was pretty good. Damn good, actually. All businesspeople need a spiel. Spiel is good. Esperanza spoke up too. She had started developing her own spiel. Well honed. The perfect complement to Myron's. Quite the partnership, this was becoming.

Win stopped by briefly as planned. If recruitment was a baseball game, Win was the big closer. People knew his name. They checked out his reputation—er, his business reputation, that is. When prospective clients learned that Windsor Horne Lockwood III himself would handle their finances, that Win and Myron further insisted that clients meet with Win at least five times a year, they started smiling. Score one for the small agency.

Lamar Richardson played it close to the vest. He nodded a lot. He asked questions but not too many. Two hours after arriving, he shook their hands and said he'd be in touch. Myron and Esperanza walked him to the elevator and bade him good-bye.

Esperanza turned to Myron. "Well?"

"Got him."

"How can you be so sure?"

"I'm all-seeing," Myron said. "All-knowing."

They moved back into Myron's office and sat down.

"If Lamar chooses us over IMG and TruPro"—she stopped, smiled—"we're baaaaack."

"Pretty much."

"And that means Big Cyndi will come back."

"That's supposed to be a good thing, right?"

"You're starting to love her, you know."

"Yeah, don't rub it in."

Esperanza studied his face. She did that a lot. Myron didn't much believe in reading faces. Esperanza did. Especially his. "What happened in that law office?" she asked. "With Chase Layton?"

"I boxed his ears once and punched him seven times."

Her eyes stayed on his face.

"You're supposed to say, 'But you saved Jeremy's life,'" Myron added.

"No, that's Win's line." She adjusted herself and faced him full. She wore an aquamarine business suit, cut low with no blouse, and it was a wonder Lamar had been able to concentrate on anything. Myron was used to her, but the effect was still there, still dazzling. He just saw the dazzle from a different angle.

"Speaking of Jeremy," she said.

"Yes."

"You still blocking?"

Myron thought about it, remembered the embrace in that cabin, stopped. "More than ever," he said.

"So what now?"

"The blood test came back. I'm the father."

Something popped onto her face—regret maybe—but it didn't stay long. "You should tell him the truth."

"Right now I just want to save his life."

She kept studying the face. "Maybe soon," she said.

"Maybe soon what?"

"You'll stop blocking," Esperanza said.

"Yeah, maybe."

"We'll chat then. In the meantime . . ."

"Don't be stupid," he finished for her.

The health club was located in a chi-chi hotel in midtown. The walls were fully mirrored. The ceiling and the trim and the front desk were whole-milk white. Same with the clothes worn by the personal trainers. The weights and exercise machines were sleek and chrome and so beautiful you didn't want to touch them. Everything about the place gleamed; you were almost tempted to work out in sunglasses.

Myron found him on a bench press, struggling without a spotter. Myron waited, watching him wage war on gravity and the barbell. Chase Layton's face was pure red, his teeth gritted, veins in his forehead doing their pop-up video. It took some time, but the attorney achieved victory. He dropped the weight onto the stand. His arms fell to his sides like he'd missed a brain synapse.

"You shouldn't hold your breath," Myron said.

Chase looked over at him. He didn't seem surprised or upset. He sat up, breathing heavily. He wiped his face with a towel.

"I won't take up much of your time," Myron said.

Chase put the towel down and looked at him.

"I just wanted to say that if you want to press charges, Win and I won't get in your way."

Chase did not reply.

"And I'm very sorry for what I did," Myron said.

"I watched the news," Chase said. "You did it to save that boy's life."

"Doesn't excuse it."

"Maybe not." He stood and added a plate to both sides of the bar. "Frankly, Mr. Bolitar, I'm not sure what to think."

"If you want to press charges—"

"I don't."

Myron was not sure what to say, so he settled for "Thank you."

Chase Layton nodded and sat back on the bench. Then he looked at Myron. "Do you want to know what the worst part of it is?"

No, Myron thought. "If you want to tell me."

"The shame," Chase said.

Myron started to open his mouth, but Chase waved him quiet.

"It's not the beating or the pain. It's the feeling of total helplessness. We were primitive. We were man to man. And there was nothing I could do but take it. You made me feel like"—he looked up, found the words, looked straight at Myron—"like I wasn't a real man."

The words made Myron cringe.

"I went to these great schools and joined all the right clubs and made a fortune in my chosen profession. I fathered three kids and raised them and loved them the best I could. Then one day you punch me—and I realize that I'm not a real man."

"You're wrong," Myron said.

"You're going to say that violence is no measure of a man. On some level you're right. But on some level, the base level that makes us men, we both know you're wrong. Don't pretend you don't know what I'm talking about. It'd just be a further insult."

Myron swallowed down the clichés. Chase took deep breaths and reached for the bar.

"Need a spotter?" Myron said.

Chase Layton gripped it and jerked it off the stand. "I don't need anybody," he said.

Thursday came. Karen Singh introduced him to a fertility expert named Dr. Barbara Dittrick. Dr. Dittrick handed Myron a small cup and told him to masturbate into it. There were more surreal and embarrassing experiences in life, Myron guessed, but being led to a small room to masturbate into a cup while everyone waited for you in the next room had to be right up there with the best of them.

"Step in here, please," Dr. Dittrick said.

Myron frowned at the cup. "I usually insist on flowers and a movie."

"Well, at least you got the movie," she said, pointing at the television. "The TV has X-rated videos." She left the room and closed the door behind her.

Myron checked the titles. *On Golden Blonde. Father Knows Breast* (starring Robert Hung). *Field of Wet Dreams* ("If you watch it, they will come"). He frowned and passed. So to speak. He stared at the swivel leather chair, one of those lean-back kind, where probably hundreds of other men had sat and . . . He covered it with paper towels and did his bit, though it took some time. His imagination was spinning in the wrong direction, generating an aura about as erotic as mole hair on an old man's buttock. When he was, uh, finished, he opened the door and handed the cup to Dr. Dittrick and tried to smile. He felt like the world's biggest doofus. She wore rubber gloves, even though the, uh, specimen was in a cup. Like it might scald her. She brought it to a lab where they "washed" (their expression, not his) the semen. The semen was declared "serviceable but slow." Like it was falling behind in algebra.

"Funny," Emily said. "I usually found Myron to be serviceable but quick."

"Ha-ha," Myron said.

A few hours later Emily was in a hospital bed. Barbara Dittrick smiled while inserting what looked suspiciously like a turkey baster into her and pressed the plunger. Myron took her hand. Emily smiled.

"Romantic," she said.

Myron made a face.

"What?"

"Serviceable?" he said.

She laughed. "But quick."

Dr. Dittrick finished her part. Emily stayed prone for another hour. Myron sat with her. They were doing this to save Jeremy's life. That was all. He didn't let the future enter the equation. He didn't consider the long-term effects or what this might one day mean. Irresponsible, sure. But first things first.

They had to save Jeremy. The hell with the rest.

Terese Collins called him from Atlanta that afternoon. "Can I come up and visit?" she asked.

"The station will give you more time off?"

"Actually, my producer encouraged me."

"Oh?"

"You, my studly friend, are part of a huge story," Terese said.

"You used the words 'studly' and 'huge' in the same sentence."

"That turn you on?"

"Well, it might a lesser man."

"And you are that lesser man."

"I thank you," he said.

"You're also the only one in this story who won't talk to the press."

"So you just want me for my mind," Myron said. "I feel so used."

"Dream on, hot buns. I want your bod. It's my producer who wants your brain."

"Your producer cute?"

"No."

"Terese?"

"Yes."

"I don't want to talk about what happened."

"Good," she said. "Because I don't want to hear it."

There was a brief silence.

"Yeah," Myron said. "I'd like it very much if you came up."

Ten days later, Karen Singh called him at home.

"The pregnancy didn't take."

Myron closed his eyes.

"We can try again next month," she said.

"Thanks for calling, Karen."

"Sure."

There was empty space. "Anything else?" Myron asked.

"There's been a lot of marrow drives," she said.

"I know."

"One donor looks like a match for an AML patient in Maryland. A young mother. She would have probably died if it weren't for these drives."

"Good news," Myron said.

"But no matches for Jeremy."

"Yeah."

"Myron?"

"What?"

"I don't think we have much time here."

Terese returned to Atlanta later that day. Win invited Esperanza to his place for a night of mindless television. The three of them sat in their customary spots. Fritos and Indian takeout were on the night's menu. Myron had the remote. He paused when he saw a familiar image on CNN. A basketball superstar simply known as "TC," one of the NBA's most controversial players and a teammate of Greg's, was on *Larry King Live*. His hair was razor-carved to spell out *Jeremy*, and both gold earrings had Jeremy's name on them. He wore a ripped T-shirt that simply read HELP OR JEREMY DIES. Myron smiled. TC was something else, but he'd get the people out in droves.

More flipping. Stan Gibbs was on some talking-head show on MSNBC. Nothing new. The only thing the press loves as much as tearing somebody down is a story of redemption. Bruce Taylor had gotten the exclusive, as promised, and he'd set the tone. The public was mixed on what Stan had done, but for the most part, they sympathized with him. In the end, Stan had risked his own life to catch a killer, saved Jeremy Downing from certain death, and been wrongly accused by a too-eager-to-convict media. The fact that Stan had been confused about turning in his own father played for him, especially since the media was anxious to wipe away the awful mar of plagiarism they'd so quickly tattooed on him. Stan got his column back. Rumor had it his show was coming back too but in a better time slot. Myron wasn't sure what to think. Stan was no hero to him. But so few people were.

Stan, too, was pounding the bone-marrow-drive

drum. "This boy needs our help," he said directly into the camera. "Please come down. We'll be here all night."

A blond talking head asked Stan about his own part in this drama, about tackling his father, about racing to the cabin. Stan played the modesty card. Wise. The man knew the media.

"Boring," Esperanza said.

"Agreed," Win said.

"Isn't there a *Partridge Family* marathon on TV Land?"

Myron suddenly stopped.

"Myron?" Win said.

He did not reply.

"Hello, world." Esperanza snapped her fingers in Myron's face. "There's a song that we're singing. Come on, get happy."

Myron switched off the television. He looked at Win, then at Esperanza. "Say one last good-bye to the boy."

Esperanza and Win exchanged a glance.

"You were right, Win."

"About what?"

"Human nature," Myron said.

40

Myron called Kimberly Green at her office. She answered the line and said, "Green."

"I need a favor," Myron said.

"Shit, I thought you were out of my life."

"But never your fantasies. You want to help me or not?"

"Not."

"I need two things."

"Not. I said 'not.' "

"Eric Ford said that the supposedly plagiarized novel was sent directly to you."

"So?"

"Who sent it?"

"You heard him, Myron. It was sent anonymously."

"You have no idea."

"None."

"Where is it now?"

"The book?"

"Yes."

"In an evidence locker."

"Ever do anything with it?"

"Like what?"

Myron waited.

"Myron?"

"I knew you guys were holding something back," he said.

"Listen to me a second—"

"The author of that novel. It was Edwin Gibbs. He

wrote it under a pseudonym after his wife died. It makes perfect sense now. You were searching for him right from the get-go. You knew, dammit. You knew the whole time."

"We suspected," she said. "We didn't know."

"All that crap about thinking he was Stan's first victim—"

"It wasn't total crap. We knew it was one of them. We just didn't know which one. We couldn't find Edwin Gibbs until you told us about the Waterbury address. By the time we got there, he was already on his way to kidnap Jeremy Downing. Maybe if you had been more forthcoming—"

"You guys lied to me."

"We didn't lie. We just didn't tell you everything."

"Jesus, you ever listen to yourself?"

"We owed you nothing here, Myron. You weren't a federal agent on this. You were just a pain in the ass."

"A pain in the ass who helped you solve the case."

"And for that I thank you."

Myron's thoughts entered the maze, turned left, turned right, circled back.

"Why doesn't the press know about Gibbs being the author?" Myron asked.

"They will. Ford wants all his ducks in a row first. Then he'll hold yet another big press conference and present it as something new."

"He could do that today," Myron said.

"He could."

"But then the story dies down. Right now the rumors keep it going. Ford gets more time in the limelight."

"He's a politician at heart," she said. "So what?"

Myron took another few turns, hit a few more walls, kept feeling for the way out. "Forget it," he said.

"Good. Can I go now?"

"First I need you to call the national bone marrow registry."

"Why?"

"I need to find out about a donor."

"This case is closed, Myron."

"I know," he said. "But I think a new one might be opening."

Stan Gibbs was at the anchor chair when Myron and Win arrived. His new cable show, *Glib with Gibbs*, was filming in Fort Lee, New Jersey, and the studio, like every television studio Myron had ever seen, looked like a room with the roof ripped off. Wires and lights hung in no discernible pattern. Studios, especially newsrooms, were always much smaller in person than on television. The desks, the chairs, the world map in the background. All smaller. The power of television. A room on a nineteen-inch screen somehow looks smaller in real life.

Stan wore a blue blazer, white shirt, red tie, jeans and sneakers. The jeans would stay under the desk and never get camera time. Classic anchorman-wear. Stan waved to them when they entered. Myron waved back. Win did not.

"We need to talk," Myron said to him.

Stan nodded. He sent away the producers and motioned Myron and Win to the guest chairs. "Sit."

Stan stayed in the anchor chair. Win and Myron sat in guest chairs, which felt pretty strange, as though a home audience were watching. Win checked his reflection in a camera glass and smiled. He liked what he saw.

"Any word on a donor?" Stan asked.

"None."

"Something will come through."

"Yeah," Myron said. "Look, Stan, I need your help."

Stan intertwined his fingers and rested both hands on the anchor desk. "Whatever you need."

"There's a lot of things that don't add up with Jeremy's kidnapping."

"For example?"

"Why do you think your father took a child this time? He never did that before, right? Always adults. Why this time a child?"

Stan mulled it over, chose his words one at a time. "I don't know. I'm not sure taking adults was a pattern or anything. His victims seemed pretty random."

"But this wasn't random," Myron said. "His choosing Jeremy Downing couldn't have been just a coincidence."

Stan thought about that one too. "I agree with you there."

"So he picked him because he was somehow connected with my investigation."

"Seems logical."

"But how would your father have known about Jeremy?"

"I don't know," Stan said. "He might have followed you."

"I don't think so. You see, Greg Downing stayed up in Waterbury after our visit. He kept his eye on Nathan Mostoni. We know he didn't travel out of town until the day before the kidnapping."

Win looked into the camera again. He smiled and waved. Just in case it was on.

"It's strange," Stan said.

"And there's more," Myron said. "Like the call where Jeremy screamed. With the others, your father told the family not to contact the cops. But he didn't this time. Why? And are you aware that he wore a disguise when he kidnapped Jeremy?"

"I heard that, yes."

"Why? If he planned on killing him, why go to the trouble of donning a disguise?"

"He kidnapped Jeremy off the streets," Stan said. "Someone might have been able to identify him."

"Yeah, okay, that makes sense. But then why blindfold Jeremy once he was in the van? He killed all the others. He would have killed Jeremy. So why worry about him seeing his face?"

"I'm not sure," Stan said. "He might have always done it that way, for all we know."

"I guess," Myron said. "But something about it all just rings wrong, don't you think?"

Stan thought about it. "It rings funny," he said slowly. "I'm not sure it rings wrong."

"That's why I came to you. All these questions have been swirling in my head. And then I remembered Win's credo."

Stan Gibbs looked over at Win. Win blinked his eyes and lowered them modestly. "What credo is that?"

"Man is into self-preservation," Myron said. "He is, above all, selfish." He paused a moment. "You agree with that, Stan?"

"To some degree, of course. We're all selfish."

Myron nodded. "You even."

"Yes, of course. And you too, I'm sure."

"The media is making you out to be this noble guy," Myron said. "Torn between family and duty and ultimately doing the right thing. But maybe you're not."

"Not what?"

"Noble."

"I'm not," Stan said. "I did wrong. I never claimed to be a saint."

Myron looked at Win. "He's good."

"Damn good," Win agreed.

Stan Gibbs frowned. "What are you talking about, Myron?"

"Follow me here, Stan. And remember Win's credo. Let's start at the beginning. When your father first contacted you. You talked to him and you decided to write the Sow the Seeds story. What was your motive at first? Were you trying to find an outlet for your fear and guilt? Was it simply to be a good reporter? Or—and here's where we're using the Win credo—did you write it because you knew it would make you a big star?"

Myron looked at him and waited.

"Am I supposed to answer that?"

"Please."

Stan looked in the air and rubbed his fingertips with his thumb. "All of the above, I guess. Yes, I was excited by the story. I thought it could very well be a big deal. If that's selfishness, okay, I'm guilty."

Myron glanced at Win again. "Good."

"Damn good."

"Let's keep following this track, Stan, okay? The story did indeed become a big deal. So did you. You became a celebrity—"

"We covered this already, Myron."

"Right. You're absolutely right. Let's skip to the part where the feds sued you. They demanded to know your source. You refused. Now again there might be several reasons for this. The First Amendment, of course. That could be it. Protecting your father would be another. The combination of the two. But—and again Win's

313

credo—what would be the selfish choice?"

"What do you mean?"

"Think selfishly and you really have only one option."

"That being?"

"If you caved in to the feds—if you said, Okay, now that I'm in legal trouble, my source is my father—well, how would that have looked?"

"Bad," Win said.

"Damn bad. I doubt you'd have been much of a hero if you sold out your father—not to mention the First Amendment—just to save your hide from vague legal threats." Myron smiled. "See what I mean about Win's credo?"

"So you think I acted selfishly by not telling the feds," Stan said.

"It's possible."

"It's also possible that the selfish thing was also the right thing."

"Possible too," Myron agreed.

"I never claimed to be a hero in all this."

"Never denied it either."

Stan smiled this time. "Maybe I didn't deny it because I'm using Win's credo."

"How's that?"

"Denying it would harm me," Stan said. "As would boasting about it."

Myron didn't have a chance to look before he heard Win say, "Damn good."

"I still don't see the relevance of any of this," Stan said.

"Stick with me, I think you will."

Stan shrugged.

"Where were we?" Myron asked.

"The feds take him to court," Win said.

"Right, thanks, the feds take you to court. You battle back. Then something happens you totally didn't foresee. The plagiarism charges. For the sake of discussion, we'll assume the Lex family sent the book to the feds. They wanted to get you off their back—what better way to do that than to ruin your reputation? So what did you do? How did you react to the charges of plagiarism?"

Stan kept quiet. Win said, "He disappeared."

"Correct answer," Myron said.

Win smiled and nodded a thank-you into the camera.

"You took off," Myron said to Stan. "Now the question again is why. Several things come to mind. It could have been because you were trying to protect your father. Or it might have been that you were afraid of the Lex family."

"Which would certainly fit Win's credo," Stan said. "Self-preservation."

"Right. You were afraid they'd harm you."

"Yes."

Myron treaded gently. "But don't you see, Stan? We have to think selfishly too. You're presented with this serious plagiarism charge. What choices did you have? Two really. You could either run off—or you could tell the truth."

Stan said, "I still don't see your point."

"Stay with me. If you told the truth, you would again look like a louse. Here you've been defending the First Amendment and your father and whoops, you get in trouble and you sell them out. No good. You'd still be ruined."

"Damned if you do," Win said. "Damned if you don't."

"Right," Myron said. "So the wise move—the selfish move—was to vanish for a while."

"But I lost everything by vanishing."

"No, Stan, you didn't."

"How can you say that?"

Myron lifted his palms to the skies and grinned. "Look around you."

For the first time, something dark flicked across Stan's face. Myron saw it. So did Win.

"Let's continue, shall we?"

Stan said nothing.

"You go into hiding and start counting your problems. One, your father is a murderer. You're selfish, Stan, but you're not inhumane. You want him off the streets, yet you can't tell on him. Maybe because you love him. Or maybe there's Win's credo."

"Not this time," Stan said.

"Pardon?"

"Win's credo doesn't apply. I kept quiet because I loved my father and because I believe in protecting sources. And I can offer proof."

"I'm listening," Myron said.

"If I wanted to turn my father in—if that would have been in my best interest—I could have done it anonymously." Stan leaned back and folded his arms.

"That's your proof?"

"Sure. I didn't do the selfish thing."

Myron shook his head. "You got to go deeper."

"Deeper how?"

"Turning your father in anonymously wouldn't help you, Stan. Not really. Yes, you needed to put your father behind bars. But more than that, you needed to be redeemed."

Silence.

"So what would answer both those needs? What would put your father away and put you back on top— maybe even more on top than before? First, you had to be patient. That meant staying hidden. Second, you couldn't be the one who turned him in. You had to set him up."

"Set up my father?"

"Yes. You had to leave a trail for the feds to follow. Something subtle, something that would lead to your father, and something you could manipulate at any time. So you took a fake ID, Stan—the same way your father had. You even took a job where people would spot the disguise your father used and hey, maybe you could also tie in your dad's old nemesis the Lex family in the process."

"What the hell are you talking about?"

"You know what bugged me? Your father had been so careful in the past. Now all of a sudden he's leaving incriminating evidence in a locker. He rents the kidnap van on a credit card and leaves a red sneaker in it. It didn't make any sense. Unless someone was setting him up."

Stan's look of disbelief was almost genuine. "You think I killed these people?"

"No," Myron said. "Your father did."

"Then what—?"

"You're the one who used the Dennis Lex identity," Myron said, "not your father."

Stan tried to look stunned, but it wasn't happening.

"You kidnapped Jeremy Downing. And you called me and pretended to be the Sow the Seeds killer."

"And why did I do that?"

"To have this heroic ending. To have your father arrested. To have yourself redeemed."

"How the hell does calling you—"

"To get me interested. You probably learned about my background. You knew I'd investigate. You needed a dupe and a witness. Someone outside the police. I was that dupe."

"The dupe du jour," Win added.

Myron shot him a look. Win shrugged.

"That's ridiculous."

"No, Stan, it adds up. It answers all my earlier questions. How did the kidnapper happen to choose Jeremy? Because you followed me after I left your condo. You saw the feds pick me up. That's how you knew I'd spoken to them. You followed me to Emily's house. From there, any old newsman worth a damn could have figured out her son was the sick kid I told you about. His illness wasn't a secret. So Jeremy's being taken is no longer a coincidence, see?"

Stan folded his arms across his chest. "I see nothing."

"Other questions get answered too now. Like why did the kidnapper wear a disguise and make Jeremy wear a blindfold? Because you couldn't let Jeremy identify you. Why didn't the kidnapper kill Jeremy right away, like he had the others? Same reason you wore the disguise. You had no intention of killing him. Jeremy had to survive the ordeal unharmed. Otherwise you're no hero. Why didn't the kidnapper make his usual demand not to contact the authorities? Because you wanted the feds in. You needed them to witness your heroics. It wouldn't work without their involvement. I wondered how the media was always in the right spot—in Bernardsville, at the cabin. But you set that part up too. Anonymous leaks probably. So the cameras could witness and replay your heroics—your tackling your father, the dramatic rescue of Jeremy Downing. Good television. You knew the power of capturing those moments for all the world to see."

Stan waited. "You finished?"

"Not yet. You see, I think you went too far in spots. Leaving that sneaker in the van, for example. That was overkill. Too obvious. It made me wonder how neatly it all came together in the end. And then I start realizing that I was your main sucker, Stan. You played me like a Stradivarius. But even if I hadn't shown up, you just would have kidnapped someone else. Your main dupes were the feds. For crying out loud, that photograph of your father by the statue was the only picture in the whole condo. It even faced the window. You knew the feds were spying on you. You threw the truth about Dennis Lex right in their faces. Surely they'd go to the sanitarium and put it together. And if not, you could somehow get it out in the end, when they had you in custody. You were all set to cave in and tell on your father when I came through in the clutch. Me, the dupe du jour, saw the truth up at the sanitarium. You must have been so pleased."

"This is crazy."

"It answers all the questions."

"That doesn't mean it's the truth."

"The Davis Taylor address you used at work. It was the same address as your father's in Waterbury. So we would trace it back to him, to Nathan Mostoni. Who else would have done that?"

"My father!"

"Why? Why would your father change identities at all? And if your father needed a new identity, wouldn't he shed the old one? Or hell, at least change addresses? Only you could have pulled it off, Stan. You could have hooked up the extra phone line with no problem. Your father was pretty far gone. He was demented, at the very least. You kidnapped Jeremy. Then you probably told your father to meet you at the house in Bernardsville. He did what you said—for love or because of dementia, I don't know which. Did you know he'd arm himself like that? I doubt it. If Greg had died, you'd probably look worse. But I don't know for sure. Maybe the fact that he fired shots just made you look more heroic in the end. Think selfishly, Stan. That's the key."

Stan shook his head.

" 'Say one last good-bye to the boy,' " Myron said.

"What?"

"That's what the Sow the Seeds killer said to me on the phone. The boy. I made a mistake when he called me. I told him a boy needed help. After that, I only used the word 'child.' When I spoke to Susan Lex. When I spoke to you. I said a thirteen-year-old child needs a transplant."

"So?"

"So when we talked in the car that night, you asked what I was really after, what my real interest in all this was. Remember?"

"Yes."

"And I said I already told you."

"Right."

"And you said, 'That boy who needs a bone marrow transplant?' You said, 'That boy.' How did you know he was a boy, Stan?"

Win turned toward Stan. Stan looked at Win's face.

"Is that your proof?" Stan countered. "I mean, is this supposed to be a Perry Mason moment or something? Maybe you slipped up, Myron. Or maybe I just assumed it was a boy. Or I heard wrong. That's not evidence."

"You're right. It's not. It just got me thinking, that's all."

"Thoughts aren't proof."

"Wow," Win said. "Thoughts aren't proof. I'll have to remember that one."

"But there is proof," Myron said. "Definitive proof."

"Impossible," Stan said, but his voice warbled now. "What?"

"I'll get to that in a moment. First let me back off on my indignation a little."

"I don't understand."

"At the end of the day, what you did was scummy, no question about it. But in its own way, it was almost ethical. Win and I often discuss the ends justifying the means. You could claim that's what happened here. You tried to turn your father in before he struck again. You did all you could to make sure nobody else was harmed. Jeremy was never in any real danger. You couldn't know that Greg would be shot. So in the end, you scared a boy, but so what? Next to the murder and destruction your father would have continued to wreak, it was nothing. So you did some good. The ends perhaps justified the means. Except for one thing."

Stan didn't bite.

"Jeremy's bone marrow transplant. He needs that to live, Stan. You know that. You also know that you're the match, not your father. That was why you slipped him that cyanide pill. Because once we dragged your father to the hospital and realized that he wasn't a match, well, we would have investigated. We would have realized that Edwin Gibbs was not Davis Taylor né Dennis Lex. So you had to have him kill himself and then you pushed for a quick cremation. I don't mean to make it sound as harsh or cold as all that. You didn't murder your father. He took the pill all on his own. He was a sick man. He wanted to die. It's yet another case of the ends justifying the means."

Myron took a moment and just looked into Stan's eyes. Stan did not look away. In a sense, this was more agenting work. Myron was negotiating here—the most important negotiation of his life. He had put his opponent in a corner. Now he needed to reach out. Not help him yet. He had to keep him in the corner. But he had to start reaching out. Just a little.

"You're not a monster," Myron said. "You just didn't count on the complication of being a bone marrow match. You want to do right by Jeremy. It's why you've gone so nuts trying to help the bone marrow drive. If they find another donor, it takes you off the hook. Because you're in this lie too deep now. You couldn't admit the truth—that you are the match. It would ruin you. I understand that."

Stan's eyes were wide and wet, but he was listening.

"Before I told you that I had proof," Myron said. "We checked the bone marrow registry. Know what we found, Stan?"

Stan didn't reply.

"You're not registered," Myron said. "Here you are telling everybody to sign up and you yourself aren't in their computer. The three of us know why. It's because you'd be a match. And if you matched, there would be those questions again."

Stan gave defiance one last shot. "That's not proof."

"Then how will you explain not registering?"

"I don't have to explain anything."

"A blood test will prove it conclusively. The registry still has the blood that Davis Taylor gave during the marrow drive. We can do a DNA test with yours, see if it matches up."

"And if I don't agree to a test?"

Win took that one. "Oh, you'll give blood," he said with just the slightest smile. "One way or another."

Something on Stan's face broke then. He lowered his head. The defiance was over. He was trapped in the corner now. No way to escape. He'd start looking for an ally. It always happened in negotiations. When you're lost, you look for an out. Myron had reached out before. It was time to do it again.

"You don't understand," Stan said.

"Strangely enough, I do." Myron moved a little closer to Stan. He made his voice soft yet unyielding. Total command mode. "Here's what we're going to do, Stan. You and I are going to make a deal."

Stan looked up, confused but also hopeful. "What?"

"You are going to agree to donate bone marrow to save Jeremy's life. You'll do it anonymously. Win and I can set that up. No one will ever know who the donor was. You do that, you save Jeremy, I forget the rest."

"How can I believe you?"

"Two reasons," Myron said. "One, I'm interested in saving Jeremy's life, not ruining yours. Two"—he tilted both palms toward the ceiling—"I'm no better. I bent rules here too. I let the ends justify the means. I assaulted a man. I kidnapped a woman."

Win shook his head. "There's a difference. His reasons were selfish. You, on the other hand, were trying to save a boy's life."

Myron turned to his friend. "Weren't you the one who said that motives are irrelevant? That the act is the act?"

"Sure," Win said. "But I meant that to apply to him, not you."

Myron smiled and faced Stan again. "I'm not your

moral superior. We both did wrong. Maybe we can both live with what we've done. But if you let a boy die, Stan, you cross the line. You can't go home again."

Stan closed his eyes. "I would have found a way," he said. "I would have gotten another fake ID, given blood under a pseudonym. I was just hoping—"

"I know," Myron said. "I know all about it."

Myron called Dr. Karen Singh. "I found a matching donor."

"What?"

"I can't explain. But he has to stay anonymous."

"I explained to you that all the bone marrow donors remain anonymous."

"No. The bone marrow registry can't know about this either. We have to find a place that can harvest the marrow without knowing the patient's identity."

"Can't be done."

"Yeah, it can."

"No doctor will agree—"

"We can't play these games, Karen. I have a donor. No one can know who he is. Make it work."

He could hear her breathing.

"He'll have to be retested," she said.

"No problem."

"And pass a physical."

"Done."

"Then okay. Let's get this started."

When Emily heard about the donor, she gave Myron a curious look and waited. He didn't explain. She never asked.

Myron visited the hospital the day before the marrow transplant was to begin. He peeked his head around the doorjamb and saw the boy sleeping. Jeremy was bald from the chemo. His skin had a ghostly glow, like something withering from a lack of sunshine. Myron watched his son sleeping. Then he turned and went home. He didn't come back.

He returned to work at MB SportsReps and lived his life. He visited his father and mother. He hung out with Win and Esperanza. He landed a few new clients and started rebuilding his business. Big Cyndi handed in her wrestling resignation and took over the front desk. His world was wobbly but back on the axis.

Eighty-four days later—Myron kept count—he got a call from Karen Singh. She asked him to visit her office. When he arrived, she wasted no time.

"It worked," she said. "Jeremy went home today."

Myron started to cry. Karen Singh moved around her desk. She sat on the arm of his chair and rubbed his back.

Myron knocked on the half-open door.

"Enter," Greg said.

Myron did so. Greg Downing was sitting up in a chair. He'd grown a beard during his long hospital stretch.

He smiled at Myron. "Nice to see you."

"Same here. I like the beard."

"Gives me that Paul Bunyan touch, don't you think?"

"I was thinking more along the lines of Sebastian Cabot as Mr. French," Myron said.

Greg laughed. "Going home on Friday."

"Great."

Silence.

"You haven't visited much," Greg said.

"Wanted to give you time to heal. And grow that beard in fully."

Greg tried another laugh, but he sort of choked on it. "My basket-ball career is over, you know."

"You'll get over it."

"That easy?"

Myron smiled. "Who said anything about easy?"

"Yeah."

"But there are more important things in life than basketball," Myron said. "Though sometimes I forget that."

Greg nodded again. Then he looked down and said, "I heard about you finding the donor. I don't know how you did it—"

"It's not important."

He looked up. "Thank you."

Myron was not sure what to say to that. So he kept quiet. And that was when Greg shocked him.

"You know, don't you?"

Myron's heart stopped.

"That was why you helped," Greg said. His voice was pure flat-line. "Emily told you the truth."

The muscles around Myron's throat tightened. There was a whooshing sound in his head.

"Did you take a blood test?" Greg asked.

Myron managed a nod this time. Greg closed his eyes. Myron swallowed and said, "How long . . . ?"

"I'm not sure anymore," Greg said. "I guess right away."

He *knows*. The words fell on Myron, smacking down like raindrops, beading and rolling off, impenetrable. *He's always known. . . .*

"For a while I fooled myself into believing it wasn't so," Greg said. "It's amazing what the mind can do sometimes. But when Jeremy was six, he had his appendix out. I saw his blood type on a chart. It pretty much confirmed what I'd known all along."

Myron didn't know what to say. The realization pushed down on him, swept away the months of blocking like so many children's toys. The mind can indeed do amazing things. He looked at Greg and it was like seeing something in the proper light for the first time and it changed everything. He thought about fathers again. He thought about real sacrifice. He thought about heroes.

"Jeremy's a good boy," Greg said.

"I know," Myron said.

"You remember my father? Screaming on the sidelines like a lunatic?"

"Yes."

"I ended up looking just like him. Spitting image of my old man. He was my blood. And he was the cruelest son of a bitch I ever knew," Greg said. Then he added, "Blood never meant much to me."

A strange echo filled the room. The background noises faded away and there was just the two of them, staring at one another from across the most bizarre chasm.

Greg moved back to the bed. "I'm tired, Myron."

"Don't you think we should talk about this?"

"Yeah," Greg said. He laid back and shut his eyes a little too tightly. "Maybe later. But right now I'm really tired."

At the end of the day, Esperanza stepped into Myron's office, sat down, and said, "I don't know much about family values or what makes a happy family. I don't know the best way to raise a kid or what you have to do to make him happy and well adjusted, whatever the hell 'well adjusted' means. I don't know if it's best to be an only child or have lots of siblings or be raised by two parents or a single parent or a gay couple or a lesbian couple or an overweight albino. But I know one thing."

Myron looked up at her and waited.

"No child could ever be harmed by having you in his life."

Esperanza stood and went home.

Stan Gibbs was playing in the yard with his boys when Myron and Win pulled into the driveway. His wife—at least, Myron guessed it was his wife—sat in a lawn chair and watched. A little boy rode Stan like a horsey. They other boy lay on the ground giggling.

Win frowned. "How very Norman Rockwell."

Myron and Win stepped out of the car. Stan the horsey looked up. The smile stayed on when he saw them, but you could see it starting to lose its grip at the edges. Stan hoisted his son off his back and said something to him Myron couldn't hear. The boy gave an "Aaaw, Dad." Stan jumped to his feet and ruffled the boy's hair. Win frowned again. As Stan jogged toward them, his smile faded away like the end of a song.

"What are you doing here?"

Win said, "Back together with the wife, are we?"

"We're giving it a go."

"Touching," Win said.

Stan turned toward Myron. "What's going on here?"

"Tell the kids to go inside, Stan."

"What?"

Another car pulled in the driveway. Rick Peck was driving. Kimberly Green was in the passenger seat. Stan's face lost color. He snapped a look at Myron.

"We had a deal," he said.

"Remember how I told you that you had two choices when the novel was discovered?"

"I'm not in the mood—"

"I said you could run or you could tell the truth. Remember?"

Stan's façade tottered, and for the first time, Myron saw the rage.

"I left out a third choice. A choice you yourself pointed out to me the first time we met. You could have said that the Sow the Seeds kidnapper was a copycat. That he had read the book. It might have helped you out. Taken some of the heat off."

"I couldn't do that."

"Because it would have led to your father?"

"Yes."

"But you didn't know your father had written the book. Isn't that right, Stan? You said you never knew about the book. I remember that from the first time we talked. I've been watching you say the same thing on TV. You claim you didn't even know your father wrote it."

"All true," Stan said, and the façade slipped back into place. "But—I don't know—maybe subconsciously I suspected something somehow. I can't explain it."

"Good," Myron said.

"Damn good," Win added.

"The problem was," Myron said, "you had to say you hadn't read it. Because if you had, well, Stan, you'd be a plagiarizer. All this work, all your big plans to regain your reputation—it would be for nothing. You'd be ruined."

"We discussed this already."

"No, Stan, we didn't. At least not this part of it." Myron held up the evidence bag with the sheet of paper inside.

Stan set his jaw.

"Know what this is, Stan?"

He said nothing.

"I found it in Melina Garston's apartment. It says 'With love, Dad.' "

Stan swallowed. "So?"

"Something about it bothered me from the beginning. First off, the word 'Dad.' "

"I don't understand—"

"Sure you do, Stan. Melina's sister-in-law called George Garston 'Papa.' When I spoke to him, he referred to himself as 'Papa.' So why would he sign a note like this 'Dad'?"

"That doesn't mean anything."

"Maybe, maybe not. The second thing that bothered me: Who writes a note like this—on the top inside of a folded card? People use the bottom half, right? But see, Stan, this wasn't a card. It was a sheet of a paper folded in half. That's the key. Then there are those tears along the left edge. See them, Stan? Like someone had ripped it out of something."

Win handed Myron the novel that had been sent to Kimberly Green. Myron opened it and laid the piece of paper inside it.

"Something like a book."

It was a perfect match.

"Your father wrote this inscription," Myron said. "To you. Years ago. You'd known about the book all along."

"You can't prove that."

"Come on, Stan. A handwriting analyst will have no trouble with this. The Lexes weren't the ones who found the book. Melina Garston did. You asked her to lie for you in court. She did. But then she started growing suspicious. So she dug around your house and found this book. She's the one who mailed it to Kimberly Green."

"You have no proof—"

"She sent it in anonymously because she still cared about you. She even tore out the inscription so no one, most especially you, would ever know where the book had come from. You had plenty of enemies. Like Susan Lex. And the feds. She probably hoped you'd think they did it. At least for a little while. But you knew right away it was Melina. She didn't count on that. Or your reaction."

Stan's hands tightened into fists. They started shaking.

"The victims' families wouldn't speak to you, Stan. And you needed that for your article. You ended up following the book more than reality. The feds thought it was to fool them. But that wasn't it. Maybe your father told you he was the killer, but nothing else. Maybe the real story wasn't as interesting, so you needed to embellish. Maybe you weren't that good of a writer and you really felt you needed those family quotes. I don't know. But you plagiarized. And the only one who could tie you to that book was Melina Garston. So you killed her."

"You'll never prove it," Stan said.

"The feds will dig hard now. The Lexes will help. Win and I will help. We'll find enough. If nothing else, the jury—and the world—will hear all you did in this. They'll hate you enough to convict."

"You son of a bitch." Stan cocked his fist and aimed it at Myron. With an almost casual movement, Win swept his leg. Stan fell down in a heap. Win pointed and laughed. Stan's sons watched it all.

Kimberly Green and Rick Peck got out of the car. Myron signaled them to wait, but Kimberly Green shook her head. They cuffed Stan hard and dragged him away. His sons still watched. Myron thought about Melina Garston and his silent vow. Then he and Win headed back to the car.

"You always intended to turn him in," Win said.

"Yes. But first I had to make sure he went along with donating the bone marrow."

"And once you knew Jeremy was okay—"

"Then I told Green, yes."

Win started the car. "The evidence is still marginal. A good attorney will be able to poke holes."

"Not my problem," Myron said.

"You'd be willing to let him walk?"

"Yes," Myron said. "But Melina's father has juice. And he won't."

"I thought you advised him against taking the law into his own hands."

Myron shrugged. "No one ever listens to me."

"That's true," Win said.

Win drove.

"I just wonder," Myron said.

"What?"

"Who was the serial killer here? Did his father really do it? Or was it all Stan?"

"Doubt we'll ever know," Win said.

"Probably not."

"It shan't matter," Win said. "They'll get him for Melina Garston."

"I guess," Myron said. Then he frowned and repeated, " 'Shan't'?"

Win shrugged. "So is it finally over, my friend?"

Myron's leg did that nervous jig again. He stopped it and said, "Jeremy."

"Ah," Win said. "Are you going to tell him?"

Myron looked out the window and saw nothing. "Win's credo about selfishness would say yes."

"And Myron's credo?"

"I don't know that it's much different," Myron said.

Jeremy was playing basketball at the Y. Myron stepped into the bleachers, the rickety kind that shake with each step, and sat. Jeremy was still pale. He was thinner than the last time Myron had seen him, but there'd been a growth spurt over the last few months. Myron realized how fast changes take place for the young and felt a deep, hard thud in his chest.

For a while, he just watched the flow of the scrimmage and tried to judge his son's play objectively. Jeremy had the tools, Myron could see that right away, but there was plenty of rust on them. That wouldn't be a problem though. Again with the young. Rust doesn't stay long on the young.

As Myron watched the practice, his eyes widened. He felt his insides shrivel. He thought again about what he was about to do, and a swelling tide rose inside of him, overwhelming him, pulling him under.

Jeremy smiled when he spotted Myron. The smile cleaved Myron's heart in two even pieces. He felt lost, adrift. He thought about what Win had said, about what a real father was, and he thought about what Esperanza had said. He thought about Greg and Emily. He wondered if he should have spoken to his own father about this, if he should have told him that this wasn't a hypothetical, that the bomb had indeed landed, that he needed his help.

Jeremy continued to play, but Myron could see that the boy was distracted by his presence. Jeremy kept sneaking quick glances toward the stands. He played a little harder, picked up the pace a bit. Myron had been there, done that. The desire to impress. It had driven Myron, maybe as much as wanting to win. Shallow, but there you have it.

The coach had his players run a few more drills and then he lined them up on the baseline. They finished up with the aptly named "suicides," which was basically a series of gut-heaving sprints broken up by bending and touching different lines on the floor. Myron might be nostalgic for many things connected to basketball. Suicides were not one of them.

Ten minutes later, with most of the kids still trying to catch their breath, the coach gathered his troops, gave out schedules for the rest of the week, and dispersed the boys with a big handclap. Most of them headed toward the exit, slinging backpacks over their shoulders. Some went into the locker room. Jeremy walked over to Myron slowly.

"Hi," Jeremy said.

"Hi."

Sweat dripped off Jeremy's hair, his face coated and flushed from exertion. "I'm going to shower," he said. "You want to wait?"

"Sure," Myron said.

"Cool, I'll be right back."

The gymnasium emptied out. Myron stood and picked up an errant basketball. His fingers found the grooves right away. He took a few shots, watching the bottom of the net dance as the ball swished through. He smiled and sat back down, still holding the ball. A janitor came in and swept the floor Zamboni-style. His keys jangled. Someone flipped off the overhead lights. Jeremy came back not long after that. His hair was still wet. He, too, had a backpack over his shoulder.

As Win would say, "Showtime."

Myron gripped the ball a little tighter. "Sit down, Jeremy. We need to talk."

The boy's face was serene and almost too beautiful. He slid the backpack off his shoulder and sat down. Myron had rehearsed this part. He had looked at it from all sides, all the pluses and minuses. He had made up his mind and changed it and made it up again. He had, as Win put it, properly tortured himself.

But in the end, he knew there was one universal truth: Lies fester. You try to put them away. You jam them in a box and bury them in the ground. But eventually they eat their way out of coffins. They dig their way out of graves. They may sleep for years. But they always wake up. When they do, they're rested, stronger, more insidious.

Lies kill.

"This is going to be hard to understand—" He stopped. Suddenly his rehearsed speech sounded so damn canned, filled with "It's nobody's fault" and "Adults make mistakes too" and "It doesn't mean your parents love you any less." It was patronizing and stupid and—

"Mr. Bolitar?"

Myron looked up at the boy.

"My mom and dad told me," Jeremy said. "Two days ago."

His chest shuddered. "What?"

"I know you're my biological father."

Myron was surprised and yet he wasn't. Some might say that Emily and Greg had made a preemptive strike, almost like a lawyer who reveals something bad about his own client because he knows the opposition will do it. Lessen the blow. But maybe Emily and Greg had

335

learned the same lesson he had about lies and how they fester. And maybe, once again, they were trying to do what was best for their boy.

"How do you feel about it?" Myron asked.

"Weird, I guess," Jeremy said. "I mean, Mom and Dad keep expecting me to fall apart or something. But I don't see why it has to be such a big deal."

"You don't?"

"Sure, okay, I see it, but"—he stopped, shrugged—"it's not like the whole world's turned inside out or anything. You know what I mean?"

Myron nodded. "Maybe it's because you've already had your world turned inside out."

"You mean being sick and all?"

"Yes."

"Yeah, maybe," he said, thinking about it. "Must be weird for you too."

"Yeah," Myron said.

"I've been thinking about it," Jeremy said. "You want to hear what I've come up with?"

Myron swallowed. He looked into the boy's eyes— serenity, yes, but not through innocence. "Very much," he said.

"You're not my dad," he said simply. "I mean, you might be my father. But you're not my dad. You know what I mean?"

Myron managed a nod

"But"—Jeremy stopped, looked up, shrugged the shrug of a thirteen-year-old—"but maybe you can still be around."

"Around?" Myron repeated.

"Yeah," Jeremy said. He smiled again and *pow*, Myron's chest took another blow. "Around. You know."

"Yeah," Myron said, "I know."

"I think I'd like that."

"Me too," Myron said.

Jeremy nodded. "Cool."

"Yeah."

The gym clock grunted and pushed forward. Jeremy looked at it. "Mom's probably outside waiting for me. We usually stop at the supermarket on the way home. Want to come?"

Myron shook his head. "Not today, thanks."

"Cool." Jeremy stood, watching Myron's face. "You okay?"

"Yeah."

Jeremy smiled. "Don't worry. It's going to work out."

Myron tried to smile back. "How did you get to be so smart?"

"Good parenting," he said. "Combined with good genes."

Myron laughed. "You might want to consider a future in politics."

"Yeah," Jeremy said. "Take it easy, Myron."

"You too, Jeremy."

He watched the boy walk out the door, again with the familiar gait. Jeremy didn't look back. There was the sound of the door closing, the echoes, and then Myron was alone. He turned toward the basket and stared at the hoop until it blurred. He saw the boy's first step, heard his first word, smelled the sweet clean of a young child's pajamas. He felt the smack of a ball against a glove, bent over to help with his homework, stayed up all night when he had a virus, all of it, like his own father had, a whirl of taunting, aching images, as irretrievable as the past. He saw himself hovering in the boy's darkened doorway, the silent sentinel to his adolescence, and he felt what remained of his heart burst into flames.

The images scattered when he blinked. His heart started beating again. He stared again at the basket and waited. This time nothing blurred. Nothing happened.

Acknowlegments

The author wishes to thank Sujit Sheth, M.D., Department of Pediatrics, Babies and Children's Hospital in New York, Anne Armstrong-Coben, M.D., Department of Pediatrics, Babies and Children's Hospital (and my love monkey), and Joachim Schulz, Executive Director, Fanconi Anemia Research Fund, all of whom offered up wonderful medical insights and then watched me take liberties with them; two fellow scribes, friends, and experts in their fields, Linda Fairstein and Laura Lippman; Larry Gerson, the inspiration; Nils Lofgren, for rocking me over the last hurdle; early reader and long-time bud Maggie Griffin; Lisa Erbach Vance and Aaron Priest for another job well done; Jeffrey Bedford, FBI Special Agent (and not a bad freshman dorm counselor); as always, Dave Bolt; and mostly, Jacob Hoye, my editor for all the Myron Bolitar books—and now a father. That dedication is for you, too, Jake. Thanks, dude.

For those interested in becoming a bone marrow donor and perhaps saving a life, I urge you to contact the National Marrow Donor Program at

> www.marrow.org
> or 1–800-MARROW2

For more information on Fanconi anemia, check out

> www.fanconi.org

This book is a work of fiction. That means I make stuff up.

No Second Chance

chapter 1

When the first bullet hit my chest, I thought of my daughter.

At least, that is what I want to believe. I lost consciousness pretty fast. And, if you want to get technical about it, I don't even remember being shot. I know that I lost a lot of blood. I know that a second bullet skimmed the top of my head, though I was probably already out by then. I know that my heart stopped. But I still like to think that as I lay dying, I thought of Tara.

FYI: I saw no bright light or tunnel. Or if I did, I don't remember that either.

Tara, my daughter, is only six months old. She was lying in her crib. I wonder if the gunfire frightened her. It must have. She probably began to cry. I wonder if the familiar albeit grating sound of her cries somehow sliced through my haze, if on some level I actually heard her. But again I have no memory of it.

What I do remember, however, was the moment Tara was born. I remember Monica—that's Tara's mother—bearing down for one last push. I remember the head appearing. I was the first to see my daughter. We all know about life's forks in the road. We all know about opening one door and closing another, life cycles, the changes in seasons. But the moment your child is born . . . it's beyond surreal. You have walked through a *Star Trek*–like portal, a full-fledged reality transformer. Everything is different. You are different, a simple element hit with a startling catalyst and metamorphosed into one far more complex. Your world is gone; it shrinks down to the dimensions of—in this case, anyway—a six-pound fifteen-ounce mass.

Fatherhood confuses me. Yes, I know that with only six months on the job, I am an amateur. My best friend, Lenny, has four kids. A girl and three boys. His oldest, Marianne, is ten, his youngest just turned one. With his face permanently set on happily harried and the floor of his SUV permanently stained with congealed fast food, Lenny reminds me that I know nothing yet. I agree. But when I get seriously lost or afraid in the realm of raising a child, I look at the helpless bundle in the crib and she looks up at me and I wonder what I would not do to protect her. I would lay down my life in a second. And truth be told, if push came to shove, I would lay down yours too.

So I like to think that as the two bullets pierced my body, as I collapsed onto the linoleum of my kitchen floor with a half-eaten granola bar clutched in my hand, as I lay immobile in a spreading puddle of my own blood, and yes, even as my heart stopped beating, that I still tried to do something to protect my daughter.

I came to in the dark.

I had no idea where I was at first, but then I heard the beeping coming from my right. A familiar sound. I did not move. I merely listened to the beeps. My brain felt as if it'd been marinated in molasses. The first impulse to break through was a primitive one: thirst. I craved water. I had never known a throat could feel so dry. I tried to call out, but my tongue had been dry-caked to the bottom of my mouth.

A figure entered the room. When I tried to sit up, hot pain ripped like a knife down my neck. My head fell back. And again, there was darkness.

When I awoke again, it was daytime. Harsh streaks of sunlight slashed through the venetian blinds. I blinked through them. Part of me wanted to raise my hand and block the rays, but exhaustion would not let the command travel. My throat was still impossibly parched.

I heard a movement and suddenly there was someone standing over me. I looked up and saw a nurse. The perspective, so different from the one I was used to, threw me. Nothing felt right. I was supposed to be the one standing looking down, not the other way around. A white hat—one of those small, harshly triangular numbers—sat like a bird's nest on the nurse's head. I've spent a great deal of my life working in a wide variety of hospitals, but I'm not sure I've ever seen a hat like that outside of TV or the movies. The nurse was heavyset and black.

"Dr. Seidman?"

Her voice was warm maple syrup. I managed a very slight nod.

The nurse must have read minds because she already had a cup of water in her hand. She put the straw between my lips and I sucked greedily.

"Slow down," she said gently.

I was going to ask where I was, but that seemed pretty obvious. I opened my mouth to find out what had happened, but again she was one step ahead of me.

"I'll go get the doctor," she said, heading for the door. "You just relax now."

I croaked, "My family . . ."

"I'll be right back. Try not to worry."

I let my eyes wander about the room. My vision had that medicated, shower-curtain haze. Still, there were enough stimuli getting through to make certain deductions. I was in a typical hospital room. That much was obvious. There was a drip bag and IV pump on my left, the tube snaking down to my arm. The fluorescent bulbs buzzed almost, but not quite, imperceptibly. A small TV on a swinging arm jutted out from the upper right-hand corner.

A few feet past the foot of the bed, there was a large glass window. I squinted but could not see through it. Still, I was probably being monitored. That meant I was in an ICU. That meant that whatever was wrong with me was something pretty bad.

The top of my skull itched, and I could feel a pull at my hair. Bandaged, I bet. I tried to check myself out, but my head really did not want to cooperate. Dull pain quietly boomed inside me, though I couldn't tell from where it originated. My limbs felt heavy, my chest encased in lead.

"Dr. Seidman?"

I flicked my eyes toward the door. A tiny woman in surgical scrubs complete with the shower cap stepped into the room. The top of the mask was untied and dangled down her neck. I am thirty-four years old. She looked about the same.

"I'm Dr. Heller," she said, stepping closer. "Ruth Heller." Giving me her first name. Professional courtesy, no doubt. Ruth Heller gave me a probing stare. I tried to focus. My brain was still sluggish, but I could feel it sputtering to life. "You are at St. Elizabeth Hospital," she said in a properly grave voice.

The door behind her opened and a man stepped inside. It was hard to see him clearly through the shower-curtain haze, but I don't think I knew him. The man crossed his arms and leaned against the wall with practiced casualness. Not a doctor, I thought. You work with them long enough, you can tell.

Dr. Heller gave the man a cursory glance and then she turned her full attention back to me.

"What happened?" I asked.

"You were shot," she said. Then added: "Twice."

She let that hang for a moment. I glanced toward the man against the wall. He hadn't moved. I opened my mouth to say something, but Ruth Heller pressed on. "One bullet grazed the top of your head. The bullet literally scraped off your scalp, which, as you probably know, is incredibly rich with blood."

Yes, I knew. Serious scalp wounds bled like beheadings. Okay, I thought, that explained the itch on top of my head. When Ruth Heller hesitated, I prompted her. "And the second bullet?"

Heller let out a breath. "That one was a bit more complicated."

I waited.

"The bullet entered your chest and nicked the pericardial sac. That caused a large supply of blood to leak into the space between your heart and the sac. The EMTs had trouble locating your vital signs. We had to crack your chest—"

"Doc?" the leaning man interrupted—and for a moment, I thought he was talking to me. Ruth Heller stopped, clearly annoyed. The man peeled himself off the wall. "Can you do the details later? Time is of the essence here."

She gave him a scowl, but there wasn't much behind it. "I'll stay here and observe," she said to the man, "if that's not a problem."

Dr. Heller faded back and now the man loomed over me. His head was too big for his shoulders so that you feared his neck would collapse from the weight of it. His hair was crew cut all around, except in the front, where it hung down in a Caesar line above his eyes. A soul patch, an ugly smear of growth, sat on his chin like a burrowing insect. All in all, he looked like a member of a boy band gone to serious seed. He smiled down at me, but there was no warmth behind it. "I'm Detective Bob Regan of the Kasselton Police Department," he said. "I know you're confused right now."

"My family—" I began.

"I'll get to that," he interrupted. "But right now, I need to ask you some questions, okay? Before we get into the details of what happened."

He waited for a response. I tried my best to clear the cobwebs and said, "Okay."

"What's the last thing you remember?"

I scanned my memory banks. I remembered waking up that morning, getting dressed. I remembered looking in on Tara. I remembered turning the knob on her black-n-white mobile, a gift from a colleague who insisted it would help stimulate a baby's brain or something. The mobile hadn't moved or bleated out its tinny song. The batteries were dead. I'd made a mental note to put in new ones. I headed downstairs after that.

"Eating a granola bar," I said.

Regan nodded as if he'd expected this answer. "You were in the kitchen?"

"Yes. By the sink."

"And then?"

I tried harder, but nothing came. I shook my head. "I woke up once before. At night. I was here, I think."

"Nothing else?"

I reached out again but to no avail. "No, nothing."

Regan flipped out a pad. "Like the doc here told you, you were shot twice. You have no recollection of seeing a gun or hearing a shot or anything like that?"

"No."

"That's understandable, I guess. You were in a bad way, Marc. The EMTs thought you were a goner."

My throat felt dry again. "Where are Tara and Monica?"

"Stay with me, Marc." Regan was staring down at the pad, not at me. I felt the dread begin to press down on my chest. "Did you hear a window break?"

I felt groggy. I tried to read the label on the drip bag to see what they were numbing me with. No go. Pain medication, at the very least.

Probably morphine in the IV pump. I tried to fight through the effects. "No," I said.

"You're sure? We found a broken window near the rear of the house. It may have been how the perpetrator gained entry."

"I don't remember a window breaking," I said. "Do you know who—"

Regan cut me off. "Not yet, no. That's why I'm here asking these questions. To find out who did this." He looked up from his pad. "Do you have any enemies?"

Did he really just ask me that? I tried to sit up, tried to gain some sort of angle on him, but there was no way that was going to happen. I did not like being the patient, on the wrong end of the bed, if you will. They say doctors make the worst patients. This sudden role reversal is probably why.

"I want to know about my wife and daughter."

"I understand that," Regan said, and something in his tone ran a cold finger across my heart. "But you can't afford the distraction, Marc. Not right yet. You want to be helpful, right? Then you need to stay with me here." He went back to the pad. "Now, what about enemies?"

Arguing with him any further seemed futile or even harmful, so I grudgingly acquiesced. "Someone who would shoot me?"

"Yes."

"No, no one."

"And your wife?" His eyes settled hard on me. A favorite image of Monica—her face lighting up when we first saw Raymondkill Falls, the way she threw her arms around me in mock fear as the water crashed around us—rose like an apparition. "Did she have enemies?"

I looked at him. "Monica?"

Ruth Heller stepped forward. "I think that might be enough for now."

"What happened to Monica?" I asked.

Dr. Heller met up with Detective Regan, standing shoulder to shoulder. Both looked at me. Heller started to protest again, but I stopped her.

"Don't give me this protect-the-patient crap," I tried to shout, fear and fury battling against whatever had put my brain in this fuzz. "Tell me what happened to my wife."

"She's dead," Detective Regan said. Just like that. Dead. My wife. Monica. It was as if I hadn't heard him. The word couldn't reach me.

"When the police broke into your home, you had both been shot. They were able to save you. But it was too late for your wife. I'm sorry."

There was another quick flash now—Monica at Martha's Vineyard, on the beach, tan bathing suit, that black hair whipping across those cheekbones, giving me the razor-sharp smile. I blinked it away. "And Tara?"

"Your daughter," Regan began with a quick throat-clear. He looked at his pad again, but I don't think he planned on writing anything down. "She was home that morning, correct? I mean, at the time of the incident?"

"Yes, of course. Where is she?"

Regan closed the pad with a snap. "She was not at the scene when we arrived."

My lungs turned to stone. "I don't understand."

"We originally hoped that maybe she was in the care of a family member or friend. A baby-sitter even, but . . ." His voice faded.

"Are you telling me you don't know where Tara is?"

There was no hesitation this time. "Yes, that's correct."

It felt as if a giant hand were pushing down on my chest. I squeezed my eyes shut and fell back. "How long?" I asked.

"Has she been missing?"

"Yes."

Dr. Heller started speaking too quickly. "You have to understand. You were very seriously injured. We were not optimistic you would survive. You were on a respirator. A lung collapsed. You also contracted sepsis. You're a doctor, so I know I don't have to explain to you how serious that is. We tried to slow down the meds, help you wake up—"

"How long?" I asked again.

She and Regan exchanged another glance, and then Heller said something that ripped the air out of me all over again. "You've been out for twelve days."

chapter 2

"**We're doing all** we can," Regan said in a voice that sounded too rehearsed, as if he'd been standing over my bed while I was unconscious, working on his delivery. "As I told you, we were not sure we had a missing child at first. We lost valuable time there, but we've recovered now. Tara's photo has been sent out to every police station, airport, tollbooth plaza, bus and train station—anything like that within a hundred-mile radius. We've run background profiles on similar abduction cases, see if we can find a pattern or a suspect."

"Twelve days," I repeated.

"We have a trace on your various phones—home, business, cell—"

"Why?"

"In case someone calls in a ransom demand," he said.

"Have there been any calls?"

"Not yet, no."

My head dropped back to the pillow. Twelve days. I'd been lying in this bed for twelve days while my baby girl was . . . I pushed the thought away.

Regan scratched at his beard. "Do you remember what Tara was wearing that morning?"

I did. I had developed something of a morning routine—wake up early, tiptoe toward Tara's crib, stare down. A baby is not all joy. I know that. I know that there are moments of mind-numbing boredom. I know that there are nights when her screams work on my nerve endings like a cheese grater. I don't want to glorify life with an infant. But I liked my new morning routine. Looking down at Tara's tiny form fortified me somehow. More than that, this act was, I guess, a form of rapture. Some people find rapture in a house of worship. Me—and yeah, I know how corny this sounds—I found rapture in that crib.

"A pink one-piece with black penguins," I said. "Monica got it at Baby Gap."

He jotted it down. "And Monica?"

"What about her?"

His face was back in the pad. "What was she wearing?"

"Jeans," I said, remembering the way they slid over Monica's hips, "and a red blouse."

Regan jotted some more.

I said, "Are there—I mean, do you have any leads?"

"We're still investigating all avenues."

"That's not what I asked."

Regan just looked at me. There was too much weight in that stare. My daughter. Out there. Alone. For twelve days. I thought of her eyes, the warm light only a parent sees, and I said something stupid. "She's alive."

Regan tilted his head like a puppy hearing a new sound.

"Don't give up," I said.

"We won't." He continued with the curious look.

"It's just that . . . are you a parent, Detective Regan?"

"Two girls," he said.

"It's stupid, but I'd know." The same way I knew the world would never be the same when Tara was born. "I'd know," I said again.

He did not reply. I realized that what I was saying—especially coming from a man who scoffs at notions of ESP or the supernatural—was ridiculous. I knew that this "sense" merely came from want. You want to believe so badly that your brain rearranges what it sees. But I clung to it anyway. Right or wrong, it felt like a lifeline.

"We'll need some more information from you," Regan said. "About you, your wife, friends, finances—"

"Later." It was Dr. Heller again. She moved forward as if to block me from his gaze. Her voice was firm. "He needs to rest."

"No, now," I said to her, upping the firm-o-meter a notch past hers. "We need to find my daughter."

Monica had been buried at the Portman family plot on her father's estate. I missed her funeral, of course. I don't know how I felt about that, but then again, my feelings for my wife, in those stark moments when I was honest with myself, have always been muddled. Monica had that beauty of privilege, what with the too-fine cheekbones, straight silk-black hair, and that country-club lockjaw that both annoyed and aroused. Our marriage was an old-fashioned one—shotgun. Okay, that's an exaggeration. Monica was pregnant. I was fence-sitting. The upcoming arrival tilted me into the matrimonial pasture.

I heard the funeral details from Carson Portman, Monica's uncle and the only member of her family who kept in touch with us. Monica had loved him dearly. Carson sat at my hospital bedside with his hands folded in his lap. He looked very much like your favorite college professor—the thick-lensed spectacles, the nearly shedding tweed coat, and the overgrown shock of Albert Einstein-meets-Don King hair. But his brown eyes glistened as he told me in his sad baritone that Edgar, Monica's father, had made sure that my wife's funeral was a "small, tasteful affair."

Of that, I had no doubt. The small part, at least.

Over the next few days I had my share of visitors at the hospital. My mother—everyone called her Honey—exploded into my room every morning as if fuel propelled. She wore Reebok sneakers of pure white. Her sweatsuit was blue with gold trim, as if she coached the St. Louis Rams. Her hair, though neatly coifed, had the brittle of too many colorings, and there was the whiff of a last cigarette about her. Mom's makeup did little to disguise the anguish of losing her only grandchild. She had amazing energy, staying by my bedside day after day and managing to exude a steady stream of hysteria. This was good. It was as though she was, in part, being hysterical for me, and thus, in a strange way, her eruptions kept me calm.

Despite the room's nearly supernova heat—and my constant protestations—Mom would put an extra blanket over me when I was asleep. I woke up one time—my body drenched in sweat, naturally—to hear my mother telling the black nurse with the formal hat about my previous stay at St. Elizabeth's when I was only seven.

"He had salmonella," Honey stated in a conspiratorial whisper that was only slightly louder than a bullhorn. "You never smelled diarrhea like that. It was just pouring out of him. His stench practically seeped into the wallpaper."

"He ain't all roses now either," the nurse replied.

The two women shared a laugh.

On Day Two of my recovery, Mom was standing over my bed when I awoke.

"Remember this?" she said.

She was holding a stuffed Oscar the Grouch someone had given me during that salmonella stay. The green had faded to a light mint. She looked at the nurse. "This is Marc's Oscar," she explained.

"Mom," I said.

She turned her attention back to me. The mascara was a little too heavy today, crinkling into the wrinkle lines. "Oscar kept you company back then, remember? He helped you get better."

I rolled and then closed my eyes. A memory came to me. I had gotten the salmonella from raw eggs. My father used to add them into milk-shakes for the protein. I remember the way pure terror had gripped me when I'd first learned that I would have to stay in the hospital overnight. My father, who had recently ruptured his Achilles tendon playing tennis, was in a cast and constant pain. But he saw my fear and as always, he made the sacrifice. He worked all that day at the plant and spent all night in a chair by my hospital bed. I stayed at St. Elizabeth's for ten days. My father slept in that chair every night of them.

Mom suddenly turned away, and I could see she was remembering the same thing. The nurse quickly excused herself. I put a hand on my mother's back. She didn't move, but I could feel her shudder. She stared down at the faded Oscar in her hands. I slowly took it from her.

"Thank you," I said.

Mom wiped her eyes. Dad, I knew, would not come to the hospital this time, and while I am sure my mother had told him what had happened, there was no way to know if he even understood. My father had had his first stroke when he was forty-one years old—one year after staying those nights with me at the hospital. I was eight at the time.

I also have a younger sister, Stacy, who is either a "substance abuser" (for the more politically correct) or "crack-head" (for the more accurate). I sometimes look at old pictures from before my dad's stroke, the ones with the young, confident family of four and the shaggy dog and the well-groomed lawn and the basketball hoop and the coal-overloaded, lighter fluid–saturated barbecue. I look for hints of the future in my sister's front-teeth-missing smile, her shadow self perhaps, a sense of fore-boding. But I see none. We still have the house, but it's like a sagging movie prop. Dad is still alive, but when he fell, everything shattered Humpty-Dumpty style. Especially Stacy.

Stacy had not visited or even called, but nothing she does surprises me anymore.

My mother finally turned to face me. I gripped the faded Oscar a little tighter as a thought struck me anew: It was just us again. Dad was pretty much a vegetable. Stacy was hollowed out, gone. I reached out and took Mom's hand, feeling both the warmth and the more recent thickening of her skin. We stayed like that until the door opened. The same nurse leaned into the room.

Mom straightened up and said, "Marc also played with dolls,"

"Action figures," I said, quick on the correction. "They were action figures, not dolls."

My best friend, Lenny, and his wife, Cheryl, also stopped by the hospital every day. Lenny Marcus is a big-time trial lawyer, though he also handles my small-time stuff like the time I fought a speeding ticket and the closing on our house. When he graduated and began working for the county prosecutor, friends and opponents quickly dubbed Lenny "the Bulldog" because of his aggressive courtroom behavior. Somewhere along the line, it was decided that the name was too mild for Lenny, so now they called him "Cujo." I've known Lenny since elementary school. I'm the godfather of his son Kevin. And Lenny is Tara's godfather.

I haven't slept much. I lie at night and stare at the ceiling and count the beeps and listen to the hospital night sounds and try very much not to let my mind wander to my little daughter and the endless array of possibilities. I am not always successful. The mind, I have learned, is indeed a dark, snake-infested pit.

Detective Regan visited later with a possible lead.

"Tell me about your sister," he began.

"Why?" I said too quickly. Before he could elaborate, I held up my hand to stop him. I understood. My sister was an addict. Where drugs roamed, so too did a certain criminal element. "Were we robbed?" I asked.

"We don't think so. Nothing seems to be missing, but the place was tossed."

"Tossed?"

"Someone made a mess. Any thoughts on why?"

"No."

"So tell me about your sister."

"You have Stacy's record?" I asked.

"We do."

"I'm not sure what I can add."

"You two are estranged, correct?"

Estranged. Did that apply to Stacy and me? "I love her," I said slowly.

"And when was the last time you saw her?"

"Six months ago."

"When Tara was born?"

"Yes."

"Where?"

"Where did I see her?"

"Yes."

"Stacy came to the hospital," I said.

"To see her niece?"

"Yes."

"What happened during that visit?"

"Stacy was high. She wanted to hold the baby."

"You refused?"

"That's right."

"Did she get angry?"

"She barely reacted. My sister is pretty flat when she's stoned."

"But you threw her out?"

"I told her she couldn't be a part of Tara's life until she was clean."

"I see," he said. "You were hoping that would force her back into rehab?"

I might have chuckled. "No, not really."

"I'm not sure I understand."

I wondered how to put this. I thought of the smile in the family photo, the one without the front teeth. "We've threatened Stacy with worse," I said. "The truth is that my sister won't quit. The drugs are part of her."

"So you hold out no hope for recovery?"

There was no way I was about to voice that. "I didn't trust her with my daughter," I said. "Let's leave it at that."

Regan headed over to the window and looked out. "When did you move into your current residence?"

"Monica and I bought the house four months ago."

"Not far from where you both grew up, no?"

"That's right."

"Had you two known each other long?"

I was puzzled by the line of questioning. "No."

"Even though you grew up in the same town?"

"We traveled in different circles."

"I see," he said. "And just so I have it straight, you bought your house four months ago and you hadn't seen your sister in six months, correct?"

"Correct."

"So your sister has never visited you at your current residence?"

"That's right."

Regan turned to me. "We found a set of Stacy's fingerprints at your house."

I said nothing.

"You don't seem surprised, Marc."

"Stacy is an addict. I don't think she's capable of shooting me and kidnapping my daughter, but I've underestimated how low she could sink before. Did you check her apartment?"

"No one has seen her since you were shot," he said.

I closed my eyes.

"We don't think your sister could pull off something like this by herself," he went on. "She might have had an accomplice—a boyfriend, a dealer, someone who knew your wife was from a wealthy family. Do you have any thoughts?"

"No," I said. "So, what, you think this whole thing was a kidnapping plot?"

Regan started clawing at his soul patch again. Then he gave a small shrug.

"But they tried to kill us both," I went on. "How do you collect ransom from dead parents?"

"They could have been so doped up that they made a mistake," he said. "Or maybe they thought they could extort money from Tara's grandfather."

"So why haven't they yet?"

Regan did not reply. But I knew the answer. The heat, especially after the shooting, would be too much for crack-heads. Crack-heads don't handle conflict well. It is one of the reasons they snort or shoot themselves up in the first place—to escape, to fade away, to avoid, to dive down into the white. The media would be all over this case. The police would be making inquiries. Crack-heads would freak under that kind of pressure. They would flee, abandon everything.

And they would get rid of all the evidence.

But the ransom demand came two days later.

Now that I had regained consciousness, my recovery from the gunshot wounds was proceeding with surprising smoothness. It could be that I was focused on getting better or that lying in a quasi-catatonic state for twelve days had given my injuries time to heal. Or it could be that I was suffering from a pain way beyond what the physical could inflict. I would think of Tara and the fear of the unknown would stop my breath. I would think of Monica, of her lying dead, and steel claws would shred me from within.

I wanted out.

My body still ached, but I pressed Ruth Heller to release me. Noting that I was proving the adage about doctors making the worst patients, she reluctantly gave me the okay to go home. We agreed that a physical therapist would come by every day. A nurse would pop by periodically, just to be on the safe side.

On the morning of my departure from St. Elizabeth, my mother was at the house—the former crime scene—getting it "ready" for me, whatever that meant. Oddly enough, I wasn't afraid to go back there. A house is mortar and brick. I didn't think the sight of it alone would move me, but maybe I was just blocking.

Lenny helped me pack and get dressed. He is tall and wiry with a face darkened by a Homer Simpson five-o'clock shadow that pops up six minutes after he shaves. As a child Lenny wore Coke-bottle glasses and too-thick corduroy, even in the summer. His curly hair had a habit of getting outgrown to the point where he'd start resembling a stray poodle. Now he keeps the curls religiously close cropped. He had laser eye surgery two years ago, so the glasses are gone. His suits lean toward the upscale side.

"You sure you won't stay with us?" Lenny said.

"You have four kids," I reminded him.

"Oh yeah, right." He paused. "Can I stay with you?"

I tried to smile.

"Seriously," Lenny said, "you shouldn't be alone in that house."

"I'll be fine."

"Cheryl cooked you some dinners. She put them in the freezer."

"That was nice of her."

"She's still the world's most godawful cook," Lenny said.

"I didn't say I was going to eat them."

Lenny looked away, busying himself with the already packed bag. I watched him. We have known each other a long time, since Mrs. Roberts's first-grade class, so it probably did not surprise him when I said, "You want to tell me what's up?"

He'd been waiting for the opening and thus quickly exploited it. "Look, I'm your lawyer, right?"

"Right."

"So I want to give you some legal advice."

"I'm listening."

"I should have said something earlier. But I knew you wouldn't listen. Now, well, now it's a different story, I think."

"Lenny?"

"Yeah?'

"What are you talking about?"

Despite his physical enhancements, I still saw Lenny as a kid. It made it hard to take his advice too seriously. Don't get me wrong. I knew that he was smart. I had celebrated with him when he got his acceptance to Princeton and then Columbia Law. We took the SATs together and were in the same AP chemistry class our junior year. But the Lenny I saw was the one I desperately cruised with on muggy Friday and Saturday nights. We used his dad's wood-paneled station wagon— not exactly a "babe trawler"—and tried to hit the parties. We were always let in but never really welcome, members of that high school majority I call the Great Unseen. We would stand in corners, holding a beer, bopping our heads to the music, trying hard to be noticed. We never were. Most nights we ended up eating a grilled cheese at the Heritage Diner or, better, at the soccer field behind Benjamin Franklin Middle School, lying on our backs, checking out the stars. It was easier to talk, even with your best friend, when you were looking at the stars.

"Okay," Lenny said, overgesturing as was his custom, "it's like this: I don't want you talking to the cops anymore without my being present."

I frowned. "For real?"

"Maybe it's nothing, but I've seen cases like this. Not *like* this, but you know what I mean. The first suspect is always family."

"Meaning my sister."

"No, meaning close family. Or clos*er* family, if possible."

"Are you saying the police suspect me?"

"I don't know, I really don't." He paused but not for very long. "Okay, yeah, probably."

"But I was shot, remember? My kid was the one taken."

"Right, and that cuts both ways."

"How do you figure that?"

"As the days pass, they're going to start suspecting you more and more."

"Why?" I asked.

"I don't know. That's just how it works. Look, the FBI handles kidnappings. You know that, right? Once a child is gone twenty-four hours, they assume it's interstate and the case is theirs."

"So?"

"So for the first, what, ten days or so, they had a ton of agents here. They monitored your phones and waited for the ransom call, that kinda thing. But the other day, they pretty much pulled up stakes. That's normal, of course. They can't wait indefinitely, so they scale back to an agent or two. And their thinking shifted too. Tara became less a possible kidnapping-for-ransom and more a straight-on abduction. But my guess is, they still have the taps on the phones. I haven't asked yet, but I will. They'll claim they're leaving them there in case a ransom demand is eventually made. But they'll also be hoping to hear you say something incriminating."

"So?"

"So be careful," Lenny said. "Remember that your phones—home, biz, cell—are probably tapped."

"And again I ask: So? I didn't do anything."

"Didn't do . . . ?" Lenny waved his hands as if preparing to take flight. "Look, just be careful is all. This might be hard for you to believe, but—and try not to gasp when I say this—the police have been known to twist and distort evidence."

"You're confusing me. Are you saying I'm a suspect simply because I'm the father and husband?"

"Yes," Lenny said. "And no."

"Well, okay, thanks, that clears it up."

A phone next to my bed rang. I was on the wrong side of the room. "You mind?" I said.

Lenny picked it up. "Dr. Seidman's room." His face clouded over as he listened. He spat out the words "Hold on," and handed the phone to me, as if it might have germs. I gave him a puzzled look and said, "Hello?"

"Hello, Marc. This is Edgar Portman."

Monica's father. That explained Lenny's reaction. Edgar's voice was, as always, way too formal. Some people weigh their words. A select few, like my father-in-law, take each one and put it on a scale before letting it leave their mouths.

I was momentarily taken aback. "Hello, Edgar," I said stupidly. "How are you?"

"I'm fine, thank you. I feel remiss, of course, for not having called you earlier. I understood from Carson that you were busy recuperating from your wounds. I felt it best if I let you be."

"Thoughtful," I said with nary a whiff of sarcasm.

"Yes, well, I understand you're being released today."

"That's right."

Edgar cleared his throat, which seemed out of character for him. "I was wondering if perhaps you could stop by the house."

The house. Meaning his. "Today?"

"As soon as possible, yes. And alone please."

There was silence. Lenny gave me a puzzled look.

"Is something wrong, Edgar?" I asked.

"I have a car waiting downstairs, Marc. We'll talk more when you arrive."

And then, before I could say another word, he was gone.

The car, a black Lincoln Town Car, was indeed waiting.

Lenny wheeled me outside. I was familiar with this area, of course. I had grown up scant miles from St. Elizabeth. When I was five years old, my father had rushed me to the emergency room here (twelve stitches) and when I was seven, well, you already know too much about my sal-monella visit. I'd gone to medical school and did my residency at what was then called Columbia Presbyterian in New York, but I returned to St. Elizabeth for a fellowship in ophthalmology for reconstruction.

Yes, I am a plastic surgeon, but not in the way you think. I do the oc-casional nose job, but you won't find me working with sacks of silicone or any of that. Not that I'm judging. It just isn't what I do.

I work in pediatric reconstructive surgery with my former medical school classmate, a fireball from the Bronx named Zia Leroux. We work for a group called One World WrapAid. Actually, Zia and I founded it. We take care of children, mostly overseas, who suffer defor-mities either through birth, poverty, or conflict. We travel a lot. I have worked on facial smashes in Sierra Leone, on cleft palates in Upper Mongolia, on Crouzon's in Cambodia, on burn victims in the Bronx. Like most people in my field, I've done extensive training. I've studied ENT—ears, nose, and throat—with a year of reconstructive, plastics, oral, and, as I mentioned above, ophthalmology. Zia's training history is similar, though she's stronger with the maxillofacial.

You may think of us as do-gooders. You'd be wrong. I had a choice. I could do boob jobs or tuck back the skin of those who were already too beautiful—or I could help wounded, poverty-stricken children. I chose the latter, not so much to help the disadvantaged, but alas, be-cause that is where the cool cases lie. Most reconstructive surgeons are, at heart, puzzle lovers. We're weird. We get jazzed on circus-sideshow congenital anomalies and huge tumors. You know those medical text-books that have hideous facial deformities that you have to dare your-self to look at? Zia and I love that stuff. We get off on repairing it—taking what's shattered and making it whole—even more.

The fresh air tickled my lungs. The sun shone as if it were the first day, mocking my gloom. I tilted my face toward the warmth and let it soothe me. Monica used to like to do that. She claimed that it "de-stressed" her. The lines in her face would disappear as if the rays were gentle masseurs. I kept my eyes closed. Lenny waited in silence, giving me the time.

I have always thought of myself as an overly sensitive man. I cry too easily at dumb movies. My emotions are easily manipulated. But with my father, I never cried. And now, with this terrible blow, I felt—I don't know—beyond tears. A classic defense mechanism, I assumed. I had to push forward. It's not so different from my business: When cracks appear, I patch them up before they become full-fledged fissures.

Lenny was still fuming from the phone call. "Any idea what that old bastard wants?"

"Not a one."

He was quiet a moment. I know what he was thinking. Lenny blamed Edgar for his father's death. His old man had been a middle manager at ProNess Foods, one of Edgar's holdings. He had slaved for the company twenty-six years and had just turned fifty-two years old when Edgar orchestrated a major merger. Lenny's father lost his job. I remember seeing Mr. Marcus sitting slump shouldered at the kitchen table, meticulously stuffing his résumé into envelopes. He never found work and died two years later of a heart attack. Nothing could convince Lenny that the two events were unrelated.

He said, "You sure you don't want me to come?"

"Nah, I'll be all right."

"Got your cell?"

I showed it to him.

"Call me if you need anything."

I thanked him and let him walk away. The driver opened the door. I winced my way in. The drive was not far. Kasselton, New Jersey. My hometown. We passed the split-levels of the sixties, the expanded ranches of the seventies, the aluminum sidings of the eighties, the McMansions of the nineties. Eventually the trees grew denser. The houses sat farther back from the road, protected by the lush, away from the great unwashed who might happen by. We were nearing old wealth now, that exclusive land that always smelled of autumn and woodsmoke.

The Portman family had first settled in this thicket immediately following the Civil War. Like most of suburban Jersey, this had been farmland. Great-great-grandfather Portman slowly sold off acreage and made a fortune. They still had sixteen acres, making their lot one of the largest in the area. As we climbed the drive, my eyes drifted left—toward the family burial plot.

I could see a small mound of fresh dirt.

"Stop the car," I said.

"Sorry, Dr. Seidman," the driver replied, "but I was told to bring you right up to the main house."

I was about to protest but thought better of it. I waited until the car stopped by the front door. I got out and headed back down the drive. I heard the driver say, "Dr. Seidman?" I kept going. He called after me again. I ignored him. Despite the lack of rain, the grass was a green usually reserved for rain forests. The rose garden was in full bloom, an explosion of color.

I tried to hurry on, but my skin still felt as if it might rip. I slowed. This was only my third visit inside the Portman family estate—I had seen it from the outside dozens of times in my youth—and I had never visited the family plot. In fact, like most rational people, I did my best to avoid it. The idea of burying your kin in your backyard like a family pet . . . it was one of those things that rich people do that we regular folk could never quite grasp. Or would want to.

The fence around the plot was maybe two feet high and blindingly white. I wondered if it'd been freshly painted for the occasion. I stepped over the superfluous gate and walked past the modest gravestones, keeping my eye on the dirt mound. When I reached the spot, a shudder tore through me. I looked down.

Yep, a recently dug grave. No stone yet. The marker on it, printed up in wedding-invitation calligraphy, read simply: OUR MONICA.

I stood there and blinked. Monica. My wild-eyed beauty. Our relationship had been turbulent—a classic case of too much passion in the beginning and not enough near the end. I don't know why that happens. Monica was different, no question. At first that crackle, that excitement, had been a draw. Later, the mood swings simply made me weary. I didn't have the patience to dig deeper.

As I looked down at the pile of dirt, a painful memory jabbed at me. Two nights before the attack, Monica had been crying when I came to the bedroom. It was not the first time. Not even close. Playing my part in the stage show that was our lives, I asked her what was wrong, but my heart was not in it. I used to ask with more concern. Monica never replied. I would try to hold her. She would go rigid. After a while the nonresponsiveness got tiresome, taking on a boy-who-cried-wolf aspect that eventually frosts the heart. Living with a depressive is like that. You can't care all the time. At some point, you have to start to resent.

At least, that was what I told myself.

But this time, there was something different: Monica did indeed reply to me. Not a long reply. One line, actually. "You don't love me," she said. That was it. There was no pity in her voice. "You don't love me." And while I managed to utter the necessary protestations, I wondered if maybe she was right.

I closed my eyes and let it all wash over me. Things had been bad, but for the past six months anyway, there had been an escape for us, a calm and warm center in our daughter. I glanced at the sky now, blinked again, and then looked back down at the dirt that covered my volatile wife. "Monica," I said out loud. And then I made my wife one last vow.

I swore on her grave that I would find Tara.

A servant or butler or associate or whatever the current term was led me down the corridor and into the library. The décor was understated though unequivocally rich—finished dark floors with simple oriental carpets, old-Americana furniture that was solid rather than ornate. Despite his wealth and large plot of land Edgar was not one for show wealth. The term *nouveau riche* was to him profane, unspeakable.

Dressed in a blue cashmere blazer, Edgar rose from behind his expansive oak desk. There was a feather quill pen on the top—his great-grandfather's, if I recall—and two bronze busts, one of Washington and one of Jefferson. I was surprised to see Uncle Carson sitting there too. When he'd visited me in the hospital, I had been too frail to embrace. Carson made up for that now. He pulled me close. I held on to him in silence. He, too, smelled of autumn and woodsmoke.

There were no photographs in the room—no family-vacation snapshots, no school portraits, no shot of the man and his missus decked out at a charity formal. In fact, I do not think I had ever seen a photograph anywhere in the house.

Carson said, "How are you feeling, Marc?"

I told him that I was as well as could be expected and turned toward my father-in-law. Edgar did not come around the desk. We did not embrace. We did not, in fact, even shake hands. He gestured toward the chair in front of the desk.

I did not know Edgar very well. We had only met three times. I do not know how much money he has, but even out of these dwellings, even on a city street or at a bus depot, hell, even naked, you could tell that the Portmans were from money. Monica had the bearing too, the one ingrained over generations, the one that cannot be taught, the one that may literally be genetic. Monica's choice to live in our relatively modest dwelling was probably a form of rebellion.

She had hated her father.

I was not a big fan of his either, probably because I had met his type before. Edgar thinks himself a pull-up-by-the-bootstraps sort, but he himself earned his money the old-fashioned way: He inherited it. I don't know many superwealthy people, but I noticed that the more things were handed to you on a silver platter, the more you complain about welfare mothers and government handouts. It is bizarre. Edgar belongs to that unique class of the entitled who have deluded themselves into believing that they somehow earned their status through hard work. We all live with self-justification, of course, and if you have never fended for yourself, if you live in luxury and have done nothing to deserve it, well, that is going to compound your insecurities, I guess. But it shouldn't make you such a prig, to boot.

I sat. Edgar followed suit. Carson remained standing. I stared at Edgar. He had the plump of the well fed. His face was all soft edges. The normal ruddy on his cheeks, so far from anything rawbone, was gone now. He laced his fingers and rested them on his paunch. He looked, I was somewhat surprised to see, devastated, drawn, and sapless.

I say *surprised*, because Edgar always struck me as pure id, a person whose own pain and pleasure trumped all others', who believed those who inhabited the space around him were little more than window dressing for his own bemusement. Edgar had now lost two children. His son, Eddie the Fourth, had died while speeding under the influence ten years ago. According to Monica, Eddie veered across the double yellow line and plowed into the semi on purpose. For some reason, she blamed her father. She blamed him for a lot of things.

There is also Monica's mother. She "rests" a lot. She takes "extended vacations." In short, she is in and out of institutions. Both times we met, my mother-in-law was propped up for some social affair, well dressed and powdered, lovely and too pale, a vacancy in her eyes, a slur in her speech, a sway in her stance.

Except for Uncle Carson, Monica had been estranged from her family. As you might imagine, I hardly minded.

"You wanted to see me?" I said.

"Yes, Marc. Yes, I did."

I waited.

Edgar put his hands on his desk. "Did you love my daughter?"

I was caught off guard, but I still said, "Very much," with no hesitation.

He seemed to see the lie. I worked hard to keep my gaze steady. "She still wasn't happy, you know."

"I'm not sure you can blame me for that," I said.

He nodded slowly. "Fair point."

But my own pass-the-buck defense didn't really work on me. Edgar's words were a fresh body blow. The guilt came roaring back.

"Did you know that she was seeing a psychiatrist?" Edgar asked.

I turned toward Carson first, then back to Edgar. "No."

"She didn't want anyone to know."

"How did you find out?"

Edgar did not reply. He stared down at his hands. Then he said: "I want to show you something."

I sneaked another look at Uncle Carson. His jaw was set. I thought I saw a tremble. I turned back to Edgar. "Okay."

Edgar opened his desk drawer, reached in, and pulled out a plastic bag. He raised it into view, gripping the bag at the corner between his forefinger and thumb. It took a moment, but when I realized what I was looking at, my eyes went wide.

Edgar saw my reaction. "You recognize it then?"

I couldn't speak at first. I glanced over at Carson. His eyes were red. I looked back at Edgar and nodded numbly. Inside the plastic bag was a small swatch of clothing, maybe three inches by three inches. The pattern was one I had seen two weeks ago, moments before being shot.

Pink with black penguins.

My voice was barely a hush. "Where did you get this?"

Edgar handed me a large brown envelope, the kind with bubble wrap on the inside. This too, was protected in plastic. I turned it around. Edgar's name and address had been printed on a white label. There was no return address. The postmark read New York City.

"It came in today's mail," Edgar said. He gestured to the swatch. "Is it Tara's?"

I think I said yes.

"There's more," Edgar said. He reached into the drawer again. "I took the liberty of putting everything in plastic bags. In case the authorities need to test it."

Again he handed me what looked like a Ziploc bag. Smaller this time. There were hairs inside. Little wisps of hair. With mounting dread, I realized what I was looking at. My breath stopped.

Baby hair.

From far away, I heard Edgar ask, "Are they hers?"

I closed my eyes and tried to picture Tara in the crib. The image of my daughter, I was horrified to realize, was already fading in the mind's eye. How could that be? I could no longer tell if I was seeing memory or something I conjured up to replace what I was already forgetting. Damn it. Tears pressed against my eyelids. I tried to bring back the feel of my daughter's soft scalp, the way my finger would trace the top.

"Marc?"

"They could be," I said, opening my eyes. "There's no way for me to know for sure."

"Something else," Edgar said. He handed me another plastic bag. Gingerly, I put down the bag with her hair on the desk. I took the new bag. There was a sheet of white paper in it. A note from some kind of laser printer.

If you contact the authorities, we disappear. You will never know what happened to her. We will be watching. We will know. We have a man on the inside. Your calls are being monitored. Do not discuss this over the phone. We know that you, Grandpa, are rich. We want two million dollars. We want you, Daddy, to deliver the ransom. You, Grandpa, will get the money ready. We are enclosing a cell phone. It is untraceable. But if you dial out or use it in any way, we will know. We will disappear and you will never see the child again. Get the money ready. Give it to Daddy. Daddy, keep the money and phone near you. Go home and wait. We will call and tell you what to do. Deviate from what we ask, and you will never see your daughter again. There will be no second chance.

The syntax was odd, to put it mildly. I read the note three times and then I looked up at Edgar and Carson. A funny calm spread over me. Yes, this was terrifying, but receiving this note . . . it was also a relief. Something had finally happened. We could act now. We could get Tara back. There was hope.

Edgar stood and headed toward the corner of the room. He opened a closet door and pulled out a gym bag with a Nike logo on it. Without preamble, he said, "It's all here."

He dropped the bag onto my lap. I stared down at it. "Two million dollars?"

"The bills are not sequential, but we have a list of all the serial numbers, just in case."

I looked at Carson and then back at Edgar. "You don't think we should contact the FBI?"

"Not really, no." Edgar perched himself on the lid of the desk, folding his arms across his chest. He smelled of barbershop bay rum, but I could sense something more primitive, more rancid, that lay just beneath. Up close, his eyes had the dark rings of exhaustion. "It's your decision, Marc. You're the father. We'll respect whatever you do. But as you know, I have had some dealings with the federal authorities. Perhaps my views are colored by my own sense of their incompetence, or perhaps I am biased because I've witnessed the degree to which they are ruled by personal agendas. If it were my daughter, I'd rather trust my own judgment than theirs."

I was not sure what to say or do. Edgar took care of that. He clapped his hands once and then gestured toward the door.

"The note says that you should go home and wait. I think it's best if we obey."

chapter 3

The same driver was there. I slid into the backseat, the Nike bag pressed against my chest. My emotions rocketed between abject fear and the strangest tinge of elation. I could get my daughter back. I could blow it all.

But first things first: Should I tell the police?

I tried to calm myself, to look at it coldly, at a distance, weigh the pros and cons. That was impossible, of course. I am a doctor. I have made life-altering decisions before. I know that the best way to do that is to remove the baggage, the ardent excess, from the equation. But my daughter's life was at stake. My own daughter. To echo what I said in the beginning: my world.

The house Monica and I bought is literally around the corner from the house I grew up in and where my parents still reside. I am ambivalent about that. I really don't like living so close to my parents, but I dislike the guilt of abandoning them even more. My compromise: Live near them and then travel a lot.

Lenny and Cheryl live four blocks away, near the Kasselton Mall, in the house where Cheryl's parents had raised her. Cheryl's parents moved to Florida six years ago. They keep a condo up here in neighboring Roseland so they can visit their grandchildren and escape the molten-lava summers of the Sunshine State.

I don't particularly like living in Kasselton. The town has changed very little over the past thirty years. In our youth, we scoffed at our parents, their materialism, their seemingly aimless values. Now we are our parents. We have simply replaced them, pushed Mom and Dad into whatever retirement village would have them. And our children have replaced us. But Maury's Luncheonette is still on Kasselton Avenue. The fire department is still mostly volunteer. The Little League still plays at Northland Field. The high-tension wires are still too close to my old elementary school. The woods behind the Brenners' house on Rockmont Terrace is still a place where kids hang out and smoke. The high school still gets between five and eight national merit finalists a year, though when I was younger the list was more Jewish while today it tilts toward the Asian community.

We turned right on Monroe Avenue and drove past the split-level where I was raised. With its white paint and black shutters, with its kitchen, living room, and dining room up three steps on the left and its den and garage entrance two steps down on the right, our house, though a bit more threadbare than most, was pretty much indistinguishable from the other cookie-cutters on the block. What did make it stand out, the only thing really, was the wheelchair ramp. We put it in after my dad's third stroke when I was twelve years old. My friends and I liked to skateboard down it. We built a jump out of plywood and cinder blocks and put it at the bottom.

The nurse's car was in the driveway. She comes in during the days. We don't have someone full time. My father has been confined to a wheelchair for more than two decades now. He cannot speak. His mouth has an ugly down-hook curve on the left side of it. Half his body is totally paralyzed and the other half is not that much better.

When the driver made the turn at Darby Terrace, I saw that my house—our house—looked the same as it had a few weeks before. I didn't know what I'd expected. Yellow crime-scene tape maybe. Or a big bloodstain. But there was nothing hinting at what had occurred two weeks earlier.

When I'd bought the house, it'd been in foreclosure. For thirty-six years the Levinsky family had lived there, but no one really knew them. Mrs. Levinsky had been a seemingly sweet woman with a facial tic. Mr. Levinsky was an ogre who always yelled at her out on the lawn. He scared us. One time, we saw Mrs. Levinsky run out of the house in a nightgown, Mr. Levinsky chasing her with a shovel. Kids cut through every yard but theirs. When I was fresh out of college, rumors surfaced that he had abused his daughter Dina, a sad-eyed, stringy-haired waif I'd gone to school with since the first grade. Looking back on it, I must have been in a dozen classes with Dina Levinsky and I don't remember ever hearing her speak above a whisper and only then when forced to by well-meaning teachers. I never reached out to Dina. I don't know what I could have done, but I still wished that I'd tried.

Sometime during that year out of college, when the rumors of Dina's abuse began to take root, the Levinskys had upped and moved away. No one knew where. The bank took over the house and began to rent it out. Monica and I made an offer a few weeks before Tara was born.

Months later, when we first settled in, I'd stay awake at night and listen for—I don't know—sounds of some sort, for signs of the house's past, of the unhappiness within. I would try to figure out which bedroom had been Dina's and try to imagine what it'd been like for her, what it was like now, but there were no clues here. As I said earlier, a house is mortar and brick. Nothing more.

Two strange cars were parked in front of my house. My mother was standing by the front door. When I got out, she rushed me like those newscasts of returning POWs. She hugged me hard, and I got a whiff of too much perfume. I was still holding the Nike bag with the money, so it was hard for me to reciprocate.

Over my mother's shoulder, Detective Bob Regan stepped out of my house. Next to him stood a large black man with a gleaming shaved head and designer sunglasses. My mother whispered, "They've been waiting for you."

I nodded and moved toward them. Regan cupped a hand over his eyes, but only for effect. The sun was not that strong. The black man remained stonelike.

"Where have you been?" Regan asked. When I didn't reply right away, he added, "You left the hospital more than an hour ago."

I thought about the cell phone in my pocket. I thought about the bag of money in my hand. For now, I'd go for the semitruth. "I visited my wife's grave," I said.

"We need to talk, Marc."

"Step inside," I said.

We all moved back into the house. I stopped in the foyer. Monica's body had been found less than ten feet from where I now stood. Still in the entranceway, my eyes scanned the walls, looking for any telltale sign of violence. There was only one. I found it fairly quickly. Above the

Behrens lithograph near the stairwell, a bullet hole—one created from the only bullet that had not hit either Monica or me—had been spackled over. The spackle was too white for the wall. It would need a coat of paint.

I stared at it for a long moment. I heard a throat being cleared. It snapped me out of it. My mother rubbed my back and then headed to the kitchen. I showed Regan and his buddy to the living room. They took the two chairs. I took the couch. Monica and I hadn't truly decorated yet. The chairs dated back to my college dorm and looked it. The couch had come from Monica's apartment, a too-formal hand-me-down that looked like something kept in storage at Versailles. It was heavy and stiff and, even in its heyday, had had very little padding.

"This is Special Agent Lloyd Tickner," Regan began, motioning toward the black man. "He's with the FBI."

Tickner nodded. I nodded back.

Regan tried to smile at me. "Good to see you're feeling better," he began.

"I'm not," I said.

He looked puzzled.

"I won't be better until I have my daughter back."

"Right, of course. About that. We have a few follow-up questions, if you don't mind."

I let them know I didn't.

Regan coughed into his fist, buying himself time. "You have to understand something. We need to ask these questions. I don't necessarily like it. I'm sure you don't either, but these questions need to be asked. You understand?"

I didn't really, but this was no time to encourage elaboration. "Go ahead," I said.

"What can you can tell us about your marriage?"

A warning light flashed across my cortex. "What does my marriage have to do with anything?"

Regan shrugged. Tickner remained still. "We're just trying to put some pieces together, that's all."

"My marriage has nothing to do with any of this."

"I'm sure you're right, but look, Marc, the truth is, the trail is getting cold here. Every day that passes hurts us. We need to explore every avenue."

"The only avenue I'm interested in is the one that leads to my daughter."

"We understand that. That's the main focus of our investigation. Finding out what happened to your daughter. And you too. Let's not forget that someone tried to kill you too, am I right?"

"I guess."

"But, see, we can't just ignore these other issues."

"What other issues?"

"Your marriage, for example."

"What about it?"

"When you got married, Monica was already pregnant, right?"

"What does that . . . ?" I stopped myself. I wanted to attack with both barrels, but Lenny's words roared back at me. Don't talk to the cops without him present. I should call him. I knew that. But something about their tone and posture . . . if I stopped now and said I wanted to call my lawyer, it would make me look guilty. I had nothing to hide. Why feed into their suspicions? It would only distract them. Of course, I also knew that this was how they worked, how the police played the game, but I'm a doctor. Worse, a surgeon. We often make the mistake of thinking we're smarter than everyone else.

I went with honesty. "Yes, she was pregnant. So?"

"You're a plastic surgeon, correct?"

The change of subjects threw me. "That's right."

"You and your partner travel overseas and repair cleft palates, serious facial trauma, burns, that kind of thing?"

"Something like that, yes."

"You travel a lot then?"

"A fair amount," I said.

"In fact," Regan said, "in the two years before your marriage, isn't it fair to say that you were probably out of the country more than you were in it?"

"Possibly," I said. I squirmed against the padless cushion. "Could you tell me what the relevance of any of this is?"

Regan gave me his most disarming smile. "We're just trying to get a complete picture here."

"Picture of what?"

"Your work partner"—he checked his notes—"a Ms. Zia Leroux."

"Dr. Leroux," I corrected.

"Dr. Leroux, yes, thank you. Where is she now?"

"Cambodia."

"She's performing surgery on deformed children over there?"

"Yes."

Regan tilted his head, feigning confusion. "Weren't you originally scheduled to take that trip?"

"A long time ago."

"How long ago?"

"I'm not sure I follow."

"How long ago did you take yourself off the schedule?"

"I don't know," I said. "Eight, nine months ago maybe."

"And so Dr. Leroux went instead, correct?"

"Yes, that's correct. And the point of that is . . . ?"

He wouldn't bite. "You like your job, don't you, Marc?"

"Yes."

"You like traveling overseas? Doing this commendable work?"

"Sure."

Regan scratched his head too dramatically, pretending in the most obvious way to be bewildered. "So if you like the traveling, why did you cancel and let Dr. Leroux go in your place?"

Now I saw where he was heading. "I was cutting back," I said.

"On travel, you mean."

"Yes."

"Why?"

"Because I had other obligations."

"Those obligations being a wife and daughter, am I correct?"

I sat up and met his eye. "Point," I said. "Is there a point to all this?"

Regan settled back. The silent Tickner did likewise. "Just trying to get a complete picture, that's all."

"You said that already."

"Yeah, hold on, give me a second here." Regan flipped through the pages of his notebook. "Jeans and a red blouse."

"What?"

"Your wife." He pointed at his notes. "You said that she was wearing jeans and a red blouse that morning."

More images of Monica flooded me. I tried to stem the tide. "So?"

"When we found her body," Regan said, "she was naked."

The tremors began in my heart. They spread down my arms, tingling my fingers.

"You didn't know?"

I swallowed. "Was she . . . ?" My voice died in my throat.

"No," Regan said. "Not a mark on her, other than the bullet holes." He did that help-me-understand head-tilt again. "We found her dead in this very room. Did she often parade in here with no clothes on?"

"I told you." Overload. I tried to process this new data, keep up with him. "She was wearing jeans and a red blouse."

"So she was dressed already?"

I remembered the sound of the shower. I remembered her coming out, throwing her hair back, lying on the bed, working the jeans over the hips. "Yes."

"Definitely?"

"Definitely."

"We've been through the whole house. We can't find a red blouse. Jeans, sure. She had several pairs. But no red blouse. Don't you think that's odd?"

"Wait a second," I said. "Her clothes weren't near her body?"

"Nope."

This made no sense. "I'll look in her closet, then," I said.

"We already did that, but sure, go ahead. Of course, I'd still like to know how clothes she was wearing ended up back in her closet, wouldn't you?"

I had no answer.

"Do you own a gun, Dr. Seidman?"

Another subject shift. I tried to keep up, but my head was spinning. "Yes."

"What kind?"

"A Smith and Wesson thirty-eight. It belonged to my father."

"Where do you keep it?"

"There's a compartment in the bedroom closet. It's on the top shelf in a lockbox."

Regan reached behind him and pulled out the metal lockbox. "This it?"

"Yes."

"Open it."

He tossed it to me. I caught it. The gray-blue metal was cold. But more than that, it felt shockingly light. I moved the wheels to the right combination and flipped it open. I poked through the legal documents—the car title, the deed on the house, the property survey—but that was just to get my bearings. I knew right away. The gun was gone.

"You and your wife were both shot with a thirty-eight," Regan said. "And yours seems to be missing."

I kept my eyes on the box, as if I expected the weapon to suddenly materialize in it. I tried to put it together, but nothing was coming to me.

"Any idea where the gun is?"

I shook my head.

"And something else strange," Regan said.

I looked up at him.

"You and Monica were shot with *different* thirty-eights."

"Excuse me?"

He nodded. "Yeah, I found it hard to believe too. I made ballistics check it twice. You and your wife were shot with two different guns, both thirty-eights—and yours seems to be missing." Regan shrugged theatrically. "Help me understand, Marc."

I looked at their faces. I didn't like what I saw. Lenny's warning came back to me again, firmer this time. "I want to call my lawyer," I said.

"You sure?"

"Yes."

"Go ahead."

My mother had been standing by the kitchen door, wringing her hands. How much had she heard? Judging by her face, too much. Mom looked at me expectantly. I nodded, and she went to call Lenny. I folded my arms, but that didn't feel right. I tapped my foot. Tickner took off the sunglasses. He met my eye and spoke for the first time.

"What's in the bag?" he asked me.

I just looked at him.

"That gym bag you been groping." Tickner's voice, belying his tough looks, had a nerdy cadence to it, a quasi-whine quality. "What's in it?"

This had all been a mistake. I should have listened to Lenny. I should have called him right away. Now I was not sure how to reply. In the background, I heard my mother urging Lenny to hurry. I was sifting through a response that might work as a semitruthful stall—none were convincing—when a sound ripped my attention away.

The cell phone, the one the kidnappers had sent to my father-in-law, began to ring.

chapter 4

Tickner and Regan waited for me to answer.

I excused myself, rising before they had a chance to react. My hand fumbled with the phone as I hurried outside. The sun hit me full in the face. I blinked and looked down at the keypad. The phone's answer button was located in a different spot from mine. Across the street, two girls donning brightly hued helmets were riding neon bikes. Ribbon strips of pink cascaded out of the handlebars of one.

When I was little, this neighborhood sheltered more than a dozen kids my age. We used to meet up after school. I don't remember what games we played—we were never organized enough for, say, a real game of baseball or anything like that—but they all involved hiding and chasing and some form of feigned (or borderline-real) violence. Childhood in suburbia is purportedly a time of innocence, but how many of those days ended in tears for at least one kid? We would argue, shift alliances, make declarations of friendship and war, and like some short-term memory case, it was all forgotten the next day. A clean slate every afternoon. New coalitions forged. A new kid running home in tears.

My thumb finally touched down on the right button. I pressed it and brought the phone to my ear, all in one move. My heart thumped against my rib cage. I cleared my throat and, feeling like a total idiot, I simply said, "Hello?"

"Answer yes or no." The voice had the robotic hum of one of those customer-care phone systems, the ones that tell you to press one for service, press two to check the status of an order. "Do you have the money?"

"Yes."

"You know the Garden State Plaza?"

"In Paramus," I said.

"In exactly two hours from now, I want you parked at the north lot. That's near Nordstrom's. Section Nine. Someone will approach your car."

"But—"

"If you're not alone, we disappear. If you're being followed, we disappear. If I smell a cop, we disappear. There will be no second chances. Do you understand?"

"Yes, but when—"

Click.

I let my hand drop to my side. Numbness seeped in. I did not fight it. The little girls across the street were quarreling now. I couldn't hear the specifics, but the word *my* popped up a lot, that simple syllable accentuated and drawn out. An SUV sped around the corner. I watched it as though from above. The brakes shrieked. The driver-side door was open before the car had come to a complete stop.

It was Lenny. He took one look at me and picked up his pace. "Marc?"

"You were right." I nodded toward the house. Regan was standing by the door now. "They think I'm involved."

Lenny's face darkened. His eyes narrowed, his pupils shrinking to pinpoints. In sports, you call it putting on your "game face." Lenny was becoming Cujo. He stared at Regan as if deciding which limb to chew off. "You talked to them?"

"A little."

Lenny jerked his gaze toward me. "Didn't you tell them you wanted counsel?"

"Not at first."

"Damn it, Marc, I told you—"

"I got a ransom demand."

That made Lenny pull up. I checked my watch. Paramus was a forty-minute ride. With traffic, it could take as much as an hour. I had time, but not much. I started filling him in. Lenny gave Regan another glare and led me farther away from the house. We stopped at the curb, those familiar cloud-gray stones that lie on property lines like sets of teeth, and then, like two children, we squatted deep and sat on them. Our knees were at our chins. I could see Lenny's skin between the argyle sock and tapered cuff. Squatting like this was uncomfortable as hell. The sun was in our eyes. We both looked off rather than at each other, again just like in our youths. It made it easier to spill it all out.

I spoke quickly. Midway through my recap, Regan began to move toward us. Lenny turned to him and shouted, "Your balls."

Regan stopped. "What?"

"Are you arresting my client?"

"No."

Lenny pointed toward Regan's crotch. "Then I'm going to have them bronzed and hanging from my rearview mirror, if you take another step."

Regan straightened his spine. "We have some questions for your client."

"Tough. Go abuse the rights of someone with a lesser lawyer."

Lenny made a dismissive gesture and nodded at me to continue. Regan did not look happy, but he took two steps back. I glanced at my watch again. Only five minutes had passed since the ransom call. I finished up while Lenny kept the laser glare aimed at Regan.

"You want my opinion?" he said.

"Yes."

Still glaring. "I think you should tell them."

"You sure?"

"Hell, no."

"Would you?" I said. "I mean, if it was one of your kids?"

Lenny gave it a few seconds. "I can't put myself in your place, if that's what you mean. But yeah, I think I would. I play the odds. The odds are better when you tell the cops. Doesn't mean it works out every time, but they're experts at this. We're not." Lenny put his elbows on his knees and rested his chin in his hands—a pose from his youth. "That's the opinion of Lenny the Friend," he went on. "Lenny the Friend would encourage you to tell them."

"And Lenny the Lawyer?" I asked.

"He would be more insistent. He would strongly urge you to come forward."

"Why?"

"If you go off with two million dollars and it vanishes—even if you get Tara back—their suspicions will be, to put it mildly, aroused."

"I don't care about that. I just want Tara back."

"Understood. Or should I say, Lenny the Friend understands."

Now it was Lenny's turn to check his watch. My insides felt hollow, scooped out canoe-style. I could almost hear the tick-tick. It was maddening. I tried again to do the rational thing, to list the pros on the right, the cons on the left, and then add them up. But the tick-tick would not stop.

Lenny had talked about playing the odds. I don't gamble. I'm not a risk taker. Across the street one of the little girls shouted, "I'm telling!" She stormed down the street. The other girl laughed at her and got back on her bike. I felt my eyes well up. I wished like hell Monica were here. I shouldn't be making this decision alone. She should be in on this, too.

I looked back at the front door. Regan and Tickner were both outside now. Regan had his arms folded across his chest, bouncing on the balls of his feet. Tickner did not move, his face the same placid pool. Were these men I could trust with my daughter's life? Would they put Tara first, or as Edgar had suggested, would they follow some unseen agenda?

The tick-tick grew louder, more insistent.

Someone had murdered my wife. Someone had taken my child. For the past few days, I had asked myself why—why us?—trying again to stay rational and not allowing myself extended forays in the deep end of the pity pool. But no answer came. I could see no motive and maybe that was most frightening of all. Maybe there was no reason. Maybe it was just pure bad luck.

Lenny stared straight ahead and waited. Tick, tick, tick.

"Let's tell them," I said.

Their reaction surprised me. They panicked.

Regan and Tickner tried to hide it, of course, but their body language was suddenly all wrong—the flutter in the eyes, the tightness at the corners of their mouths, the unduly modulated, FM-soft-rock timbre in their tones. The time frame was simply too close for them. Tickner quickly dialed up the FBI specialist on kidnapping negotiations to enlist his help. He cupped his hand around the mouthpiece while he spoke into it. Regan got hold of his police colleagues in Paramus.

When Tickner hung up, he said to me, "We'll get people to cover the mall. Discreetly, of course. We're going to try to get men in cars near every exit and on Route Seventeen in both directions. We'll have people inside the mall by all the entrances. But I want you to listen to me closely, Dr. Seidman. Our expert tells us that we should try to stall him. Maybe we can get the kidnapper to postpone—"

"No," I said.

"They won't just run away," Tickner said. "They want the money."

"My daughter has been with them for almost three weeks," I said. "I'm not putting this off."

He nodded, not liking it, trying to keep up with the placid. "Then I want to put a man in the car with you."

"No."

"He can duck down in the back."

"No," I said again.

Tickner tried another avenue. "Or better yet—we've done this before—we tell the kidnapper that you can't drive. Hell, you're just out of the hospital. We have one of our men drive instead. We say it's your cousin."

I frowned and looked at Regan. "Didn't you say you thought my sister might be involved?"

"It's possible, yes."

"Don't you think she'd know if this guy was a cousin or not?"

Tickner and Regan both hesitated and then nodded in unison. "Good point," Regan said.

Lenny and I exchanged a glance. These were the professionals I was trusting with Tara's life. The thought was not comforting. I started for the door.

Tickner put a hand on my shoulder. "Where are you going?"

"Where the hell do you think?"

"Sit down, Dr. Seidman."

"No time," I countered. "I have to start heading up there. There could be traffic."

"We can clear the traffic."

"Oh, and that won't look suspicious," I said.

"I highly doubt he's going to follow you from here."

I spun on him. "And you'd be willing to risk your child's life on that?"

He paused just long enough.

"You don't get it," I went on, in his face now. "I don't care about the money or if they get away. I just want my daughter back."

"We understand that," Tickner said, "but there is something you're forgetting."

"What?"

"Please," he said. "Sit down."

"Look, do me a favor, okay? Just let me stand. I'm a doctor. I know the delivering-bad-news drill as well as anyone. Don't try to play me."

Tickner held his palms up and said, "Fair enough." He proceeded to take a long, lingering breath. Stall tactic. I was not in the mood.

"So what is it?" I said.

"Whoever did this," he began, "they shot you. They killed your wife."

"I understand that."

"No, I don't think you do. Think about it a second. We can't just let you go in on your own. Whoever did this tried to end your life. They shot you twice and left you for dead."

"Marc," Regan said, moving closer, "we threw some wild theories at you before. The problem is, that's all they are. Theories. We don't know what these guys are really after. Maybe this is just a simple kidnapping, but if it is, it's not like any we've seen before." His interrogation face was gone now, replaced with an aw-shucks, eyebrow-raised attempt at openness. "What we do know with certainty is that they tried to kill you. You don't try to kill the parents, if you're just after ransom."

"Maybe they planned on getting the money from my father-in-law," I said.

"Then why did they wait so long?"

I had no answer.

"Maybe," Tickner went on, "this isn't about kidnapping at all. At least, not at first. Maybe that's become a sideline. Maybe you and your wife were the targets all along. And maybe they want to finish the job."

"You think this is a setup?"

"It's a strong possibility, yes."

"So what are you advising?"

Tickner took that one. "Don't go alone. Buy us some time so we can prepare properly. Let them call you back."

I looked at Lenny. He saw it and nodded. "That's not possible," Lenny said.

Tickner turned at him hard. "With all due respect, your client is in grave danger here."

"So is my daughter," I said. Simple words. This decision was a no-brainer when you kept it simple. I pulled away and started toward my car. "Keep your people at a distance."

chapter 5

There was no traffic, so I made it to the mall with plenty of time to spare. I turned the engine off and sat back. I glanced around. I figured that the feds and cops were probably still on me, but I couldn't see them. That was a good thing, I guess.

Now what?

No idea. I waited some more. I fiddled with the radio, but nothing caught my attention. I turned on the CD player/tape deck. When Donald Fagan of Steely Dan began singing "Black Cow," I felt a slight jerk. I had not listened to this particular tape since, what, my college days. Why did Monica have it? And then, with a renewed pang, I realized that Monica had been the last to use this car, that this may have been the last song she ever heard.

I watched the shoppers prepare for mall entry. I concentrated on the young mothers; the way they flipped open the back door of the minivan; the way they unfolded the baby strollers midair with a magician's flourish; the way they struggled to release their offspring from safety seats that reminded me of Buzz Aldrin's on *Apollo 11*; the way the mothers skirted forward, heads high, smartly pressing the remote control that slid the minivan door to a close.

The mothers, all of them, looked so blasé. Their children were with them. Their safety, what with the five-star side-collision rating and NASA-sleek car seats, was a given. And here I sat with a bag of ransom money, hoping to get my daughter back. The thin line. I wanted to roll down the window and shout out a warning.

We were getting close to drop time. The sun beat down on my windshield. I reached for my sunglasses but then thought better of it. I don't know why. Would putting on my sunglasses somehow make the kid-napper uneasy? No, I don't think so. Or maybe it would. Better to just leave them off. Take no chances.

My shoulders bunched up. I kept trying to look around without, for some odd reason, looking conspicuous about it. Whenever someone parked near me or walked anywhere in the vicinity of my car, my stomach tightened and I wondered:

Was Tara nearby?

We were at the two-hour mark now. I wanted this over. The next few minutes would decide everything. I knew that. Calm. I needed to stay calm. Tickner's warning reverberated in my head. Would someone simply walk up to my car and blow my brains out?

It was, I realized, a very real possibility.

When the cell phone rang, I started forward. I brought it to my ear and barked a too-quick hello.

The robotic voice said, "Pull out by the west exit."

I was confused. "Which way is west?"

"Follow the signs for Route Four. Take the overpass. We're watch-ing. If someone follows, we disappear. Keep the phone near your ear."

I obeyed with gusto; my right hand pressed the phone against my ear to the point where I started losing circulation. My left hand gripped the wheel as if preparing to tear it off.

"Get on Route Four heading west."

I took the right turn and jug-handled onto the highway. I looked in my rearview mirror to see if anyone was following me. Hard to tell.

The robotic voice said, "You'll see a strip mall."

"There's a million strip malls," I said.

"It's on the right, next to a store selling baby cribs. In front of the Paramus Road exit."

I saw it. "Okay."

"Pull in there. You'll see a driveway on the left. Take it to the back and kill the engine. Have the money ready for me."

I understood immediately why the kidnapper had picked this spot. There was only one way in. The stores were all for rent, except for the baby-crib place. That was on the far right. In other words, it was self-contained and directly off a highway. There was no way anyone could come around back or even slow down without being noticed.

I hope the feds understood that.

When I reached the back of the building, I saw a man standing by a van. He wore a red-and-black flannel shirt with black jeans, dark sunglasses, and a Yankee baseball cap. I tried to find something distinct, but the word that came to mind was *average*. Average height, average build. The only thing was his nose. Even from this distance I could see it was misshapen, like an ex-boxer's. But was that real or some kind of disguise? I didn't know.

I checked out the van. There was a sign for "B & T Electricians" of Ridgewood, New Jersey. No phone number or address. The license plate was from New Jersey. I memorized it.

The man raised a cell phone to his lips walkie-talkie style, and I heard the mechanical voice say, "I'm going to approach. Pass the money through the window. Do not get out of the car. Do not say a word to me. When we're safely away with the money, I'll call and tell you where to pick up your daughter."

The man in red flannel and black jeans lowered the phone and approached. His shirt was untucked. Did he have a gun? I couldn't tell. And even if he did, what could I do about it now? I hit the button to open the windows. They didn't budge. The key needed to be turned. The man was getting closer. The Yankee cap was pulled down until the brim touched the sunglasses. I reached for the key and gave it a tiny twist. The lights on the dashboard sprung to life. I pressed the button again. The window slid down.

Again I tried to find something about the man that was distinct. His walk was slightly off balance, as though maybe he'd had a drink or two, but he didn't look nervous. His face was unshaven and patchy. His hands were dirty. His black jeans were ripped in the right knee. His sneakers, canvas high-tops from Converse, had seen better days.

When the man was only two steps from the car, I pushed the bag up to the window and braced myself. I held my breath. Without breaking stride, the man took the money and swirled toward the van. He hurried his step now. The van's back doors opened and he leapt in, the door immediately closing behind him. It was as if the van had swallowed him whole.

The driver gunned the engine. The van sped off and now, for the first time, I realized that there was a back entrance onto a side road. The van shot down it and was gone.

I was alone.

I stayed where I was and waited for the cell phone to ring. My heart pounded. My shirt was drenched in sweat. No other car traveled back here. The pavement was cracked. Cardboard boxes jutted out of the garbage Dumpster. Broken bottles littered the ground. My eyes stared hard at the ground, trying to make out the words on faded beer labels.

Fifteen minutes passed.

I kept picturing my reunion with my daughter, how I would find her and pick her up and cradle her and hush her with gentle sounds. The cell phone. The cell phone was supposed to ring. That was part of what I was picturing. The phone ringing, the robotic voice giving me instructions. Those were parts one and two. Why wasn't the damn phone cooperating?

A Buick Le Sabre pulled into the lot, keeping a decent distance away from me. I did not recognize the driver, but Tickner was in the passenger seat. Our eyes met. I tried to read something in his expression, but he was still pure stoic.

I stared now at the cell phone, not daring to look away. The tick-tick was back, this time slow and thudding.

Ten more minutes passed before the phone grudgingly issued its tinny song. I had it to my ear before the sound had a chance to travel.

"Hello?" I said.

Nothing.

Tickner watched me closely. He gave me a slight nod, though I had no idea why. His driver still had both hands on the wheel at ten and two o'clock.

"Hello?" I tried again.

The robotic voice said, "I warned you about contacting the cops."

Ice flooded my veins.

"No second chance."

And then the phone went dead.

chapter 6

There was no escape.

I longed for the numb. I longed for the comatose state of the hospital. I longed for that IV bag and the free flow of anesthetics. My skin had been torn off. My nerve endings were exposed now. I could feel everything.

Fear and helplessness overwhelmed me. The fear locked me in a room, while the helplessness—the awful knowing that I had blown it and could do nothing to alleviate my child's pain—wrapped me in a straitjacket and turned out the lights. I may very well have been losing my mind.

Days passed in a syrupy haze. Most of the time I sat by the phone—by several phones, actually. My home phone, my cell phone, and the kidnapper's cell phone. I bought a charger for the kidnapper's cell, so I could keep it working. I stayed on the couch. The phones sat on my right. I tried to look away, to watch television even, because I remembered that old saying about a watched kettle never boiling. I still stole glances at those damn phones, fearing that they might somehow flee, willing them to ring.

I tried to mine that supernatural father-daughter connection again, the one that had insisted earlier that Tara was still alive. The pulse was still there, I thought (or at least, made myself believe), beating faintly, the connection now tenuous at best.

"No second chance . . ."

To add to my guilt, I had dreamt last night of a woman other than Monica—my old love, Rachel. It was one of those time-and-reality warp dreams, the ones where the world is totally alien and even contradictory and yet you don't question any of it. Rachel and I were together. We had never broken up yet we had been apart all these years. I was still thirty-four, but she hadn't aged since the day she left me. Tara was still my daughter in the dream—she had, in fact, never been kidnapped—but somehow she was also Rachel's, though Rachel wasn't the mother. You've probably had dreams like this. Nothing really makes sense, but you don't challenge what you see. When I woke up, the dream faded into smoke the way dreams always do. I was left with an aftertaste and a longing that pulled with unexpected force.

My mother hung around too much. She had just plopped another tray of food in front of me. I ignored it and for the millionth time, Mom repeated her mantra: "You have to keep up your strength for Tara."

"Right, Mom, strength is the key here. Maybe if I do enough bench presses, that'll bring her back."

Mom shook her head, refusing to rise to the bait. It was a cruel thing to say. She was hurting too. Her granddaughter was missing and her son was in horrific shape. I watched her sigh and head back to the kitchen. I didn't apologize.

Tickner and Regan visited frequently. They reminded me of Shakespeare's sound and fury signifying nothing. They told me about all the technological wonders that were being utilized in the quest to find Tara—stuff involving DNA and latent prints and security cameras and airports and tollbooths and train stations and tracers and surveillance and labs. They trotted out the tried-and-true cop clichés like "no stone unturned" and "every possible avenue." I nodded at them. They had me look at mug shots, but the bagman in flannel was not in any of the books.

"We ran a trace on B and T Electricians," Regan told me that first night. "The company exists, but they use magnetic signs, the kind you can just peel off a truck. Someone stole one two months ago. They never thought it was worth reporting."

"What about the license plate?" I asked.

"The number you gave us doesn't exist."

"How can that be?"

"They used two old license plates," Regan explained. "See, what they do is, they cut the license plates in half and then they weld the left half of one with the right half of the other."

I just stared at him.

"There is something of a bright side to that," Regan added.

"Oh?"

"It means we're dealing with professionals. They knew that if you contacted us, we'd be set up at the mall. They found a drop spot that we couldn't get to without being seen. They have us tracking down useless leads with the fake sign and welded license plates. Like I said, they're pros."

"And that's good because . . . ?"

"Pros usually aren't bloodthirsty."

"So what are they doing?"

"Our theory," Regan said, "is that they're softening you up, so they can ask for more money."

Softening me up. It was working.

My father-in-law called after the ransom fiasco. I could hear the disappointment in Edgar's voice. I don't want to sound unkind here—Edgar was the one who provided the money and made it clear he would do so again—but the disappointment sounded more aimed at me, at the fact that I had not taken his advice about not contacting the police, than at the final outcome.

Of course, he was right about that. I had messed up big time.

I tried to participate in the investigation, but the police were far from encouraging. In the movies the authorities cooperate and share information with the victim. I naturally asked Tickner and Regan a lot of questions about the case. They didn't answer. They never discussed specifics with me. They treated my interrogatories with near disdain. I wanted to know, for example, more about how my wife was found, about why she'd been naked. They stonewalled.

Lenny was at the house a lot. He had trouble meeting my eye because he, too, blamed himself for encouraging me to come forward. The faces of Regan and Tickner fluctuated between guilt because everything had gone so wrong and guilt of another kind, like maybe I, the grieving husband and father, had been behind this from the get-go. They wanted to know about my shaky marriage to Monica. They wanted to know about my missing gun. It was exactly as Lenny had predicted. The more time passed, the more the authorities aimed their sights on the only available suspect.

Yours truly.

After we hit the one-week mark, the police and FBI presence started fading. Tickner and Regan no longer came by very much. They checked their watches more often. They excused themselves for phone calls involving other cases. I understood that, of course. There had been no new leads. Things were quieting down. Part of me welcomed the respite.

And then, on the ninth day, everything changed.

At ten o'clock, I began to get undressed and ready for bed. I was alone. I love my family and friends, but they began to realize that I needed some time by myself. They had all left before dinner. I ordered delivery from Hunan Garden and, per Mom's earlier instructions, ate for strength.

I looked at the bedside alarm clock. That's how I knew that the time was exactly 10:18 P.M. I glanced at the window, just a casual land sweep. In the dark, I almost missed it—nothing consciously registered anyway—but something snagged my gaze. I stopped and looked again.

There, standing on my walk like a stone, staring at my house, was a woman. I assume that she was staring. I did not know for certain. Her face was lost in the shadows. She had long hair—that much I could see in the silhouette—and she wore a long coat. Her hands were jammed into her pockets.

She just stood there.

I was not sure what to make of it. We were in the news, of course. Reporters stopped by at all hours. I looked up and down the street. No cars, no news vans, nothing. She had come on foot. Again that was not unusual. I live in a suburban neighborhood. People take walks all the time, usually with a dog or spouse or both, but it was hardly earth shattering for a woman to be walking alone.

Then why had she stopped?

Morbid curiosity, I figured.

She looked tall from here, but that was pretty much a guess. I wondered what to do. An uneasy feeling slithered up my back. I grabbed my sweatshirt and threw it over my pajama top. Ditto with a pair of sweatpants and the bottoms. I looked out the window again. The woman stiffened.

She had seen me.

The woman turned and began to hurry away. My chest felt tight. I tried to open the window. It was stuck. I hit the sides to loosen it and tried again. It grudgingly gave me an inch. I lowered my mouth to the opening.

"Wait!"

She picked up the pace.

"Please, hold up a second."

She broke into a run. Damn. I turned away and sprinted after her toward the door. I had no idea where my slippers were and there was no time for shoes. I ran outside. The grass tickled my feet. I sprinted in the direction she had gone. I tried to follow, but I lost her.

When I got back inside my house, I called Regan and told him what had happened. It sounded stupid even as I said it. A woman had been standing in front of my house. Big deal. Regan, too, sounded thoroughly unimpressed. I convinced myself that it was nothing, just a nosy neighbor. I climbed back into bed, flipped the television, and eventually I closed my eyes.

The night, however, was not over.

It was four in the morning when my phone rang. I was in the state I now refer to as sleep. I never fall into true slumber anymore. I hang above it with my eyes shut. The nights struggle by like the days. The separation between the two is the flimsiest of curtains. At night, my body manages to rest, but my mind refuses to shut down.

With my eyes closed, I was replaying the morning of the attack for the umpteenth time, hoping to stir a new memory. I started where I am now: in the bedroom. I remembered my alarm clock going off. Lenny and I were going to play racquetball that morning. We'd started playing every Wednesday about a year before, and so far, we had progressed to the point where our games had improved from "pitiful" to "almost remedial." Monica was awake and in the shower. I was scheduled for surgery at 11:00 A.M. I got up and looked in on Tara. I headed back to the bedroom. Monica was out of shower now and putting on her jeans. I went down to the kitchen, still in my pajamas, opened the cabinet to the right of the Westinghouse refrigerator, chose the raspberry granola bar over the blueberry (I had actually told this detail to Regan recently, as if it might be relevant), and bent over the sink while I ate. . . .

Bam, that was it. Nothing until the hospital.

The phone rang a second time. My eyes opened.

My hand found the phone. I picked it up and said, "Hello?"

"It's Detective Regan. I'm with Agent Tickner. We'll be over in two minutes."

I swallowed. "What is it?"

"Two minutes."

He hung up.

I got out of bed. I glanced out the window, half expecting to see that woman again. No one was there. My jeans from yesterday were crumpled on the floor. I slid them on. I pulled a sweatshirt over my head and made my way down the stairs. I opened the front door and peered out. A police car turned the corner. Regan was driving. Tickner was in the passenger seat. I don't think that I had ever seen them arrive in the same vehicle.

This, I knew, would not be good news.

The two men stepped out of the car. Nausea swept over me. I had prepared myself for this visit since the ransom had gone wrong. I'd even gone so far as to rehearse in my mind how it would all happen—how they would deliver the hammer blow and how I would nod and thank them and excuse myself. I practiced my reaction. I knew precisely how it would all go down.

But now, as I watched Regan and Tickner head toward me, those defenses fled. Panic set in. My body began to shiver. I could barely stand. My knees wobbled, and I leaned against the door frame. The two men moved in step. I was reminded of an old war movie, the scene where the officers come to the mother's house with solemn faces. I shook my head, wishing them away.

When they reached the door, the two men pushed inside.

"We have something to show you," Regan said.

I turned and followed. Regan flicked on a lamp, but it didn't provide much light. Tickner moved to the couch. He opened his laptop computer. The monitor sprang to life, bathing him in an LCD-blue.

"We had a break," Regan explained.

I moved closer.

"Your father-in-law gave us a list of the serial numbers on the ransom bills, remember?"

"Yes."

"One of those bills was used at a bank yesterday afternoon. Agent Tickner is bringing up a video feed right now."

"From the bank?" I asked.

"Yes. We downloaded the video onto his laptop. Twelve hours ago, someone brought a hundred-dollar bill to this bank in order to get smaller notes. We want you to take a look at the video."

I sat next to Tickner. He pressed a button. The video started up immediately. I expected black-and-white or poor, grainy quality. This feed had neither. The angle was shot from above in almost too-brilliant color. A bald man was talking to a teller. There was no sound.

"I don't recognize him," I said.

"Wait."

The bald man said something to the teller. They appeared to be sharing a good-natured chuckle. He picked up a slip of paper and waved a good-bye. The teller gave a small wave back. The next person in line approached the booth. I heard myself groan.

It was my sister, Stacy.

The numb I had longed for suddenly flooded me. I don't know why. Perhaps because two polar emotions pulled at me simultaneously. One, dread. My own sister had done this. My own sister, whom I loved dearly, had betrayed me. But, two, hope—we now had hope. We had a lead. And if it was Stacy, I could not believe that she would harm Tara.

"Is that your sister?" Regan asked, pointing his finger at her image.

"Yes." I looked at him. "Where was this taken?"

"The Catskills," he said. "A town called—"

"Montague," I finished for him.

Tickner and Regan looked at each other. "How do you know that?" But I was already heading for the door. "I know where she is."

chapter 7

My grandfather had loved to hunt. I always found this strange because he was such a gentle, soft-spoken soul. He never talked about his passion. He didn't hang deer heads over the fireplace mantel. He did not keep trophy pictures or souvenir antlers or whatever else hunters liked to do with carcasses. He did not hunt with friends or family members. Hunting was a solitary activity for my grandfather; he did not explain, defend, or share it with others.

In 1956, Grandpa purchased a small cabin in the hunting woods of Montague, New York. The cost, or so I am told, was under three thousand dollars. I doubt that it would fetch much more today. There was only one bedroom. The structure managed to be rustic without any of the charm associated with that term. It was almost impossible to find—the dirt road stopped two hundred yards before the cabin. You had to hike along a root-infested trail the rest of the way.

When he died four years ago, my grandmother inherited it. At least, that is what I assumed. No one really thought about it much. My grandparents had retired to Florida almost a decade before. My grandmother was in the murky throes of Alzheimer's now. The old cabin, I guessed, was part of her estate. In terms of taxes and whatever expenses, it was probably deep in arrears.

When we were children, my sister and I spent one weekend each summer with our grandparents at the cabin. I did not like it. Nature to me was boredom occasionally broken up by an onslaught of mosquito bites. There was no TV. We went to bed too early and in too much darkness. During the day, the deep silence was too often shattered by the charming echo of shotgun blasts. We spent most of our time taking walks, an activity I find tedious to this very day. One year, my mother packed me only khaki-colored clothes. I spent two days terrified that a hunter would mistake me for a deer.

Stacy, on the other hand, found solace out there. Even as a young child, she seemed to revel in the escape from our suburban rat-maze of school and extracurricular activities, of sport teams and popularity. She would wander for hours. She would pick leaves off the trees and collect inchworms in a jar. She would shuffle her feet across carpets of fallen pine needles.

I explained about the cabin to Tickner and Regan as we sped up Route 87. Tickner radioed the police department in Montague. I still remembered how to find the cabin, but describing it was harder. I did my best. Regan kept his foot on the gas pedal. It was four-thirty in the morning. There was no traffic and no need for the siren. We reached Exit 16 on the New York Thruway and sped past the Woodbury Common Outlet Center.

The woods were a blur. We were not far now. I told him where to turn off. The car wound up and down back roads that had not changed one iota in the past three decades.

Fifteen minutes later, we were there.

Stacy.

My sister had never been very attractive. That may have been part of her problem. Yes, that sounds like nonsense. It is silly, really. But I lay it out for you anyway. No one asked Stacy to any prom. Boys never called. She had very few friends. Of course, there are many adolescents with such hardships. Adolescence is always a war; no one gets out unscathed. And yes, my father's illness was a tremendous burden on us. But that doesn't explain it.

In the end, after all the theories and psychoanalyzing, after all the combing through her childhood traumas, I think what went wrong with my sister was more basic. She had some kind of chemical imbalance in her brain. Too much of one compound flowing here, not enough of another flowing there. We did not recognize the warning signs soon enough. Stacy was depressed in an era when such behavior was mistaken for sullen. Or maybe, yet again, I use this sort of convoluted rationale to justify my own indifference to her. Stacy was just my weird younger sister. I had my own problems, thank you very much.

I had the selfishness of a teenager, a truly redundant description if ever I've heard one.

Either way, be the origins of my sister's unhappiness physiological, psychological, or the deluxe combo plan, Stacy's destructive journey was over.

My little sister was dead.

We found her on the floor, curled up in a tight fetal position. That was how she had slept when she was a child, her knees up to her chest, her chin tucked. But even though there was not a mark on her, I could see that she was not sleeping. I bent down. Stacy's eyes were open. She stared straight at me, unblinking, questioning. She still looked so very lost. That wasn't supposed to be. Death was supposed to bring solitude. Death was supposed to bring the peace she had found so elusive in life. Why, I wondered, did Stacy still look so damn lost?

A hypodermic needle lay on the floor by her side, her companion in death as in life. Drugs, of course. Intentional or otherwise, I did not yet know. I had no time to dwell on it either. The police fanned out. I wrested my eyes away from her.

Tara.

The place was a mess. Raccoons had found their way in and made a little home for themselves. The couch where my grandfather had taken his naps, always with his arms folded, was torn up. The stuffing had bled onto the floor. Springs popped up looking for someone to stab. The entire place smelled like urine and dead animals.

I stopped and listened for the sound of a crying baby. There was none. Nothing in here. Only one other room. I dived into the bedroom behind a policeman. The room was dark. I hit the light switch. Nothing happened. Flashlights sliced through the black like saber swords. My eyes scanned the room. When I saw it, I nearly cried out.

There was a playpen.

It was one of those modern Pack 'N Plays with the mesh sides that fold up for easy transport. Monica and I have one. I don't know anyone with a baby who doesn't. The product tag dangled off the side. It had to be new.

Tears came to my eyes. The flashlight cut past the Pack 'N Play, giving it a strobe-light effect. It appeared to be empty. My heart sank. I ran over anyway, in case the light had caused an optical illusion, in case Tara was nestled so sweetly that she—I don't know—barely made a bump.

But there was only a blanket inside.

A soft voice—a voice from a whispery, inescapable nightmare—floated across the room: "Oh Christ."

I swiveled my head toward the sound. The voice came again, weaker this time. "In here," a policeman said. "In the closet."

Tickner and Regan were already there. They both looked inside. Even in the dim glow, I saw their faces lose color.

My feet stumbled forward. I crossed the room, nearly falling, grabbing the closet doorknob at the last moment to regain my balance. I looked through the doorway and saw it. And then, as I looked down at the frayed fabric, I could actually feel my insides implode and crumble into ash.

There, lying on the floor, torn and discarded, was a pink one-piece outfit with black penguins.

eighteen months later

chapter 8

Lydia saw the widow sitting alone at Starbucks.

The widow was on a stool seat, gazing absently at the gentle trickle of pedestrians. Her coffee was near the window, the steam forming a circle on the glass. Lydia watched her for a moment. The devastation was still there—the battle-scarred, thousand-yard stare, the posture of the defeated, the hair with no sheen, the shake in the hands.

Lydia ordered a grande skim latte with an extra shot of espresso. The *barista*, a too-skinny black-clad youth with a goatee, gave her the shot "on the house." Men, even ones this young, did stuff like that for Lydia. She lowered her sunglasses and thanked him. He nearly wet himself.

Lydia moved toward the condiment table, knowing he was checking out her ass. Again she was used to it. She added a packet of Equal to her drink. The Starbucks was fairly empty—there were plenty of seats—but Lydia slid up on the stool immediately next to the widow. Sensing her, the widow startled out of her reverie.

"Wendy?" Lydia said.

Wendy Burnet, the widow, turned toward the soft voice.

"I'm very sorry for your loss," Lydia said.

Lydia smiled at her. She had, she knew, a warm smile. She wore a tailored gray suit on her petite, tight frame. The skirt was slit fairly high. Business sexy. Her eyes had that shiny-wet thing going, her nose small and slightly upturned. Her hair was auburn ringlets, but she could—and often did—change that.

Wendy Burnet stared just long enough for Lydia to wonder if she'd been recognized. Lydia had seen that stare plenty of times before, that unsure I-know-you-from-somewhere expression, even though she had not been on TV since she turned thirteen. Some people would even comment, "Hey, you know who you look like?" but Lydia—she had been billed as Larissa Dane back then—would shrug it away.

But alas, this hesitation was not like that. Wendy Burnet was still shell-shocked from the horrible death of her beloved. It simply took her a while to register and assimilate unfamiliar data. She was probably wondering how to react, if she should pretend she knew Lydia or not.

After another few seconds, Wendy Burnet went for the noncommittal. "Thank you."

"Poor Jimmy," Lydia followed up. "Such an awful way to go."

Wendy fumbled for the paper coffee cup and downed a healthy sip. Lydia checked out the little boxes on the side of the cup and saw that the Widow Wendy had ordered a grande latte too, though she'd chosen half decaf and soy milk. Lydia slid a little closer to her.

"You don't know who I am, do you?"

Wendy gave her a weak got-me smile. "I'm sorry."

"No need to be. I don't think we ever met."

Wendy waited for Lydia to introduce herself. When she didn't, Wendy said, "You knew my husband then?"

"Oh yes."

"Are you in the insurance business too?"

"No, I'm afraid not."

Wendy frowned. Lydia sipped her beverage. The awkwardness grew, at least for Wendy. Lydia was fine with it. When it became too much, Wendy rose to leave.

"Well," she said, "it was nice meeting you."

"I . . ." Lydia began, hesitating until she was sure that she had Wendy's full attention, "I was the last person to see Jimmy alive."

Wendy froze. Lydia took another sip and closed her eyes. "Nice and strong," she said, gesturing toward the cup. "I love the coffee here, don't you?"

"Did you say . . . ?"

"Please," Lydia said with a small sweep of her arm. "Have a seat so I can explain properly."

Wendy glanced over at the *baristas*. They were busy gesticulating and whining about what they thought was the great world conspiracy that kept them from the most amazing of lives. Wendy slid back onto the stool. For a few moments, Lydia just stared at her. Wendy tried to hold her gaze.

"You see," Lydia began, offering up a fresh, warm smile and tilting her to the side, "I'm the one who killed your husband."

Wendy's face went pale. "That isn't funny."

"True, yes, I'd have to agree with you on that, Wendy. But then again humor was not really my aim. Would you like to hear a joke instead? I'm on one of those joke e-mail lists. Most are duds, but every once in a while, they send a howler."

Wendy sat stunned. "Who the hell are you?"

"Calm down a second, Wendy."

"I want to know—"

"Shhh." Lydia put her finger to Wendy's lip with too much tenderness. "Let me explain, okay?"

Wendy's lips trembled. Lydia kept her finger there for a few more seconds.

"You're confused. I understand that. Let me clarify a few things for you. First off, yes, I'm the one who put the bullet in Jimmy's head. But Heshy"—Lydia pointed out the window in the direction of an enormous man with a misshapen head—"he did the earlier damage. Personally, by the time I shot Jimmy, well, I think I might have been doing him in a favor."

Wendy just stared.

"You want to know why, am I right? Of course, you do. But deep down inside, Wendy, I think you know. We're women of the world, aren't we? We know our men."

Wendy said nothing.

"Wendy, do you know what I'm talking about?"

"No."

"Sure you do, but I'll say it anyway. Jimmy, your dearly departed husband, owed a great deal of money to some very unpleasant people. As of today, the amount is just under two hundred thousand dollars." Lydia smiled. "Wendy, you're not going to pretend you know nothing about your husband's gambling woes, are you?"

Wendy had trouble forming the words in her mouth. "I don't understand. . . ."

"I hope your confusion has nothing to do with my gender."

"What?"

"That would be really narrow and sexist on your part, don't you think? This is the twenty-first century. Women can be whatever they want."

"You"—Wendy stopped, tried again—"you murdered my husband?"

"Do you watch much television, Wendy?"

"What?"

"Television. You see, on television, whenever someone like your husband owes money to someone like me, well, what happens?"

Lydia stopped as if she really expected her to answer. Wendy finally said, "I don't know."

"Sure you do, but again I'll answer for you. The someone-like-me—okay, usually the *male* someone-like-me—is sent to threaten him. Then maybe my cohort Heshy out there would beat him up or break his legs, something like that. But they never kill the guy. That's one of those TV-bad-guy rules. 'You can't collect from a dead man.' You've heard that, haven't you, Wendy?"

She waited. Wendy finally said, "I guess."

"But, see, that's wrong. Let's take Jimmy, for example. Your husband had a disease. Gambling. Am I right? It cost you everything, didn't it? The insurance business. That had been your father's. Jimmy took it over for him. It's gone now. Wiped out. The bank was ready to foreclose on your house. You and the kids barely had enough money for groceries. And still Jimmy didn't stop." Lydia shook her head. "Men. Am I right?"

There were tears in Wendy's eyes. Her voice, when she was able to speak, was so weak. "So you killed him?"

Lydia looked up, shaking her head gently. "I'm really not explaining this well, am I?" She lowered her gaze and tried again. "Have you ever heard the expression that you can't squeeze blood from a stone?"

Again Lydia waited for an answer. Wendy finally nodded. Lydia seemed pleased.

"Well, that's the case here. With Jimmy, I mean. I could have Heshy out there work him over—Heshy is good at that—but what good would that do? Jimmy didn't have the money. He would never be able to get his hands on that kind of cash." Lydia sat a little straighter and put out her hands. "Now, Wendy, I want you to think like a businessman—check that, a business*person*. We don't have to be raving feminists, but I think we should at least keep ourselves on equal footing."

Lydia gave Wendy another smile. Wendy cringed.

"Okay, so what am I—as a wise business*person*—what am I supposed to do? I can't let the debt go unpaid, of course. In my line of work, that's professional suicide. Someone owes my employer money, they have to pay. No way around that. The problem here is, Jimmy doesn't have a cent to his name but"—Lydia stopped and widened her smile—"but he does have a wife and three kids. And he used to be in the insurance business. Do you see where I'm going with this, Wendy?"

Wendy was afraid to breathe.

"Oh, I think you do, but again I'll say it for you. Insurance. More specifically, *life* insurance. Jimmy had a policy. He didn't admit it right away, but eventually, well, Heshy can be persuasive." Wendy's eyes drifted toward the window. Lydia saw the shiver and hid a smile. "Jimmy told us he had two policies, in fact, with a total payout of nearly a million dollars."

"So you"—Wendy was struggling to comprehend—"you killed Jimmy for the insurance money?"

Lydia snapped her fingers. "You go, girlfriend."

Wendy opened her mouth but nothing came out.

"And, Wendy? Let me make this crystal clear. Jimmy's debts don't die with him. We both know that. The bank still wants you to pay the mortgage, am I right? The credit-card companies don't stop mounting the interest." Lydia shrugged her small shoulders, palms to the sky. "Why should my employer be any different?"

"You can't be serious."

"Your first insurance check should come in about a week. By that time, your husband's debt will be two hundred eighty thousand dollars. I'll expect a check for that amount on that day."

"But the bills he left alone—"

"Shhh." Again Lydia silenced her with a finger to her lips. Her voice dropped to an intimate whisper. "That doesn't really concern me,

Wendy. I have given you the rare opportunity to get out from under. Declare bankruptcy, if you must. You live in a ritzy area. Move out. Have Jack—that's your eleven-year-old, correct?"

Wendy jolted at the sound of her son's name.

"Well, no summer camp for Jack this year. Have him get a job after school. Whatever. None of that concerns me. You, Wendy, will pay what you owe, and that will be the end of this. You will never see or hear from me again. If you don't pay, however, well, take a good look at Heshy over there." She paused, letting Wendy do just that. It had the desired effect.

"We'll kill little Jack first. Then, two days later, we'll kill Lila. If you report this conversation to the police, we'll kill Jack and Lila and Darlene. All three, in age order. And then, after you bury your children—please listen, Wendy, because this is key—I'll still make you pay."

Wendy couldn't speak.

Lydia followed up a deep, caffeinated sip with an "Ahh" of satisfaction. "Dee-lightful," she said, rising from her seat. "I really enjoyed our little girl chat, Wendy. We should get together again soon. Say, your house at noon on Friday the sixteenth?"

Wendy kept her head down.

"Do you understand?"

"Yes."

"What are you going to do?"

"I'm going to pay the debt," Wendy said.

Lydia smiled at her. "Again, my sincerest condolences."

Lydia headed outside and breathed in the fresh air. She looked behind her. Wendy Burnet had not moved. Lydia waved good-bye and met up with Heshy. He was nearly six six. She was five one. He weighed 275 pounds. She was 105. He had a head like a misshapen pumpkin. Her features seemed to have been made in the Orient out of porcelain.

"Problems?" Heshy asked.

"Please," she said with a dismissive wave. "On to more profitable ventures. Did you find our man?"

"Yes."

"And the package is already out?"

"Sure, Lydia."

"Very good." She frowned, felt a gnawing.

"What's wrong?" he asked.

"I have a funny feeling, that's all."

"You want to back out?"

Lydia smiled at him. "Not on your life, Pooh Bear."

"Then what do you want to do?"

She thought about it. "Let's just see how Dr. Seidman reacts."

chapter 9

"**Don't drink any** more apple juice," Cheryl told her two-year-old, Conner.

I stood on the sidelines with my arms folded. It was a bit nippy, the frosty, damp chill of late New Jersey autumn, so I pulled the hood of my sweatshirt over my Yankee cap. I also had on a pair of Ray-Bans. Sunglasses and hood. I looked very much like the police sketch of the Unabomber.

We were at a soccer game for eight-year-old boys. Lenny was the head coach. He needed an assistant and recruited me because, I assume, I am the only one who knows even less about soccer than he does. Still our team was winning. I think the score was about eighty-three to two, but I am not certain.

"Why can't I have more juice?" Conner asked.

"Because," Cheryl answered with the patience of a mother, "apple juice gives you diarrhea."

"It does?"

"Yes."

To my right, Lenny drowned the kids in a steady stream of encouragement. "You're the best, Ricky." "Way to go, Petey." "Now *that's* what I call hustle, Davey." He always added a *y* to the end of their names. And yes, it is annoying. Once, in a pitch of overexcitement, he called me Marky. Once.

"Uncle Marc?"

I feel a tug at my leg. I look down at Conner, who is twenty-six months old. "What's up, pal?"

"Apple juice gives me a diarrhea."

"Good to know," I said.

"Uncle Marc?"

"Yeah?"

Conner gave me his gravest look. "Diarrhea," he said, "is not my friend."

I glanced at Cheryl. She smothered a smile, but I saw the concern there too. I looked back at Conner. "Words to live by, kid."

Conner nodded, pleased by my response. I love him. He breaks my heart and brings me joy in equal measure and at exactly the same time. Twenty-six months old. Two months older than Tara. I watch his development with awe and a longing that could heat a furnace.

He turned back to his mother. Littered about Cheryl was the product of her mommy-as-pack-mule harvest. There were Minute Maid juice boxes and Nutri-Grain bars. There were Pampers Baby-Dry diapers (as opposed to Baby-Wet?) and Huggies wipes containing aloe vera for the discriminating buttock. There were angled baby bottles from Evenflo. There were cinnamon Teddy Grahams and well-scrubbed baby carrots and sectioned oranges and cut-up grapes (sliced the long way so as to make them chokeproof) and cubes of what I hoped was cheese, all hermetically sealed in their own Ziploc bags.

Lenny, the head coach, was yelling out key, game-winning strategy to our players. When we are on offense, he tells them to "Score!" When we are on defense, he advises them to "Stop him!" And then sometimes, like right now, he offers keen insight into the subtleties of the game:

"Kick the ball!"

Lenny glanced at me after he'd shouted that for the fourth time in a row. I gave him a thumbs-up and way-to-go nod. He wanted to give me the finger, but there were too many underage witnesses. I refolded my arms and squinted at the field. The kids were geared up like the pros. They wore cleats. Their socks were pulled up over their shin guards. Most wore that black grease under their eyes, even though there was nary a hint of sunshine. Two even had those breathing strip-bandages across their noses. I watched Kevin, my godson, try, per his father's instructions, to kick the ball. And then it hit me like a body blow.

I staggered back.

That was how it always happened. I will be watching the game or I'll be having dinner with friends or I'll be working on a patient or listening to a song on the radio. I'll be doing something normal, average, feeling pretty decent, and then, wham, I get blindsided.

My eyes welled up. That never used to happen to me before the murder and kidnapping. I am a doctor. I know how to play poised in both my professional and personal life. But now I wear sunglasses all the time like some self-important B movie star. Cheryl looked up at me and again I saw the concern. I straightened and forced a smile. Cheryl was becoming beautiful. That happened sometimes. Motherhood agreed with certain women. It gave their physical appearance a wonder and richness that borders on the celestial.

I don't want to give you the wrong impression. I don't spend every day crying. I still live my life. I am bereaved, sure, but not all the time. I am not paralyzed. I work, though I haven't yet had the courage to travel overseas. I keep thinking that I need to stay close by, in case there is a new development. That kind of thinking is, I know, not rational and perhaps even delusional. But I am still not ready.

What gets me—what gives me that surprise wham—is the way grief seems to relish in catching you unawares. Grief, when spotted, can be, if not handled, somewhat manipulated, finessed, concealed. But grief likes to hide behind bushes. It enjoys leaping out of nowhere, startling you, mocking you, stripping away your pretense of normalcy. Grief lulls you to sleep, thus making that blindside hit all the more jarring.

"Uncle Marc?"

It was Conner again. He talked pretty well for a kid his age. I wondered what Tara's voice would have sounded like, and behind my sunglasses, my eyes closed. Sensing something, Cheryl reached out to pull him away. I shook her off. "What is it, pal?"

"What about poop?"

"What about it?"

He looked up and closed one eye in concentration. "Is poop my friend?"

Hell of a question. "I don't know, pal. What do you think?"

Conner considered his own query so hard it appeared as if he might explode. Finally he replied, "It's more my friend than diarrhea."

I nodded sagely. Our team scored another goal. Lenny shot his fists into the air and shouted, "Yes!" He nearly cartwheeled out to congratulate Craig (or should I say Craigy), the goal scorer. The players followed

him. There was much high-fiving. I didn't join in. My job, I figured, was
to be the quiet partner to Lenny's histrionics, the Tonto to his Lone
Ranger, the Abbott to his Costello, the Rowan to his Martin, the Captain to his Tennille. Balance.

I watched the parents on the sidelines. The mothers became clusters.
They talked about their kids, about their child's achievements and extracurricular activities, and no one listened much because other people's
children are boring. The fathers offered more variety. Some videotaped.
Some yelled encouragement. Some rode their kids in a way that borders
on the unhealthy. Some gabbed on cell phones and constantly fiddled
with handheld electronics of one kind or another, experiencing a bit of
the bends after spending all week immersed in their work.

Why did I go to the police?

I have been told countless times since that terrible day that I am not
to blame for what happened. On one level, I realize that my actions may
have changed nothing. In all likelihood, they had never intended to let
Tara come home. She might even have been dead before the first ransom
call. Her death may have been accidental. Maybe they just panicked or
were strung out. Who knows? I certainly don't.

And, ah, there's the rub.

I cannot, of course, be certain that I am not responsible. Basic science: For every action, there is a reaction.

I do not dream about Tara—or if I do, the gods are generous enough
to not let me remember. That is probably giving them too much credit.
Let me rephrase. I may not dream about Tara specifically, but I do
dream about the white van with the mix-and-match license plate and
the stolen magnetic sign. In the dreams I hear a noise, muffled, but I'm
pretty sure it is the sound of a baby crying. Tara, I know now, was in
the van, but in my dream, I don't go toward the sound. My legs are
buried deep in that nightmare muck. I can't move. When I finally wake
up, I cannot help but ponder the obvious. Was Tara that close to me?
And more important: Had I been a little braver, could I have saved her
then and there?

The referee, a lanky high-school boy with a good-natured grin, blew
the whistle and waved his hands over his head. Game over. Lenny
shouted, "Woo, yeah!" The eight-year-olds stared at one another, confused. One asked a teammate, "Who won?" and the teammate shrugged.
They lined up, Stanley Cup hockey style, for the postgame handshakes.

Cheryl stood up and put a hand on my back. "Great win, Coach."

"Yeah, I carry this team," I said.

She smiled. The boys started rambling back toward us. I congratulated them with my stoic nod. Craig's mother had brought a fifty-pack of Dunkin' Donuts Munchkins in a box with a Halloween design. Dave's mom had boxes of something called Yoo-hoo, a perverse excuse for chocolate milk that tastes like chalk. I popped a Munchkin in my mouth and skipped the washdown. Cheryl asked, "What flavor was that?"

I shrugged. "They come in different flavors?" I watched the parents interact with their children and felt tremendously out of place. Lenny came toward me.

"Great win, wasn't it?"

"Yeah," I said. "We're the balls."

He gestured for us to step away. I complied. When we were out of earshot, Lenny said, "Monica's estate is almost wrapped up. It shouldn't be too much longer now."

I said, "Uh-huh," because I didn't really care.

"I also have your will drawn up. You need to sign it."

Neither Monica nor I had made up a will. For years, Lenny had warned me about that. You need to put in writing who gets your money, he'd remind me, who is going to raise your daughter, who is going to care for your parents, yadda, yadda, yadda. But we didn't listen. We were going to live forever. Last wills and testaments were for, well, the dead.

Lenny changed subjects on the fly. "You want to come back to the house for a game of foosball?"

Foosball, for those of you who lack a basic education, is that tabletop bar game with the soccer-type men skewered on sticks. "I'm already champion of the world," I reminded him.

"That was yesterday."

"Can't a man revel in his title for little while? I'm not yet ready to let go of the feeling."

"Understood." Lenny headed back to his family. I watched his daughter, Marianne, corner him. She was gesturing like mad. Lenny slumped his shoulders, took out his wallet, peeled out a bill. Marianne took it, kissed him on the cheek, ran off. Lenny watched her disappear, shaking his head. There was a smile on his face. I turned away.

The worst part—or should I say the best part—was that I have hope.

Here was what we found that night at Grandpa's cabin: my sister's corpse, hairs belonging to Tara in the Pack 'N Play (DNA confirmed), and a pink one-piece with black penguins that matched Tara's.

Here was what we did not find and, in fact, still have not found: the ransom money, the identity, if any, of Stacy's accomplices—and Tara.

That's right. We never found my daughter.

The forest is big and sprawling, I know. The grave would be small and easily hidden. There could be rocks over it. An animal might have found it and dragged the contents deeper into the thicket. The contents could be miles from my grandfather's cabin. They could be somewhere else entirely.

Or—though I keep this thought to myself—maybe there is no grave at all.

So you see, the hope is there. Like grief, hope hides and pounces and taunts and never leaves. I am not sure which of the two is the crueler mistress.

The police and FBI theorize that my sister acted in conjunction with some very bad people. While no one is quite sure if their original intention was kidnapping or robbery, most everyone agrees that someone panicked. Maybe they thought that Monica and I would not be home. Maybe they thought that they would just have to contend with a baby-sitter. Whatever, they saw us, and acting in some drugged or crazed state, someone fired a shot. Then someone else fired a shot, ergo the ballistic tests showing Monica and I were shot by different .38's. They then kidnapped the baby. Eventually they double-crossed Stacy and killed her with an overdose of heroin.

I keep saying "they" because the authorities also believe that Stacy had at least two accomplices. One would be the professional, the cool head who knew how to work the drop and weld the license plates and disappear without a trace. The other accomplice would be the "panicker," if you will, the one who shot us and probably caused the death of Tara.

Some, of course, don't buy that theory. Some believe that there was only one accomplice—the cool professional—and that the one who panicked was Stacy. She, this theory goes, was the one who fired the first bullet, probably at me since I don't remember any shots, and then the professional killed Monica to cover the mistake. This theory is backed up by one of the few leads we had following that night in the cabin: a drug dealer who, in some bizarre plea bargain on another charge, told authorities that Stacy had purchased a gun from him, a .38, a week before the murder-kidnapping. This theory is further backed up by the fact that the only unexplained hairs and fingerprints found at the murder scene were Stacy's. While the cool pro would know to wear gloves and be careful, a drugged-out accomplice would probably not.

Still others do not embrace that theory either, which is why certain members of the police department and FBI cling to and support a more obvious third scenario:

I was the mastermind.

The theory goes something like this: first caveat, the husband is always suspect number one. Second, my Smith & Wesson .38 is still missing. They press me on this question all the time. I wish I had an answer. Third, I never wanted a child. Tara's birth forced me into a loveless marriage. They believe that they have evidence that I was considering divorce (something that yes, I did indeed contemplate) and so I planned the whole thing, top to bottom. I invited my sister over to my house and perhaps enlisted her help so that she would take the fall. I have the ransom money hidden away. I killed and buried my own daughter.

Awful, yes, but I am past anger. I am past exhaustion. I am not sure where I am anymore.

The main problem with their hypothesis is, of course, that it is hard to finesse my being left for dead. Did I kill Stacy? Did she shoot me? Or—drum roll here—is there a third possibility out there, a blending of the two different theories into one? Some believe that yes, I was behind it, but I had another accomplice besides Stacy. That accomplice killed Stacy, perhaps against my wishes, perhaps as part of my grand scheme to deflect my guilt and avenge my own shooting. Or something like that.

And round and round we go.

In sum, when you cut through it all, they—and I—have nothing. No ransom money. No idea who did it. No idea why. And most important: no small corpse.

That is where we are today—a year and a half after the abduction. The file is still technically open, but Regan and Tickner have moved on to new cases. I haven't heard a word from either in nearly six months.

The media gnawed on us for a few weeks, but with nothing new to feed on, they too, slithered toward juicier troughs.

The Dunkin' Donuts Munchkins were gone. Everyone started heading to a parking lot overloaded with minivans. After the game we coaches take our budding athletes to Schrafft's Ice Cream Parlor, a tradition in our town. Every coach in every other league in every other age group follows the same tradition. The place was packed. Nothing like an ice cream cone in the autumn frost to burrow the chill into the bone.

I stood with my Cookies-n-Cream cone and surveyed the scene. Children and fathers. It was getting to be too much for me. I checked my watch. Time for me to leave anyway. I met Lenny's eye and motioned that I was going. He mouthed the words *Your will* at me. In case I didn't get the drift, he even made a signing motion with his hand. I waved that I understood. I got back into my car and flipped on the radio.

For a long while, I sat there and watched the flow of families. I kept my eyes on the fathers mostly. I gauged their reactions to this most domestic of activities, hoping to see a flicker of doubt, something in the eyes that might comfort me. But I didn't.

I'm not sure how long I stayed like that. Not more than ten minutes, I suppose. An old favorite by James Taylor came on the radio. It brought me back. I smiled, started up the car, and made my way toward the hospital.

An hour later, I was scrubbing up to perform surgery on an eight-year-old boy with—to use terminology familiar to both layman and professional—a facial smash. Zia Leroux, my medical partner, was there.

I'm not sure why I first chose to be a plastic surgeon. It was neither the siren song of easy dollars nor the ideal of helping my fellowman. I had wanted to be a surgeon pretty much from the get-go, but I saw myself more in the vascular or cardiac fields. Life's turns come in funny ways though. During my second year of residency, the cardiac surgeon who ran our rotation was—what's the phrase?—a total prick. On the other hand, the doctor in charge of the cosmetic surgery, Liam Reese, was incredible. Dr. Reese had that enviable have-it-all feel to him, that combination of good looks, calm confidence, and internal warmth that naturally drew people. You wanted to please him. You wanted to be like him.

Dr. Reese became my mentor. He showed how reconstructive surgery was creative, a Humpty-Dumpty process that forced you to find new ways to put back together what had been destroyed. The bones in the face and skull are the most complex stretch of skeletal landscape in the human body. We who repair them are artists. We are jazz musicians. If you talk to orthopedic or thoracic surgeons, they can be pretty specific about their procedures. Our work—reconstruction—is never exactly the same. We improvise. Dr. Reese taught me that. He appealed to my inner techno-weenie with talk of microsurgery and bone grafts and synthetic skin. I remember visiting him in Scarsdale. His wife was long legged and beautiful. His daughter was school valedictorian. His son was captain of the basketball team and the nicest kid I've ever met. At the age of forty-nine Dr. Reese was killed in a car crash on Route 684 heading to Connecticut. Somebody might find something poignant in that, but that person wouldn't be me.

When I was finishing up residency, I landed a one-year fellowship to train in oral surgery overseas. I didn't apply to be a do-gooder; I applied because it sounded pretty cool. This trip would be, I hoped, my version of backpacking through Europe. It was not. Things went wrong right away. We got caught up in a civil war in Sierra Leone. I handled wounds so horrible, so unfathomable, that it was hard to believe the human mind could conjure up the necessary cruelty to inflict them. But even in the midst of this destruction, I felt a strange exhilaration. I don't try to figure out why. Like I said before, this stuff gets me jazzed. Maybe part of it was the satisfaction of helping people truly in need. Or maybe I was drawn to this work the same way some are drawn to extreme sports, who need the risk of death to feel whole.

When I came back, Zia and I set up One World, and we were on our way. I love what I do. Perhaps our work is like an extreme sport, but it also has a very—pardon the pun—human face. I like that. I love my patients and yet I love the calculating distance, the necessary coldness, of what I do. I care about my patients so much, but then they are gone—intense love mixed with fleeting commitment.

Today's patient presented us with a rather complicated challenge. My patron saint—the patron saint of many in reconstructive surgery—is the French researcher René LeFort. LeFort tossed cadavers off a tavern roof onto their skulls to see the natural pattern of fracture lines in the face. I bet this impressed the ladies. Today we name certain fractures for him—more specifically, LeFort type I, LeFort type II, LeFort type III. Zia and I checked the films again. The Water view gave us the best look, but the Caldwell and lateral backed it up.

Simply put, the fracture line on this eight-year-old was a LeFort type III, causing a complete separation of the facial bones and the cranium. I could pretty much rip off the boy's face like a mask if I wanted to.

"Car accident?" I asked.

Zia nodded. "Father was drunk."

"Don't tell me. He's fine, right?"

"He even remembered to put on his own seat belt."

"But not his son's."

"Too much trouble. What with him being tired from raising a glass so many times."

Zia and I started our life's journey in two very different places. Like the Story's classic seventies song "Brother Louie," Zia is black as the night while I am whiter than white (my skin tone, as described by Zia: "underwater fish belly"). I was born at Beth Israel Hospital in Newark and grew up on the suburban streets of Kasselton, New Jersey. Zia was born in a mud hut in a village outside of Port-au-Prince, Haiti. Sometime during the reign of Papa Doc, her parents became political prisoners. No one knows too many details. Her father was executed. Her mother, when released, was damaged goods. She grabbed her daughter and escaped on what might liberally be dubbed a raft. Three passengers died on the journey. Zia and her mother survived. They made their way to the Bronx where they took up residence in the basement of a beauty parlor. The two spent their days quietly sweeping hair. The hair, it seemed to Zia, was inescapable. It was on her clothes, clinging to her skin, in her throat, in her lungs. She lived forever with that feeling that a stray strand was in her mouth and she couldn't quite pull it out. To this day, when Zia gets nervous, her fingers play with her tongue, as though trying to pluck out a memento of her past.

When the surgery was over, Zia and I collapsed onto a bench. Zia untied her surgical mask and let it fall to her chest.

"Piece of cake," she said.

"Amen," I agreed. "How did your date go last night?"

"It sucked," she said. "And I don't mean that literally."

"Sorry."

"Men are such scum."

"Don't I know it."

"I'm getting so desperate," she said, "I'm thinking of sleeping with you again."

"Gasp," I said. "Woman, have you no standards?"

Her smile was blinding, the bright white against the dark skin. She was a shade under six feet tall with smooth muscles and cheekbones so high and sharp you feared they might pierce her skin. "When are you going to start dating?" she asked.

"I date."

"I mean, long enough to have a sexual encounter."

"Not all women are easy as you, Zia."

"Sad," she said, giving my arm a playful punch.

Zia and I slept together once—and we both knew that it would never happen again. It was how we met. We hooked up during my first year of medical school. Yep, a one-night stand. I have had my fair share of one-night stands, but only two have been memorable. The first led to disaster. The second—this one—led to a relationship I will cherish forever.

It was eight o'clock at night by the time we got out of our scrubs. We took Zia's car, a tiny thing called a BMW Mini, to the Stop & Shop on Northwood Avenue and picked up some groceries. Zia chatted without letup as we wheeled carts down the aisles. I liked when Zia talked. It gave me energy. At the deli counter Zia pulled a call number. She looked at the specials board and frowned.

"What?" I said.

"Boar's Head ham on sale."

"What about it?"

"Boar's Head," she repeated. "What marketing genius came up with that name? 'Say, I have an idea. Let's name our premium cold cuts after the most disgusting animal imaginable. No, check that. Let's name it after its head.' "

"You always order it," I said.

She thought about it. "Yeah, I guess."

We moved to the checkout line. Zia put her stuff up front. I placed the divider down and unloaded my cart. A portly cashier began to ring up her items.

"You hungry?" she asked me.

I shrugged. "Guess I could go for a couple of slices at Garbo's."

"Let's do it." Zia's eyes drifted over my shoulder and then jerked to a stop. She squinted and something crossed her face. "Marc?"

"Yeah."

She waved it off. "Nah, can't be."

"What?"

Still staring over my shoulder, Zia gestured with her chin. I turned slowly and when I saw her, I felt it in my chest.

"I've only seen her in pictures," Zia said, "but isn't that . . . ?"

I managed a nod.

It was Rachel.

The world closed in around me. It shouldn't feel this way. I knew that. We had broken up years ago. Now, after all this time, I should be smiling. I should feel something wistful, a passing nostalgia, a poignant remembrance of a time when I was young and naïve. But no, that was not what was going on here. Rachel stood ten yards away and it all flooded back. What I felt was a still-too-powerful yearning, a longing that tore through me, that made both the love and heartbreak feel fresh and alive.

"You okay?" Zia said.

Another nod.

Are you one of those who believe that we all have one true soul mate—one and only one preordained love? There, across three Stop & Shop checkout lanes and under a sign reading EXPRESS LANE—15 ITEMS OR LESS, stood mine.

Zia said, "I thought she got married."

"She did," I said.

"No ring." Then Zia punched my arm. "Oooh, this is exciting, isn't it?"

"Yeah," I said. "Exhilaration city."

Zia snapped her fingers. "Hey, you know what this is like? That crappy old album you used to play. The song about meeting the old lover in the grocery store. What's the name of it?"

The first time I'd seen Rachel, when I was a lad of nineteen years, the effect was relatively gentle. There was no big boom. I'm not even sure that I found her overly attractive. But as I'd soon learn, I like a woman whose looks grow on you. You start off thinking, Okay, she's pretty decent looking, and then, a few days later, maybe it's something she says or the way she tilts her head when she says it, but then, wham, it's like getting hit by a bus.

It felt like that again now. Rachel had changed but not by much. The years had made that sneaky beauty harden maybe, more brittle and angled. She was thinner. Her dark blue-black hair was pulled back and tied into a ponytail. Most men like the hair down. I've always liked it tied back, the openness and exposure of it, I guess, especially with Rachel's cheekbones and neck. She wore jeans and a gray blouse. Her hazel eyes were down, her head bent in that pose of concentration I knew so well. She had not seen me yet.

" 'Same Old Lang Syne,' " Zia said.

"What?"

"The song about the lovers in the grocery store. By Dan Somebody. That's the title. 'Same Old Lang Syne.' " Then she added: "I think that's the title."

Rachel reached into her wallet and plucked out a twenty. She began to hand it to the cashier. Her gaze lifted—and that was when she saw me.

I can't say exactly what crossed her face. She did not look surprised. Our eyes met, but I did not see joy there. Fear, perhaps. Maybe resignation. I don't know. I also don't know how long we both stood there like that.

"Maybe I should move away from you," Zia whispered.

"Huh?"

"If she thinks you're with a chick this hot, she'll conclude that she has no chance."

I think I smiled.

"Marc?"

"Yeah."

"The way you're standing like that. Gaping like a total whack job. It's a little scary."

"Thanks."

I felt her hand push on my back. "Go over and say hello."

My feet started moving, though I don't remember the brain issuing any commands. Rachel let the cashier bag her groceries. She stepped toward me and tried to smile. Her smile had always been spectacular, the kind that makes you think of poetry and spring showers, a dazzler that can change your day. This smile, however, was not like that. It was tighter. It was pained. And I wondered if she was holding back or if she could no longer smile like she used to, if something had dimmed the wattage permanently.

We stopped a yard away from each other, neither sure if the proper protocol called for a hug, a kiss, a handshake. So we did none of the above. I stood there and felt the hurt everywhere.

"Hi," I said.

"Good to see you still have all the smooth lines, " Rachel replied.

I feigned a rakish grin. "Hey, baby, what's your sign?"

"Better," she said.

"Come here often?"

"Good. Now say, 'Haven't we met before?' "

"Nah." I arched an eyebrow. "No way I'd forget meeting a foxy lady like you."

We both laughed. We were both trying too hard. We both knew it.

"You look good," I said.

"So do you."

Brief silence.

"Okay," I said, "I'm out of uncomfortable clichés and forced banter."

"Whew," Rachel said.

"Why are you here?"

"I'm buying food."

"No, I mean—"

"I know what you meant," she interrupted. "My mother moved into a condo development in West Orange."

A few of the strands had escaped her ponytail and fell across her face. It took all my willpower to stop from pushing them away.

Rachel glanced away and then back at me. "I heard about your wife and daughter," she said. "I'm sorry."

"Thank you."

"I wanted to call or write but . . ."

"I heard you got married," I said.

She wiggled the fingers on her left hand. "Not anymore."

"And that you were an agent with the FBI."

Rachel put her hand back down. "Also not anymore."

More silence. Again I don't know how long we stood there. The cashier had moved on to the next shopper. Zia came up behind us. She cleared her throat and jammed her hand toward Rachel. "Hi, I'm Zia Leroux," she said.

"Rachel Mills."

"Good to meet you, Rachel. I'm Marc's practice partner." Then, thinking about it, she added: "We're just friends."

"Zia," I said.

"Oh, right, sorry. Look, Rachel, I'd love to stay and chat, but I have to run." She jerked her thumb toward the exit to emphasize the point. "You two talk. Marc, I'll meet you back here later. Great meeting you, Rachel."

"Same here."

Zia rushed off. I shrugged. "She's a great doctor."

"I bet she is." Rachel took hold of her cart. "I have someone waiting in the car, Marc. It was good seeing you."

"You too." But surely, with all I'd lost, I must have learned something, right? I couldn't just let her go. I cleared my throat and said, "Maybe we should get together."

"I'm still living in Washington. I head back tomorrow."

Silence. My insides turned to jelly. My breathing was shallow.

"Good-bye, Marc," Rachel said. But those hazel eyes were wet.

"Don't go yet."

I tried to keep the pleading out of my voice, but I don't think I was successful. Rachel looked at me, and she saw everything. "What do you want me to say here, Marc?"

"That you want to get together too."

"That's all?"

I shook my head. "You know that's not all."

"I'm not twenty-one anymore."

"Neither am I."

"The girl you loved is dead and gone."

"No," I said. "She's right in front of me."

"You don't know me anymore."

"So let's get reacquainted. I'm not in a rush."

"Just like that?"

I tried to smile. "Yeah."

"I live in Washington. You live in New Jersey."

"So I'll move," I said.

But even before the impetuous words came out, even before Rachel made that face, I could recognize my own false bravado. I couldn't just leave my parents or dump my business with Zia or—or abandon my ghosts. Somewhere between my lips and her ears the sentiment crashed and burned.

Rachel turned to leave then. She did not say good-bye again. I watched her push the cart toward the door. I saw it automatically swing open with an electric grunt. I saw Rachel, the love of my life, disappear again without so much as a backward glance. I stayed still. I did not follow her. I felt my heart tumble and shatter, but I did nothing to stop her.

Maybe I hadn't learned anything, after all.

chapter 10

I drank.

I am not a big drinker—pot had been my elixir of choice during my younger days—but I found an old bottle of gin in a cabinet over the sink. There was tonic in the fridge. I have an automatic icemaker in the freezer. You do the math.

I still lived in the old Levinsky house. It is much too big for me, but I don't have the heart to let it go. It feels like a portal now, a lifeline (albeit a fragile one) to my daughter. Yes, I know how that sounds, but selling it now would be like closing a door on her. I can't do that.

Zia wanted to stay with me, but I begged off. She did not push it. I thought about the corny Dan Fogelberg (not Dan Somebody) song where the old lovers talk until their tongues get tired. I thought about Bogie questioning the gods who would allow Ingrid Bergman into his, of all possible, gin joints. Bogie drank after she left. It seemed to help him. Maybe it would help me too.

The fact that Rachel could still pack this kind of wallop annoyed the hell out of me. It was stupid and childish really. Rachel and I had first met during summer break between my sophomore and junior years of college. She was from Middlebury, Vermont, and supposedly a distant cousin of Lenny's wife, Cheryl, though no one could ascertain the exact relationship. That summer—the summer of all summers—Rachel stayed with Cheryl's family because Rachel's folks were going through a nasty divorce. We were introduced, and like I said before, it took some time for the bus to smack into me. Maybe that's what made it all the more potent when it did.

We began to date. We doubled a lot with Lenny and Cheryl. The four of us spent every weekend at Lenny's summer house on the Jersey shore. It was indeed a glorious summer, the kind of summer everyone should experience at least once in a lifetime.

If this were a movie, we'd be cueing up the montage music. I went to Tufts University while Rachel was starting out at Boston College. First scene of the montage, well, they'd probably have us on a boat on the Charles, me paddling, Rachel holding a parasol, her smile tentative then mocking. She'd splash me and then I'd splash her and then the boat would tip. It never happened, but you get the point. Next maybe there would be a picnic scene on campus, a shot of us studying in the library, our bodies entwined on a couch, me staring mesmerized as Rachel reads from her textbook, her glasses on, absentmindedly tucking a hair behind her ear. The montage would probably close on two bodies tussling under a white satin sheet, even though no college student uses satin sheets. Still, I'm thinking cinematic here.

I was in love.

During one Christmas break, we visited Rachel's grandmother, a card-carrying yenta from the old school, in a nursing home. The old woman took both our hands in hers and declared us *beshert* which is a Yiddish word that means predestined or fated.

So what happened?

Our ending was not an uncommon one. We were young, I guess. During my senior year, Rachel decided that she wanted to spend a semester in Florence. I was twenty-two. I got pissed off and while she was away, I slept with another woman—a one-night stand with a featureless coed from Babson. It meant absolutely nothing. I understand that makes it no better, but maybe it should. I don't know.

Anyway, someone at the party told someone else and eventually it got back to Rachel. She called me from Italy and broke it off, just like that, which I saw as something of an overreaction. Like I said, we were young. At first, I was too proud (read: too stupid) to beg and then, when I started soaking in the repercussions, I called and wrote letters and sent flowers. Rachel never responded. It was over. We were done.

I stood and stumbled to my desk. I fished out the key I had taped under the credenza and unlocked the bottom drawer. I lifted off the files and found my secret stash underneath. No, not drugs. The past. Rachel things. I found the familiar photo and pulled it into view. Lenny and Cheryl still have this picture in their den, which had, understandably enough, angered Monica to no end. It was a photograph of the four of us—Lenny, Cheryl, Rachel, and I—at a formal during my senior year. Rachel is wearing a spaghetti-strap black dress and the thought of the way it clung to her shoulders still takes my breath away.

A long time ago.

I've moved on, of course. Per my life plan, I went to medical school. I always knew that I wanted to be a doctor. Most doctors I know will tell you the same. It is rarely a decision you come to late.

And I dated too. I even had other one-night stands (remember Zia?), but—and this is going to sound pitiful—even after all these years, I never go through a day without thinking, at least fleetingly, about Rachel. Yes, I know that I've romanticized the romance, if you will, completely out of proportion. Had I not made that stupid blunder, I would probably not be living in some blissful alternative universe, still entwined on the couch with my beloved. As Lenny once pointed out in a moment of naked honesty, if my relationship with Rachel had been that great, it surely could have survived this most hackneyed of speed bumps.

Am I saying that I never loved my wife? No. At least, I think the answer is no. Monica was beautiful—right-away beautiful, nothing slow about the way her looks hit you—and passionate and surprising. She was also wealthy and glamorous. I tried not to compare—that is a terrible way to live your life—but I could not help but love Monica in my smaller, less bright, post-Rachel world. Given time, the same might have happened had I stayed with Rachel, but that's using logic and in matters of the heart, logic need not apply.

Over the years, Cheryl grudgingly kept me informed on what Rachel was up to. Rachel, I'd learned, had gone into law enforcement and become a federal agent in Washington. I can't say I was totally surprised. Three years ago, Cheryl told me that Rachel had gotten married to an older guy, a senior fed. Even after all this time—Rachel and I had been broken up eleven years by then—I felt my insides cave in. I realized with a heavy thud just how badly I'd messed up. I'd always assumed somehow that Rachel and I were biding our time, living in some sort of suspended animation, until we inevitably came to our senses and got back together. Now she had married someone else.

Cheryl saw my face and has never again spoken to me about Rachel.

I stared at the picture and heard the familiar SUV pull up. No surprise there. I did not bother walking to the door. Lenny had a key. He never knocked anyway. He'd know where I was. I put away the photograph as Lenny entered the room carrying two enormous, brightly clad paper cups.

Lenny held up the Slurpees from 7-Eleven. "Cherry or cola?"

"Cherry."

He handed it to me. I waited.

"Zia called Cheryl," he said in way of explanation.

I had figured that. "I don't want to talk about it," I said.

Lenny hopped onto the couch. "Me neither." He reached into his pocket and took out a thick sheaf of papers. "The will and the final stuff on Monica's estate. Read it whenever." He picked up the remote control and began to flip. "Don't you have any porno?"

"No, sorry."

Lenny shrugged and settled on a college basketball game on ESPN. We watched a few minutes in silence. I broke it.

"Why didn't you tell me Rachel was divorced?"

Lenny grimaced in pain and raised his palm as if stopping traffic.

"What?" I said.

"Brain freeze." He rode it out. "I always drink these things too fast."

"Why didn't you tell me?"

"I thought we weren't going to talk about it."

I looked at him.

"It's not that simple, Marc."

"What's not?"

"Rachel has been through some tough times."

"So have I," I said.

Lenny watched the game a little too closely.

"What happened to her, Lenny?"

"It's not my place." He shook his head. "You haven't even seen her in, what, fifteen years?"

Fourteen actually. "Something like that."

His eyes scanned the room and rested on a photograph of Monica and Tara. He looked away and sipped his Slurpee. "Have to stop living in the past, my friend."

We both settled back and pretended to watch the game. Stop living in the past, he'd said. I looked at the photograph of Tara and wondered if Lenny was talking about more than Rachel.

Edgar Portman picked up the leather dog leash. He jingled the end. Bruno, his champion bull mastiff, clattered toward the sound at full speed. Bruno had won a Best in Breed at the Westminster Dog Show six years ago. Many believed that he had what it took to earn Best in Show. Edgar chose instead to retire Bruno. A show dog is never home. Edgar wanted Bruno with him.

People disappointed Edgar. Dogs never.

Bruno stuck out his tongue and wagged his tail. Edgar clipped the leash onto the collar. They would go for an hour. Edgar looked down at his desk. There, on the shiny veneer, sat a cardboard package, identical to the one he had received eighteen months earlier. Bruno whimpered. Edgar wondered if it was a whimper of impatience or if he could sense his master's dread. Maybe both.

Either way, Edgar needed air.

The package from eighteen months ago had undergone every possible forensic test. The police had learned nothing. Edgar was relatively certain, based on that past experience, that the incompetents in law enforcement would find nothing again. Eighteen months ago, Marc had not listened to him. That mistake, Edgar hoped, would not be repeated.

He started for the door. Bruno led the way. The air felt good. He stepped outside and sucked in a deep breath. It did not change his outlook, but it helped. Edgar and Bruno started down the familiar route, but something made Edgar veer to the right. The family plot. He saw it every day, so often that he no longer saw it, so to speak. He never visited the stones. But today, suddenly, he felt drawn. Bruno, surprised by the deviation in his routine, grudgingly followed.

Edgar stepped over the small fence. His leg throbbed. Old age. These walks were getting more difficult. He had begun using a walking stick a lot of the time—he had purchased one purportedly used by Dashiell Hammet during a TB stint—but for some reason, Edgar never took it with him when he was with Bruno. It felt wrong somehow.

Bruno hesitated and then leapt the fence. They both stood in front of the two most recent headstones. Edgar tried not to ponder about life and death, about wealth and its relativity to happiness. That sort of lint picking was best left to others. He realized now that he had probably not been a very good father. He had learned, however, from his father, who learned from his. And in the end, perhaps his aloofness had saved him. Had he loved his children fully, had he been deeply involved in their lives, he doubted that he could have survived their deaths.

The dog began to whimper again. Edgar looked down at his companion, deep into his eyes. "Time to go, boy," he said softly. The front door of the house opened. Edgar turned and spotted his brother Carson, rushing toward him. Edgar saw the look on his brother's face.

"My God," Carson called out.

"I assume you saw the package."

"Yes, of course. Did you call Marc?"

"No."

"Good," Carson said. "It's a hoax. It has to be."

Edgar did not reply.

"You don't agree?" Carson said.

"I don't know."

"You can't possibly think that she's still alive."

Edgar gave the leash a gentle tug. "Best to wait for the tests to come back," he said. "Then we'll know for certain."

I like to work night hours. I always have. I am lucky in my career choice. I love my job. It is never a chore or drudgery or something I do simply to put food on the table. I disappear into my work. Like a troubled athlete, I forget everything when I'm playing my game. I enter the zone. I am at my best.

This night, however—three nights after seeing Rachel—I was off duty. I sat alone in my den and flipped stations. I, like most males of our species, hit the remote too frequently. I can watch several hours of nothing. Last year, Lenny and Cheryl got me a DVD player, explaining to me that my VCR was heading the way of the eight-track. I checked the clock on it now. A few minutes after nine. I could pop in a DVD and still get to bed by eleven.

I had just removed the rental DVD from its box and was about to stick it into the machine—they do not have a remote that does that yet—when I heard a dog bark. I rose. A new family had moved in two houses down. They had four or five young kids, something like that. Hard to say when a family has that many. They seem to blur into one another. I had not introduced myself yet, but I had seen in their yard an Irish wolfhound, who was approximately the size of a Ford Explorer. The bark, I believed, was his.

I pushed the curtain aside. I looked out the window, and for some reason—a reason I cannot properly articulate—I was not surprised by what I saw.

The woman stood in the exact same spot where I had seen her eighteen months earlier. The long coat, the long hair, the hands in the pockets—all the same.

I was afraid to let her out of my sight, but then again, I did not want her to see me. I dropped to my knees and slid to the side of the window, super-sleuth-style. With my back and cheek pressed against the wall, I considered my options.

First off, I was now not watching her. That meant she could leave and I wouldn't notice. Hmm, not good. I had to risk a look. That was the first thing.

I turned my head and sneaked a peek. Still there. The woman was still out front, but she had moved a few steps closer to my front door. I had no idea what that meant exactly. So now what? How about going to the door and confronting her? That seemed a pretty good move. If she ran, well, I guess that I would pursue.

I risked another glimpse, just a quick head turn, and when I did, I realized that the woman was staring directly at my window. I fell back. Damn. She'd seen me. No way around it. My hands grabbed the bottom of the window, readying to open it, but she had already started hurrying up the block.

Oh no, not this time.

I was wearing surgical scrubs—every doctor I know has a few pairs for lounge-wear use—and I was barefoot. I sprinted to the door and threw it open. The woman was almost to the top of the block. When she saw me at the door, she stopped the hurry-walk and broke into an all-out run.

I gave chase. To hell with my feet. Part of me felt ridiculous. I am not the fastest fellow on two legs. I am probably not even the fastest on one leg—and here I was running down a strange woman because she was standing in front of my house. I don't know what I hoped to find here. The woman was probably taking a walk, and I had spooked her. She would probably call the police. I could see their reaction. Bad enough I killed my own family and got away with it. Now I was chasing strange women around my neighborhood.

I did not stop.

The woman turned right onto Phelps Road. She had a big lead. I pumped my arms and willed my legs to pick up the pace. The pebbles on the sidewalk dug into the soles of my feet. I tried to stay on grass. She was out of view now, and I was out of shape. I had gone maybe a hundred yards and I could already hear the wheeze in my breath. My nose started running.

I reached the end of my street and made the right.

But there was no one.

The road was long and straight and well enough lit. In other words, she should still be visible. For some dumb reason I looked the other way too, behind me. But the woman was not there either. I ran the route she'd taken. I looked down Morningside Drive, but there was no sign of her.

The woman was gone.

But how?

She could not have been that fast. Carl Lewis was not that fast. I stopped, put my hands on my knees, sucked in some very necessary oxygen. Think. Okay, could she live in one of these houses? Perhaps. And if she did, so what? That meant that she was taking a walk in her own neighborhood. She had seen something that had struck her as curious. She stopped to take a look.

Like she did eighteen months ago?

Okay, first off, we don't know if it was the same woman.

So two women stopped in front of your house in the exact same spot and stood like statues?

It was possible. Or maybe it was the same woman. Maybe she liked looking at houses. Maybe she was into architecture or something.

Oh yes, the ever-desirable architecture of the seventies suburban split-level. And if her visit was totally innocent, why did she run away?

I don't know, Marc, but maybe—and this is just a stab in the dark—maybe because some lunatic chased her?

I shook the voice away and started running again, looking for I-don't-know-what. But when I passed the Zuckers' house, I came to a halt.

Was that possible?

The woman had simply disappeared. I had checked both exit roads. She was not on either one of them. So that meant, A, she lived in one of the houses, B, she was hiding.

Or C, she had taken the Zucker path in the woods.

When I was a kid, we sometimes used to cut through the Zuckers' backyard. There was a path to the middle-school fields. It was not easy to find, and Old Lady Zucker really didn't like us going through her lawn. She would never say anything, but she would stand by the window, her beehive hair glazed like a Krispy Kreme, and glare us down. After a while, we stopped using the path and took the long way.

I looked left and right. No sign of her.

Could the woman know about the path?

I sprinted into the blackness of the Zuckers' backyard. I half expected Old Lady Zucker to be at her kitchen window, glaring at me, but she had moved out to Scottsdale years ago. I don't know who lived here anymore. I didn't even know if the path was still there.

It was black-hole dark in the yard. No lights were on in the house. I tried to remember where exactly the path was. Actually, that took no time. You remember stuff like that. It's automatic. I ran toward it and something whacked me in the head. I felt the thud and fell on my back.

My head swam. I looked up. In the faint moonlight, I could see a swing set. One of those fancy wooden ones. It hadn't been there in my childhood, and in the dark, I hadn't seen it. I felt woozy, but time was key here. I leapt to my feet with too much bravado, reeling back.

The path was still there.

I headed along it as fast as I could. Branches whipped my face. I did not care. I stumbled on a root. I did not care. The Zucker path was not long, maybe forty, fifty feet. It opened into a big clearing of soccer fields and baseball diamonds. I was still making good enough time. If she had taken this route, I would be able to spot her in the recreational expanse.

I could see the smoky haze from the fluorescent lights drifting down from the field's parking lots. I burst out into the opening and quickly scanned my surroundings. I saw several sets of soccer posts and one chain-link backstop.

But no woman.

Damn.

I had lost her. Again. My heart fell. I don't know. I mean, when you thought about it, what was the point? This whole thing was stupid, really. I looked down at my feet. They hurt like hell. I felt a trickle of what was probably blood on my right sole. I felt like an idiot. A defeated idiot, at that. I started to turn away. . . .

Hold the phone.

In the distance, under the lights of the parking lot, there was a car. One solitary car, all by its lonesome. I nodded to myself and followed my thoughts. Let's say that the car belonged to the woman. Why not? If it doesn't, well, nothing lost, nothing gained. But if it did, if she had parked here, it made sense. She parks, she goes through the woods, she stands in front of my house. Why she would do any of this, I had no idea. But for right now, I decided to go with it.

Okay, if that was the case—if that was her car—then I could conclude that she had not yet departed. No flies on me. So what had happened here? She's spotted, she runs, she starts heading down the path. . . .

. . . and she realizes that I might follow.

I almost snapped my fingers. The mystery woman would know that I had grown up in this neighborhood and thus might remember the path. And if I did, if I somehow put together (as I had) that she would use the path, then I would spot her in the opening. So what would she do?

I thought about it and the answer came pretty quickly.

She would hide in the woods along the path.

The mystery woman was probably watching me at this very moment.

Yes, I know that this argument barely reached the level of flimsy conjecture. But it felt right. Very right. So what to do? I gave a heavy sigh and said out loud, "Damn." I slumped my shoulders as though deflated, trying hard not to oversell this, and started trudging back through the path to the Zucker place. I lowered my head, my eyes swerving left and right. I walked delicately, my ears alert, straining to hear a rustle of some sort.

The night remained silent.

I reached the end of the path and kept walking as if I were heading home. When I was deep in the thicket of darkness, I dropped to the ground. I commando-crawled back under the swing set toward the path's opening. I stopped and waited.

I don't know how long I stayed there. Probably not more than two or three minutes. I was about to give up when I heard the noise. I was still on my stomach, my head raised. The silhouette rose and started down the path.

I scrambled to my feet, trying to stay quiet, but that was a major no-go. The woman spun toward the sound, spotting me.

"Wait," I shouted. "I just want to talk to you."

But she had already darted back into the woods. Off the path, the woods were thick and yep, it was plenty dark. I could lose her easily. I was not about to risk that. Not again. Maybe I couldn't *see* her, but I could still *hear* her.

I jumped into the thicket and almost immediately hit a tree. I saw stars. Man, that had been a dumb move. I stopped now and listened.

Silence.

She had stopped. She was hiding again. So now what?

She had to be nearby. I considered my options and then thought, Ah, the hell with it. Remembering where I had last heard a noise, I leapt at the spot, spread-eagle, my hands and legs stretched to the max so that my body would cover as much territory as possible. I landed on a shrub.

But my left hand touched something else.

She tried to crawl away, but my fingers closed tight around her ankle. She kicked at me with her free leg. I held on like a dog digging his teeth in.

"Let go of me!" she shouted.

I did not recognize the voice. I did not let go of her ankle.

"What the—let go of me!"

No. I got some leverage and pulled her toward me. It was still too dark, but my eyes were beginning to adjust. I gave another tug. She rolled onto her back. We were close enough now. I was finally able to see her face.

It took a few moments to register. The memory was an old one, for one thing. The face, or what I could see of it, had changed. She looked different. What gave it away, what helped me recognize her, was the way her hair had fallen in front of her face during our tussle. That was almost more familiar than the features—the vulnerability of the pose, the way she now avoided eye contact. And of course, living in that house, that house I had always so closely associated with her, had kept her image in the forefront of my memory banks.

The woman pushed her hair to the side and looked up at me. I fell back to school days, the brick building barely two hundred yards from where we now lay. Now maybe it made some sort of sense. The mystery woman had been standing in front of the house where she used to live.

The mystery woman was Dina Levinsky.

chapter 11

We sat at the kitchen table. I made tea, a Tazo blend of Chinese green I'd bought at Starbucks. It was supposed to soothe. We'd see. I handed Dina a cup.

"Thank you, Marc."

I nodded and sat across from her. I had known Dina my whole life. I knew her in the way only a kid can know another kid, the way only elementary-school classmates know each other, even—bear with me here—even though I don't think we ever really spoke to one another.

We all have a Dina Levinsky in our past. She was the class victim, the girl so much an outcast, so often teased and abused, you wonder how she stayed sane. I never picked on her, but I stood on the sidelines plenty of times. Even if I didn't reside in her childhood home, Dina Levinsky would still live in me. She lives in you too. Quick: Who was the most picked-on kid in your elementary school? Right, exactly, you remember. You remember their first and last name and what they looked like. You remember watching them walk home alone or sitting in the cafeteria in silence. Whatever, you remember. Dina Levinsky stays with you.

"I hear you're a doctor now," Dina said to me.

"Yes. And you?"

"A graphic designer and artist. I have a show in the Village next month."

"Paintings?"

She hesitated. "Yes."

"You were always a good artist," I said.

She cocked her head, surprised. "You noticed?"

There was a brief pause. Then I found myself saying, "I should have done something."

Dina smiled. "No, I should have."

She looked good. No, she had not grown into a beauty like those ugly-duckling-swans you see in the movies. First off, Dina had never been ugly. She had been plain. Maybe she still was. Her features were still too narrow, but they worked better on an adult face. Her hair, so drippy in her youth, had body now.

"Do you remember Cindy McGovern?" she asked me.

"Sure."

"She tortured me more than anyone."

"I remember."

"Well, this is funny. I had an exhibit a few years back at a gallery in midtown—and Cindy shows up. She comes up to me and gives me a big hug and kiss. She wants to talk about old times, you know, like 'Remember how dorky Mr. Lewis was?' She's all smiles and I swear, Marc, she didn't remember what she'd been like. She wasn't pretending either. She just totally blocked out how she'd treated me. I find that sometimes."

"Find what?"

Dina raised the cup with two hands. "No one remembers being the bully." She hunched over, her eyes darted about the room. I wondered about my own remembrance. Had I just been on the sidelines—or was that, too, some sort of revisionist history?

"This is so messed up," Dina said.

"Being back in this house?"

"Yeah." She put down the cup. "I guess you want an explanation."

I waited.

Her eyes started darting again. "You want to hear something bizarre?"

"Sure."

"This is where I used to sit. I mean, when I was a kid. We had a rectangular table too. I always sat in the same spot. When I came in here now, I don't know, I just naturally gravitated to this chair. I guess—I guess that's part of the reason why I was here tonight."

"I'm not sure I understand."

"This house," she said. "It still has a pull on me. A hold." She leaned forward. Her eyes met mine for the first time. "You've heard the rumors, haven't you? About my father and what happened here."

"Yes."

"They're true," she said.

I forced myself not to wince. I had no idea what to say. I thought about the hell of school. I tried to add on to that the hell of this house. It was unfathomable.

"He's dead now. My father, I mean. He died six years ago."

I blinked and looked away.

"I'm okay, Marc. Really. I was in therapy—well, I mean, I still am. Do you know Dr. Radio?"

"No."

"That's his real name. Stanley Radio. He's pretty famous for the Radio Technique. I've been with him for years. I'm much better. I'm over the self-destructive tendencies. I'm past feeling worthless. It's funny though. I got over it. No, I mean it. Most victims of abuse have commitment and sex issues. I never did. I'm able to be intimate, no problem. I'm married now. My husband is a great guy. It's not happily-ever-after, but it's pretty damn good."

"I'm glad," I said, because I had no idea what else to say.

She smiled again. "Are you superstitious, Marc?"

"No."

"Me neither. Except, I don't know, when I read about your wife and daughter, I started to wonder. About this house. Bad karma and all that. Your wife was so lovely."

"You knew Monica?"

"We'd met."

"When?"

Dina did not reply right away. "Are you familiar with the term *trigger*?"

I remembered it from my medical school rotations. "You mean, in terms of psychiatry?"

"Yes. You see, when I read about what happened here, it was a trigger. Like with an alcoholic or anorexic. You're never fully cured. Something happens—a trigger—and you fall back into bad patterns. I started biting my nails. I started doing physical harm to myself. It was like—it was like I had to face down this house. I had to confront the past in order to defeat it."

"And that's what you were doing tonight?"

"Yes."

"And when I spotted you eighteen months ago?"

"Same thing."

I sat back. "How often do you stop by?"

"Once every couple of months, I guess. I park at the school lot and come through the Zucker path. But there's more to it than that."

"More to what?"

"My visits. See, this house still holds my secrets. I mean that literally."

"I'm not following."

"I keep trying to work up the courage to knock on the door again, but I can't do it. And now I'm inside, in this kitchen, and I'm okay." She tried to smile, as if to prove the point. "But I still don't know if I can do it."

"Do what?" I asked.

"I'm babbling." Dina started scratching the back of her hand, hard and fast, digging her nails in and nearly breaking skin. I wanted to reach out to her, but it felt too forced. "I wrote it all down. In a journal. What happened to me. It's still here."

"In the house?"

She nodded. "I hid it."

"The police went through here after the murder. They searched this place pretty good."

"They didn't find it," she said. "I'm sure of it. And even if they did, it's just an old journal. There'd be no reason for them to disturb it. Part of me wants it to stay put. It's over and done with it, you know what I mean? Let sleeping dogs lie. But another part wants to let it out into the light. Like it's a vampire and the sunshine will kill it."

"Where is it?" I asked.

"In the basement. You have to stand on the dryer to get to it. It's behind one of the ducts in the crawl space." She glanced at the clock. She looked at me and hugged herself. "It's getting late."

"Are you okay?"

The eyes were darting again. Her breathing was suddenly uneven. "I don't know how much longer I can stay here."

"Do you want to look for your journal?"

"I don't know."

"Do you want me to get it for you?"

She shook her head hard. "No." She stood, gulping air now. "I better go now."

"You can always come back, Dina. Anytime you want."

But she wasn't listening. She was in full panic mode and heading for the door.

"Dina?"

She suddenly spun toward me. "Did you love her?"

"What?"

"Monica. Did you love her? Or was there someone else?"

"What are you talking about?"

Her face drained of color. She stared at me now, backing away, petrified. "You know who shot you, don't you, Marc?"

I opened my mouth, but nothing came out. By the time I found my voice, Dina had turned away.

"I'm sorry, I have to go."

"Wait."

She flung the door open and ran out. I stood by the window and watched her scurry back up toward Phelps Road. This time, I chose not to follow.

Instead, I turned and with her words—*"You know who shot you, don't you, Marc?"*—still reverberating in my ears, I sprinted to the basement door.

All right, let me explain something here. I was not going down into the dingy, unfinished subdwelling to invade Dina's privacy. I did not pretend to know what was best for her, what might salve her horrendous pain. Many of my psychiatry colleagues would disagree, but sometimes I wonder if the past is better left buried. I don't have the answer, of course, and as my psychiatry colleagues would remind me, I don't ask them for their take on the best way to handle a cleft palate. So in the end, all I know for certain is that it is not my place to decide for Dina.

And I was not going in the basement out of curiosity about her past either. I had no interest in reading the details of Dina's torment. In fact, I actively did not want to know them. To speak selfishly, I was creeped out plenty just knowing such horrors had occurred in the place I call home. It was already enough in my face, thank you very much. I needed to hear or read no more.

So what exactly was I after?

I hit the light switch. A bare bulb came on. I was putting the pieces together even as I started to descend. Dina had said several curious things. Putting aside the most dramatic for a moment, I was starting to pick up on the more subtle ones. It was a night of spontaneous behavior on my part. I decided to let the trend continue.

First off, I remembered how Dina, when she was still the mystery woman on the sidewalk, had taken a step toward the door. I know now, as Dina herself had told me, that she'd been "trying to work up the courage to knock on the door again."

Again.

Knock on the door *again.*

The obvious implication was that Dina had, on at least one other occasion, worked up the courage to knock on my door.

Second, Dina had told me that she had "met" Monica. I could not imagine how. Yes, Monica, too, had grown up in this town, but from all I knew of her, she might as well have grown up in a different, more opulent era. The Portman estate was on the opposite end of our rather sprawling suburb. Monica had started boarding school at a young age. No one in town knew her. I remember seeing her once at the Colony movie theater over the summer of my sophomore year in high school. I had stared. She had studiously ignored me. Monica had that whole remote-beauty thing down pat by then. When I met her years later—she actually coming on to me—the flattery turned my head. Monica had seemed so fabulous at a distance.

So how, I wondered now, had my wealthy, remote, beautiful wife met poor, drab Dina Levinsky? The most likely answer, when you consider the "again" comment, was that Dina had knocked on the door and Monica had answered. They met then. They probably talked. Dina probably told Monica about the hidden journal.

"You know who shot you, don't you, Marc?"

No, Dina. But I plan on finding out.

I had reached the cement floor. Boxes that I would never throw away and never open were piled everywhere. I noticed, perhaps for the first time, that there were paint splatters on the floor. A large variety of hues. They'd probably been here since Dina's time, a reminder of her sole escape.

The washer and dryer were in the corner on the left. I moved slowly toward them in the shadowy light. I tiptoed, actually, as though I were afraid of waking Dina's sleeping dogs. Stupid really. As I said before, I am not superstitious and even if I were, even if I believed in evil spirits and the like, there was no reason to fear angering them. My wife was dead and my daughter was missing—what else could they do to me? In fact, I should disturb them, make them act, hope they let me know what really happened to my family, to Tara.

There it was again. Tara. Everything circled back to her eventually. I don't know how she fitted into all this. I don't know how her kidnapping was connected to Dina Levinsky. It probably wasn't. But I was not turning back.

You see, Monica never mentioned meeting Dina Levinsky.

I found that odd. True, I am building this ridiculous theory on pure foam. But if Dina had indeed knocked on the door, if Monica had indeed opened it, you would think that my wife would have mentioned it to me at some point. She knew that Dina Levinsky had gone to school with me. Why keep her visit—or the fact that they had met—a secret?

I hopped up on the dryer. I had to both crouch and look above me. Dust city. Spider webs were everywhere. I saw the duct and reached up. I felt around. It was difficult. There was a web of pipes, and my arm was having trouble fitting between them. It would have been much easier for a young girl with thin arms.

Eventually I worked my hand through the copper. I slid my fingertips to the right and pushed up. Nothing. My hand crawled a few more inches over and pushed again. Something gave way.

I pulled up my sleeve and twisted my arm in another inch or two. Two pipes pressed against my skin, but they gave enough. I was able to reach into the crawl space. I felt around, found something, pulled it into view.

The journal.

It was a classic school notebook with the familiar black marble cover. I opened and paged through it. The handwriting was minuscule. It reminded me of that guy in the mall who writes names on a grain of rice. Dina's immaculate penmanship—belying, no doubt, the content—started at the very top of the sheet and ran all the way to the bottom. There were no left or right margins. Dina had used both sides of every sheet.

I did not read it. Again that was not what I had come down for. I reached back up and put the journal back in its place. I don't know how this would set me with the gods—if just touching it would unleash a King Tut–like curse—but again I didn't care very much either.

I felt around again. I knew. I don't know how, but I just knew. Eventually my hand hit something else. My heart thumped. It felt smooth. Leather. I pulled it into view. Some dust followed. I blinked the particles out of my eyes.

It was Monica's DayRunner.

I remembered when she bought it at some chic boutique in New York. Something to organize her life, she'd told me. It'd had the customary calendar and datebook. When had we bought it? I wasn't sure. Maybe eight, nine months before she died. I tried to remember the last time I'd seen it. Nothing came to me.

I jammed the leather planner between my knees and put the ceiling panel back in place. I grabbed the datebook and climbed down from the dryer. I considered waiting until I got upstairs into better light, but, uh-uh, no way. The datebook had a zipper. Despite the dust it opened smoothly.

A CD fell out and landed on the floor.

It glittered in the low light like a jewel. I picked it up by the edges. There was no label on it. Memorex had manufactured it. "CD-R," it said, "80 Minutes."

What the hell is this?

One way to find out. I hurried upstairs and booted up my computer.

chapter 12

When I put the disk into the CD drive, the following screen appeared:

Password: _ _ _ _ _ _
MVD
Newark, NJ

Six-digit password. I typed in her birthday. No go. I tried Tara's birthday. No go. I put in our anniversary and then my birthday. I tried the code for our ATM. Nothing worked.

I sat back. So now what?

I debated calling Detective Regan. By now it was closing in on midnight, and even if I could reach him, what exactly would I say? "Hi, I found a CD hidden in my basement, rush over"? No. Hysterics would not work here. Better to show calm, to feign rationality. Patience was key. Think it through. I could call Regan in the morning. Nothing he could or would do tonight anyway. Sleep on it.

Fine, but I was not about to give up quite yet. I logged on to the Internet and brought up a search engine. I typed in MVD in Newark. A listing popped up.

"MVD—Most Valuable Detection."

Detection?

There was a link to a Web site. I clicked it, and the MVD Web site came up. My eyes did a quick scan. MVD was a "group of professional private investigators" who "provided confidential services." They offered online background checks for less than a hundred dollars. Their ads exclaimed, "Find out if that new boyfriend has a criminal record!"

and "Where is your old sweetheart? Maybe she's still pining for you!" Stuff like that. They also did more "intense, discreet investigations" for those who required such things. They were, per the top banner, a "full-service investigative entity."

So, I asked myself, what had Monica needed investigated?

I picked up the phone and dialed MVD's 800 number. A machine picked up—no surprise considering the hour—and told me how much they appreciated my call and that their office opened at nine in the morning. Okay. I'd call back then.

I hung up the phone and pressed the e: drive's eject button. The CD slid into view. I lifted up by the edges and checked for, I don't know, clues, I guess. Nothing new. Time to think here. It seemed pretty clear that Monica had hired MVD to investigate something and that this CD contained whatever it was she wanted investigated. Not exactly a brilliant deduction on my part, but it was a start.

Let's go back then. Fact is, I had no idea what Monica wanted investigated or why or any of that. But if I was right, if this CD did indeed belong to Monica, if she had hired a private investigator for whatever reason, it would naturally follow that she would have had to pay MVD for said services.

I nodded. Okay, a better start.

But—and here is where confusion immediately set in—the police had thoroughly combed through our bank accounts and financial records. They had scrutinized every transaction, every Visa purchase, every written check, every ATM withdrawal. Had they seen one to MVD? If so, they decided not to tell me. Of course, I had not been a potted plant here. My daughter was gone. I, too, had examined those financial statements. There was nothing to any detective agency nor were there any cash withdrawals out of the ordinary.

So what did that mean?

Maybe this CD was old.

That was a possibility. I don't think any of us checked transactions going back more than six months before the attack. Maybe her relationship with Most Valuable Detection predated that. I could probably check through the old statements.

But I wasn't buying it.

This CD was not old. I was fairly certain of that. And it didn't matter much anyway. Time frame, when I thought about it, was irrelevant.

Recent or otherwise, the key questions remained: Why would Monica hire a private investigator? What was password protected on that damn CD? Why had she hidden it in that creepy space in the basement? What, if anything, did Dina Levinsky have to do with any of this? And most important, did it have anything to do with the attack—or was this all a big exercise in wishful thinking on my part?

I looked out the window. The street was clear and silent. Suburbia sleeps. No more answers would come tonight. In the morning, I would take my father for our weekly walk and then I would call MVD and maybe even Regan.

I climbed into bed and waited for sleep.

The phone next to Edgar Portman's bed rang at four-thirty in the morning. Edgar jerked awake, pulled out in middream, and fumbled with the phone.

"What?" he barked.

"You said to call as soon as I knew."

Edgar rubbed his face. "You have the results."

"I do."

"And?"

"It's a match."

Edgar closed his eyes. "How certain are you?"

"It's preliminary. If I were taking it to court, I'd need a few more weeks to line up all the arrows. But that would just be following proper protocol."

Edgar could not stop shaking. He thanked the man, put the phone back in its cradle, and began to prepare.

chapter 13

At six the next morning, I left my house and walked down the block. Using a key I've had since college, I unlocked the door and slipped into my childhood home.

The years had not been a friend to this dwelling, but then again, it hadn't been featured in *House and Garden* (except maybe as one of their "before" photos) to begin with. We'd replaced the shag carpet four years ago—the blue-white speck had been so faded and thread-bare, it practically replaced itself—and went with close-cropped office-gray so that my father's wheelchair could move with ease. Other than that, nothing had been changed. The overvarnished side tables still held Lladró porcelain knickknacks from a long-ago trip to Spain. Holiday Inn–like oils of violins and fruit—none of us are the least bit musical or, uh, fruity—still adorned the white-painted wood paneling.

There were photos on the fireplace mantel. I always stopped and looked at the ones of my sister, Stacy. I don't know what I was looking for. Or maybe I do. I was searching for clues, for foreshadowing. I was searching for any hint that this young, fragile, damaged woman would one day buy a gun off the street, shoot me, harm my daughter.

"Marc?" It was Mom. She knew what I was doing. "Come help me, okay?"

I nodded and headed toward the back bedroom. Dad slept on the ground floor now—easier than trying to get up the stairs with a wheelchair. We dressed him, which was a bit like dressing wet sand. My father lolls from side to side. His weight has a tendency toward sudden shifts. My mother and I were used to that, but it doesn't make the task less arduous.

When my mother kissed me good-bye, the faint and familiar whiff of breath mint and cigarette smoke came off her. I had urged her to quit. She kept promising, but I knew that it would never happen. I noticed how loose the skin on her neck was getting, her gold chains almost embedded in their folds. She leaned down and kissed my father on the cheek, holding her lips to him a few seconds too long.

"Be careful," she told us. Then again, that was what she always told us.

We began our journey. I pushed Dad past the train station. We live in a commuter town. Mostly men but yes, women, too, were lined up in long coats, briefcase in one hand, coffee cup in the other. This might sound odd, but even before 9/11, these people were heroes to me. They board that damn train five times a week. They take it to Hoboken and switch to the PATH. That train takes them into New York City. Some will head up to Thirty-third Street and change to hit midtown. Others will take it to the financial center, now that it's opened up again. They make the everyday sacrifice, stifling their own wants and dreams in order to provide for those they love.

I could be doing cosmetic plastic surgery and making a mint. My parents would be able to afford better care for my dad. They could move someplace nice, get that full-time nurse, find a place that could cater more to their needs. But I don't do that. I don't help them by taking the more traveled route because, frankly, working such a job would bore me. So I choose to do something more exciting, something I love to do. For that, people think I'm the heroic one, that I am the one making the sacrifice. Here's the truth. The person who works with the poor? They are usually more selfish. We are not willing to sacrifice our needs. Working a job that provides for our families is not enough for us. Supporting those we love is secondary. We need personal satisfaction, even if our own family is made to do without. Those suits I now watch numbingly board the NJ Transit train? They often hate where they are going and what they are doing, but they do it anyway. They do it to take care of their families, to provide a better life for their spouses, their children, and maybe, just maybe, their aging and ill parents.

So, really, which one of us is to be admired?

Dad and I followed the same route every Thursday. We took the path around the park behind the library. The park was chockful—and you'll notice a suburban theme here—of soccer fields. How much quality real estate was tied up in this supposedly second-tier foreign sport? My father seemed comforted by the playground, by the sights and sounds of children at play. We stopped and took deep breaths. I glanced to my left. Several healthy women jogged by clad in your finest, sheer-clingy Lycra. Dad seemed very still. I smiled. Maybe Dad's liking this spot had nothing to do with soccer.

I no longer remember what my father used to be like. When I try to think back that far, my memories are snapshots, flashes—a man's deep laugh, a little boy clinging to his bicep, dangling off the ground. That was pretty much it. I remember that I loved him deeply, and I guess that has always been enough.

After his second stroke sixteen years ago, Dad's speech became extremely labored. He'd get stuck midsentence. He'd drop words. He'd go silent for hours and sometimes days. You'd forget that he was there. No one really knew for sure if he understood, if he had classic "expressive aphasia"—you understand but you can't really communicate—or something even more sinister.

But on a hot June day during my senior year of high school, my father suddenly reached out and grabbed hold of my sleeve with an eagle-talon grip. I'd been heading out to a party at the time. Lenny was waiting for me by the door. My father's surprisingly strong grasp stopped me cold. I looked down. His face was pure white, the tendons of his neck taut, and more than anything, what I saw was naked fear. That look on his face haunted my sleep for years afterward. I slid into the chair next to him, his hand still clutching my arm.

"Dad?"

"I understand," he pleaded. His grip on my sleeve tightened. "Please." Every word was a struggle. "I still understand."

That was all he said. But it was enough. What I took it to mean was this: "Even though I can't speak or respond, I comprehend. Please don't shut me out." For a while, the doctors agreed. He had expressive aphasia. Then he had another stroke, and the doctors became less sure of what he did and did not understand. I don't know if I apply my own version of Pascal's Wager here—if he understands me, then I should talk to him, if he doesn't, what's the harm?—but I figure that I owe him that. So I talk to him. I tell him everything. And right now, I was telling him about Dina Levinsky's visit—"Do you remember her, Dad?"—and the hidden CD.

Dad's face was locked, immobile, the left side of his mouth turned down in an angry slash-hook. I often wished that he and I never had that "I understand" conversation. I don't know which is worse: to be beyond comprehension, or to understand how trapped you really are. Or maybe I do know.

I was making the second turn, the one by the new skateboard run, when I spotted my former father-in-law. Edgar Portman sat on a bench, splendid in his casual best, his legs crossed, his pants crease sharp enough to slice tomatoes. After the shootings, Edgar and I tried to keep up a relationship that had never existed when his daughter was alive. We had hired a detective agency together—Edgar, of course, knew the best—but they came up with nothing. After a while, Edgar and I both grew weary of the pretense. The only bond between us was one that conjured up the worst moment of my life.

Edgar's being here could, of course, have been a coincidence. We live in the same town. It would only be natural to bump into one another from time to time. But that wasn't the case. I knew that. Edgar was not one for casual park visits. He was here for me.

Our eyes met, and I wasn't sure I liked what I saw. I wheeled the chair toward the bench. Edgar kept his eyes on me, never glancing down at my father. I might as well have been pushing a shopping cart.

"Your mother told me I'd find you here," Edgar said.

I stopped a few feet away from him. "What's up?"

"Sit with me."

I set my father's chair on my left. I lowered the brake. My father stared straight out. His head lolled toward his right shoulder, the way it does when he gets tired. I turned and faced Edgar. He uncrossed his legs.

"I've been wondering how to tell you this," he began.

I gave him a little space. He looked off. "Edgar?"

"Hmm."

"Just tell me."

He nodded, appreciating my directness. Edgar was that kind of man. Without preamble, he said, "I got another ransom demand."

I reeled back. I don't know what I had expected to hear—maybe that Tara had been found dead—but what he was saying . . . I couldn't quite comprehend it. I was about to ask a follow-up question when I saw that he now had a satchel in his lap. He opened it and pulled something into view. It was in a plastic bag—just like the last time we went through this. I squinted. He handed it to me. Something ballooned in my chest. I blinked and looked at the bag.

Hairs. There were hairs inside it.

"This is their proof," Edgar said.

I could not speak. I just looked at the hairs. I laid the bag gently on my lap.

"They understood that we would be skeptical," Edgar said.

"Who understood?"

"The kidnappers. They said they'd give us a few days. I immediately brought the hairs to a DNA laboratory."

I looked up at him and then back at the hairs.

"The preliminary results came in two hours ago," Edgar said. "Nothing they could use in court, but it's still pretty conclusive. The hairs match the ones sent to us a year and a half ago." He stopped and swallowed. "The hairs belong to Tara."

I heard the words. I didn't understand them. For some reason, I shook my head no. "Maybe they just saved them from before. . . ."

"No. They have aging tests too. Those hairs came from a child around two years old."

I guess that I knew that already. I could look and see that these were not my daughter's wispy baby hairs. She wouldn't have them anymore. Her hair would have darkened and thickened. . . .

Edgar handed me a note. Still in a fog, I took it from him. The font was the same as from the note we'd gotten eighteen months before. The top line over the fold said:

WANT ONE LAST CHANCE?

I felt the thud deep in my chest. Edgar's voice seemed suddenly far away. "I probably should have told you immediately, but it seemed an obvious hoax. Carson and I didn't want to get your hopes up unnecessarily. I have friends. They were able to rush through the DNA results. We still had hairs from the last mailing." He put a hand on my shoulder. I did not move.

"She's alive, Marc. I don't know how or where, but Tara is alive."

My eyes stayed on the hairs. Tara. They belonged to Tara. The sheen, that golden-wheat hue. I petted them through the plastic. I wanted to reach inside the bag, to touch my daughter, but I thought my heart would burst.

"They want another two million dollars. The note warns us again about calling the police—they claim to have an inside source. They sent another cell phone for you. I have the money in the car. We have another twenty-four hours maybe. That was the window they gave us for the DNA testing. You'll have to be ready."

I finally read the note. Then I looked over at my father in his wheelchair. He still stared straight ahead.

Edgar said, "I know you think I'm rich. I am, I guess. But not like you'd think. I'm leveraged and . . ."

I turned toward him. His eyes were wide. His hands shook.

"What I mean to say is that I don't really have that many liquid assets left. I'm not made of money. This is it."

"I'm surprised you're doing this at all," I said.

The words, I could see immediately, wounded him. I wanted to take them back, but for some reason I didn't. I let my eyes drift back toward my father. Dad's face remained frozen, but—I looked closer—there was a tear on his cheek. That didn't mean anything. Dad has teared up before, usually with no apparent provocation. I did not take this as any kind of sign.

And then, I don't know why, I followed his gaze. I looked across the soccer field, past the goalposts, past two women with Baby Joggers, all the way to the street nearly a hundred yards away. My stomach dropped. There, standing on the sidewalk, looking back at me with his hands in his pockets, was a man wearing a flannel shirt and black jeans and a Yankee cap.

I couldn't say for sure that it was the same man from the ransom drop. Red-and-black flannel is hardly an uncommon pattern. And maybe it was my imagination—I was pretty far away—but I think he was smiling at me. I felt my whole body jerk.

Edgar said, "Marc?"

I barely heard him. I rose and kept my eyes up. At first, the man in the flannel stayed perfectly still. I ran toward him.

"Marc?"

But I knew that it was no mistake. You don't forget. You close your eyes and you still see him. He never leaves you. You wish for moments like this. I knew that. And I knew what wishes could bring. But I ran straight toward him. Because there was no mistake. I knew who it was.

When I was still a good distance away, the man lifted his hand and waved to me. I kept moving, but I could already see that it was futile. I was only halfway across the park when a white van drove up. The man in flannel snapped a salute in my direction before disappearing into the back.

The van was out of sight before I reached the street.

chapter 14

Time started playing games with me. Going in and out. Speeding up and slowing down. In focus and suddenly blurred. But that did not last long. I let the surgeon side of me take over. He, Marc the Doctor, knew how to compartmentalize. I have always found this easier to do at work than in my personal life. The skill—to partition, to separate, to detach—has never translated. At work, I am able to take my emotional excess and channel it, allow it to converge into a constructive focus. I have never been successful at doing this at home.

But this crisis had forced a change. Compartmentalizing wasn't a question of desire as much as survival. To get emotional, to allow myself to wallow in doubt or consider the implications of a child missing for eighteen months . . . it would paralyze me. That was probably what the kidnappers wanted. They wanted me to come apart. But I work well under pressure. I am at my best. I know that. I had to do that now. The walls came up. I could look at the situation rationally.

First thing: No, I would not contact the police this time.

But that did not mean I had to wait around helplessly.

By the time Edgar handed me the duffel bag stuffed with money, I had an idea.

I called Cheryl and Lenny's house. There was no answer. I checked my watch. Eight-fifteen in the morning. I didn't have Cheryl's cell phone, but it would be better to do this in person anyway.

I drove over to Willard Elementary School and arrived at eight twenty-five. I parked behind a line of SUVs and minivans and got out. This elementary school, like so many others, has the bricks, the cement back steps, the one level, the architectural design made shapeless by the many additions. Some additions try to blend in, but then there are the others, usually built between 1968 and 1975, that were faux-sleek with blue glass and odd tiling. They looked like post-apocalyptic greenhouses.

Kids scrambled around the playground as they always do. The difference was, the parents now stayed and watched. They chatted with one another and when the bell rang, they made sure that their charges were safely ensconced inside the brick or sleek blue glass before departing. I hated to see the fear in the eyes of the parents. But I understood it. The day you become a parent, fear becomes your constant companion. It never lets you go. My life was Exhibit A in the why.

Cheryl's blue Chevy Suburban pulled into the drop-off line. I started toward her. She was unharnessing Justin from his car seat when she spotted me. Justin gave her a dutiful kiss, an act he takes for granted which, I guess, is how it should be, and then he ran off. Cheryl watched him as though afraid he could vanish on the short concrete trek. Kids can never understand that fear, but that's okay. Hard enough to be a kid without having that weight on you.

"Hey," Cheryl said to me.

I said hi back. Then: "I need something."

"What?"

"Rachel's phone number."

Cheryl was already back at the driver-side door. "Get in."

"My car is parked over there."

"I'll bring you back. Swim practice ran late. I've got to get Marianne to school."

She had already started the car. I hopped up into the front passenger seat. I turned and smiled at Marianne. She wore headphones and quick-fingered her Game Boy Advance. She gave me an absentminded wave, barely glancing up. Her hair was still wet. Conner was in the child seat next to her. The car reeked of chlorine, but I found the smell oddly comforting. Lenny, I know, cleans out the car religiously, but you can't possibly keep up. There were French fries in the crevice between the seats. Crumbs of unknown origin clung to the upholstery. On the floor by my feet lay a potpourri of school notices and children's artwork that had been subjected to onslaughts of rain boots. I sat on a small action figure, the kind that McDonald's gives away with their Happy Meals. A

CD case reading NOW THAT'S WHAT I CALL MUSIC 14 sat between us, providing listeners with the latest from Britney and Christina and Generic Boy Band. The windows in the back were smeared with greasy fingerprints.

The kids were only allowed to play with the Game Boy in the car, never in the house. They were never, under any circumstance, allowed to watch a PG-13 movie. I asked Lenny about how he and Cheryl went about deciding such matters and he responded, "It's not the rules themselves, but the fact that there are rules." I think I know what he meant.

Cheryl kept her eyes on the road. "It's not my nature to pry."

"But you want to know my intentions."

"I guess."

"And if I don't want to tell you?"

"Maybe," she said, "it's better if you don't."

"Trust me here, Cheryl. I need the number."

She flipped on her signal light. "Rachel is still my closest friend."

"Okay."

"It took her a long time to get over you." She hesitated.

"And vice versa."

"Exactly. Look, I'm not saying this right. It's just . . . there are some things you need to know."

"Like?"

She kept her eyes on the road, two hands on the wheel. "You asked Lenny why we never told you she got divorced."

"Yes."

Cheryl glanced in the rearview mirror, not at the road, but at her daughter. Marianne seemed wrapped up in her game. "She didn't get divorced. Her husband is dead."

Cheryl glided to a stop in front of the middle school. Marianne took off the headphones and slid out. She did not bother with the dutiful kiss, but she did say good-bye. Cheryl put the car back in drive.

"I'm sorry to hear that," I said, because that was what people said under these circumstances. I almost added, because the mind works in very strange and even macabre ways: Hey, Rachel and I have something else in common.

And then, as if Cheryl could read these thoughts, she said, "He was shot."

This eerie parallel sat between us for several seconds. I stayed quiet.

"I don't know the details," she quickly added. "He was with the FBI too. Rachel was one of the highest-ranking women in the bureau at the time. She resigned after he died. She stopped taking my calls. It hasn't been good for her since." Cheryl pulled up to my car and stopped. "I'm telling you this because I want you to understand. A lot of years have passed since college. Rachel isn't the same person you loved all those years ago."

I kept my tone steady. "I just need her phone number."

Without another word, Cheryl grabbed a pen from the visor, uncapped it with her teeth, and jotted the number on a Dunkin' Donuts napkin.

"Thanks," I said.

She barely nodded as I got out.

I did not hesitate. I had my cell phone. I slipped into my car and dialed the number. Rachel answered with a tentative hello. My words were simple enough.

"I need your help."

chapter 15

Five hours later, Rachel's train pulled into Newark Station.

I couldn't help but think of all those old movies where trains separate lovers, steam billowing from beneath, the conductor calling a last warning, the whistle sounding, the chug-chug as the wheels begin to move, one lover hanging out and waving, the other running along the platform. I don't know why I thought of this. The Newark train station is about as romantic as a pile of hippo dung with head lice. The train approached with nary a whisper and nothing you'd want to see or smell wafted in the air.

But when Rachel stepped off, I still felt the hum in my chest. She was dressed in faded blue jeans and a red turtleneck. Her overnight bag dangled from one shoulder, and she hoisted it up as she stepped down. For a moment, I just stared. I'd just turned thirty-six years old. Rachel was thirty-five. We had not been together since our very early twenties. We had lived our entire adult lives apart. Odd when you think of it that way. I told you before about our breakup. I try to unearth the whys, but maybe it is that simple. We were kids. Kids do dumb things. Kids don't understand repercussions, don't think long term. Kids don't understand that the hum may never really leave your chest.

Yet today, when I realized that I needed help, I thought first of Rachel. And she had come.

She moved toward me with no hesitation. "You okay?"

"Fine."

"Did they call?"

"Not yet."

She nodded and started walking down the platform. Her tone was no nonsense. She, too, had slipped into her role as a professional. "Tell me more about the DNA test."

"I don't know anything else."

"So it's not definitive?"

"Not court-evidence definitive, no, but they seem pretty sure."

Rachel shifted her bag from her right shoulder to her left. I tried to keep up with her pace. "We have to make some tough decisions, Marc. You ready for that?"

"Yes."

"First off, are you certain that you don't want to contact the cops or FBI?"

"The note said they had an inside source."

"That's probably bull," she said.

We walked a few more steps.

"I contacted the authorities last time," I said.

"Doesn't mean it was the wrong move."

"But it certainly wasn't the right one."

She made a yes-no gesture with her head. "You don't know what happened last time. Maybe they spotted the tail. Maybe they watched your house. But most likely, they never intended to give her back. You understand that?"

"Yes."

"But you still want them left out."

"It's why I called you."

She nodded and finally stopped, waiting for me to signal which way. I pointed to the right. She started up again. "Another thing," she said.

"What?"

"We can't let them dictate the tempo this time. We have to insist on assurances that Tara is alive."

"They'll say the hairs prove it."

"And we'll say the tests were inconclusive."

"You think they'll buy that?"

"I don't know. Probably not." She kept walking, the cut of her jaw held high. "But this is what I mean by tough decisions. That flannel-shirt guy in the park? That's about head games. They want to intimidate and weaken you. They want you to follow blindly again. Tara is your child. If you want to just hand over the money again, that's up to you. But I wouldn't advise it. They vanished before. There's no reason to think they won't again."

We entered the parking garage. I handed the attendant my ticket. "So what do you suggest?" I asked her.

"A few things. First, we have to demand an exchange. No 'Here's the money, call us later.' We get your daughter when they get the money."

"And if they don't agree?"

She looked at me with those eyes. "Tough decisions. You understand?"

I nodded.

"I also want a total electronic surveillance hookup, so I can stay with you. I want to strap on a fiber-optic camera and see what this guy looks like, if possible. We don't have manpower, but there are still things we can do."

"Suppose they catch on?"

"Suppose they run away again?" she countered. "We're taking chances here no matter what we do. I'm trying to learn from what happened the first time. There are no guarantees. I'm simply trying to improve our odds."

The car arrived. We slid in and started up McCarter Highway. Rachel suddenly grew very quiet. The years again melted away. I knew this posture. I had seen it before.

"What else?" I said.

"Nothing."

"Rachel."

Something in my tone made her look away. "There are some things you should know."

I waited.

"I called Cheryl," she said. "I know she filled you in on most of it. You understand that I'm not a fed anymore."

"Yes."

"There's a limit to what I can do."

"I understand that." She sat back. The posture was still there. "What else?"

"You need a reality check here, Marc."

We pulled to a red light. I turned and looked at her—really looked at her—for the first time. The eyes still had that hazel with gold flakes. I know the years had been tough, but it didn't show in the eyes.

"The odds that Tara is still alive are minuscule," she said.

"But the DNA test," I countered.

"I'll handle that later."

"Handle it?"

"Later," she said again.

"What the hell does that mean? It's a match. Edgar said the final confirmation is a formality."

"Later," she repeated with steel in her voice. "Right now we might as well assume that she's alive. We should go through with the ransom drop-off as if there is a healthy child on the other end. But somewhere along the line, I need you to understand that this could be an elaborate con."

"How do you figure?"

"That's not relevant."

"Like hell it isn't. Are you saying, what, they faked a DNA test?"

"I doubt it." Then she added, "But it's a possibility."

"How? There was a match between the two sets of hairs."

"The hairs matched each other."

"Yes."

"But," she said, "how do you know the first set of hairs—the ones you got a year and a half ago—belonged to Tara?"

It took a few moments for the meaning to reach me.

"Did you ever run a test on the first set, see if the DNA matched yours?" she asked.

"Why would we?"

"So for all you know, the original kidnappers sent you the hairs of another kid."

I tried to shake my head clear. "But they had a snippet of her clothes," I said. "The pink with black penguins. How do you explain that?"

"You don't think the Gap sold more than one of those? Look, I don't know what the story is yet, so let's not get bogged down in hypotheticals. Let's just concentrate on what we can do here and now."

I sat back. We fell into silence. I wondered if I had made the right move by calling her. There was so much excess baggage here. But at the end of the day, I trusted her. We needed to maintain the professional, to keep compartmentalizing.

"I just want my daughter back," I said.

Rachel nodded, opened her mouth as if to say something, and then grew silent again. And that was when the ransom call came in.

chapter 16

Lydia liked to stare at old photographs.

She did not know why. They offered her little comfort. The nostalgia factor was, at best, limited. Heshy never looked back. For reasons that she could never properly articulate, Lydia did.

This particular photograph had been taken when Lydia was eight years old. It was a black-and-white still from the beloved classic TV sitcom *Family Laughs*. The show ran for seven years—in Lydia's case, from the age of six until just near her thirteenth birthday. *Family Laughs* starred ex–movie hunk Clive Wilkins as the widowed father of three adorable children: twin boys, Tod and Rod, who were eleven when the series began, and an adorable pixie of a little sister named, cutely enough, Trixie, played by the irrepressible Larissa Dane. Yes, the show was at least three steps beyond precious. Old repeats of *Family Laughs* still run on TV Land.

Every once in a while, the *E! True Hollywood Story* runs a piece on the old cast of *Family Laughs*. Clive Wilkins died from pancreatic cancer two years after the show ended. The narrator would note that Clive was "just like a father on the set," which, Lydia knew, was a load of crap. The guy drank and smelled liked tobacco. When she hugged him for the cameras, it took all her considerable young acting skills not to gag from the stench.

Jarad and Stan Frank, the real-life identical twins who played Tod and Rod, had been trying to get a music career going since the show's cancellation. On *Family Laughs*, they had a groovy garage band with a repertoire of songs written by others, instruments played by others, and voices so echoed and distorted by synthesizers that even Jarad and Stan, who could not hold a key if it was tattooed into their palms, started to believe that they were genuine musical artistes. The twins were both nearing forty now, both clearly clients of the Hair Club, both deluding themselves that, even though they claimed to be "tired of the fame," they were one break away from the return to stardom.

But the true draw here, the gripping enigma of the *Family Laughs* saga, involved the fate of the adorable "Pixie named Trixie," Larissa Dane. Here is what is known about her: During the show's final season, Larissa's parents got divorced and fought bitterly over her earnings. Her dad ended up blowing his brains out. Her mother remarried a con artist who disappeared with the money. Like most child actors, Larissa Dane became an immediate has-been. Rumors of promiscuity and drug abuse swirled, though—this being before the nostalgia craze—no one really cared enough to be interested. She overdosed and nearly died when she was just fifteen. She was sent to a sanitarium of some sort and seemingly dropped off the face of the earth. No one really knows what became of her. Many believe that she died from a second drug overdose.

But of course, she had not.

Heshy said, "You ready to make the call, Lydia?"

She did not answer right away. Lydia moved to the next photograph. Another shot from *Family Laughs*, this time Season Five, Episode 112. Little Trixie wore a cast on her arm. Tod wanted to draw a guitar on it. Father didn't really approve. Tod protested, "But, Dad, I promise only to draw it, not play it!" The laugh track howled. Young Larissa didn't understand the joke. Grown-up Lydia didn't either. What she did remember, however, was how she had broken her arm that day. Typical kid stuff really. She was horsing around and fell down the stairs. The pain was tremendous, but they needed to get this show in the can. With that in mind, the studio doctor shot her up with Lord-knows-what and two hack screenwriters incorporated the injury into the script. She was barely conscious when they filmed.

But please, do not start up the violins.

Lydia had read Danny Partridge's book. She had listened to the whining of Willis on *Diff'rent Strokes*. She had heard all about the plight of the child star, the abuse, the stolen money, the long hours. She had seen all the talk shows, heard all the complaints, seen all the crocodile tears from her colleagues—and their dishonesty sickened her.

Here was the truth about the child star dilemma. No, it's not the abuse, though when Lydia was young and foolish enough to believe a shrink could help, he kept telling her how she must be "blocking," that she had in all likelihood been molested by one of the show's producers. And no, don't blame parental neglect for what child stars become. Or, in reverse, parental pushing. It's not the lack of friends, the long hours, the poor socialization skills, the stream of studio tutors. No, it is none of that.

It is, quite simply, the loss of the spotlight.

Period. The rest are excuses because no one wants to admit that they are that shallow. Lydia began working on the show when she was six. She had few memories that dated back before then. All she remembers, thus, is being a star. A star is special. A star is royalty. A star is the closest thing on earth to a god. And for Lydia, there had never been anything else. We teach our children that they are special, but Lydia lived it. Everyone thought she was adorable. Everyone thought she was the perfect daughter, loving and kind and yet properly sassy. People stared at her with a bizarre longing. People wanted to be near her, to know about her life, spend time with her, touch the hem of her cloak.

And then, one day, poof—all gone.

Fame is more addictive than crack. Adults who lose fame—one-hit wonders, for example—usually tailspin into depression, though they try to act like they're above it. They don't want to admit the truth. Their whole life is a lie, a desperate scramble for another dose of that most potent of drugs. Fame.

Those adults had a mere sip of the nectar before it was snatched away. But for a child star, that nectar is mother's milk. It's all they've ever known. They can't comprehend that it's fleeting, that it won't last. You can't explain that to a child. You can't prepare them for the inevitable. Lydia had never known anything but adulation. And then, pretty much overnight, the spotlight went out. She was, for the first time in her life, alone in the dark.

That was what screws you up.

Lydia recognized that now. Heshy had helped her. He had gotten her off the junk once and for all. She had hurt herself, had been a slut, had snorted and shot up more narcotics than one could imagine. She did none of these things to escape. She did them to lash out, to hurt something or someone. Her mistake, she realized in rehab after a truly horrific and violent incident, was that she was hurting *herself*. Fame raises you up. It makes others lesser. So why on earth was she hurting the one who should be on top? Instead, why not hurt the pitiful masses, those who had worshiped her, who had given her such heady power, who had turned on her? Why harm the superior species, the one who'd been worthy of all this praise?

"Lydia?"

"Hmm."

"I think we should call now."

She turned to Heshy. They had met in the loony bin, and right away, it was as if their mutual misery could reach out and embrace. Heshy had rescued her when two orderlies had pinned her down. At the time, he had merely pushed them off her. The orderlies threatened them, and they both promised not to say anything. But Heshy understood how to bide his time. He waited. Two weeks later, he ran over one of the goons with a stolen car. While the goon lay wounded, Heshy backed up over his head and then, positioning the tire near the base of the neck, hit the accelerator. A month later, the second goon—the lead orderly—was found in his home. Four of his fingers had been ripped off. Not cut or sliced, but twisted. The ME could tell by the rotation tears. The fingers had been rotated around and around until the tendons and bone finally snapped. Lydia still had one of the fingers somewhere in the basement.

Ten years ago, they ran off together and changed their names. They altered their appearances just enough. They both started over, avenging angels, damaged but superior, above the riffraff. She didn't hurt anymore. Or at least, when she did, she found an outlet.

They had three residences. Heshy purportedly lived in the Bronx. She had a place in Queens. They both had working addresses and working phones. But that was all for show. Business offices, if you will. Neither of them wanted anyone to know that they were, in fact, a team, connected, lovers. Lydia, using an alias, had bought this bright yellow house four years ago. It had two bedrooms and one and a half baths. The kitchen, where Heshy now sat, was airy and happy. They were on a lake in the tippy north corner of Morris County, New Jersey. It was peaceful here. They loved the sunsets.

Lydia kept staring at the pictures of "Pixie Trixie." She tried to remember what she'd felt like back then. The memories were pretty much gone. Heshy stood behind her now and waited with his usual patience. There were those who would claim that she and Heshy were cold-blooded killers. That, Lydia quickly realized, was pretty much a misnomer, another Hollywood creation. Like the wonderfulness of Pixie Trixie. No one enters this violent business merely because it is profitable. There are easier ways to make a living. You may act like a professional. You may keep your emotions in check. You may even delude yourself into thinking it's just another day at the office, but when you look at it honestly, the reason you walk on this wrong side of the line is because you enjoy it. Lydia understood that. Hurting someone, killing someone, fading or turning out the light in a person's eyes . . . no, she did not need that. She did not crave it as she had the spotlight. But yes, no question, there was that pleasant jolt, that unmistakable thrill, a lessening of her own pain.

"Lydia?"

"I'm on it, Pooh Bear." She picked up the cell phone with the stolen number and the scramble. She turned and faced Heshy. He was hideous, but she didn't see that. He nodded at her. She flipped on the voice changer and dialed the number.

When Lydia heard Marc Seidman's voice, she said, "Shall we try this again?"

chapter 17

Before I answered the phone, Rachel put her hand over mine. "This is a negotiation," she said. "Fear and intimidation are tools in that. You have to stay strong. If they intend to let her go, they will be flexible."

I swallowed and flicked on the phone. I said hello.

"Shall we try this again?"

The voice had the same robotic hum. I felt a tick in my blood. I closed my eyes and said, "No."

"Pardon me?"

"I want assurances that Tara is alive."

"You received hair samples, did you not?"

"Yes."

"And?"

I looked over at Rachel. She nodded. "The match was inconclusive."

"Fine," the voice said. "I might as well hang up now."

"Wait," I said.

"Yes?"

"You drove off last time."

"So we did."

"How do I know you won't do that again?"

"Did you call the police this time?"

"No."

"Then you have nothing to worry about. Here is what I want you to do."

"It's not going to work like that," I said.

"What?"

I could feel my body begin to quake. "We make a swap. You don't get the money until I get my daughter."

"You're not in any position to bargain."

"I get my daughter," I said, my words coming out slowly, dead weights. "You get your money."

"It's not going to work like that."

"Yes," I said, trying to force bravado into my voice. "This ends here and now. I don't want you running away again and then coming back for more. So we make an exchange and end this."

"Dr. Seidman?"

"I'm here."

"I want you to listen to me carefully."

The silence was too long, straining my nerves.

"If I hang up now, I won't call back for another eighteen months."

I closed my eyes and hung on.

"Think about the repercussions for a moment. Aren't you wondering where your daughter has been? Aren't you wondering what will become of her? If I hang up, you won't know anything for another eighteen months."

It felt like a steel belt was being tightened around my chest. I couldn't breathe. I looked at Rachel. She stared back steadily, urging me to stay strong.

"How old would she be then, Dr. Seidman? I mean, if we keep her alive."

"Please."

"Are you ready to listen?"

I squeezed my eyes shut. "I'm just asking for assurances."

"We sent you the hair samples."

"I bring the money. You bring my daughter. You get the money when I see her."

"Are you trying to dictate terms, Dr. Seidman?"

The robotic voice had a funny lilt now.

"I don't care who you are," I said. "I don't care why you did any of this. I just want my daughter back."

"Then you'll make the drop exactly as I tell you."

"No," I said. "Not without assurances."

"Dr. Seidman?"

"Yes."

"Good-bye."

And then the phone went dead.

chapter 18

Sanity is a thin string. Mine snapped.

No, I did not scream. Just the opposite. I grew impossibly calm. I pulled the phone away from my ear and looked at it as if it'd just materialized there and I had no idea what it was.

"Marc?"

I looked at Rachel. "They hung up."

"They'll call back," she said.

I shook my head. "They said not for another eighteen months."

Rachel studied my face. "Marc?"

"Yes?"

"I need you to listen to me closely."

I waited.

"You did the right thing here."

"Thanks. Now I feel better."

"I've had experience with this. If Tara is still alive and if they have any intention of giving her back, they'll give on this issue. The only reason not to make this exchange is because they don't want to—or can't."

Can't. The tiny part of my brain that remained rational understood that. I reminded myself of my training. Compartmentalize. "So now what?"

"We get ready just as we planned before. I have enough equipment with me. We'll wire you up. If they call back, we'll be ready."

I nodded dumbly. "Okay."

"Meanwhile, is there anything else we can do here? Did you recognize the voice at all? Do you remember anything new about the man in flannel, about the van, anything?"

"No," I said.

"On the phone, you mentioned finding a CD in your basement."

"Yes." I quickly told her the story about the disk and the label reading MVD. She took out a pad and jotted down notes.

"Do you have the disk with you?"

"No."

"Doesn't matter," she said. "We're in Newark now. We might as well see what we can learn from this MVD."

chapter 19

Lydia lifted the Sig-Sauer P226 into the air.

"I don't like how that went," she said.

"You made the right move," Heshy said. "We cut out now. This is over."

She stared at the weapon. She wanted very much to pull the trigger.

"Lydia?"

"I heard you."

"We were doing this because it was simple."

"Simple?"

"Yes. We thought that it would be easy money."

"Lots of money."

"True," he said.

"We can't just walk away."

Heshy saw the wetness in her eyes. This was not about the money. He knew that. "He's tortured either way," he said.

"I know."

"Think about what you just did to him," Heshy said. "If he never hears from us again, he will spend the rest of his life wondering, blaming himself."

She smiled. "Are you trying to turn me on?"

Lydia moved onto Heshy's lap, curled into him like a kitten. He wrapped his giant arms around her and for a moment, Lydia calmed. She felt safe and quiet. She closed her eyes. She loved the feeling. And she knew—as did he—that it would never last. That it would never be enough.

"Heshy?"

"Yes."

"I want to get that money."

"I know you do."

"And then, I think, it would be best if he died."

Heshy pulled her close. "Then that's what will happen."

chapter 20

I don't know what I expected from the offices of Most Valuable Detection. A pebbled-glass door à la Sam Spade or Philip Marlowe maybe. A soiled building of faded brick. A walk-up, for sure. A buxom secretary with a bad dye job.

But the office of Most Valuable Detection had none of that. The building was shiny and bright, part of the "urban renewal" program of Newark. I keep hearing about Newark's renaissance, but I don't see it. Yes, there are several beautiful office buildings—like this one—and a stunning Performing Arts Center conveniently located so that those who can afford to attend (read: those who don't live in Newark) can get to it without, well, driving through the city. But these sleek edifices are flowers among the weeds, scant stars in an otherwise black sky. They do not change the basic color. They do not blend or bleed. They remain removed. Their sterile beauty is not contagious.

We stepped off the elevator. I still held the bag with two million dollars in it. It felt weird in my hand. There were three headphone-clad receptionists behind a wall of glass. Their desk was high. We stated our names into an intercom. Rachel showed an ID that listed her as a retired FBI agent. We were buzzed in.

Rachel pushed open the door. I trailed behind her. I felt empty, but I was functioning. The horror of what had happened—the hang-up—was so great that I had pushed beyond paralysis to a strange state of focus. Again I compare all this to the surgery room. I enter that room, I cross that gateway, and I shed the world. I had a patient once, a six-year-old boy, who was getting a fairly routine cleft palate repair. While on the table, his vitals dropped suddenly. His heart stopped. I didn't panic. I fell into a state of focus, not unlike this one. The boy pulled through.

Still flashing the ID, Rachel explained that we wanted to see some-one in charge. The receptionist smiled and nodded in that way people do when they aren't listening. She never took off the headphones. Her fingers pressed some buttons. Another woman appeared. She led us down the corridor and into a private office.

For a moment, I couldn't tell if we were in the presence of a man or a woman. The bronze nameplate on the desk read Conrad Dorfman. Conclusion: a man. He rose theatrically. He was too slim in a blue suit with *Guys and Dolls*–wide pinstripes, tapered at the waist so that the bottom of the jacket flared out almost enough to be mistaken for a skirt. His fingers were thin like a pianist's, his hair slicked down like Julie Andrews's in *Victor/Victoria*, and his face had a blotchy smooth-ness I usually associate with a cosmetic foundation.

"Please," he said in a voice with too much affect. "My name is Con-rad Dorfman. I'm the executive vice president of MVD." We shook his hand. He held our hands a second too long, putting the free hand over the shake and peering intently into our eyes. Conrad invited us to sit. We did. He asked us if we'd enjoy a cup of tea. Rachel, taking the lead, said that we would.

There were a few more minutes of chitchat. Conrad asked Rachel questions about her time with the FBI. Rachel was vague. She implied that she, too, worked in the private detection biz and was thus his col-league and worthy of professional courtesy. I said nothing, letting her work. There was a knock on the door. The woman who had escorted us down the corridor opened the door and wheeled in a silver teacart. Conrad began to pour. Rachel got to the point.

"We were hoping you could help us," Rachel said. "Dr. Seidman's wife was a client of yours."

Conrad Dorfman concentrated on the tea. He used one of those screen-door sifters that seemed all the rage nowadays. He shook out some leaves and slowly poured.

"You folks provided her with a CD that's password protected. We need to get into it."

Conrad handed a cup of tea to Rachel first, then me. He settled back and took a deep sip. "I'm sorry," he said. "I can't help you. The password is set by the client on their own."

"The client is dead."

Conrad Dorfman did not blink. "That really doesn't change anything."

"Her husband here is next of kin. That makes the CD his."

"I wouldn't know," Conrad said. "I don't practice estate law. But we have no control over any of that. As I said before, the client sets the password. We may have given her the CD—I really can't confirm or deny that at this stage—but we would have no idea what numbers or letters she programmed in for the password."

Rachel waited a beat. She stared at Conrad Dorfman. He stared back but dropped his eyes first. He picked up his tea and took another sip. "Can we find out why she came to you in the first place?"

"Without a court order? No, I don't think so."

"Your CD," she said. "There's a back entry."

"Excuse me?"

"Every company has one," Rachel said. "The info isn't lost forever. Your company programs in its own password so that you folks can get on the CD."

"I don't know what you're talking about."

"I used to be an FBI agent, Mr. Dorfman."

"So?"

"So I know these things. Please don't insult my intelligence."

"That was not my intent, Ms. Mills. But I simply can't help."

I looked at Rachel. She seemed to be weighing her options. "I still have friends, Mr. Dorfman. In the department. We can ask questions. We can poke around. The feds don't much like private eyes. You know that. I don't want trouble. I just want to know what's on the CD."

Dorfman put down his cup. He strummed his fingers. There was a knock, and the same woman opened the door. She beckoned Conrad Dorfman. He rose, again too theatrically, and practically leapt across the floor. "Excuse me a moment."

When he left the office, I looked at Rachel. She wouldn't turn toward me. "Rachel?"

"Let's just see how it plays out, Marc."

But there really wasn't much more to play. Conrad came back into the office. He crossed the room and stood over Rachel, waiting for her to look up. She wouldn't give him the satisfaction.

"Our president, Malcolm Deward, is a former federal agent himself. Did you know that?"

Rachel said nothing.

"He made some calls while we chatted." Conrad waited. "Ms. Mills?" Rachel finally looked up. "Your threats are impotent. You have no friends at the agency. Mr. Deward, alas, does. Get out of my office. Now."

chapter 21

I said, "What the hell was that all about?"

"I told you before. I'm not an agent anymore."

"What happened, Rachel?"

She kept her eyes forward. "You haven't been a part of my life in a long time."

There was nothing to add. Rachel drove now. I held on to the cell phone, again willing it to ring. When we arrived back at my house, dusk had settled in. We went inside. I debated calling Tickner or Regan, but what good would that do now?

"We need to get that DNA checked," Rachel said. "My theory might sound implausible, but does the idea of your daughter being held all this time sound any more so?"

So I called Edgar. I told him that I wanted to run some additional tests on the hair. He said that would be fine. I hung up without telling him that I had already endangered the drop by enlisting the help of a former FBI agent. The less said on that, the better. Rachel called someone she knew to pick up the samples from Edgar, as well as a blood sample from me. He ran a private lab, she said. We would know something within twenty-four to forty-eight hours, which would probably be, in terms of a ransom demand, too late.

I settled into a chair in the den. Rachel sat on the floor. She opened her bag and pulled out wires and electronic contraptions of all sorts. Being a surgeon makes me pretty good with my hands, but when it comes to high-tech gizmos, I'm totally lost. She carefully spread the contents of the bag across the carpet, giving this action her full attention. Again I was reminded of the way she'd do the same thing with textbooks when we were in college. She reached into the bag and pulled out a razor.

"The bag of money?" she said.

I handed it to her. "What are you going to do?"

She opened it. The money was in packs of hundred-dollar bills. She grabbed a wad and slowly slipped the money out, not breaking the band around it. She cut the bills like they were a deck of cards.

"What are you doing?" I asked.

"I'm going to cut a hole."

"In the actual currency?"

"Yup."

She did it with the straight razor. She dug out a circle about the perimeter of a silver dollar, maybe a quarter inch thick. She scanned the floor, found a black device that was about the same size, fit it into the bills. Then she put the wrapping back on it. The device was totally hidden in the middle of the money wad.

"A Q-Logger," she said in way of explanation. "It's a GPS device."

"You say so."

"GPS stands for Global Positioning System. Put simply, it will track the money. I'll put one in the lining of the bag too, but most criminals know about that. They usually dump the cash into a bag of their own. But with all this money, they won't have time right away to search through every pack."

"How small do those things come?"

"The Q-Loggers?"

"Yes."

"They can make them even thinner, but the problem is the power source. You need a battery. That's where we lose out. I need something that can travel at least eight miles. This will do it."

"And where does it go to?"

"You mean where do I keep track of the movements?"

"Yes."

"Most of the time it goes to a laptop, but this is state of the art." Rachel lifted a device into the air, one I see too often in the world of medicine. In fact, I think I'm the only doctor on the planet without one.

"A Palm Pilot?"

"Designed with a special tracking screen. I'll have it on me if I have to move." She went back to work.

"What's all the other stuff?" I asked.

"Surveillance equipment. I don't know how much I'll be able to use, but I'd like to put a Q-Logger in your shoe. I want to get a camera on the car. I'd like to see if I can hook up some fiber-optics on you, but that could be riskier." She started to organize her equipment, lost in the activity. Her eyes were down when she spoke again. "Something else I want to explain to you."

I leaned forward.

"Do you remember when my parents got divorced?" she asked.

"Yeah, sure." It had been when we first met.

"Close as we were, we never talked about it."

"I always got the impression you didn't want to."

"I didn't," she said too quickly.

And, I thought, neither had I. I was selfish. We were supposedly in love for two years—and yet I never so much as nudged her to open up about her parents' divorce. It was more than an "impression" that made me hold my tongue. I knew something dark and unhappy lay there. I did not want to poke at it, disturb it, have it possibly turn its attention in my direction.

"It was my father's fault."

I almost said something really stupid like "It's never anyone's fault" or "There are two sides to every story," but a flyby of good sense kept my tongue in check. Rachel still hadn't looked up. "My father destroyed my mother. Crushed her soul. Do you know how?"

"No."

"He cheated on her."

She lifted her head and held my gaze. I did not look away. "It was a destructive cycle," she said. "He'd cheat, he'd get caught, he'd swear he'd never do it again. But he always did. It wormed into my mother, ate away at her." Rachel swallowed, turned back to her high-tech toys. "So when I was away in Italy and I heard you'd been with someone else . . ."

I thought of a million different things to say, but they were all meaningless. Frankly so was what she was telling me. It explained a lot, I guess, but it was the ultimate too-little-too-late. I stayed where I was, not moving from the chair.

"I overreacted," she said.

"We were young."

"I just wanted . . . I should have told you about this back then."

She was reaching out. I started to say something, but I pulled up short. Too much. Just all too much. It had been six hours since the ransom call. The seconds tick-ticked, a deep, painful pounding in the well of my chest.

I jumped when the phone rang, but it was my regular line, not the kidnapper's cell. I picked it up. It was Lenny.

"What's wrong?" he said without preamble.

I looked at Rachel. She shook her head. I nodded back that I understood. "Nothing," I said.

"Your mom told me you saw Edgar in the park."

"Don't worry."

"That old bastard will screw you, you know that."

There was no reasoning with Lenny when it came to Edgar Portman. He also might be right. "I know."

There was brief silence.

"You called Rachel," he said.

"Yes."

"Why?"

"Nothing important."

There was another pause. Then Lenny said, "You're lying to me, right?"

"Like a Vegas toupee."

"Yeah, okay. Hey, we still on for racquetball tomorrow morning?"

"I better cancel."

"No problem. Marc?"

"Yeah."

"If you need me . . ."

"Thanks, Lenny."

I hung up. Rachel was busy with her electronic gizmos. The words she had said were gone now, dissipated smoke. She looked up and saw something in my face.

"Marc?"

I didn't speak.

"If your daughter is alive, we'll bring her home. I promise."

And for the first time, I was not sure that I believed her.

chapter 22

Special Agent Tickner stared down at the report.

The Seidman murder-kidnapping had been beyond back-burner. The FBI had realigned its priorities in recent years. Terrorism was number one on the most wanted list. Numbers two through ten were, well, terrorism. The Seidman case had only involved him when it became a kidnapping issue. Despite what you see on television, the local police are usually anxious to have the FBI involved. The feds have the resources and the know-how. Calling them too late can cost a life. Regan had been smart enough not to wait.

But once the kidnapping issue was—and he hated to use this term for it—"resolved," Tickner's job (unofficially at least) was to back off and leave it to the locals. He still thought about it a lot—you don't forget the sight of a baby's clothing in a cabin like that—but in his mind, the case had been inactive.

Until five minutes ago.

He read the brief report for the third time. He wasn't trying to put it together. Not yet. This was too weird for that. What he was trying to do, what he hoped to accomplish, was to find some kind of angle, some sort of handle he could grip. Nothing came to him.

Rachel Mills. How the hell did she fit into this?

A young subordinate—Tickner couldn't remember if his name was Kelly or Fitzgerald, something Irish like that—stood in front of the desk, hands not sure what to do. Tickner leaned back in the chair and crossed his legs. He tapped the pen against his lower lip.

"There has to be a connection between them," he told Sean or Patrick.

"She claimed to be a private detective."

"Is she licensed?"

"No, sir."

Tickner shook his head. "There's more to it than that. Check phone records, find some friends, whatever. Trace it down for me."

"Yes, sir."

"Call that detective agency. The MVD. Tell them I'm on my way."

"Yes, sir."

The Irish kid left. Tickner stared off. He and Rachel had gone through training together at Quantico. They'd both had the same mentor. Tickner thought about what to do here. While he didn't always trust the locals, he liked Regan. The guy was just off enough to be an asset. He picked up the phone and dialed Regan's cell.

"Detective Regan."

"Long time, no speak."

"Ah, Federal Agent Tickner. You still wearing the sunglasses?"

"You still stroking that soul patch—uh, among other things?"

"Yes. And maybe."

Tickner could hear sitar music in the background. "You busy?"

"Not at all. I was just meditating."

"Like Phil Jackson?"

"Exactly. Except I don't have all those pesky championship rings. You should join me sometime."

"Yeah, I'll put that on my list of must-dos."

"It would relax you, Agent Tickner. I hear tremendous strain in your voice." Then: "I assume that there was a reason for this call?"

"Remember our favorite case?"

There was a funny pause. "Yes."

"How long has it been since we had something new?"

"I don't think we ever had anything new."

"Well, we may now."

"I'm listening."

"We just got a strange call from an ex–FBI agent. Guy named Deward. He's a private dick in Newark now."

"So?"

"It seems our friend Dr. Seidman paid his office a visit today. And he had someone very special with him."

*   *   *

Lydia dyed her hair black—the better to blend in with the night.

The plan, as it were, was simple.

"We confirm that he has the money," she told Heshy. "Then I kill him."

"You sure?"

"Positive. And the beauty of it is, the murder will automatically get tied to the original shooting." Lydia smiled at him. "Even if something goes wrong, nothing ties back to us."

"Lydia?"

"Something the matter?"

Heshy shrugged his giant shoulders. "Don't you think it would be better if I kill him?"

"I'm the better shot, Pooh Bear."

"But"—he hesitated, shrugged again—"I don't need a weapon."

"You're trying to protect me," she said.

He said nothing.

"That's sweet." And it was. But one of the reasons she wanted to do it herself was to protect Heshy. He was the vulnerable one here. Lydia never worried about getting caught. Part of it was classic overconfidence. Dumb people get caught, not those who were careful. But more than that, she knew if she did get nabbed, they'd never convict her. Forget her still girl-next-door looks, though that would undoubtedly be an asset. What no prosecutor would ever overcome would be the weepy Oprahization of her case. Lydia would remind them of her "tragic" past. She would claim abuses in many forms. She would cry on the talk shows. She would talk about the plight of the child star, of the calamity of being forced into the world of Pixie Trixie. She would look adorably victimized and innocent. And the public—not to mention the jury—would lap it up.

"I think it's best this way," she told him. "If he sees you approach, well, he is apt to run. But if he catches sight of lil' ol' me . . ." Lydia let her voice die out with a small shrug.

Heshy nodded. She was right. This should be cake. She stroked his face and handed him the car keys.

"Does Pavel understand his part?" Lydia asked.

"He does. He'll meet us there. And yes, he'll be wearing the flannel shirt."

"Then we might as well start on our way," she said. "I'll call Dr. Seidman."

Heshy used the remote to unlock the car doors.

"Oh," she said, "I have to check something before we go."

Lydia opened the back door. The child was fast asleep in the car seat. She checked the straps and made sure that they were secure. "I better sit in the back, Pooh Bear," she said. "Just in case a little someone wakes up."

Heshy angled his way into the driver's seat. Lydia took out the phone and voice changer and dialed the number.

chapter 23

We ordered a pizza, which I think was a mistake. Late-night pizzas are college. It was yet another not-so-subtle reminder of the past. I kept staring at the mobile phone, wishing it to ring. Rachel was quiet, but that was okay. We had always been good with silence. That, too, was weird. In many ways, we were falling back, picking up where we'd left off. But in many more ways, we were strangers with a tenuous, awkward connection.

What was odd was that my memories were suddenly hazy. I'd thought that once I saw her again, they'd head straight to the surface. But few specifics came to me. It was more a feeling, an emotion, like the way I remembered the ruddy cold of New England. I don't know why I couldn't remember. And I wasn't sure what it meant.

Rachel's brow creased as she toyed with the electronic equipment. She took a bite of pizza and said, "Not as good as Tony's."

"That place was awful."

"A little greasy," she agreed.

"A little? Didn't the large come with a coupon for a free angioplasty?"

"Well, there was that sludge-through-the-veins feel to it."

We looked at each other.

"Rachel?"

"Yeah."

"Suppose they don't call."

"Then they don't have her, Marc."

I let that settle in. I thought about Lenny's son, Conner, the things he could say and do, and I tried to apply it to the baby I'd last laid eyes on in her crib. It wouldn't compute, but that didn't mean anything. There was hope. I held on to that. If my daughter was dead, if that phone never rang again, the hope would, I know, kill me. But I didn't care. Better to go down this way than try to go the distance.

So I had hope. And I, the cynic, let myself believe the best.

When the cell phone finally did ring, it was nearly ten. I did not even glance over to Rachel and wait for her nod. My finger was on the answer button before the first chirp could die off.

"Hello?"

"Okay," the robotic voice said, "you'll get to see her."

I couldn't breathe. Rachel moved over closer and put her ear near mine.

"Good," I said.

"You have the money?"

"Yes."

"All of it?"

"Yes."

"Then listen closely. Deviate from what I tell you and we disappear. Do you understand?"

"Yes."

"We checked with our police sources. So far, so good. It appears that you haven't contacted the authorities. But we need to make sure. You will drive alone toward the George Washington Bridge. Once there, we will be in range. Use the two-way radio feature on the phone. I will tell you where to go and what to do. You will be searched. If we find any weapons or wires, we will disappear. Do you understand?"

I could feel Rachel's breath quicken.

"When do I see my daughter?"

"When we meet."

"How do I know you won't just take the money?"

"How do you know I'm not going to hang up on you now?"

"I'm on my way," I said. Then I quickly added, "But I won't hand over the money until I see Tara."

"Then we are in agreement. You have an hour. Signal me then."

chapter 24

Conrad Dorfman did not appear happy to be dragged back into the MVD office this late. Tickner didn't care. If Seidman had come here alone, that would be an important lead, no doubt about it. But the fact that Rachel Mills had been here, too, that she was somehow involved, well, let's just say that Tickner's curiosity was more than piqued.

"Did Ms. Mills show you an ID?" he asked.

"Yes," Dorfman replied. "But it was stamped 'Retired.' "

"And she was with Dr. Seidman?"

"Yes."

"They arrived together."

"I think so. I mean, yes, when they came in here, they were together."

Tickner nodded. "What did they want?"

"A password. For a CD-ROM."

"I'm not sure I follow."

"They claimed that they had a CD-ROM we provided to a client. Our CDs are password protected. They wanted us to give them the password."

"Did you?"

Dorfman looked properly shocked. "Of course not. We had a call put in to your agency. They explained to us ... well, they never quite explained to us anything really. They just stressed that we should not cooperate with Agent Mills in any way."

"*Ex*-agent," Tickner said.

How? Tickner wondered. How the hell had Rachel Mills hooked up with Seidman? He had tried to give her the benefit of the doubt. Unlike his fellow agents, he had known her, had seen her in action. She'd been a good agent, maybe even a great one. But now he wondered. He wondered about the timing. He wondered about her being here. He wondered about her flashing her badge and trying to apply pressure.

"Did they tell you how they came by this CD-ROM?"

"They claimed that it belonged to Dr. Seidman's wife."

"Does it?"

"I believe so, yes."

"Are you aware that his wife died more than a year and a half ago, Mr. Dorfman?"

"I know that now."

"But you didn't when they were here?"

"Right."

"Why did Seidman wait eighteen months to ask for the password?"

"He didn't say."

"Did you ask?"

Dorfman shifted in his seat. "No."

Tickner smiled, buddy-to-buddy. "No reason you should," he said, faux-genteel. "Did you give them any information at all?"

"None."

"You didn't tell them why Mrs. Seidman hired your agency in the first place?"

"That's correct."

"Okay, very good." Tickner leaned forward, his elbows on his knees now. He was about to ask another question when his cell phone rang. "Excuse me," he said, reaching into his pocket.

"Is this going to take much longer?" Dorfman asked. "I have plans."

He didn't even bother responding. Rising, he put the phone to his ear. "Tickner."

"It's Agent O'Malley," the young kid said.

"Did you find anything?"

"Oh yeah."

"I'm listening."

"We checked the phone records going back three years. Seidman never called her—at least, not from his house or office—until today."

"Am I about to hear a *but*?"

"You are. But Rachel Mills called him—once."

"When?"

"June two years ago."

Tickner did the math. That would have been about three months before the murder and kidnapping. "Anything else?"

"Something big, I think. I had one of our agents check Rachel's apartment in Falls Church. He's still poking around, but guess what he found in her night-table drawer?"

"Does this look like a quiz show, O'Ryan?"

"O'Malley."

Tickner rubbed the bridge of his nose. "What did the agent find?"

"A prom photo."

"What?"

"I mean, I don't know if it's from the prom exactly. It's some kind of old formal. Photo gotta be fifteen, twenty years old. She's wearing her hair in some flip-style and she's got one of those flower bands on her arm. What do you call those?"

"A corsage?"

"Right."

"What the hell does this have to do with—"

"The guy in the picture."

"What about him?"

"Our agent is sure. The guy she's with—her date, I mean—is our own Dr. Seidman."

Tickner felt the thrum rush through him. "Keep digging," he said. "Call me when you get more."

"On it."

He hung up the phone. Rachel and Seidman went to a prom together? What the hell was going on? She was from Vermont, if he remembered correctly. Seidman lived in New Jersey. They didn't go to high school together. How about college? They'd have to look into it.

"Something wrong?"

Tickner turned. It was Dorfman. "Let me see if I have this straight, Mr. Dorfman. This CD-ROM belonged to Monica Seidman?"

"That's what we were told, yes."

"Yes or no, Mr. Dorfman."

He cleared his throat. "We believe the answer is yes."

"So she was a client here?"

"Yes, that we've been able to confirm."

"So to sum up, a murder victim was a client of yours."

Silence.

"Her name was in every paper in the state," Tickner went on, giving him the hard stare. "How come you never came forward?"

"We didn't know."

Tickner kept with the hard stare.

"The guy who handled that case is no longer employed by us," he added quickly. "See, he was gone by the time Mrs. Seidman was killed. So no one here put the pieces together."

Defensive. Tickner liked that. He believed him, but he didn't show it. Make the guy anxious to please.

"What was on the CD?"

"Photographs, we think."

"Think?"

"That's usually the case. Not always. We use the CD to store photographs, but there could be some scanned documents too. I really couldn't tell you."

"Why the hell not?"

He put up both hands. "Don't worry. We have a backup. But any file more than a year old is stored in the basement. The office was closed, but when I heard you were interested, I got someone to come in. He's running off the material on the backup CD right now."

"Where?"

"He's on the lower level." Dorfman checked his watch. "He should be done or just about by now. Do you want to go down and see?"

Tickner stood. "Let's rumble."

chapter 25

"There are still things we can do," Rachel said. "This stuff is state of the art. Even if they pat you down, we can get away with it. I have a bulletproof vest that has a pinhole camera right in the center."

"And you don't think they'll find that with a pat-down?"

"Yeah, okay, look, I know you're worried about them finding out, but let's be realistic here. There's an excellent chance this is all a setup. Don't give up the money until you see Tara. Don't get yourself stuck somewhere alone. Don't worry about the Q-Logger—if they're being up front, we'll have Tara before they can search the stacks of money. I know this isn't an easy decision, Marc."

"No, you're right. I played it safe last time. I think we need to take some chances. But the vest is out."

"Okay, here's what we're going to do. I'm going to be in the trunk. They may check the backseat to see if someone is lying there. The trunk will be a safer bet. I'll disconnect the wires back there so when the trunk opens, no lights will come on. I'll try to keep up with you, but I have to stay at a safe distance. Make no mistake here. I'm not Wonder Woman. I might lose you, but remember: Don't look for me. Not even casually. These guys are probably pretty good. They'll spot that."

"I understand." She was dressed totally in black. I said, "You look like you're going to do a reading in the Village."

"Kumbaya, my Lord. You ready?"

We both heard the car pull up. I looked out the window and felt my panic needle jump. "Damn," I said.

"What?"

"That's Regan, the cop on the case. I haven't seen him in more than a month." I looked at her. Her face was stark white against the black outfit. "Coincidence?"

"No coincidence," she said.

"How the hell did he find out about the ransom?"

She moved back from the window. "He's probably not here for that."

"Then what?"

"My guess would be that they got word of my involvement from MVD."

I frowned. "So?"

"No time to explain. Look, I'm going to go out to the garage and hide. He's going to ask about me. Tell him I went back to D.C. If he presses, tell him I'm an old friend and leave it at that. He's going to want to interrogate you."

"Why?"

But she was already moving away from me. "Just be firm and get him out of there. I'll wait for you by the car."

I didn't like it, but now was not the time. "Okay."

Rachel headed to the garage via the door in the den. I waited until she was out of sight. When Regan hit my front walkway, I opened the door, trying to cut him off at the pass.

Regan smiled. "Were you expecting me?" he asked.

"I heard your car."

He nodded as if I'd said something that required serious analysis. "Do you have a few moments, Dr. Seidman?"

"Actually, it's a bad time."

"Oh." Regan did not break stride. He slid past me and into my front foyer, his eyes taking in everything. "Heading out, are we?"

"What do you want, Detective?"

"Some new information has come to our attention."

I waited for him to say more.

"Don't you want to know what it is?"

"Of course."

Regan had a strange, almost serene look on his face. He looked up at the ceiling, as if he were considering what color to paint it. "Where have you been today?"

"Get out, please."

His eyes were still on the ceiling. "Your hostility surprises me." But he did not look surprised.

"You said you had some new information. If you do, say it. If not, get out. I'm not in the mood to be questioned."

He made a well-well face. "We hear that you visited a private detective agency in Newark today."

"So?"

"So what were you doing there?"

"Tell you what, Detective. I'm going to ask you to leave because I know answering your questions will bring me no closer to finding my daughter."

He looked at me. "You sure about that?"

"Kindly get the hell out of my house. Now."

"Suit yourself." Regan started for the door. When we reached it, he asked, "Where's Rachel Mills?"

"Don't know."

"She's not here?"

"Nope."

"No idea at all where she could be?"

"I think she's on her way back to Washington."

"Hmm. How do you two know each other?"

"Good night, Detective."

"Okay, sure. But one last question."

I stifled a sigh. "You've watched too many episodes of *Columbo*, Detective."

"Indeed I have." He smiled. "But let me ask it anyway."

I spread my hands for him to go ahead.

"Do you know how her husband died?"

"He was shot," I said too quickly, and immediately regretted it. He leaned a little more into my space and kept on me.

"And do you know who shot him?"

I stood without moving.

"Do you, Marc?"

"Good night, Detective."

"She killed him, Marc. A bullet to the head at close range."

"That," I said, "is a load of bull."

"Is it? I mean, are you sure?"

"If she killed him, why isn't she in jail?"

"Good question," Regan said, backing down the walkway. When he reached the end of the walkway, he added, "Maybe you should ask her."

chapter 26

Rachel was in the garage. She looked up at me. She suddenly looked small, I thought. And I saw fear in her face. The car trunk was open. I moved toward the driver-side door.

"What did he want?" she asked.

"What you said."

"He knew about the CD?"

"He knew we'd been at MVD. He didn't say anything about the CD."

I slid into the car. She let it drop. Now was not the time to raise any new issues. We both knew that. But again I questioned my judgment here. My wife had been murdered. So had my sister. Someone had tried very hard to kill me. Stripping it bare, I was trusting a woman I really didn't know. I was trusting her not only with my life, but with my daughter's. How stupid when you think about it. Lenny had been right. It was not so simple. In truth, I had no idea who she was or what she'd become. I had deluded myself into making her something she might not be, and now I wondered what it might cost me.

Her voice cut through my haze. "Marc?"

"What?"

"I still think you should wear the bulletproof vest."

"No."

My tone was firmer than I'd wanted. Or maybe not. Rachel climbed into the trunk and closed it. I put the duffel bag with the money on the seat next to me. I hit the garage-door opener under the sun-visor and started the car.

We were on our way.

* * *

When Tickner was nine years old, his mother bought him a book of optical illusions. You'd look at a drawing of, say, an old lady with a big nose. You'd look a little longer and then, poof, it appeared now to be a young woman with her head turned. Tickner had loved the book. When he got a little older, he moved on to those Magic Eyes, staring for however long it took for the horsey or whatever to appear in the swirling colors. Sometimes it would take a long time. You'd even start to wonder if there was anything there at all. And then, suddenly, the image surfaced.

That was what was happening here.

There were moments in a case, Tickner knew, that altered everything—just like those old optical illusions. You are viewing one reality and then, with a gentle tilt, reality changes. Nothing is as it appeared.

He had never really bought the conventional theories on the Seidman murder-kidnapping. They all felt too much like reading a book with missing pages.

Over the years, Tickner had not dealt with that many murders. They were, for the most part, left to the local cops. But he knew plenty of homicide investigators. The best ones were always off center, overly theatrical, ridiculously imaginative. Tickner had heard them talk about a point in the case where the victim "reaches out" from the grave. The victim "talks" to them somehow, pointing them toward the killer. Tickner would listen to his nonsense and nod politely. It always sounded like a load of hyperbole, just one of those meaningless things cops say because the general public laps it up.

The printer still whirred. Tickner had seen twelve photos already.

"How many more?" he asked.

Dorfman looked at the computer screen. "Six more."

"Same as these?"

"Pretty much, yeah. I mean, same person."

Tickner stared down at the photographs. Yes, the same person was featured in all of them. They were all in black and white, all taken without the subject knowing, probably from a distance with a zoom lens.

The reach-from-the-grave stuff—it no longer sounded so silly. Monica Seidman had been dead for eighteen months. Her murderer had gone free. And now, with all hope lost, she seemed to have risen from the dead to point a finger. Tickner looked again and tried to understand.

The subject of the pictures, the person Monica Seidman was pointing at, was Rachel Mills.

* * *

When you take the eastern spur of the New Jersey Turnpike north, the night skyline of Manhattan beckons. Like most people who see it nearly every day, I used to take it for granted. No more. For a while afterward, I thought I could still see the Towers. It was as though they were bright lights I'd stared at for a long time, so that even when I closed my eyes, their images were still there, imbedded. But like any sunspot, the images eventually began to fade. It is different now. When I drive this route, I still make myself look for them. Even tonight. But sometimes I forget precisely where those towers stood. And that angers me more than I can express.

Out of habit, I took the lower level of the George Washington Bridge. There was no traffic at this hour. I drove through the E-ZPass. I had managed to keep myself distracted. I flipped stations between two talk radio shows. One was a sports station where lots of guys named Vinny from Bayside called up and complained about inept coaches and how much better they'd be at the job. The other station featured two beyond-puerile Howard Stern rip-offs who thought it was funny for a college freshman to call his mother and tell her he had testicular cancer. Both were, if not entertaining, mildly distracting.

Rachel was in the trunk, which was totally weird if I thought about it. I reached for the cell phone and flipped on the two-way radio feature. My finger pressed down on the call button and almost instantly I heard the robotic voice say, "Take the Henry Hudson north."

I put the phone to mouth, walkie-talkie style. "Okay."

"Tell me the moment you get on the Hudson."

"Right."

I got into the left lane. I knew the way. This area was familiar to me. I had done a fellowship at New York Presbyterian, which resided about ten blocks south. Zia and I had roomed with a cardiac resident named Lester in an Art Deco building at the tail end of Fort Washington Avenue in upper, upper Manhattan. When I lived here, this section of the city was known as the far northern point of Washington Heights. Now I had noticed several realtors redubbing it "Hudson Heights" so as to differentiate it, in both substance and cost, from its lower-class roots.

"Okay, I'm on the Hudson," I said.

"Take your next exit."

"Fort Tryon Park?"

"Yes."

Again I knew it. Fort Tryon floats cloudlike high above the Hudson River. It is a quiet and restful jagged cliff, New Jersey on its west, Riverdale-Bronx on its east. The park is a mishmash of terrains—walkways of harsh stone, fauna from a bygone era, terraces of stone, nooks and crannies of cement and brick, thick brush, rocky slopes, open grass. I had spent plenty of summer days on her green lawns, adorned in shorts and T-shirt, Zia and unread medical books my companions. My favorite time here: summer, right before dark. The orange glow bathing the park in something almost ethereal.

I put on my blinker and glided onto the exit ramp. There were no cars and few lights. The park was closed at night, but the roadway stayed open for through traffic. My car chugged up the steep road and entered what felt like a medieval fortress. The Cloisters, a former quasi-French monastery that was now part of the Metropolitan Museum of Art, held middle ground. It houses a fabulous collection of medieval artifacts. Or so I'm told. I've been in this park a hundred times. I've never been inside the Cloisters.

It was, I thought, a smart place for a ransom drop—dark, quiet, filled with serpentine trails, stone cliffs, sudden drops, thick woods, paved and unpaved walks. You could get lost here. You could hide here for a very long time and never be found.

The robotic voice asked, "Are you there yet?"

"I'm in Fort Tryon, yes."

"Park near the café. Get out and walk up to the circle."

Riding in the trunk was noisy and jarring. Rachel had brought a padded blanket, but there was not much she could do about the noise. A flashlight stayed in her satchel. She had no interest in turning it on. Rachel had never minded the dark.

Sight could be distracting. The dark was a good place to think.

She tried to keep her body loose, riding bumps, and wondered about Marc's behavior right before they left. The cop at the house had, no doubt, said something that shook him. About her? Probably. She wondered what exactly he had said and how she should react.

Didn't matter now. They were on their way. She had to concentrate on the task at hand.

Rachel was falling back into a familiar role. There was a pang here.

She missed being with the FBI. She had loved her job. Yes, perhaps it was all she had. It was more than her escape—it was the only thing she really enjoyed doing. Some people pushed through the nine-to-five so they could go home and live their lives. For Rachel, it was the opposite.

After all these years apart, here was something that she and Marc had in common: They'd both found careers they loved. She wondered about that. She wondered if there was a connection, if their careers had become some kind of true-love substitute. Or was that looking at it too deeply?

Marc still had his job. She did not. Did that make her more desperate? No. His child was gone. Game, set, match.

In the darkness of the trunk, she smeared her face with black make-up, enough to take the shine away. The car started climbing upward. Her gear was packed and ready.

She thought about Hugh Reilly, the son of a bitch.

Her breakup with Marc—and everything after—was his fault. Hugh had been her dearest friend in college. That was what he wanted, he told her. Just to be her friend. No pressure. He understood that she had a boyfriend. Had Rachel been naïve or purposefully naïve? Men who want to "just be friends" do so because they hope to be next in line, as though friendship were an on-deck circle, a good place for practice swings before heading to the plate. Hugh had called her in Italy that night with nothing but the best of intentions. "I just think you should know," he said, "as your friend." Right. And then he told her what Marc had done at some stupid frat party.

Yes, enough blaming herself. Enough blaming Marc. Hugh Reilly. If that son of a bitch had just minded his own business, what would her life be like right now? She couldn't say. Ah, but what had her life become? That was easier to answer. She drank too much. She had a bad temper. Her stomach bothered her more than it should. She spent too much time reading *TV Guide*. And let's not forget the pièce de résistance: She had gotten herself ensnared in a self-destructive relationship—and gotten herself out of it in the worst way possible.

The car veered and climbed upward, forcing Rachel to roll back. A moment or two later, the car stopped. Rachel lifted her head. The cruel musings fled.

It was game time.

* * *

From the old fort's lookout tower, some two hundred fifty feet above the Hudson River, Heshy had one of the most stunning views of the Jersey Palisades, stretching from the Tappan Zee Bridge on the right to the George Washington Bridge on his left. He actually took the time to appreciate it before he got to the matter at hand.

As though on cue, Seidman took the exit off the Henry Hudson Parkway. No one followed. Heshy kept his eyes on the road. No car slowed. No car sped up. No one was trying to make it look as though they weren't following.

He spun around, lost sight of the car for a brief moment, then spotted it again as it came back into view. He could see Seidman in the driver's seat. No one else was visible. That didn't mean much—someone could be ducking down in the back—but it was a start.

Seidman parked the car. He turned off the engine and opened the door. Heshy lifted the microphone to his mouth.

"Pavel, you ready?"

"Yes."

"He's alone," he said, speaking now for Lydia's benefit. "Proceed."

"Park near the café. Get out and walk up to the circle."

The circle, I knew, was Margaret Corbin Circle. When I reached the clearing, the first thing I spotted, even in the dark, was the bright colors of the children's playground near Fort Washington Avenue at 190th Street. The colors still leapt out. I'd always liked this playground, but tonight the yellows and blues taunted me. I thought of myself as a city boy. When I lived near here, I'd imagined staying in this neighborhood— too sophisticated was I for the vanilla suburbs—and of course, that meant that I would bring my children to this very park. I took that as an omen, but I didn't know of what.

The phone squawked. "There's a subway station on the left."

"Okay."

"Take the stairs down toward the elevator."

I might have suspected this. He would put me on the elevator and then on the A train. It would be difficult, if not impossible, for Rachel to follow me.

"Are you on the stairs?"

"Yes."

"At the bottom, you'll see a gate on the right."

I knew where it was. It led to a smaller park and was locked except for weekends. It had been set aside as something of a small picnic area. There were Ping-Pong tables, though you had to bring your own net and paddles to play. There were benches and eating areas. Kids used it for birthday parties.

The wrought-iron gate, I remember, was always locked.

"I'm there," I said.

"Make sure no one sees you. Push open the gate. Slip through and quickly close it."

I peered inside. The park was black. Distant streetlights reached out and gave the area no more than a dull glow. The duffel bag felt heavy. I adjusted it up my shoulder. I looked behind me now. No one. I looked to my left. The subway elevators were still. I put my hand on the gate door. The padlock had been cut. I gave the area one more quick glance because that was what the robotic voice had told me to do.

No sign of Rachel.

The gate creaked when I pushed it open. The echo ripped through the still night. I slipped through the opening and let the dark swallow me whole.

Rachel felt the car rock as Marc got out.

She made herself wait a full minute, which felt like two hours. When she thought that it was probably safe, Rachel lifted the trunk an inch and peeked out.

She saw no one.

Rachel had a gun with her, a fed-issue Glock .22 40-caliber semiautomatic, and she carried her night-vision goggles, Rigel 3501 military-grade Gen. 2+. The Palm Pilot that could read the Q-Logger transmitter was in her pocket.

She doubted that anyone would see her, but she still only opened the trunk wide enough so she could roll out. She huddled down low. Her hand reached back and grabbed the semiautomatic and night-vision goggles. Then she quietly closed the trunk.

Field operations had always been her favorite—or at least, the training for them. There had been very few missions that required this sort of cloak-and-dagger reconnaissance. For the most part, stakeouts were high-tech. You had vans and spy planes and fiber-optics. You rarely found yourself crawling through the night in black clothes and greasepaint.

She made herself small against the back tire. In the distance, she saw Marc heading up the drive. She put the gun in its holster and strapped the night-vision goggles to her belt. Keeping low, Rachel moved up the grass to higher ground. There was still enough light. She didn't need the goggles yet.

A sliver of moon sliced through the sky. There were no stars tonight. Up ahead, she could see that Marc had the cell phone near his ear. The duffel bag was on his shoulder. Rachel looked around, saw no one. Would the drop take place here? It wasn't a bad place, if you had a planned escape route. She started to think about the possibilities.

Fort Tryon was hilly. The secret would be to try to get higher. She started climbing and was just about to settle in when Marc exited the park.

Damn. She'd have to move again.

Rachel commando-crawled down the hill. The grass was prickly and smelled like hay, the cause being, she assumed, the recent water shortage. She tried to keep her eyes on Marc, but she lost him when he left the park grounds. She took a risk and moved quicker. At the park gate, she ducked behind a stone pillar.

Marc was there. But not for very long.

With the phone back to his ear, Marc veered to the left and vanished down the steps leading to the A train.

Up ahead, Rachel saw a man and a woman walking a dog. They could be part of this—or they could be a man and a woman walking a dog. Marc was still out of sight. No time for debate now. She ducked low at a stone wall.

Leaning her back against it, Rachel made her way toward the stairs.

Tickner thought that Edgar Portman looked like something out of a Noël Coward production. He wore silk pajamas under a red robe that appeared to have been tied with great care. There were velvet slippers on his feet. His brother, Carson, on the other hand, looked properly ruffled. His pajamas were askew. His hair was all over the place. His eyes were bloodshot.

Neither Portman could take his eyes off the photographs from the CD.

"Edgar," Carson said, "let's not jump to conclusions."

"Not jump . . . ?" Edgar turned to Tickner. "I gave him money."

"Yes, sir," Tickner said. "A year and a half ago. We know about that."

"No." Edgar tried to make the word snap with impatience, but he didn't have the strength. "I mean, recently. Today, in fact."

Tickner sat up. "How much?"

"Two million dollars. There was another ransom demand."

"Why didn't you contact us?"

"Oh sure." Edgar made a sound that was half chortle, half sneer. "You all did such a wonderful job last time."

Tickner felt the tick in his blood. "Are you saying that you gave your son-in-law an additional two million dollars?"

"That is precisely what I'm saying."

Carson Portman was still staring at the photographs. Edgar glanced at his brother, then back at Tickner. "Did Marc Seidman kill my daughter?"

Carson stood up. "You know better."

"I'm not asking you, Carson."

Both men looked at Tickner now. Tickner was not having any of it. "You said you met with your son-in-law today?"

If Edgar was upset about his question being ignored, he did not show it. "Early this morning," he said. "At Memorial Park."

"That woman in the pictures." Tickner gestured toward them. "Was she with him?"

"No."

"Has either of you ever seen her before?"

Both Carson and Edgar answered in the negative. Edgar picked up one of the photographs. "My daughter hired a private investigator to take these?"

"Yes."

"I don't understand. Who is she?"

Tickner again ignored his question. "The ransom note came to you, like last time?"

"Yes."

"I'm not sure I follow. How did you know that it wasn't a hoax? How did you know that you were dealing with the real kidnappers?"

Carson took that one. "We did think it was a hoax," he said. "At first, I mean."

"So what changed your mind?"

"They sent hairs again." Carson quickly explained about the tests and about Dr. Seidman's request for additional tests.

"You gave him all the hairs, then?"

"We did, yes," Carson said.

Edgar seemed lost in the photographs again. "This woman," he spat. "Was Seidman involved with her?"

"I can't answer that."

"Why else would my daughter want these pictures taken?"

A mobile phone rang. Tickner excused himself and put the receiver to his ear.

"Bingo," O'Malley said.

"What?"

"We got a hit on Seidman's E-ZPass. He crossed the George Washington Bridge five minutes ago."

The robotic voice told me, "Walk down the path."

There was still enough light to see the first few steps. I started down them. The darkness gathered around, closed in. I started to use my foot to feel my way, like a blind man swinging a cane. I didn't like this. I didn't like this at all. I wondered again about Rachel. Was she near here? I tried to follow the path. It curved to the left. I stumbled on the cobblestone.

"Okay," the voice said. "Stop."

I did so. I could see nothing in front of me. Behind me, the street was a faded glow. On my right was a steep incline. The air had that city-park smell to it, a swirling potpourri of fresh and stale. I listened for some sort of clue, but there was nothing other than the distant humming swish of traffic.

"Put down the money."

"No," I said. "I want to see my daughter."

"Put down the money."

"We had a deal. You show me my daughter, I show you the money."

There was no reply. I could hear the blood roaring in my ears. The fear was crippling. No, I did not like this. I was too exposed. I checked the path behind me. I could still break into a run and scream like a psycho. This neighborhood was tighter than most in Manhattan. Someone might call the police or try to help.

"Dr. Seidman?"

"Yes?"

And then a flashlight hit my face. I blinked and raised a hand to block my eyes. I squinted, trying to see past it. Someone lowered the flashlight beam. My eyes quickly adjusted, but there was no need. The beam was cut off by a silhouette. There was no mistake. I could see immediately what was being highlighted.

There was a man. I may have even seen flannel, I'm not sure. As I said, it was in silhouette. I couldn't really make out features or colors or design. So that part could have been my imagination. But not the rest. I saw the shapes and outlines clear enough to know.

Standing next to the man, gripping his leg just above the knee, was a small child.

chapter 27

Lydia wished that there was more light. She would very much like to see the look on Dr. Seidman's face right now. Her desire to see his expression had nothing to do with the cruelty that was about to come down. It was curiosity. It was deeper than the slow-to-see-the-car-accident aspect of human nature. Imagine. This man had had his child taken away. For a year and a half, he had been left to wonder about her fate, tossing through sleepless nights, conjuring up horrors best left in the dark abyss of our subconscious.

Now he had seen her.

It would be unnatural *not* to want to see the expression on his face.

Seconds ticked away. She wanted that. She wanted to stretch the tension, pull him beyond what a man could handle, soften him for the final blow.

Lydia took out her Sig-Sauer. She held it to her side. Peering out from behind the bush she judged the distance between her and Seidman at thirty, maybe forty feet. She put the voice changer and phone back to her mouth. She whispered into it. Whisper or scream, it made no difference. The voice changer made it all sound the same.

"Open the money bag."

From her perch, she watched him move like a man in a trance. He did what she asked—now without question. This time, she was the one using the flashlight. She shone it at his face and then dropped the beam to the bag.

Money. She could see the stacks. She nodded to herself. They were good to go.

"Okay," she said. "Leave the money on the ground. Walk slowly down the path. Tara will be waiting for you."

She watched Dr. Seidman drop the bag. He was squinting at the spot where he believed his daughter would be waiting. His movements were stiff, but then again his vision had probably been affected by the lights in his eyes. That again would make it easier.

Lydia wanted a close shot. Two quick bullets to the head, in case he was wearing a flap jacket. She was a good shot. She could probably hit him in the head from here. But she wanted the sure thing. No mistakes. No chance to run.

Seidman moved toward her. He was twenty feet away. Then fifteen. When he was only ten feet away, Lydia raised the pistol and took aim.

If Marc took the subway, Rachel knew that it'd be near impossible to follow him without being spotted.

Rachel hurried toward the stairwell. When she got there, she looked down into the dark. Marc was gone. Damn. She scanned the surroundings. There was a sign for elevators leading down to the A train. On the right was a closed wrought-iron gate. Nothing else.

He had to be in an elevator heading down to the subway.

Now what?

She heard footsteps behind her. With her right hand, Rachel quickly wiped the greasepaint, hoping to make herself look at least semi-presentable. With her left hand, she slid the goggles behind her and out of sight.

Two men trotted down the stairs. One caught her eye and smiled. She wiped her face again and smiled back. The men jogged the rest of the way down the steps and turned toward the elevator bank.

Rachel quickly considered her options. Those two men could be her cover. She could follow them down, get into the same elevator, get off with them, maybe even engage them in conversation. Who'd suspect her then? Hopefully Marc's subway car hadn't left yet. If it had . . . well, no use in thinking negative.

Rachel started toward the men when something made her stop. The wrought-iron gate. The one she had seen on her right. It was closed. The sign on it read: OPEN ON WEEKENDS AND MAJOR HOLIDAYS ONLY.

But through the thicket, Rachel saw the beam of a flashlight.

She pulled up. She tried to peer through the fence, but all she could see was the light beam. The brush was too thick. On her left, she heard the ding of an elevator. The doors slid open. The men stepped inside. No time to pull out the Palm Pilot and check the GPS. Besides, the elevator and beam of flashlight were too close. It would be hard to pinpoint the difference.

The man who had smiled at her put his hand against the side, keeping the door open. She wondered what to do.

The flashlight beam went out.

"Are you coming?" the man asked.

She waited for the flashlight beam to come back on. It didn't. She shook her head. "No, thank you."

Rachel quickly broke back up the stairs, trying to find a dark spot. It had to be dark for the goggles to work. The Rigels came with a built-in overlight sensor system to protect from bright lights, but Rachel still found that the fewer artificial lights, the better. Street level looked down over the park. Okay, the positioning was pretty good, but there was still too much light from the street.

She moved to the side of the stone hut that housed the elevators. On the left, there was a spot that—if she pressed herself against the wall— would give her total darkness. Perfect. The trees and bushes were still too heavy to get a clear view. But it would have to do.

Her goggles were supposedly lightweight but they still felt bulky. She should have bought a model you could just hold up to your face, binocular style. Most have that feature. This model didn't. You could not just hold it to up your eyes. You had to strap it on as a mask. The advantage, however, was obvious: If you attached it like a mask, you could keep your hands free.

As she pulled them over her head, the flashlight beam appeared again. Rachel tried to follow it, see where it was coming from. It seemed to her that it was a different spot this time. Over on the right now. Closer.

And then, before she could pinpoint it, the beam was gone.

Her eyes locked on the spot where she thought the beam had come from. Dark. Very dark now. Still keeping her eyes looking there, she finished getting the night-vision goggles in place. Night-vision goggles are not magic. They don't really see in the dark. Night-vision optics work by intensifying existing light, even very small amounts. But here, there was pretty much nothing. That used to be a problem, but now most brands came with an infrared illuminator standard. The illuminator cast a beam of infrared light that was not visible to the human eye.

But it was visible to the night-vision goggles.

Rachel flipped on the illuminator. The night lit up in full green. She was looking not through a lens, but at a phosphor screen, not unlike the one on your TV set. The eyepiece magnified the picture—you were looking at a picture, not the actual site—and the picture was green because the human eye can differentiate more shades of green than any other phosphor color. Rachel stared.

Got something.

The view was hazy, but it looked to Rachel like a small woman. The woman seemed to be hiding behind a bush. She held something up to her mouth. A phone maybe. Peripheral vision is nearly nonexistent with these goggles, though these claimed to give you a thirty-seven-degree angle. She had to swivel her head to the right, and there, putting down the duffel bag with the two million dollars in it, was Marc.

Marc started walking toward the woman. His steps were short, probably because he was on cobblestones in the dark.

Rachel swiveled her head from the woman, to Marc, back to the woman. Marc was approaching, getting closer. The woman was still crouched in hiding. There was no way Marc could see her. Rachel frowned and wondered what the hell was going on.

Then the woman swung her arm up.

It was hard to see clearly—there were trees and branches in the way—but the woman seemed to be pointing her finger at Marc. They were not far apart anymore. Rachel squinted at the screen attached to her face. And it was then that she realized that the woman was not pointing a finger. The image was too big for a hand.

It was a gun. The woman was pointing a gun at Marc's head.

A shadow crossed over Rachel's vision. She started back, opening her mouth to call out a warning, when a hand like a baseball glove covered her mouth and smothered all sound away.

Tickner and Regan hooked up on the New Jersey Turnpike. Tickner drove. Regan sat next to him and stroked his face.

Tickner shook his head. "Can't believe you still have that soul patch."

"You don't like it?"

"You think you're Enrique Iglesias?"

"Who?"

"Exactly."

"What's wrong with the soul patch?"

"It's like wearing a T-shirt that says, 'I Had a Middle-Age Crisis in 1998.' "

Regan thought about it. "Yeah, okay, fair point. By the way, those sunglasses you always wear. I was wondering if they were FBI issue."

Tickner grinned. "Helps me land the chicks."

"Yeah, those and your stun gun." Regan shifted in the chair. "Lloyd?"

"Uh-huh."

"I'm not sure I get it."

They weren't talking about eyewear or facial hair anymore.

"We don't have all the pieces," Tickner said.

"But we're getting close?"

"Oh yeah."

"Let's go through it then, cool?"

Tickner nodded. "First off, if the DNA lab Edgar Portman used is correct, the child is still alive."

"Which is weird."

"Very. But it explains a lot. Who would be most likely to keep a kid-napped child alive?"

"Her father," Regan said.

"And whose gun mysteriously vanished from the murder scene?"

"Her father's."

Tickner made a gun with his forefinger and thumb, aimed it at Re-gan, dropped the hammer. "Righto."

"So where has the kid been all this time?" Regan asked.

"Hidden."

"Well, gee, that helps."

"No, think about it. We've been looking at Seidman. We've looked closely. He knows that. So who would be the best person to hide his kid?"

Regan saw where he was going. "The girlfriend we didn't know about."

"More than that, a girlfriend who used to work for the feds. A girlfriend who would know how we work. How to do a ransom drop. How to hide a child. Someone who would know Seidman's sister, Stacy, and be able to enlist her help."

Regan thought about it. "Okay, let's assume I believe all that. They commit this crime. They get two million dollars and the kid. But then what? They bide their time for eighteen months? They decide they need more cash? What?"

"They need to wait to avoid suspicion. Maybe they wanted the wife's estate to clear. Maybe they need another two million dollars to run away, I don't know."

Regan frowned. "We're still trying to finesse away the same point."

"What's that?"

"If Seidman was behind this, how come he was nearly killed? This was no wound-me-so-it-looks-good injury. He was flatlined. The paramedics were sure they had a goner when they first got there. Hell, we quietly called it a double homicide for almost ten days."

Tickner nodded. "It's a problem."

"And more than that, where the hell is he going right now? I mean, crossing the George Washington Bridge. Do you think he decided now was the time to flee with the two million dollars?"

"Could be."

"If you were fleeing, would you use your E-ZPass to pay the toll?"

"No, but he might not know how easy it is to trace."

"Hey, everyone knows how easy it is to trace. You get the bill in the mail. It tells you what time you hit what tollbooth. And even if he was dumb enough to forget that, your federal agent Rachel Whatshername isn't."

"Rachel Mills." Tickner nodded slowly. "Good point, though."

"Thank you."

"So what conclusions can we draw?"

"That we still don't have a clue what the hell is going on," Regan said.

Tickner smiled. "Nice to be in familiar territory."

The cell phone rang. Tickner picked it up. It was O'Malley. "Where are you?" O'Malley asked.

"A mile from the George Washington Bridge," Tickner said.

"Hit the accelerator."

"Why? What's up?"

"NYPD just spotted Seidman's car," O'Malley said. "It's parked at Fort Tryon Park—a mile, maybe mile and a half, from the bridge."

"Know it," Tickner said. "We'll be there in less than five."

Heshy had thought that it was all going a little too smoothly.

He'd watched Dr. Seidman leave his car. He waited. No one else had come out. He'd started down from the old fort's tower.

That was when he spotted the woman.

He paused, watching her head down toward the subway elevators. Two guys were with her. Nothing suspicious in that. But then, when the woman sprinted back up alone, well, that was when things had changed.

He kept a close eye from then on. When she moved into the darkness, Heshy started creeping toward her.

Heshy knew that his appearance was intimidating. He also knew that much of the circuitry inside of his brain was not wired normally. He didn't much care, which, he assumed, was part of the wiring problem. There were those who would tell you that Heshy was pure evil. He had killed sixteen people in his life, fourteen of them slowly. He had left six men alive who still wished that he hadn't.

Supposedly, people like Heshy did not understand what they were doing. Other people's pain did not reach them. That was not true. His victims' pain was not something distant to him. He knew what pain was like. And he understood love. He loved Lydia. He loved her in ways most people could never fathom. He would kill for her. He would die for her. Many people say that about their loved ones, of course—but how many are willing to put it to the test?

The woman in the dark had binoculars strapped onto her head. Night-vision goggles. Heshy had seen them on the news. Soldiers in battle wore them. Having them did not necessarily mean she was a cop. Most weaponry and military gizmos were available online to anyone with the proper dollars. Heshy watched her. Either way, cop or no cop, if the goggles worked, this woman would be a witness to Lydia committing murder.

So she had to be silenced.

He closed in slowly. He wanted to hear if she was talking to anyone, if she had some kind of radio control to other units. But the woman was silent. Good. Maybe she was indeed on her own.

He was about two yards away from her when her body stiffened.

The woman gave a little gasp. And Heshy knew that it was time to close her down.

He hurried over, moving with a grace that defied his bulk. He snaked one hand around her face and clasped it over her mouth. His hand was big enough to cover her nose too. Cut off the air supply. With his free hand, he cupped the back of her skull. He pushed his hands together.

And then, with both hands firmly placed on the woman's head, Heshy lifted her all the way off the ground.

chapter 28

A sound made me stop. I turned to my right. I thought that maybe I heard something up there, near the street level. I tried to see, but my eyes were still suffering from the onslaught of the flashlight. The trees also helped cut off my view. I waited, seeing if I heard a follow-up. Nothing. The sound was gone now. It wasn't important anyway. Tara should be waiting for me at the end of this path. Whatever else might go on, that was all that counted.

Focus, I thought again. Tara, end of the path. All else was extraneous.

I started up again, not even glancing behind me to check on the fate of the duffel bag with the two million dollars in it. It, too, was, like everything else but Tara, irrelevant. I tried to conjure up the shadowy image again, the silhouette made by the flashlight. I trudged on. My daughter. She could be right here, scant steps from where I now walked. I had been given a second chance to rescue her. Focus on that. Compartmentalize. Let nothing stop me.

I continued down the path.

While with the Federal Bureau of Investigation, Rachel had been well trained in weapons and hand-to-hand combat. She had learned much during her four months at Quantico. She knew that true fighting was nothing like you saw on TV. You would never, for example, mess around with a high kick to the face. You would never try anything involving turning your back on an opponent, spinning, leaping—none of that.

Successful hand-to-hand combat could be broken down pretty simply.

You aimed for the vulnerable spots on the body. The nose was good—it usually made your opponent's eyes well up with tears. The eyes, of course. The throat was good too—anyone who has ever been struck there knew how it could shut down your will to fight. The groin, well, obvious. You always hear that. The groin, however, is a difficult target, probably because a man is prone to defend it. It's usually better as a decoy move. Fake there and then go to one of the other more exposed, vulnerable spots.

There were other areas—the solar plexus, the instep, the knee. But there was also a problem with all these techniques. In the movies, a smaller opponent might beat a larger one. In reality, yes, that can happen, but when the woman is as small as Rachel and the man as large as her current attacker, the odds of her coming out on the winning end are very small. If the attacker knows what he is doing, very small becomes pretty close to nonexistent.

The other problem for a woman is that fights never go as they do in the movies. Think about any physical altercation you may have seen in a bar or at a sporting event or even on a playground. The battle almost always ends up in a grapple on the floor. On TV or in a boxing ring, sure, people stand and hit each other. In real life, one or the other ducks down and grabs the opponent and they go down to the ground and wrestle. It didn't matter how much training you had. If the fight reached that stage, Rachel would never defeat an opponent this large.

Lastly, while Rachel had practiced and trained and been in simulated dangerous situations—Quantico went so far as to have a "mock town" for these purposes—she had never been involved in a real physical altercation before. She was not ready for the pure panic, the tingly, unpleasant numbness in the legs, the way adrenaline mixed with fear saps your strength.

Rachel could not breathe. She felt the hand on her mouth and, out of her element, reacted wrong. Instead of immediately kicking behind her—trying to take out his knee or stomping down on the instep—Rachel worked on instinct and used both her hands to pry her mouth free. It did not work.

Within seconds, the man had his other hand on the base of her head, holding her skull in a viselike grip. She could feel his fingers dig into her gums, push in her teeth. His hands seemed so powerful that Rachel was sure he could crush her skull like an eggshell. He didn't. Instead he wrenched up. Her neck took the brunt of it. It felt as if her head was being torn off. The hand against her mouth and nostrils effectively cut off her air supply. He lifted more. Her feet fully left the ground. She took hold of his wrists and tried to pull up, tried to lessen the strain on her neck.

But she still could not breathe.

There was a roaring in her ears. Her lungs burned. Her feet kicked out. They landed on him, blows so tiny and impotent he didn't bother to block them. His face was close to her now. She could feel the spit in his breath. Her night-vision goggles had been knocked askew but not all the way off. They blocked her sight.

The pressure in her head was pounding. Trying to remember her training, Rachel dug her nails into the pressure point on his hand beneath the thumb. No effect. She kicked harder. Nothing. She needed a breath. She felt like a fish on the line, flailing, dying. Panic took hold.

Her gun.

She could reach for it. If she could just control herself long enough, to have the courage to release her hand, she could go for her pocket, pull out the weapon, and fire it. It was her only chance. Her brain was going groggy. Consciousness was starting to ebb away.

With her skull seconds away from exploding, Rachel dropped her left hand away. Her neck stretched so taut, she was sure it would snap like a rubber band. Her hand found her holster. Her fingers touched the gun.

But the man saw what she was doing. With Rachel still dangling in the air like a rag doll, he kneed her hard in the kidney. Pain exploded in a flash of red. Her eyes rolled back. But Rachel did not give in. She kept going for the gun. The man had no choice. He put her down.

Air.

Her breathing passage was finally opened. She tried not to gulp it down, but her lungs had other ideas. She couldn't stop.

Her relief, however, was short lived. With one hand, the man stopped her from pulling out her gun. With the other, he delivered a dartlike blow to her throat. Rachel gagged and went down. The man took hold of her weapon and tossed it away. He dropped hard on top of her. The little wind she had managed to gather was gone now. He straddled her chest and moved his hands toward her throat.

That was when the police car sped past.

The man suddenly sat up. She tried to take advantage, but he was simply too big. He grabbed a cell phone from his pocket and put it to his mouth. In a harsh whisper, he said, "Abort! Cops!"

Rachel tried to move, tried to do something. But there was nothing left. She looked up in time to see the man cock his fist. It started toward her. She tried to turn away. But there was no place to go.

The blow jarred her head back against the cobblestone. And then darkness flooded in.

When Marc walked past her, Lydia stepped out of the bush from behind him with the gun up. She was aiming at the back of the head and had her finger on the trigger. The "Abort! Cops!" call in her earpiece startled her so, she almost pulled the trigger. But her mind worked fast. Seidman was still heading down the path. Lydia saw everything. Saw it clearly. She dumped the gun. No gun on her, no proof of any wrongdoing. The weapon could never be tied to her as long as it was not in her possession. Like most weapons, it was untraceable. She wore gloves, of course, so there would be no fingerprints.

But—her mind was still working fast here—what was there to prevent her from taking the money?

She was just Miss Citizen taking a stroll through the park. She could spot the duffel bag, right? If she was caught with it, well, she was just being a good Samaritan. Given the chance, she would have brought the bag to the police. No crime there. No risk.

Not when you consider that two million dollars was inside it.

Her mind quickly ran through the pros and cons. Simple when you think about it. Take the money. If they caught her with it, so what? There was absolutely nothing to tie her to this crime. She had dumped the gun. She had dumped the cell phone. Sure, someone might find it. But it would not lead to either her or Heshy.

She heard a noise. Marc Seidman, who'd been about fifteen feet in front of her, broke into a sprint. Fine, no problem. Lydia started toward the money. Heshy appeared around the corner. She continued toward him. Without hesitation, Lydia scooped up the bag.

Then Lydia and Heshy headed down the path, fading into the night.

I continued to stumble forward. My eyes were beginning to adjust, but they were still several minutes from being particularly useful. The path slid downward. There were small cobblestones. I tried not to trip. The route grew steeper now, and I let the momentum carry me so that I could move faster without appearing to be running.

On my right, I could see the abrupt slope that overlooked the Bronx. Lights twinkled from way below.

I heard a child's yelp.

I stopped. It was not loud, but the sound was unmistakably that of a small child. I heard rustling. The child yelped again. It was farther away now. The rustling sound was gone, but I could hear the steady slap of footsteps on the pavement. Someone was running. Running with a child. Away from me.

No.

I broke into a sprint. The faraway lights provided enough illumination so that I could stay on the path. Up ahead, I saw the chain-link fence. It had always been locked. When I reached it, I saw that someone had used a bolt cutter on it. I pushed through and was back on the path now. I looked to my left, which led back up to the park.

No one.

Damn, what the hell had gone wrong? I tried to think rationally. Focus. Okay, if I were the one running away, which way would I go? Simple. I would veer to the right. The paths were confusing, dark, windy. You could easily hide in the shrubs. That would be the way to go if one were a kidnapper. I stopped for only an instant, hoping to pick up the sounds of a child. I didn't. But I did hear someone say, "Hey!" with what sounded like genuine surprise.

I cocked my head. The sound had indeed come from my right. Good. I sprinted again, searching the horizon for a flannel shirt. Nothing. I continued down the hill. I lost my footing and almost tumbled down the hill. From my time living in this area, I knew the homeless found sanctuary on the off-path inclines too steep for the casual trekker. They made shelter out of branches and caves. Every once in a while, you could hear a rustling too loud for a squirrel. Sometimes a homeless guy would emerge out of seemingly nowhere—long haired, matted beard, the stench coming off him in waves. There was a spot not far from here where the male street prostitutes plied their trade to the businessmen getting off the A train. I used to jog by that area during the quiet of the day. Condom wrappers often littered the walkway.

I kept running, trying to keep my ears open. I hit a fork in the path.

Damn. Again I asked, What way was the more twisty? I didn't know. I was about to veer right again when I heard a sound.

Rustling in the bush.

Without thinking, I dived in. There were two men. One in a business suit. Another, much younger and dressed in jeans, was on his knees. The business suit yelled an expletive. I did not back away. Because I had heard the man's voice before. Seconds ago.

He had been the one who yelled "Hey."

"Did you see a man and a little girl go by here?"

"Get the hell out—"

I crossed over and slapped him in the face. "Did you see them?"

He looked far more shocked than hurt. He pointed to the left. "They went up that way. He was carrying the kid."

I jumped back on the path. Okay, right. They were heading back up toward the green. If they stayed that route, they would come out not far from where I'd parked. I started running again, pumping my arms. I ran past the male prostitutes sitting on the wall. One of them caught my eye—he had a blue kerchief on his head—nodded, and pointed to stay on the path. I nodded a thanks back. I kept running. In the distance, I could see the lights of the park. And there, crossing in front of the lamp-post, I caught a fleeting glimpse of the man in the flannel shirt carrying Tara.

"Stop!" I shouted. "Someone stop him!"

But they were gone.

I swallowed and started up the path, still shouting for help. No one reacted or shouted back. When I reached the outpost where lovers often gazed at the eastern view, I again spotted the flannel shirt. He was jumping over the wall into the woods. I started to follow but when I turned the corner, I heard someone yell, "Freeze!"

I looked behind me. It was a cop. He had his gun drawn.

"Freeze!"

"He has my kid! This way!"

"Dr. Seidman?"

The familiar voice came to my right. It was Regan.

What the . . . ? "Look, just follow me."

"Where's the money, Dr. Seidman?"

"You don't understand," I said. "They just jumped over that wall."

"Who did?"

I saw where this was going. Two cops had their guns pointed. Regan was staring at me with his arms crossed. Tickner appeared behind him.

"Let's talk about this, okay?"

Not okay. They wouldn't shoot. Or if they did, I didn't much care. So I started running. They took chase. The cops were younger and no doubt in better shape. But I had something going for me. I was crazed. I jumped the fence and fell down the incline. The cops pursued, but they were moving more gingerly, with normal human care.

"Freeze!" the cop yelled again.

I was breathing too fast to try to yell out more explanation. I wanted them to stay with me—I just didn't want them to catch up.

I curled up my body and rolled down the hill. Dried glass clung to me and got caught up in my hair. The dust kicked up. I stifled a cough. Just as I was picking up speed, my rib cage slammed into the trunk of tree. I could hear the hollow thud. I gasped, the wind almost knocked out of me, but I hung on. Sliding to the side, I reached the path. The cops' flashlights pursued. They were within sight but far enough behind. Fine.

On the path, my eyes swerved right, then left. No sign of the flannel shirt or Tara. I tried again to figure out which way he might run. Nothing came to me. I stopped. The police were coming closer.

"Freeze!" the cop yelled yet again.

Fifty-fifty chance.

I was about to break to my left, to head back into the darkness, when I saw the young man with the blue kerchief, the one who had nodded at me earlier. He shook his head this time and pointed in the direction behind me. "Thank you," I said.

He might have said something in return, but I was already on my way. I cut back up and headed through the same chain-link fence I had pushed through earlier. I heard footsteps, but they were too far away. I looked up and again spotted the flannel shirt. He was standing near the lights of the subway steps. He seemed to be trying to catch his breath.

I ran faster.

So did he.

There was probably fifty yards that separated us. But he had to carry a child. I should be able to close in on him. I started running. The same cop yelled "Halt!" this time, I guess for the sake of variety. I hoped like hell they didn't decide to shoot.

"He's back on the street!" I shouted. "He has my daughter."

I don't know if they were listening or not. I reached the steps and took them three at a time. I was out of the park again, back on Fort Washington Avenue at Margaret Corbin Circle. I looked ahead at the playground. No movement. I glanced down Fort Washington Avenue and spotted someone running near Mother Cabrini High School, near the chapel.

The mind flashes to odd things. Cabrini Chapel was one of the most surreal stops in all of Manhattan. Zia had dragged me to Mass there once to see without telling why the chapel was something of a tourist spot. I immediately understood the draw. Mother Cabrini died in 1901, but her embalmed body is kept in what looks like a lucite block. That's the altar. The priests conduct mass over her body/table. No, I'm not making that up. The same guy who preserved Lenin in Russia worked on Mother Cabrini. The chapel is open to the public. It even has a gift shop.

My legs felt heavy, but I kept moving. I no longer heard the police. I quickly glanced behind me. The flashlights were far away.

"Over here!" I shouted. "Near Cabrini High!"

I started sprinting again. I reached the entrance to the chapel. It was locked. There was no sign of flannel shirt anywhere. I looked around, eyes wide, panicked. I had lost them. They were gone.

"This way!" I shouted, hoping that either (or both) the police and Rachel would hear me.

But my heart sank. My chance. My daughter was gone again. I felt the weight on my chest. And that was when I heard the car start up.

My head jerked to the right. I scanned the street and started running. A car started moving. It was about ten yards in front of me. A Honda Accord. I memorized the license plate, even as I knew that would be futile. The driver was still trying to maneuver out of a parking spot. I couldn't see who it was. But I wasn't about to take any chances.

The Honda had just cleared the bumper of the car in front of it and was about start up when I grabbed the driver's side door handle. Lucky break finally—he hadn't locked the door. No time, I assumed, because he'd been in a rush.

Several things happened in a very short period of time. As I started pulling the door open, I was able to see through the window. It was indeed the flannel-shirt man. He reacted quickly. He grabbed the door and tried to hold it closed. I pulled harder. The door opened a crack. He hit the accelerator.

I tried to run with the car, like you see in the movies. The problem is, cars move faster than people. But I would not let go. You hear those stories about people gaining extraordinary strength in certain circumstances, about average men being able to lift cars off the ground to rescue trapped loved ones. I scoff at those stories. You probably do too.

I am not saying that I lifted a car. But I held on. I wedged my fingers in and wrapped them around the divide between the front door and back. I used both hands and willed my fingers into vises. I would not let go. No matter what.

If I hold on, my daughter lives. If I let go, my daughter dies.

Forget focus. Forget compartmentalizing. This thought, this equation, was as simple as breathing.

The man in the flannel shirt pushed down on the gas. The car was picking up speed now. I kicked my legs off the ground, but there was no place to perch them. They slid down the back door and landed with a clunk. I felt the skin of my ankles being scraped off on the pavement. I tried to regain my footing. No go. The pain was tremendous but inconsequential. I held on.

The status quo, I knew, was working against me. I couldn't hang on much longer, no matter how much I willed it. I had to make a move. I tried to pull myself into the car, but I wasn't strong enough. I hung on and let my arms go straight. I tried hopping up again. My body was horizontal now, parallel to the ground. I extended my body. My right leg reached up and curled around something. The antenna on the top of the car. Would that hold me? I didn't think so. My face was pressed against the backseat window. I saw the little car seat.

It was empty.

Panic seized me again. I felt my hands slipping. We had only driven maybe a twenty, thirty yards. With my face against the glass, my nose bouncing against the window, my body and face scraped and battered, I looked at the child in the front seat and a crushing truth pried my hands off the car window.

Again the mind works in odd ways. My first thought was classically doctor: The child should be sitting in the back. The Honda Accord has a passenger-side airbag. No child under the age of twelve should ever sit in the front. Also, small children should be in a proper car seat. That was, in fact, the law. Riding out of a car seat and in the front . . . that was doubly unsafe.

Ridiculous thought. Or maybe natural. Either way, that was not the thought that ripped the fight out of me.

The flannel-shirted man yanked the steering wheel to the right. I heard the tires squeak. The car jerked, and my fingers slipped away. My grip was gone now. I went airborne. My body landed hard, skidding across the pavement like a stone. I could hear the police sirens behind me. They would, I thought, follow the Honda Accord. But it wouldn't matter. I had only gotten a brief glimpse. But it had been enough to know the truth.

The child in the car was not my daughter.

chapter 29

Again I was in a hospital, this time New York Presbyterian—my old stomping grounds. They hadn't yet run X rays, but I was pretty sure they'd find a cracked rib. Nothing you could really do about it other than shoot yourself up with painkillers. It would hurt. That was okay. I was pretty scraped up. There was a gash on my right leg that looked like the work of a shark attack. Skin had been ripped off both elbows. None of that mattered.

Lenny arrived in record time. I wanted him here because I was not really sure how to handle this. At first, I almost convinced myself that I had made a mistake. A child changes, right? I had not seen Tara since she was six months old. A lot of growth occurs in that period. She'd have matured from wee infancy to an older toddler. I'd been hanging on to a moving car, for crying out loud. I had only gotten the briefest of glimpses.

But I knew.

The child in the front seat of the car looked to be a boy. He was probably closer to three years old than two. His skin, his coloring, was simply too pale.

It was not Tara.

I knew that Tickner and Regan had questions. I wanted to cooperate. I also wanted to know how the hell they had found out about the ransom drop. I hadn't seen Rachel yet either. I wondered if she were in the building. I also wondered about the fate of the ransom money, the Honda Accord, the man in the flannel shirt. Had they caught him? Had he kidnapped my daughter originally—or had that first ransom drop been a con job too? If so, how had my sister, Stacy, fitted into it?

In short, I was confused. Enter Lenny aka Cujo.

He burst through the door dressed in baggy khakis and a pink La-coste shirt. His eyes had that scared, wild look that again brought back memories of our childhood. He pushed past a nurse and approached my bed.

"What the hell happened?"

I was about to give Lenny an overview when he stopped me with a raised finger. He turned to the nurse and asked her to leave. When we were alone he nodded for me to go ahead again. Starting with seeing Edgar in the park, I ran through calling Rachel, her arrival, her prepara-tion with all the electronic gizmos, the ransom calls, the drop, my dive on the car. I backtracked and told him about the CD. Lenny interrupted—he always interrupted—but not as often as usual. I saw something cross his face, and maybe—I don't want to read too much into it here—but maybe he was hurt that I hadn't confided in him. The look didn't last long. Lenny gathered himself a piece at a time.

"Any chance that Edgar has been playing you?" he asked.

"To what end? He's the one who's lost four million dollars."

"Not if he's the one who set it up."

I made a face. "That doesn't make any sense."

Lenny didn't like it, but he didn't have a response either. "So where is Rachel now?"

"She's not here?"

"I don't think so."

"I don't know, then."

We both went quiet a second.

"Maybe she went back to my house," I said.

"Yeah," Lenny said. "Maybe."

There was nary a trace particle of conviction in his voice.

Tickner pushed open the door. His sunglasses sat atop his shaved head, a look I found disconcerting; if he bent his neck and drew a mouth on the lower part of his pate, it would look like a second face. Regan followed in a sort of hip-hop step, or maybe the soul patch was affecting the way I viewed him. Tickner took the lead.

"We know about the ransom demand," he said. "We know your father-in-law gave you another two million dollars. We know that you visited a private detective agency today called MVD and asked about the password to a CD-ROM owned by your late wife. We know that

Rachel Mills was with you and that she did not, as you told Detective Regan earlier, return to the Washington, D.C., area. So we can skip all that."

Tickner moved closer. Lenny watched him, ready to pounce. Regan folded his arms and leaned against the wall. "So let's start with the ransom money," Tickner said. "Where is it?"

"I don't know."

"Did someone take it?"

"I don't know."

"What do you mean, you don't know?"

"He told me to put it down."

"Who is 'he'?"

"The kidnapper. Whoever was on the cell phone."

"Where did you put it down?"

"In the park. On the path."

"And then what?"

"He said to start walking forward."

"Did you?"

"Yes."

"And then?"

"That's when I heard a child cry and someone start running. Everything went crazy after that."

"And the money?"

"I told you. I don't know what happened to the money."

"How about Rachel Mills?" Tickner asked. "Where is she?"

"I don't know."

I looked at Lenny, but he was studying Tickner's face now. I waited.

"You lied to us about her returning to Washington, D.C., isn't that correct?" Tickner asked.

Lenny put a hand on my shoulder. "Let's not start by mischaracterizing my client's statements."

Tickner made a face as if Lenny were a turd that had plopped down from the ceiling. Lenny stared back, unfazed. "You told Detective Regan that Ms. Mills was on her way back to Washington, did you not?"

"I said I didn't know where she was," I corrected him. "I said she *might* have gone back."

"And where was she at the time?"

Lenny said, "Don't answer."

I let him know that it was okay. "She was in the garage."

"Why didn't you tell Detective Regan that?"

"Because we were getting ready for the ransom drop. We didn't want anything slowing us down."

Tickner folded his arms. "I'm not sure I understand."

"Then ask another question," Lenny snapped.

"Why would Rachel Mills be involved in the ransom drop?"

"She's an old friend," I said. "And I knew she'd been a special agent with the FBI."

"Ah," Tickner said. "So you thought maybe her experience could help you here?"

"Yes."

"You didn't call Detective Regan or myself?"

"That's correct."

"Because?"

Lenny took that one. "You know damn well why."

"They told me no cops," I said. "Like last time. I didn't want to risk it again. So I called Rachel."

"I see." Tickner looked back at Regan. Regan looked off as if trying to follow a stray thought. "You chose her because she used to be a federal agent?"

"Yes."

"And because you two were"—Tickner made vague hand gestures—"close."

"A long time ago," I said.

"Not anymore?"

"No. Not anymore."

"Hmm, not anymore," Tickner repeated. "And yet you chose to call her in a matter involving your child's life. Interesting."

"Glad you think so," Lenny said, "By the way, is there a point to any of this?"

Tickner ignored him. "Before today, when was the last time you saw Rachel Mills?"

"What difference does that make?" Lenny said.

"Please just answer my question."

"Not until we know—"

But my hand was on Lenny's arm now. I knew what he was doing. He had automatically snapped into his adversarial pose. I appreciated it, but I wanted to get past this as quickly as possible.

"About a month ago," I said.

"Under what circumstances?"

"I bumped into her at the Stop & Shop on Northwood Avenue."

"Bumped into her?"

"Yes."

"You mean, as in a coincidence? As in not knowing the other was going to be there, out of the blue?"

"Yes."

Tickner turned around and looked at Regan again. Regan kept perfectly still. He wasn't even toying with the soul patch.

"And before that?"

"What before that?"

"Before you 'bumped' "—Tickner's sarcasm spit the word across the room—"into Ms. Mills at the Stop & Shop, when was the last time you'd seen her?"

"Not since college," I said.

Again Tickner spun toward Regan, his face lit up with incredulity. When he turned back, the glasses dropped down to his eyes. He pushed them back up onto his forehead. "Are you telling us, Dr. Seidman, that the only time you've seen Rachel Mills between your college days and today was just that one time at the supermarket?"

"That's exactly what I'm telling you."

For a moment, Tickner seemed at a loss. Lenny looked as if he might have something to add, but he kept himself in check.

"Have you two spoken on the phone?" Tickner asked.

"Before today?"

"Yes."

"No."

"Not ever? You never talked to her on the phone before today? Not even when you were dating?"

Lenny said, "Jesus Christ, what kind of question is that?"

Tickner snapped his head toward Lenny. "You have a problem?"

"Yeah, your questions are moronic."

They started again with the death stares. I broke the silence. "I hadn't spoken to Rachel on the phone since college."

Tickner turned to me. His expression was openly skeptical now. I glanced behind him at Regan. Regan was nodding to himself. While they both looked off balance, I tried to press it. "Did you find the man and child in the Honda Accord?" I asked.

Tickner considered the question a moment. He looked back at Regan, who shrugged a why-not. "We found the car abandoned on Broadway near 145th Street. It'd been stolen a few hours earlier." Tickner took out his notebook but didn't look at it. "When we spotted you at the park, you began yelling about your daughter. Do you believe that she was the child in the car?"

"I thought so at the time."

"But not anymore?"

"No," I said. "It wasn't Tara."

"What made you change your mind?"

"I saw him. The child, I mean."

"It was a he?"

"I think so."

"When did you see him?"

"When I jumped on the car."

Tickner spread his hands. "Why don't you start at the beginning and tell us exactly what happened?"

I told them the same story I'd told Lenny. Regan never moved from the wall. He still hadn't said a word. I found that odd. As I spoke, Tickner seemed to be growing more and more agitated. The skin on his cleanly shaven head tightened, making the sunglasses, which still sat perched on the top of his skull, start sliding forward. He kept readjusting them. I saw the pulse near his temples flutter. His jaw was locked.

When I was done, Tickner said, "You're lying."

Lenny slid between Tickner and my bed. For a moment, I thought that they might come to blows, which, let's face it, would not be good for Lenny. But Lenny never gave an inch. It reminded me of the time in third grade when Tony Merullo picked a fight with me. Lenny had stepped between us then, faced Tony bravely, and gotten clobbered.

Lenny stayed nose-to-nose with the larger man. "What the hell is wrong with you, Agent Tickner?"

"Your client is a liar."

"Gentlemen, this interview is over. Get out."

Tickner bent his neck so that his forehead pressed against Lenny's. "We have proof he's lying."

"Let's see it," Lenny said. Then, "No, wait, forget it. I don't want to see it. Are you arresting my client?"

"No."

"Then get your sorry butt out of this hospital room."

I said, "Lenny."

With one more glare at Tickner to show he wasn't intimidated, Lenny looked back at me.

"Let's finish this now," I said.

"He's trying to hang you for this."

I shrugged because I didn't really care. I think Lenny saw that. He slid away. I nodded for Tickner to do his worst.

"You've seen Rachel before today."

"I told you—"

"If you hadn't seen or spoken to Rachel Mills, how did you know she'd been a federal agent?"

Lenny started to laugh.

Tickner quickly spun toward him. "What are you laughing at?"

"Because, numb-nuts, my wife is friends with Rachel Mills."

That confused him. "What?"

"My wife and I talk to Rachel all the time. We introduced them." Lenny laughed again. "That's your proof?"

"No, that's not my proof," Tickner snapped, defensive now. "Your story about getting this ransom call, about reaching out to an old girlfriend like that. You expect that to fly?"

"Why," I said, "what do you think happened?"

Tickner said nothing.

"You think I did it, right? That this was yet another elaborate scheme to, what, get another two million from my ex–father-in-law?"

Lenny tried to slow me down. "Marc . . ."

"No, let me just say something here." I tried to get Regan into it, but he still looked off, so I locked eyes with Tickner. "Do you really think I staged all this? Why go through all the machinations of having this meeting in the park? How did I know you'd track me down there—hell, I still don't know how you did that. Why would I bother leaping on a car like that? Why wouldn't I have just taken the money and hidden it and come up with a story for Edgar? If I was just running a scam, did I hire this guy with the flannel shirt? Why? Why involve another person or a stolen car? I mean, come on. It makes no sense."

I looked at Regan, who still wasn't biting. "Detective Regan?"

But all he said was "You're not being straight with us, Marc."

"How?" I asked. "How am I not being straight with you?"

"You claim that before today you and Ms. Mills haven't spoken on the phone since college."

"Yes."

"We have phone records, Marc. Three months before your wife was murdered, there was a call from Rachel's house to yours. Do you want to explain that?"

I turned to Lenny for help, but he was staring down at me. This made no sense. "Look," I said, "I have Rachel's cell phone number. Let's call her and find out where she is."

"Do that," Tickner said.

Lenny picked up the hospital phone next to my bed. I gave him the number. I watched him dial it, all the while trying to put it together. The phone rang six times before I heard Rachel's voice tell me she could not answer her phone and that I should leave a message. I did so.

Regan finally peeled himself off the wall. He pulled a chair to the side of my bed and sat. "Marc, what do you know about Rachel Mills?"

"Enough."

"You dated in college?"

"Yes."

"How long?"

"Two years."

Regan spread his arms, all open and wide eyed. "See, Agent Tickner and I still aren't sure why you called her. I mean, okay, you dated a long time ago. But if you haven't been in touch at all"—he shrugged—"why her?"

I thought about how to put this and chose the direct route. "There's still a connection."

Regan nodded as if that explained a lot. "You were aware that she got married?"

"Cheryl—that's Lenny's wife—she told me."

"And you knew her husband was shot?"

"I learned about it today." Then, realizing that it had to be after midnight, "I mean, yesterday."

"Rachel told you?"

"Cheryl told me." Regan's words from his late-night visit to my abode came back to me. "And then you said Rachel shot him."

Regan looked back at Tickner. Tickner said, "Did Ms. Mills mention that to you?"

"What, that she shot her husband?"

"Yes."

"You're kidding, right?"

"You don't believe it, do you?"

Lenny said, "What's the difference what he believes?"

"She confessed," Tickner said.

I looked at Lenny. Lenny looked away. I tried to sit up a little more. "Then why isn't she in jail?"

Something dark crossed Tickner's face. His hands clenched into fists. "She claimed the shooting was accidental."

"And you don't believe that?"

"Her husband was shot in the head at point-blank range."

"So again I ask: Why isn't she in jail?"

"I'm not privy to all the details," Tickner said.

"What does that mean?"

"The local cops handled the case, not us," Tickner explained. "They decided not to pursue it."

I am neither a cop nor a great student of psychology, but even I could see that Tickner was holding something back. I looked at Lenny. His face was emotionless, which, of course, is not at all like Lenny. Tickner took a step away from the bed. Regan filled the void.

"You said you still felt a connection with Rachel?" Regan began.

"Asked and answered," Lenny said.

"Did you still love her?"

Lenny couldn't let that one go without comment. "Are you Ann Landers now, Detective Regan? What the hell does any of this have to do with my client's daughter?"

"Bear with me."

"No, Detective, I will not bear with you. Your questions are nonsense." Again I put my hand on Lenny's shoulder. He turned to me. "They want you to say yes, Marc."

"I know that."

"They're hoping to use Rachel as a motive for killing your wife."

"I know that too," I said. I looked at Regan. I remembered the feeling when I first saw Rachel at the Stop & Shop.

"You still think about her?" Regan asked.

"Yes."

"Does she still think about you?"

Lenny was not about to surrender. "How the hell would he know that?"

"Bob?" I said. It was the first time I had used Regan's first name.

"Yes."

"What are you trying to get at here?"

Regan's voice was low, almost conspiratorial. "Let me ask you one more time: Before the incident at the Stop & Shop, had you seen Rachel Mills since you broke up in college?"

"Jesus Christ," Lenny said.

"No."

"You're sure?"

"Yes."

"No communication at all?"

"They didn't even pass notes during study hall," Lenny said. "I mean, get on with it."

Regan leaned away. "You went to a private detective agency in Newark to ask about a CD-ROM."

"Yes."

"Why today?"

"I'm not sure I understand."

"Your wife has been dead for a year and a half. Why the sudden interest in the CD?"

"I'd just found it."

"When?"

"The day before yesterday. It was hidden in the basement."

"So you had no idea that Monica had hired a private detective?"

It took me a moment to answer. I thought about what I had learned since my beautiful wife's death. She had been seeing a psychiatrist. She had hired a private detective. She had hidden his findings in our basement. I hadn't known about any of it. I thought about my life, my love of work, my wanting to keep traveling. Sure, I loved my daughter. I cooed on command and marveled at the wonder of her. I would die—and kill—to protect her, but in my honest moments, I knew that I had not accepted all the changes and sacrifices she'd brought to my life.

What kind of husband had I been? What kind of father?

"Marc?"

"No," I said softly. "I had no idea she had hired a private investigator."

"Do you have any idea why she did?"

I shook my head. Regan faded back. Tickner pulled out a manila folder.

"What's that?" Lenny said.

"The contents of the CD." Tickner looked at me one more time. "You never saw Rachel, right? Just that time in the supermarket."

I did not bother answering.

Without fanfare, Tickner withdrew a photograph and handed it to me. Lenny snapped on his half-moon reading glasses and stood over my shoulder. He did that thing where you tilt your head up to look down. The photograph was black and white. It was a shot of Valley Hospital in Ridgewood. There was a date stamped on the bottom. The photograph had been taken two months before the shooting.

Lenny frowned. "The lighting is pretty good, but I'm not sure about the overall composition."

Tickner ignored the sarcasm. "That's where you work, is it not, Dr. Seidman?"

"We have an office there, yes."

"We?"

"My partner and I. Zia Leroux."

Tickner nodded. "There's a date stamped on the bottom."

"I can see that."

"Were you in the office on that day?"

"I really don't know. I'd have to check my calendar."

Regan pointed to near the hospital entrance. "Do you see that figure over there?"

I looked harder, but I couldn't make much out. "No, not really."

"Just notice the length of the coat, okay?"

"Okay."

Then Tickner handed me a second glossy. The photographer had used the zoom lens on this one. Same angle. You could see the person in the coat clearly now. She wore sunglasses, but there was no mistake. It was Rachel.

I looked up at Lenny. I saw the surprise on his face too. Tickner pulled out another photo. Then another. They were all taken in front of Valley Hospital. In the eighth one, Rachel entered the building. In the ninth one, taken one hour later, I exited alone. In the tenth, taken six minutes after that, Rachel went out the same doors.

At first, my mind could simply not soak in the implications. I was one big, swirling "Huh?" of bewilderment. There was no time to process. Lenny seemed stunned too, but he recovered first.

"Get out," Lenny said.

"You don't want to explain these photographs first?"

I wanted to argue, but I was too dazed.

"Get out," Lenny said again, more forcefully this time. "Get out now."

chapter 30

I sat up in the bed. "Lenny?"

He made sure the door was closed. "Yes," he said. "They think you did it. Check that, they think you and Rachel did it together. You two were having an affair. She killed her husband—I don't know if they think you were involved with that or not—and then you both killed Monica, did who-knows-what with Tara, and came up with this scheme to rip off her father."

"That makes no sense," I said.

Lenny kept quiet.

"I was shot, remember?"

"I know."

"So what, they think I shot myself?"

"I don't know. But you can't talk to them anymore. They have evidence now. You can deny a relationship with Rachel to the skies, but Monica was suspicious enough to hire a private detective. Then, Jesus, think about it. The private detective delivers. He takes those photographs and gives them to Monica. Next thing you know, your wife is dead, your kid is gone, and her father is out two million bucks. Skip ahead a year and a half. Her father is out another two million and you and Rachel are lying about being with one another."

"We're not lying."

Lenny would not look at me.

"What about all I was saying," I tried, "about how no one would go through all this? I could have just taken the ransom money, right? I didn't have to hire that guy with the car and the kid. And what about my sister? Do they think I murdered her too?"

"Those pictures," Lenny said softly.

"I never knew about them."

He could barely look at me, but that didn't stop him from reverting to our youth. "Well, duh."

"No, I mean I don't know anything about them."

"You really haven't seen her except for that time at the supermarket?"

"Of course not. You know all this. I wouldn't hide it from you."

He weighed that statement for too long. "You might hide it from Lenny the Friend."

"No, I wouldn't. But even if I would, there's no way I could keep it from Lenny the Lawyer."

His voice was soft. "You didn't tell either one of us about this ransom drop."

So there it was. "We wanted to keep it contained, Lenny."

"I see." But he didn't. I couldn't blame him. "Another thing. How did you find that CD in the basement?"

"Dina Levinsky came by the house."

"Dina the fruitcake?"

"She's had it rough," I said. "You have no idea."

Lenny waved off my sympathy. "I don't understand. What was she doing at your house?" I filled him on the story. Lenny started making a face. When I finished, I was the one who said, "What?"

"She told you she was better now? That she was married?"

"Yes."

"That's bull."

I stopped. "How do you know that?"

"I do some legal work for her aunt. Dina Levinsky has been in and out of asylums since she was eighteen. She even served time for aggravated assault a few years back. She's never been married. And I doubt she's ever had an art exhibit."

I did not know what to make of that. I remembered Dina's haunting face, the way the color ebbed away when she said, *"You know who shot you, don't you, Marc?"*

What the hell had she meant by that anyway?

"We need to think this through," Lenny said, rubbing his chin. "I'm going to check with some of my sources, see what I can learn. Call me if anything comes up, okay?"

"Yeah, okay."

"And promise me you won't say another word to them. There is an excellent chance they'll arrest you." He raised a hand before I could protest. "They have enough for an arrest and maybe even an indictment. True, the *t*'s aren't all crossed and the *i*'s aren't all dotted. But think about that Skakel case. They had less there and they convicted him. So if they come back in here, promise me you won't say a word."

I promised because, yet again, the authorities were on the wrong track. Cooperating with them would not help find my daughter. That was the bottom line. Lenny left me alone. I asked him to shut off the lights. He did. But the room did not grow dark. Hospital rooms never get totally dark.

I tried to understand what was happening. Tickner had taken those strange photographs with him. I wished he hadn't. I wanted to take another look because no matter how I laid it out, those pictures of Rachel at the hospital made no sense. Were they for real? Trick photography was a strong possibility, especially in this digital day and age. Could that be the explanation? Were they phonies, a simple cut-and-paste job? My thoughts veered toward Dina Levinsky again. What had her bizarre visit really been about? Why had she asked if I loved Monica? Why did she think I knew who shot me? I was considering all of this when the door opened.

"Is this the room belonging to the Stud in Scrubs?"

It was Zia. "Hey."

She entered, gestured at my supine position with a sweep of her hand. "This supposed to be your excuse for missing work?"

"I was on call last night, wasn't I?"

"Yep."

"Sorry."

"They woke my ass up instead, interrupting, I might add, a rather erotic dream." Zia pointed with her thumb toward the door. "That big black man down the hall."

"The one with the sunglasses on top of a shaved head?"

"That's him. He a cop?"

"An FBI agent."

"Any chance you can introduce us? Might make up for interrupting my dream."

"I'll try to do that," I said, "before he arrests me."

"After is okay too."

I smiled. Zia sat on the edge of the bed. I told her what had happened. She didn't offer a theory. She didn't throw up a question. She just listened, and I loved her for it.

I was just getting to the part about being a serious suspect when my cell phone started ringing. Both of us, because of our training, were surprised. Cell phones in the hospital were a no-no. I reached it for quickly and brought it to my ear.

"Marc?"

It was Rachel. "Where are you?"

"Following the money."

"What?"

"They did exactly what I thought," she said. "They dumped the bag, but they haven't spotted the Q-Logger in the pack of bills. I'm heading up the Harlem River Drive right now. They're maybe a mile ahead of me."

"We need to talk," I said.

"Did you find Tara?"

"It was a hoax. I saw the kid they had with them. It wasn't my daughter."

There was a pause.

"Rachel?"

"I'm not doing so good, Marc."

"What do you mean?"

"I took a beating. At the park. I'm okay, but I need your help."

"Wait a second. My car is still at the scene. How are you following them?"

"Did you notice a Parks Department van on the circle?"

"Yes."

"I stole it. It's an old van, easy to hot-wire. I figured it wouldn't be missed until the morning."

"They think we did it, Rachel. That we were having an affair or something. They found photos on that CD. You in front of where I work."

Cell-phone-static silence.

"Rachel?"

"Where are you?" she asked.

"I'm at New York Presbyterian Hospital."

"Are you okay?"

"Banged up. But I'm fine, yeah."

"The cops there?"

"The feds too. A guy named Tickner. You know him?"

Her voice was soft. "Yes." Then, "How do you want to play it?"

"What do you mean?"

"Do you want to keep following them? Or do you want to turn it over to Tickner and Regan?"

I wanted her back here. I wanted to ask her about those photos and the phone call to my house. "I'm not sure it matters," I said. "You were right from the beginning. It was a con job. They must have used someone else's hair."

More static.

"What?" I said.

"You know anything about DNA?" she asked me.

"Not much," I said.

"I don't have time to explain it, but a DNA test goes layer by layer. You start seeing things match up. It takes at least twenty-four hours before we can really say with any degree of certainty that there's a match."

"So?"

"So I just spoke to my lab guy. We've only had about eight hours. But so far, that second set of hairs that Edgar got?"

"What about them?"

"They match yours." I wasn't sure I heard correctly. Rachel made a sound that might have been a sigh. "In other words, he hasn't ruled out that you're the father. Just the opposite, in fact."

I nearly dropped the phone. Zia saw it and moved closer. Again I focused and compartmentalized. Process. Rebuild. I considered my options. Tickner and Regan would never believe me. They would not allow me to go. They'd probably arrest us. At the same time, if I told them, I might be able to prove our innocence. On the other hand, proving my innocence was irrelevant.

Was there a chance my daughter was still alive?

That was the only question here. If she was, then I had to resort to our original plan. Confiding in the authorities, especially with their fresh suspicions, would not work. Suppose there was, as the ransom note said, a mole? Right now, whoever had picked up that bag of money had no idea that Rachel was onto them. But what would happen if the cops and feds got involved? Would the kidnappers run, panic, do something rash?

There was something else here that I should be considering: Did I still trust Rachel? Those photographs had shaken my faith. I didn't know what to believe anymore. But in the end, I had no choice but to treat those doubts as a distraction. I needed to focus on one goal. Tara. What would give me the best chance of finding out what really happened to her?

"How badly hurt are you?" I asked.

"We can do this, Marc."

"I'm on my way, then."

I hung up and looked at Zia.

"You have to help me get out of here."

Tickner and Regan sat in the doctors' lounge down the hall. A lounge seemed a strange name for this threadbare dwelling with too much light and a rabbit-ear TV set. There was a minifridge in the corner. Tickner had opened it. There were two brown-bag lunches in it, both with names written on them. It reminded him of elementary school.

Tickner collapsed on a couch with absolutely no springs. "I think we should arrest him now."

Regan said nothing.

"You were awfully quiet in there, Bob. Something on your mind?"

Regan started scratching the soul patch. "What Seidman said."

"What about it?"

"Don't you think he had a point?"

"You mean that stuff about him being innocent?"

"Yes."

"No, not really. You buy it?"

"I don't know," Regan said. "I mean, why would he go through all this with the money? He couldn't have known we'd learn about that CD and decide to track him with E-ZPass and find him at Fort Tryon Park. And even if he had, why go through all that? Why jump on a moving car? Christ, he's lucky he wasn't killed. Again. Which brings us back to the original shooting and our original problem. If he and Rachel Mills did this together, why was he nearly killed?" Regan shook his head. "There are too many holes."

"Which we are filling in one by one," Tickner said.

Regan made a yes-no with a head tilt.

"Look at how many we plugged today by learning about Rachel Mills's involvement," Tickner said. "We just need to get her in here and sweat them both."

Regan looked off again.

Tickner shook his head. "What now?"

"The broken window."

"The one at the crime scene?"

"Yeah."

"What about it?"

Regan sat up. "Play along with me, okay? Let's go back to the original murder-kidnapping."

"At the Seidman house?"

"Right."

"Okay, go."

"The window was broken from the outside," Regan said. "That could be how the perp gained entry to the house."

"Or," Tickner added, "Dr. Seidman broke the window to throw us off."

"Or he had an accomplice do it."

"Right."

"But either way, Dr. Seidman would have been in on the broken window, right? If he was involved, I mean."

"Where are you going with this?"

"Just stay with me, Lloyd. We think Seidman was involved. Ergo, Seidman knew that the window had been broken to make it look like, I don't know, a random break-in. Agreed?"

"I guess."

Regan smiled. "Then how come he never mentioned the broken window?"

"What?"

"Read his statement. He remembers eating a granola bar and then—bam—nothing. No sound. No one sneaking up on him. Nothing." Regan spread his hands. "Why doesn't he remember hearing the window break?"

"Because he broke it himself to make it look like an intruder."

"But see, if that's the case, he would have kept the broken window in his story. Think about it. He breaks the window to convince us the perp broke in and shot him. So what would you say if you were him?"

Now Tickner saw where he was heading. "I'd say, 'I heard the window break, I turned and bam, the bullets hit me.' "

"Exactly. But Seidman did none of that. Why?"

Tickner shrugged. "Maybe he forgot. He was seriously injured."

"Or maybe—just stay with me—maybe he's telling the truth."

The door opened. An exhausted-looking kid in scrubs looked in. He saw the two cops, rolled his eyes, left them alone. Tickner turned back toward Regan. "But wait a second, you've caught yourself in a Catch-22."

"How so?"

"If Seidman didn't do it—if it really was a perp who broke the window—why didn't Seidman hear it?"

"Maybe he doesn't remember. We've seen this a million times. A guy getting shot and hurt that seriously loses some time." Regan smiled, warming up to this theory. "Especially if he saw something that totally shocked him—something he wouldn't want to remember."

"Like his wife being stripped down and killed?"

"Like that," Regan said. "Or maybe something worse."

"What's worse?"

A beeping sound came from the corridor. They could hear the nearby nurse's station. Someone was bitching about a shift time or schedule change.

"We said we're missing something," Regan said slowly. "We've been saying that from the beginning. But maybe it's just the opposite. We've been *adding* something."

Tickner frowned.

"We keep adding Dr. Seidman. Look, we both know the score. In cases like this, the husband is always involved. Not nine times out of ten—ninety-nine times out of a hundred. Every scenario we've devised includes Seidman."

Tickner said, "And you think that's wrong?"

"Listen to me a second. We've had Seidman in our sights from the get-go. His marriage was not idyllic. He got married because his wife was pregnant. We seized on all that. But if their marriage had been friggin'

Ozzie and Harriet, we'd still say, 'Nah, no one is that happy,' and leap on that. So whatever we've stumbled across, we've tried to fit it into that reality: Seidman had to be involved. So for just a second, let's take him out of the equation. Let's pretend he's innocent."

Tickner shrugged. "Okay, so?"

"Seidman talked about a connection with Rachel Mills. One that's lasted all these years."

"Right."

"He sounded a little obsessed with her."

"A little?"

Regan smiled. "Suppose the feeling was mutual. Check that. Suppose it was more than mutual."

"Okay."

"Now remember. We're assuming Seidman didn't do it. That means he's telling us the truth. About everything. About when he last saw Rachel Mills. About those photographs. You saw his face, Lloyd. Seidman isn't that great an actor. Those pictures shocked him. He didn't know about them."

Tickner frowned. "Hard to say."

"Well, there was something else I noticed about those pictures."

"What?"

"How come that private eye didn't get any pictures of the two of them together? We have her outside the hospital. We have him coming out. We have her going out. But none of them together."

"They were careful."

"How careful? She was hanging outside his place of work. If you're being careful, you don't do that."

"So what's your theory?"

Regan smiled. "Think about it. Rachel had to know Seidman was inside the building. But did he have to know she was outside?"

"Wait a second," Tickner said. A smile started coming to his face. "You think she was stalking him?"

"Maybe."

Tickner nodded. "And—whoa—we're not talking about just any woman here. We're talking about a well-trained federal agent."

"So one, she would know how to run a professional kidnapping operation," Regan added, raising a finger. He raised another. "Two, she would know how to kill someone and get away with it. Three, she would know how to cover her tracks. Four, she would know Marc's sister, Stacy. Five"—the thumb now—"she'd be able to use her old contacts to find and set the sister up."

"Holy Christ." Tickner looked up. "And what you said before. About seeing something so horrible Seidman doesn't remember."

"How about seeing the love of your life shooting you? Or your wife. Or . . ."

They both stopped.

"Tara," Tickner said. "How does the little girl fit into all this?"

"A way of extorting money?"

Neither one of them liked that. But whatever other answers they came up with, they liked those even less.

"We can add something else," Tickner said.

"What?"

"Seidman's missing thirty-eight."

"What about it?"

"His gun was in a lockbox in his closet," Tickner said. "Only someone close to him would know where it was hidden."

"Or," Regan added, seeing something else now, "maybe Rachel Mills brought her own thirty-eight. Remember that two were used."

"But that raises another question: Why would she need two guns?"

Both men frowned, ran a few new theories through their heads, and came up with a solid conclusion. "We're still missing something," Regan said.

"Yep."

"We need to go back and get some answers."

"Like?"

"Like why did Rachel skate on the murder of her first husband?"

"I can ask around," Tickner said.

"Do that. And let's get a man on Seidman. She has four million dollars now. She might want to eliminate the only guy who can still tie her to this."

chapter 31

Zia found my clothes in the closet. Bloodstains darkened my jeans, so we decided to go with surgical scrubs. She ran down the hall and found me a pair. Wincing from the cracked ribs, I slipped them on and tied the string waist. It would be a slow go. Zia checked to see if the coast was clear. She had a backup plan in case the feds were still watching. Her friend, Dr. David Beck, had been involved in a major federal case a few years ago. He knew Tickner from that. Beck was on call. If it came to it, he was waiting at the end of the hall and would try to slow them down with some sort of reminiscence.

In the end, we didn't need Beck. We simply walked out. No one questioned us. We made our way through the Harkness Pavilion and out into the courtyard north of Fort Washington Avenue. Zia's car was parked in the lot on 165th and Fort Washington. I moved gingerly. I felt sore as hell, but basically all right. Marathon running and heavy lifting would be out, but the pain was controllable and I had full range of motion. Zia had slipped me a bottle of Vioxx, the fifty-milligram big-boys. They'd be good because they worked without making you drowsy.

"If anyone asks," she said, "I'll tell them I took public transportation and that my car is home. You should be okay for a while."

"Thanks," I said. "Actually, can I also trade cell phones?"

"Sure, why?"

"They might try, I don't know, to track me down using mine."

"They can do that?"

"Beats the hell out of me."

She shrugged and dug out her cell. It was a tiny thing, the size of a compact mirror. "You really think Tara is alive?"

"I don't know."

We hurried up the parking garage's cement steps. The stairwell stank, as always, of urine.

"This is insane," she said. "You know that, right?"

"Yeah."

"I got my pager. You need me, you page me."

"I will."

We stopped at the car. Zia handed me the keys.

"What?" I said to her.

"You got a pretty big ego, Marc."

"This your idea of a pep talk?"

"Just don't let it get you hurt or anything," Zia said. "I need you."

I hugged her and slipped into the driver's seat. I started north on the Henry Hudson, dialing Rachel's number. The night was clear and still. The lights from the bridge made the dark water look like a star-filled sky. I heard two rings and then Rachel picked up. She didn't say anything and then I realized why. She probably had Caller ID and didn't recognize the number.

"It's me," I said. "I'm using Zia's phone."

Rachel asked, "Where are you?"

"About to get on the Hudson."

"Keep going north to the Tappan Zee. Cross it and start heading west."

"Where are you now?"

"By that huge Palisades Mall."

"In Nyack," I said.

"Right. Keep in phone touch. We'll find a place to hook up."

"I'm on my way."

Tickner was on his mobile phone, filling in O'Malley. Regan hurried back into the lounge. "Seidman's not in his room."

Tickner looked annoyed. "What do you mean, he's not in his room?"

"How many different ways are there to interpret that, Lloyd?"

"Did he go down to X ray or something?"

"Not according to the nurse," Regan said.

"Damn. The hospital has security cameras, right?"

"Not on every room."

"But they have to cover the exits."

"They must have a dozen exits here. By the time we get the tapes and review them—"

"Yeah, yeah, yeah." Tickner thought about it. He put the phone back to his ear. "O'Malley?"

"I'm here."

"You heard?"

"Yup."

"How long will it take you to get phone logs from both Seidman's hospital room and cell phone?" Tickner asked.

"Immediate calls?"

"It would have to have been in the past fifteen minutes, yeah."

"Give me five."

Tickner pressed the "end" button. "Where's Seidman's lawyer?"

"I don't know. I think he said he was leaving."

"Maybe we should give him a ring."

"He didn't hit me as the helpful type," Regan said.

"That was before, when we thought his client was a wife-and-baby killer. We're now theorizing that an innocent man's life is in danger." Tickner handed Regan the business card Lenny had given him.

"Worth a shot," Regan said, and began dialing.

I caught up with Rachel just over the north New Jersey–south New York border town of Ramsey. Using our phones we managed to hook up in the parking lot of the Fair Motel on Route 17 in Ramsey, New Jersey. The motel was a no-tell, complete with a sign proudly reading COLOR TV! (as if most motels were still using black and white) where all the letters (and the exclamation point) are a different color, in case you don't know what the word *color* means. I always liked the name. The Fair Motel. We're not great, we're not terrible. We're, well, Fair. Honesty in advertising.

I pulled into the lot. I was scared. I had a million questions for Rachel, but in the end, it all boiled down to different variations of the same thing. I wanted to know about her husband's death, sure, but more than that, I wanted to know about those damn private-eye pictures.

The lot was dark, most of the light coming off the highway. The stolen Parks Department van sat by a Pepsi machine on the far right side. I pulled next to it. I never saw Rachel leave the van, but the next thing I knew she had slid into the passenger seat next to me.

"Start moving," she said.

I turned to confront her, but her face made me pull up short. "Jesus, are you all right?"

"I'm fine."

Her right eye was swollen over like a boxer's who had gone the distance. There were yellow-purple bruises around her neck. Her face had a giant red mark across both cheeks. I could see scarlet indentations from where her attacker had dug in his fingers. The fingernails had even broken the skin. I wondered if there was deeper trauma to her face, if whatever blow she took to the eye had been powerful enough to break a bone. I doubted it. A break like that would normally knock someone out of commission. Then again, best-case scenario and these were only surface wounds: It was amazing she was still upright.

"What the hell happened?" I asked.

She had her Palm Pilot out. The screen was dazzlingly bright in the dark of the car. She looked down at it and said, "Take Seventeen south. Hurry, I don't want to get too far behind."

I put the car in reverse, backed up, started down the highway. I reached into my pocket and pulled out the bottle of Vioxx. "These should help deaden the pain."

She pulled off the top. "How many should I take?"

"One."

Her index finger scooped it out. Her eyes never left the Palm Pilot's screen. She swallowed it down and said thanks.

"Tell me what happened," I said.

"You first."

I filled her in as best I could. We stayed on Route 17. We passed the Allendale and Ridgewood exits. The streets were empty. The shops— and, man, there were lots of them, the entire highway pretty much one continuous strip mall—were all closed up. Rachel listened without interrupting. I glanced at her as I drove. She looked in pain.

When I finished, she asked, "Are you sure it wasn't Tara in the car?"

"Yes."

"I called my DNA guy again. The layers are still matching up. I don't get that."

Neither did I. "What happened to you?"

"Somebody jumped me. I was watching you through the night-vision goggles. I saw you put down the money bag and start walking. There was a woman in the bushes. Did you see her?"

"No."

"She had a gun. I think she planned on killing you."

"A woman?"

"Yes."

I wasn't sure how to react to that. "Did you get a good look at her?"

"No. I was about to call out a warning when this monster grabbed me from behind. Strong as hell. He lifted me off my feet by my head. I thought he was going to rip my skull off."

"Jesus."

"Anyway, a cop car drove by. The big guy panicked. He punched me here"—she pointed to the swollen eye—"and it was lights-out. I don't know how long I was lying on the pavement. When I woke up, the cops were all over the place. I was huddled in a corner in the dark. I guess they didn't see me or figured I was a homeless guy sleeping one off. Anyway, I checked the Palm Pilot. I saw the money was on the move."

"Which direction?"

"South, walking near 168th Street. Then suddenly they went still. See, this thing"—she gestured to the screen—"works two ways. I zoom in, I can get as close as a quarter mile. I go out a little farther, like right now, I get more an idea than an exact address. Right now, based on the speed, I figure they're driving about six miles ahead of us still on Route Seventeen."

"But when you first spotted them, they were on 168th Street?"

"Right. Then they start heading downtown fast."

I thought about it. "The subway," I said. "They took the A train from the 168th Street stop."

"That's what I figured. Anyway, I stole the van. I started downtown. I was near the seventies when all of a sudden they started going east. This time it was more stop and go."

"They were stopping for lights. They had a car now."

Rachel nodded. "They sped up on the FDR and Harlem River Drive. I tried to cut across town, but that took too long. I fell behind by five, six miles. Anyway, you know the rest."

We slowed for night construction near the Route 4 interchange. Three lanes became one. I looked at her, at the bruises and the swelling, at the giant handprint on her skin. She looked back at me and didn't say a word. My fingers reached out and caressed her face as gently as I knew how. She closed her eyes, the tenderness seemingly too much, and even in the midst of all this we both knew that it felt right. A stirring, an old one, a dormant one, started deep inside of me. I kept my eyes on that lovely, perfect face. I pushed back her hair. A tear escaped her eye and ran down her cheek. She put her hand on my wrist. I felt the warmth start there and spread.

Part of me—and, yes, I know how this will sound—wanted to forget this quest. The kidnapping had been a hoax. My daughter was gone. My wife was dead. Someone was trying to kill me. It was time to start again, a new chance, a way, this time, to get it right. I wanted to turn the car around and start heading in the other direction. I wanted to drive—keep driving—and never ask about her dead husband and those pictures on the CD. I could forget all that, I knew I could. My life was filled with surgical procedures that altered the surface, that helped people begin anew, that improved what was visible and thus what was not. That could be what would happen here. A simple face-lift. I would make my first incision the day before that damn frat party, pull the fourteen-year-old folds across time, close the suture at now. Stick the two moments together. Nip and tuck. Make those fourteen years disappear, as though they'd never happened.

Rachel opened her eyes now and I could see that she was thinking pretty much the same thing, hoping I'd call it off and turn around. But of course, that could not be. We blinked. The construction cleared. Her hand left my forearm. I risked another glance at Rachel. No, we were not twenty-one years old anymore, but that didn't matter. I saw that now. I still loved her. Irrational, wrong, stupid, naïve, whatever. I still loved her. Over the years, I might have convinced myself otherwise, but I had never stopped. She was still so damn beautiful, so damn perfect, and when I thought of how close she'd just come to death, those giant hands smothering away her breath, those niggling doubts began to soften. They wouldn't go away. Not until I knew the truth. But no matter what the answers were, they would not consume me.

"Rachel?"

But she suddenly sat up, her eyes back on the Palm Pilot.

"What is it?" I asked.

"They've stopped," Rachel said. "We'll be on them in two miles."

chapter 32

Steven Bacard replaced the phone's receiver.

You slip-slide into evil, he thought. You cross the line for just one moment. You cross back. You feel safe. You change things, you believe, for the better. The line is still there. It's still intact. Okay, maybe there's a smudge there now, but you can still see it clearly. And next time you cross, maybe that line smudges a little more. But you have your bearings. No matter what happens to that line, you remember where it is.

Don't you?

There was a mirror above the fully stocked bar in Steven Bacard's office. His interior decorator had insisted that all people of prestige had to have a place to toast their successes. So he had one. He didn't even drink. Steven Bacard stared at his reflection and thought, not for the first time in his life: Average. He had always been average. His grades in school, his SAT and LSAT scores, his law-school ranking, his bar score (he passed it on the third attempt). If life were a game where children choose sides for kickball, he'd be picked in the middle of the pack, after the good athletes and before the really bad ones—in that cusp for those who leave no mark.

Bacard became a lawyer because he believed that being a JD would give him a level of prestige. It didn't. No one hired him. He opened up his own pitiful office near the Paterson courthouse, sharing space with a bail bondsman. He ambulance-chased, but even as a member of this small-time pack, he couldn't distinguish himself. He managed to marry a woman slightly above his station, though she reminded him of that as often as she could.

Where Bacard had indeed been below average—*way* below average—

was in sperm count. Try as he might—and Dawn, his wife, didn't really like him to try—he could not impregnate his wife. After four years, they tried to adopt. Again, Steven Bacard fit into the abyss of the great unspectacular, which made finding a white baby—something Dawn truly craved—nearly impossible. He and Dawn traveled to Romania, but the only children available were too old or born drug addled.

But it was there, overseas in that god-deserted place, that Steven Bacard finally came up with an idea that, after thirty-eight years, made him rise above the crowd.

"Problem, Steven?"

The voice startled him. He turned away from his reflection. Lydia stood in the shadows.

"Staring in the mirror like that," Lydia said, adding a tsk-tsk at the end. "Wasn't that Narcissus's downfall?"

Bacard could not help it. He began to tremble. It wasn't just Lydia, though, in truth, she often had that effect on him. The phone call had set him on edge. Lydia popping up like that—that was the clincher. He had no idea how she'd gotten in or how long she'd been standing there. He wanted to ask what had happened tonight. He wanted details. But there was no time.

"We do indeed have a problem," Bacard said.

"Tell me."

Her eyes chilled him. They were big and luminous and beautiful and yet you sensed nothing behind them, only a cold chasm, windows to a house long abandoned.

What Bacard had discovered while in Romania—what had finally helped him rise above the pack—was a way to beat the system. Suddenly, for the first time in his life, Bacard was on a roll. He stopped chasing ambulances. People started looking up to him. He was invited to fund-raisers. He became a sought-after speaker. His wife, Dawn, started to smile at him again and ask him about his day. He even appeared on News 12 New Jersey when the cable station needed a certain kind of legal expert. He stopped, however, when a colleague overseas reminded him of the danger of too much publicity. Besides, he no longer needed to attract clients. They found him, these parents searching for a miracle. The desperate have always done that, like plants stretching through the dark for any sliver of sunlight. And he, Steven Bacard, was that sunlight.

He pointed to the phone. "I just got a call."

"And?"

"The ransom money is bugged," he said.

"We switched bags."

"Not just the bags. There's some kind of device in the money. Between the bills or something."

Lydia's face clouded over. "Your source didn't know about this before?"

"My source didn't know about any of it until just now."

"So what you're telling me," she said slowly, "is that while we stand here the police know exactly where we are?"

"Not the police," he said. "The bug wasn't planted by the cops or the feds."

That seemed to surprise her. Then Lydia nodded. "Dr. Seidman."

"Not exactly. He has a woman named Rachel Mills helping him. She used to be a fed."

Lydia smiled as if this explained something. "And this Rachel Mills—this ex-fed—she's the one who bugged the money?"

"Yes."

"Is she following us right now?"

"No one knows where she is," Bacard said. "No one knows where Seidman is either."

"Hmm," she said.

"The police think this Rachel woman is involved."

Lydia lifted her chin. "Involved in the original kidnapping?"

"And the murder of Monica Seidman."

Lydia liked that. She smiled and Bacard felt a fresh shiver slink down his back. "Was she, Steven?"

He teetered. "I wouldn't know."

"Ignorance is bliss, that it?"

Bacard chose to say nothing.

Lydia said, "Do you have the gun?"

He stiffened. "What?"

"Seidman's gun. Do you have it?"

Bacard did not like this. He felt as if he were sinking. He considered lying, but then he saw those eyes. "Yes."

"Get it," she said. "How about Pavel? Have you heard from him?"

"He's not happy with any of this. He wants to know what's going on."

"We'll call him in the car."

"We?"

"Yes. Now let's hurry, Steven."

"I'm coming with you?"

"Indeed."

"What are you going to do?"

Lydia put her fingers to her lips. "Shh," she said. "I have a plan."

Rachel said, "They're on the move again."

"How long did they stop?" I asked

"Maybe five minutes. They could have met up with someone and transferred the money. Or maybe they were just getting gas. Turn right here."

We pulled up on Centuro Road off Route 3. Giants Stadium loomed in the distance. About a mile up, Rachel pointed out the window. "They were somewhere over there."

The sign read METROVISTA and the parking lot appeared to be a never-ending expanse, disappearing in the distant marsh. MetroVista was a classic New Jersey office complex, built during the great expanse of the eighties. Hundreds of offices, all cold and impersonal, sleek and robotic, with too many tinted windows not letting in enough sunlight. The vapor lights buzzed and you could imagine, if not actually hear, the drone of worker bees.

"They weren't stopping for gas," Rachel muttered.

"So what do we do?"

"Only thing we can," she said. "Let's keep following the money."

Heshy and Lydia headed west toward the Garden State Parkway. Steven Bacard followed in the car behind them. Lydia ripped open the wads of bills. It took her ten minutes to find the tracking device. She dug it out from the money crevice.

She held it up, so Heshy could see it. "Clever," she said.

"Or we're slipping."

"We've never been perfect, Pooh Bear."

Heshy did not reply. Lydia opened the car window. She stuck her hand out and signaled for Bacard to follow them. He waved back that he understood. When they slowed for the toll, Lydia quickly pecked

Heshy's cheek and got out of the car. She took the money with her. Heshy was now left alone with just the tracking device. If this Rachel woman still had any juice or if the police got wind of what was happening, they would pull Heshy over. He would toss the tracking device into the street. They would find the device, sure, but they wouldn't be able to prove it had come from his car. And even if they could, so what? They would search Heshy and his car and find nothing. No kid, no ransom note, no ransom money. He was clean.

Lydia hurried over to Steven Bacard's car and slipped into the passenger's side. "You got Pavel on the line?" she asked.

"Yes."

She took the phone. Pavel started screaming in whatever the hell language was native to him. She waited and then told him the meeting place. When Bacard heard the address, his head snapped toward her. She smiled. Pavel, of course, didn't understand the significance of the location, but then again, why should he? He ranted a little more, but eventually Pavel calmed enough to say he'd be there. She hung up the phone.

"You can't be serious," Bacard said to her.

"Shh."

Her plan was simple enough. Lydia and Bacard would race ahead to the meeting spot while Heshy, who had the tracker on him, would stall. When Lydia was set up and fully prepared, she would call Heshy on the cell phone. Then and only then would Heshy go to the meeting spot. He would have the tracking device with him. The woman, this Rachel Mills, would hopefully follow.

She and Bacard arrived in twenty minutes. Lydia spotted a car parked up the block. Pavel's, she figured. A stolen Toyota Celica. Lydia didn't like that. Strange cars parked on streets like these were noticed. She glanced over at Steven Bacard. His face was moon pale. It almost seemed detached, floating. The scent of fear came off him in waves. His fingers gripped the wheel, tense. Bacard didn't have the stomach for this. That would be a liability.

"You can just drop me off," she said.

"I want to know," he began, "what you plan on doing here."

She just looked at him.

"My God."

"Spare me the indignant act."

"No one was supposed to be hurt."

"You mean like Monica Seidman?"

"We had nothing to do with that."

Lydia shook her head. "And the sister, what was her name, Stacy Seidman?"

Bacard opened his mouth as though he might counter. Then he lowered his head. She knew what he had planned on saying. Stacy Seidman had been a drug addict. She was expendable, a waste, a danger, heading for death, whatever justification floated his boat. Men like Bacard needed justification. In his mind, he wasn't selling babies. He really believed that he was helping. And if he made money—lots of money— from it and broke the law, well, he was taking tremendous risk to better lives. Shouldn't he be well compensated?

But Lydia had no interest in digging into his psyche nor comforting it. She had counted the money in the car. He had hired her. Her take was a million dollars. Bacard got the other million. She shouldered the duffel bag with her—and Heshy's—money. She stepped out of the car. Steven Bacard stared straight ahead. He did not refuse the money. He did not call her back and say that he wanted to wash his hands of this. There was a million dollars sitting in the seat next to him. Bacard wanted it. His family had a big house in Alpine now. His kids went to private school. So no, Bacard did not back off. He simply stared ahead and put the car in drive.

When he was gone, Lydia called Pavel with the two-way radio portion of the cell phone. Pavel was hiding behind some shrubs up the block. He still wore the flannel shirt. His walk was a labored lumber. His teeth had suffered under a lifetime of cigarettes and ill care. He had a squashed-from-too-many-fights nose. He was Balkan rough trade. He had seen a lot in his life. Didn't matter, though. When you don't know what's happening, you are in over your head.

"You," he said, spitting the word. "You no tell me."

Pavel was right. She no tell him. In other words, he'd known nothing. His English was beyond broken, which was why he had been the perfect front man for this crime. He'd come over from Kosovo two years ago with a pregnant woman. During the first ransom drop, Pavel had been given specific instructions. He'd been told to wait for a certain car to pull into the lot, to approach the car without speaking to the man, to take a bag from him, to get into the van. Oh, and to confuse matters a little more, they told Pavel to keep a phone in front of his mouth and pretend to talk into it.

That was it.

Pavel had no idea who Marc Seidman was. He had no idea about what was in the bag, about a kidnapping, about a ransom, nothing. He didn't wear his gloves—his fingerprints were not on file in the United States—and he didn't carry ID.

They paid him two thousand dollars and sent him back to Kosovo. Based on Seidman's rather specific description, the police circulated a sketch of a man who, for all practical purposes, was impossible to find. When they decided to rerun the ransom drop, Pavel was the natural go-to guy. He would dress the same, look the same, play with Seidman's head in case he decided to fight back this time.

Still, Pavel was a realist. He would adapt. He had spent time selling women in Kosovo. White slavery in the guise of strip clubs was a big market over there, though Bacard had come up with another way of using those women. Pavel, no stranger to sudden change, would do what needed to be done. He gave Lydia some attitude, but once she handed him a wad of bills adding up to five thousand dollars, he grew quiet. The fight was out of him. It was only a question of how.

She handed Pavel a gun. He knew how to use it.

Pavel set up near the driveway, keeping his two-way radio channel open. Lydia called Heshy and told them they were ready. Fifteen minutes later, Heshy drove past them. He tossed the tracking device out the car window. Lydia caught it and threw back a kiss. Heshy kept driving. Lydia brought the tracking device into the backyard. She took out her gun and waited.

The night air was starting to give way to the morning dew. That tingle was there, lighting up her veins. Heshy, she knew, was not far away. He wanted to join in, but this was her game. The street was silent. It was 4:00 A.M.

Five minutes later, she heard the car pull up.

chapter 33

Something was very wrong here.

The roads were becoming so familiar I barely noticed them. I was wired, jazzed, the pain in my ribs barely noticeable. Rachel was absorbed in her Palm Pilot. She'd click screens with her little wand, tilt her head, change viewing angles. She dug through the backseat and found Zia's road atlas. With the cap of the Flair pen in her mouth, Rachel started marking up the route, trying to discern a pattern, I guess. Or maybe she was just stalling, so I wouldn't ask the inevitable.

I called her name softly. She flicked her eyes at me and then back to the screen.

"Did you know about that CD-ROM before you got here?" I said.

"No."

"There were photos of you in front of the hospital where I work."

"So you told me."

She clicked the screen again.

"Are the photos real?" I asked.

"Real?"

"I mean, were they digitally altered or something—or were you really in front of my office two years ago?"

Rachel kept her head down, but out of the corner of my eye, I could see her shoulders slump. "Make a right," she said. "Up here."

We were on Glen Avenue now. This was getting creepy. My old high school was up on the left. They'd refurbished it four years ago, adding a weight room, a swimming pool, and a second gymnasium. The façade had been intentionally scuffed up and aged with ivy, giving the place a proper collegiate feel, reminding the youth of Kasselton what was expected of them.

"Rachel?"

"The pictures are real, Marc."

I nodded to myself. I don't know why. Maybe I was trying to buy myself some time. I was heading into something worse than unchartered waters here. I knew that the answers would alter everything again, make it all go topsy-turvy, just when I hoped to set the world right. "I think I'm owed an explanation," I said.

"You are." She kept her head down on the screen. "But not right now."

"Yeah, right now."

"We need to concentrate on what we're doing."

"Don't hand me that crap. We're just driving here. I can handle two things at the same time."

"Maybe," she said softly, "I can't."

"Rachel, what were you doing in front of that hospital?"

"Whoa."

"Whoa what?"

We were approaching the traffic lights at Kasselton Avenue. Because of the hour, they were blinking yellow and red. I frowned and turned to her. "Which way?"

"Right."

My heart iced. "I don't understand."

"The car has stopped again."

"Where?"

"Unless I'm reading this wrong," Rachel said, and finally she looked up and met my gaze, "they're at your house."

I made the right turn. Rachel no longer needed to direct me. She kept her eyes on the screen. We were less than a mile away now. My parents had taken this route to the hospital on the day I was born. I wondered how many times I'd been on this road since. Weird thought, but the mind goes where it must.

I made the right on Monroe. My parents' house was on the left. The lights were off except, of course, for the lamp downstairs. We had it on a timer. It stayed on from 7:00 P.M. to 5:00 A.M. every day. I'd put in one of those long-life, energy-saving light bulbs that look like soft-ice-cream swirls. Mom bragged about how long it lasted. She'd read somewhere that keeping a radio on was also a good way to scare away burglars, so she had an old AM radio constantly tuned into a talk station. The problem was, the sound of the radio kept her up at night, so now Mom put the volume so low that a burglar would have to press his ear against it to be warded off.

I started making the turn onto my road, onto Darby Terrace, when Rachel said, "Slow down."

"They moving?"

"No. The signal is still coming from your house."

I looked up the block. I started thinking about it. "They didn't exactly take a direct route here."

She nodded. "I know."

"Maybe they found your Q-Logger," I said.

"That's exactly what I was thinking."

The car inched forward. We were in front of the Citrons' house now, two away from mine. No lights were on—not even a timer lamp. Rachel chewed on her lower lip. We were at the Kadisons' house now, nearing my driveway. It was one of those situations people describe as "too quiet," as if the world had frozen, as if all you saw, even animate objects, were trying to stay still.

"This has to be a setup," she said.

I was just about to ask her what we should do—pull back, park and walk, call the cops for help?—when the first bullet shattered the front windshield. Shards of glass smacked my face. I heard a short scream. Without conscious thought, I ducked my head and raised my forearm. I looked down and saw blood.

"Rachel!"

The second shot zinged so close to my head that I felt it in my hair. The impact hit my seat with a sound like a pillowy wallop. Instincts took over again. But this time it had a mission, a direction of sorts. I hit the accelerator. The car lurched forward.

The human brain is an amazing instrument. No computer can duplicate it. It can process millions of stimuli in hundredths of a second. That was, I guess, what was going on now. I was hunched over in the driver's seat. Someone was taking shots at me. The base part of my brain wanted to flee, but something farther along the evolutionary path realized that there might be a better way.

The thought process took—and this is just a rough estimate—less than a tenth of a second. I had my foot on the accelerator. The tires shrieked. I thought about my house, the familiar setup of it, the direction the bullets had come from. Yes, I know how that sounds. Maybe panic speeds up those brain functions, I don't know, but I realized that if I were the one doing the shooting, if I had been lying in wait for this car to approach, I'd have hidden behind the three shrubs that divide my property from the Christies' next door. The shrubs were big and bushy and right on our driveway. If I had pulled all the way in, bam, you could have blown us away from the passenger side. When I hesitated, when the shooter had seen that we might back away, he was still in position, though not as good, to take us from the front.

So I looked up, turned the wheel, and aimed the car for those bushes.

A third bullet rang out. It hit something metal, probably the front grill, with a *ka-ping*. I sneaked a glance at Rachel long enough to take a visual snapshot: her head was down, her hand pressed against the side of her head, blood seeping through the fingers. My stomach fell, but my foot stayed on the pedal. I moved my head back and forth, as if that might throw off the shooter's aim.

My headlights illuminated the bushes.

I saw flannel.

Something happened to me. I talked before about sanity being a thin string and that mine had snapped. In that case, I went quiet. This time, a mix of rage and dread roared through my body. I pressed the pedal harder, almost through the floor. I heard a yell of surprise. The man in the flannel shirt tried to leap to the right.

But I was ready.

I turned the steering wheel toward him like we were playing bumper cars. There was a crash, a dull thud. I heard a scream. The bushes were caught up in the bumper. I looked for the man in the flannel. Nothing. I had my hand on the door handle, about to open it and go after him, when Rachel said, "No!"

I stopped. She was alive!

Her hand reached up and shifted the car into reverse. "Go back!"

I listened. I don't know what I'd been thinking. The man was armed. I wasn't. Despite the impact, I didn't know if he was dead or injured or what.

I started back. I noticed that my dark suburban street was lit up now. Shots and shrieking tires are not common noises here on Darby Terrace. People had woken up and turned on the lights. They'd be dialing 911.

Rachel sat up. Relief flooded me. She had a gun in one hand. The other was still over her wound. "It's my ear," she said, and again, the mind working in funny ways, I had already started thinking about what procedure I would use to repair the damage.

"There!" she shouted.

I turned. The man in the flannel was hobbling down the driveway. I turned the wheel and aimed the car lights in his direction. He disappeared around back. I looked over at Rachel.

"Back up," she said. "I'm not sure he's alone."

I did. "Now what?"

Rachel had her gun out, her free hand on the door handle. "You stay."

"Are you out of your mind?"

"You keep revving the engine and moving a little. Let them think we're still in the car. I'll sneak up on them."

Before I could protest any further, she rolled out. With blood still flowing down her side, she darted away. I, per her instructions, revving the engine and feeling like a total dweeb, shifted the car into drive, moved forward, shifted the car into reverse, went back.

A few seconds later, I lost sight of Rachel.

A few seconds after that, I heard two more shots.

Lydia had watched it all from her spot in the backyard.

Pavel had shot too early. It was a mistake on his part. From her vantage point behind a wall of firewood, Lydia could not see who was in the car. But she'd been impressed. The driver had not only flushed Pavel out but wounded him as well.

Pavel limped into view. Lydia's eyes adjusted enough to see the blood on his face. She raised her arm and waved him toward her. Pavel fell and then started crawling. Lydia kept her eyes on the routes to the backyard. They would have to come from the front. There was a fence behind her. She was near the back neighbor's gate in case she needed to escape.

Pavel kept crawling. Lydia urged him on while keeping watch. She wondered how this ex-fed would play it. The neighbors were awake now. Lights were going on. The cops would be on their way.

Lydia would have to hurry.

Pavel made it to the pile of firewood and rolled next to her. For a moment, he stayed on his back. His breathing was wheezy and wet. Then he forced himself up. He knelt next to Lydia and looked out into the yard. He winced and said, "Leg broken."

"We'll take care of it," she said. "Where's your gun?"

"Dropped."

Untraceable, she thought. Not a problem. "I have another weapon you can use," she told him. "Keep a lookout."

Pavel nodded. He squinted into the dark.

"What?" Lydia said. She moved a little closer to him.

"Not sure."

As Pavel stared out, Lydia pressed the barrel of her gun against the hollow spot behind his left ear. She squeezed the trigger, firing two shots into his head. Pavel dropped to the ground like a marionette with his strings cut.

Lydia looked down at him. In the end, this might be best. Plan B was probably better than Plan A anyway. Had Pavel killed the woman—an ex–FBI agent—that would not have ended it. They'd probably search even harder for the mysterious man in flannel. The investigation would have continued. There wouldn't be closure. This way, with Pavel dead—dead by the gun used at the original Seidman crime scene—the police would conclude that either Seidman or this Rachel (or both) was behind it. They'd be arrested. The charges might not stick, but no matter. The police would stop looking for anyone else. They could disappear with the money now.

Case closed.

Lydia suddenly heard the shriek of tire wheels. She tossed the weapon into the neighbor's yard. She didn't want it in plain sight. That would be too obvious. She quickly checked Pavel's pockets. There was money, of course, the wad of bills she'd just given him. She'd let him keep that. One more thing to tie it all up nice and neat.

There was nothing else in his pockets—no wallet, no slip of paper, no identification or anything that could trace back to anything. Pavel had been good about that. More lights in windows now. Not much time. Lydia rose.

"Federal agent! Drop your weapon!"

Damn! A woman's voice. Lydia fired toward where she thought the voice had originated from and ducked back behind the firewood. Shots came back in her direction. She was pinned down. What now? Still behind the firewood, Lydia stretched up behind her and released the gate hatch.

"All right!" Lydia shouted. "I'm surrendering!"

Then she jumped up with the semiautomatic already going. She pulled the trigger as fast as she could. Bullets flew, the sound ringing in her ears. She didn't know if the shots were being returned or not. She didn't think so. There was no hesitation, though. The gate was open. She darted through it.

Lydia ran hard. A hundred yards away, Heshy was waiting in a neighbor's yard. They met up. Keeping low, they followed a trail of recently pruned shrubs. Heshy was good. He always tried to prepare for the worst. His car was hidden in a cul-de-sac two blocks down.

When they were safely on their way, Heshy asked, "You okay?"

"Fine, Pooh Bear." She took a deep breath, closed her eyes, and settled back. "Just fine."

It wasn't until they were near the highway that Lydia wondered what had happened to Pavel's cell phone.

My first reaction, naturally enough, was panic.

I opened the car door to give chase, but my brain finally kicked in and made me pull up. It was one thing to be brave or even foolhardy. It was another to be suicidal. I did not have a gun. Both Rachel and her assailant did. Rushing to her aid unarmed would be, at best, fruitless.

But I couldn't just stay here.

I closed the car door. Once again, my foot stamped down on the accelerator. The car bolted forward. I spun the wheel and veered across my front lawn. The shots had come from the back of the house. I aimed the car there. I tore through the flower beds and shrubs. They had been here so long that I almost cared.

My headlights danced through the dark. I started toward the right, hoping that I could work around the big elm. No go. The tree was too close to the house. The car wouldn't fit. I floored it in reverse. The tires ripped into dewy lawn, taking a second or two to catch. I headed toward the Christies' property line. I took out their new gazebo. Bill Christie would be pissed.

I was in the backyard now. The headlights slipped along the Grossmans' stockade fence. I swung the steering wheel toward the right. And then I saw her. I hit the brake. Rachel stood by the pile of firewood. The wood had been there when we bought the house. We hadn't used any. It was probably rotten and bug infested. The Grossmans had complained that it was so close to their fence that the bugs would start eating into it. I had promised to get rid of it, but I hadn't yet gotten around to it.

Rachel had her gun drawn and pointing down. The man in the flannel was lying at her feet like yesterday's refuse. I didn't have to roll down a window. The windshield was gone from the earlier gunshots. I heard nothing. Rachel lifted her hand. She waved to me, signaling that it was okay. I hurried out of the car.

"You shot him?" I asked, almost rhetorically.

"No," she said.

The man was dead. You didn't have to be a doctor to see that. The back of his skull had been blown off. Brain matter, congealed and pink-white, clung to the firewood. I am not on expert on ballistics but the damage was severe. It was either a very large bullet or from very close range.

"Someone was with him," Rachel said. "They shot him and escaped through that gate."

I stared down at him. The rage boiled up again. "Who is he?"

"I checked his pockets. He has a wad of bills but no ID."

I wanted to kick him. I wanted to shake him and ask what he had done with my daughter. I looked at his face, damaged yet handsome, and wondered what had led him here, why our life paths had crossed. And that was when I noticed something odd.

I tilted my head to the side.

"Marc?"

I dropped to my knees. Brain matter did not bother me. Bone splinters and bloody tissue did not faze me in the least. I had seen worse trauma. I examined his nose. It was practically putty. I remembered that from last time. A boxer, I'd thought. Either that or he'd lived some rough years. His head lolled back at a funny angle. His mouth was open. That was what had drawn my eye.

I put my fingers on his jaw and palate and pulled his mouth farther open.

"What the hell are you doing?" Rachel asked.

"Do you have a flashlight?"

"No."

Didn't matter. I lifted his head up and aimed his mouth toward the
car. The headlights did the trick. I could see clearly now.

"Marc?"

"It always bothered me that he let me see his face." I lowered my
head toward his mouth, trying to do so without casting too much of a
shadow. "They were so careful about everything else. The altered voice,
the stolen van sign, the welding together of license plates. Yet he lets me
see his face."

"What are you talking about?"

"I thought maybe he'd worn an elaborate disguise the first time I'd
seen him. That would make sense. But now we know that's not the case.
So why would he let me see him?"

She seemed taken aback that I was asserting myself, but that didn't
last long. She joined in. "Because he had no record."

"Maybe. Or . . ."

"Or what? Marc, we don't have time for this."

"His dental work."

"What about it?"

"Look at his crowns. They're tin cans."

"They're what?"

I lifted my head. "On his upper right molar and upper left cuspid.
See, our crowns used to be made of gold, though most are now porcelain. Your dentist makes a mold so you can get an exact fitting. But this
is just an aluminum, ready-made cap. You put it over the teeth and
squeeze it on with pliers. I did two oral rotations overseas, mostly dealing with reconstruction, but I saw lots of mouths with these things in
them. They call them tin cans. And they don't do it here in the USA, except maybe as a temporary."

She took a knee next to me. "He's foreign?"

I nodded. "I'd bet he's from the old Soviet bloc, something like that.
The Balkans, maybe."

"That would make sense," she said. "Whatever prints they'd find they'd send down to NCIC. Same with any sort of face ID. Our files and computers wouldn't pick him up. Hell, it'll take the police forever to ID him unless someone comes forward."

"Which probably won't happen."

"My God, that's why they killed him. They know that we won't be able to trace him back."

The sirens sounded. Our eyes locked.

"You got a choice to make here, Marc. We stay, we're going to jail. They'll think he was part of our plot and we killed him. My guess is, the kidnappers knew that. Your neighbors will claim it was quiet until we drove up. Suddenly there's shrieking tires and gunfire. I'm not saying that we won't be able to explain it eventually."

"But it will take time," I said.

"Yes."

"And whatever opening we have here, it will close. The cops will pursue it their own way. Even if they can help, even if they believe us, they'll make a lot of noise."

"One more thing," she said.

"What?"

"The kidnappers set us up. They knew about the Q-Logger."

"We figured that out already."

"But now I'm wondering, Marc. How did they find it?"

I looked up, remembering the warning in the ransom note. "A leak?"

"I wouldn't rule it out anymore."

We both started toward the car. I put my hand on her arm. She was still bleeding. Her eye was almost swollen shut now. I looked at her, and again something primitive took over: I wanted to protect her. "If we run, it'll make us look guilty," I said. "I don't mind that—I don't have anything to lose here—but what about you?"

Her voice was soft. "I don't have anything to lose either."

"You need a doctor," I said.

Rachel almost smiled. "Aren't you one?"

"True enough."

There was no time to discuss the pros and cons. We had to act. We got into Zia's car. I swerved it around and headed out the back way, the Woodland Road exit. Thoughts—rational, clear thoughts—were starting to filter in now. When I really considered where we were and what we were doing, the truth nearly crushed me. I almost pulled over. Rachel saw it.

"What?" she said.

"Why are we running?"

"I don't understand."

"We hoped to find my daughter or at least who did this to her. We said there was a small opening."

"Yes."

"But don't you see? The opening, if there ever really was one, is gone. That guy back there is dead. We know he's foreign, but so what? We don't know who he is. We've reached a dead end. We don't have any other clues."

There was suddenly a trace of mischief on Rachel's face. She reached into her pocket and pulled something into a view. A cell phone. It wasn't mine. It wasn't hers. "Maybe," she said, "we do."

chapter 34

"First thing," Rachel said, "we need to get rid of this car."

"The car," I said, shaking my head at the damage. "If this search doesn't kill me, Zia will."

Rachel managed another smile. We were in the zone now, so deep in, so far past scared that we had found a little quiet. I debated where we should go, but really there was only one alternative.

"Lenny and Cheryl," I said.

"What about them?"

"They live four blocks from here."

It was five in the morning. Dark had begun to surrender to the inevitable. I dialed Lenny's home number and hoped that he hadn't gone back to the hospital. He answered on the first ring and barked a hello.

"I got a problem," I said.

"I hear sirens."

"That would be part of the problem."

"The police called me," he said. "After you took off."

"I need your help."

"Is Rachel with you?" he asked.

"Yes."

There was an awkward silence. Rachel fiddled with the dead man's cell phone. I had no idea what she was looking for. Then Lenny said, "What are you trying to do here, Marc?"

"Find Tara. Are you going to help me or not?"

Now there was no hesitation. "What do you need?"

"To hide the car we're using and borrow another."

"And then what are you going to do?"

I turned the car to the right. "We'll be there in a minute. I'll try to explain it to you then."

Lenny wore a pair of old gray sweatpants, the kind with the tie waist, a pair of slippers, and a Big Dog T-shirt. He pressed a button and the garage door slid to a smooth close as soon as we entered. Lenny looked exhausted, but then again, I don't think Rachel and I were ready for our close-ups either.

When Lenny saw the blood on Rachel, he took a step back. "What the hell happened?"

"Do you have any bandages?" I asked.

"Cabinet over the kitchen sink."

Rachel still had the cell phone in her hand. "I need to get on the Internet," she said.

"Look," Lenny said, "we have to discuss this."

"Discuss it with him," Rachel said. "I need Web access."

"In my office. You know where it is."

Rachel hurried inside. I followed, staying in the kitchen. She continued on to the den. We both knew this house well. Lenny stayed with me. They had recently renovated the kitchen into something French Farmesque and added a second refrigerator because four kids ate like four kids. The fronts of both fridges were overloaded with artwork and family photos and a brightly colored alphabet. The new one had one of those magnetic poetry sets. The words I STAND ALONE AROUND THE SEA ran down the handle. I started going through the cabinet over the sink.

"You want to tell me what's going on?"

I found Cheryl's first aid kit and pulled it out. "There was a shooting at our house."

I gave him the bare bones, opening the first aid kit and checking the supplies. There'd be enough in here for now. I finally glanced at him. Lenny just gaped at me. "You ran away from a murder scene?"

"If I stayed, what would have happened?"

"The police would have picked you up."

"Exactly."

He shook his head and kept his voice low. "They don't think you did it anymore."

"What do you mean?"

"They think it was Rachel."

I blinked, not sure how to react.

"Has she explained those photos to you?"

"Not yet," I said. Then, "I don't understand. How did they figure it was Rachel?"

Lenny rapidly outlined a theory involving jealousy and rage and my forgetting key moments before the shooting. I stood there too stunned to respond. When I did, I said, "That's nuts."

Lenny did not reply.

"That guy with the flannel shirt just tried to kill us."

"And what ended up happening to him?"

"I told you. Someone else was with him. He was shot."

"You saw someone else?"

"No. Rachel . . ." I saw where he was going. "Come on, Lenny. You know better."

"I want to know about those photos on the CD, Marc."

"Fine, let's go ask her."

When we left the kitchen, I spotted Cheryl on the stairwell. She looked down at me, arms crossed. I don't think I had ever seen that look on her face before. It made me pause. There was some blood on the carpet, probably from Rachel. On the wall was one of those studio photos of all four kids, trying to look casual in matching white turtlenecks against a white background. Children and all that white.

"I'll take care of it," Lenny told her. "You stay upstairs."

We hurried through the den. A DVD case from the latest Disney movie lay splayed on top of the television. I nearly tripped over a Wiffle Ball and plastic bat. A game of Monopoly featuring Pokemon characters was spread across the floor in midgame clutter. Someone, one of the kids I assumed, had scrawled DO NOT TOUCH A THING! on a piece of paper and laid it over the board. As we passed the fireplace mantel, I noticed that they'd recently updated the photographs. The kids were older now, in those images as in real life. But the oldest photograph, the "formal dance" image of the four of us, was gone. I don't know what that meant. Probably nothing. Or maybe Lenny and Cheryl were taking their own advice: It was time to move on.

Rachel sat at Lenny's desk, hovering over the keyboard. The blood had dried down the left side of her neck. Her ear was a mess. She glanced up when she saw us and then went back to typing. I examined her ear. Severe damage. The bullet had scraped along the upper region. It had skimmed the side of her head too. Another inch—hell, another quarter inch—and she'd probably be dead. Rachel ignored me, even when I applied the Bactine and threw on a bandage. It would be good enough for now. I'd fix it for real when we had the chance.

"Bang," Rachel said suddenly. She smiled and hit a key. The printer began to whir. Lenny nodded toward me. I put the finishing touches on the bandage and said, "Rachel?"

She looked up at me.

"We need to talk," I said.

"No," she countered, "we need to get out of here. I just found us a major lead."

Lenny stayed where he was. Cheryl slipped into the room now, her arms still folded. "What lead?" I asked.

"I checked the logs on the cell phone," Rachel said.

"You can do that?"

"They're in plain view, Marc," she said, and I could hear the impatience. "The dialed and received call logs. It's pretty much standard on every phone."

"Right."

"The dial log didn't help. No numbers were listed, which means, if the guy did dial out, it was to a blocked number."

I was trying to stay with her. "Okay."

"But the received log is another story. There was only one incoming call on the list. According to the internal timer, it came in at midnight. I just checked the phone number in the reverse directory at Switchboard dot-com. It's a residence. One Verne Dayton in Huntersville, New Jersey."

Neither the name nor the city rang any bells. "Where is Huntersville?"

"I MapQuested it. It's near the Pennsylvania border. I zoomed in to within a few hundred yards. The house is all by itself out there. Acres of land in the heart of Nowheresville."

The chill started in my center and spread. I turned to Lenny. "I need to borrow your car."

"Hold up a second," Lenny said. "What we need here are some answers."

Rachel stood. "You want to know about the photos on the CD."

"For starters, yes."

"It's me in the pictures. Yes, I was there. The rest is none of your business. I owe Marc an explanation, not you. What else?"

For once, Lenny didn't know what to say.

"You also want to know if I killed my husband, right?" She looked at Cheryl. "Do you think I killed Jerry?"

"I don't know what to think anymore," Cheryl said. "But I want you both out of here."

"Cheryl," Lenny said.

She shot him a look that could have downed a charging rhino. "They shouldn't have brought this to our doorstep."

"He's our best friend. He's the godfather of our son."

"Which makes it that much worse. He drags this danger into our home? Into the lives of our children?"

"Come on, Cheryl. You're exaggerating."

"No," I said. "She's right. We should get out of here now. Let me have the keys."

Rachel grabbed the sheet out of the printer. "Directions," she explained.

I nodded and looked at Lenny. His head was down. His feet rocked back and forth. Again, I thought of our childhood. "Shouldn't we call Tickner and Regan?" he said.

"And tell them what?"

"I can explain it to them," Lenny said. "If Tara is at this place"—he stopped, shook his head as if he suddenly saw how ridiculous the thought was—"they'll be better equipped to go in."

I moved right up next to him. "They found out about Rachel's tracking device."

"What?"

"The kidnappers. We don't know how. But they found it. Add it up, Lenny. The ransom note warned us that they had an inside source. First time out, they knew I'd told the cops. Second time out, they learn about the tracking device."

"That doesn't prove anything."

"Do you think I have time to look for proof?"

Lenny's face sank.

"You know I can't risk that."

"Yeah," he said. "I know."

Lenny reached into his pocket and handed me the keys. We were off.

chapter 35

When Regan and Tickner got the call about the shooting at the Seidman residence, both men leapt to their feet. They were nearing the elevator when Tickner's cell phone rang.

A stiff, overly formal female voice said, "Special Agent Tickner?"

"Speaking."

"This is Special Agent Claudia Fisher."

Tickner knew the name. He may have even met her once or twice. "What's up?" he asked.

"Where are you right now?" she asked.

"New York Presbyterian Hospital, but I'm heading out to New Jersey."

"No," she said. "Please come down to One Federal Plaza immediately."

Tickner checked the time. It was only five in the morning. "Now?"

"That is what immediately means, yes."

"May I ask what this is about?"

"Assistant Director in Charge Joseph Pistillo would like to see you."

Pistillo? That made him pause. Pistillo was the top agent on the East Coast. He was the boss of Tickner's boss's boss. "But I'm on the way to a crime scene."

"This isn't a request," Fisher said. "Assistant Director Pistillo is waiting. He expects you here within the half hour."

The phone went dead. Tickner lowered his hand.

"What the hell was that about?" Regan asked.

"I gotta go," Tickner said, heading down the corridor.

"Where?"

"My boss wants to see me."

"Now?"

"Right now." Tickner was already halfway down the hall. "Call me when you know something."

"This isn't easy to talk about," Rachel said.

I drove. The unanswered questions had started to gather, weighing us both down, sapping our energy. I kept my eyes on the road and waited.

"Was Lenny with you when you saw the photos?" she asked.

"Yes."

"Was he surprised by them?"

"Looked that way to me."

She settled back. "Cheryl probably wouldn't have been."

"Why's that?"

"When you asked for my number, she called to warn me."

"About what?" I asked.

"About us."

No further explanation required. "She warned me too," I said.

"When Jerry died—that was my husband's name, Jerry Camp—when he died, let's just say it was a very hard time for me."

"I understand."

"No," she said. "Not like that. Jerry and I, we hadn't worked in a very long time. I don't know if we ever did. When I went for training at Quantico, Jerry was one of my instructors. More than that, he was a legend. One of the best agents ever. You remember that KillRoy case a few years back?"

"He was a serial killer, right?"

Rachel nodded. "That capture was mostly due to Jerry. He had one of the most distinguished records in the bureau. With me . . . I don't know how it happened exactly. Or maybe I do. He was older. Something of a father figure maybe. I loved the FBI. It was my life. Jerry had a crush on me. I was flattered. But I don't know if I ever really loved him."

She stopped. I could feel her eyes on me. I kept mine on the road.

"Did you love Monica?" she asked. "I mean, really love her?"

The muscles in my shoulder bunched. "What the hell kind of a question is that?"

She was still. Then she said, "I'm sorry. That was out of line."

The silence grew. I tried to slow my breathing. "You were telling me about the photos?"

"Yes." Rachel started fidgeting. She only wore one ring. Now she twisted and tugged at it. "When Jerry died—"

"Was shot," I interjected.

Again I could feel her eyes on me. "Was shot, yes."

"Did you shoot him?"

"This isn't good, Marc."

"What isn't?"

"You're already angry."

"I just want to know if you shot your husband."

"Let me tell it my way, okay?"

There was a touch of steel in her voice now. I backed down, gave her a suit-yourself shrug. "When he died, I pretty much lost it. I was forced to resign. Everything I had—my friends, my work, hell, my life—was wrapped in the bureau. Now it was gone. I started drinking. I sank deeper into a funk. I hit bottom. And when you hit bottom, you look for a way to bounce back up. You look for anything. You get desperate."

We slowed at an interchange.

"I'm not saying this right," she said.

I surprised myself then. I reached through the red and put my hand on hers. "Just tell me, okay?"

She nodded, keeping her gaze down, staring at my hand on hers. I kept it there. "One night, when I had too much to drink, I dialed your number."

I remembered what Regan had told me about the phone records. "When was this?"

"A few months before the attack."

"Did Monica answer?" I asked.

"No. Your machine picked up. I—I know how stupid this sounds—I left a message for you."

I slowly took my hand back. "What did you say exactly?"

"I don't remember. I was drunk. I was crying. I think I said that I missed you and hoped you'd call back. I don't think I went further than that."

"I never got the message," I said.

"I realize that now."

Something clicked. "That means," I said, "that Monica listened to it."

A few months before the attack, I thought. When Monica was feeling her most insecure. When we were starting to have serious problems. I remembered other things too. I remembered how often Monica had cried at night. I remembered how Edgar had told me that she'd started seeing a psychiatrist. And there I was, in my oblivious little world, taking her to Lenny and Cheryl's house, subjecting her to that picture with my old lover in it—my old lover who had called our house late at night and said she missed me.

"My God," I said. "No wonder she hired a private investigator. She wanted to know if I was cheating on her. She probably told him about your call, about our past."

She said nothing.

"You still haven't answered the question, Rachel. What were you doing in front of the hospital?"

"I came to New Jersey to see my mother," she began. There was a hitch in her voice now. "I told you that she has a condo now in West Orange."

"So? Are you trying me to tell me she was a patient there?"

"No." She went quiet again. I drove. I almost flipped on the radio, just out of habit, just to do something. "Do I really have to say this?"

"I think so, yeah," I said. But I knew. I understood exactly.

Her voice was stripped off all passion. "My husband is dead. My job is gone. I've lost everything. I'd been talking to Cheryl a lot. I could tell from what she said that you and your wife were having problems." She turned to me full. "Come on, Marc. You know we never got over each other. So that day I went to the hospital to face you. I don't know what I expected. Was I really naïve enough to think you'd sweep me into your arms? Maybe, I don't know. So I hung around and tried to work up the courage. I even went up to your floor. But in the end, I couldn't go through with it—not because of Monica or Tara. I wish I could say I was that noble. I wasn't."

"So why then?"

"I walked away because I thought you'd reject me and I wasn't sure I could handle that."

We fell into silence then. I had no idea what to say. I don't even know how I felt.

"You're angry," she said.

"I don't know."

We drove some more. I wanted so very much to do the right thing. I thought about it. We both stared straight ahead. The tension pressed against the windows. Finally I said, "It doesn't matter anymore. All that matters is finding Tara."

I glanced at Rachel. I saw a tear on her cheek. The sign was up ahead now—small, discreet, nearly indiscernible. It read simply: HUNTERS-VILLE. Rachel brushed the tear away and sat up. "Then let's concentrate on that."

Assistant Director in Charge Joseph Pistillo was at his desk, writing. He was large, barrel chested, big shouldered, and bald, the sort of old-timer that makes you think of dock workers and city-saloon fights—power without the show muscle. Pistillo was probably on the wrong side of sixty. Rumor had it that he'd be retiring soon.

Special Agent Claudia Fisher showed Tickner into the office and closed the door as she left. Tickner took his sunglasses off. He stood with his hands behind his back. He was not invited to sit. There was no greeting, no handshake, no salute, or anything such.

Without looking up, Pistillo said, "I understand you've been asking about the tragic death of Special Agent Jerry Camp."

Alarm bells rang in Tickner's head. Whoa, that was fast. He'd only started his inquiries a few hours ago. "Yes, sir."

More scribbling. "He taught you at Quantico, isn't that right?"

"Yes, sir."

"He was a great teacher."

"One of the best, sir."

"*The* best, Agent."

"Yes, sir."

"Your inquiries into his death," Pistillo went on, "do they have anything to do with your past relationship with Special Agent Camp?"

"No, sir."

Pistillo stopped writing. He put down the pen and folded his rock-breaking hands on his desk. "Then why are you asking about it?"

Tickner looked for the traps and pitfalls he knew lurked in his answer. "His wife's name has arisen in another case I'm working on."

"That would be the Seidman murder-kidnapping case?"

"Yes, sir."

Pistillo frowned. His forehead crinkled. "You think there's a connection between the accidental shooting death of Jerry Camp and the Tara Seidman kidnapping?"

Careful, Tickner thought. Careful. "It's an avenue I need to explore."

"No, Agent Tickner, it is not."

Tickner stayed still.

"If you can tie Rachel Mills to the Seidman murder-kidnapping, do it. Find evidence that connects her to the case. But you don't need Camp's death to do that."

"They could be related," Tickner said.

"No," Pistillo said in a voice that left little room for doubt, "they're not."

"But I need to look—"

"Agent Tickner?"

"Yes, sir."

"I've looked into the file already," Pistillo said. "More than that, I helped investigate the death of Jerry Camp personally. He was my friend. Do you understand?"

Tickner did not reply.

"I am completely satisfied that his shooting was a tragic accident. That means you, Agent Tickner"—Pistillo pointed a meaty finger at Tickner's chest—"are completely satisfied too. Do I make myself clear?"

The two men stared at each other. Tickner was not a foolish man. He liked working for the bureau. He wanted to rise up the ladder. It would not pay to upset someone as powerful as Pistillo. So in the end, Tickner was the first to look away.

"Yes, sir."

Pistillo relaxed. He picked up his pen. "Tara Seidman has been missing for over a year now. Is there any proof she is still alive?"

"No, sir."

"Then the case doesn't belong to us anymore." He started writing now, making no bones about the fact that this was a dismissal. "Let the locals handle it."

New Jersey is our most densely populated state. That doesn't surprise people. New Jersey has cities, suburbs, and plenty of industry.

That doesn't surprise people either. New Jersey is called the Garden State and has plenty of rural areas. That surprises people.

Even before we hit the border of Huntersville, signs of life—human life, that is—had already started fading away. There were few houses. We had passed one general store straight out of *Mayberry RFD*, but that was boarded up. During the next three miles we hit six different roads. I saw no houses. I passed no cars.

We were in the thick of the woods. I made my final turn and the car climbed up the side of a mountain. A deer—the fourth I'd seen by my count—sprinted out of the road, far enough up so I wasn't in any danger of hitting it. I was beginning to suspect that the name Huntersville was to be taken literally.

"It'll be on the left," Rachel said.

A few seconds later, I could see the mailbox. I began to slow, searching for a house or building of some kind. I saw nothing but trees.

"Keep driving," Rachel said.

I understood. We couldn't just pull into the driveway and announce ourselves. I found a small indentation off the road about a quarter of a mile up. I parked and turned off the engine. My heart started to trip-hammer. It was six in the morning. Dawn was here.

"Do you know how to use a gun?" Rachel asked me.

"I used to fire my dad's at the range."

She jammed a weapon into my hand. I stared down at it as if I'd just discovered an extra finger. Rachel had her gun out too. "Where did you get this?" I asked.

"At your house. Off the dead guy."

"Jesus."

She shrugged as if to say, *Hey, you never know.* I looked at the gun again and suddenly a thought hit me: Was this the weapon used to shoot me? To kill Monica? I stopped there. There was no time for this squeamish nonsense. Rachel was already out the door. I followed. We started into the woods. There was no path. We made our own. Rachel took the lead. She tucked her weapon into the back of her pants. For some reason, I didn't do the same. I wanted to hold the gun. Faded orange signs tacked to trees warned trespassers to stay away. They had the word NO in giant font and a surprising amount of finer print, over-explaining what seemed to me to be pretty obvious.

We angled closer to where we thought the driveway was. When we spotted it, we had our guiding star. We stayed near the unpaved stretch and continued on our way. A few minutes later, Rachel stopped. I nearly bumped into her. She pointed ahead.

A structure.

It looked like a barn of some sort. We were more careful now. We kept low. We darted from tree to tree and tried to stay out of sight. We did not speak. After a bit, I started hearing music. Country, I think, but I'm no expert. Up ahead, I spotted a clearing. There was indeed a barn that appeared to be in mid-demolition. There was another structure too—a ranch or maybe extended trailer.

We moved a little closer, right to the end of the woods. We pressed ourselves against trees and peeked out. There was a tractor in the yard. I saw an old Trans Am up on cement blocks. Directly in front of the ranch was a white, overly sporty car—some might call it a "hot rod," I guess—with a thick black stripe up the hood. It looked like a Camaro.

The woods had ended, but we were still at least fifty feet from the ranch house. The grass was high, knee level. Rachel took out her gun. I still held mine. She dropped to the ground and began to commando-crawl. I did the same. On television commando-crawling looks pretty easy. You simply crawl with your butt down. And for about ten feet, it is pretty easy. Then it gets a lot harder. My elbows ached. The grass kept getting caught up in my nose and mouth. I do not suffer from hay fever or allergies, but we were kicking up something. Gnats and the like rose vengefully as we disturbed their slumber. The music was louder now. The singer—a man hitting nary a note—complained about his poor, poor heart.

Rachel stopped. I crawled to her right and pulled up even. "You okay?" she whispered.

I nodded, but I was panting.

"We may have to do something once we get there," she said. "I can't have you exhausted. We can slow down if you need to."

I shook her off and started moving. I was not going to slow down. Slowing down was simply not on the menu. We were getting closer. I could see the Camaro more clearly now. There were black mud flaps with the silver silhouette of a shapely girl behind the rear tires. There were bumper stickers on the back. One read: GUNS DON'T KILL PEOPLE, BUT THEY SURE MAKE IT EASIER.

Rachel and I were near the end of the grass, almost exposed, when the dog started barking. We both froze.

There are several varieties of dog barks. The yap of an annoying toy dog. The call of a friendly golden retriever. The warning of a basically harmless pet. And then there is that guttural, junkyard, rip-out-the-thorax bark that makes the blood thin.

This bark fit into the last category.

I was not particularly scared of the dog. I had a gun. It'd be easier, I guess, to use it on a dog than a human being. What did frighten me, of course, was that the barking would be heard by the ranch's occupant. So we waited. A minute or two later, the dog stopped. We kept our eyes on the ranch door. I was not sure what we would do if someone came out. Suppose we were spotted. We couldn't shoot. We still didn't know anything. The fact that a call had been made from the residence of Verne Dayton to the cell phone of a dead man did not add up to much. We didn't know if my daughter was here or not.

We knew, in fact, nothing.

There were hubcaps in the yard. The rising sun gleamed off them. I spotted a bunch of green boxes. And something about them held my gaze. Forgetting caution, I started moving closer.

"Wait," Rachel whispered.

But I couldn't. I needed to get a better look at those boxes. Something about them . . . but I couldn't put my finger on it. I crawled to the tractor and then hid behind it. I peered out toward the boxes again. Now I saw it. The boxes were indeed green. They also had a graphic featuring a smiling baby.

Diapers.

Rachel was next to me now. I swallowed. A big box of diapers. The kind you buy in bulk at a price club. Rachel saw it too. She put her hand on my arm, warning me to stay calm. We got back down on the ground. She signaled that we were going to make our way to a side window. I nodded that I understood. There was a long fiddle solo blaring from the stereo now.

We were both on our stomachs when I felt something cold against the back of my neck. I slid my eyes toward Rachel. There was a rifle barrel there too, pressed against the base of her skull.

A voice said, "Drop your weapons!"

It was a man. Rachel's right hand was bent in front of her face. The gun was in it. She let it go. A work boot stepped forward and kicked it away. I tried to discern the odds. One man. I could see that now. One man with two rifles. I could conceivably make a move here. No way I'd make it in time, but it might free up Rachel. I met her eyes and saw panic in them. She knew what I was thinking. The rifle suddenly dug deeper into my skull, pushing my face into the dirt.

"Don't try it, Chief. I can splatter two sets of brains as easy as one."

My mind scurried, but it kept hitting dead ends. So I let the gun drop from my hand and watched this man kick away our hope.

chapter 36

"Stay on your stomachs!"

"I'm an agent with the Federal Bureau of Investigation," Rachel said.

"Shut the hell up."

With our faces still in the dirt, he had us both put our hands on top of our head, fingers laced. He put a knee in my spine. I grimaced. Using his body for leverage, the man pulled my arms back, nearly popping my shoulders out of their sockets. My wrists were expertly bound together with nylon flex cuffs. They felt like those ridiculously complicated plastic ties they use to package toys so they can't be shoplifted.

"Put your feet together."

Another cuff fastened my ankles together. He pushed down on my back to get up. Then he moved over to Rachel. I was going to say something stupidly chivalric like *Leave her alone!* but I knew that this would be, at best, futile. I kept still.

"I'm a federal agent," Rachel said.

"I heard you the first time."

He put a knee in her back and pulled her hands together. She grunted in pain.

"Hey," I said.

The man ignored me. I turned and took my first real look at him, and it was like I'd been dropped into a time warp. No doubt about it— the Camaro belonged to him. His hair was eighties-hockey-player long, maybe permed, the color a strange offshoot of orange-blond, tucked back behind his ears and styled into the kind of mullet cut I hadn't seen since a Night Ranger music video. He had a cheesy blond mustache that could have been a milk stain. His T-shirt read UNIVERSITY OF SMITH AND WESSON. His jeans were unnaturally dark blue and looked stiff.

After he bound Rachel's hands, he said, "Get up, missy. You and me are taking a walk."

Rachel tried to make her voice stern. "You're not listening," she said, her hair falling down over her eyes. "I'm Rachel Mills—"

"And I'm Verne Dayton. So what?"

"I'm a federal agent."

"Your ID says retired." Verne Dayton smiled. He wasn't toothless, but he wasn't exactly an orthodontic poster boy either. His right incisor was totally turned in like a door off its hinge. "Kinda young to be retired, don't you think?"

"I still work special cases. They know I'm here."

"Really? Don't tell me. There's a bunch of agents waiting down yonder and if they don't hear from you in three minutes, they're all gonna come storming in. That about it, Rachel?"

She stopped. He had read her bluff. She had nowhere else to go.

"Get up," he said again, this time pulling on her arms.

Rachel stumbled to her feet.

"Where are you taking her?" I asked.

He did not reply. They started walking toward the barn. "Hey!" I called out, my voice booming with impotence. "Hey, come back!" But they kept walking. Rachel struggled, but her hands were tied behind her back. Every time she moved too much, he lifted the hands up, forcing her to bend forward. Eventually she complied and just walked.

Fear lit my nerves. In a frenzy, I looked for something, anything, that would get me free. Our guns? No, he had picked them up already. And even if he hadn't, what would I do? Fire with my teeth? I debated rolling over onto my back, but I wasn't sure how that would help yet. So now what? I started moving inchworm-style toward the tractor. I looked for a blade or anything that I might use to cut myself free.

In the distance, I heard the barn door creak open. My head swerved in time to see them disappear inside. The door closed behind them. The sound echoed into silence. The music—it must have been a CD or tape—had stopped. It was quiet now. And Rachel was gone from sight.

I had to get my hands free.

I started crawling forward, lifting my butt, pushing off with my legs.

I made it to the tractor. I searched for some kind of blade or sharp edge. Nothing. My eyes darted to the barn.

"Rachel!" I shouted.

My voice echoed through the stillness. That was the only reply. My heart started doing flip-flops.

Oh God, now what?

I rolled onto my back and sat up. Pushing with my legs, I pressed against the tractor. I had a clear view of the barn. I don't know what the hell that did for me. There was still no movement, no sound. My eyes darted all over the place, desperately hunting for something that could bring salvation. But there was nothing.

I thought about going for the Camaro. A gun nut like this probably had two, three concealed weapons on him at all times. There might be something in there. But again, even if I managed to get there in time, how would I open the door? How would I search for a gun? How would I fire it when I found one?

No, I had to get this cuff off me first.

I looked on the ground for . . . I don't even know. A sharp rock. A broken beer bottle. Something. I wondered how much time had passed since they disappeared. I wondered what he was doing to Rachel. My throat felt as if it might close up.

"Rachel!"

I heard the desperation in the echo. It scared me. But again there was no reply.

What was going on in there?

I looked again for some kind of edge on the tractor, something I could use to break free. There was rust. Lots of rust. Would that work? If I rubbed the cuff against a rusty corner, would it eventually cut through? I doubted it, but there was nothing else.

I managed to get on my knees. I leaned my wrists against the rusted corner and moved up and down like a bear using a tree to scratch his back. My arms slipped. The rust bit into my skin, and the sting ran up my arm. I looked back over at the barn, listened hard, still heard nothing.

I kept going.

The problem was, I was doing this by feel. I turned my head as far as I could, but I couldn't see my wrists. Was this having any effect at all? I had no idea. But it was all I had to work with. So I continued moving up and down, trying to break free by pulling my arms apart like Hercules in a B movie.

I don't know how long I kept it up. Probably no more than two or three minutes, though it felt like a lot longer. The cuff did not break or even loosen. What finally made me stop was a sound. The barn door had opened. For a moment, I saw nothing. Then the Hick with the Hair came out. Alone. He started walking toward me.

"Where is she?"

Without speaking, Verne Dayton bent down and checked my cuffs. I could smell him now. He smelled of dried grass and work sweat. He was studying my hands. I glanced back. There was blood on the ground. My blood, no doubt. An idea suddenly came to me.

I reared back and aimed a head butt in his direction..

I know how devastating a proper head-butt can be. I had performed surgeries on faces crushed by such blows.

This would not be the case here.

My body position was awkward. My hands and feet were both bound. I was on my knees. I was twisting behind me. My skull didn't land on the nose or softer part of his face. It caught him on the forehead. There was a hollow *klunk* like something out of a Three Stooges soundtrack. Verne Dayton rolled back, cursing. I was totally off balance now, in free fall with nothing but my face to cushion my landing. My right cheek took the brunt of it, rattling my teeth. But I was beyond pain. I slid my eyes in his direction. He sat shaking out the cobwebs. There was a small laceration on his forehead.

Now or never.

Still tied up, I flailed toward him. But I was too slow.

Verne Dayton leaned back and raised a work boot. When I was close enough, he stomped my face as if he were beating back a brushfire. I fell back. He backpedaled to a safe distance and grabbed the rifle.

"Don't move!" His fingers checked the gash on his head. He looked at the blood in disbelief. "You out of your mind?"

I was flat on my back, my breaths coming in deep heaves. I didn't think anything was broken, but then again, I wasn't sure it was going to matter. He walked over to me and kicked me hard in the ribs. I rolled over. He grabbed my arms and started dragging me. I tried to get my feet under me. He was strong as hell. The steps to the trailer didn't slow him down. He pulled me up them, shouldered the door open, and tossed me in like bag of peat moss.

I landed with a thud. Verne Dayton stepped inside and closed the door. My eyes took in the room. It was half what you'd expect, half not. The expected: There were guns mounted on the wall, antique muskets, hunter's rifle. There was the obligatory deer head, a framed NRA membership made out to Verne Dayton, a quilted American flag. The unexpected: The place was spotless and what some might call tastefully furnished. I spotted a playpen in the corner, but it wasn't cluttered. The toys were in one of those fiberglass chests with different color drawers. The drawers were categorized and labeled.

He sat down and looked at me. I was still on my stomach. Verne Dayton toyed with his hair a little, pushing back the strands, tucking the long sides behind his ears. His face was thin. Everything about him screamed yokel.

"You the one beat her up?" he said.

For a moment I didn't know what he was talking about. Then I remembered that he'd seen Rachel's injuries. "No."

"That get you off, huh? Beating up a woman?"

"What did you do with her?"

He took out a revolver, opened the chamber, slid a bullet into it. He spun it to a close and pointed it at my knee. "Who sent you?"

"No one."

"You want to get capped?"

I'd had enough. I rolled onto my back, waiting to hear him pull the trigger. But he didn't shoot. He let me move, keeping the gun on me. I sat up and stared him down. That seemed to confuse him. He took a step back.

"Where's my daughter?" I said.

"Huh?" He tilted his head. "You trying to be funny?"

I looked into his eyes and I saw it. This was no act. He had no idea what I was talking about.

"You come here with guns," he said, his face reddening. "You want to kill me? My wife? My kids?" Verne raised the gun to my face. "Give me one good reason I don't blow you both away and bury you in the woods?"

Kids. He said kids. Something about this whole setup suddenly wasn't making sense. I decided to take a chance. "Listen to me," I said. "My name is Marc Seidman. Eighteen months ago, my wife was murdered and my daughter abducted."

"What are you babbling about?"

"Please, just let me explain."

"Wait a second." Verne's eyes narrowed. He rubbed his chin. "I remember you. From the television. You were shot too, right?"

"Yes."

"So why do you want to steal my guns?"

I closed my eyes. "I'm not here to steal your guns," I said. "I'm here"—I wasn't sure how to say this—"I'm here to find my daughter."

It took this a second to register. Then his mouth dropped open. "You think I had something to do with that?"

"I don't know."

"You better start explaining."

So I did. I told him all of it. The story sounded insane in my ears, but Verne listened. He gave me his full attention. Toward the end, I said, "The man who did this. Or was somehow involved. I don't know anymore. We got his cell phone. He only had one incoming call. It came from here."

Verne thought about it. "This man. What's his name?"

"We don't know."

"I call a lot of people, Marc."

"We know the call was made sometime last night."

Verne shook his head. "Nope, no way."

"What do you mean?"

"I wasn't home last night. I was on the road, making a delivery. I only got home about half an hour before you got here. Spotted you when Munch—that's my dog—started the low growl. The bark, that don't mean much. It's the low growl tells me someone's there."

"Wait a second. No one was here last night?"

He shrugged. "Well, my wife and boys. But the boys are six and three. I don't think they were calling anyone. And I know Kat. She wouldn't be making any calls that late either."

"Kat?" I said.

"My wife. Kat. It's short for Katarina. She's from Serbia."

* * *

"Get you a beer, Marc?"

I surprised myself by saying, "That would be nice, Verne."

Verne Dayton had cut off the plastic cuffs. I rubbed my wrists. Rachel was next to me. He hadn't harmed her. He'd just wanted us separated, in part, he said, because he thought that I'd beaten her up and forced her to help me. Verne had a valuable gun collection—many of them still in working condition—and people were a little too interested in them. He'd figured that was the case with us.

"A Bud, okay?"

"Sure."

"You, Rachel?"

"No thanks."

"Soft drink? Some ice water maybe?"

"Water would be great, thanks."

Verne smiled, which wasn't the most pleasant sight. "No problem." I rubbed my wrists again. He spotted it and grinned. "We used those in the Gulf War. Kept them Iraqis under control, I can tell you."

He disappeared into the kitchen. I looked at Rachel. She shrugged. Verne came back with two Buds and a glass of water. He passed out the drinks. He raised the bottle for us to clink. I did. He sat down.

"I got two kids of my own. Boys. Verne Junior and Perry. If something ever happened to them . . ." Verne whistled low and shook his head. "I don't know how you even get out of bed in the morning."

"I think about finding her," I said.

Verne nodded hard at that. "I can relate, I guess. Long as a man ain't fooling himself, you know what I mean?" He looked over at Rachel. "You absolutely sure the phone number is mine?"

Rachel took out the cell phone. She pressed some digits and then showed him the small screen. Using his mouth, Verne extracted a Winston from the pack. He shook his head. "I don't understand it."

"We're hoping your wife can help."

He nodded slowly. "She wrote a note, says she went food shopping. Kat likes to do that early in the morning. At the twenty-four-hour A and P." He stopped. I think Verne was torn here. He wanted to be able to help, but he didn't want to hear that his wife had called a strange man at midnight. He raised his head. "Rachel, how about I get you some fresh bandages?"

"I'm fine."

"You sure?"

"Really, thank you." She held the glass of water with both hands. "Verne, do you mind if I ask you how you and Katarina met?"

"Online," he said. "You know, one of those Web sites for foreign brides. Cherry Orchid, it's called. They used to call it mail order. I don't think they do that anymore. Anyway, you go to the site. You look at these pictures of women from all over—Eastern Europe, Russia, the Philippines, wherever. They list measurements, a little bio, likes and dislikes, that kinda thing. You see one that strikes your fancy, you can buy her address. They got package deals too, if you want to write to more than one."

Rachel and I gave each other a quick glance. "How long ago was this?"

"Seven years ago. We started sending each other e-mails and stuff. Kat was living on a farm in Serbia. Her parents had nothing. She used to walk four miles to get computer access. I wanted to call too, you know, talk on the phone. But they didn't even have one. She had to call me. Then one day, she says she's coming over. To meet me."

Verne put his hands up, as if to silence an interruption. "Now see, this is where the girls usually hit you up for some money, you know, dollars to buy a plane ticket and stuff. So I was ready for that. But Kat didn't. She came over on her own. I drove up to New York City. We met. We were married three weeks later. Verne Junior came in a year. Perry three years after that."

He took a deep sip of his beer. I did the same. The coldness felt wonderful sliding down my throat.

"Look, I know what you're thinking," Verne said. "But it ain't like that. Kat and me, we're real happy. I was married before to a grade-A American ball-buster. All she did was whine and complain. I wasn't making enough money for her. She wanted to stay at home and do nothing. Ask her to do a load of laundry, she'd go all ballistic on me with that feminazi crap. Always tearing me down, telling me I'm a loser. With Kat, it ain't like that. Do I like the fact that she makes a nice house and home? Sure, okay, that's important to me. If I'm working outside and it's hot, Kat'll fetch me a beer without giving me a *Ms.* magazine lecture. Is there anything wrong with that?"

Neither of us replied.

"Look, I want you to think about it, okay? Why are any two people attracted to each other? Looks maybe? Money? Because you have an important job? We all join up because we want to get something out of it. Give and take, am I right? I wanted a loving wife who'd help me raise children and take care of a home. I wanted a partner too, someone, I don't know, who'd just be nice to me. I get that. Kat, she wanted out of a terrible life. I mean, they were so poor, dirt was a luxury. She and me, we got it good here. In January, we took the kids and went down to Disney World. We like hiking and canoeing. Verne Junior and Perry, they're good kids. Hey, maybe I'm simple. Hell, I'm *definitely* simple. I like my guns, my hunting and fishing—and most of all, my family."

Verne lowered his head. His mullet hair dropped like a curtain blocking his face. He started ripping the label off the beer. "Some places—probably most, I don't know—marriages are arranged. That's the way it's always been. The parents decide. They force them. Well, no one forced Kat and me. She could walk away anytime. Me too. But it's been seven years now. I'm happy. So is she."

Then he shrugged his shoulders. "At least, I thought she was."

We drank in silence.

"Verne?" I said.

"Yeah?"

"You're an interesting man."

He laughed, but I could see the fear. He took a swig of beer to hide it. He'd carved out a life for himself. A nice life. It's funny. I am not a very good judge of people. My initial impressions are usually wrong. I see this gun-toting redneck with his hair and his bumper stickers and his monster-truck-rally 'tude. I hear he has a mail-order bride from Serbia. How can you not judge? But the more I listened to him, the more I liked him. I must be at least as alien to him. I'd crept up on his house with a gun. Yet as soon as I had started telling my story, Verne had acted. He knew that we were telling the truth.

We heard the car pull up. Verne moved to the window and looked out. There was a small, sad smile on his face. His family was pulling into the drive. He cherished them. Intruders had come to his home with guns, and he had done what he could to protect it. And now, maybe, in my attempt to bring my family together, I might tear apart his.

"Look! Daddy's home!"

That had to be Katarina. The accent was unmistakably foreign, something in the Balkan–East European–Russian family. I am not linguist enough to know which. I heard the happy squeals of little children. Verne's smile widened a bit. He stepped out onto the porch. Rachel and I stayed where we were. We could hear running feet on the steps. The greeting lasted a minute or two. I stared at my hands. I heard Verne say something about presents in the truck. The kids sprinted for them.

The door opened. Verne entered with his arm around his wife.

"Marc, Rachel, this here's my wife, Kat."

She was lovely. She wore her long hair straight down. Her yellow sundress left her shoulders exposed. Her skin was pure white, her eyes blue ice. She had that certain bearing so that I could have told, even if I hadn't known, that she was foreign. Or maybe I was projecting. I tried to guess her age. She could pass for mid-twenties, but the age lines around the eyes told me I was probably a decade off.

"Hi," I said.

We both stood and shook her hand. It was dainty, but there was steel in the grip. Katarina held on to the hostess smile, but it wasn't easy. Her eyes stayed on Rachel, on the wounds. The sight, I guess, was rather shocking. I was almost getting used to it.

Still smiling, Katarina turned to Verne as if to ask a question. He said, "I'm trying to help them out."

"Help them?" she repeated.

The children had located the presents and were hooting and hollering. Verne and Katarina didn't seem to hear. They were looking at each other. He held her hand. "That man over there"—he gestured with his chin toward me—"somebody murdered his wife and took away his little girl."

She put a hand to her mouth.

"They're here trying to find his daughter."

Katarina did not move. Verne turned to Rachel and nodded a go-ahead.

"Mrs. Dayton," Rachel began, "did you make a phone call last night?"

Katarina's head jerked as though she'd just been startled. She looked at me first, as if I were some kind of circus oddity. Then she turned her attention to Rachel. "I don't understand."

"We have a phone record," Rachel said. "Last night at midnight, someone placed a call from this house to a certain cell phone. We assume it was you."

"No, that's not possible." Katarina's eyes started shifting as if seeking out an escape route. Verne still held her hand. He tried to meet her gaze, but she kept avoiding it. "Oh wait," she said. "Maybe I know."

We waited.

"Last night, when I was sleeping, the phone rang." She tried the smile again, but it was having trouble staying anchored. "I don't know what time it was. Very late. I thought maybe it was you, Verne." She looked at him and now the smile held. He smiled back. "But when I answered it, there was no one there. So I remembered something I saw on the television. Star, six, nine. You hit those numbers and it dials the number. So I did that. A man answered. It wasn't Verne, so I hung up."

She looked at us expectantly. Rachel and I exchanged a glance. Verne was still smiling, but I saw his shoulders drop. He let go of her hand and half collapsed onto the couch.

Katarina started toward the kitchen. "You need another beer, Verne?"

"No, darling, I don't. I want you to sit here next to me."

She was hesitant but she listened. She sat with her spine still ramrod. Verne, too, sat up tall and again took her hand.

"I want you to listen to me, okay?"

She nodded. The children were wailing with delight outside. Corny to say, but there are few sounds like the unimpeded laughter of children. Katarina looked at Verne with an intensity that almost made me turn away.

"You know how much we love our boys, right?"

She nodded.

"Imagine if someone took them away from us. Imagine if that happened more than a year ago. Think about it. Imagine if someone stole, say, Perry and for more than a year, we didn't know where he was." He pointed to me. "That man over there. He doesn't know what happened to his little girl."

Her eyes were brimming with tears.

"We have to help him, Kat. Whatever you know. Whatever you done. I don't care. If there are secrets, you tell them now. We wipe the slate clean. I can forgive just about anything. But I don't think I can forgive if you don't help that man and his little girl."

She lowered her head and said nothing.

Rachel ratcheted up a notch. "If you're trying to protect the man you called, don't bother. He's dead. Someone shot him a few hours after you called."

Katarina's head stayed down. I rose and started pacing. From outside, there was another squeal of laughter. I walked over to the window and looked out. Verne Junior—the boy looked to be about six—shouted, "Ready or not, here I come!" It wouldn't be too hard to find him. I couldn't see Perry, but the hiding child's laughter was clearly coming from behind the Camaro. Verne Junior pretended to look elsewhere but not for very long. He sneaked up on the Camaro and yelled, "Boo!"

Perry popped out still laughing and ran. When I saw the boy's face, I felt my world, already teetering, take another hit. See, I recognized Perry.

He was the little boy I'd seen in the car last night.

chapter 37

Tickner parked in front of the Seidman house. They hadn't put up the yellow crime-scene tape yet, but he counted six squad cars and two news vans. He wondered if it'd be a good idea to approach, what with the cameras rolling. Pistillo, his boss's boss, had made it pretty clear where he stood. In the end, Tickner figured that it was safe enough to stay. If he was caught on camera, he could always opt for the truth: He had come to let the locals know that he was off the case.

Tickner found Regan in the backyard with the body. "Who is he?"

"No ID," Regan said. "We'll send in the prints, see what we come up with."

They both looked down.

"He matches that sketch Seidman gave us last year," Tickner said.

"Yup."

"So what does that mean?"

Regan shrugged.

"What have you learned so far?"

"Neighbors heard shots first. That was followed by screeching tires. They saw a BMW Mini driving across the grass. More shots. They spotted Seidman. One neighbor said he might have seen a woman with him."

"Probably Rachel Mills," Tickner said. He looked up in the morning sky. "So what does it mean?"

"Maybe the victim worked for Rachel. She silenced him."

"In front of Seidman?"

Regan shrugged. "The BMW Mini struck a chord though. I remembered that Seidman's partner had one. Zia Leroux."

"That would be who helped him get out of the hospital."

"We have an APB on the car."

"I'm sure they switched vehicles."

"Yeah, probably." Then Regan stopped. "Uh-oh."

"What?"

He pointed at Tickner's face. "You're not wearing your sunglasses."

Tickner smiled. "Bad omen?"

"The way this case is going? Maybe it's a good one."

"I came to tell you I'm off the case. Not just me. The bureau. If you can prove the girl is still alive—"

"—which we both know she ain't—"

"—or that she was transported across state lines, I can probably get back in. But this case is no longer a priority."

"Back to terrorism, Lloyd?"

Tickner nodded. He looked back up in the sky. It felt weird without the sunglasses.

"What did your boss want, anyway?"

"To tell me what I just told you."

"Uh-huh. Anything else?"

Tickner shrugged. "The shooting of Federal Agent Jerry Camp was accidental."

"Your big boss called you into his office before six in the morning to tell you that?"

"Yep."

"Yowza."

"Not only that, he investigated the case personally. He and the victim were friends."

Regan shook his head. "Does this mean Rachel Mills has powerful friends?"

"Not at all. If you can nail her for the Seidman murder or kidnapping, go to it."

"Just don't involve the death of Jerry Camp."

"There you go."

Someone called out. They looked over. A gun had been found in the neighbor's yard. A quick sniff told them that it had been fired recently.

"Convenient," Regan added.

"Yup."

"Any thoughts?"

"Nope." Tickner turned to him. "It's your case, Bob. Always was. Good luck."

"Thanks."

Tickner walked away.

"Hey, Lloyd?" Regan called out.

Tickner stopped. The gun had been bagged. Regan stared at it, then at the body by his feet.

"We still don't know what's going on here, do we?"

Tickner continued toward his car. "Not a clue," he said.

Katarina had her hands in her lap. "Is he really dead?"

"Yes," Rachel said.

Verne stood, fuming, his arms folded over his chest. He had been that way since I told him that Perry had been the child I saw in the Honda Accord.

"His name is Pavel. He was my brother."

We waited for her to say more.

"He was not a good man. I always knew that. He could be cruel. Kosovo makes you that way. But kidnapping a small child?" She shook her head.

"What happened?" Rachel asked.

But her eyes were on her husband. "Verne?"

He would not look at her.

"I lied to you, Verne. I lied to you about so much."

He tucked his hair behind his ears and blinked. I saw him wet his lip with his tongue. But he would still not look at her.

"I didn't come from a farm," she said. "My father died when I was three. My mother took any job she could. But we couldn't get by. We were too poor. We'd steal rinds out of the garbage. Pavel, he stayed on the streets, begging and stealing. I started working in sex clubs when I was fourteen. You can't imagine what it was like, but there is no way out of that life in Kosovo. I wanted to kill myself, I can't tell you how many times."

She raised her head toward her husband, but Verne still wouldn't meet her gaze. "Look at me," she said to him. When he didn't she leaned forward, "Verne?'

"This ain't about us," he said. "Just tell them what they need to know."

Katarina put her hands in her lap. "After a while, when you live like that, you don't think about escape. You don't think about pretty things or happiness or any of that. You become like an animal. You just hunt and survive. And I don't even know why you do that. But one day, Pavel came to me. He told me he knew a way out."

Katarina stopped. Rachel moved closer to her. I let her handle this. She had experience with interrogation and at the risk of sounding sexist, I thought that Katarina would have an easier time being drawn out by a fellow female.

"What was the way out?" Rachel asked.

"My brother said he could get us some money—and to America—if I could get pregnant."

I thought—check that: I hoped—I'd heard wrong. Verne whipped his head toward her. This time Katarina was ready. She looked at him steadily.

"I don't understand," Verne said.

"I'm worth something as a prostitute. But a baby is worth more. If I get pregnant, someone can get us to America. They will pay us money."

The room went silent. I could still hear the children outside, but the sound suddenly seemed far away, a distant echo. I was the one who spoke next, reaching through the numb. "They pay you," I said, hearing the horror and disbelief in my own voice, "for the baby?"

"Yes."

Verne said, "Sweet Jesus."

"You can't understand."

"Oh, I understand," Verne said. "Did you go through with it?"

"Yes."

Verne turned away as if he'd been slapped. His hand reached up and took hold of the curtain. He stared out at his own children.

"In my country, if you have a baby, they put it in a horrible orphanage. American parents, they want so much to adopt. But it's hard. It takes a long time. More than a year sometimes. Meanwhile, the baby lives in squalor. The parents, they must pay government officials. The system is so corrupt."

"I see," Verne said. "You were doing it for the good of mankind?"

"No, I did it for me. For me only, okay?"

Verne winced. Rachel put her hand on Katarina's knee. "So you flew over here?"

"Yes. Pavel and I."

"Then what?"

"We stayed at a motel. I would visit a woman with white hair. She would check on me, make sure I was eating okay. She gave me money to buy food and supplies."

Rachel nodded, encouraging. "Where did you have the baby?"

"I don't know. A van with no windows came. The woman with white hair, she was there. She delivered the baby. I remember hearing it cry. Then they took it away. I don't even know if it was a boy or a girl. They drove us back to the motel. The woman with the white hair, she gave us our money."

Katarina shrugged.

It felt as if my circulation had stopped. I tried to think this through, get past the horror. I looked at Rachel and started to ask how, but she shook her head. Now was not the time to make deductions. Now was the time to gather information.

"I loved it here," Katarina said after some time had passed. "You think you have a wonderful country. But you really have no idea. I wanted so much to stay. But the money started running low. I looked for ways. I met a woman who told me about the Web site. You put your name and men write you. They wouldn't want a whore, she told me. So I made up a biography with a farm. When men asked, I gave them an e-mail address. I met Verne three months later."

Verne's face fell even farther. "You mean the whole time we were writing . . . ?"

"I was in America, yes."

He shook his head. "Was anything you told me the truth?"

"Everything that mattered."

Verne made a scoffing sound.

"What about Pavel?" Rachel asked, trying to get us back on topic. "Where did he go?"

"I don't know. He went back home sometimes, I know. He would re- cruit other girls to bring over. For the finder's fee. Time to time, he would contact me. If he needed a few dollars, I'd give it to him. It was really no big deal. Until yesterday."

Katarina looked up at Verne. "The children, they will be hungry."

"They can wait."

"What happened yesterday?" Rachel asked.

"Pavel called late in the afternoon. He says he needs to see me right away. I don't like that. I ask him what he wants. He says he'll tell me when he gets here, not to worry. I don't know what to say."

"How about no?" Verne snapped.

"I couldn't say no."

"Why not?"

She didn't answer.

"Oh, I see. You were afraid he'd tell me the truth. Isn't that it?"

"I don't know."

"What the hell's that supposed to mean?"

"Yes, I was terrified he'd tell you the truth." Again she looked up at her husband. "And I prayed he would."

Rachel tried to get us back on course. "What happened when your brother got here?"

She started welling up.

"Katarina?"

"He said he needed to take Perry with him."

Verne's eyes widened.

Katarina's chest started hitching, as if it was hard to get air. "I said to him no. I said I wouldn't let him touch my children. He threatened me. He said he'd tell Verne everything. I said I didn't care. I wasn't going to let him take Perry. Then he punched me in the stomach. I fell down. He promised me he'd bring Perry back in a few hours. He promised me no one would get hurt unless I said something. If I called Verne or the police, he'd kill Perry."

Verne's hand were balled into tight fists. His face was scarlet.

"I tried to stop him. I tried to stand up, but Pavel pushed me back down. And then"—her voice caught—"then he drove away. With Perry. The next six hours were the longest of my life." She sneaked a guilty glance in my direction. I knew what she was thinking. She had experienced this terror for six hours. I'd been living with it for a year and half.

"I didn't know what to do. My brother is a bad man. I know that. But I couldn't believe he'd ever hurt my children. He was their uncle."

I thought about Stacy then, my sister, my words of sibling defense echoing in hers.

"For hours, I stayed by the window. I couldn't stand it. Finally, at midnight, I called his cell phone. He told me he was on his way back.

Perry was fine, he said. Nothing had happened. He tried to sound light, but there was something in his voice. I asked him where he was. He told me he was on Route Eighty near Paterson. I couldn't just sit in the house and wait. I told him I'd meet him halfway. I packed Verne Junior and we went. When we got to the gas station by the Sparta exit. . . ." She looked at Verne. "He was fine. Perry. I felt such relief, you can't imagine."

Verne was tugging on his bottom lip with his thumb and index finger. He looked away again.

"Before I left, Pavel grabbed my arm hard. He pulled me close to him. I could see how scared he was. He said no matter what, never tell anybody about what happened. That if they found out about me—if they knew he had a sister—they would kill us all."

"Who is they?" Rachel asked.

"I don't know. Whoever he was working for. The people who bought the babies, I think. He said they were crazy."

"What did you do then?"

Katarina opened her mouth, closed it, tried again. "I went to the supermarket," she said with a sound that might have even been a laugh. "I bought the kids juice boxes. I let them drink while we shopped. I just wanted to do something normal. To, I don't know, to put it all behind me."

Katarina looked up at Verne then. I followed her gaze. I again studied this man with the long hair and the bad teeth. After a moment, he turned to her.

"It's all right," Verne said in the gentlest voice I'd ever heard. "You were scared. You've been scared your whole life."

Katarina started sobbing.

"I don't want you to be scared anymore, okay?"

He moved toward her. He took her in his arms. She settled enough to say, "He said they'd come after us. The whole family."

"Then I'll protect us," Verne said simply. He looked at me over her shoulder. "They took my kid. They threatened my family. You hear what I'm saying?"

I nodded.

"I'm in this now. I'm with you till it's over."

Rachel sat back. I saw her grimace. Her eyes closed. I didn't know how much longer she could go. I moved toward her. She held up her palm. "Katarina, we need you to help us here. Where was your brother staying?"

"I don't know."

"Think. Do you have any of his possessions, something that can lead us to who he worked for?"

She let go of her husband. Verne stroked her hair with a blend of tenderness and strength I envied. I turned to Rachel. I wondered if I had the courage to do the same.

"Pavel just arrived from Kosovo," Katarina said. "And he would not come here empty handed."

Rachel nodded. "You think he brought a pregnant woman with him?"

"He always did before."

"Do you know where she's staying?"

"The women always stay at the same place—the same place I stayed. It's in Union City." Katarina looked up. "You'll want this woman to help you, right?"

"Yes."

"Then I'll have to go with you. She most likely won't speak English."

I looked at Verne. He nodded. "I'll watch the kids."

No one moved for several moments. We needed to gather our strength, adjust as if we'd entered a no-gravity zone. I used the time to step outside and call Zia. She answered on the first ring and started right in.

"The cops might be listening in, so let's not stay on the line too long," Zia said.

"Okay."

"Our friend Detective Regan came to my house. He told me that he thought you used my car to leave the hospital. I called Lenny. Lenny told me to neither confirm nor deny any allegation. You can probably guess the rest."

"Thanks."

"You being careful?"

"Always."

"Sure. By the way, the cops aren't stupid. They figure that if you used one friend's car, maybe they would look for another."

I got her meaning—don't use Lenny's car.

"Better hang up now," she said. "Love you."

The phone went dead. I moved back inside. Verne had unlocked his gun cabinet using a key. He was checking weapons. On the other side of the room, he had a safe with ammunition. It opened by combination. I looked over his shoulder. Verne wiggled his eyebrows at me. He had enough firepower to overthrow a European country.

I told them about my conversation with Zia. Verne did not hesitate. He slapped my back and said, "I have just the vehicle for you."

Ten minutes later, Katarina, Rachel, and I drove off in a white Camaro.

chapter 38

We found the pregnant girl right away.

Before we vroomed off in Verne's ride, Rachel jumped in the shower to rinse off the blood and grime. I quickly changed her bandage. Katarina loaned her a summer dress with a flower print, the kind that fits loose but clings just right. Rachel's hair was wet and kinky, still dripping when we reached the car. Forget the bruises and swelling—I am not sure that I ever saw a more beautiful woman in my life.

We started driving. Katarina insisted on taking the fold-down seat in the back. That left Rachel and me in the front. For a few minutes, nobody spoke. We were, I think, decompressing.

"What Verne said," Rachel began. "About getting the secrets out of the way and wiping the slate clean."

I kept driving.

"I didn't kill my husband, Marc."

She didn't seem to care that Katarina was in the car. Neither did I. "The official word is that it was an accident," I said.

"The official word is a lie." She let out a long breath. She needed time to gather herself. I gave it to her.

"It was Jerry's second marriage. He had two kids from his first. His son, Derrick, has cerebral palsy. The expenses are ridiculous. Jerry was never good with finances or anything like that, but he did his best there. He even set up a large life-insurance policy in case something happened to him."

In my peripheral vision, I could see her hands. They didn't move or tighten into fists. They just sat primly in her lap.

"Our marriage fell apart. There were a lot of reasons. I mentioned some before. I really didn't love him. I think he sensed that. But most of all, Jerry was a manic depressive. When he stopped taking his medication, it got worse. So I finally filed for divorce."

I peeked over at her. She was biting her lip and blinking.

"On the day they served him papers, Jerry shot himself in the head. I was the one who found him slumped over our kitchen table. There was an envelope with my name on it. I recognized Jerry's handwriting right away. I opened it up. There was just a single sheet of paper with one word written on it. 'Bitch.' "

Katarina put a comforting hand on Rachel's shoulder. I concentrated hard on the road.

"I think Jerry did it like that on purpose," she said, "because he knew what I'd have to do."

"What was that?" I asked

"A suicide would mean that the life insurance wouldn't pay. Derrick would be financially devastated. I couldn't let that happen. I called one of my old bosses, a friend of Jerry's named Joseph Pistillo. He's a big deal in the FBI. He brought down a few of his men, and we made it look like an accident. The official line was, I mistook him for a burglar. The local cops and the insurance company were both pressured into signing off on it." She shrugged.

"So why did you leave the bureau?" I asked.

"Because the rank-and-file never bought it. They all thought that I must be sleeping with someone powerful. Pistillo couldn't protect me. It would look bad. I couldn't defend myself, for that matter. I tried to tough it out, but the FBI is not a place for the unwanted."

Her head dropped back against the pad. She looked out the passenger window. I didn't know what to make of the story. I didn't know what to make of any of this yet. I wished that I could say something comforting. I couldn't. I just kept driving until we mercifully arrived at the motel in Union City.

Katarina approached the check-in desk, pretending to speak only Serbian, gesturing like mad, until the clerk, figuring that it was the only way to settle her down, told her the room number of the only other person on the premises who seemed to speak that language. We were in business.

The pregnant girl's room was more a low-end efficiency unit than something you'd find in a normal highway motel. I refer to her as a pregnant "girl" because Tatiana—that was what she said her name was—claimed to be sixteen. I suspected that she was younger. Tatiana had the sunken eyes of a child who'd just stepped out of a war newsreel, which in this situation, may have literally been the case.

I stayed back, almost out of the room. So did Rachel. Tatiana did not speak English. We let Katarina handle it. The two of them talked for about ten minutes. After that, there was a brief silence. Tatiana sighed, opened the drawer under the phone, and gave Katarina a piece of paper. Katarina kissed her cheek and then came over to us.

"She's scared," Katarina said. "She only knew Pavel. He left her yesterday and said not to leave the room under any circumstances."

I glanced over at Tatiana. I tried to give her a reassuring smile. It fell, I'm certain, way short.

"What did she say?" Rachel asked.

"She doesn't know anything, of course. Like me. She only knows that her baby will find a good home."

"What was that piece of paper she gave you?"

Katarina lifted the slip of paper into view. "It's a phone number. If there is an emergency, she's supposed to call and dial in four nines."

"A beeper," I said.

"Yes, I believe so."

I looked at Rachel. "Can we trace it?"

"I doubt it will lead anywhere. It's easy to get beepers using a phony name."

"So let's call it," I said. I turned to Katarina. "Has Tatiana met anyone else besides your brother?"

"No."

"Then you make the call," I said to her. "You say you're Tatiana. You tell whoever answers that you're bleeding or in pain or something."

"Whoa," Rachel said. "Slow down a second."

"We need to get someone here," I said.

"And then what?"

"What do you mean, then what? You interrogate them. Isn't that what you do, Rachel?"

"I'm not a fed anymore. And even if I was, we can't just bulldoze them over like that. Pretend you're one of them for a second. You show up and I confront you. What would you do if you were involved in something like this?"

"Cut a deal."

"Maybe. Or maybe you'd just clam up and ask for a lawyer. Then where would we be?"

I thought about that. "If the person asks for a lawyer," I said, "you leave them alone with me."

Rachel stared at me. "Are you serious?"

"We're talking about my daughter's life."

"We're talking about a lot of children now, Marc. These people buy babies. We need to put them out of business."

"So what are you suggesting?"

"We page them. Like you said. But Tatiana will have to do the talking. She'll have to say whatever to get them here. They'll examine her. We check their license plate. We follow them when they leave. We find out who they are."

"I don't understand," I said. "Why can't Katarina make the call?"

"Because whoever comes will want to examine the person they talked to on the phone. Katarina and Tatiana don't sound alike. They'll know what we're up to."

"But why do we need to go through all that? We'll have them here. Why risk following them home?"

Rachel closed her eyes, then opened them again. "Marc, think. If they find out we're on to them, how will they react?"

I stopped.

"And I want to be clear about something else. This isn't about just Tara anymore. We need to bring these guys down."

"And if we just jump them here," I said, seeing her true point now, "they'll be forewarned."

"That's right."

I wasn't sure how much I cared about that. Tara was my priority. If the FBI or cops want to build a legal case against these people, I was all for it. But that sat way off my personal radar.

Katarina talked to Tatiana about our plan. I could see it wasn't taking. The young girl was petrified. She kept shaking her head no. Time passed—time we really didn't have. I snapped and decided to do something fairly stupid. I picked up the phone, dialed the beeper number, and pressed the nine button four times. Tatiana went still.

"You'll do it," I said.

Katarina translated.

No one spoke for the next two minutes. We all just stared at Tatiana. When the phone rang, I did not like what I saw in the young girl's eyes. Katarina said something, her tone urgent. Tatiana shook her head and crossed her arms. The phone rang a third time. Then a fourth.

I took out my gun.

Rachel said, "Marc."

I kept the gun at my side. "Does she know we're talking about my daughter's life?"

Katarina burst off something in Serbian. I looked Tatiana hard in the eyes. There was no reaction. I raised the gun and fired. The lamp exploded, the sound reverberating too loudly in the room. Everyone jumped. Another stupid move. I knew that. I just wasn't sure I cared.

"Marc!"

Rachel put her hand on my arm. I shook it off. I looked at Katarina. "Tell her if the caller hangs up . . ."

I never finished the thought. Katarina started talking quickly. I gripped the gun, but it was back at my side now. Tatiana still had her eyes on me. Sweat popped up on my forehead. I felt my body shake. As Tatiana watched me, something in her face began to soften.

"Please," I said.

On the sixth ring Tatiana snatched up the receiver and started talking.

I glanced over at Katarina. She listened to the conversation and then she nodded at me. I moved back to the other side of the room. I still had the gun in my hand. Rachel stared at me. But I stared back.

Rachel blinked first.

We parked the Camaro in a restaurant lot next door and waited.

There was not a lot of chitchat. The three of us looked everywhere but at each other, as if we were all strangers on an elevator. I wasn't sure what to say. I wasn't sure what I felt. I had fired a gun and come pretty close to threatening a teenage girl. Worse, I don't think I cared very much. The repercussions, if there were any, seemed far away, storm clouds that might gather and then again might disperse.

I flipped on the radio and dialed into the local news station. I half expected someone to say, "We interrupt this program with this special bulletin," and then announce our names and give out descriptions and maybe warn that we were armed and dangerous. But there were no stories on a shooting in Kasselton or a police search for us.

Rachel and I were still in the front while Katarina lay across the fold-down seat in the back. Rachel had her Palm Pilot out. The stylus was in her hand, poised to tap. I debated calling Lenny, but I remembered Zia's warning. They'd be listening in. I had nothing much to report anyway—just that I had threatened a pregnant sixteen-year-old girl with an illegal handgun taken off the corpse of a man who'd been murdered in my backyard. Lenny the Lawyer would certainly not relish the details.

"Do you think she'll cooperate?" I said.

Rachel shrugged.

Tatiana had promised that she was now with us. I didn't know if we could believe her or not. To be on the safe side, I unplugged her phone and took the cord with me. I searched the room for papers and writing material, so she couldn't sneak her visitor a note. I found nothing. Rachel also put her cell phone on the window ledge to be used as a listening device. Katarina had the phone to her ear now. Again she would translate.

Half an hour later, a gold-toned Lexus SC 430 roared into the lot. I whistled low. A colleague at the hospital had just bought the same car. It put him back sixty grand. The woman who emerged sported a short, spiky shock of white hair. She wore a too-tight, hair-matching white shirt and, keeping with the theme, white pants so tight they seemed to be hovering below skin level. Her arms were toned and tan. The woman had that look. You know the one. She brought on memories of the hot mother strutting around the tennis club.

Rachel and I both turned to Katarina. Katarina nodded solemnly. "That's her. That's the woman who delivered my baby."

I saw Rachel begin working her Palm Pilot. "What are you doing?" I asked.

"Putting in the license plate and make. We should know who the car is registered to in a matter of minutes."

"How do you do that?"

"It's not hard," Rachel said. "Every law enforcement officer makes connections. And if you don't, you pay off someone at the DMV. Five hundred bucks usually."

"Are you online or something?"

She nodded. "Wireless modem. A friend of mine named Harold Fisher, he's a tech geek who works freelance. He didn't like how the feds pushed me out."

"So he helps you now?"

"Yes."

The white-haired woman leaned back in and pulled out what might have been a medical bag. She threw on a pair of designer sunglasses and hurried toward Tatiana's room. The woman knocked, the door opened, Tatiana let her in.

I turned around in my seat and watched Katarina. She had the phone on mute. "Tatiana is telling her that she feels better now. The woman is annoyed she called for nothing." She paused.

"Have you heard a name yet?"

Katarina shook her head. "The woman is going to examine her."

Rachel stared at her tiny Palm Pilot screen as if it were a magic eight ball. "Bang."

"What?"

"Denise Vanech, Forty-seven Riverview Avenue, Ridgewood, New Jersey. Forty-six years of age. No outstanding parking violations."

"You got it that fast?"

She shrugged. "All Harold has to do is type the license plate. He's going to see what he can dig up on her." Her stylus started up again. "Meanwhile I'm going to plug the name into Google."

"The search engine?"

"Yup. You'd be surprised what you can find."

I knew about that, actually. I once put my own name in. I don't remember why. Zia and I were drunk and did it for fun. She calls it "ego surfing."

"Not much speaking now." Katarina's face was a mask of concentration. "Maybe she's examining her?"

I looked over at Rachel. "Two hits on Google," she said. "The first is a Web site for the Bergen County planning board. She requested a variance to subdivide her lot. It was rejected. The second, however, is more interesting. It's an alumni site. It lists past graduates that they're trying to locate."

"What school?" I asked.

"University of Philadelphia Family Nurse and Midwifery."

That fit.

Katarina said, "They're done."

"Fast," I said.

"Very."

Katarina listened some more. "The woman is telling Tatiana to take care of herself. That she should eat better, for the baby. That she should call if she feels any further discomfort."

I turned to Rachel. "Sounds more pleasant than when she arrived."

Rachel nodded. The woman we assumed was Denise Vanech came out. She walked with her head high, her rear end twitching in that cocky way. The stretched white shirt was ribbed and, I couldn't help but notice, rather see-through. She got in her car and took off.

I started up the Camaro, the engine roaring like a lifetime smoker with a hacking cough. I followed at a safe distance. I wasn't too worried about losing her. We knew where she lived now.

"I still don't understand," I said to Rachel. "How do they get away with buying babies?"

"They find desperate women. They lure them here with promises of money and a stable, comfortable home for their child."

"But in order to adopt," I said, "there's a whole procedure you have to go through. It's a pain in the ass. I know some children overseas—physically deformed children—people tried to bring over. You can't believe the paperwork. It's impossible."

"I don't have the answer to that, Marc."

Denise Vanech veered onto the New Jersey Turnpike north. That would be the way back to Ridgewood. I let the Camaro drop back another twenty, thirty feet. The right blinker came on, and the Lexus turned off at the Vince Lombardi rest stop. Denise Vanech parked and headed inside. I pulled the car to the side of the ramp and looked at Rachel. She was biting her lip.

"Could be she's using the bathroom," I said.

"She washed up after examining Tatiana. Why didn't she go then?"

"Maybe she's hungry?"

"Does she look like she eats much Burger King to you, Marc?"

"So what do we do?"

There was little hesitation. Rachel gripped the door handle. "Drop me off by the door."

* * *

Denise Vanech was pretty sure that Tatiana was faking.

The girl had claimed to be hemorrhaging. Denise checked the sheets. They hadn't been changed, yet there was no blood on them. The tiles on the bathroom floor were clean. The toilet seat was clean. There was no blood anywhere.

That alone, of course, wouldn't mean all that much. There was a chance the girl had cleaned up. But there were other things. The gynecological examination showed no signs of distress. Nothing. Not the slightest red tint. Her vaginal hairs, too, had no traces of blood. Denise checked the shower when she finished up. Dry as bone. The girl had called less than an hour before. She claimed to be bleeding heavily.

It didn't add up.

Lastly, the girl's demeanor was wrong. The girls are always scared. That goes without saying. Denise had moved out of Yugoslavia when she was nine, during Tito's reign of relative peace, and she knew what a hellhole it was. To this girl, from where she had come, the United States must seem like Mars. But her fear had a different quality to it. Usually the girls stare at Denise as if she were some kind of parent or savior, looking up to her with a mix of trepidation and hope. But this girl averted her gaze. She fidgeted too much. And there was something else. Tatiana had been brought in by Pavel. He was usually good about watching them. But he hadn't been there. Denise was about to ask about that, but she decided to wait and play it out. If nothing was wrong, the girl would certainly raise Pavel's name.

She hadn't.

Yes, something was definitely wrong.

Denise did not want to raise suspicion. She finished the exam and hurried out. Behind her sunglasses, she checked for possible surveillance vans. There were none. She looked for obvious unmarked police cars. Again nothing. Of course, she was no expert. Though she had been working with Steven Bacard for nearly a decade, there had never been any complications. Perhaps that was why she'd let her guard down.

As soon as she got back into her car, Denise reached for her cell phone. She wanted to call Bacard. But no. If they were somehow on to them, they'd be able to trace that back. Denise debated using a pay phone at the nearest gas station. But they'd be expecting that too. When she saw the sign for the rest stop, she remembered that they had a huge bank of pay phones. She could call from there. If she moved fast enough, they wouldn't see her or know what phone she used.

But was that safe either?

She quickly sorted through the possibilities. Suppose she was indeed being followed. Driving to Bacard's office would definitely be the wrong move. She could wait and call him when she got home. But they might have a tap on her phone. This—calling from the large bank of pay phones—seemed the least risky.

Denise grabbed a napkin and used it to keep her fingerprints off the receiver. She was careful not to wipe it off. There were probably dozens of fingerprints already on it. Why make their job any easier?

Steven Bacard picked up. "Hello?"

The obvious strain in his voice made her heart sink. "Where is Pavel?" she asked.

"Denise?"

"Yes."

"Why are you asking?"

"I just visited his girl. Something isn't right."

"Oh God," he moaned. "What happened?"

"The girl called the emergency number. She said she was hemorrhaging, but I think she was lying."

There was silence.

"Steve?"

"Go home. Don't talk to anyone."

"Okay." Denise saw the white Camaro pull up. She frowned. Hadn't she seen it before?

"Are there any records in your house?" Bacard asked.

"No, of course not."

"You're sure?"

"Positive."

"Okay, good."

A woman was getting out of the Camaro. Even from this distance, Denise could see the bandage on the woman's ear.

"Go home," Bacard said.

Before the woman could turn around, Denise hung up the phone and slipped into the bathroom.

* * *

Steven Bacard had loved the old *Batman* TV show as a kid. Every episode, he remembered, started out pretty much the same way. A crime would be committed. They would flash to Commissioner Gordon and Chief O'Hara. The two law-enforcement buffoons would be grim faced. They would discuss the situation and realize that there was only one way out. Commissioner Gordon would then pick up the red Batphone. Batman would answer, promise to save the day, turn to Robin and say, "To the Batpoles!"

He stared at the phone with that creepy feeling in the pit of his stomach. This was no hero he was calling. Just the opposite, in fact. But in the end, survival was what mattered. Pretty words and justification were great during times of peace. In times of war, in times of life and death, it was simpler: Us or Them. He picked up the phone and dialed the number.

Lydia answered sweetly. "Hello, Steven."

"I need you again."

"Bad?"

"Very."

"We're on our way," she said.

chapter 39

"When I got in there," Rachel said, "she was in the bathroom. But I have a feeling she made a call first."

"Why?"

"There was a line in the bathroom. She was only three people ahead of me. She should have been more."

"Any way of figuring out who she called?"

"Not in the near future, no. Every phone in that place is taken. Even if I had full FBI access, it would take some time."

"So we keep following."

"Yes." She turned behind her. "Do you have an atlas in the car?"

Katarina smiled. "Many. Verne likes maps. World, country, state?"

"State."

She dug into the pocket behind my seat and handed Rachel the atlas. Rachel uncapped a pen and started marking it up.

"What are you doing?" I asked.

"I'm not sure."

The cell phone rang. I picked it up.

"You guys all right?"

"Yeah, Verne, we're fine."

"Got my sister to watch the kids for me. I'm in the pickup heading east. What's your ten-forty?"

I told him we were heading to Ridgewood. He knew the town.

"I'm about twenty minutes away," he said. "I'll meet you at the Ridgewood Coffee Company on Wilsey Square."

"We may be at this midwife's house," I said.

"I'll wait."

"Okay."

"Hey, Marc," Verne said, "not to get sentimental or anything, but if somebody needs shooting—"

"I'll let you know."

The Lexus turned off at Linwood Avenue. We dropped farther back. Rachel kept her head down, alternating between the stylus on the Palm Pilot and the marker on the atlas. We hit the suburbs. Denise Vanech turned left on Waltherly Road.

"She's definitely heading home," Rachel said. "Let her go. We need to think this through."

I couldn't believe what she was suggesting. "What do you mean, think this through? We need to approach her."

"Not yet. I'm working on something."

"What?"

"Just give me a few minutes."

I slowed my speed and turned down Van Dien, right near Valley Hospital. I looked back at Katarina. She gave me a small smile. Rachel kept working at whatever. I checked the dashboard clock. Time to meet Verne. I took North Maple to Ridgewood Avenue. A parking spot opened in front of a store named Duxiana. I grabbed it. Verne's pickup truck was parked across the street. It had mag wheels and two bumper stickers, one reading, CHARLTON HESTON FOR PRESIDENT and the other: DO I LOOK LIKE A HEMORRHOID? THEN GET OFF MY ASS.

Ridgewood's town center was a blend of turn-of-the-century picture-postcard splendor and modern-day extravagant food-court mall. Most of the old mom-n-pop shops were gone now. Sure, the independent bookstore still thrived. There was an upscale mattress store, a cute place that sold sixties paraphernalia, a smattering of boutiques, beauty parlors, and jewelry stores. And, yes, a few of the chains—Gap, Williams-Sonoma, the prerequisite Starbucks—had gobbled up space. But more than anything, the town center had become a veritable smorgasbord, a potpourri of eateries for too many tastes and budgets. Name a country, they had a bistro here. Throw a stone, even pathetically, in any direction, you would hit three such eateries.

Rachel took the atlas and Palm Pilot with her. She worked as we walked. Verne was already inside the coffee shop, chatting up the burly guy behind the counter. Verne wore a Deere baseball cap with a T-shirt that read: MOOSEHEAD: A GREAT BEER AND A NEW EXPERIENCE FOR A MOOSE.

We grabbed a table.

"So what's the deal?" Verne said.

I let Katarina fill him in. I was watching Rachel. Every time I started to speak, she held up a finger to silence me. I told Verne that he should take Katarina home. We didn't need their help anymore. They should be with their children. Verne was reluctant.

The time was sneaking up on 10:00 A.M. I wasn't really tired. Lack of sleep—even for reasons far less adrenaline generating than this—does not bother me. I credit my medical residency and the many nights on call for that.

"Bang," Rachel said again.

"What?"

With her eyes still on the Palm Pilot, Rachel put out her hand. "Let me use your phone."

"What is it?"

"Just give it to me, okay?"

I handed her the cell phone. She dialed and moved to the corner of the café. Katarina excused herself to use the bathroom. Verne poked me with his elbow and pointed at Rachel.

"You two in love?"

"It's complicated," I said.

"Only if you're a dumb-ass."

I may have shrugged.

"You either love her or you don't," Verne said. "The rest? That's for dumb-asses."

"Is that how you dealt with what you heard this morning?"

He thought about that. "What Kat said. What she did in the past. It don't matter much. There's a core. I've slept with that woman for eight years. I know the core."

"I don't know Rachel that well."

"Yeah, you do. Look at her." I did. And I felt something airy and light travel all the through me. "She got beaten up. She got shot, for Chrissake." He paused. I wasn't looking, but I bet he shook his mane in disgust. "You let that go, you know what you are?"

"A dumb-ass."

"A *professional* dumb-ass. You give up your amateur status."

Rachel hung up the phone and hurried back over. Maybe it was something Verne said, but I could swear that I saw a bit of fire back in her eyes. In that dress, with her hair mussed, with the confident lick-the-world smile, I was transported back. It didn't last long. No more than a moment or two. But maybe it was enough.

"Bang?" I asked.

"Cannon-fire, Fourth-of-July bang." She starting tapping with the stylus again. "I just need to do one more thing. In the meantime, look at this atlas."

I pulled it over. Verne looked over my shoulder. He smelled like motor oil. There were all kinds of markings on the atlas—little stars, crosses, but the thickest line was a circuitous route. I recognized enough of it.

"That's the route the kidnappers took last night," I said. "When we were following them."

"Right."

"What's with all the stars and stuff?"

"Okay, first thing. Look at the actual route they took. Up north over the Tappan Zee. Then west. Then south. Then west again. Then back east and north."

"They were stalling," I said.

"Right. It's like we said. They were setting up that trap for us at your house. But think about it a second. Our theory is that someone from law enforcement warned them about the Q-Logger, right?"

"So?"

"So no one knew about the Q-Logger until you were at the hospital. That means, for at least part of the journey, they wouldn't have known I was tailing them."

I wasn't sure I followed, but I said, "Okay."

"Do you pay your phone bill online?" she asked.

The subject change threw me for a moment. "Yes," I said.

"So you get a statement, right? You click on the link, you sign in, you can see all your calls. It probably has a reverse directory link too—so you can click on the number and see who you called."

I nodded. It did.

"Well, I got Denise Vanech's last phone bill." She held up a hand.

"Don't worry about how. Again it's fairly easy. Harold could probably do it by hacking, if he had more time, but having a connection or a giving a bribe is easier. Now with the Internet billing, it's easier than ever."

"Harold sent you her bill online?"

"Yep. Anyway, Ms. Vanech makes a fair amount of calls. That's what took me so long. We've been sorting through them, finding the names, then the addresses."

"And a name popped out?"

"No, an address did. I wanted to see if she called anybody on the kidnapper's route."

Now I saw where she was going. "And I assume the answer is yes?"

"Better than yes. Remember when they stopped at the MetroVista office complex?"

"Sure."

"Over the past month, Denise Vanech placed six calls to the law office of a Steven Bacard." Rachel pointed to the star she'd drawn on the map. "At MetroVista."

"A lawyer?"

"Harold is going to see what he can dig up, but again I just used Google. The name Steven Bacard pops up frequently."

"In what context?"

Rachel smiled again. "His expertise is adoption."

Verne said, "Sweet mother of God."

I sat back and tried to digest it all. Warning lights flashed, but I wasn't sure what they meant. Katarina came back to the table. Verne told her what we'd found. We were getting close. I knew that. But I felt adrift. My cell phone—or should I say, Zia's—rang. I looked down at the Caller ID. It was Lenny. I debated not answering, remembering what Zia had said. But of course, Lenny would know about the possibility of a tap. He had been the one who warned Zia.

I hit the answer button.

"Let me talk first," Lenny said before I could even utter a hello. "For the record, if this is being taped, this conversation is between an attorney and his client. It is thus protected. Marc, don't tell me where you are. Don't tell me anything that would force me to lie. You understand?"

"Yes."

"Did your trip bear fruit?" he asked.

"Not the fruit we wanted. Not yet anyway. But we're getting very close."

"Any way I can help?"

"I don't think so." Then, "Wait." I remembered that Lenny had handled my sister's arrests. He had been her main legal advisor. "Did Stacy ever say anything to you about adoption?"

"I'm not following."

"Did she ever think about giving up a baby for adoption, or in any way mention adoption to you?"

"No. Is this somehow connected with the kidnapping?"

"Could be."

"I don't remember anything like that. Look, they might be taping us, so let me tell you why I called. They found a dead body at your house— a man shot twice in the head." Lenny knew that I was already aware of this. I assumed that he was saying this for the benefit of whoever might be eavesdropping. "They haven't made an ID, but they did locate the murder weapon in the Christies' backyard."

I was not surprised. Rachel had figured that they'd plant the gun somewhere.

"The thing is, Marc, the murder weapon is your old gun, the one that's been missing since the shooting at your house. They already ran a ballistics test. You and Monica were shot with two different thirty-eights, remember?"

"Yes."

"Well, that gun—*your* gun—was one of the two used that morning."

I closed my eyes. Rachel mouthed a "what?" at me.

"I better go," Lenny said. "I'll look into Stacy and an adoption angle, if you want. See what I can dig up."

"Thanks."

"Stay safe."

He hung up. I turned to Rachel and told her about the gun discovery and the ballistics test. She leaned back and bit down on her lower lip, another familiar habit from our dating days. "So that means," she said, "that Pavel and the rest of these people are definitely linked to the first attack."

"You still had doubts?"

"A few hours ago, we thought it was a total hoax, remember? We thought that maybe these guys knew enough to fake like they had Tara, just to con some ransom money out of your father-in-law. But now we know different. These people were there that morning. They were part of the original abduction."

It made sense, but something about it still felt wrong. "Where do we go from here?" I asked.

"The logical step is to visit this lawyer, Steven Bacard," Rachel said. "The problem is, we don't know if he's the boss or just another employee. For all we know, Denise Vanech is the mastermind and he works for her. Or they both work for a third party. And if we go busting in there, Bacard is just going to clam up. He's a lawyer. He's too smart to talk to us."

"So what do you suggest?"

"I'm not sure," she said. "It might be time to call in the feds. Maybe they can raid his office."

I shook my head. "That'll take too long."

"We might be able to get them to move fast."

"Assuming they believe us—which is a big assumption—how fast?"

"I don't know, Marc."

I didn't like it. "Suppose Denise Vanech was suspicious back there. Suppose Tatiana gets scared and calls her again. Suppose there is indeed a leak. There are too many variables here, Rachel."

"So what do you think we should do?"

"A two-prong attack," I said, the words coming out without much thought. There was a problem. I suddenly had a solution. "You take Denise Vanech. I take Steven Bacard. We coordinate it so that we hit them at the same time."

"Marc, he's a lawyer. He's not going to open up to you."

I looked at her. She saw it. Verne sat up a little and made a small *woo-ee* noise.

"You're going to threaten him?" Rachel asked.

"We're talking about my child's life."

"And you're talking about taking the law into your own hands." Then she added, "Again."

"So?"

"You threatened a teenage girl with a gun."

"I was trying to intimidate, that's all. I would have never really hurt her."

"The law—"

"The law hasn't done squat to help my daughter," I said, trying not to shout. In the corner of my eye, I saw Verne nodding along with my outrage. "They're too busy wasting time on you."

That made her straighten up. "Me?"

"Lenny told me at the house. They think you did it. Without me. That you were obsessed with having me back or something."

"What?"

I rose from the table. "Look, I'm going to see this Bacard guy. I don't plan on hurting anyone, but if he knows something about my daughter, I'm going to find out what it is."

Verne raised his fist. "Right on."

I asked Verne if I could keep borrowing the Camaro. He reminded me that he was behind me all the way. I expected Rachel to argue some more. She didn't. Maybe she knew that I would not change my mind. Maybe she knew I was right. Or maybe—perhaps most likely—she had been stunned to learn that her old colleagues had zeroed in on her as the sole serious suspect.

"I'll come with you," Rachel said.

"No." My voice left no wiggle room. I had no idea what I would do when I got there, but I knew that I was capable of plenty. "What I said before makes sense." I could hear my familiar surgeon-tone taking over. "I'll call you when I get to Bacard's office. We hit him and Denise Vanech at the same time."

I didn't wait for a response. I got back in the Camaro and started toward the MetroVista office complex.

chapter 40

Lydia checked her surroundings. She was a little more in the open than she liked to be, but that couldn't be helped. She had on the spiky blond wig—the one not unlike Steven Bacard's description of Denise Vanech. She knocked on the door of the efficiency.

The curtain next to the door moved. Lydia smiled. "Tatiana?"

No reply.

She had been warned that Tatiana spoke very little English. Lydia had debated how to play this. Time was critical. Everything and everyone needed to be shut down. When someone who dislikes blood as much as Bacard says that, you immediately understand the ramifications. Lydia and Heshy had split up. She had come down here. They would meet up afterward.

"It's okay, Tatiana," she said through the door. "I'm here to help."

There was no movement.

"I'm a friend of Pavel's," she tried. "You know Pavel?"

The curtain moved. A young woman's face appeared for a brief moment, gaunt and childlike. Lydia nodded at her. The woman still did not open the door. Lydia scanned her surroundings. Nobody looking, but she still felt too exposed. This had to end fast.

"Wait," Lydia said. Then, looking at the curtain, she reached into her purse. She pulled out a piece of paper and pen. She wrote something down, making sure that if someone was still at the window, they would see exactly what she was doing. She capped the pen and stepped close to the window. Lydia held the piece of paper up to the pane of glass so Tatiana could read it.

It was like drawing a scared cat out from under the sofa. Tatiana moved slowly. She came toward the window. Lydia stayed still, so as not to startle her. Tatiana leaned closer. Here, kitty, kitty. Lydia could see the girl's face now. She was squinting, trying to see what was on the piece of paper.

When Tatiana came close enough, Lydia pressed the barrel of the gun against the glass and aimed between the young girl's eyes. At the last second, Tatiana tried to veer away. Too little, too late. The bullet went clean through the glass and into Tatiana's right eye. Blood appeared. Lydia fired again, automatically tilting the gun downward. It caught the falling Tatiana in the top of the forehead. But the second bullet had been superfluous. The first shot, the one in the eye, had ripped into the brain and killed the young girl instantly.

Lydia hurried away. She risked a glance behind her. No one. When she reached the neighboring mall, she dumped the wig and the white coat. She found her car in a lot another half mile away.

I called Rachel when I arrived at MetroVista. She was parked down the street from Denise Vanech's house. We were both ready to go.

I'm not sure what I expected to happen here. I guess I figured that I would explode into Bacard's office, stick my gun in his face, and demand answers. What I hadn't foreseen was a regular, state-of-the-state office setup—that is, Steven Bacard had a well-appointed reception area. There were two people waiting—a married couple, by all appearances. The husband had his face stuck in a waiting-room-laminated *Sports Illustrated*. The wife looked to be in pain. She tried to smile at me, but it was as if the effort would wound her.

I realized how shoddy I must look. I was still in my hospital scrubs. I was unshaven. My eyes were undoubtedly red from lack of sleep. My hair, I imagined, was probably sticking up in a textbook case of bedhead.

The receptionist was behind one of those sliding glass windows I usually associate with a dental practice. The woman—a small nameplate read AGNES WEISS—smiled at me sweetly.

"May I help you?"

"I'm here to see Mr. Bacard."

"Do you have an appointment?" She kept the tone sweet, but there was a rhetorical twang there too. She already knew the answer.

"This is an emergency," I said.

"I see. Are you a client of ours, Mr. . . . ?"

"Doctor," I snapped back automatically. "Tell him Dr. Marc Seidman needs to see him immediately. Tell him it's an emergency."

The young couple was watching us now. The receptionist's sweet smile began to falter. "Mr. Bacard's schedule is very full today." She opened her appointment ledger. "Let me see when we have something available, okay?"

"Agnes, look at me."

She did.

I gave her my gravest, you-might-die-if-I-don't-operate-right-away expression. "Tell him Dr. Seidman is here. Tell him it's an emergency. Tell him if he doesn't see me now, I will go to the police."

The young couple exchanged a glance.

Agnes adjusted herself in the chair. "If you'll just have a seat—"

"Tell him."

"Sir, if you don't step back, I'll call security."

So I stepped back. I could always step forward again. Agnes did not pick up the phone. I moved to a nonthreatening distance. She slid the little window closed. The couple looked at me. The husband said, "She's covering for him."

The wife said, "Jack!"

Jack ignored her. "Bacard ran out of here half an hour ago. That receptionist keeps telling us he'll be right back."

I noticed a wall of photographs. Now I took a closer look. The same man was in all of them with a potpourri of politicos, quasi celebrities, gone-to-flab athletes. Steven Bacard, I assumed. I stared at the man's face—pudgy, weak chinned, country-club shiny.

I thanked the man named Jack and started for the door. Bacard's office was on the first floor, so I decided to wait by the entrance. This way, I could catch him unawares on neutral ground and before Agnes had a chance to warn him. Five minutes passed. Several suits came and went, all harried from their days of printer toner and paperweights, dragged down by briefcases the size of car trunks. I paced the corridor.

Another couple entered. I could tell right away by their tentative steps and shattered eyes that they, too, were heading for Bacard's office. I watched them and wondered what path they had taken here. I saw them getting married, holding hands, kissing freely, making love in the morning. I saw their careers begin to thrive. I saw them feel the pang and segue toward the initial attempts at conceiving, the wait-till-next-month shrug when the home tests were negative, the slowly blossoming worry. A year passes. Still nothing. Their friends are starting to have children now and talk about them incessantly. Their parents are wondering when they'll have grandkids. I see them visiting the doctor—"a specialist"—the endless probing for the woman, the humiliation of masturbating into a beaker for the man, the personal questions, the blood and urine samples. More years pass. Their friends drift away. Making love is now strictly about procreation. It is calculated. It is always tinged with sadness. He stops holding her hand. She rolls over at night unless it's the right time in her cycle. I see the drugs, the Pergonal, the ridiculously expensive in-vitro fertilization, the time off from work, the checking of calendars, the same home tests, the crushing disappointments.

And now they were here.

No, I didn't know if any of this was really the case. But somehow I suspected that I was close. How far, I wondered, would they go to end this pain? How much would they pay?

"Oh my God! Oh my God!"

I jerked my head toward the scream. A man banged through the door.

"Call nine-one-one!"

I ran toward him. "What is it?"

I heard another scream. I ran through the door and outside. Yet another scream, this one more high pitched. I turned to my right. Two women were running out of the lower-level parking garage. I sprinted down the ramp. I slipped past the gate where you pick up your parking ticket. Someone else was calling for help, begging people to call 911.

Up ahead, I saw a security guard shouting into a walkie-talkie of some sort. He broke into a full gallop too. I followed him. When we turned the corner, the security guard pulled up. There was a woman next to him. She had her hands on her cheeks and was screaming. I ran next to them and looked down.

The body was jammed between two cars. His eyes stared open at nothing. His face was still pudgy, weak chinned, country-club shiny. The blood flowed from the wound in his head. The world teetered again.

Steven Bacard, maybe my last hope, was dead.

chapter 41

Rachel rang the doorbell. Denise Vanech had one of those preten-
tious chimes that ring up and then down the scale. The sun was all the
way up now. The sky was blue and clear. On the street, two women
power-walked carrying tiny mauve dumbbells. They nodded at Rachel,
never missing a step. Rachel nodded back.

The intercom sounded. "Yes?"

"Denise Vanech?"

"Who is this please?"

"My name is Rachel Mills. I used to work with the FBI."

"Did you say, used to?"

"Yes."

"What do you want?"

"We need to talk, Ms. Vanech."

"About what?"

Rachel sighed. "Could you please just open the door?"

"Not until I know what this is about."

"The young girl you just visited in Union City. It's about her. For
starters."

"I'm sorry. I don't discuss my patients."

"I said, for starters."

"Why would a former FBI agent be interested in any of this
anyway?"

"Would you prefer I call a current agent?"

"I don't care what you do, Ms. Mills. I have nothing else to say to
you. If the FBI has questions, they can call my lawyer."

"I see," Rachel said. "And would your lawyer be Steven Bacard?"

There was a brief silence. Rachel glanced back at the car.

"Ms. Vanech?"

"I don't have to talk to you."

"No, that's true. I'll start going door-to-door maybe. Talk to your neighbors."

"And say what?"

"I'll ask them if they know anything about a baby-smuggling operation that runs out of this house."

The door opened quickly. Denise Vanech with her tan skin and white hair pushed her head through the door. "I'll sue you for libel."

"Slander," Rachel said.

"What?"

"Slander. Libel is for the printed word. Slander is for the spoken. You mean slander. But either way, you'd have to prove what I'm saying is untrue. And we both know better."

"You have no evidence I've done anything wrong."

"Sure I do."

"I was treating a woman who claimed to be ill. That's all."

Rachel pointed up the lawn. Katarina stepped out of the car. "And what about this former patient?"

Denise Vanech put a hand to her mouth.

"She'll testify that you paid her money for her baby."

"No, she won't. They'll arrest her."

"Oh sure, right, the FBI would much rather crack down on a poor Serbian woman than break up a baby-smuggling ring. That's rich."

When Denise Vanech paused, Rachel pushed open the door. "Mind if I come in?"

"You have it wrong," she said quietly.

"Cool." Rachel was inside now. "You can correct me on all my misgivings."

Denise Vanech seemed suddenly unsure what to do. With one more look at Katarina, she slowly closed the front door. Rachel was already heading into the den. It was white. Totally white. White sectional couches against a white carpet. White porcelain statues of naked women riding horses. White coffee table, white side tables, and two of those white ergonomic-looking chairs with no backs. Denise followed her in. Her white clothes blended into the background, camouflagelike, making it look like her head and arms were floating.

"What do you want?"

"I'm looking for a specific child."

Denise let her eyes wander toward the door. "Hers?"

She was talking about Katarina.

"No."

"It wouldn't matter. I don't know anything about placement."

"You're a midwife, correct?"

She folded the smooth, muscular arms under her bosom. "I'm not answering any of your questions."

"See, Denise, I know most of it. I just need you to fill in a few blanks." Rachel sat on the vinyl couch. Denise Vanech didn't move. "You have people in a foreign country. Maybe more than one country, I don't know. But I know about Serbia. So let's start there. You have people there who recruit girls. The girls come over pregnant, but they don't mention that at customs. You deliver the baby. Maybe here, maybe you have another spot, I don't know."

"You don't know a lot."

Rachel smiled. "I know enough."

Denise put her hands on her hips now. Her poses all seemed unnatural, as if she practiced them in front of a mirror.

"Anyway, the women have the babies. You pay them. You turn the baby over to Steven Bacard. He works for desperate couples who might be willing to bend the rules. They adopt the child."

"That's a nice story."

"Are you saying it's fiction?"

Denise grinned. "Total fiction."

"Cool, fine." She took out her cell phone. "Then let me call the feds. I'll introduce them to Katarina. They can go down to Union City and grill Tatiana. They can start going through your phone records, your finances—"

Denise started waving her hands. "Okay, okay, tell me what you want. I mean, you said you're not an FBI agent anymore. So what do you want with me?"

"I want to know how it works."

"You trying to cut yourself in?"

"No."

Denise waited a beat. "You said before that you're looking for a specific kid."

"Yes."

"You're working for someone, then?"

Rachel shook her head. "Look, Denise, you don't have a lot of options here. You either tell me the truth or you do serious jail time."

"And if I do tell you what I know?"

"Then I'll leave you out of it," Rachel said. It was a lie. But it was an easy one. This woman was involved in baby selling. There was no way Rachel was just going to let that go.

Denise sat. The tan seemed to be leaving her face. She looked suddenly older. The lines around her mouth and eyes deepened. "It's not what you think," she began.

Rachel waited.

"We aren't hurting anyone. The truth is, we're helping."

Denise Vanech picked up her purse—white, of course—and dug out a cigarette. She offered one to Rachel. Rachel shook her off.

"Do you know anything about orphanages in poor countries?" Denise asked.

"Just what I see on PBS documentaries."

Denise lit the cigarette and drew a deep breath. "They are beyond awful. They may house forty babies to one nurse. The nurse is uneducated. The job is often a political favor. Some of the children are abused. Many are born drug dependent. The medical care—"

"I get the picture," Rachel said. "It's bad."

"Yes."

"And?"

"And we've found a way to save some of these children."

Rachel sat back and crossed her legs. She could see where this was going. "You pay pregnant women to fly over and sell you their babies?"

"That's hyperbole," she said.

Rachel shrugged. "How would you put it?"

"Put yourself in their position. You are a poor woman—and I mean poor—maybe a prostitute or somehow involved in white slavery. You are dirt. You have nothing. Some man knocks you up. You can abort or, if your religion forbids that, you can stick the kid in a godforsaken orphanage."

"Or," Rachel added, "if they're lucky, they end up with you?"

"Yes. We will give them adequate medical care. We will offer financial restitution. And most importantly, we will make sure that their baby is placed in a loving home with caring, financially stable parents."

"Financially stable," Rachel repeated. "As in wealthy?"

"The service is expensive," she admitted. "But let me ask you something now. Take your friend out there. Katarina you said her name was?"

Rachel kept still.

"What would her life be like right now if we hadn't brought her here? What would her child's life be like?"

"I don't know. I don't know what you did with her child."

Denise smiled. "Fine, be argumentative. But you know what I mean. Do you think the baby would be better off with a dirt-poor prostitute in a war-torn hellhole—or with a caring family here in the United States?"

"I see," Rachel said, trying not to squirm. "So you're sort of like the world's most wonderful social worker. This is charity work you're doing?"

Denise chuckled. "Look around you. I have expensive taste. I live in a ritzy neighborhood. I have a kid in college. I like to vacation in Europe. We have a house in the Hamptons. I do this because it's incredibly profitable. But so what? Who cares about my motives? My motives don't change the conditions in those orphanages."

"I still don't understand," Rachel said. "The women sell you their babies."

"They give us their babies," she corrected. "In return, we offer financial restitution—"

"Yeah, yeah, whatever. You get the baby. They get money. But then what? There has to be paperwork on the child, otherwise the government would step in. They wouldn't just let Bacard keep running adoptions like this."

"True."

"So how do you work it?"

She smiled. "You plan on busting me, don't you?"

"I don't know what I'm going to do."

She was still smiling. "You'll remember I cooperated, right?"

"Yes."

Denise Vanech pressed her palms together and closed her eyes. It looked as if she might be praying. "We hire American mothers."

Rachel made a face. "Excuse me?"

"For example, let's say Tatiana is about to have the baby. We might hire you, Rachel, to pose as the mother. You'd go to vital records at your town hall. You'd tell them you're pregnant and going to have a home birth, so there won't be a hospital record. They give you forms to fill out. They never check to see if you're really pregnant. How would they? It's not like they can give you a gynecological exam."

Rachel sat back. "Jesus."

"It's pretty simple when you think about it. There is no record that Tatiana is going to have a baby. There is a record that you are. I deliver the baby. I sign as the attending witness to your child being born. You become the mother. Bacard has you fill in the paperwork for adoption. . . ." She shrugged.

"So the adopting parents never learn the truth?"

"No, but they don't look too hard either. They're desperate. They don't want to know."

Rachel suddenly felt drained.

"And before you turn us in," Denise went on, "consider something else. We've been doing this for almost ten years now. That means there are children who've been happily placed with families that long. Dozens. All of those adoptions will be considered null and void. The birth mothers can come over here and demand their children back. Or take a payoff. You'd be ripping apart a lot of lives."

Rachel shook her head. It was too much to consider right now. Another time. She was getting off track. Had to keep her eye on the prize. She turned and squared her shoulders. She looked Denise deep in the eye.

"So how does Tara Seidman fit into all this?"

"Who?"

"Tara Seidman."

Now it was Denise's turn to look confused. "Wait a second. Wasn't that the little girl kidnapped in Kasselton?"

Rachel's cell phone rang. She checked the Caller ID and saw it was Marc. She was just about to press the answer button when a man stepped into view. Her breath stopped. Sensing something, Denise turned around. She jumped back at the sight.

It was the man from the park.

His hands were huge, making the gun he now pointed at Rachel look like a child's toy. He wiggled his fingers in her direction. "Give me the phone."

Rachel handed it to him, trying her best to avoid his touch. The man put the barrel of the gun against her head. "Now give me your gun."

Rachel reached into her handbag. He told her to lift it into view with two fingers. She complied. The phone rang for the fourth time.

The man hit the answer button and said, "Dr. Seidman?"

Even Rachel could hear the reply. "Who is this?"

"We're all at Denise Vanech's house now. You will come here unarmed and alone. I will tell you all about your daughter then."

"Where's Rachel?"

"She's right here. You have thirty minutes. I will tell you what you need to know. You have a tendency to try to be cute in these situations. But not this time or your friend Ms. Mills dies first. Do you understand?"

"I understand."

The man hung up the phone. He looked down at Rachel. His eyes were brown with a gold center. They looked almost gentle, the eyes of a doe. Then the big man swung his gaze toward Denise Vanech. She flinched. A smile came to the man's lips.

Rachel saw what he was about to do.

She shouted, "No!" as the big man aimed the gun at Denise Vanech's chest and fired three shots. All three hit dead center. Denise's body went slack. She slid off the couch and onto the floor. Rachel started to stand, but now the gun was pointed at her.

"Stay put."

Rachel obeyed. Denise Vanech was clearly dead. Her eyes were open. Her blood streamed down, the color startlingly red against a sea of white.

chapter 42

Now what do I do?

I had been calling to tell Rachel about the shooting death of Steven Bacard. Now this man was holding her hostage. Okay, so what's my next step? I tried to think it through, to analyze the data carefully, but there was not enough time. The man on the phone had been right. I had been "cute" in the past. During the first ransom drop, I had let the police and FBI in on it. During the second, I'd enlisted the aid of an ex–federal agent. For a long time, I blamed the first drop-gone-wrong on my decision. Not anymore. I had played the odds both times, but now I think the game was fixed from the get-go. They had never intended to give me back my daughter. Not eighteen months ago. Not last night.

And not now.

Maybe I had been on a search for an answer that I knew all along. Verne had understood my quest with one caveat: "Long as a man ain't fooling himself." But maybe I had been. Even now, even as we were uncovering this baby-smuggling scam, I had allowed myself fresh hope. Perhaps my daughter was alive. Perhaps she had gotten ensnared in this adoption con. Would that be horrible? Yes. But the obvious alternative—that Tara is dead—was a hell of a lot worse.

I no longer knew what to believe.

I checked my watch. Twenty minutes had passed. I wondered about how to play it. First things first. I called Lenny on the private line at his office.

"A man named Steven Bacard was just murdered in East Rutherford," I said.

"Bacard the lawyer?"

"You know him?"

"I worked a case with him a few years ago," Lenny said. Then: "Oh damn."

"What?"

"You asked before about Stacy and an adoption. I didn't see a connection. But now that you say Bacard's name . . . Stacy asked me about him, what, three, four years ago."

"What about him?"

"I don't remember anymore. Something about being a mother."

"What does that mean?"

"I don't know. I really didn't pay that much attention. I just told her not to sign anything without showing it to me." Then Lenny asked, "How do you know he's been murdered?"

"I just saw his body."

"Whoa, don't say anything else. This line might not be secure."

"I need your help. Call the cops. They need to get Bacard's records. He ran an adoption scam. There's a possibility that he had something to do with Tara's kidnapping."

"How?"

"I don't have time to explain."

"Yeah, okay, I'll call Tickner and Regan. Regan's been searching for you pretty much nonstop, you know."

"I figured."

I hung up before he could ask more. I am not really sure what I expected them to find. I couldn't make myself believe that the answer to Tara's fate lay in some file cabinet in a law office. But maybe. And if something went wrong here—and there was certainly a decent chance of that happening—I wanted someone to be able to follow up.

I was in Ridgewood now. I did not believe for a second that the man on the phone was telling the truth. They were not in the trade-information business. They were here to clean house. Rachel and I knew too much. They were drawing me there so that they could kill us.

So what do I do?

There was very little time. If I stalled—if it took me much longer than a half an hour—the man on the phone would start getting antsy. That would be bad. I thought again about calling the police, but I remembered his warning about being "cute" and I still worried about a leak. I had a gun. I knew how to use it. I was a pretty good shot, but that was at a range. Shooting at people would, I assumed, be different. Or maybe not. I no longer had qualms about killing these people. I'm not sure I ever had.

A block away from Denise Vanech's house, I parked the car, grabbed the gun, and started down the street.

He called her Lydia. She called him Heshy.

The woman had arrived five minutes ago. She was petite and pretty, her baby-doll eyes wide with excitement. She stood in front of Denise Vanech's corpse and watched the blood still trickling out. Rachel sat still. Her hands had been bound behind her back with duct tape. The woman named Lydia turned to Rachel.

"That stain is going to be a bitch to get out."

Rachel stared at her. Lydia smiled.

"You don't think that's funny?"

"Inside," Rachel said. "Inside I'm cracking up."

"You visited a young girl named Tatiana today, yes?"

Rachel said nothing. The big man named Heshy began to pull down the shades.

"She's dead. Just thought you'd like to know." Lydia sat next to Rachel. "Do you remember the TV show *Family Laughs*?"

Rachel wondered how to play this. This Lydia was insane, no doubt about it. Tentatively she said, "Yes."

"Were you a fan?"

"The show was puerile nonsense."

Lydia threw back her head and laughed. "I played Trixie."

She smiled at Rachel. Rachel said, "You must be very proud."

"Oh I am. I am." Lydia stopped, tilted her face, moved it closer to Rachel's. "You know, of course, that you're going to die soon."

Rachel did not blink. "Then how about telling me what you did with Tara Seidman?"

"Oh please." Lydia stood. "I was an actress, remember? I was on television. So, what, is this the part of the show where we tell all so that the audience can catch up and your hero can sneak up on us? Sorry, sweetie." She turned to Heshy. "Gag her, Pooh Bear."

Heshy used the duct tape and wrapped it around Rachel's mouth and the back of her head. He moved back toward the window. Lydia bent close to Rachel's ear. Rachel could feel the woman's breath.

"I will tell you this," she whispered, "because it's funny." Lydia bent in a little closer. "I have no idea what happened to Tara Seidman."

Okay, I wasn't about to drive up and knock on the door.

Let's face it. They were out to kill us. My only chance was to surprise them. I didn't know the layout of the house, but I figured that I could find a side window and try to sneak in. I was armed. I was confident I could shoot without hesitation. I really wished that I had a better plan, but even if I had more time, I doubt that I'd come up with anything.

Zia had mentioned my surgeon's ego. I admit that it scared me. I actually felt confident that I could pull this off. I was smart. I knew how to be careful. I would look for an opening. If I didn't see one, I would offer them a trade—me for Rachel. I would not be sucked in by talk of Tara. Yes, I wanted to believe that she was still alive. Yes, I wanted to believe that they knew where she was. But I would no longer risk Rachel's life for a pipe dream. My life? Sure. But not Rachel's.

I moved closer to Denise Vanech's house, trying to duck behind trees while not looking conspicuous. In an upscale suburban neighborhood, this was impossible. People don't skulk. I imagined the neighbors watching me from behind the blinds, their fingers on the auto-911 dial button. I couldn't worry about it. Whatever was going to happen, one way or the other, would happen before any police could get here.

When my cell phone rang, I nearly jumped out my skin. I was three houses away now. I cursed under my breath. Dr. Cool—Dr. Confident—had forgotten to put his phone on vibrate. I realized with a sinking certainty that I was deluding myself. I was out of my element here. Suppose, for example, the phone had rung when I was right up against the house. What then?

I leapt behind a shrub and answered it with a snap of my wrist.

"You got a lot to learn about sneaking up on places," Verne whispered. "I mean, you're godawful at it."

"Where are you?"

"Check out the second-floor window, far back."

I peeked out at Denise Vanech's house. Verne was in the window. He waved to me.

"Back door was unlocked," Verne whispered. "I let myself in."

"What's going on in there?"

"Stone-cold killing. I heard them say they killed that girl at the motel. They blew away that Denise woman. She's lying dead not three feet from Rachel."

I closed my eyes.

"This is a trap, Marc."

"Yeah, I figured that."

"There's two of them—one man, one woman. I want you to hustle back to your car. I want you to drive and park on the street. You'll be far enough away so that they won't get a clear shot at you. Stay there. Don't get any closer. I just want you to draw their attention, you got me?"

"Yes."

"I'll try to keep one alive, but I can't make any promises."

He hung up. I hurried back to the car and did as he said. I could feel my heart pounding against my chest. But there was hope now. Verne was there. He was inside the house and armed. I pulled up to the front of Denise Vanech's house. The blinds and curtains were drawn. I took a deep breath. I opened the car door and stood.

Silence.

I expected to hear shots. But that was not what came first. The first sound was shattering glass. And then I saw Rachel fall out the window.

"His car just pulled up," Heshy said.

Rachel's hands were still bound behind her back, the duct tape over her mouth. She knew that this was it. Marc would come to the door. They would let him in, this mutant version of Bonnie and Clyde, and then they would shoot them both.

Tatiana was already dead. Denise Vanech was already dead. There was no other way to play this. Heshy and Lydia could not let them survive. Rachel had hoped that Marc would realize this and go to the police. She hoped that he wouldn't show up, but of course, that would not be an option for him. So he was here. He would probably try something foolhardy or maybe he was still so blinded by hope that he would simply walk into the trap.

Either way, Rachel had to stop him.

Her only chance was to surprise them. Even then, even if everything fell into place, the best she could realistically hope for was to save Marc. The rest was fool's gold.

Time to act.

They hadn't bothered to tie her feet. With her hands behind her back and her mouth taped shut, what harm could she do? Trying to run at them would be suicide. She'd make an easy target.

And that was what she was counting on.

Rachel got to her feet. Lydia turned around and pointed the gun at her. "Sit down."

She didn't. And now Lydia had a dilemma. If she fired the gun, Marc would hear it. He would know something was wrong. A stalemate. But it wouldn't last. An idea—a pretty lame idea—came to Rachel. She broke into a run. Lydia would either have to shoot or give chase or . . .

The window.

Lydia saw what Rachel was doing, but there was no way to stop her. Rachel lowered her head like a battering ram and dived straight toward the picture window. Lydia raised her gun to shoot. Rachel braced herself. She knew that this would hurt. The glass broke with surprising ease. Rachel flew through it, but what she hadn't counted on was how far off the ground she was. Her hands were still tied behind her back. There was no way to break the fall.

She turned to the side and took the impact on her shoulder. Something popped. She felt a stabbing pain run down her leg. A shard of glass stuck out of her thigh. The sound would warn Marc, no question about it. He could be saved. But as Rachel rolled over, dread—deep, heavy dread—hit her next. Yes, she had warned Marc. He had seen her fall out the window.

But now, without thinking of the danger, Marc was running toward her.

Verne was crouched on the stairs.

He'd been about to make his move when Rachel suddenly stood up. Was she crazy? But no, he realized, she was just a brave lady. After all, she had no idea that he was hiding upstairs. She couldn't just sit there and let Marc walk in on this setup. She wasn't built that way.

"Sit down."

The woman's voice. The pert thing named Lydia. She started to swing her gun up. Verne panicked. He wasn't in position yet. He wouldn't have a clear shot. But Lydia didn't pull the trigger. Verne watched in amazement as Rachel ran and jumped through the window.

Talk about a distraction.

Verne moved now. He had heard countless times about how time stands still in moments of extreme violence, that brief seconds can drag so that you can see everything clearly. In reality, that was total bull. When you looked back, when you ran it through your mind in safety and comfort, that's when you imagine it went by slowly. But in the heat of the moment, when he and three buddies had gotten into a firefight with some of Saddam's "elite" soldiers, time had actually sped up. That was what was happening here.

Verne spun around the corner. "Drop it!"

The big man had his gun aimed at the window where Rachel had fallen out. There was no time to call out another warning. Verne fired twice. Heshy went down. Lydia screamed. Verne ducked into a roll and disappeared behind the couch. Lydia screamed again.

"Heshy!"

Verne peered out, expecting to see Lydia aiming the gun at him. But that wasn't the case. She ditched the weapon. Still crying out, Lydia dropped to her knees and gently cradled Heshy's head.

"No! Don't die. Please, Heshy, please don't leave me!"

Verne kicked her gun away. He kept his pointed at Lydia.

Her voice was low now, soft and motherly. "Please, Heshy. Please don't die. Oh God, please don't leave me."

Heshy said, "I never will."

Lydia looked at Verne, her eyes pleading. He didn't bother calling 911. He could hear the sirens now. Heshy grabbed Lydia's hand. "You know what you have to do," he said.

"No," she said, her voice small.

"Lydia, we planned for this."

"You're not going to die."

Heshy closed his eyes. His breathing was labored.

"The world will think you were a monster," she said.

"I only care what you think. Promise me, Lydia."

"You're going to be fine."

"Promise me."

Lydia shook her head. The tears were flowing freely now. "I can't do it."

"You can." Heshy managed a final smile. "You're a great actress, remember?"

"I love you," she said.

But his eyes were closed. Lydia kept sobbing. She kept pleading with him not to leave her. The sirens came closer. Verne stepped back. The police arrived. When they came inside, they stood around her in a circle. Lydia suddenly lifted her head off Heshy's chest.

"Thank God," she said to them—and the tears started rolling again. "My nightmare is finally over."

Rachel was rushed to the hospital. I wanted to follow, but the police had other ideas. I spoke to Zia. I asked her to look in on Rachel for me.

The police questioned us for hours. They questioned Verne, Katarina, and me separately and then together. I think they believed us. Lenny was there. Regan and Tickner showed up, but it took some time. They'd been going through Bacard's files per Lenny's phone call.

Regan took the lead with me. "Long day, huh, Marc?"

I sat across from him. "Do I look in the mood for chitchat, Detective?"

"The woman goes by the name Lydia Davis. Her real name is Larissa Dane."

I made a face. "Why does that name sound familiar?"

"She was a child actor."

"Trixie," I said, remembering. "On *Family Laughs*."

"Yep, that's her. Or at least, that's what she says. Anyway, she claims this guy—we only know him as Heshy—kept her locked up and abused her. She said he forced her to do things. Your friend Verne thinks it's all a scam. But that's not important right now. She claims that she doesn't know anything about your daughter."

"How can that be?"

"She says they were just hired hands. That Bacard came to Heshy with this scheme about asking for ransom for a kid they hadn't kidnapped. Heshy loved the idea. Lot of money—and since they didn't really have the kid, there was almost no risk."

"She says they had nothing to do with the shooting at my house?"

"That's right."

I looked at Lenny. He saw the problem too. "But they had my gun. The one they used on Katarina's brother."

"Yeah, we know. She claims that Bacard gave it to Heshy. To set you up. Heshy shot Pavel and planted the gun so you and Rachel would take the fall."

"How did they get Tara's hair for the ransom drop? How did they get her clothes?"

"According to Ms. Dane, Bacard provided them."

I shook my head. "So Bacard was the one who kidnapped Tara?"

"She claims not to know."

"How about my sister? How did she get involved?"

"Again she claims it was Bacard. He gave them Stacy's name as a fall guy. Heshy gave Stacy the money and told her to cash it at a bank. Then he killed her."

I looked over at Tickner, then back at Regan. "It doesn't add up."

"We're still working on it."

Lenny said, "I have a question. Why did they come back after a year and a half and try it again?"

"Ms. Dane claims not to know for sure, but she suspects it was simple greed. She says Bacard called and asked if Heshy would want to make another million. He said yes. Going through Bacard's records, he was clearly in financial trouble. We think she's right. Bacard simply decided to take another bite of the apple."

I rubbed my face. My ribs began to ache. "Did you find Bacard's adoption records?"

Regan glanced at Tickner. "Not yet."

"How can that be?"

"Look, we just got on this. We'll find them. We're going to check every adoption he's ever made, especially anything involving a female eighteen months ago. If Bacard had Tara adopted, we'll find out."

I shook my head again.

"What is it, Marc?"

"That doesn't make any sense. The guy has a decent thing going with this adoption scam. Why shoot me and Monica and up the ante to kidnapping and murder?"

"We don't know," Regan said. "I think we can all agree that there's more to the story. But the truth is, the most likely scenario right now is that your sister and an accomplice shot you and Monica and took the baby. She then brought it to Bacard."

I closed my eyes and replayed it in my head. Could Stacy have really done that? Could she have broken into my house and shot me? I still couldn't make myself believe. And then I thought of something.

Why hadn't I heard the window break?

More than that, before I was shot, why hadn't I heard *anything*? A window break, a doorbell, heck, a door opening. Why hadn't I heard any of that? The answer, according to Regan, had been that I was blocking. But now I saw that wasn't it.

"The granola bar," I said.

"Pardon me?"

I turned to him. "Your theory is that I'm forgetting something, right? Stacy and her accomplice either broke the window or, I don't know, rang the doorbell. I would have heard either one of those. But I didn't. I remember eating my granola bar and then going down."

"Right."

"But see, I was pretty specific. I had the granola bar in my hand. When you found me, it was on the floor. How much had been eaten?"

"Maybe a bite or two," Tickner said.

"Then your amnesia theory is wrong. I was standing over the sink eating the granola bar. I remember that. When you found me, that's what I was doing. There is no time unaccounted for. And if it was my sister, why would she strip Monica, for Chrissake . . . ?" I stopped.

Lenny said, "Marc?"

Did you love her?

I stared straight ahead.

You know who shot you, don't you, Marc?

Dina Levinsky. I thought about her bizarre visits to the house she'd grown up in. I thought about the two guns—one being mine. I thought about the CD-ROM hidden in the basement, in the spot Dina had told me about. I thought about those pictures taken in front of the hospital. I thought about what Edgar said about Monica seeing a psychiatrist.

And then an awful thought, one so terrible I might indeed have suppressed it, began to surface.

chapter 43

I feigned illness and excused myself. I went to the bathroom and dialed Edgar's phone number. My father-in-law himself answered. "Hello?"

"You said Monica was seeing a psychiatrist?"

"Marc? Is that you?" Edgar cleared his throat. "I just heard from the police. Those pissant fools had me convinced that you were behind all this—"

"I don't have time for that now. I'm still trying to find Tara."

"What do you need?" Edgar asked.

"Did you ever find out the name of her psychiatrist?"

"No."

I thought about it. "Is Carson there?"

"Yes."

"Put him on."

There was a brief pause. I tapped my foot. Uncle Carson's rich voice came over the line. "Marc?"

"You knew about those pictures, didn't you?"

He didn't reply.

"I checked our accounts. The money didn't come from us. You paid for the private detective."

"It had nothing to do with the shooting or kidnapping," Carson said.

"I think it did. Monica told you the name of her psychiatrist, didn't she? What was it?"

Again he did not reply.

"I'm trying to find out what happened to Tara."

"She only saw him twice," Carson said. "How can he help you?"

"He can't. His name can."

"What?"

"Just tell me, yes or no. Was his name Stanley Radio?"

I could hear him breathing.

"Carson?"

"I already spoke to him. He knows nothing—"

But I had already hung up. Carson wouldn't say any more.

But Dina Levinsky might.

I asked Regan and Tickner if I was under arrest. They said no. I asked Verne if I could still borrow the Camaro.

"No problemo," Verne said. Then squinting, he added, "Do you need my help?"

I shook my head. "You and Katarina are out of this now. It's over for you."

"I'm still here, if you need me."

"I don't. Go home, Verne."

He surprised me with a big hug then. Katarina kissed my cheek. I let go and watched them drive off in the pickup. I headed toward the city. There was heavy traffic at the Lincoln Tunnel. It took me over an hour to get through the tolls. That gave me time to make some phone calls. I learned that Dina Levinsky shared an apartment in Greenwich Village with a friend.

Twenty minutes later, I knocked on her door.

When Eleanor Russell returned from lunch, there was a plain manila envelope on her chair. It was addressed to her boss, Lenny Marcus, and marked PERSONAL AND CONFIDENTIAL.

Eleanor had worked with Lenny for eight years. She loved him dearly. Having no family of her own—she and her husband, Saul, who had died three years before, had never been blessed with children—she had become something of a surrogate grandmother to the Marcuses. Eleanor even had photographs of Lenny's wife, Cheryl, and their four children on her desk.

She studied the envelope and frowned. How had it gotten here? She peeked into Lenny's office. He looked so harried. That was because Lenny had just returned from a homicide scene. The case involving his best friend, Dr. Marc Seidman, had exploded back into the headlines. Normally Eleanor would not bother Lenny at a time like this. But the return address . . . well, she thought he should see it for himself.

Lenny was on the phone. He saw her enter and put his hand over the receiver. "I'm kinda busy," he said.

"This came for you."

Eleanor handed him the envelope. Lenny almost ignored it. Then Eleanor watched as he spotted the return address. He turned it over, then back again.

The return address simply read, *From a friend of Stacy Seidman.*

Lenny put down the phone and tore open the envelope.

I don't think Dina Levinsky was surprised to see me.

She let me in without a word. The walls were blanketed with her paintings, many hung at odd angles. The effect was dizzying, giving the entire apartment a Salvador Dalí feel. We sat in the kitchen. Dina offered to make tea. I said no. She put her hands on the table. I could see that her fingernails were bitten down past the cuticle. Had they been that way at my house? She seemed different now, sadder somehow. Her hair was straighter. Her eyes were downcast. It was as if she was transforming back to the pitiful girl I had known in elementary school.

"You found the pictures?" she asked.

"Yes."

Dina closed her eyes. "I should have never led you to them."

"Why did you?"

"I lied to you before."

I nodded.

"I'm not married. I don't enjoy sex. I do have troubles with relationships." She shrugged. "I even have problems with telling the truth."

Dina tried to smile. I tried to smile back.

"In therapy we're taught to confront our fears. The only way to do that is to let the truth in, no matter how much it hurts. But see, I wasn't even sure what the truth was. So I tried to lead you there."

"You were back in the house before the night I saw you, weren't you?"

She nodded.

"And that's how you met Monica?"

"Yes."

I kept going. "You two became friends?"

"We had something in common."

"That being?"

Dina looked up at me, and I saw the pain.

"Abuse?" I said.

She nodded.

"Edgar sexually abused her?"

"No, not Edgar. Her mother. And it wasn't sexual. It was more physical and emotional. The woman was very ill. You knew that, right?"

"I guess I did," I said.

"Monica needed help."

"So you introduced her to your therapist?"

"I tried. I mean, I set up an appointment for her with Dr. Radio. But it didn't work out."

"How come?"

"Monica was not the sort of woman who believed in therapy. She thought that she could best handle her own problems."

I nodded. I knew. "At the house," I said, "you asked me if I loved Monica."

"Yes."

"Why?"

"She thought you didn't." Dina put her finger in her mouth, searching for a sliver of nail to bite. There was none. "Of course, she thought herself unworthy of love. Like me. But there was a difference."

"What was that?"

"Monica felt that there was one person who could love her forever."

I knew the answer here. "Tara."

"Yes. She trapped you, Marc. You probably realize that. It wasn't an accident. She wanted to get pregnant."

Sadly, I was not surprised. Again I tried, as in surgery, to put the pieces together. "So Monica believed that I no longer loved her. She was afraid I wanted a divorce. She was troubled. She was crying at night." I paused. I was saying this as much for my benefit as Dina's. I didn't want to keep following this train of thought, but there was no way to stop me. "She's fragile. Her mind is frayed. And then she hears that phone message from Rachel."

"That's your ex-girlfriend?"

"Yes."

"You still keep her picture in your desk drawer. Monica knew about that too. You keep mementos of her."

I closed my eyes, remembering the Steely Dan CD in Monica's car. College music. Music I had listened to with Rachel. I said, "So she hired a private detective to see if I was having an affair. He took those photographs."

Dina nodded.

"So now she has proof. I'm going to leave her for another woman. I'm going to claim she's unstable. I'll say she's an unfit mother. I'm a well-respected doctor, and Rachel has connections with law enforcement. We'd end up with custody of the only thing that really mattered to Monica. Tara."

Dina rose from the table. She washed out a glass in the sink and then filled it with water. I thought again about what had happened that morning. Why hadn't I heard the window break? Why hadn't I heard the doorbell ring? Why hadn't I heard the intruder enter?

Simple. Because there was no intruder.

Tears filled my eyes. "So what did she do, Dina?"

"You know, Marc."

I squeezed my eyes shut.

"I didn't think she'd really do it," Dina said. "I thought she was just acting out, you know? Monica was so despondent. When she asked me if I knew how to get a gun, I thought she wanted to kill herself. I never thought . . ."

"She would shoot me?"

The air was suddenly heavy. Exhaustion overwhelmed me. I was too tired to cry anymore. But there was still more to unearth here. "You said she asked you to help her get a gun?"

Dina wiped her eyes and nodded.

"Did you?"

"No. I wouldn't know how to get one. She said you had a gun at home, but she didn't want something that could trace back. So she went to the only person she knew with seedy enough contacts to help."

I saw it now. "My sister."

"Yes."

"Did Stacy get her a gun?"

"No, I don't think so."

"What makes you say that?"

"The morning you were both shot, Stacy came to see me. See, Monica and I had come up with the idea of going to Stacy together. So Monica mentioned me to her. She came and asked what Monica needed a gun for. I didn't tell her because, well, I really wasn't all that sure. Stacy ran out. I was in a panic. I wanted to ask Dr. Radio what to do, but my next session was that afternoon. I figured it could wait."

"And then?"

"I still don't know what happened, Marc. That's the truth. But I know Monica shot you."

"How?"

"I got scared. So I called your house. Monica answered. She was crying. She told me you were dead. She kept saying, 'What have I done, what have I done?' And then suddenly she hung up. I called back. But no one answered. I really didn't know what to do. Then the TV had the story. When they said your daughter was missing . . . I didn't understand. I thought they'd find her right away. But they never did. And I never heard anything about those pictures either. I hoped, I don't know, I hoped leading you to those photographs might shed some light on what really happened. Not so much for the two of you. But for your daughter."

"Why did you wait so long?"

Her eyes closed and for a moment, I thought that she might be praying. "I had a bad spell, Marc. Two weeks after you were shot, I was hospitalized with a breakdown. The truth is, I was so far gone I forgot about it. Or maybe I wanted to forget, I don't know."

My cell phone rang. It was Lenny. I picked it up.

"Where are you?" he asked.

"With Dina Levinsky."

"Get over to Newark Airport. Terminal C. Now."

"What's going on?"

"I think," Lenny said. Then he slowed down, caught his breath. "I think I may know where we can find Tara."

chapter 44

By the time I arrived at Terminal C, Lenny was already standing by the Continental check-in desk. It was six o'clock at night now. The airport was jammed with the weary. He handed me the anonymous note that had been found in his office. It read:

Abe and Lorraine Tansmore
26 Marsh Lane
Hanley Hills, MO

That was it. Just the name and address. Nothing else.

"It's a suburb near St. Louis," Lenny explained. "I did some research already."

I just kept staring down at the name and address.

"Marc?"

I looked up at him.

"The Tansmores adopted a daughter eighteen months ago. She was six months old when they got her."

Behind him, a Continental service rep said, "Next please." A woman pushed past me. She might have said, "Excuse me," but I'm not sure.

"I have us booked on the next flight to St. Louis. We're leaving in an hour."

When we reached the departure gate, I told him about my meeting with Dina Levinsky. We sat, as we often do, next to each other, facing out. When I finished, he said, "You have a theory now."

"I do."

We watched a plane take off. An old couple sitting across from us shared a tin of Pringles. "I'm a cynic. I know that. I hold no illusions about drug addicts. If anything, I overestimate their depravity. And that, I think, is what I did here."

"How do you figure?"

"Stacy wouldn't shoot me. And she would never hurt her niece. She was an addict. But she still loved me."

"I think," Lenny said, "that you're right."

"I look back. I was so wrapped up in my own world that I never saw . . ." I shook my head. Now was not the time for this. "Monica was desperate," I said. "She couldn't get a gun and maybe, she decided, she didn't have to."

"She used yours," Lenny said.

"Yes."

"And then?"

"Stacy must have guessed what was up. She ran to the house. She saw what Monica had done. I don't know how it played exactly. Maybe Monica tried to shoot her too—that could explain the bullet hole near the stairs. Or maybe Stacy just reacted. She loved me. I was lying there. She probably thought I was dead. So I don't know, but either way Stacy came armed. And she shot Monica."

The gate attendant announced that the flight would soon be boarding but those with special needs or One Pass Gold and Platinum members could board now.

"You said on the phone that Stacy knew Bacard?"

Lenny nodded. "She mentioned him, yeah."

"Again I'm not sure how it played exactly. But think about it. I'm dead. Monica is dead. And Stacy is probably freaking out. Tara is crying. Stacy can't just leave her. So she takes Tara with her. Later she realizes that she can't raise a kid on her own. She's too messed up. So she turns her over to Bacard and tells him to find her a good family. Or, if I want to be cynical, maybe she gives Tara over for the money. We'll never know."

Lenny was nodding.

"From there, well, we just follow what we already learned. Bacard decides to rake in extra money by pretending it was a kidnapping. He hires those two lunatics. Bacard would be able to get hair samples, for example. He double-crossed Stacy. He set her up to take the fall."

I saw something cross Lenny's face.

"What?"

"Nothing," he said.

They called our row.

Lenny stood. "Let's board."

The flight was delayed. We didn't arrive in St. Louis until past midnight local time. It was too late to do anything tonight. Lenny booked us a room at the Airport Marriott. I bought clothes at their all-night boutique. When we got to the room, I took a very long, very hot shower. We settled in and stared at the ceiling.

In the morning, I called the hospital to check on Rachel. She was still sleeping. Zia was in her room. She assured me that Rachel was doing fine. Lenny and I tried to eat the hotel's buffet breakfast. Nothing would stay down. Our rental car was waiting for us. Lenny had gotten directions to Hanley Hills from the desk clerk.

I don't remember what we saw on the drive. Aside from the Arch in the distance, there was nothing distinct. The United States has a strip-mall sameness about it now. It's easy to criticize that—I often do—but maybe the appeal is that we all like what we already know. We claim to embrace change. But in the end, especially in these times, what truly draws us is the familiar.

When we reached the town limits, I felt a tingling in my legs. "What do we do here, Lenny?"

He had no answer.

"Do I just knock on the door and say, 'Excuse me, I think that's my daughter?' "

"We could call the police," he said. "Let them handle it."

But I didn't know how that would play out. We were so close now. I told him to keep on driving. We made a right onto Marsh Lane. I was shaking now. Lenny tried to give me a buck-up look, but his face was pale too. The street was more modest than I'd expected. I had assumed that all of Bacard's clients were wealthy. That was clearly not the case with this couple.

"Abe Tansmore works as a schoolteacher," Lenny said, reading my thoughts as usual. "Sixth grade. Lorraine Tansmore works for a day-care center three days a week. They're both thirty-nine years old. They've been married for seventeen years."

Up ahead, I saw a house with a cherry-wood sign that read 26—THE TANSMORES. It was a small, one-level, what I think they called "bungalow" style. The rest of the houses on the block seemed tired. This one did not. The paint glistened like a smile. There were lots of clusters of color, of flowers and shrubs, all trimly laid out and perfectly pruned. I could see a welcome mat. A low picket fence encircled the front yard. A station wagon, a Volvo model from several years back, sat in the driveway. There was a tricycle, too, and one of those bright-hued plastic Big Wheels.

And there was a woman outside.

Lenny pulled over in front of an empty lot. I barely noticed. The woman was in the flower beds, on her knees. She was working a small digging spade. Her hair was tied back with a red bandanna. Every few digs she would wipe her forehead with her sleeve.

"You say she works at a day-care center?"

"Three days a week. The daughter goes with her."

"What do they call the daughter?"

"Natasha."

I nodded. I don't know why. We waited. The woman, this Lorraine, worked hard, but I could see she enjoyed it. There was a serenity about her. I opened the car window. I could hear her whistling to herself. I don't know how many minutes passed. A neighbor walked by. Lorraine rose and greeted her. The neighbor gestured toward the garden. Lorraine smiled. She wasn't a beautiful woman, but she had a great smile. The neighbor left. Lorraine waved good-bye and turned back to her garden.

The front door opened.

I saw Abe. He was a tall man, thin and wiry, slightly balding. He had a neatly trimmed beard. Lorraine stood and looked over at him. She gave him a small wave.

And then Tara ran outside.

The air around us stopped. I felt my insides shut down. Next to me, Lenny stiffened and muttered, "Oh my God."

For the last eighteen months, I had never really believed that this moment was possible. What I had done instead was convince myself— no, trick myself—into believing that maybe, somehow, Tara was still alive and okay. But my subconscious knew it was only a self-delusion. It winked at me. It nudged me in my sleep. It whispered the obvious truth: that I would never see my daughter again.

But it was my daughter. She was alive.

I was surprised at how little Tara had changed. Oh she'd grown, of course. She was able to stand. She was even able, as I now saw, to run. But her face . . . there was no mistake. No being blinded by hope. It was Tara. It was my little girl.

With a huge smile, Tara ran with total abandon toward Lorraine. Lorraine bent low, her face lighting up in that celestial way only a mother's can. She swept my child into her arms. Now I could hear the melodious sound of Tara's laughter. The sound pierced my heart. Tears streamed down my face. Lenny put a hand on my arm. I could hear him sniffling. I saw the husband, this Abe, walk toward them. He was smiling too.

For several hours, I watched them in their small, perfect yard. I saw Lorraine patiently point out the flowers, explaining what each one was. I saw Abe give her a horsey ride on his back. I saw Lorraine teach her how to pat the dirt down with her hand. Another couple dropped by. They had a little girl about Tara's age. Abe and the other father pushed the girls on the metal swing-set in the backyard. Their giggles pounded in my ears. Eventually they all went inside. Abe and Lorraine were the last to disappear. They walked through the door with their arms around each other.

Lenny turned to me. I let my head drop back. I had hoped that today would be the end of my journey. But it wasn't.

After a while, I said, "Let's go."

chapter 45

When we got back to the Airport Marriott, I told Lenny to go home. He said he would stay. I told him that I could handle this on my own—that I *wanted* to handle this on my own. He reluctantly agreed.

I called Rachel. She was doing well. I told her what had happened. "Call Harold Fisher," I said. "Ask him to do a thorough background check on Abe and Lorraine Tansmore. I want to know if there's something there."

"Okay," she said softly. "I wish I could be there."

"Me too."

I sat on my bed. My head dropped into my hands. I don't think I cried. I don't know what I felt anymore. It was over. I had learned as much as I would. When Rachel called back two hours later, nothing she told me was a surprise. Abe and Lorraine were solid citizens. Abe was the first person in his family to graduate college. He had two younger sisters who lived in the area. Both had three children. He had met Lorraine during their freshman year at Washington University in St. Louis.

Night fell. I stood and looked in the mirror. My wife had tried to kill me. Yes, she was unstable. I knew that now. Hell, I probably knew it then. I didn't much care, I guess. When a child's face breaks, I put it back together. I can do miracles in the surgical room. But my own family fell apart and I did nothing but watch.

I thought now about what it meant to be a father. I loved my daughter. I know that. But when I saw Abe today, when I see Lenny coaching soccer, I wonder. I wonder about my fitness. I wonder about my commitment. And I wonder if I am worthy.

Or do I already know the answer?

I wanted so badly to have my little girl back with me. I also wanted so badly for this not to be about me or my wants.

Tara had looked so damn happy.

It was midnight now. I looked at myself in the mirror again. What if leaving this alone—letting her stay with Abe and Lorraine—was the right thing? Was I really brave enough, strong enough, to walk away? I kept staring in the mirror, challenging myself. Was I?

I lay back. I think I fell asleep. A knock on the door startled me awake. I glanced at the digital clock next to my bed. It read 5:19 A.M.

"I'm sleeping," I said.

"Dr. Seidman?"

It was a male voice.

"Dr. Seidman, my name is Abe Tansmore."

I opened the door. He was handsome up close, in a sort of James Taylor way. He wore jeans and a tan shirt. I looked at his eyes. They were blue but tinged with red. So, I knew, were mine. For a long time, we just stared at one another. I tried to speak, but I couldn't. I stepped back and let him in.

"Your lawyer stopped by. He"—Abe stopped, swallowed hard—"he told us the whole story. Lorraine and I stayed up all night. We talked it out. We cried a lot. But I think we knew right from the get-go that there was only one decision here." Abe Tansmore was trying to hold on, but he was losing it now. He closed his eyes. "We have to give you your daughter back."

I didn't know what to say. I shook my head. "We have to do what's best for her."

"That's what I'm doing, Dr. Seidman."

"Call me Marc. Please." It was a dumb thing to say. I know that. But I wasn't ready for this. "If you're worried about a long, drawn-out court case, Lenny shouldn't have—"

"No, that's not it."

We stood there a little longer. I pointed toward the chair in the room. He shook his head. Then he looked at me. "All night, I've been trying to imagine your pain. I don't think I can. I think there are places a man just can't get to without experience. Maybe this is one of them. But your pain, awful as it must be, that's not why Lorraine and I came to this decision. And it's not because we blame ourselves either. In hindsight, maybe we should have wondered what was going on. We went to

Mr. Bacard. But the fees would have added up to over a hundred thousand dollars. I'm not a rich man. I couldn't afford that. Then a few weeks later, Mr. Bacard calls us. He said he had a baby that needed immediate placing. She wasn't a newborn, he said. The mother had just abandoned her. We knew something was not quite right, but he said that if we wanted this, we'd have to go in no questions asked."

He looked off then. I watched his face. "I think deep down, maybe we always knew. We just couldn't face it. But that's not the reason we came to this decision either."

I swallowed. "What then?"

His eyes drifted toward mine. "You can't do the wrong thing for the right reason." I must have looked confused. "If Lorraine and I don't do this, we're not fit to raise her. We want Natasha to be happy. We want her to be a good person."

"You might be the best ones to make that happen."

He shook his head. "That's not how it works. We don't give children to whatever parents would be best to raise them. You and I can't make that judgment. You don't know how hard this is for us. Or maybe you do."

I turned away. I caught my reflection in the mirror. Just for a second. Less maybe. But it was enough. I saw the man I was. I saw the man I wanted to be. I turned to him and said, "I want us both to raise her."

He was stunned. So was I. "I'm not sure I understand," he said.

"Neither do I. But that's what we're going to do."

"How?"

"I don't know."

Abe shook his head. "It can't work. You know that."

"No, Abe, I don't know that. I came here to bring my daughter home—and I find that maybe she already is. Is it right for me to rip her away from that? I want you both in her life. I'm not saying it'll be easy. But kids are raised by single parents, by stepparents, in foster homes. There are divorces and separations and who-knows-what. We all love this little girl. We'll make it work."

I saw the hope return to the man's thin face. He couldn't speak for a few seconds. Then he said, "Lorraine is in the lobby. Can I go talk to her?"

"Of course."

They didn't take long. There was a knock on my door. When I

opened it, Lorraine threw her arms around me. I hugged her back, this woman I had never met. Her hair smelled of strawberry. Behind her, Abe came into the room. Tara was sleeping in his arms. Lorraine let go of me and moved away. Abe stepped closer. He handed me my daughter carefully. I held her, and my heart burst into flame. Tara began to stir. She started to fuss. I still held her. I rocked her back and forth and made shushing sounds.

And soon she settled on me and fell back to sleep.

chapter 46

It started to all go wrong again when I looked at the calendar.

The human brain is amazing. It is a curious mix of electricity and chemicals. It is, in effect, pure science. We understand more about the workings of the great cosmos than we do about the curious circuitry of the cerebrum, cerebellum, hypothalamus, medulla oblongata, and all the rest. And like any tricky compound, we are never sure how it will react to a certain catalyst.

There were several things that gave me reason to pause. There was the question of leaks. Rachel and I had thought that someone in either the FBI or police department had told Bacard and his people what was happening. But that never fit in with my theory about Stacy shooting Monica. There was the fact that Monica was found with no clothes on. I think I understood why now, but the thing is, Stacy wouldn't have.

But the main catalyst occurred, I think, when I looked at the calendar and realized that today was Wednesday.

The shootings and original abduction had taken place on a Wednesday. Of course, there had been plenty of Wednesdays in the past eighteen months. The day of the week was a pretty innocuous thing. But this time, after we had learned so much, after my brain had digested all the fresh data, something meshed. All those little questions and doubts, all those idiosyncrasies, all those moments I took for granted and never really examined . . . they all shifted a little. And what I saw was even worse than what I had originally imagined.

I was back in Kasselton now—at my house where it had all started. I called Tickner for confirmation.

I said, "My wife and I were shot with thirty-eights, right?"

"Yes."

"And you're sure they were two different guns?"

"Positive."

"And my Smith and Wesson was one of them?"

"You know all this, Marc."

"Did you get all the ballistic reports back yet?"

"Most of them."

I licked my lips and readied myself. I hoped to hell that I was wrong. "Who was shot with my gun—me or Monica?"

He turned coy on me. "Why are you asking me this now?"

"Curiosity."

"Yeah, right. Hold on a second." I could hear him shuffling papers. I felt my throat constrict. I almost hung up. "Your wife was."

When I heard the car pull up outside, I put the receiver back in the cradle. Lenny turned the knob and opened the door. He didn't knock. After all, Lenny never knocked, right?

I was sitting on the couch. The house was still, all the ghosts sleeping now. He had a Slurpee in either hand and a broad smile. I wondered how many times I had seen that smile. I remembered it more crooked. I remembered it jammed to overflowing with braces. I remembered it bleeding after he hit a tree when we went sledding down the Gorets' backyard. I thought again about when big Tony Merruno picked a fight with me in third grade, how Lenny jumped on his back. I remembered now that Tony Merruno broke Lenny's glasses. I don't think Lenny cared.

I knew him so well. Or maybe I hadn't known him at all.

When Lenny saw my face, his smile faded away.

"We were supposed to play racquetball that morning, Lenny. Remember?"

He lowered the cups and put them on the end table.

"You never knock. You always just open the door. Like today. So what happened, Lenny? You came to pick me up. You opened the door."

He started shaking his head, but I knew now.

"The two guns, Lenny. That's what gave it away."

"I don't know what you're talking about." But there was no conviction in his voice.

"We figured that Stacy didn't get Monica a gun—that Monica used mine. But you see, she didn't. I just checked with ballistics. It's funny. You never told me that Monica was shot with my gun. I was shot with the other weapon."

"So?" Lenny said, suddenly the attorney again. "That doesn't mean anything. Maybe Stacy got her a gun, after all."

"She did," I said.

"So fine, okay, it still adds up."

"Tell me how."

He shifted his feet. "Maybe Stacy helped Monica get a gun. Monica shot you with it. When Stacy arrived a few minutes later, Monica tried to shoot her." Lenny moved over to the staircase as if to demonstrate. "Stacy ran upstairs. Monica fired—that would explain the bullet hole." He pointed to the spackled area by the stairs. "Stacy grabbed your gun out of the bedroom, came downstairs, and shot Monica."

I looked at him. "Is that how it happened, Lenny?"

"I don't know. I mean, it could be."

I waited a beat. He turned away. "One problem," I said.

"What?"

"Stacy didn't know where I hid the gun. She didn't know the lockbox's combination either." I took a step closer. "But you did, Lenny. I kept all my legal documents there. I trusted you with everything. So now I want the truth. Monica shot me. You came in. You saw me lying on the floor. Did you think I was dead?"

Lenny closed his eyes.

"Make me understand, Lenny."

He shook his head slowly. "You think you love your daughter," he said. "But you have no idea. What you feel, it grows every day. The longer you have a child, the more attached you get. The other night I came home from work. Marianne was crying because some girls were teasing her in school. I went to bed feeling sick, and I realized something. I can only be as happy as my saddest child. Do you understand what I'm saying?"

"Tell me what happened," I said.

"You have it pretty much right. I came to your house that morning. I opened the door. Monica was on the phone. She was still holding the gun in her hand. I ran over to you. I couldn't believe it. I felt for a pulse but . . ." He shook his head. "Monica started screaming at me, about how she wouldn't let anyone take away her baby. She pointed the gun at me. I mean, Jesus Christ. I thought for sure I was going to die. I rolled away and then I ran for the stairs. I remembered you had a gun up there. She fired at me." He pointed again. "That's the bullet hole."

He stopped. He took a few breaths. I waited.

"I grabbed your gun."

"Did Monica follow you up the stairs?"

His voice was soft. "No." He started blinking. "Maybe I should have tried to use the phone. Maybe I should have sneaked out. I don't know. I've gone through it hundreds of times. I try to imagine how I should have played it. But you were lying there, my best friend, dead. That crazy bitch was shouting about running away with your daughter—my godchild. She had already taken a shot at me. I didn't know what she would do next."

He looked away.

"Lenny?"

"I don't know what happened, Marc. I really don't. I sneaked back down the stairs. She still had the gun. . . ." His voice tailed.

"So you shot her."

He nodded. "I didn't mean to kill her. At least, I don't think I did. But suddenly you were both lying there, dead. I was going to call the police. But now I wasn't sure how it would look. I had shot Monica at a funny angle. They could claim her back was turned."

"You thought maybe they'd arrest you?"

"Of course. The cops hate me. I'm a successful defense attorney. What do you think would have happened?"

I didn't reply. "You broke the window?"

"From the outside," he said. "So it would look like an intruder.

"And you took Monica's clothes off?"

"Yes."

"Same reason?"

"I knew that there would be gunpowder residue on the clothes. They'd realize she fired a gun. I was trying to make it look like a random attacker. So I got rid of her clothes. I used a baby wipe to clean off her hand."

That was another thing that had bothered me. Monica being stripped down. There had been the possibility that Stacy would have done it to throw off the police, but I couldn't imagine her thinking of that. Lenny was the defense attorney—him I could see.

We were getting to the heart of it now. We both knew that. I crossed my arms. "Tell me about Tara."

"She was my godchild. It was my job to protect her."

"I don't understand."

Lenny spread his hands. "How many times did I beg you to write a will?"

I was confused. "What does that have to do with anything?"

"Think it through for a second. During all this, when you were in trouble, you resorted to your surgical training, right?"

"I guess."

"I'm an attorney, Marc. I did the same. You were both dead. Tara was wailing in the other room. And I, Lenny the Lawyer, realized instantly what would happen."

"What?

"You hadn't made out a will. You hadn't named guardians. Don't you see? That meant Edgar would get your daughter."

I looked at his face. I hadn't thought of that.

"Your mother might contest, but she wouldn't stand a chance against his finances. She had your father to worry about. She had a drunk driving conviction six years ago. Edgar would get custody."

I saw it now. "And you couldn't allow that."

"I'm Tara's godfather. It was my job to protect her."

"And you hated Edgar."

He shook his head. "Was I clouded by what he did to my dad? Yeah, maybe subconsciously, a little. But Edgar Portman is evil. You know that. Look at how Monica turned out. I couldn't let him destroy your daughter like he did his own."

"So you took her."

He nodded.

"You brought her to Bacard."

"He had been a client. I knew some of what he did, though not to what extent. I also knew that he would keep it confidential. I told him I wanted the best family he had. Forget money, forget power. I wanted good people."

"So he placed her with the Tansmores."

"Yes. You have to understand. I thought you were dead. Everyone did. And then it looked like you might end up a vegetable. By the time you were okay, it was too late. I couldn't tell anybody. I would go to prison for sure. Do you know what that would do to my family?"

"Gee, I can't imagine," I said.

"That's not fair, Marc."

"I don't have to be fair here."

"Hey, I didn't ask for any of this." He was shouting now. "I walked in on a terrible situation. I did what I thought best—for your daughter. But you can't expect me to sacrifice my family."

"Better to sacrifice mine?"

"The truth? Yes, of course. I'd give up anything to protect my children. Anything. Wouldn't you?"

Now I was the one who stayed silent. I had said it before: I would lay down my life in a second for my daughter. And truth be told, if push came to shove, I would lay down yours too.

"Believe it or not, I tried to think through this coldly," Lenny said. "A cost-benefit analysis. If I come forward with the truth, I destroy my wife and four children and you take your daughter from a loving home. If I keep quiet . . ." He shrugged. "Yeah, you suffered. I didn't want to do that. It hurt me to watch you. But what would you have done?"

I didn't want to think about it. "You're leaving something out," I said.

He closed his eyes and muttered something unintelligible.

"What happened to Stacy?"

"She wasn't supposed to be hurt. It was like you said. She had sold Monica the gun and when she realized why, she rushed to stop her."

"But she arrived too late?"

"Yes."

"She saw you?"

He nodded. "Look, I told her everything. She wanted to help, Marc. She wanted to do the right thing. But in the end, the habit was too strong."

"She blackmailed you?"

"She asked for money. I gave it to her. That wasn't important. But she was there. And when I went to Bacard, I told him everything that had happened. You have to understand. I thought you were going to die. When you didn't, I knew that you'd go nuts without closure. Your daughter was gone. I talked to Bacard about it. He came up with the idea of a fake kidnapping. We'd all make a lot of money."

"You took money for this?"

Lenny leaned back as if I'd just slapped him. "Of course not. I put my share into a trust fund for Tara's college. But the idea of this fake kidnapping appealed to me. They'd set it up so in the end, it would look like Tara was dead. You'd have closure. We'd also be taking money from Edgar and funneling at least some of it to Tara. It seemed like a win-win."

"Except?"

"Except when they heard about Stacy, they decided that they couldn't depend on a drug addict to keep quiet. The rest you know. They lured her with money. They made sure she got caught on tape. And then, without telling me, they killed her."

I thought about that. I thought about Stacy's last minutes in the cabin. Did she know that she was going to die? Or did she just drift off, thinking she was merely getting yet another fix?

"You were the leak, weren't you?"

He didn't reply.

"You told them about the police being involved."

"Don't you see? It made no difference. They never intended to give Tara back. She was already with the Tansmores. After the ransom drop, I thought it was over. We all tried to move on."

"So what happened?'

"Bacard decided to run the ransom again."

"Were you in on it?" I asked.

"No, he kept me out of the loop."

"When did you learn about it?"

"When you told me in the hospital. I was furious. I called him. He told me to relax, that there was no way it could be traced back to us."

"But we did it trace it back."

He nodded.

"And you knew that I was getting close to Bacard. I told you on the phone."

"Yes."

"Wait a minute." A fresh chill ran up my neck. "In the end, Bacard wanted to clean house. He called those two lunatics. The woman, that Lydia, she went out and killed Tatiana. Heshy was sent to take care of Denise Vanech. But"—I thought it through—"but when I saw Steven

Bacard, he had just been shot. He was still bleeding. There was no way either of them could have done it."

I looked up. "You killed him, Lenny."

Rage seeped into his voice. "You think I wanted to?"

"Then why?"

"What do you mean, why? I was Bacard's get-out-of-jail-free card. When it all started to go wrong, he said he would turn state's evidence against me. He'd claim I shot you and Monica and brought him Tara. Like I said before, the cops hate me. I've gotten too many bad guys off. They'd go for the deal in a second."

"You'd have gone to jail?"

Lenny looked near tears.

"Your kids would have suffered?"

He nodded.

"So you killed a man in cold blood."

"What else could I do? You're looking at me like that, but deep down, you know the truth. This was your mess. I got stuck cleaning it up. Because I cared about you. I wanted to help your child." He stopped, closed his eyes, and added, "And I knew that if I killed Bacard, maybe I could save you too."

"Me?"

"Another cost-benefit analysis, Marc."

"What are you talking about?"

"It was over. Once Bacard was dead, he could take the fall. For everything. I was in the clear." Lenny came over and stood in front of me. For a moment I thought he was going to try to hug me. But he just stood there.

"I wanted you to have peace, Marc. But that would never be. I knew that now. Not until you found your daughter. With Bacard dead, my family was safe. I could let you know the truth."

"So you wrote up that anonymous note and left it on Eleanor's desk."

"Yes."

I nodded and Abe's words came back to me. "You did the wrong thing for the right reason."

"Put yourself in my place. What would you have done?"

"I don't know," I said.

"I did it for you."

And the saddest part was, he was telling the truth. I looked at him.

"You were the best friend I ever had, Lenny. I love you. I love your wife. I love your children."

"What are you going to do?"

"If I say I'm going to talk, will you kill me too?"

"Never," he said.

But I wasn't sure, much as I loved him, much as he loved me, that I believed him.

epilogue

A year has passed.

During the first two months, I racked up the frequent flier miles coming out to St. Louis every week, trying to figure out with Abe and Lorraine what we were going to do. We started slowly. For the first few visits, I asked Abe and Lorraine to stay in the room. Eventually, Tara and I started going places alone—the park, the zoo, the merry-go-round at the mall—but she looked over her shoulder a lot. It took some time for my daughter to get comfortable with me. I understood that.

My father passed away in his sleep ten months ago. After his funeral, I bought a house on Marsh Lane, two down from Abe and Lorraine, and moved out here permanently. Abe and Lorraine are remarkable people. Get this: We call "our" daughter Tasha. Think about it. It's short for Natasha and close to Tara. The reconstructive surgeon in me likes that. I keep waiting for things to go wrong. They haven't. It's weird, but I don't question it much.

My mother bought a condo and moved out here too. With Dad gone, there was no reason for her to stay in Kasselton anymore. After all the tragedies—my father's poor health, Stacy, Monica, the attack, the abduction—we both needed a second act. I'm glad she's near us. Mom has a new boyfriend, a guy named Cy. She's happy. I like him, and not just because he has season tickets to the Rams. They laugh a lot. I almost forgot how hard my mom could laugh.

I talk to Verne a fair amount. He and Katarina brought Verne Junior and Perry out in an RV during the spring. We had a great week together. Verne took me fishing, a first for me. I liked it. Next time he wants to hunt. I told him no way, but Verne can be pretty persuasive.

I don't talk much to Edgar Portman. He sends presents on Tasha's birthday. He's called twice. I'm hoping he'll come out and see his granddaughter soon. But there is simply too much guilt there for both of us. It's like I said before. Maybe Monica was unstable. Maybe it was just a chemical thing. I know that a great deal of psychiatry problems stem more from the physical, from hormonal imbalances, than life experiences. Chances are there was nothing we could have done. But in the end, whatever may have been the origin, we both let Monica down.

Zia was initially hit hard by my leaving, but then she saw it as an opportunity. She has a new doctor in the practice. I hear he's pretty good. I've opened up a One World WrapAid branch office in St. Louis. So far, it seems to be going well.

Lydia—or Larissa Dane, if you prefer—is going to get off. She did a double-flip off a murder rap and stuck the "I was abused" landing with both feet. She is a celebrity again, what with the mysterious return of the Pixie named Trixie. Lydia appeared on *Oprah*, crying on cue about the years of torment at the hands of Heshy. They flashed his picture up on the screen. The audience gasped. Heshy is hideous. Lydia is beautiful. So the world believes. Rumor has it she is set to appear in a TV movie based on her life story.

As for the baby-smuggling case, the FBI decided to "enforce the law," which meant bringing the bad guys to justice. Steven Bacard and Denise Vanech were the bad guys here. They're both dead. Officially, authorities are still searching for the records, but nobody wants to look too closely at what child ended up where. I think that's best.

Rachel fully recovered from her injuries. I ended up doing the reconstructive work on her ear myself. Her bravery got major play in the press. She received credit for smashing the baby-smuggling ring. The FBI rehired her. She requested and received a post in St. Louis. We live together. I love her. I love her more than you can imagine. But if you are expecting a totally happy ending, I'm not sure I can give you one.

As of now, Rachel and I are still together. I cannot imagine living without her. I think about losing her and it makes me physically ill. Yet I'm not sure that's enough. There is a lot of baggage here. It confuses things. I understand about her making that late-night call and showing up outside the hospital—and yet, I know those acts eventually led to death and destruction. I don't blame Rachel, of course. But there is something there. Monica's death has given our relationship a second chance. That feels strange. I tried explaining all of this to Verne when he visited. He told me that I'm a dumb-ass. I think he's probably right.

The doorbell rings. There is a tug on my leg. Yes, it's Tasha. She is fully acclimated to having me in her life now. Children, after all, adapt better than adults. Across the room, Rachel is on the couch. She is sitting with her legs curled under her. I look at her, then at Tasha, and I feel the wondrous blend of bliss and fear. They—bliss and fear—are constant companions. Rarely does one venture out without the other.

"One second, pumpkin," I say to her. "Let's go answer the door, okay?"

"Okay."

The UPS man is there. He has packages. I bring them inside. When I look at the return address, I feel the familiar ache. The little sticker tells me that they are from Lenny and Cheryl Marcus of Kasselton, New Jersey.

Tasha looks up at me. "My present?"

I never told the police about Lenny. There was no evidence anyway—only his confession to me. That wouldn't stand up in court. But that's not why I decided not to say anything.

I suspect Cheryl knows the truth. I think maybe she knew from the beginning. I flash back to her face on the stairs, the way she snapped when Rachel and I arrived at their house that night, and now I wonder if it was out of anger or fear. I suspect the latter.

The fact is, Lenny was right. He did do it for me. What would have happened if he had just left the house? I don't know. It might have been even worse. Lenny asked me if I would have done the same in his place. Back then, probably not. Because maybe I wasn't that good a man. Verne, I bet, would have. Lenny was trying to protect my daughter without sacrificing his own family. He just messed up.

But man, I miss him. I think about how big a part of my life he was. There are times I reach for the phone and begin dialing his number. But I never finish the call. I won't speak to Lenny again. Not ever. I know that. And it hurts like hell.

But I also think about little Conner's inquisitive face at the soccer game. I think about Kevin playing soccer and Marianne's hair smelling of chlorine from her morning swim practice. I think about how beautiful Cheryl had become since she had the children.

I look down at my daughter now, safe and with me. Tasha is still gazing up. It is indeed a present for her from her godfather. I remember the first time I met Abe, that strange day at the Airport Marriott. He told me that you shouldn't do the wrong thing for the right reason. I thought about that a lot before deciding what to do about Lenny.

In the end, well, chalk it up as "too close to call."

I mix it up sometimes. Is it the wrong thing for the right reason or the right thing for the wrong reason? Or are they same? Monica needed to feel love, so she deceived me and got pregnant. That was how it all started. But if she hadn't done that, I wouldn't be staring down at the most wonderful creation I would ever know. Right reason? Wrong reason? Who's to say?

Tasha tilts her head and twitches her nose at me. "Daddy?"

"It's nothing, sweetheart," I say softly.

Tasha gives me a big, elaborate kid shrug. Rachel looks up. I see the concern on her face. I take the package and place it high up in the closet. Then I close that door and pick up my daughter.

acknowledgments

The author—man, I love referring to myself in the third person—would like to thank the following for their technical expertise: Steven Miller, M.D., Director of Pediatric Emergency Medicine, Children's Hospital of New York Presbyterian, Columbia University; Christopher J. Christie, United States Attorney for the state of New Jersey; Anne Armstrong-Coben, M.D., Medical Director of Covenant House Newark; Lois Foster Hirt, R.D.H.; Jeffrey Bedford, FBI; Gene Riehl, FBI (retired); Andrew McDade, brother-in-law extraordinaire and renaissance man. Any mistakes are theirs and theirs alone. After all, they're the experts, right? Why should I take the heat?

I also want to acknowledge Carole Baron, Mitch Hoffman, Lisa Johnson, and everyone at Dutton and Penguin Group (USA); Jon Wood, Susan Lamb, Malcolm Edwards, Anthony Cheetham, Juliet Ewers, Emily Furniss, and everyone at Orion; and the always reliable Aaron Priest, Lisa Erbach Vance, Maggie Griffin, and Linda Fairstein.

Oh, and of course, a big thanks to Katharine Foote and Rachel Cooke for freeing me up so I could get over that final hurdle.